Roland Yorke by Mrs Henry Wood

"And Deering's Woods are fresh and fair,
And with joy that is almost pain
My heart goes back to wander there,
And among the dreams of the days that were

I find my lost youth again.
And the strange and beautiful song,
The groves are repeating it still:
'A boy's will is the wind's will,
And the thoughts of youth are long, long thoughts.'"
Longfellow

Ellen Price was born on 17th January 1814 in Worcester.

In 1836 she married Henry Wood, whose career in banking and shipping meant living in Dauphiné, in the South of France, for two decades. During their time there they had four children.

Henry's business collapsed and he and Ellen together with their four children returned to England and settled in Upper Norwood near London.

Ellen now turned to writing and with her second book 'East Lynne' enjoyed remarkable popularity. This enabled her to support her family and to maintain a literary career.

It was a career in which she would write over 30 novels including 'Danesbury House', 'Oswald Cray', 'Mrs. Halliburton's Troubles', 'The Channings' and 'The Shadow of Ashlydyat'.

Sadly, her husband, Henry died in 1866.

Ellen though continued to strive on. In 1867, she purchased the magazine 'Argosy', founded two years previously by Alexander Strahan. She was a prolific writer and wrote much of the magazine herself although she had some very respected contributors, amongst them Hesba Stretton and Christina Rossetti. Although she would gradually pare down writing for the magazine she continued to write novel after novel. Such was her talent that for a time she was, in Australia, more popular than Charles Dickens.

Apart from novels she was an excellent translator and a writer of short stories. 'Reality or Delusion?' is a staple of supernatural anthologies to this day.

Ellen Wood died of bronchitis on 10th February 1887. He estate was valued at a very considerable £36,000.

She is buried in Highgate Cemetery, London.

A monument to her in Worcester Cathedral was unveiled in 1916.

Index of Contents

ROLAND YORKE

PROLOGUE

CHAPTER I

IN THE MOONLIGHT

The scene of this Prologue to the story about to be written was a certain cathedral town, of which most of you have heard before, and the time close upon midnight.

It was a warm night at the beginning of March. The air was calm and still; the bright moon was shedding her pure light with unusual brilliancy on the city, lying directly underneath her beams. On the pinnacles of the time-honoured cathedral; on the church-spire, whose tapering height has made itself a name; on the clustering roofs of houses; on the trees of what people are pleased to call the Park; on the river, silently winding its course along beneath the city walls; and on the white pavement of its streets: all were steeped in the soft and beautiful light of the Queen of Night.

Surely at that late hour people ought to have been asleep in their beds, and the town hushed to silence! Not so. A vast number of men—and women too, for the matter of that—were awake and abroad. At least, it looked a good number, stealing quietly in one direction along the principal street. A few persons, comparatively speaking, assembled together by daylight, will look like a crowd at night. They went along for the most part in silence, one group glancing round at another, and being glanced at, back again: whether drawn out by curiosity, by sympathy, by example, all seemed very much as if they were half ashamed to be seen there.

Straight through the town, past the new law-courts, past the squares and the good houses built in more recent years, past the pavements and the worn highway, telling of a city's bustle, into the open country, to where a churchyard abuts upon a side-road. A rural, not much frequented churchyard, dotted with old graves, its small, grey church standing in the middle. People were not buried there now. On one side of the church yard, open to the side way, the boundary hedge had disappeared, partly through neglect. The entrance was on the other side, facing the city; and where was the use of raising up again the trodden-down hedge, destroyed gradually and in process of time by boys and girls at play? So, at least, argued the authorities—when they argued about it at all.

People were not buried there now: and yet a grave was being dug. At the remotest corner of this open side of the churchyard, so close to the consecrated ground that you could scarcely tell whether they were on it or off it, two men with torches were working at the nearly finished, shallow, hastily-made grave. A pathway, made perhaps more of custom than of plan, led right over it into the churchyard—if any careless person chose to enter it by so unorthodox a route—and the common side-road, wide enough to admit of carts and other vehicles, crossed it on the exact spot where the grave was being dug. So that a spectator might have said the grave's destined occupant was to lie in a cross-road.

Up to this spot came the groups, winding round the front hedge silently, save from the inevitable hum which attends a number, their footsteps grating and shuffling on the still air. That there was some kind of reverence attaching to the feeling in general, was proved by the absence of all jokes and light words; it may be almost said by the absence of conversation altogether, for what little they said was spoken in whispers. The open space beyond the grave was a kind of common, stretching out into the country, so that there was room and to spare for these people to congregate around, without pressing inconveniently on the sides of the shallow grave. Not but what every soul went close to give a look in, taking a longer or shorter time in the gaze as curiosity was slow or quick to satisfy itself.

The men threw out the last spadeful, patted the sides well, and ascended to the level of the earth. Not a minute too soon. As they stamped their feet, like men who have been in a cramped position, and put their tools away back, the clock of the old grey church struck twelve. It was a loud striker at all times; it sounded like a gong in the stillness of the night, and a movement ran through the startled spectators.

With the first stroke of the clock there came up a wayfarer. Some traveller who had missed his train at Bromsgrove, and had to walk the distance. He advanced with a jaunty though somewhat tired step along the highway, and did not discern the crowd until close upon them, for the road wound just there. To say that he was astonished would be saying little. He stood still, and stared, and rubbed his eyes, almost questioning whether the unusual scene could be real.

"What on earth's the matter?" demanded he of someone near him. "What does it all mean?"

The man addressed turned at the question, and recognized the speaker for Mr. Richard Jones, an inhabitant of the town.

At least he was nearly sure it was he, but he knew him by sight but slightly. If it was Mr. Jones, why this same crowd and commotion had to do with him, in one sense of the word. Its cause had a great deal to do with his home.

"Can't you answer a body?" continued Mr. Jones, finding he got no reply.

"Hush!" breathed the other man. "Look there."

Along the middle of the turnpike-road, on their way from the city, came eight men with measured and even tread, bearing a coffin on their shoulders. It was covered with what looked like a black cloth shawl, whose woollen fringe was clearly discernible in the moonlight. Mr. Jones had halted at the turning up to the churchyard, where he first saw the assembly of people; consequently the men bearing the coffin, whose heavy tread and otherwise silent presence seemed to exhale a kind of unpleasant thrill, passed round by Mr. Jones, nearly touching him.

"What is it?" he repeated in a few seconds, nearly wild to have his understanding enlightened.

"Don't you see what it is?—a coffin. It's going to be buried in that there cross grave up yonder."

"But who is in the coffin?"

"A gentleman who died by his own hand. The jury brought it in self-murder, and so he's got to be put away without burial service."

"Lawk a mercy!" exclaimed Mr. Jones, who though a light shallow, unstable man, given to make impromptu excursions from his home and wife, and to spend too much money in doing it, was not on the whole a bad-hearted one. "Poor gentleman! Who was it?"

"One of them law men in wigs that come in to the 'sizes."

Mr. Jones might have asked more but for two reasons. The first was, that his neighbour moved away in the wake of those who were beginning to press forward to see as much as they could get to see of the closing ceremony; the next was, that in a young woman who just then walked past him, he recognized his wife's sister. Again Mr. Jones rubbed his eyes, mentally questioning whether this second vision might be real. For she, Miss Rye, was a steady, good, superior young woman, not at all likely to come out of her home at midnight after a sight of any sort, whether it might be a burying or a wedding. Mr. Jones really doubted whether his sight and the moonlight had not played him false. The shortest way to solve this doubt would have been to accost the young woman, but while he had been wondering, she disappeared. In truth it was Miss Rye, and she had followed the coffin from whence it was brought, as a vast many more had followed it. Not mixing with them; walking apart and alone, close to the houses, in the deep shade cast by their walls. She was a comely young woman of about seven-and-twenty, tall and fair, with steady blue eyes, good features, and a sensible countenance. In deep mourning for her mother, she wore on this night a black merino dress, soft and fine, and a black shawl trimmed with crape, that she held closely round her. But she had disappeared; and amidst so many Mr. Jones thought it would be useless to go looking for her.

A certain official personage or two, perhaps deputies from the coroner, or from the parish, or from the undertaker furnishing the coffin and the two sets of bearers—who can tell?—whose mission it was to see the appointed proceedings carried out, cleared by their hands and gestures a space around the grave. The people fell back obediently. They pressed and elbowed each other no doubt, and grumbled at others crushing them; but they kept themselves back in their places. A small knot, gentlemen evidently, and probably friends of the deceased, were allowed to approach the grave. The grave-diggers stood near, holding the torches. But for those flaring torches, the crowd would have seen better: they saw well enough, however, in the bright moonlight.

In the churchyard, having taken up his station there behind an upright tombstone, where tombstones were thick, stood an officer connected with the police. He was in plain clothes—in fact, nobody remembered to have seen him in other ones—and had come out tonight not officially but to gratify himself personally. Ensconced behind the stone, away from everybody, he could look on at leisure through its upper fretwork and take his own observations, not only of the ceremony about to be performed, but of those who were attending it. He was a middle-sized, spare man, with a pale face, deeply sunk green eyes, that had a habit of looking steadily at people, and a small, sharp, turned-up nose. Silent by nature and by habit, he imparted the idea of possessing a vast amount of astute keenness as a detector of crime: in his own opinion he had not in that respect an equal. Nobody could discern him, and he did not intend they should.

Amidst a dead silence, save for the creaking of the cords, amidst a shiver of sympathy, of pity, of awful thoughts from a great many of the spectators, the black covering was thrown aside and the coffin was lowered. There was a general lifting off of hats; a pause; and then a rush. One in the front rank—a fat woman, who had fought for her place—stepped forward in her irrepressible curiosity to take a last look inside the grave; another followed her; the movement was contagious, and there was a commotion. Upon which the men holding the torches swept them round; it threw out the flame rather dangerously, and the rushers drew back again with half a cry. Not quite all. A few, more adventurous than the rest, slipped round to the safer side, and were in time to read the inscription on the lid:

"JOHN OLLIVERA.
Aged 28."

Short enough, and simple enough, for the sad death. Only a moment after the cords were drawn away did it remain visible; for the grave-diggers, flinging their torches aside, threw in the earth, spadeful upon spadeful, and covered it up from sight.

The shallow grave was soon filled in; the grave-diggers flattened it down level with spades and feet: no ceremony accorded, you see, to such an end as this poor man had made. Before it was quite accomplished, those officially connected with the burial, or with the buried, left the ground and departed. Not so the mob of people: they stayed to see the last; and would have stayed had it been until morning light. And they talked freely now, one with another, but were orderly and subdued still.

Mr. Jones stayed. He had not mixed with the people, but stood apart in the churchyard, under the shade of the great yew-tree. Soon he began to move away, and came unexpectedly upon the detective officer standing yet behind the gravestone. Mr. Jones halted in surprise.

"Halloo!" cried he. "Mr. Butterby!"

"Just look at them idiots!" rejoined Mr. Butterby, with marked composure, as if he had seen Richard Jones from the first, and expected the address. "So you are back!" he added, turning his head sharply on the traveller.

"I come in from Bromsgrove on my legs; missed the last train there," said Mr. Jones, rather addicted to a free-and-easy kind of grammar in private life: as indeed was the renowned gentleman he spoke to. "When I got past the last turning and see these here folks, I thought the world must be gone mad."

"Did you come back on account of it?" asked Mr. Butterby. "Did they write for you?"

"On account of what? As to writing for me, they'd be clever to do that, seeing I left 'em no address to write to. I have been going about from place to place; today there, tomorrow yonder."

"On account of that," answered the detective, nodding his head in the direction of the grave, to which the men were then giving the last finishing strokes and treads of flattening.

To Mr. Jones's ear there was something so obscure in the words that he only stared at their speaker, almost wondering whether the grave officer had condescended to a joke.

"I don't understand you, sir."

Mr. Butterby saw at once how the matter stood: that Dicky Jones—the familiar title mostly accorded him in the city—was ignorant of recent events.

"The poor unfortunate man just put in there, Jones,"—with another nod to the grave—"was Mr. Ollivera, the counsel."

"Mr. Ollivera!" exclaimed the startled Jones.

"And he took his life away at your house."

"Lawk a mercy!" cried Mr. Jones, repeating his favourite expression, one he was addicted to when overwhelmed with surprise. "Whatever did he do it for?"

"Ah, that's just what we can't tell. Perhaps he didn't know himself what."

"How was it, sir? Poison?"

"Shot himself with his own pistol," briefly responded the officer.

"And did it knowingly?—intentional?"

"Intentional for sure, or he'd not have been put in here tonight. They couldn't have buried a dog with much less ceremony."

"Well, I never knew such a thing as this," cried Mr. Jones, scarcely taking in the news yet. "When I went away Mr. Ollivera, hadn't come; he was expected; and my wife—Halloa!"

The cause of the concluding exclamation was a new surprise, great as any the speaker had met with yet. Mr. Butterby, his keen eyes strained forward from their enclosed depths, touched him on the arm with authority to enjoin silence.

The young woman—it would be no offence against taste to call her a lady, with her good looks, her good manners, her usually calm demeanour—whom Mr. Jones had recognized as his wife's sister, had come forward to the grave. Kneeling down, she bent her face in her hands, perhaps praying; then lifted it, rose, and seemed about to address the crowd. Her hands were clasped and raised before her; her bonnet had fallen back from her face and her bright flaxen hair.

"It is Alletha Rye, isn't it, sir?" he dubiously cried.

"Hold your noise!" said Mr. Butterby.

"I think it would be a wicked thing to let you disperse this night with a false belief on your minds," began Miss Rye, her clear voice sounding quite loud and distinct in the hushed silence. "Wicked in the sight of God; unkind and unjust to the dead. Listen to my words, please, all you who hear me. I believe that a dreadful injury has been thrown upon Mr. Ollivera's memory; I solemnly believe that he did not die by his own hand. Heaven hears me assert it."

The solemn tone, the strange words, the fair appearance of the young woman, with her good and refined face deathly pale now, and the moonlight playing on her light hair, awed the listeners into something like statues. The silence continued unbroken until Miss Rye moved away, which she did at once and with a rather quick step in the direction of the road, pulling her bonnet on her head as she went, drawing her shawl round her. Even Mr. Jones made neither sound nor movement until she had disappeared, so entire was his astonishment.

"Was there ever heard the like of that?" he exclaimed, when he at length drew breath. "Do you think she's off her head, sir?"

He received no answer, and turned to look at Mr. Butterby. That gentleman had his note-book out, and was pencilling something down in it by moonlight.

"I never see such a start as this—take it for all in all," continued Mr. Jones to himself and the air, thus thrown upon his own companionship.

"And I'd not swear that you've seen the last of it," remarked Mr. Butterby, closing his note-case with a click.

"Well, sir, goodnight to you," concluded Mr. Jones. "I must make my way home afore the house is locked up, or I shall get a wigging from my wife. Sure to get that in any case, now this has happened," he continued, ruefully. "She'll say I'm always away when I'm wanted at home in particular."

He went lightly enough over the graves to the opposite and more frequented side of the churchyard, thus avoiding the assemblage; and took his departure. There being nothing more to see, the people began to take theirs. Having gazed their fill at the grave—just as if the silent, undemonstrative earth could give them back a response—they slowly made their way down the side-path to the high-road, and turned towards the city, one group after another.

By one o'clock the last straggler had gone, and Mr. Butterby came forth from his post behind the sheltering gravestone. He had his reasons, perhaps, for remaining behind the rest, and for wishing to walk home alone.

However that might be, he gave their progress a good margin of space, for it was ten minutes past one when he turned out of the churchyard. He had just gained the houses, when he saw before him a small knot of people emerge from a side-turning, as if they had not taken the direct route in coming from the heart of the city. Mr. Butterby recognized one or two of them, and whisked into a friendly doorway until they had passed by.

Letting them get on well ahead, he turned back and followed in their wake. That they were on their way to the grave, appeared evident: and the acute officer wondered why. A thought crossed him that possibly they might be about to take up what had been laid there.

He went into the churchyard by the front gate, and made his way cautiously across it, keeping under the shadow of the grey church walls. Thence, stooping as he crossed the open ground, and dodging behind first one grave then another, he took up his former position against the high stone. They were at the grave now, and he began to deliberate whether, if his thought should prove correct, he should or should not officially interrupt proceedings. Getting his eyes to the open fretwork of the stone, Mr. Butterby looked out. And what he saw struck him with a surprise equal to any recently exhibited by Mr. Jones: he, the experienced police official, who knew the world so thoroughly as to be surprised at little or nothing.

Standing at the head of the grave was a clergyman in his surplice and hood. Four men were grouped around him, one of whom held a lantern so that its light fell upon the clergyman's book. He was beginning to read the burial service. They stood with bowed heads, their hats off. The night had grown cold, but Mr. Butterby took off his.

"I am the resurrection and the life, saith the Lord: he that believeth in me, though he were dead, yet shall he live: and whosoever liveth and believeth in me shall never die."

The solemn words doubly solemn at that time and place, came distinctly to the official ears. Perhaps in all the times he had heard them during his whole life—many and many that it had been—they had never so impressed him. But habit is strong; and Mr. Butterby found himself taking observations ere the psalm had well commenced, even while he was noticing how heartily the alternate verses were given by the spectators.

Three of them around the grave he recognized; the other one and the clergyman he did not. Of those three, one was a tall, fine man of forty years, Kene, the barrister; the next was a cousin of the deceased, Frank Greatorex, whom Mr. Butterby only knew by seeing him in the inquest-room, where he tendered some slight evidence; the third was a gentleman of the city. Neither the clergyman nor the one who held the light did Mr. Butterby remember to have seen before. The elder and other cousin of the deceased was not present, though Mr. Butterby looked for him; he had been the principal witness on the inquest—Mr. Bede Greatorex.

The officer could but notice also how singularly solemn, slow, and impressive was the clergyman's voice as he read those portions of the service that relate more particularly to the deceased and the faith in which he has died. "In sure and certain hope of the Resurrection to eternal life." He almost made a pause between each word, as if he would impress on his hearers that it was his own belief the deceased had so died. And again, "Blessed are the dead which die in the Lord." And towards the end, in the collect, in the beseeching prayer that when we depart this life we may rest in Christ, "as our hope is this our brother doth." It was not to be mistaken that the clergyman, at least, held firm faith in the absence of guilt of the deceased in regard to his own death. As indeed the reading of the service over him proved.

With the Amen of the concluding benediction, there ensued a silence; every head was bowed in prayer. The clergyman was the first to look up. He waited until the rest did.

"Allow me to say a word ere we depart," he began then, in a low tone; which nevertheless quick-eared Mr. Butterby distinctly caught. "From the bottom of my heart, I believe a foul deed of murder to have been committed on my good and dear brother. It shall be the business of my life to endeavour to bring it to light, to clear his name from the cruel stain pronounced upon it; and my whole time apart from what must be spent in my appointed duties, shall be devoted to this end. So help me, Heaven!"

"Amen!" responded the young man who stood by Mr. Kene.

"So! he's the deceased man's brother" was Mr. Butterby's comment on the clergyman, as he saw him take off his surplice and roll it up.

Blowing out the light in the lantern, they silently took their departure. Mr. Butterby watched them away, and then finally took his, his mind in full work.

"Just the same thing that the girl, Alletha Rye, said! It's odd. I didn't see any doubt about the business: in spite of what Kene said at the inquest; neither did the coroner; and I'm sure the jury didn't. Dicky Jones was right, though. Take it for all in all, it's the queerest start we've had in this town for many a day."

CHAPTER II

UP TO THE MONDAY EVENING

On the Saturday previous to the events recorded in the last chapter, the cathedral city had been the scene of unusual bustle. The judges came in from Oxford to hold the Spring Assize, bringing in their wake the customary multiplicity of followers: attendants, officers, barristers, and others. Some of the witnesses in the different cases to be tried, civil and criminal also came in that day, to remain until they should be wanted the following week: so that the town was full.

Amidst the barristers who arrived was Mr. Ollivera. He was a young man; and it was only the second time he had come on circuit. After leaving college he had travelled a good deal, and also sojourned in different foreign countries, acquiring legal experience, and did not take up his profession at home as early as some do. A fresh-coloured, pleasing, bright looking man was he, his curly hair of a light auburn, his eyes blue, his figure elastic and of middle height. All the world liked John Ollivera. He was essentially of a practical nature, of sound sense, of pure mind and habits, holding a reverence for all things holy; and in every respect just the last man who could have been suspected of a tendency to lay violent hands on himself.

He had written to secure his former lodgings at Mr. Jones's in High Street, and proceeded to them at once on arriving at the station. It was the third time he had lodged there. At the previous assizes in July he had gone there first; and the whole of the month of October, during the long vacation, he had been there again, having, as people supposed, taken a liking to the town. So that this was the third time.

He got in between six and seven on the Saturday evening. Ordered tea and two mutton chops, which were got for him at once, and then went out to pay a visit to a lady who lived within the precincts of the cathedral. She was a widow; her husband, Colonel Joliffe, having died about a year before, leaving her with a slender income and three expensive daughters. During the colonel's lifetime they had lived in good style, about two miles from the town; but a great part of his means died with him, and Mrs. Joliffe then took a small house in the city and had to retrench in all her ways. Which was a terrible mortification to the young ladies.

To this lady's house Mr. Ollivera took his way when his frugal dinner was over. He spent a couple of hours with them, and then returned to his rooms and got out his law papers, over which he remained until twelve o'clock, when he went to bed. He occupied the drawing-room, which was on the first floor over the shop, and looked to the street; and the bedroom behind it. On the following day, Sunday, he attended early prayers in the cathedral at eight o'clock, staying to partake of the Sacrament, and also the later service at eleven, when the judges and corporation were present. In the afternoon he attended the cathedral again, going to it with the Miss Joliffes; dined at home at five, which was also Mrs. Joliffe's dinner hour, and spent the rest of the evening at her house. Mrs. Jones, his landlady, who had a vast amount of shrewd observation—and a shrewd tongue too on occasions, as well as a sharp one—gave it as her opinion that he must be courting one of the Miss Joliffes. He had been with them a little in his few days' sojourn at the July assizes, and a great deal with them during his stay in October.

On Monday morning the trials commenced, and Mr. Ollivera, though he had no cause on, was in court a great portion of the day. He left it in the afternoon, telling Mr. Kene that he had an appointment for half-past three, a disagreeable commission that had been entrusted to him, he added, and must go and keep it. About half-past four he appeared at his rooms; Mrs. Jones met him in the hall, and spoke to him as he went upstairs. When his dinner was sent up at five, the maid found him buried in a heap of law papers. Hastily clearing a space at one end of the table, he told her to put the dinner there. In less than half an hour the bell was rung for the things to be taken away, and Mr. Ollivera was then bending over his papers again.

The papers no doubt related to a cause in which he was to appear the following day. It was a civil action, touching some property in which Mrs. Joliffe was remotely though not actively interested. The London solicitors were the good old firm of Greatorex and Greatorex; Mr. Ollivera was a relative of the house; nephew of old Mr. Greatorex, in fact; and to him had been confided the advocacy of the cause. The name of the local solicitor it does not signify to mention. It was not a very important cause: but a new barrister thinks all his causes important, and Mr. Ollivera was an earnest, painstaking man, sparing himself no trouble that could conduce to success. He had declined a proffered dinner engagement for that evening, but accepted an invitation for the next. So much was known of his movements up to the Monday evening.

On that same evening, Mr. Bede Greatorex arrived at the station by the six o'clock train from London; took a fly, and was driven to the Star and Garter Hotel. He was the son of old Mr. Greatorex, and the second partner in the firm. His journey down had reference to the next day's action: something new had unexpectedly arisen; some slight information been gained of a favourable nature, and Mr. Greatorex, senior, had despatched his son to confer with Mr. Ollivera in preference to writing or telegraphing. Bede Greatorex was nothing loth, and entered on his flying journey with high good-humour, intending to be back in London by the following midday. He was a tall, fine-looking man, in face not unlike Mr. Ollivera, except that his hair and eyes were dark, and his complexion a clear, pale olive; his age about thirty-four. The cousins were cordial friends.

On arriving at the Star and Garter he declined refreshment then, having taken an early dinner before leaving town and asked to be directed to Mr. Ollivera's lodgings in High Street: which was readily done, High Street being in a direct line with the hotel. Mr. Bede Greatorex gained the house, and found it to be one of commodious proportions, the lower part occupied as a hosier's shop, whose windows were of plate-glass. Over the door in the middle was inscribed "Richard Jones, hosier and patent shirt-front maker." There was a side entrance, wide and rather handsome; the house altogether being a good one. Ringing at the side bell, he inquired of the answering servant for Mr. Ollivera, and was at once shown up to him.

Mr. Ollivera was seated at the table, his back to the door. The papers he had been engaged upon were neatly stacked now, as if done with; he appeared to be writing a note; and a pistol lay at his elbow. All this was shown both to Mr. Bede Greatorex and the maid, by the bright flame of the moderator lamp; then lighted.

"Well, John!" cried the visitor, in a gay, laughing tone, before the girl could speak. "Don't be surprised at seeing me."

Mr. Ollivera turned round at the voice and evidently was surprised: surprised and pleased.

"Why, Bede!" he cried, starting up. "I'd as soon have expected to see a ghost."

They shook hands heartily, and Mr. Bede Greatorex sat down. The maid, to save coming up again to ask, took the opportunity of inquiring when Mr. Ollivera would like tea; and was answered that he might not want any; if he did, he'd ring: he might be going out. As the servant shut the door she heard the visitor begin to explain his errand, and that his father had sent him in preference to writing. Her ears were always full of curiosity.

In about an hour's time, Mr. Bede Greatorex departed. A young man belonging to the house, Alfred Jones, who happened to be passing up the stairs when Mr. Greatorex was quitting the drawing-room, heard that gentleman make an appointment with Mr. Ollivera for the morning.

Mr. Bede Greatorex walked back to the hotel, ordered a fire made in his bedroom against night, took a glass of brandy-and-water, for he felt cold, washed the travelling dust off his face and hands, which he had not done before, had his coat brushed, and went out again. It was nine o'clock then, and he bent his steps quickly towards the cathedral to call on Mrs. Joliffe, having to inquire the way. It took him through High Street again, and as he passed his cousin's lodgings, the same servant who had shown him in was standing at the front-door, recognized him and dropped a curtsey.

In the drawing-room with Mrs. Joliffe were her three daughters, Louisa, Clare, and Mary; some three or four friends were also assembled. They were astonished to see Mr. Bede Greatorex: none of them knew him well, except Louisa, who had paid a long visit to his father's house the previous year. She changed colour when he was announced: and it may have been that his voice took a tenderer tone as it addressed her; his hand lingered longer in clasping hers than it need have done. She was an excessively fashionable young lady: not very young, perhaps six or seven-and-twenty: and if Bede Greatorex coveted her for a wife it was to be hoped his pockets were well lined. He spoke just a word to Mrs. Joliffe of having come down on a mission to Mr. Ollivera; not stating explicitly what it was; and said he was going back home in the morning.

"We are expecting Mr. Ollivera here tonight," observed Mrs. Joliffe. "He is late."

"Are you?" was the reply of Mr. Greatorex. "John said he might be going out, I remember, but I did not know it was to your house. Don't make too sure of him, Mrs. Joliffe, he seemed idle, and complained of headache."

"I suppose he is busy," remarked Mrs. Joliffe. "All you law people are busy at assize time."

"Louisa, is it as it should be between us?" whispered Bede Greatorex, in an opportunity that occurred when they were alone near the piano.

"Don't be silly, Mr. Greatorex," was the answer.

"Silly!"

She bent her bead, not speaking.

"What do you mean, Louisa? Our engagement was entered upon deliberately: you gave me every hope. You cannot play with me now. Speak, Louisa."

He had taken possession of her hand, and was keeping her before him; his dark eyes, gleaming with their doubt and love, looked straight into hers.

"What?" she faintly asked. "Why do you question it?"

"Because your manner is strange: you have avoided me ever since I came in."

"The surprise was so great."

"Surely a pleasant surprise. I intended it as such. Do you suppose I should have cared to come down on this business to Mr. Ollivera, when writing would have answered every purpose? No: I came to see you. And to learn why—"

"Not now. Don't you see mamma is looking at me?"

"And what though she is? I should have liked to speak to your mother tonight, but for—"

"Not tonight. I pray you not tonight. Take another opportunity."

The words reassured him.

"Then, Louisa, it is all right between us."

"Yes, yes, of course it is. You offended me, Bede, last January, and I—I have been vexed. I'll write to you as soon as you get back home, and explain everything."

He pressed her hand with a lingering touch, and then released it. There was nothing in the wide world so coveted by Bede Greatorex as that false hand of hers: as many things, fair outside, false within, are coveted by us poor mortals, blind at the best. But Miss Joliffe looked half scared as she left him for a safer part of the room; her eyes and manner were alike restless. Bede followed her, and they were talking together at intervals in an undertone during the rest of the evening. Louisa being evidently ill at ease, but striving to conceal it.

At a quarter to eleven Mr. Bede Greatorex took his departure. In passing up High Street, his cousin's lodgings were on the opposite side of the way. He momentarily halted and stepped off the pavement as if he would have crossed to go in, and then hesitated, for the sitting-room was in darkness.

"The light's out: he's gone to bed, I dare say," said Mr. Greatorex, speaking aloud. "No good to disturb him." And a tradesman, who happened to be fastening his side-door and had got it about an inch open, overheard the words Mr. Greatorex having doubtless been quite unaware that he spoke to an auditor.

Towards the top of High Street he met Mr. Kene, the barrister. The latter, after expressing some surprise at seeing him, and assuming he had come direct from Mr. Ollivera's, asked whether the latter was in.

"In and in bed," replied Mr. Greatorex.

"Indeed! Why it's not eleven o'clock."

"At any rate, there's no light in his room, or I should have gone up. He complained of headache: perhaps he has gone to bed early to sleep it off."

"I want to see him particularly," said the barrister. "Are you sure he is in bed?"

"You can go and ascertain, Kene. Ring the people of the house up, should they have gone to bed too. I could see no light anywhere."

Mr. Kene did not care to ring people up, and decided to leave his business with Mr. Ollivera until the morning. He had been dining with some fellows he said, and had no idea how the time was running on. Linking his arm within that of Bede Greatorex, they walked together to the Star, and there parted. Mr. Greatorex went up at once to his chamber, stirred the fire into a blaze, rang for the waiter, and ordered another glass of hot brandy-and-water.

"I think I must have taken cold," he observed to the man when it was brought to him. "There has been a chill upon me ever since I came here."

"Nothing more likely, sir," returned the waiter. "Them trains are such draughty things."

However Mr. Greatorex hoped he should be all right in the morning. He gave directions to be called at a quarter before eight, and the night wore on.

Some time before that hour chimed out from the cathedral clock, when the morning had come, he found himself aroused by a knocking at his door. A waiter, speaking from the outside, said that something had happened to Mr. Ollivera. Mr. Bede Greatorex, thinking the words odd, and not best pleased to be thus summarily disturbed, possibly from dreams of Louisa Joliffe, called out from the downy pillow (in rather a cross tone, it must be confessed) to know what had happened to Mr. Ollivera: and was answered that he was dead.

Springing out of bed, and dressing himself quickly, Bede Greatorex went downstairs, and found that Kene, who had brought the news, was gone again, leaving word that he had gone back to High Street. Mr. Greatorex hastened to follow.

The tale to be told was very singular, very sad, and Bede Greatorex could not help shivering as he heard it. His cold was upon him still. It appeared that nothing more had been seen or heard of Mr. Ollivera after Mr. Greatorex left him the previous evening. Mrs. Jones, the mistress of the house, had gone out at seven, when the shop closed, to sit by the bed-side of a dying relative; her sister, Miss Rye, was also out: the maid left in charge, the only servant the house kept, had taken the opportunity to spend her time in the street; standing now at her own door, now at other doors half a score yards off, as she could get neighbours' servants to gossip with. About half-past ten it occurred to the maid that she might as well go up and inquire if Mr. Ollivera wanted anything: perhaps the fact of his not having rung at all struck her as singular. She knew he had not gone out, or she must have seen him, for she had contrived to keep a tolerably steady lookout on the street door, however far she had wandered from it. Up she went, knocked at the door, got no answer, opened it, saw that the room was in darkness, and regarded it as a sure proof that Mr. Ollivera had left the room for the night, for he never put the lamp out in any other case.

"He's gone to bed early tonight," thought the girl, shutting the door again. "I hope to goodness he didn't ring, and me not hear it. Wouldn't missis fly out at me!"

And when Mrs. Jones came in, as she did soon after the girl got downstairs again, and inquired after Mr. Ollivera, she was told he had gone to bed.

Now it appeared that Miss Rye sat over the sitting-room fire (a parlour behind the shop, underneath Mr. Ollivera's bedroom) for some time after the rest of the house had retired to rest. When at length she went to bed, she was unable to sleep. Towards morning she dropped into a doze and was awakened (according to her own account) by a dream. A very vivid dream, that startled and unnerved her. She dreamt she saw Mr. Ollivera in his sitting-room—dead. And, as she seemed to look at him, a terrible amount of self-reproach, far greater than any she could ever experience in life, rushed over her mind, for not having gone in earlier to discover him. It was this feeling that awoke her: it had seemed that he cast it on her, that it came out direct to her from his dead presence, cold and lifeless though he was. So real did it all appear, that for some minutes after Miss Rye awoke, she could not believe it to be only a dream. Turning to look at her watch she saw it was half-past six, and the sun had risen. An early riser always, for she had to get her living by dressmaking, Miss Rye got up and dressed herself: but she could not throw off the impression made upon her; and a little before seven she went down and opened the door of Mr. Ollivera's sitting-room. Not so much to see whether it might be true or not, as to show to herself by ocular demonstration that it was not true: she might forget the impression then.

But it was true. What was Miss Rye's horror and astonishment at seeing him, Mr. Ollivera, there! At the first moment of opening the door, she observed nothing unusual. The white blinds were down before the windows; the tables, chairs, and other furniture were as customary; but as she stood looking in, she saw in an easy-chair near the table, whose back was towards her, the head of Mr. Ollivera. With a strange bounding-on of all her pulses; with a dread fear at her heart, that caused it to cease beating, Miss Rye went in and looked at him, and then flew out of the room, uttering startled cries.

The cries arose the house. Mrs. Jones, the young man Alfred Jones, and the servant-maid came flocking forth: the two former were nearly dressed; the maid had been about her work downstairs. Mr. Ollivera lay back in the easy-chair, dead and cold. The right arm hung down over the side, and immediately underneath it on the carpet, looking as if it had dropped from the hand, lay the discharged pistol.

The servant and Alfred Jones ran two ways: the one for a doctor, the other to Mr. Kene the barrister, who had been intimate with Mr. Ollivera; Mrs. Jones, a shrewd, clever woman, locking the room up exactly as it was, until they should arrive.

But now, by a singular coincidence, it happened that Mr. Butterby, abroad betimes, was the first to meet the running servant-maid, and consequently, he was first on the scene. The doctor and Mr. Kene came next, and then Bede Greatorex. Such was the story as it greeted Bede's ears.

On the table, just as both he and the servant had seen them the night before, were the neatly-stacked law papers. Also a folded legal document that had been brought from town by himself, Bede Greatorex. There were also pens, ink, and a sheet of note-paper, on which some lines were written. They were as follows:—

"My Dear Friend,—It is of no use. Nothing more can be done. Should I never see you again, I beg you once for all to believe me when I say that I have made efforts, though they have been ineffectual. And when

"The pistol is ready to my hand. Goodbye."

The first portion of this letter, up to the point of the abrupt breaking off, was written in Mr. Ollivera's usual steady hand. The latter portion was scrawling, trembling, and blotted; the writing bearing but a faint resemblance to the rest. Acute Mr. Butterby remarked that it was just the kind of writing an agitated man might pen, who was about to commit an evil deed. There was no clue as to whom the note had been intended for, but it appeared to point too evidently to the intention of self-destruction. Nevertheless, there was one at least who doubted.

"Is it so, think you?" asked Mr. Kene, in a low tone, as he stood by the side of Bede Greatorex, who was mechanically turning over the papers on the table one by one.

"Is it what?" asked Bede, looking up, his tone sharp with pain.

"Self-destruction. There never lived a man less likely to commit it than your cousin, John Ollivera."

"As I should have thought," returned Mr. Greatorex. "But if it is not that, what else can it be?"

"There is one other possible solution, at least: putting any idea of accident aside."

The supposition of accident had not occurred to Bede Greatorex. A gleam of surprised cheerfulness crossed his face.

"Do you indeed think it could have been an accident, Kene? Then—"

"No; I think it could not have been," interrupted the barrister. "I said, putting the idea of that aside: it is the most improbable of any. I alluded to the other alternative."

Mr. Greatorex understood his meaning, and shrunk from its unpleasantness. "Who would harm Ollivera, Kene? He had not an enemy in the world."

"So far as we know. But I declare to you, Greatorex, I think it the more likely thing of the two."

Bede Greatorex shook his head. The facts, so far as they were yet disclosed, seemed decisive and unmistakable.

They passed into the bedroom. It was all just as the servant had left it the past evening, ready for the occupation of Mr. Ollivera. On a small table lay his Prayer-book, and the pocket Bible he was wont to carry with him in travelling. Bede Greatorex felt a sudden faintness steal over him as he looked, and leaned for a few moments against the wall.

But he had no time for indulging grief. He went out, inquiring for the telegraph office, and sent a message with the news to his father in town, softening it as well as circumstances allowed: as we all like to do at first when ill news has to be told. He simply stated that John (the familiar name Mr. Ollivera was known by at home) had died suddenly. The message brought down his brother, Frank Greatorex, some hours later.

To say that the town was thrown into a commotion almost equal to that of Mrs. Jones's house, would be superfluous. A young barrister, known to many of the inhabitants, who had come in with the judges only on Saturday; who was to have led in a cause in the Nisi Prius Court on that very morning, Tuesday, and to be junior in another cause set down for Wednesday, in which Mr. Kene, the experienced and renowned Queen's Counsel, led, had been found dead! And by such a death! It took the public by storm. Mrs. Jones's shop was besieged to an extent that she had to put up her shutters; High Street was impassable: and all those in the remotest degree connected with the deceased or with the circumstances, were followed about and stared at as though they were wild animals. Five hundred conjectures were hazarded and spoken: five hundred tales told that had no foundation. Perhaps the better way to collect the various items of fact together for the reader, will be to transcribe some of the evidence given before the coroner. The inquest was fixed to take place on the Wednesday morning, in the club-room of an inn lying conveniently near.

CHAPTER III

BEFORE THE CORONER

The coroner and jury assembled at an unusually early hour, for the convenience of Mr. Kene, who wished to be present. It had been thought that the only brother of the deceased, a clergyman, would have come down; but he had not arrived. After viewing the body, which lay still at Mrs. Jones's, the proceedings commenced. Medical testimony was given as to the cause of death—a pistol-shot that had penetrated the heart. The surgeon, Mr. Hurst, who had been called in at the first discovery on Tuesday morning, stated that to the best of his belief, death (which must have been instantaneous) had taken place early the previous evening, he should say about seven or eight o'clock. And this view was confirmed in rather a singular manner. Upon examining the quantity of oil in the lamp, which Mrs. Jones had herself filled, it was seen that it could not have burnt very much more than an hour: thus leaving it to be inferred that the deceased had put it out before committing the rash deed, and that it must have been done shortly after Mr. Bede Greatorex left him.

Alletha Rye was called. She spoke to the fact of finding Mr. Ollivera, dead; and electrified the court, when questioned as to why she had gone to the sitting-room, seeing that it was an entirely unusual thing for her to do, by saying that she went in to see whether Mr. Ollivera was there dead, or not. In the quietest, most composed manner possible, she related her singular dream, saying it had sent her to the room.

"Surely," said the coroner, "you did not expect to see Mr. Ollivera dead?"

"I cannot say I did! I went rather to convince myself that he was not there dead," was the witness's answer. "But the dream had been so vivid that I could not shake it from my mind; it made me uneasy, although my better reason did not put any faith in it whatever that it could be true. That is why I went to the room. And Mr. Ollivera lay dead in his chair, exactly as I had seen him in my dream."

The coroner, a practical man, did not know what to make of this statement: such evidence had never been tendered him before, and he eyed the witness keenly. To see her stand there in her black robes, tall, upright, of really dignified demeanour, with her fair features and good looks—but there were dark circles round her eyes today, and the soft colour had left her cheeks—to hear her tell of this in her sensible, calm accents, was something marvellous.

"Were you at home on Monday night?" asked the coroner. And it may as well be remarked that some of the questions put by him during the inquest, miscellaneous queries that did not appear to be quite in order, or have much to do with the point in question, had very probably their origin in the various rumours that had reached him, and in the doubt breathed into his ears by Mr. Kene. The coroner did not in the least agree with Mr. Kene; rather pitied the barrister as a visionary, for allowing himself to glance at such a doubt; but he was fond of diving to the bottom of things. Living in the same town, knowing all the jury personally, in the habit of exchanging a word of news with Mrs. Jones whenever he met her, the coroner may have been excused if the proceedings were slightly irregular, involving some gossip as well as law.

"No," replied the witness. "Except that I ran in for a few minutes. I had been at work that afternoon at a neighbour's, helping her to make a gown. I went in home to get a pattern."

"What time was that?"

"I cannot be particular as to the exact time. It must have been nearly eight."

"Did you see the deceased then?"

"No. I did not see any one except the servant. She was standing at the open street door. When I had been upstairs to get what I wanted I went out again."

"Did you hear any noise as you passed Mr. Ollivera's rooms?"

"Not any. I do not know anything more of the details, sir, than I have told you."

The next witness called was Mr. Bede Greatorex. He gave his evidence clearly, but at portions of it was evidently under the influence of some natural emotion, which he contrived to suppress. A man does not like to show such.

"My name is Bede Greatorex. I am the son of Mr. Greatorex, the well-known London solicitor, and second partner in the firm Greatorex and Greatorex. The deceased, John Ollivera, was my cousin, his father and my mother having been brother and sister. A matter of business arose connected with a cause to be tried in the Nisi Prius Court, in which Mr. Ollivera was to be the leading counsel, and my father despatched me down on Monday to communicate with him. I arrived by the six o'clock evening train, and was with him before half-past six. We held a business conference together; I stayed about an hour with him, and then went back to my hotel. I never afterwards saw him alive."

"I must put a few questions to you with your permission, Mr. Greatorex, for the satisfaction of the jury," observed the coroner.

"Put as many as you like, sir; I will answer them to the best of my ability," was the reply.

"First of all—what was the exact hour at which you reached Mr. Ollivera's rooms?"

"I should think it must have been about twenty minute after six. The train got in to time, six o'clock; I took a fly to the Star and Garter, and from thence walked at once to Mr. Ollivera's lodgings, the people at the hotel directing me. The whole could not have taken above twenty minutes."

"And how long did you remain with him?"

"An hour: perhaps rather more. I should think I left him about half-past seven. I was back at the hotel by quarter to eight, having walked slowly, looking at the different features of the streets as I passed. I had never been in the town before."

"Well, now, Mr. Greatorex, what was the manner of the deceased while you were with him? Did you perceive anything unusual?"

"Nothing at all. He was just as he always was, and very glad to see me. We"—the witness paused to swallow his emotion—"we had ever been the best of friends and companions. I thought him a little quiet, dull. As he sat, he bent his forehead on his hand and complained of headache, saying it had been close in court that day."

("True enough," murmured Mr. Kene.)

"The news you brought down to him was not bad news?" questioned the coroner.

"Quite the contrary. It was good: favourable to our cause."

"Did you see him write the note found on his table, or any portion of it?"

"When the servant showed me into the room, he appeared to be writing a note. As he sat down after shaking hands with me, he put the blotting paper over what he had written. He did not take it off again, or write at all while I remained."

"Was it the same note, think you, that was afterwards found?"

"I should think it likely. I noticed that some few lines only were written. About"—the witness paused a moment—"about the same quantity as in the first portion of the note."

"Did he put the blotting paper over it to prevent you seeing it, do you suppose, Mr. Greatorex?"

"I do not know. I thought he was only afraid it might get blotted. The ink was wet."

"Did any one come in while you were with him?"

"No. I wished him goodnight, intending to see him in the morning, and was shown out by some young man."

"Do you know to whom that note was written?"

"I have not the slightest idea. Neither do I know to what it alludes."

"Then—your theory, I presume, is—that he added that blotted concluding line after your departure? In fact, just when he was on the point of committing the rash act?"

"I do not see what else can be believed. The pen lay across the words when found, as if thrown there after writing them, and appeared to have caused the blots."

"Did he say anything to you about any appointment he had kept that afternoon?"

"Not anything."

"And now about the pistol, Mr. Greatorex. Did you see one on the table!"

"Yes."

"Did it not strike you as singular that it should be there?"

"Not at all. Mr. Ollivera never travelled anywhere without a pistol; it was a fancy he had. Some years ago, when in a remote part of Spain, he was attacked in his chamber at night, robbed, and rather seriously hurt; since then he has when travelling taken a pistol with him. I asked him what brought it on the table, and he said he had been putting a drop of oil on the lock.

"Did you know that it was loaded?"

"I did not. I really did not think much about it one way or the other. We were busy over the business on which I came down: and I knew as I have said, that he used to carry a pistol with him when travelling."

"Then—in point of fact, Mr. Greatorex, you can throw no positive light on this affair for us?"

The witness shook his head. "I wish I could. I have told you all I know."

"Do you think there can be any reasonable doubt—any doubt whatever—that he committed suicide?"

"I fear there can be none," replied Mr. Greatorex, in a low tone, and he shivered perceptibly as he gave it. It was a crime which Bede Greatorex had always held in shrinking, pitying abhorrence.

"One question more, and then we will release you and thank you for the clear manner in which you have given your evidence," said the coroner. "Did you see cause to suspect in that last interview that his mind was otherwise than in a sane state?"

"Oh no; certainly not."

"It was calm and clear as usual, for all you saw?"

"Quite so."

"Stay. There is one other point. Was the deceased in any kind of embarrassment, so far as your cognizance goes, pecuniary, or else?"

"I feel quite sure that he was in no pecuniary embarrassment whatever," returned the witness warmly, anxious to do justice to his cousin's memory. "As to any other kind of embarrassment, I cannot speak. I am aware of none; and I think he was one of the least likely men to get into any."

That was all. Mr. Greatorex bowed to the coroner and gave place to another witness. A little dark woman in black, with an old-fashioned black chip bonnet on, and silver threads beginning to mix with her black hair; but her eyebrows were very black still. Certainly no two women could present a greater contrast in appearance than she and Miss Rye, although they were sisters.

"Your name is Julia Jones," began the coroner's man, who knew Mrs. Jones intimately in private life.

"Yes, it is Julia Jones," in a tart voice, and with an accent on the "Jones," as if the name grated on her tongue. And Mrs. Jones was sworn.

After some preliminary evidence, touching Mr. Ollivera's previous visits to her, and the length of time he had stayed, which she entered upon of her own accord and was not checked, Mrs. Jones was asked what she knew of the calamity. How it was first brought to her knowledge.

"The first was through my sister, Alletha Rye shrieking out from the first-floor landing below, a little before seven o'clock on Tuesday morning," responded Mrs. Jones, in the same tart tone; which was, in fact, habitual to her. "I was in my bedroom, the front room on the second floor, dressed up to my petticoat, and out I flew, thinking she must be on fire. She said something about Mr. Ollivera, and I ran down, and saw him lying in the chair. Jones's nephew, in his waistcoat and shirtsleeves, and his face all in a lather, for he was shaving, got into the room when I did."

"When did you see the deceased last, Mrs. Jones?" was the next question put, after the witness had described the appearance of the room, the pistol on the carpet, the blotted note on the table, the quantity of oil in the lamp, and so forth.

"When did I see him last? why on the Monday afternoon, when he came in from court," responded Mrs. Jones. "I was crossing the hall at the foot of the stairs, between the parlour and the shop, as he came in. He looked tired, and I said so; and he answered that he had been about all day, in the court and elsewhere, and was tired. That's when I saw him last: never after, till I saw him in his chair, dead."

"You heard nothing of his movements on that evening?"

"I wasn't likely to hear it, seeing I went out as soon as the shop was shut. Before it, in fact, for I left Jones's nephew to put up the shutters. Old Jenkins is dying, as all the parish knows, and I went to sit with him and take him some beef-tea. Jones's nephew, he went out too, to his debating club, as he calls it. And precious debating it must be," continued Mrs. Jones, with additional tartness, "if the debaters are all as green and soft as he! Alletha Rye, she was at work at Mrs. Wilson's: and so, as ill-luck had it, all the house was out."

"Except your servant, Susan Marks," observed one of the jury. "She was left at home to keep house, we hear."

"And in a very pretty manner she did keep it!" retorted Mrs. Jones, as if she had taken a pint of vinegar to set her teeth on edge; when Susan Marks, at the back, gave a kind of groan, and burst into fresh tears. "Up the street here, down the street there, over the way at the doors yonder, staring, and gossiping, and gampusing—that's how she kept it. And on an assize night, of all nights in the year, to be airing her cap in the street, when barristers and other loose characters are about!"

The gratuitous compliment paid to the barristers raised a laugh, in spite of the sad inquiry the court had met upon. Mrs. Jones's epithet sounded, however, worse to others than to herself.

"And she could tell me, when I got in just before eleven, that Mr. Ollivera had gone to bed!" resumed that lady, in intense aggravation: "which, of course, I believed, and we all went up to our rooms, suspecting nothing. Let me ever catch her out at the street door again! home she'll go to Upton Snodsbury."

Groans from the back, in the vicinity of Susan Marks.

"Had you known previously, Mrs. Jones, that Mr. Ollivera was in the habit of bringing with him a loaded pistol?"

"Yes; for he told me. One day last October, when I was up dusting his drawing-room, he had got it out of the case. I said I should not like to have such a weapon near me, and he laughed at that. He used to keep it on the chest of drawers in his bedroom: that is, the case; and I suppose the thing itself was inside."

"Your husband was not at home when this unfortunate event happened, Mrs. Jones?"

"No, he was not," assented Mrs. Jones; and it was as if she had swallowed a whole gallon of vinegar now. "He has been off to Wales last week and this, and is as likely as not to be there next."

Another question or two, not of much import, and Mrs. Jones gave place to her husband's nephew. He was known in the town for a steady, well-conducted young man, quite trustworthy. He had not very much to tell.

"My name is Alfred Jones," he said, "and I live with my uncle, Richard Jones, as assistant in the shop—"

"—Which wouldn't want any assistant at all, if Jones stayed at home and stuck to his duties," put in Mrs. Jones's sharp voice from the back. Upon which she was admonished to hold her tongue: and the witness continued.

"On Monday night, I put up the shutters at seven, as usual in the winter season; I changed my coat, washed my hands, and went to the debating club in Goose Lane. Soon after I got there I found I had forgotten a book that I ought to have taken back to the club's library. The time for my keeping it was up, and as we are fined twopence if we keep a book over time, I went back to get it. It was then half-past seven. The street door was open, and Susan, the servant, was standing at it outside. As I ran up the stairs, the book being in my bedroom at the top of the house, I heard the drawing-room door open just after I passed it; I turned my head, and saw a gentleman come out. He—"

"Did you know him, witness?"

"No, sir, he was a stranger to me. I know him now for Mr. Greatorex. He was talking to Mr. Ollivera. They were making an appointment for the next morning."

"Did you hear what was said?"

"Yes, sir. As I looked round at the gentleman he was turning his head back to the room, and said, 'Yes, you may rely upon my coming early; I'll be here before nine o'clock. Goodnight, John.' Those were, I think, the exact words, sir."

"Did you see Mr. Ollivera?"

"No, sir, he did not come out, and the gentleman only pushed the door back a little while he spoke. If it had been wide open I couldn't have seen in; I was too far, some two or three steps up the stairs. I turned back then to attend Mr. Greatorex to the street door. After that I ran up for my book, and left the house again. I was not two minutes in it altogether."

"Did you see Mr. Ollivera as you came down?"

"No, sir. The drawing-room door was closed, as Mr. Greatorex had left it. I never saw or heard of Mr. Ollivera again until Miss Rye's screams brought me down the next morning. That is all I know."

"At what hour did you go home on Monday evening?"

"It was close upon eleven, sir. We generally disperse at half-past ten but we stayed late that night. Mrs. Jones and Miss Rye had not long come in, and were in the sitting-room."

The next witness called was Susan Marks. The young woman, what with her own heinous offences on the eventful night, the dreadful calamity itself, and the reproaches of her mistress, had been in a state of tears ever since, fresh bursts breaking forth at the most unseasonable times.

Susan Marks, aged nineteen, native of Upton Snodsbury, cook and servant-of-all-work to Mrs. Jones. Such was the young woman's report of herself, as well as could be heard for her sobs and tears. She was attired neatly and well; in a print mourning gown and straw bonnet trimmed with black; her face, that would otherwise have been fresh and clear, had small patches of red upon it, the result of the many tears and of perpetual rubbing.

"Now, young woman," said the coroner briskly, as if he thought time was being lost, "what have you to tell us of the events of Monday night?"

"Nothing, sir," replied the young woman, in a fresh burst of grief that could be called nothing less than a howl. "I never see Mr. Ollivera at all after I showed the gentleman up to him."

"Well, let us hear about that. What time was it?"

"It was past six, sir; I don't know how much. I had washed up Mr. Ollivera's dinner things, and was putting the plates and dishes on the dresser shelves, when Mr. Ollivera's bell rang. It was for his lamp, which I lighted and took in: he always wanted it afore daylight was well over when he was busy. He seemed in a hurry, and drew down the window-blinds himself. I lighted the gas-burner outside the drawing-room door, and went back to the kitchen. No sooner was I there—leastways it couldn't have been five minutes—when there came a ring at the street door bell. I went to answer it, and saw a tall gentleman, who asked for Mr. Ollivera, and I showed him upstairs to the drawing-room."

"Who was that gentleman?"

"It was Mr. Greatorex. But I didn't know him then, sir. I thought it was a barrister; he didn't give no name."

"Did you see Mr. Ollivera when you took this gentleman up?"

"Yes, sir. He was sitting with his back towards us, writing at the table, and I see the things on it. I hadn't noticed them much when I took the lamp in. I see the papers put together tidy, which had been all about when he was at his dinner. I think he was very busy that evening," urged the witness, as if the fact might plead an excuse for what afterwards took place: "when I removed the dinner things he told me to put the sherry wine away on the sideboard; sometimes if he wanted to drink any, he'd have it left on the table."

"Did he seem glad to see Mr. Greatorex?"

"Yes, sir, very. They shook hands, and Mr. Greatorex began telling him what he had come down about, and said his father had sent him in place of telegrumming. I asked Mr. Ollivera what time he'd like to have tea, but he said he didn't know whether he should take any, he might be going out; if he wanted it, he'd ring. How was I to think, after that, that I ought to have went up to him, to see how he might be getting on, which missis has been a going on at me ever since for not doing?" demanded the witness with a stream of tears.

"Come, come! there, wipe your face," said one of the jury, with gruff kindness. And the questions went on, and the witness's replies.

It was about an hour that Mr. Greatorex stayed, she thought She saw him come out at the street door, and go away. Well, yes, she was a yard or two off, at a neighbour's door, next house but one. After missis went out and the shop was shut, and Alfred Jones went out, and there wasn't nobody indoors to want her, she thought it no harm to stand at the street door a bit: and if she did go a step or two away from it, she never took her eyes off the door, and no person could go in or out without her seeing them and that she'd swear. She saw Mr. Greatorex come out and walk away up High Street; and she never heard no sound in the house whatsoever.

"Did any one go in?" the coroner asked.

"No, sir, not a soul—barring Alfred Jones and Miss Rye Alfred Jones came back after he first went out, saying that he had forgot something, and he went upstairs to fetch it. He wasn't there no time; and it was while he was up there that Mr. Greatorex came down and left. Soon after that, Miss Rye, she come in, and went upstairs, and was there ever so long."

"What do you call 'ever so long'?"

"Well, sir, I'm sure she was there a quarter of an hour," returned the witness, in a quick, positive sort of tone, as if the fact of Miss Rye's being there so long displeased her. "I ought to know; and me a-standing inside the doorsill, afraid to move off it for fear she should come out."

"Were you alone?"

"Well, yes, sir, I was. Mary, the housemaid at the big linendraper's next door but one, can bear me out that I was, for she was there all the time, talking to me."

Perhaps the coroner thought the answer savoured of Hibernianism, for something like a smile crossed his face.

"And you heard no sound whatever upstairs all the evening, Susan Marks? You saw no one, except the persons mentioned, go in or come out; no stranger?"

"I never heard no sound, and never saw no stranger at all," said the witness, earnestly. "I never even saw Godfrey Pitman leave. But I b'lieve he was away earlier."

The concluding assertion fell with some surprise on the room; there ensued a pause, and the coroner lifted his head sharply. Godfrey Pitman? Who was Godfrey Pitman?

"Who is Godfrey Pitman, witness?"

"It was the lodger at the top of the house, sir. He had the front bedroom there—and a fine dance it was to carry his meals up. Missis gave him the offer of eating them in the little room off the kitchen, but I suppose he was too proud to come down. Anyway, he didn't come."

"Is he lodging there now?"

"Oh no, sir, he was only there a week and a day, and left on the Monday. He was a traveller in the spectacles line, he told me, passing through the town; which he likewise wore himself sometimes. Well, sir, I never see him go at all, and he didn't never give me a shilling for having waited on him and carried his trays up all them stairs."

The girl had told apparently what she knew, and the coroner requested Mrs. Jones to come in again. He questioned her about the lodger.

"It was a person of the name of Pitman," she answered, readily. "He was only passing through the town, and occupied the room for a week."

"Who was he?" asked the coroner. "Did you know him?"

"I didn't know him from Adam," answered Mrs. Jones, tartly; "I didn't know anything about him. I called him Alletha Rye's lodger, not mine, for it was she who picked him up. He may have told her all about himself, for aught I can say: she seemed to take a desperate fancy to him, and mended his travelling bag. He didn't tell me. Not but what he seemed a civil, respectable man."

"When did he leave you, Mrs. Jones?"

"On Monday, about half-past four, when he took the five o'clock train for Birmingham. He came to the inner shop door as he was going out, and thanked me for my kindness, as he called it, in taking him in at a pitch; he said it was not what every one would do for a stranger. Neither is it."

"You are sure he left you at that hour?"

"Have I got the use of my eyes and senses?" demanded Mrs. Jones. "Sure! I walked to the side door after him, and saw him go up the street towards the railway with his blue bag. Of course I am sure. It was as I crossed the hall, on my way back, that Mr. Ollivera came in, and I spoke to him as I have told you."

It was therefore placed beyond doubt that the lodger, Mr. Pitman, could have no part or act in what took place in the house later. The coroner would have dismissed the subject summarily, but that one of the jury, a man who liked to hear himself talk, expressed an opinion that it might be satisfactory if they questioned Miss Rye. With a gesture of impatience the coroner called for her.

She came in, was asked what she knew of Mr. Pitman, and stood before them in silence, her face a little bent, her forefinger, encased in its well-fitting black kid glove, pressed lightly on her lip, her clear blue eye looking out straight before her. It was as if she were trying to recall something to her memory.

"I recollect now," she said, after a minute "I could not remember what took me up by the railway station where I met him. It was on last Sunday week, in the afternoon. Mrs. Hillman, who lives up there, was ill, and I had been to see her. As I was leaving her house, towards dusk, a few passengers were coming down from the station. I stood on the doorstep until they should have passed; and one of them, who had a blue bag in his hand, like those that lawyers' clerks carry, stopped and asked me if I had a room in my house that I could let him occupy for a week. I supposed he took the house where I stood for mine. He went on to say he was a traveller and stranger, had never before been to the town, felt very poorly, and would very much wish to be spared the bustle of an hotel. I knew that my sister, Mrs. Jones had a bedroom ready for letting," continued Miss Rye, "and I thought she might not object to oblige him; he spoke quite as a gentleman, and I felt rather sorry for him, for he looked haggard and ill. That is how it happened."

"And your sister admitted him, and he stayed the week?" cried the juror.

"Strictly speaking, I admitted him; for when we reached home I found Mrs. Jones had gone to sit with old Jenkins for the rest of the day. So I took it upon myself to do so. On Saturday last Mr. Pitman said he would, with our permission, remain a day over the week, and leave on Monday.

"And did he pay the rent, Miss Rye?" asked the juror, who perhaps had a doubt on the point.

"He paid the first week's rent as soon as he was admitted to the house, and gave a sovereign towards the purchase of his provisions," was the answer. "What remained he settled for on the Monday, previous to his departure by the five o'clock train for Birmingham."

"Who was he, witness? Where did he come from?"

"I really cannot tell much about him," was Miss Rye's reply. "I understood him to say he was a traveller; his name, as he wrote it down for us, was Godfrey Pitman. He was laid up with a bad cold and relaxed throat all the time he stayed, and borrowed some books of me to read."

There appeared to be no further scope for the exercise of the juror's powers; no possible loophole for bringing this departed Mr. Godfrey Pitman into connection with the death of Mr. Ollivera; and Miss Rye was allowed to depart.

Little more evidence was to be gleaned. Mr. Kene, tendering evidence, spoke of his long intimacy with the deceased, and of their last interview, when he was just the same that he ever had been: calm, cheerful, earnest-purposed. He could not understand, he added, how it was possible for Mr. Ollivera to have laid violent hands on himself—unless, indeed, the headache, of which he had complained, had proceeded from some derangement of the functions of the brain, and induced temporary insanity.

But this suggested theory was wholly incompatible with the letter that had been found, and with Mr. Bede Greatorex's testimony of the sane mind of the deceased when he quitted him. The jury shook their heads: keen-eyed Mr. Butterby, looking on unobtrusively from a remote nook of the room, shook his.

The inquest drew to a close; the one fatal element in the evidence being the letter found on the table. The coroner and jury debated upon their verdict with closed doors, and only re-admitted the public when they had decided: It did not take them long.

"Felo-de-se."

In accordance with the customary usage, a mandate was issued for a night interment, without Christian rites; and the undertaker promised to be ready for that same night.

The crowd filed out of the room, talking eagerly. That it was undoubtedly a case of self-murder, and that in the most unhappy sense of the word, none doubted. No, not one: even Mr. Kene began to waver.

As they were dispersing hither and thither along the street, there came hastily up a young man in the garb of a clergyman. It was the Reverend Henry William Ollivera, brother of the deceased gentleman. He had just arrived by train. In as few words as possible, his cousin, Frank Greatorex, and Mr. Kene imparted to him some hasty particulars of the unhappy event.

"He never did it," said the clergyman, solemnly. "Bede"—for at that moment Bede Greatorex joined the speakers—"how could you suffer them to bring in a verdict so horrible?"

But Mr. Ollivera had not heard the full details yet. By common consent, as it were, they had not at first told him of the letter. Bede would not tell it now. Let the worst come out to him by degrees thought he.

"I am going up to town," said Bede Greatorex. "If—"

"And not stay for tonight?" interrupted one of them, in an accent that savoured of reproach.

"Nay, I must consider my father," was the grave reply of Bede. "He is in suspense all this while, waiting for news."

So they parted. Bede Greatorex hastened to catch the departing train for London. And the others remained to see the last of the ill-fated John Ollivera.

He was carried out of Mr. Jones's in the bright moonlight, soon after eleven o'clock had struck. Whether intentionally, as best befitting the scanty ceremony to be performed, or whether in accidental forgetfulness the undertaker had failed to provide a covering for the coffin. And Mrs. Jones, with sundry sharp and stinging words of reprimand to the man, as it was in the nature of Mrs. Jones's tongue to give, brought down a long woollen black scarf-shawl, and helped to spread it over the coffin with her own hands.

Thus the procession started, preceded by many curious gazers, followed by more, Alletha Rye stealing on amidst the latter number; and so went on to the place of interment.

You have seen what took place there.

CHAPTER IV

GOING HOME WITH THE NEWS

In the vicinity of Bedford Square, so near to it that we may as well designate the locality by that name throughout the story, stood the large professional residence of Greatorex and Greatorex. It was large in every sense of the word; both as to the size of the house, and to the extent of the business transacted in it. A safe, good, respectable firm was that of Greatorex and Greatorex, standing as well in the public estimation as any solicitors could stand; and deservedly so, Mr. Greatorex was a man of nice honour; upright, just, trustworthy. He would not have soiled his hands with what is technically called dirty work; if any client wanted underhand business done, swindling work (although it might be legal) that would not bear the light of day, he need not take it to Greatorex and Greatorex.

The head of the firm, John Greatorex, was still in what many call the prime of life. He was fifty-eight, active and energetic. Marrying when he was very young, he really did not look a great deal older than his son Bede. And Bede was not his first-born. The eldest son had entered the army; he was in India now, Captain Greatorex. He also had married young, and his little daughter and only child had been sent home to her grand-parents in accordance with the prevailing custom.

The wife of Mr. Greatorex had been Miss Ollivera, sister to the father of John Ollivera, the barrister, whose sad end has been lately recorded. Mrs. Greatorex had fallen into ill-health or some time past now; in fact, she was slowly dying of an incurable complaint. But for not liking to leave her, Mr. Greatorex might have hastened down as soon as the sad news reached him of his nephew's premature end. I say he "might;" but Mr. Greatorex was, himself, only recovering from an attack of illness, and was scarcely strong enough to travel. And so he waited at home with all the patience he could call up, understanding nothing but that his nephew John, who had been as dear to him as were his own children, was dead. His children had been many: eight. James (Captain Greatorex), the eldest; Bede the second, one year younger; next came two daughters, who were married and away; then a son, Matthew, who was working his way to competency in Spain; the two next had died, and Francis was the youngest. The latter, called Frank always, was in the house in Bedford Square, but not yet made a partner.

The young barrister just dead, John Ollivera, left no relations to mourn for him, except his brother Henry William, and the Greatorex family. The two brothers had to make their own way in the world, their uncle Mr. Greatorex helping them to do it; the elder one choosing the Bar (as you have seen); Henry William, the Church. John had his chambers in Lincoln's Inn, and would certainly have risen into note had he lived: Henry William was a curate.

Three o'clock was striking in London on Wednesday afternoon, as a train slackened its speed and drew into the Paddington terminus. One of the first of its passengers to alight was Mr. Bede Greatorex. He had a small black bag in his hand, and jumped with it into a hansom cab.

"Bedford Square!"

The cabman answered with a nod as he touched his hat. He had driven Mr. Bede Greatorex before, who was sufficiently well known in London. Instead, however, of being permitted to dash up to the well-known door, the man found himself stopped a few yards short of it.

"I'll get out here," said Bede Greatorex.

Paying the fare, he went on with his bag, and glanced up at the windows as he crossed to the house. All the blinds were down. It was a very large house: it had been two originally. In the old, old days, some thirty or more years ago, Mr. Greatorex had rented only one of the houses. As his family and business increased, he bought the one he occupied and the next adjoining, and made them into one. There were two entrances still; the one pertained to the house and Mrs. Greatorex; the other was the professional entrance. The rooms on the ground floor—and there were several—were taken up by the business; one of them, looking to the garden, was the sitting-room of Mr. Greatorex.

Bede went to the private entrance, and let himself in with his latchkey. Lodging his small bag at the foot of the handsome staircase, he walked through some passages to his father's sitting-room, which was empty. Retracing his steps he went upstairs; a maidservant happened to meet him on the first landing; he handed her the bag and opened the door of the dining-room. A spacious, well-fitted up apartment, its paper white and gold, with streaks of crimson slightly intermingled to give it colour.

Mr. Greatorex was there. He sat over the fire and had fallen asleep. It surprised Bede: for Mr. Greatorex was a man not given to idleness or indulgence of any kind. Indeed, to see him sitting upstairs in the day time was an event almost unknown. Bede closed the door again softly. There was a haggard look in the elder man's face, partly the effect of his recent illness; and Bede would not disturb him.

Outside the door, he stood a moment in hesitation. It was a spacious landing-place, something like an upper hall. The floor was carpeted with dark green; painted windows—yellow, blue, crimson—threw down a bright light of colour; there was a small conservatory at one end, containing odoriferous plants on which the sun was shining; and a chaste statue or two imparted still life to the whole.

Bede hesitated. None but himself knew how horribly he hated and dreaded the tale he had to tell about poor John Ollivera. All the way up he had been rehearsing to himself the manner in which he should break it for the best, but the plan had gone clean out of his head now.

"I'll go up and wash my hands first, at any rate," decided Bede. "The dust was worse than we had it on Monday."

Ascending to the second landing, he was quietly crossing it to his own room, when a door was flung open, and a pretty little girl in blue, her curling hair bound back with ribbons, came flying out. It was the daughter of Captain Greatorex. The young lady had naturally a will of her own; and since her arrival from India, the indulgence lavished on her had not tended to lessen it. But she was a charming child, and wonderfully keen.

"Oh, Bede, have you come back! Grandmamma has been asking for you all the day."

"Hush, Jane! I'll go in to grandmamma presently."

Miss Jane did not choose to "hush." She evaded Bede's hand, flew across the soft carpet of the landing, and threw open a bedroom door, calling out that Bede had come. As to styling him Uncle Bede, she had never done anything of the kind.

He heard his mother's voice, and could almost have boxed the child's ears. Back she came again, laying hold of him this time, her saucy dark brown eyes, grave now, lifted up to his face.

"Bede, how came John Ollivera to die?"

"Hush, Jane," he said again. This was precisely the point on which he did not care to hold present communication with his mother. He wished, if possible, to spare her; but the little girl was persistent.

"Is he dead, Bede?"

"Yes, child, he is dead."

"Oh, dear! And he can never kiss me again, or bring me new dolls! I broke the last one in two, and threw it at him."

Her eyes filled with tears. Bede, deep in thought, put away the little hands that had fastened on his arms.

"I liked him better than you, Bede. What made him die?"

"Bede! Bede! is that you?" called out his mother.

Bede had to go in. Mrs. Greatorex was on the sofa, dressed, her back supported by pillows. Her complexion was of dark olive, showing her Spanish extraction; a capable, kindly woman she had ever been in life; and was endeavouring now to meet the death that she knew could not be far off, as a

Christian should. He stooped and kissed her. In features he resembled her more than any of her children.

"Do you feel better, mother?"

"My dear, you know that there can be no 'better' for me here. The pain is not heavy today. Have you just come up to town?"

"Just got in now."

"And what have you to tell me? I cannot believe that John is dead. When the telegram came yesterday morning, your father happened to be with me, and they brought it up. But for that, I dare say he would not have told me yet. He spares me all the trouble that he can, you know, dear. I fainted, Bede; I did indeed. The death must have been very sudden."

"Yes," replied Bede.

"Was it a fit? Jane, run to the schoolroom. Your governess will be angry at your staying away so long."

Jane's answer to this mandate was to perch herself on the arm of the sofa, side by side with the speaker, and to fix her eyes and her attention on the face of Bede.

"None of the Olliveras have been subject to fits; remember that, Bede," continued Mrs. Greatorex. "Neither did John himself look at all likely for one. To think that he should go before me! Jane, my little dear one, you must indeed go to Miss Ford."

"I am going to stay here, grand'ma, and to hear about John."

"There's nothing much to hear, or to tell," spoke Bede, as much perhaps for his mother's ear as for the child's. "If you do not obey your grandmamma, Jane, I shall take you myself to the schoolroom.

"No, you won't, Bede. Why don't you answer grand'ma about John?"

Mrs. Greatorex had nearly left off contending with Miss Jane; weary, sick, in pain, it was too much effort, and she generally yielded to the dominant little will. As she appeared to do now, for it was to Bede she spoke.

"Bede, dear, you are keeping me in suspense. Was it a fit?"

"No; it could not be called a fit."

"The heart, perhaps?"

"His death must have been quite sudden," said Bede, with pardonable evasion. "Instantaneous, the doctors thought: and therefore without pain."

"Poor John! poor John! The veil is lifted for him. Bede!"

Bede had begun to turn his attention to the young lady, and was putting her down from the sofa. He wheeled round at the word, and Miss Jane mounted again.

"What, mother?"

Mrs. Greatorex dropped her voice reverently: and her dark eyes, looking large from illness, had a bright, hopeful, yearning light in them as she spoke.

"I think he was fit to go."

"Yes," answered Bede, swallowing a lump of emotion. "It is the one drop of comfort amidst much darkness. At least—. But I must keep my word," he added, breaking suddenly off, and seizing the child again, as if glad of an excuse to cease; "you go now to Miss Ford, young lady."

She set up a succession of cries. Bede only carried her away the faster.

"You'll come back and tell me more, Bede," said Mrs. Greatorex.

"I will come by-and-by," he turned to say. "I have pressing things to do; and I have not yet spoken with my father. Try and get your afternoon's sleep, mother dear."

Miss Ford, a nursery governess, stood at the schoolroom door, and began to scold her pupil as she received her from the hands of Mr. Bede Greatorex. He shut himself into his room for a few minutes, and then descended the stairs in deep thought. He had begun to ask himself whether the worst could not be kept from his mother; not for very long could she be spared to them now.

Mr. Greatorex was then coming out of the dining-room. He shook hands with his son, and they went back and sat down together. Bede grew quite agitated at the task before him. He hated to inflict pain; he knew that John Ollivera had been dear to his father, and that the blow would be keenly felt. All the news as yet sent up by him to Bedford Square was, that John was dead.

Whence, then, that grey look on his father's face?—the haggard mouth, the troubled, shrinking eyes going searchingly out to Bede's? Mr. Greatorex was a fresh-looking man in general, with a healthy colour and smooth brown hair, tall and upright as his son. He looked short and shrinking and pale now.

"Bede, how came he to do it?"

Something like a relief came into Bede's heart as he heard the words. It was so much better for the way to have been paved for him!—the shock would not be so great.

"Then you know the particulars, sir.

"I fear I know the truth, Bede; not the particulars. The Times had a short paragraph this morning, saying that John Ollivera had died by his own hand. Was it so?"

Bede gravely nodded. His breath was coming and going faster than is consistent with inward calmness.

"My God!" cried Mr. Greatorex, from between his quivering lips, as he sank into a chair, and covered his face with his hands. But the sacred word was not spoken in irreverence; no, nor in surprise; rather, as it seemed, in the light of an appealing prayer.

"And what could have induced it?" came the question presently, as he let his hands fall.

"I had better tell you the whole from the beginning," said Bede, "you will then—"

"Tell it, of course," interrupted Mr. Greatorex. "Begin at the beginning."

Bede stood up, facing the fire; his elbow on the mantelpiece, his back partially turned to his father, while he told it: he did not care to watch the anguish and horror of the usually placid face. He concealed nothing: relating how he had reached the City and held an interview with his cousin; how he had left him after the lapse of an hour, promising to be with him in the morning before starting for town; and how he had been aroused from his bed by the tidings that John was dead. He described the state of the room when found; the pistol lying underneath the hand; the note on the table. As well as Bede Greatorex could repeat the details, as testified to before the coroner—and we may be very sure they were implanted with painful exactitude on his memory—he gave them all faithfully.

"It might have been an accident," urged Mr. Greatorex, in an imploring kind of tone, as if he wanted to be assured that it was.

Bede did not answer.

"I forgot the writing, Bede; I forgot the writing," said Mr. Greatorex, with a groan.

"Whatever it might be, whether accident or self-intended, it is an awful shame to bury him as they are going to do," burst forth Bede, in a sudden access of anger.

And the words served to tell Mr. Greatorex what the verdict had been.

"It is a sin, sir; yes, it is. I could not stay to see it."

"So it may be, Bede; but that's the least of it—that's the least of it. I'd as soon have believed myself capable of such a thing as that John Ollivera was. Oh, John! John!"

A painful silence. Bede felt glad that his task was so far over.

"His motive, Bede? What could have been his motive?"

"There was no motive, father; as far as I can see."

"You were young men together, Bede; of the same pursuits—frequent companions; did you ever suspect he had any care, or embarrassment, or trouble?"

"No. He had none, I feel sure."

"Those first words of the note, as you have related them, sound curious," resumed Mr. Greatorex. "What was it that he was trying to accomplish?"

"We cannot discover; no clue whatever has come to light. It would almost seem as though he had written them to the air, without foundation."

"That would be to say his senses had deserted him."

"Kene thinks that the headache of which he had complained may have proceeded from some disordered function of the brain, and induced insanity."

"Do you think it?" asked Mr. Greatorex, looking at his son. "You were the last person who saw him alive."

"I should be glad to think it if I could. He was quite calm and collected when I was with him; just as usual."

"The extraordinary thing to me is, that nobody should have heard the discharge of the pistol."

"The people of the house were all out. Even the servant-girl had gone about the neighbourhood gossiping."

"It might have been heard in the street."

"If the street were quiet, perhaps yes. But on assize nights, they tell me, there is an unusual deal of outdoor bustle."

Mr. Greatorex sat looking at the fire, and revolving the different points of the dreadful history. Bede resumed.

"I was wondering whether the worst of the details could be kept from my mother. They would try her terribly. She only thinks as yet, I find, that he died suddenly."

"Because she only knows as much as your telegram said. It will be impossible to keep it from her; the newspapers will be full of it. Three times today has your mother sent down for The Times, and I have returned an excuse. There's no help for it, Bede."

"Then you shall tell her, sir. I can't. It must be broken to her by degrees. How was it William Ollivera was so late in coming down?" he suddenly resumed. "He only arrived today as I was departing."

"William Ollivera was out of town, and did not return until last night. You have said nothing about our cause, Bede."

"That's all right. It was taken yesterday afternoon. Kene led in the place of John, and we got the verdict."

"Where are John's papers and things?"

"His brother and Frank will take charge of them. I have his private letters. I thought it best to come up to you at once, knowing you were in suspense."

"A suspense that has been grievous since I read that paragraph this morning, Bede. I have been fit for nothing."

Neither was Bede that day. Mr. Greatorex rose to go to his wife's room, there to enter upon his task—just as his son had been entering upon it with him. Bede paced the carpet for a few minutes alone. It was a long room; the furniture not dark and heavy, but light-looking and pleasant to the eye, though comprising all the requisites for a well-appointed dining-room. Bede took a look at himself in the pier-glass, and pushed his hair off his forehead—his sisters used to accuse him of inordinate vanity. And then quitted the room and the house.

He was bending his steps to Lincoln's Inn, to the chambers occupied by his cousin. Not many yards had he gone, before someone darted across the street and pounced upon him.

"Halloa, Greatorex! What's this, that's up about Ollivera?"

It was a Chancery barrister, who had known John Ollivera well. Bede Greatorex explained in a few short words, and hurried off.

"I can't stay to tell you more now," he said in apology. "There's a great deal to do and to be thought of, and I hardly know whether our heads are on our shoulders or off. I'm on my way to his chambers to search if there may be any paper, or aught else, that can throw light on it."

A hansom passed at the moment, and Bede jumped into it. He might have met fifty questioners, else, and reached his destination after dark. The chambers were on the third floor, and he went up to them. Mr. Ollivera's clerk, a small youth of nineteen, was at his post; and the laundress, who waited on Mr. Ollivera, was there also. The news had brought her up in tears.

Perhaps it was excusable that they should both begin upon Mr. Bede Greatorex in their thirst for information. Respectfully, of course, but eagerly. He responded in a few quiet words, and passed into the rooms, the woman's sobs following him.

Here was the sitting-room where John saw people; next to it his bedroom; all in neat order. Near the bed was a small mahogany stand, and a cushioned chair. On the stand lay his Bible—just as the other one was seen but yesterday resting on its stand elsewhere. Bede knew that his cousin never failed to read that Bible, and to fall on his knees before the chair morning and evening. He turned away with a groan, and proceeded to his work of search.

Only a casual search today; there was no time for minute examination. Just a look here and there, lest haply he might come upon some paper or letter of elucidation. But he could not find any.

"I am going to lock the rooms up, Jenner," he said to the clerk. "Things must be left as they are until the Reverend Mr. Ollivera comes to town. He will have the arrangement of matters. I don't suppose there's any will."

"Am I to leave the service at once, sir?—now?" asked Mr. Jenner, in excessive surprise.

"You must leave the rooms now—unless you would like to be locked up in them," returned Bede Greatorex. "Call in Bedford Square tomorrow morning; we may be able to recommend something you to: and perhaps you will be wanted here again for a few days."

They quitted the chambers together; and Mr. Bede Greatorex took possession of the key. "I suppose," he said to the clerk, as they went down, "that you never observed any peculiarity of manner in Mr. Ollivera that might tend to induce suspicion of aberration of mind?"

The young man turned round and stared, scarcely taking in the sense of the question. Certainly there had not been anything of the kind observable in Mr. Ollivera.

"He was cheerful and sensible always, sir: he didn't seem to have a care."

Bede sighed, and proceeded homeward. A recollection came over him, as he went along in the dusk, of the last evening he had walked home from his cousin's chambers; it was only the night before John had gone on circuit. Oh, the contrast between that time and this! And Bede thought, in the bitter grief and sorrow of the moment, that he would willingly forfeit his own life could he recall that of John Ollivera.

CHAPTER V

MR BUTTERBY IN PRIVATE LIFE

The bustle of the assizes was over; the tramp and tread and hum had gone out of the streets; the judges, the barristers, and the rest of the transitory visitors had departed, to hold their assize at the next county town.

A great deal of the bustle and the hum of another event had also subsided. It does not linger very long when outward proceedings are over, and sensational adjuncts have ceased; and Mr. Ollivera, at the best, had been but a stranger. The grave where he lay had its visitors still; but his brother and other friends had left for London, carrying his few effects with them. Nothing remained to tell of the fatal act of the past Monday evening; but for that grave, it might have seemed never to have had place in reality.

The Reverend Mr. Ollivera had been firm in refusing to admit belief in his brother's guilt. He did not pretend to judge how it might have happened, whether by accident or by some enemy's hand; but he felt convinced the death could not have been deliberately self-inflicted. It was an impossibility, he avowed to Mr. Butterby—and he was looked upon, by that renowned officer, as next door to a lunatic for his pains. There was no more shadow of a doubt on Mr. Butterby's mind that the verdict had been in accordance with the facts, than there was on other people's.

Always excepting Alletha Rye's. She had been silent to the public since the avowal at the grave; but, in a dispute with Mrs. Jones, had repeated her assertion and belief. Upon a report of the display coming to Mrs. Jones's ears, that discreet matron—who certainly erred on the side of hard, correct, matter-of-fact propriety, if on any—attacked her sister in no measured terms. There were several years between them, and Mrs. Jones considered she had a right to do it. Much as Mrs. Jones had respected Mr. Ollivera in life, she entertained no doubt whatever on the subject of his death.

"My opinion is, you must have been crazy," came the sharp reprimand. "Go off after that tramping tail to the grave! I wish I'd seen you start. A good name is easier lost than regained, Alletha Rye."

"I am not afraid of losing mine," was the calm rejoinder.

"Folks seldom are till they find it gone," said Mrs. Jones, tartly. "My goodness! not content with trapesing off there in the middle of the night, you must go and make an exhibition of yourself besides!— kneeling down on the damp earth to pray, in the face and eyes of all the people; and then rising to make a proclamation, just as if you had been the town bellman! Jones says it struck him dumb."

Alletha Rye was silent. Perhaps she had felt vexed since, that the moment's excitement had led her to the act.

"Who are you, that you should put yourself up against the verdict?" resumed Mrs. Jones. "Are you cleverer and sharper than the jury, and the coroner, and me, and Mr. Ollivera's friends, and the rest of the world, all of us put together? There can't be a doubt upon the point, girl."

"Let it drop," said Alletha, with a shiver.

"Drop! I'd like to see it drop. I'd like the remembrance of it to drop out of men's minds, but you've took care that shan't be. What on earth induced you to go and do it?"

"It was a dreadful thing that Mr. Ollivera should lie under the imputation of having killed himself," came the answer, after a pause.

"Now, you just explain yourself, Alletha Rye. You keep harping on that same string, about Mr. Ollivera; what grounds have you for it?"

The girl's pale face flushed all over. "None," she presently answered. "I never said I had grounds. But there's that vivid dream upon me always. He seemed to reproach me for not having sooner gone into the room to find him; and I'm sure no self-murderer would do that. They'd rather lie undiscovered for ever. Had I kept silence," she passionately added, "I might have become haunted."

Mrs. Jones stared at the speaker with all the fiery fervour of her dark, dark eyes.

"Haunted! Haunted by what?"

"By Mr. Ollivera's spirit; by remorse. Remorse for not doing as I am sure he is wishing me to do—clear his memory."

Mrs. Jones lifted her hands in wonder, and for once made no retort. She began to question in real earnest whether the past matters had not turned her sister's brain.

Dicky Jones was present during this passage-at-arms, which took place on the Thursday, after breakfast. He had just been enduring a battery of tongue on his own score; various sins, great and small, being placed before him in glaring colours by his wife; not the least heinous of which was the having arrived home from his pleasure trip at the unseasonable hour of half after one o'clock in the morning. In recrimination he had intimated that others of the family could come in at that hour as well as himself; not to do Alletha Rye harm, for he was a good-natured man, as people given to plenty of peccadilloes are apt to be; but to make his own crime appear the less. And then it all came out; and Mrs. Jones's ears were regaled with Alletha Rye's share in the doings at the interment.

On this same Thursday, but very much later in the day, Frank Greatorex and the Reverend Mr. Ollivera departed from the city, having stayed to collect together the papers and other effects of the deceased gentleman. Which brings us (the night having passed, and a great portion of the ensuing day) to the opening of the chapter.

Mr. Butterby sat in his parlour: one of two rooms he occupied on the ground floor of a private house very near a populous part of the city. He was not a police-sergeant; he was not an inspector; people did not know what he was. That he held sway at the police-station, and was a very frequent visitor to it, everybody saw. But Mr. Butterby had been so long in the town that speculation though rife enough at first upon the point, had ceased as to what special relations he might hold with the law. When any one wanted important assistance, he could, if he chose, apply to Mr. Butterby, instead of to the regular police-inspector; and, to the mind of the sanguine inquirer, that application appeared to constitute a promise of success.

Mr. Butterby's parlour faced the street. Its one sash window, protected by shutters thrown back in the day, and by green dwarf venetian blinds and a white roller-blind inside, was not a very large one. Nevertheless, Mr. Butterby contrived to keep a tolerable lookout from it on those of his fellow citizens who might chance to pass. He generally had the white blinds drawn down to meet, within an inch, the mahogany top of the venetian ones; and from that inch of outlet, Mr. Butterby, standing up before the window, was fond of taking observations. It was an unpretending room, with a faded carpet and rug on the floor; a square table in the middle, a large bureau filled with papers in a corner; some books in a case opposite, and a stock of newspapers on the top of that; and a picture over the mantelpiece representing Eve offering the apple to Adam.

Mr. Butterby sat by the fire at his tea, taking it thoughtfully. He wore an old green coat with short tails sprouting out from the waist, not being addicted to fashion in private life, and a red-and-black check waistcoat. It was Friday evening and nearly dusk. He had been out on some business all the afternoon but his thoughts were not fixed on that, though it was of sufficient importance; they rested on the circumstances attending the death of Mr. Ollivera.

Before the brother of the deceased had quitted the town, he had made an appointment with Mr. Butterby, and came to it accompanied by Frank Greatorex; the fly, conveying them to the station, waiting at the door. The purport of his visit was to impress upon that officer his full conviction that the death was not a suicide, and to request that, if anything should arise to confirm his opinion, it might be followed up.

"He was a good, pure-minded man; he was of calm, clear, practical mind, of sound good sense; he was fond of his profession, anxious to excel in it; hopeful, earnest, and without a care in the world," urged the Reverend Mr. Ollivera, with emotion. "How, sir, I ask you, could such a man take away his own life?"

Mr. Butterby shook his head. It might be unlikely, he acknowledged; but it was not impossible.

"I tell you it is impossible," said Mr. Ollivera. "I hold a full, firm, positive conviction that my brother never died, or could have died, by his own wilful hands: the certainty of it in my mind is so clear as to be like a revelation from heaven. Do you know what I did, sir? I went to the grave at night after he was put into it, and read the burial service over him."

"I see you doing it," came the unexpected answer of Mr. Butterby. "The surplice you wore was too long for you and covered your boots."

"It belonged to a taller man than I am—the Reverend Mr. Yorke," the clergyman explained. "But now, sir, do you suppose I should have dared to hold that sacred service over a man who had wilfully destroyed himself?"

"But instead of there being proof that he did not wilfully destroy himself, there's every proof that he did," argued Mr. Butterby.

"Every apparent proof; I admit that; but I know—I know that the proofs are in some strange way false; not real."

"The death was real; the pistol was real; the writing on the note-paper was real."

"I know. I cannot pretend to explain where the explanation may be hidden; I cannot see how or whence the elucidation shall come. One suggestion I will make to you, Mr. Butterby it is not clear that no person got access to the drawing-room after the departure from it of Mr. Bede Greatorex. At least, to my mind. I only mentioned this thought," concluded Mr. Ollivera, rising to close the interview; for he had no time to prolong it. "Should you succeed in gleaning anything, address a communication to me, to the care of Greatorex and Greatorex."

"Stop a moment," cried Mr. Butterby, as they were going out. "Who holds the paper that was found on the table?"

"I do," said Frank Greatorex. "Some of them would have had it destroyed; Kene and my brother amidst them; they could not bear to look at it. But I thought my father might like to see it first, and took it into my own possession."

A smile crossed the lip of the police agent. "Considering the two gentlemen you mention are in the law, it doesn't say much for their forethought, to rash at destroying the only proof there may remain to us of anybody else's being guilty."

"But then, you know, they do not admit that any one else could have been guilty," replied Frank Greatorex. "At least my brother does not; and Kene only looks upon it as a possible case of insanity. Do you want to see the paper? I have it in my pocket."

"Perhaps you'd not mind leaving it with me for a day or two," said Mr. Butterby. "I'll forward it up safe to you when I've done with it."

Frank Greatorex took the paper from his pocketbook and handed it to the speaker. It was folded inside an envelope now. Mr. Butterby received possession of it and attended his guests to the door, where the fly was waiting.

"You'll have to drive fast, Thompson," he said to the man. And Thompson, touching his hat to the officer, who was held in some awe by the city natives, whipped his horse into a canter.

It was upon this interview that Mr. Butterby ruminated as he took his tea on the Friday evening. In his own opinion it was the most unreasonable thing in the world, that anybody should throw doubt upon the verdict. Nothing but perversity. He judged it—and he was a keen-sighted man—to be fully in accordance with the facts, as given in evidence. Excepting perhaps in one particular. Had he been on the jury he should have held out for a verdict of insanity.

"They are but a set of bumble-heads at the best," soliloquised Mr. Butterby, respectfully alluding to the twelve men who had returned the verdict, as he took a large bite out of his last piece of well-buttered pikelet. "Juries for the most part always are: if they have got any brains they send them a wool-gathering then. Hemming, the butter-and-cheese man, told me he did say something about insanity; and he was foreman, too; but the rest of 'em and the coroner wouldn't listen to it. It don't much matter, for he got the burial rites after all, poor fellow: but if I'd been them, I should have gave him the benefit of the doubt."

Stopping in his observations to put the rest of the pikelet in his mouth, Mr. Butterby went on again as he ate it.

"It might have been that, insanity; but as to the other suspicion, there's no grounds whatever for it on the face of things at present. If such is to be raised I shall have to set to work and hunt 'em up. Create 'em as it were. 'Don't spare money,' says that young clergyman last night when he sat here; 'your expenses shall be reimbursed to you with interest.' As if I could make a case out of nothing! I'm not a French Procureur-Imperial."

Drinking down his tea at a draught, Mr. Butterby tried the teapot, lest a drop might be left in it still, turning it nearly upside down in the process. The result was, that the lid came open and a shower of tea-leaves descended on the tray.

"Bother!" said Mr. Butterby, as he hastily set the teapot in its place, and went on with his arguments.

"There's something odd about the case, though, straightforward as it seems; and I've thought so from the first. That girl's dream, for example, which she says she had; and her conduct at the grave. It was curious that Dicky Jones should just be looking on at her," added Mr. Butterby, slightly diverging from the direct line of consecutive thought: "curious that Dicky should have come up then at all. First, Alletha Rye vows he didn't do it; and, next, the parson vows it, Reverend Ollivera. Kene, too—but he points to insanity; and now the young fellow, Francis Greatorex. Suppose I go over the case again?"

Stretching out his hand, Mr. Butterby pulled the bell-rope—an old-fashioned twisted blue cord with a handle at the end; and a young servant came in.

"Shut the shutters," said he.

While this was in process, he took two candles from the mantelpiece, and lighted them. The girl went away with the tea-tray. He then unlocked his bureau, and from one of its pigeon-holes brought forth a few papers, memoranda, and the like, which he studied in silence, one after the other.

"The parson's right," he began presently; "if there is a loophole it's where he said—that somebody got into the room after the departure of Mr. Greatorex. Let's sum the points up."

Drawing his chair close to the table on which the papers lay, Mr. Butterby began to tell the case through, striking his two forefingers alternately on the table's edge as each point came flowing from his tongue. Not that "flowing" is precisely the best word to apply, for his speech was thoughtfully slow, and the words dropped with hesitation.

"John Ollivera, counsel-at-law. He comes in on the Saturday with the other barristers, ready for the 'sizes. Has a cause or two coming on at 'em, in which he expects to shine. Goes to former lodgings at Jones's, and shows himself as full of sense and sanity as usual; and he'd got his share of both. Spends Saturday evening at his friend's, Mrs. Joliffe's, the colonel's widow; is sweet, Mrs. Jones thinks, on one of the young ladies; thought so when he was down last October. Gets home at ten like a decent man, works at his papers till twelve, and goes to bed."

Mr. Butterby made a pause here, both his fingers resting on the table. Giving a nod, as if his reflections were satisfactory, he lifted his hands and began again.

"Sunday. Attends public worship and takes the sacrament. That's not like the act of one who knows he is on the eve of a bad deed. Attends again after breakfast, with the judges, and hears the sheriff's chaplain preach. (And it was not a bad sermon, as sermons go," critically pronounced Mr. Butterby in a parenthesis). "Attends again in the afternoon to hear the anthem, the Miss Joliffes with him. Dines at Jones's at five, spends evening at Joliffes'. Home early, and to bed."

Once more the hands were lifted. Once more their owner paused in thought. He gave two nods this time, and resumed.

"Monday. Up before eight. Has his breakfast (bacon and eggs), and goes to the Nisi Prius Court. Stays there till past three in the afternoon, tells Kene he must go out of court to keep an appointment that wasn't a particularly pleasant one, and goes out. Arrives at Jones's at half-past four; passes Mrs. Jones in that there small back hall of theirs; she tells him he looks tired; answers that he is tired and has got a headache; court was close. Goes up to his sitting-room and gets his papers about; (papers found afterwards, on examination, to relate to the cause coming on on Tuesday morning). Girl takes up his dinner; he eats it, gets to his papers again, and she fetches things away. Rings for his lamp early, quarter-past six may be, nearly daylight still; while girl puts it on table, draws down blinds himself as if in a hurry to be at work again. Close upon this Mr. Bede Greatorex calls, (good firm that, Greatorex and Greatorex," interspersed Mr. Butterby, with professional candour). "Bede Greatorex has come down direct from London (sent by old Greatorex) to confer with Ollivera on the Tuesday's cause. Stays with him more than an hour. Makes an appointment with him for Tuesday morning. Jones's nephew, going upstairs at the time, hears them making it, and shows Mr. Bede Greatorex out. Might be half-past seven then, or two or three minutes over it; call it half-past. Ollivera never seen again alive. Found dead next morning in arm-chair; pistol fallen from right hand, shot penetrated heart. Same chair he had been sitting in when at his papers, but drawn aside now at corner of table. Alletha Rye finds him. Tells a cock-and-bull of having been frightened by a dream. Dreamt he was in the sitting-room dead, and goes to see (she says) that he was not there, dead. Finds him there dead, however, just as (she says) she saw him in her dream. Servant rushes out for doctor, meets me, and I am the first in the room. Doctor comes, Hurst; Kene comes, Jones's nephew fetching him; then Kene fetches Bede Greatorex. Doctor says death must have took place previous evening not later than eight o'clock. Mrs. Jones says lamp couldn't have burnt much more than an hour: is positive it didn't exceed an hour and a half; but she's one of the positive ones at all times, and women's judgment is fallible. Now then, let's stop."

Mr. Butterby put his hands one over the other, and looked down upon them, pausing before he spoke again.

"It draws the space into an uncommon narrow nutshell. When Bede Greatorex leaves at half-past seven, Ollivera is alive and well—as he and Jones's nephew both testify to—and, according to the evidence of the surgeon, and the negative testimony of the oil in the lamp, he is dead by eight. If he did not draw the pistol on himself, somebody came in and shot him.

"Did he draw it on himself? I say Yes. Coroner and jury say Yes. The public say Yes. Alletha Rye and the Reverend Ollivera say No. If we are all wrong—and I don't say but that there's just a loophole of possibility of it—and them two are right, why then it was murder. And done with uncommon craftiness. Let's look at the writing.

"Those high-class lawyers are not good for much in criminal cases, can't see an inch beyond their noses; they don't practise at the Old Bailey, they don't," remarked Mr. Butterby, as he took from the papers before him the unfinished note found on Mr. Ollivera's table, the loan of which he had begged from Frank Greatorex. "The idea of their proposing to destroy this, because 'they couldn't bear to look at it!' Kene, too; and Bede Greatorex! they might have known better. I'll take care of it now."

Holding it close to one of the candles, the detective scanned it long and intently, comparing the concluding words, uneven, blotted, as if written with an agitated hand, with the plain collected characters of the lines that were undoubtedly Mr. Ollivera's. When he did arrive at a conclusion it was a summary one, and he put down the paper with an emphatic thump.

"May I be shot myself if I believe the two writings is by the same hand!"

Mr. Butterby's surprise may plead excuse for his grammar. He had never, until this moment, doubted that the writing was all done by one person.

"I'll show this to an expert. People don't write the same at all times; they'll make their capitals quite different in the same day, as anybody with any experience knows. But they don't often make their small letters different—neither do men study to alter their usual formation of letters when about to shoot themselves; the pen does its work then, spontaneous; naturally. These small letters are different, several of them, the r, the p, the e, the o, the d; all them are as opposite as light and dark, and I don't think the last was written by Mr. Ollivera."

It was a grave conclusion to come to; partially startling even him, who was too much at home with crime and criminals to be startled easily.

"Let's assume that it is so for a bit, and see how it works that way," resumed the officer. "We've all been mistaken, let's say; Ollivera did not shoot himself, someone goes in and shoots him. Was it man or woman; was it an inmate of the house, or not an inmate? How came it to be done? what was the leading cause? Was the pistol (lying convenient on the table) took up incidental in the course of talking and fired by misadventure?—Or did they get to quarrelling and the other shot him of malice?—Or was it a planned, deliberate murder, one stealing in to do it in cold blood? Halt a bit here, Jonas Butterby. The first—done in misadventure? No: if any honest man had so shot another, he'd be the first to run out and get a doctor to him. No. Disposed of. The second—done in malice during a quarrel? Yes; might have been. The third—done in planned deliberation? That would be the most likely of all, but for the fact (very curious fact in the supposition) of the pistol's having been Mr. Ollivera's, and put (so to say) ready there to hand. Looking at it in either of these two views, there's mystery. The last in regard to the point now mentioned; the other in regard to the secrecy with which the intruder must have got in. If that dratted girl had been at her post indoors, as she ought to have been, with the chain of the door up, it might never have happened," concluded Mr. Butterby, with acrimony.

"Between half-past seven and eight? Needn't look much before or much beyond that hour. Girl says nobody went into the house at all, except Jones's nephew and Jones's sister-in-law. Jones's nephew did not stay; he got his book and went off again at half-past seven, close on the heels of Bede Greatorex, Mr. Ollivera being then alive. Presently, nearer eight, Alletha Rye goes in, for a pattern, she says, and she stays upstairs, according to the girl's statement, a quarter of an hour."

Mr. Butterby came to a sudden pause. He faced the fire now, and sat staring into it as if he were searching for what he could not see.

"It does not take a quarter of an hour to get a pattern. I should say not. And there was her queer dream, too. Leastways, the queer assertion that she had a dream. Dreams, indeed!—moonshine. Did she invent that dream as an excuse for having gone into the room to find him? And then look at her persistence from the first that it was not a suicide! And her queer state of mind and manners since! Dicky Jones told me last night when I met him by the hop-market, that she says she's haunted by Mr. Ollivera's spirit. Why should she be, I wonder? I mean, why should she fancy it? It's odd; very odd. The young woman, up to now, has always shown out sensible, in the short while this city has known her.

"That Godfrey Pitman," resumed the speaker. "The way that man's name got brought up by the servant-girl was sudden. I should like to know who he is, and what his business might have been. He was in hiding; that's what he was. Stopping indoors for a cold and relaxed throat! No doubt! But it does not follow that because he might have been in some trouble of his own, he had anything to do with the other business; and, in fact, he couldn't have had, leaving by the five o'clock train for Birmingham. So we'll dismiss him.

"And now for the result?" concluded Mr. Butterby, with great deliberation. "The result is that I feel inclined to think the young parson may be right in saying it was not a suicide. What it was, I can't yet make my mind up to give an opinion upon. Suppose I inquire into things a bit in a quiet manner?—and, to begin with, I'll make a friendly call on Dicky Jones and madam. She won't answer anything that it does not please her to, and it never pleases her to be questioned; on the other hand, what she does choose to say is to be relied upon, for she'd not tell a lie to save herself from hanging. As to Dicky—with that long tongue of his, he can be pumped dry."

Mr. Butterby locked up his papers, changed his ornamental coat for a black one, flattened down the coal on his fire, blew out the candles, took his hat, and went away.

CHAPTER VI

Mrs. Jones was in her parlour, doing nothing: with the exception of dropping a tart observation from her lips occasionally. As the intelligent reader cannot have failed to observe, tartness in regard to tongue was essentially an element of Mrs. Jones's nature; when anything occurred to annoy her, its signs increased four-fold; and something had just happened to annoy her very exceedingly.

The parlour was not large, but convenient, and well fitted-up. A good fire burnt in the grate, throwing its ruddy light on the bright colours of the crimson carpet and hearthrug; on the small sideboard, with its array of glass; on the horsehair chairs, on the crimson cloth covering the centre table, and finally on Mrs. Jones herself and on her sister.

Mrs. Jones sat at the table, some work before her, in the shape of sundry packages of hosiery, brought in from the shop to be examined, sorted, and put to rights. But she was not doing it. Miss Rye sat on the other side the table, stitching the seams of a gown-body by the light of the moderator lamp. The shop was just closed.

It had happened that Dicky Jones, about tea-time that evening, had strayed into his next-door neighbour's to get a chat: of which light interludes to business Dicky Jones was uncommonly fond. The bent of the conversation fell, naturally enough, on the recent calamity in Mr. Jones's house: in fact, Mr. Jones found his neighbour devouring the full account of it in the Friday evening weekly newspaper, just damp from the press. A few minutes, and back went Dicky to his own parlour, his mouth full of news: the purport of which was that the lodger, Godfrey Pitman, who had been supposed to leave the house at half-past four, to take the Birmingham train, did not really quit it until some two or three hours later.

It had not been Mrs. Jones if she had refrained from telling her husband to hold his tongue for a fool; and of asking furthermore whether he had been drinking or dreaming. Upon which Dicky gave his authority for what he said. Their neighbour, Thomas Cause, had watched the lodger go away later, with his own eyes.

Mr. Cause, a quiet tradesman getting in years, was fetched in, and a skirmish ensued. He asserted that he had seen the lodger come out of the house and go up the street by lamplight, carrying his blue bag; and he persisted in the assertion, in spite of Mrs. Jones's tongue. She declared he had not seen anything of the sort; that either his spectacles or the street lights had deceived him. And neither of them would give in to the other.

Leaving matters in this unsatisfactory state, the neighbour went out again. Mrs. Jones exploded a little, and then had leisure to look at her sister, who had sat still and silent during the discussion. Still and silent she remained; but her face had turned white, and her eyes wore a wild, frightened expression.

"What on earth's the matter with you?" demanded Mrs. Jones.

"Nothing," said Miss Rye, catching hold of her work with nervous, trembling fingers. "Only I can't bear to hear it spoken of."

"If Mr. Pitman didn't go away till later, that accounts for the tallow-grease in his room," suddenly interposed Susan Marks, who, passing into the parlour, caught the thread of the matter in dispute.

Mrs. Jones turned upon her. "Tallow-grease!"

"I didn't see it till this afternoon," explained the girl. "With all the commotion there has been in the house, I never as much as opened the room-door till today since Mr. Pitman went out of it. The first thing I see was the carpet covered in drops of tallow-grease; a whole colony of them: and I know they were not there on the Monday afternoon. They be there still."

Mrs. Jones went upstairs at once, the maid following her. Sure enough the grease drops were there. Some lay on the square piece of carpet, some on the boarded floor; but all were very near together. The candlestick and candle, from which they had no doubt dropped, stood on the wash-hand-stand at Mrs. Jones's elbow, as she wrathfully gazed.

"He must have been lighting of his candle sideways," remarked the girl to her mistress; "or else have held it askew while hunting for something on the floor. If he stopped as late as old Cause says, why in course he'd need a candle."

Mrs. Jones went down again, her temper by no means improved. She did not like to be deceived or treated as though she were nobody; neither did she choose that her house should be played with. If the lodger missed his train (as she now supposed he might have done) and came back to wait for a later one, his duty was to have announced himself, and asked leave to stay. In spite, however, of the tallow and of Mr. Cause, she put but little faith in the matter. Shortly after this there came a ring at the side-door, and Mr. Butterby's voice was heard in the passage.

"Don't say anything to him about it," said Miss Rye hastily, in a low tone.

"About what?" demanded Mrs. Jones, aloud.

"About that young man's not going away as soon as we thought he did. It's nothing to Butterby."

There was no time for more. Mr. Butterby was shown in and came forward with a small present for Mrs. Jones. It was only a bunch of violets; but Mrs. Jones, in spite of her tartness, was fond of flowers, and received them graciously: calling to Susan to bring a wine-glass of water.

"I passed a chap at the top of High Street with a basketfull; he said he'd sold but two bunches all the evening, so I took a bunch," explained Mr. Butterby. "It was that gardener's man, Reed, who met with the accident and has been unfit for work since. Knowing you liked violets, Mrs. Jones, I thought I'd just call in with them."

He sat down in the chair, offered him, by the fire, putting his hat in the corner behind. Miss Rye, after saluting him, had resumed work, and sat with her face turned to the table, partially away from his view; Mrs. Jones, at the other side of the table, faced him.

"Where's Jones?" asked Mr. Butterby.

"Jones is off, as usual," replied Jones's wife. "No good to ask where he is after the shop's shut; often not before it."

It was an unlucky question, bringing back all the acrimony which the violets had partially soothed away. Mr. Butterby coughed, and began talking of recent events in a sociable, friendly manner, just as if he had been Mrs. Jones's brother, and never in his life heard of so rare an animal as a detective.

"It's an uncommon annoying thing to have had happen in your house, Mrs. Jones! As if it couldn't as well have took place in anybody else's! There's enough barristers lodging in the town at assize time, I hope. But there! luck's everything. I'd have given five shillings out of my pocket to have stopped it."

"So would I; for his sake as well as for mine," was Mrs. Jones's answer. And she seized one of the parcels of stockings and jerked off the string.

"Have you had any more dreams, Miss Rye?"

"No," replied Miss Rye, holding her stitching closer to the light for a moment. "That one was enough."

"Dreams is curious things; not to be despised," observed crafty Mr. Butterby; than whom there was not a man living despised dreams, as well as those who professed to have them, more than he. "But I've knowed so-called dreams to be nothing in the world but waking thoughts. Are you sure that one of yours was a dream, Miss Rye?"

"I would rather not talk of it, if you please," she said. "Talking cannot bring Mr. Ollivera back to life."

"What makes you persist in thinking he did not kill himself?"

Mr. Butterby had gradually edged his chair forward on the hearthrug, so as to obtain a side view of Miss Rye's face. Perhaps he was surprised, perhaps not, to see it suddenly flush, and then become deadly pale.

"Just look here, Miss Rye. If he did not do it, somebody else did. And I should like to glean a little insight as to whether or not there are grounds for that new light, if there's any to be gleaned."

"Why, what on earth! are you taking up that crotchet, Butterby?"

The interruption came from Mrs. Jones. That goes without telling, as the French say. Mr. Butterby turned to warm his hands at the blaze, speaking mildly enough to disarm an enemy.

"Not I. I should like to show your sister that her suspicions are wrong: she'll worrit herself into a skeleton, else. See here: whatever happened, and however it happened, it must have been between half-past seven and eight. You were in the place part of that half-hour, Miss Rye, and heard nobody."

"I have already said so."

"Shut up in your room at the top of the house; looking for—what was it?—a parcel?"

"A pattern—a pattern of a sleeve. But I had to open parcels, for I could not find it, and stayed searching. It had slipped between one drawer and another at the back."

"It must have took you some time," remarked Mr. Butterby, keeping his face on the genial fire and his eyes on Miss Rye.

"I suppose it did. Susan says I was upstairs a quarter of an hour, but I don't think it was so long as that. Eight o'clock struck after I got back to Mrs. Wilson's."

Mr. Butterby paused. Miss Rye resumed after a minute.

"I don't think any one could have come in legitimately without my hearing them on the stairs. My room is not at the top of the house, it is on the same floor as Mrs. Jones's; the back room immediately over the bedroom that was occupied by Mr. Ollivera. My door was open, and the drawers in which I was searching stood close to it. If any—"

"What d'ye mean by legitimate?" interrupted Mr. Butterby, turning to take a full look at the speaker.

"Openly; with the noise one usually makes in coming upstairs. But if any one crept up secretly, of course I should not have heard it. Susan persists in declaring she never lost sight of the front door at all; I don't believe her."

"Nobody does believe her," snapped Mrs. Jones, with a fling at the socks. "She confesses now that she ran in twice or thrice to look at the fires."

"Oh! she does, does she," cried Mr. Butterby. "Leaving the door open, I suppose?"

"Leaving it to take care of itself. She says she shut it; I say I know she didn't. Put it at the best, it was not fastened; and anybody might have opened it and walked in that had a mind to and robbed the house."

The visitor, sitting so unobtrusively by the fire, thought he discerned a little glimmer of possibility breaking in amidst the utter darkness.

"But, as the house was not robbed, why we must conclude nobody did come in," he observed. "As to the verdict—I don't see yet any reason for Miss Rye's disputing it. Mr. Ollivera was a favourite, I suppose."

The remark did not please Miss Rye. Her cheek flushed, her work fell, and she rose from her seat to turn on Mr. Butterby.

"The verdict was a wrong verdict. Mr. Ollivera was a good and brave and just man. Never a better went out of the world."

"If I don't believe you were in love with him!" cried Mr. Butterby.

"Perhaps I was," came the unexpected answer; but the speaker seemed to be in too much agitation to heed greatly what she said. "It would not have hurt either him or me."

Gathering her work, cotton, scissors in her hands, she went out of the room. At the same moment there arrived an influx of female visitors, come, without ceremony, to get an hour's chat with Mrs. Jones. Catching up his hat, Mr. Butterby dexterously slipped out and disappeared.

The street was tolerably empty. He took up his position at the edge of the facing pavement, and surveyed the house critically. As if he did not know all its aspects by heart! Some few yards higher up, the dwellings of Mr. Cause and the linendraper alone intervening, there was a side opening, bearing the euphonious title of Bear Entry, which led right into an obscure part of the town. By taking this, and executing a few turnings and windings, the railway station might be approached without touching on the more public streets.

"Yes," said the police agent to himself, calculating possibilities, "that's how it might have been done. Not that it was, though: I'm only putting it. A fellow might have slipped out of the door while that girl was in at her fires, cut down Bear Entry, double back again along Goose Lane, and so gain the rail."

Turning up the street with a brisk step, Mr. Butterby found himself face to face with Thomas Cause, who was standing within the shade of his side door. Exceedingly affable when it suited him to be so, he stopped to say a good evening.

"How d'ye do Cause? A fine night, isn't it?"

"Lovely weather; shall pay for it later. Has she recovered her temper yet?" continued Mr. Cause. "I saw you come out."

Which was decidedly a rather mysterious addition to the answer. Mr. Butterby naturally inquired what it might mean, and had his ears gratified with the story of Godfrey Pitman's later departure, and of Mrs. Jones's angry disbelief in it. Never had those ears listened more keenly.

"Are you sure it was the man?" he asked cautiously.

"If it wasn't him it was his ghost," said Mr. Cause. "I was standing here on the Monday night, just a step or two for'arder on the pavement, little thinking that a poor gentleman was shooting himself within a few yards of me, and saw a man come out of Jones's side door. When he was close up, I knew him in a moment for the same traveller, with the same blue bag in his hand, that I saw go in with Miss Rye on the Sunday week previous. He came out of the house cautiously, his head pushed forward first, looking up the street and down the street, and then turned out sharp, whisked past me as hard as he could walk, and went down Bear Entry. It seemed to me that he didn't care to be seen."

But that detectives' hearts are too hard for emotion, this one's might have beaten a little faster as he listened. It was so exactly what he had been fancifully tracing to himself as the imaginary course of a guilty man. Stealing out of the house down Bear Entry, and so up to the railway station!

"What time was it?"

"What time is it now?" returned Mr. Cause: and the other took out his watch.

"Five-and-thirty minutes past seven."

"Then it was as nigh the same time on Monday night, as nigh as nigh can be. I shut up my shop at the usual hour, and I'd stood here afterwards just about as long as I've stood here now. I like to take a breath of fresh air, Mr. Butterby, when the labours of the day are over."

"Fresh air's good for all of us—that can get it," said Mr. Butterby, with a sniff at the air around him. "What sort of a looking man was this Godfrey Pitman?"

"A well-grown, straight man; got a lot of black hair about his face; whiskers, and beard, and moustachios."

"Young?"

"Thirty. Perhaps not so much. In reading the account in the Herald this evening, I saw Jones's folks gave evidence that he had left at half-past four to catch the Birmingham train. I told Jones it was a mistake, and he told his wife; and didn't she fly out! As if she need have put herself in a tantrum over that! 'twas a matter of no consequence."

In common with the rest of the town, not a gleam of suspicion that the death was otherwise than the verdict pronounced it to be, had been admitted by Mr. Cause. He went on enlarging on the grievance of Mrs. Jones's attack upon him.

"She'd not hear a word: Jones fetched me in there. She told me to my face that, between spectacles and the deceitful rays of street lamps, one, come to my age, was unable to distinguish black from white, round from square. She said I must have mistaken the gentleman, Mr. Greatorex, for Godfrey Pitman or else Jones's nephew, both of them having gone out about the same time. I couldn't get in a word edgeways, I assure you Mr. Butterby, and Dicky Jones can bear me out that I couldn't. Let it go, 'tis of no moment; I don't care to quarrel with my neighbours' wives."

Mr. Butterby thought it was of a great deal of moment. He changed the conversation to something else with apparent carelessness, and then took a leisurely departure. Turning off at the top of High Street, he increased his pace, and went direct to the railway station.

The most intelligent porter employed there was a man named Hall. It was his duty to be on the platform when trains were starting and, as the detective had previous cause to know, few of those who departed by them escaped his observation. The eight o'clock train for London was on the point of departure. Mr. Butterby waited under some sheds until it had gone.

Now for Hall, thought he. As if to echo the words the first person to approach the sheds was Hall himself. In a diplomatic way, Mr. Butterby, when he had made known his presence, began putting inquiries about a matter totally foreign to the one he had come upon.

"By the way, Hall," he suddenly said, when the man thought he was done with, "there was a friend of mine went away last Monday evening, but I'm not sure by which train. I wonder if you happened to see him here? A well-grown, straight man, with black beard and whiskers—about thirty."

Hall considered, and shook his head. "I've no recollection of any one of that description, sir."

"Got a blue bag in his hand. He might have went by the five o'clock train, or later. At eight most likely; this hour, you know."

"Was he going to London, or the other way, sir?"

"Can't tell you. Try and recollect."

"Monday?—Monday?" cried Hall, endeavouring to recal what he could. "I ought to remember that night, sir, the one of the calamity in High Street; but the fact is, one day is so much like another here, it's hard to single out any in particular."

"Were you on duty last Sunday week, in the afternoon?"

"Yes, sir; it was my Sunday on."

"The man I speak of arrived by train that afternoon, then. You must have seen him."

"So I did," said the porter, suddenly. "Just the man you describe, sir; and I remember that it struck me I had seen his face somewhere before. It might have been only fancy; I had not much of a look at him; he got mixed with the other passengers, and went away quickly. I recollect the blue bag."

"Just so; all right. Now then, Hall: did you see him leave last Monday evening?"

"I never saw him, to my recollection, since the time of his arrival. Stop a bit. A blue bag? Why, it was a blue bag that—And that was Monday evening. Wait an instant, sir. I'll fetch Bill."

Leaving the detective to make the most of these detached sentences, Hall hurried off before he could be stopped. Mr. Butterby turned his face to the wall, and read the placards there.

When Hall came back he had a lad with him. And possibly it might have been well for that lad's equanimity, that he was unconscious the spare man, studying the advertisements, was the city's renowned detective, Jonas Butterby.

"Now then," said Hall, "you tell this gentleman about your getting that there ticket, Bill."

"'Twas last Monday evening," began the boy, thus enjoined, "and we was waiting to start the eight o'clock train. In that there dark corner, I comes upon a gentleman set down upon the bench; which he called to me, he did, and says, says he, 'This bag's heavy,' says he, 'and I don't care to carry it further nor I can help, nor yet to leave it,' says he, 'for it's got val'able papers in it,' says he; 'if you'll go and get my ticket for me,' says he, 'third class to Oxford,' says he, 'I'll give you sixpence,' says he: which I did, and took it to him," concluded the speaker; "and he gave me the sixpence."

"Did he leave by the train?"

"Why in course he did," was the reply. "He got into the last third class at the tail o' the train, him and his bag; which were blue, it were."

"An old gentleman, with white hair, was it?" asked Mr. Butterby, carelessly.

The boy's round eyes opened. "White hair! Why, 'twas black as ink. And his beard, too. He warn't old; he warn't."

Mr. Butterby walked home, ruminating; stirred up his fire when he arrived, lighted his candles, for he had a habit of waiting on himself, and sat down, ruminating still. Sundry notes and bits of folded paper had been delivered for him from his confrères at the police-station—if Mr. Butterby will not be offended at our classing them with him as such—but he pushed them from him, never opening one. He did not even change his coat for the elegant green-tailed habit, economically adopted for home attire, and he was rather particular in doing so in general. No: Mr. Butterby's mind was ill at ease: not in the sense, be it understood, as applied to ordinary mortals; but things were puzzling him.

To give Mr. Butterby his due, he was sufficiently keen of judgment; though he had made mistakes occasionally. Taking the surface of things only, he might have jumped to the conclusion that a certain evil deed had been committed by Godfrey Pitman; diving into them, and turning them about in his practised mind, he saw enough to cause him to doubt and hesitate.

"The man's name's as much Pitman as mine is," quoth he, as he sat looking into the fire, a hand on each knee. "He arrives here on a Sunday, accosts a stranger he meets accidentally in turning out of the station, which happened to be Alletha Rye, and gets her to accommodate him with a week's private lodgings. Thought, she says, the house she was standing at was hers: and it's likely he did. The man was afraid of being seen, was flying from pursuit, and dare not risk the publicity of an inn. Stays in the house nine days, and never stirs out all the mortal time. Makes an excuse of a cold and relaxed throat for stopping in; which was an excuse," emphatically repeated the speaker. "Takes leave on the Monday at half-past four, and goes out to catch the Birmingham train. Is seen to go out. What brought him back?"

The question was not, apparently, easy to solve, for Mr. Butterby was a long while pondering it.

"He couldn't get back into the house up through the windows or down through the chimneys; not in anyway but through the door. And the chances were that he might have been seen going in and coming out. No: don't think he went back to harm Mr. Ollivera. Rather inclined to say his announced intention of starting by the five o'clock train to Birmingham was a blind: he meant to go by the one at eight t'other way, and went back to wait for it, afeared of hanging about the station itself or loitering in the streets. It don't quite wash, neither, that; chances were he might have been seen coming back," debated Mr. Butterby.

"Wonder if he has anything to do with that little affair that has just turned up in Birmingham?" resumed the speaker, deviating to another thought. "Young man's wanted for that, George Winter: might have been this very selfsame Godfrey Pitman; and of course might not. Let's get on.

"It don't stand to reason that he'd come in any such way into a town and stop a whole week at the top of a house for the purpose of harming Mr. Ollivera. Why 'twas not till the Tuesday after Pitman was in, that the Joneses got the barrister's letter saying he was coming and would occupy his old rooms if they were vacant. No," decided Mr. Butterby; "Pitman was in trouble on his own score, and his mysterious movements had reference to that: as I'm inclined to think."

One prominent quality in Mr. Butterby was pertinacity. Let him take up an idea of his own accord, however faint, and it took a vast deal to get it out of him. An obstinate man was he in his self-conceit. Anybody who knew Mr. Butterby well, and could have seen his thoughts as in a glass, might have known he would be slow to take up the doubts against Godfrey Pitman, because he had already them up against another.

"I don't like it," he presently resumed. "Look at it in the best light, she knows something of the matter; more than she likes to be questioned about. Put the case, Jonas Butterby. Here's a sober, sensible, steady young woman, superior to half the women going, thinking only of her regular duties, nothing to conceal, open and cheerful as the day. That's how she was till this happened. And now? Goes home on the Monday night at nigh eleven o'clock (not to speak yet of what passed up to that hour), sits over the parlour-fire after other folks had went to bed, 'thinking,' as she puts it. Goes up later; can't sleep; drops asleep towards morning, and dreams that Mr. Ollivera's dead. Gets flurried at inquest (I saw it, though others mightn't); tramps to see him buried, stands on the fresh grave, and tells the public he did not commit suicide. How does she know he didn't? Come. Mrs. Jones is ten times sharper-sighted, and she has no doubt. Says, next, to her sister in confidence (and Dicky repeats it to me as a choice bit of gossip) that she's haunted by Ollivera's spirit.

"I don't like that," pursued Mr. Butterby, after a revolving pause. "When folks are haunted by dead men's spirits—leastways, fancy they are—it bodes a conscience not at rest in regard to the dead. To-night her face was pale and red by turns; her fingers shook so they had to clutch her work; she won't talk of it; she left the room to avoid me. And," continued Mr. Butterby, "she was the only one, so far as can be yet seen, that was for any length of time in the house between half-past seven and eight on Monday evening. A quarter of an hour finding a sleeve-pattern!

"I don't say it was her; I've not got as far as that yet, by a long way. I don't yet say it was not as the jury brought it in. But she was in the house for that quarter of an hour, unaccounting for her stay in accordance with any probability; and I'm inclined to think that Godfrey Pitman must have been out of it before the harm was done. Nevertheless, appearances is deceitful, deductions sometimes wrong, and while I keep a sharp eye on the lady, I shall look you up, Mr. Godfrey Pitman."

One drawback against the "looking up" was—and Mr. Butterby felt slightly conscious of it as he rose from his seat before the fire—that he had never seen Godfrey Pitman in his life; and did not know whence he came or whither he might have gone.

PART THE SECOND

THE STORY

CHAPTER VII

IN THE OFFICE

The morning sun was shining on the house of Greatorex and Greatorex. It was a busy day in April. London was filling; people were flocking to town; the season was fairly inaugurated, the law courts were full of life.

The front door stood open; the inner door, closed, could be pushed back at will. It bore a brass plate with the inscription, "Greatorex and Greatorex, Solicitors," and it had a habit, this inner door, of swinging-to upon clients' heels as they went out, for the spring was sharp. In the passage which the door closed in, was a room on either hand. The one on the left was inscribed outside, "Clerks' Office "; that on the right, "Mr. Bede Greatorex."

Mr. Bede Greatorex was in his room today: not his private room; that lay beyond. It was a moderate-sized apartment, the door in the middle, the fireplace opposite to it. On the right, between the door and the near window, was the desk of Mr. Brown; opposite to it, between the fireplace and far window, stood Mr. Bede Greatorex's desk; two longer desks ran along the walls towards the lower part of the room. At the one, in a line with that of Mr. Bede Greatorex, the fireplace being between them, sat Mr. Hurst, a gentleman who had entered the house for improvement; at the one on the other side the door, in a line with Mr. Brown's, sat little Jenner, a paid clerk. Sundry stools and chairs stood about; a huge map hung above the fireplace; a stone bottle of ink, some letter-scales, and various other articles more useful than ornamental, were on the mantel-shelf: altogether, the room was about as bare and dull as such offices usually are. The door at the end, marked "Private," opened direct to the private room of Mr. Bede Greatorex, where he held consultations with clients.

And he generally sat there also. It was not very often that he came to his desk in the front office: but he chose to be there on occasions, and this was one. This side of the house was understood to comprise the department of Mr. Bede Greatorex; some of the clients of the firm were his exclusively; that is, when they came they saw him, not his father; and Mr. Brown was head-clerk and manager under him.

Bede Greatorex (called generally in the office, "Mr. Bede," in contradistinction to his father, Mr. Greatorex) sat looking over some papers taken out of his locked desk. Four years have gone by since you saw him last, reader; for that prologue to the story with its sad event, was not enacted lately. And the four years have aged him. His father was wont to tell him that he had not got over the shock and grief of John Ollivera's death; Bede's private opinion was that he never should get over it. They had been as close friends, as dear brothers; and Bede had been a changed man since. Apart from this grief and regret and the effect it might have left upon him, suspicions had also arisen latterly that Bede Greatorex's health was failing; in short there were indications, fancied or real, that the inward complaint of which his mother died, might, unless great care were used, creep upon him. Bede had seen a physician, who would pronounce no very positive opinion, but believed on the whole that the fears were without foundation, certainly they were premature.

Another cause that tended to worry Mr. Bede Greatorex, lay in his domestic life. More than three years ago now, he had married Miss Joliffe; and the world, given you know to put itself into everybody's business and whisper scandal of the best of us, said that in marrying her, Bede Greatorex had got his pill. She was wilful as the wind; spent his money right and left; ran him in debt; plunged into gaiety, show, whirl, all of which her husband hated: she was in fact a perfect, grave exemplification of that undesirable but expressive term that threatens to become a household word in our once sober land—"fast." Three parts of Bede's life—the life that lay apart from his profession, his routine of office duties—was spent in striving to keep from his father the extravagance of his wife, and the sums of money he had to draw for personal expenditure. Bede had chivalric ideas upon the point; he had made her his wife, and would jealously have guarded her failings from all: he would have denied, had he been questioned, that she had any. So far as he was able he would indulge her whims and wishes; but there was one of them that he could not and did not: and that related to their place of dwelling. Bede had brought his wife to the home that had been his mother's, to be its sole mistress in his late mother's place. It was a large, convenient, handsome residence (as was previously seen), replete with every comfort; but after a time Mrs. Bede Greatorex grew discontented. She wanted to be in a more fashionable quarter; Hyde Park, Belgrave Square; anywhere amidst the great world. After their marriage Bede had taken her abroad; and they remained so long there that Mr. Greatorex began to indulge a private opinion that Bede was never coming back again. They sojourned in Paris, in Switzerland, in Germany; and though, when they at length did return, Bede laughingly said he could not get Louisa home, he had in point of fact been as ready to linger away from it as she was. The Bedford Square house had been done up beautifully, and for two years Mrs. Bede found no fault with it; she had taken to do that lately, and it seemed to grow upon her like a mania.

Upstairs now, now at this very moment, when her husband is poring over his law-puzzles with bent brow, she is studying the advertisements of desirable houses in the Times, almost inclined to go out and take one on her own account. A charming one (to judge by the description) was to be had in Park Lane, rent only six hundred a-year, unfurnished. Money was as plentiful as sand in the idea of Mrs. Bede Greatorex.

You can go and see her. Through the passages and the intervening door to the other house; or else go out into the street and make a call of state at the private entrance. Up the wide staircase to the handsome landing-place already told of, with its rich green carpet, its painted windows, its miniature conservatory, and its statues; on all of which the sun is shining as brightly as it was that other day four years ago, when Bede Greatorex came home, fresh from the unhappy scenes connected with the death of Mr. Ollivera. Not into the dining-room; there's no one in it; there's no one in the large and beautiful drawing-room; enter, first of all, a small apartment on the side that they call the study.

At the table sat Jane Greatorex, grown into a damsel of twelve, but exceedingly little and childlike in appearance. She was writing French dictation. By her side, speaking the words in a slow, distinct tone, with a good and pure accent, sat a young lady, her face one of the sweetest it was ever man's lot to look upon. The hazel eyes were deep, honest, steady; the auburn hair lay lightly away from delicate and well-carved features; the complexion was pure and bright. A slender girl of middle height, and gentle, winning manners, whose simple morning dress of light cashmere sat well upon her.

Surely that modest, good, thoughtful young woman could not be Mrs. Bede Greatorex! No: you must wait yet an instant for introduction to her. That is only Miss Jane's governess, a young lady who has but recently entered on her duties as such, and is striving to perform them conscientiously. She is very patient, although the little girl is excessively tiresome, with a strong will of her own, and a decided objection to lessons of all kinds. She is the more patient because she remembers what a tiresome child she was herself, at that age, and the vast amount of trouble she gave wilfully to her sister-governess.

"No, Jane; it is not facture; it is facteur. We are speaking of a postman, you know. The two words are essentially different; different in meaning, in spelling, and in sound. I explained this to you yesterday."

"I don't like doing dictation, Miss Channing," came the answering response.

"Go on, please. Le facteur, qui—"

"I'm tired to death. I know I've done a whole page."

"You have done three lines. One of these days I will give you a whole page to do, and then you'll know what a whole page is. Le facteur, qui arrive—"

Miss Jane Greatorex suddenly took a large penful of ink, and shook it deliberately on the copy-book. Leaving them to the contest, in which be you very sure the governess would conquer, for she was calm, kind, and firm, we will go to an opposite room, one that Mrs. Bede called her boudoir. A beautiful room, its paper and panelling of white and gold, its velvet carpet of delicate tints, its silk curtains of a soft rose-colour. But neither Mrs. Bede Greatorex, who sat there, nor her attire was in accordance with the room.

And, to say the truth, she had only come down from her chamber to get something left in it the night before: it was her favourite morning room, but Mrs. Bede was not wont to take up her position in it until made up for the day. And that was not yet accomplished. Her dark hair was untidy, her face pale and pasty, her dressing-gown, of a dull red with gold sprigs on it, sat loose. Seeing the Times on the table, she had caught it up, and thrown herself back in a reclining chair of satin-wood and pink velvet, while she looked over the advertisements. Mrs. Bede Greatorex was tall and showy, and there her beauty ended. As Louisa Joliffe, she had exercised a charm of manner that fascinated many, but she kept it for rare occasions now; and, they, always public ones. She had no children, and her whole life and being were wrapt in fashion, frivolity, and heartlessness. The graver duties of existence were wholly neglected by Louisa Greatorex: she seemed to live in ignorance that such things were. She never so much as glanced at the solemn thought that there must come a life after this life; she never for a moment strove to work on for it, or to help another on the pilgrimage: had she chosen to search her memory, it could not have returned to her the satisfaction of having ever performed a kind action.

One little specimen of her selfishness, her utter disregard for the claims and feelings of others, shall be given, for it occurred opportunely. As she sat, newspaper in hand, a young woman opened the door, and asked leave to speak to her. She was the lady's-maid, and, as Mrs. Bede looked at her, knitting her brow at the request, she saw tears stealing down from the petitioning eyes.

"Could you please let me go out, madam? A messenger has come to say that my mother is taken suddenly worse: they think she is dying."

"You can go when I am dressed," replied Mrs. Bede Greatorex.

"Oh, madam, if you could please to let me go at once! I may not be in time to see her. Eliz a says she will take my place this morning, if you will allow her."

"You can go when I am dressed," was the reiterated, cold, and decisive answer. "You hear me, Tallet. Shut the door." And the maid withdrew, her face working with its vain yearning.

"She's always wanting to go out to her mother," harshly spoke Mrs. Bede Greatorex, as she settled herself to the newspaper again.

"One; two; three; four; five. Five houses that seem desirable. Bede may say what he chooses: in this miserable old house, with its professional varnish, we don't stay. I'll write at once for particulars," she added, going to her writing-table, a costly piece of furniture inlaid with mother-of-pearl.

The writing for particulars took her some little time, three-quarters of an hour about, and then she went up to be dressed; which ceremony occupied nearly an hour longer. Tallet might depart then. And thus you have a specimen of the goodness of heart of Louisa Greatorex.

But this has been a digression from the morning's business, and we must return to the husband, whose wish and will she would have liked to defy, and to the office where he sat. The room was very quiet; nothing to be heard in it but the scratching of three pens; Mr. Brown's, Mr. Hurst's, and Mr. Jenner's. This room was not entered indiscriminately by callers; the opposite door inscribed "Clerks' Office," was on the swing perpetually. This room was a very sedate one: as a matter of course so in the presence of Mr. Bede Greatorex; and the head of it in his absence, Mr. Brown, allowed no opportunity for discursive gossip. He was as efficient a clerk as Greatorex and Greatorex had ever possessed; young yet: a tall, slender, silent man, devoted to his business; about three years, or so, with them now. He wore a wig of reddish brown, and his whiskers and the hair on his chin were sandy.

Bede Greatorex shut some papers into his desk with a click, and began opening another parchment. "Did you get an answer yesterday, from Garnett's people, Mr. Hurst?" he suddenly asked.

"No, sir. I could not see them."

"Their clerk came in last evening to say we should hear from them today," interposed Mr. Brown, looking up from his writing to speak.

It was in these moments—when the clerk's eyes unexpectedly met those of Mr. Bede Greatorex—that the latter would feel a kind of disagreeable sensation shoot through him. Over and over again had it occurred: the first time when Mr. Brown had been in the office but a day. They were standing talking together on that occasion, when a sudden fancy took Bede that he had seen the man somewhere before. It was not to be called a recognition; but a kind of semi-recognition, vague, indefinite, uncertain, and accompanied by a disagreeable feeling, which had its rise perhaps in the very uncertainty.

"Have we ever met before?" Mr. Bede Greatorex had questioned; but Mr. Brown shook his head, and could not say. A hundred times since then, when he met the steady gaze of those remarkably light grey eyes (nearly always bent on their work), had Bede stealthily continued to study the man; but the puzzle was always there.

Mr. Brown's eyes and face were bent on his desk again today. His master, holding a sheet of parchment up before him, as if to study the writing better, suffered his gaze to wander over its top and fix itself on Mr. Brown. The clerk, happening to glance up unguardedly, caught it.

He was one of the most observant men living, quiet though he seemed, and could not fail to be aware that he was thus occasionally subjected to the scrutiny of his master—but he never appeared to see it.

"Did you speak, sir?" he asked, as if he had looked up to put the question.

"I was about to speak," said Mr. Bede Greatorex. "There's a new clerk coming in today to replace Parkinson. Nine o'clock was the hour fixed, and now it is half-past ten. If this is a specimen of his habits of punctuality, I fear he'll not do much good. You will place him at Mr. Hurst's desk."

"Very good, sir," replied Mr. Brown, making no comment. The out-going clerk, Parkinson, had been at Jenner's desk.

"I am going over to Westminster," continued Mr. Bede Greatorex, gathering some papers in his hand. "If Garnett's people come in, they must wait for me. By the way, what about that deed—"

The words were cut short by a clatter. A clatter and bustle of feet and doors; someone was dashing in from the street in a desperate hurry, with a vast deal of unnecessary noise. First the swing-door gave a bang, then the clerks' door opened and banged; now this one was sent back with a breeze; and a tall fine-looking young man came bustling in, head foremost—Mr. Roland Yorke.

Not so very young, either. For more than seven years have elapsed since he was of age, and went careering off on a certain hopeful voyage of his to Port Natal, told of in history. He is changed since then. The overgrown young fellow of twenty-one, angular and awkward, has become quite a noble-looking man in his great strength and height. The face is a fine one, good-nature the predominant expression of the somewhat rough features, which are pale and clear and healthy: the indecision that might once have been detected in his countenance, has given place to earnestness now. Of regular beauty in his face, as many people count beauty, there is none; but you would scarcely pass him in the street without turning to look at him. In manner he is nearly as much of a boy as a grown man can be, just as he ever was, hasty, thoughtless, and impulsive.

"I know I'm late," he began. "How d'ye do, Mr. Greatorex?"

"Yes, you are late, Mr. Yorke," was the response of Mr. Bede Greatorex, submitting to the hearty handshake offered. "Nine was the hour named."

"It was the boat's fault," returned Roland, speaking with loud independence, just as he might had he been a ten thousand a-year client of the house. "I went down to see Carrick off at eight o'clock, and if you'll believe me, the vessel never got away before ten. They were putting horses on board. Carrick says they'll lose their tide over yonder; but he didn't complain, he's as easy as an old shoe. Since then I've had a pitch out of a hansom cab."

"Indeed!"

"I told the fellow to drive like mad; which he did; and down went the horse, and I out atop of him, and the man atop-faced of me. There was no damage, only it all served to hinder. But I'm ready for work now, Mr. Greatorex. Which is to be my place?"

To witness a new clerk announce himself in this loud, familiar kind of way, to see him grasp and shake the hand of Mr. Bede Greatorex: above all to hear him speak unceremoniously of the Earl of Carrick, one of the house's noble clients, as if the two were hail-fellow-well-met, caused the whole office to look up, even work-absorbed Mr. Brown. Bede Greatorex indicated the appointed desk.

"This is where you will be, by the side of Mr. Hurst, a gentleman who is with us for improvement. Mr. Brown, the manager in this room"—pointing out the clerk with the end of his pen—"will assign you your work. Mr. Hurst, Mr. Roland Yorke."

Roland took his seat at once, and turned up his coat-cuffs as a preliminary step to industry. Mr. Bede Greatorex, saying no more, passed through to his private room, and after a minute was heard to go out.

"What's to do?" asked Roland.

Mr. Brown was already giving him something; a deed to be copied. He spoke a few instructions in a concise, quiet tone, and Roland Yorke set to work.

"What ink d'ye call this?" began Roland.

"It is the proper ink," said Mr. Brown.

"It's uncommon bad."

"Have you ever been used to the kind of work, Mr. Yorke?" inquired the manager, wondering whether the new comer might be a qualified solicitor, brought to grief, or a gentleman-embryo just entering on his noviciate.

"Oh, haven't I!" returned Mr. Yorke; "I was in a proctor's office once, where I was worked to death."

"Then you'll soon find that to be good ink."

"I had all the care of the office on my shoulders," resumed Roland, holding the pen in the air, and sitting back on his stool while he addressed Mr. Brown. "There were three of us in the place altogether, not counting the old proctor himself, and we had enough work for six. Well, circumstances occurred to take the other two out of the office, and I, who was left, had to do it all. What do you think of that?"

Mr. Brown did not say what he thought. He was writing steadily, giving no encouragement for the continuance of the conversation. Mr. Hurst, his elbow on the desk, had his face turned to the speaker, surveying him at leisure.

"I couldn't stand it; I should have been in my grave in no time; and so I thought I'd try a part of the world that might be more desirable—Port Natal. I say, what are you staring at?"

This was to Mr. Hurst. The latter dropped his elbow as he answered.

"I was looking whether you were much altered. You are: and yet I think I should hare known you, after a bit, for Roland Yorke. When the name was mentioned I might have been at fault, but for your speaking of Lord Carrick."

"He's my uncle," said Roland. "Who are you?"

"Jos Hurst, from Helstonleigh. Have you forgotten me? I was at the college school with your brothers, Gerald and Tod."

Roland stared. He had not forgotten Josiah Hurst; but the rather short and very broad young man by his side, as broad as he was high, bore no resemblance to the once slim college boy. Roland never doubted: he got off his stool, upsetting it in the process, to shake heartily the meeting hand. Mr. Brown began to think the quiet of the office would not be much enhanced through its new inmate.

"My goodness! you are the first of the old fellows I've seen. And what are you, Hurst,—a lawyer?"

"Yes; I've passed. But the old doctor (at home, you know) won't buy me a practice, or let me set up for myself, or anything, until I've had some experience: and so I've come to Greatorex and Greatorex to get it," concluded Mr. Hurst, ruefully.

"And who's he?" continued Roland, pointing to Jenner. "Greatorex said nothing about him."

He was one of the least men ever seen, but he had a vast amount of work in him. Mr. Hurst explained that Jenner was only a clerk, but a very efficient one.

"He'd do twice the amount of work that I could, Yorke: I'm slow and sure; Jenner is sure and quick. How long have you been home from Port Natal?"

"Don't bother about that now," said Roland.

"Did you make your fortune out there?"

"What a senseless question! If I'd made a fortune there, it stands to reason I should not have come into an office here."

"How was I to know? You might have made a fortune and dissipated it?"

"Dissipated it in what?" cried Roland, with wide-open eyes. And to Mr. Hurst, who had gained some knowledge of what is called life, the look and the question bore earnest that Roland Yorke, in spite of his travelling experiences, was not much tainted by the world and its ways.

"Oh, in many things. Horse-racing, for instance."

Roland threw back his head in the old emphatic manner. "If ever I do get a fortune, Jos,—which appears about as likely as that Port Natal and Ireland should join hands and spin a waltz with each other—I'll take care of it."

Possibly in the notion occurring to him that idleness was certainly not the best way to acquire a fortune, Roland tilted his stool on its even legs, and began to work in earnest. When he had accomplished two lines, he took it to the manager.

"Will this do, Mr. Brown? I'm rather out of practice."

Mr. Brown signified that it would. He knew his business better than to give anything of much consequence to an unknown and untried clerk.

"Are you related to Sir Richard Yorke?" he asked of Roland.

"Yes, I am; and I'm ashamed of him. Old Dick's my uncle, my late father's brother; and his son and heir, young Dick, is my cousin. Old Dick is the greatest screw alive; he'd not help a fellow to save him from hanging. He's as poor as Carrick; but I don't call that an excuse for him; his estate is mortgaged up to the neck."

Mr. Brown needed not the additional information, which Roland proffered so candidly. His nature had not changed a whit. Nay, perhaps the free and easy life at Port Natal, about which we may hear somewhat later, had only tended to render him less reticent, if that were possible. Greatorex and Greatorex were the confidential solicitors to Sir Richard Yorke, and Mr. Brown was better acquainted than Roland with the baronet's finances.

"I thought it must be so," remarked Mr. Brown. "I knew there was some connection between Sir Richard and Lord Garrick. Are you likely to stay in our office long?" he questioned, inwardly wondering that Roland with two uncles so puissant should be there at all.

"I am likely to stay for ever, for all I know. They are going to give me twenty shillings a week. I say, Mr. Brown, why do you wear a wig?"

Doubtless Mr. Brown thought the question a tolerably pointed one upon so brief an acquaintance. He settled to his work again without answering it. A hint that the clerk, just come under his wing, might return and settle to his. Which was not taken.

"My hair is as plentiful as ever it was," said Roland, giving his dark hair a push backwards. "I don't want a wig; and you can't be so very much my senior; six or seven years, perhaps. I am eight-and-twenty."

"And I am three-and-thirty, sir. My hair came off in a fever a few years back, and it does not grow again. Be so good as to get on with what you have to do, Mr. Yorke."

Thus admonished, Roland obediently sought his place. And what with renewed questions to Mr. Brown—that came ringing out at the most unexpected moments—what with a few anecdotes of life at Port Natal with which he confidently regaled Mr. Hurst, what with making the acquaintance of little Jenner, which Roland accomplished with great affability, and what with slight interludes of writing, a line here and a line there, the morning wore away agreeably.

CHAPTER VIII

ARRIVAL FROM PORT NATAL

Mr. Roland Yorke's emigration to Port Natal cannot be said to have turned out a success. He had gone off in high spirits, a chief cabin passenger, Lord Carrick having paid the passage money, forty pounds. He had carried with him, from the same good-natured source, fifty pounds, to begin life with when he should land, a small but sufficient outfit, and a case of merchandize consisting of frying-pans. Seven years, before, when Roland resolved to emigrate and run away from work at home, he became imbued with the conviction (whence derived, he scarcely knew, but it lay on his mind as a positive certainty) that frying-pans formed the best and most staple article on which to commence trading at Port Natal, invariably the foundation of a fortune. Some friend of his, a Mr. Bagshaw, who had previously emigrated, had imparted this secret to him; at least, Roland was impressed with the belief that he had; a belief which nothing could shake. Frying-pans and fortune were associated together in his dreams. He stood out strongly for the taking out forty dozen, but Lord Carrick declined to furnish them, allowing only the miserable number of four-and-twenty. "When ye see for ye'reself out there that there's a market for them, send me word, and I'll dispatch loads to ye by the first steamer, me boy," said his lordship sensibly; and Roland was fain to put up with the advice and with the two dozen accorded. He arrived at Port Natal, all youth and joy and buoyancy. Seen from the deck of the vessel, when she anchored in the beautiful harbour, calm as a lake, Natal looked a very paradise. Ranges of hills on the west of the fair town were dotted with charming houses and pleasure grounds; and Roland landed fresh and full of hope as a summer's morning: just as too many an emigrant from the dear old mother-country does land, at other parts besides Natal. And he bought experience as they do.

In the first place, Roland began life there as he had been accustomed to do it in England; that is, as a gentleman. In the second place there proved to be no especial market for frying-pans. That useful culinary article might be bought in sufficient abundance, he found, when inquired for, without bringing into requisition the newly-arrived supply. The frying-pans being thus left upon his hands, lying like a dead weight on them, metaphorically speaking, brought the first check to his hopes; for they had been relied upon (as the world knows) to inaugurate and establish the great enterprizes, commercial or otherwise, that had floated in rose-coloured visions through Roland's brain. He quitted the port town, Durban, and went to Maritzburg, fifty miles off, and then came back to Durban. Thrown upon his own resources (through the failure of the frying-pans), Roland had leisure to look about him, for some other fertile source in which to embark his genius and energy, and lead him on to speedy fortune. Such resources did not appear to be going begging; they were coyly shy; or at least came not flowing in Roland's way; and meanwhile his money melted. Partly in foolish expenditure on his own account, partly in helping sundry poor wights, distressed steerage passengers with whom he had made acquaintance on board (for Roland had brought out his good-nature with him), the money came to a summary end. One fine morning, Roland woke up from a dream of idle carelessness, to find himself changing the last sovereign of all the fifty. It did not dismay him very much: all he said was, "I must set about money-making in earnest now."

Of course the great problem was—how to do it. You, my reader, may be, even now, trying to solve it. Thousands of us are, every day. Roland Yorke made but one more of a very common experience; and he had to encounter the usual rubs incidental to the process. He came to great grief and was reduced to a crust; nay, to the not knowing where the crust could be picked up from. The frying-pans went first, disposed of in a job lot, almost literally for an old song. Some man who owned a shed had, for a consideration, housed the case that contained them, and they were eating their handles off. Roland's wardrobe went next, piece-meal; and things fell to the pass that Roland was not sure but he himself would have to go after it. It came to one of two things—starvation or work. To do Roland justice, he was ready and willing to work; but he knew no mechanical trade; he had never done an hour's hard labour, and in that lay the difficulty of getting it. He would rush about from office to store, hunger giving him earnestness, from store to workshop, from workshop to bench, and say, Employ me. For the most part, the answer would be that he was not wanted; the labour market of all kinds was overstocked; but if the application appeared, by rare chance, likely to be entertained, and Roland was questioned of his experience and capabilities, rejection was sure to follow. He was too honest, too shallow in the matter of tact, to say he had been accustomed to work when he had not; and the experience in copying which he acknowledged and put forth, was somehow never required to be tested. To hear Roland tell of what he had accomplished in this line at home, must have astonished the natives of Port Natal.

Well, time went on; it does not stand still for any one; and Roland went on with it, down and down and down. Years went on; and one rainy day, when about four winters had gone by from the date of his departure, Roland returned to England. He landed in St. Katharine's Docks, his coat out at elbows and ninepence in his pocket: as an old friend of his, Mr. Galloway, had once prophesied he would land, if he lived to get back at all.

Mr. Roland Yorke had sailed for Port Natal in style, a first-class cabin passenger; he came home in the steerage, paying twelve pounds for the passage, and working out part of that. From thence he made his way to Lord Carrick in Ireland, very much like a bale of returned goods.

The best account he gave of his travels to Lord Carrick, perhaps the best account he could give, was that he had been "knocking about." Luck had not been with him, he said; and there really did seem to have been a good deal in that. To hear him tell of his adventures was something rich; not consecutively as a history, he never did that: but these chance recollections were so frequent and diffuse, that a history of his career at Natal might have been compiled from them. The Earl would hold his sides, laughing at Roland's lamentations for the failure and sacrifice of his frying-pans, and at the reminiscences in general. A life of adventure one week, a life of starvation the next. Roland said he had tried all kinds of things. He had served in stores; at bars where liquor was dispensed; he had been a hired waiter at half the hotels in Natal; he had worked on the shore with the half-naked Zulu Kaffirs at lading and unlading boats; once, for a whole week, when he was very hard up, or perhaps very low down, he had cried hot potatoes in the streets. He had been a farmer's labourer and driven a waggon, pigs, and cattle. He had been sub-editor in a newspaper office, The Natal Mercury, and one unlucky day sent the journal out with its letters printed upside down. He had hired himself out as chemist's assistant, and half ruined his master by his hopeless inability to distinguish between senna and tincture of laudanum, so that the antidotes obliged to be supplied to the hapless customers who came rushing for them, quite outweighed the profits. Occasionally he met with friends who assisted him, and then Roland was at ease—for his propensity to live as a gentleman was for ever cropping up. Up and down; down and up; now fortune smiling a little, but for the most part showing herself very grim, and frowning terribly. Roland had gone (as he called it) up the country, and amidst other agreeable incidents came to a fight with the Kaffirs. He took out a licence, the cost thirty shillings, and opened a retail store for pickled pork, candles, and native leeches, the only articles he could get supplied him on trust. His fine personal appearance, ready address, evident scholarship, and hearty frank manners, obtained for him a clerkship in the Commercial and Agricultural Bank, recently opened, and he got into so hopeless a maze with the books and cash by the week's end, that he was turned off without pay. Architecture was tried next. Roland sent in a graphic plan as competitor for the erection of a public building; and the drawing—which he had copied from a model, just as he used to copy cribs in the college school at Helstonleigh—looked so well upon paper that the arbitrators were struck with admiration at the constructive talent displayed, until one of them made the abrupt discovery that there were no staircases and no room left to build any. So, that hope was abandoned for a less exalted one; and Roland was glad to become young man at a general store, where the work was light: alternating between dispensing herrings and treacle (called there golden syrup) to customers over the counter, and taking out parcels in a wheelbarrow.

But there was good in Roland. And a great deal of it too, in spite of his ill-luck and his careless improvidence. The very fact of his remaining away four years, striving manfully with this unsatisfactory life of toil and semi-starvation, proved it. The brown bread and pea-soup Mr. Galloway had foreseen he would be reduced to live on, was often hungered for by Roland in vain. He put up with it all; and not until every chance seemed to have failed, would he go home to tax his uncle's pocket, and to disappoint his mother. A sense of shame, of keen, stinging mortification, no doubt lay at the bottom of this feeling against return. He had been so sanguine, as some of my readers may remember; and as he, sitting one day on a roadside stone in the sand, towards the close of his stay in Natal, recalled; so full of hopeful, glowing visions in the old home, that his mother, the Lady Augusta Yorke, had caught their reflection. Roland's castles in the air cannot have slipped yet out of people's memory. He had represented to his mother; aye, and believed it too; that Port Natal was a kind of Spanish El Dorado, where energetic young men might line their pockets in a short while, and come home millionaires for life. He had indulged large visions and made magnificent promises on the strength of them, beginning with a case of diamonds to his mother, and ending—nobody but Roland could have any conception where. Old debts were to be paid, friends benefited, enemies made to eat humble-pie. Mr. Galloway was to be passed in the street by Mr. Roland Yorke, the millionaire; the Reverend William Yorke to have the cold shoulder turned upon him. Arthur Channing was to be honoured; Jenkins, the hard-working clerk, who had thought nothing of doing Roland's work as well as his own, to be largely patronised; within three months after his arrival in Port Natal, funds were to be dispatched home to settle claims that might be standing against Roland in Helstonleigh. That there could be the slightest doubt he should come back "worth millions," Roland never supposed; he had talked of it everywhere—and talked faithfully. Poor Jenkins had long gone where worldly patronage and gifts could not follow him, but others had not. Roland remembered how his confident anticipations had so won upon his mother, that she went to bed and dreamt of driving about a charming city, whose streets were paved with Malachite marble.

And so, recalling these visions and promises, Roland, for very disappointment and shame, was not in a hurry to go back, but rather lingered on in Port Natal, struggling manfully with his ill-luck, as he called it. Pride and good-feeling alike prevented him. To appear before Lady Augusta, poor, starving, hatless, and bootless, would be undoubtedly a worse blow to her than that other alternative which he (forgetting his height and weight) had laid before her view: the one, he said, might happen if he did not get to Port Natal—the riding as a jockey on Helstonleigh race-course, in a pink silk jacket and yellow breeches.

No. He did try heartily with all his might and main; tried at it for four mortal years. Beyond a scrap of writing he now and again sent home, in which he always said he was "well, and happy, and keeping straight, and getting on," but which never contained a request for home news, or an address to which it might be sent, Lady Augusta heard nothing. Nobody else heard. One letter, indeed, reached a bosom friend of his, Arthur Channing, which was burnt when read, as requested, and Arthur looked grieved for a month after. He had told Arthur the truth; that he was not getting on; but under an injunction of secrecy, and giving no details. Beyond that, no news reached home of Roland.

His fourth year of trial at Port Natal was drawing to a close when illness seized hold of him, and for the first time Roland felt as if he were losing heart. It was not serious illness, only such as is apt to attack visitors to the country, and from which Roland's strength of frame, sound constitution, and good habits—for he had no bad ones, unless a great appetite might be called such—had hitherto preserved him. But, what with the wear and tear of his chequered life, its uncertain food, a plentiful dinner today, bread and beans tomorrow, nothing the following one, and its harassing and continuous disappointments, Roland felt the illness as a depressing calamity; and he began to say he could not make head against the tide any longer, and must get away from it. He might have to eat humble-pie on landing in England; but humble-pie seems tolerable or nauseous according to the existing state of mind; and it is never utterly poisonous to one of the elastic temperament of Roland Yorke. In a fit of impulse he went down to the ships and made the best bargain for getting home that circumstances allowed. He had been away more than four years, and never once, during that time, had he written home for money.

And so, behold him, out at pocket (except for ninepence) and out at elbows, but wonderfully improved in tone and physique, arriving in London early one rainy morning from Port Natal, and landing in the docks.

The first thing he did was to divide the ninepence with one who was poorer than he; the second was to get a cup of coffee and a slice of bread at a street coffee-stall; the third was to hasten to Lord Carrick's tailor—and a tremendous walk it was, but that was nothing to Roland—and get rigged out in any second-hand suit of clothes returned on hand that might be decent. There ill news awaited him; it was the time of year when Lord Carrick might, as a rule, be found in London; but he had not come; he was, the tailor believed, in Ireland. Roland at once knew, as sure as though it had been told him, that his uncle was in some kind of pecuniary hot water. Borrowing the very smallest amount of money that would take him to Ireland, he went off down the Thames in a return cattleboat that very day.

Since that period, hard upon three years, he had been almost equally "knocking about," and experienced nearly as many ups and downs in Ireland as at Port Natal. Sometimes living in clover with Lord Carrick, at others thrown on his own resources and getting on somehow. Lord Carrick's will was good to help him, but not always his ability; now and again it had happened that his lordship (who was really more improvident than his nephew, and had to take flights to the Continent on abrupt emergencies and without a day's warning) was lost to society for a time, even to Roland. Roland hired himself out as a kind of overlooker to some absentee's estate, but he could not get paid for it. This part of his career need not be traced; on the whole, he did still strive to do something for himself as strenuously as he had at Port Natal, and not to be a burthen to anybody, even to Lord Carrick.

To this end he came over to London, and presented himself one day to his late father's brother, Sir Richard Yorke, and boldly asked him if he could not "put him into something." The request caused Sir Richard (an old gentleman with a fat face) to stare immensely; he was very poor and very selfish, and had persistently held himself aloof from his late brother's needy family, keeping them always at arm's length. His son and heir had been content to do the same: in truth, the cousins did not know each other by sight. Sir Richard's estate was worth four thousand a-year, all told; and as he was wont to live at the rate of six, it will be understood that he was never in funds. Neither had he patronage or influence in anyway. To be thus summarily applied to by a stalwart young man, who announced himself as his nephew, took the baronet aback; and if he did not exactly turn Roland out of the house, his behaviour was equivalent to it "I'll be shot if I ever go near him again," cried Roland. "I'd rather cry hot pies in Poplar streets."

A day or two previously, in sauntering about parts of London least frequented by men of the higher class—for when we are very much down in the world we don't exactly choose the region of St. James's for our promenades, or the sunny side of Regent Street—Roland had accidentally met one of the steerage passengers with whom he had voyaged home from Port Natal. Ever open-hearted, he had frankly avowed the reason of being unable to treat his friend; namely, empty pockets: he was not sure, he added, but he must take to crossing-sweeping for a living; he heard folks made fortunes at it. Upon this the gentleman, who wore no coat and very indifferent pantaloons, confided to him the intelligence that there was a first-rate opening in the perambulating hot-pie trade, down in Poplar, for an energetic young man with a sonorous voice. Roland, being great in the latter gift, thought he might entertain it.

Things were at a low ebb just then with Roland. Lord Carrick, as usual, was totally destitute of ready money; and Roland, desperately anxious though he was to get along of his own accord, was fain to write to his mother for a little temporary help. One cannot live upon air in London, however that desirable state of things may be accomplished at Port Natal. But the application was made at an inopportune moment. Every individual boy Lady Augusta possessed was then tugging at her purse-strings; and she returned a sharp answer to Roland, telling him he ought to be ashamed of himself not to be helping her, now that he was the eldest, instead of wanting her to keep him. George, the eldest son, had died in India, which brought Roland first.

"It's true," said Roland, in a reflective mood, "I ought to be helping her. I wonder if Carrick could put me into anything, as old Dick won't. Once let me get a start, I'm bound to go on, and the mother should be the first to benefit by it."

A short while after this, and when Roland was far more at his wits' end for a shilling than he had ever been at Port Natal—for there he had no appearance to keep up, and here he had; there he could encamp out in the sand, here he couldn't—Lord Carrick arrived suddenly in London, in a little trouble as usual. Some warm-hearted friend had induced his good-natured lordship to accept a short bill, and afterwards treacherously left him to meet it. So Lord Carrick was again en route for the Continent, until his men of business, Greatorex and Greatorex, could arrange the affair for him by finding the necessary money. Halting in London a couple of days, to confer with them on that and other matters—for Lord Carrick's affairs altogether were complicated and could not be touched upon in an hour—Roland seized on the opportunity to prefer the application. And this brings us to the present time.

When under a cloud, and not quite certain that the streets were safe, the Earl was wont to eschew his hotel at the west end, and put up at a private one in a more obscure part. Roland, having had notice of his arrival, clattered in to breakfast with him on the morning of the second day, and entered on his petition forthwith—to be put into something.

"Anything for a start, Uncle Carrick," he urged. "No matter how low I begin: I'll soon go along swimmingly, once I get the start. I can't go about here, you know, with my toes out, as I have over yonder. It's awful work getting a dinner only once a week. I've had thoughts of crying hot pies in Poplar."

To judge by the breakfast Roland was eating, he had been a week without that meal as well as dinner. Lord Carrick, looking at the appetite with admiration, sat pulling his white whiskers in perplexity; for the grey hair of seven years ago had become white now. His heart was good to give Roland the post of Prime Minister, or any other trifling office, but he did not see his way clear to accomplish it.

"Me boy, there's only one thing I can do for ye just now," he said after silently turning the matter about in all its bearings, and hearing the explanation of the Poplar project. "Ye know I must be off tomorrow by the early French steamer, and I can't go about looking after places today, even if I knew where they could be picked up, which I don't. I must leave ye to Greatorex and Greatorex."

"What will they do?" asked Roland.

"You can come along with me there, and see."

Accordingly, when the Earl of Carrick went forth to his appointed interview that day with Mr. Greatorex, he presented Roland; and simply told the old lawyer that he must put him in a way of getting along, until he, Lord Carrick, was in funds again. Candid and open as ever Roland could be, the Earl made no secret whatever of that gentleman's penniless state, enlarging on the fact that to go dinnerless, as a rule, could not be good for him, and that he should not exactly like to see him set up as a hot-pie man in Poplar. Mr. Greatorex, perhaps nearly as much taken to as Sir Richard Yorke had been on a similar occasion, glanced at his son Bede who was present, and hesitated. He did not refuse point blank—as he might have done by almost anybody else. Lord Carrick was a valuable client, his business yearly bringing in a good share of feathers to the Greatorex nest, and old Mr. Greatorex was sensible of the fact. Still, he did not see what he could do for one who, like Roland, was in the somewhat anomalous position of being nephew to an earl and a baronet, but reduced to contemplate the embarking in the hot-pie trade.

"We might give him a stool in our office, Lord Carrick, for it happens that we are a clerk short: and pay him—pay him—twenty shillings a week. As a temporary thing, of course."

To one who had not had a dinner for days, twenty shillings a week seems an ample fortune; and Roland started up and grasped the elder lawyer's hand.

"I'll earn it," he said, his tone and eyes alike beaming with gratitude. "I'll work for you till I drop."

Mr. Greatorex smiled. "The work will not be difficult, Mr. Yorke; writing, and going on errands occasionally. If you do come," he pointedly added, "you must be ready to perform anything you may be directed to do, just as a regular clerk does."

"Ready and willing too," responded Roland.

"We have room for a certain number of clerks only," proceeded Mr. Greatorex, who was desirous that there should be no misunderstanding in the bargain; "each one has his appointed work and must get through it. Can you copy deeds?"

"Can't I," unceremoniously replied Roland. "I was nearly worked to death with old Galloway, of Helstonleigh."

"Were you ever with him?" cried Mr. Greatorex in surprise to whom Mr. Galloway was known.

"Yes, for years; and part of the time had all the care of the office on my shoulders," was Roland's ready answer. "There was only Galloway then, beside myself, and he was not good for much. Why! the amount of copying I had to do was so great, I thought I should have dropped into my grave. Lord Carrick knows it."

Lord Carrick did, in so far as that he had heard Roland repeatedly assert it, and nodded assent. Mr. Greatorex thought the services of so experienced a clerk must be invaluable to any house, and felt charmed to have secured them.

And that is how it arose that Roland Yorke, as you have seen, was entering the office of Greatorex and Greatorex. He was to be a clerk there to all intents and purposes; just as he had been in the old days at Mr. Galloway's; and yet, when he came in that morning, after his summerset out of the hansom cab, with a five-pound note in his pocket that Lord Carrick had contrived to spare for him, and an order for unlimited credit at his lordship's tailor's, hatter's, and bootmaker's, Roland's buoyant heart and fate were alike radiant, as if he had suddenly come into a fortune.

CHAPTER IX

UNEXPECTED MEETINGS

"You can go to your dinner, Mr. Yorke."

The clocks were striking one, as Brown, the manager, gave the semi-order. Roland, to whom dinner was an agreeable interlude, especially under the circumstances of having money in his pocket to pay for it, leaped off his stool forthwith, and caught up his hat.

"Are you not coming, Hurst?"

Mr. Hurst shook his head. "Little Jenner goes now. I stay until he comes back."

Little Jenner had been making preparation to go of his own accord, brushing his hat, drawing down his waistcoat, pushing gingerly in order his mass of soft fair hair. He was remarkably small; and these very small men are often very great dandies. Roland, who had shaken off the old pride in his rubs with the world, waited for him outside.

"Jenner, d'ye know of a good dining-place about here?" he asked, as they stood together, looking like a giant and a dwarf.

The clerk hesitated whether to say he did or did not. The place that he considered good might not appear so to the nephew of Sir Richard Yorke.

"I generally go to a house in Tottenham Court Road, sir. It's a kind of cook's shop, clean, and the meat excellent; but one sees all kinds of people there, and you may not think it up to you."

"Law, bless you!" cried Roland. "When a fellow has been knocked about for four years in the streets of Port Natal, he doesn't retain much ceremony. Let's get on to it. Do you know of any lodgings to be let in these parts, Jenner?" he continued again. "I shall get some as near to Greatorex's as I can. One does not want a three or four miles' dance night and morning."

Jenner said he did not know of any, but would help Mr. Yorke to look for some that evening if he liked. And they had turned into Tottenham Court Road, when Jenner halted to speak to someone he encountered: a little woman, very dark, who was bustling by with a black and white flat basket in her hand.

"How d'ye do, Mrs. Jones? How's Mr. Ollivera?"

"Now, I've not got the time to stand bothering with you, Jenner," was the tart retort. "Call in any evening you like, as I've told you before; but I'm up to my eyes in errands now."

Roland Yorke, whose attention had been attracted to something in a shop-window, wheeled round on his heel at the voice, and stared at the speaker. Jenner had called her Mrs. Jones; but Roland fully believed no person in the world could own that voice, save one. A voice that struck on every chord of his memory, as connected with Helstonleigh.

"It is Mrs. Jenkins!" cried Roland, seizing the stranger's hands. "What on earth does he mean by calling you Mrs. Jones?"

"Ah," she groaned, "I am Mrs. Jones, more's the shame and pity. Let it pass for now, young Mr. Yorke. I should have known you anywhere."

"You don't mean to say you are living in London?" returned Roland.

"Yes, I am. In Gower Street. Come and see me, Mr. Yorke; Jenner will show you the house. Did you make your fortune at Port Natal? You'd always used to be telling Jenkins, you know, that you should."

"And I thought I should," said Roland, with emphasis; "but I got no luck, and it turned out a failure. Won't I come and see you! I say, Mrs. Jenkins, do you remember the toasted muffins that Jenkins wouldn't eat?"

Mrs. Jones nodded twice to the reminiscence. She went bustling on her way, and they on theirs. Roland for once was rather silent. Mingling with the satisfaction he experienced in meeting any one from Helstonleigh, especially one so associated with the old familiar daily life as Mrs. Jenkins had been, came the thoughts of the years since; of the defeats and failures; of the mortification that invariably lay on his heart when he had to tell of them and of what they had brought him. He had now met two of the old people in one day; Hurst and Mrs. Jones; or, as Roland still called her, Mrs. Jenkins. Cords would not have dragged Roland to Helstonleigh: his mother, with the rest of them at home, had come over to Ireland to stay part of the summer at Lord Carrick's, soon after Roland's return from Port Natal; but he would not go to see them at the old home city. With the exception of scraps of news learnt from Hurst that day, Roland knew nothing about Helstonleigh's later years.

"Look here, Jenner! What brings her name Jones? It used to be Jenkins."

"I think I have heard that it was Jenkins once," replied Jenner, reflectively. "She must have married Jones after Jenkins died. Did you know him?"

"Did I know him?" echoed Roland, to whom the question sounded a very superfluous one. "I should just think I did know him. Why, he was chief clerk for years to Galloway, that cantankerous old proctor I was with. Jenkins was a good fellow as ever lived, meek and patient, and of course Mrs. J. put upon him. She'd not allow him to have his will in the smallest way: he couldn't dress himself in a morning unless she chose to let him. Which she didn't always."

"Not let him dress himself?"

"It's true," affirmed Roland, diving down into the depth of the old grievances. "Our office was in an awful state of work at that time; and because Jenkins had a cough she'd lock up his pantaloons to keep him at home. It wasn't his fault; he'd have come in his coffin. Jones whoever he may be, must have had the courage of a wolf to venture on her. Does he look like one?"

"I never saw him," said Jenner. "I think he's dead, too."

"Couldn't stand it, I suppose? My opinion is, it was her tongue took off poor Jenkins. He was mild as honey. Not that she's a bad lot at bottom, mind you, Jenner. I wonder what brought her to London?"

"I don't know anything about her affairs," said Jenner. "The Rev. Henry William Ollivera has his rooms in her house. And I go to see him now and then. That's all."

"Who is the Rev. William Ollivera?"

"Curate of a parish hard by. His brother, a barrister, had chambers in Lincoln's Inn, and I was his clerk. Four years ago he went the Oxford circuit, and came to his death at Helstonleigh. It was a shocking affair, and happened in the Joneses' house. They lived at Helstonleigh then. Mrs. Jones's sister went in one morning and found him dead in his chair."

"My goodness!" cried Roland. "Was it a fit?"

"Worse than that. He took away his own life. And I have never been able to understand it from that hour to this, for he was the most unlikely man living to do such a thing—as people all said. The Greatorexes interested themselves to get me a fresh place, giving me some temporary work in their office. It ended in my remaining with them. They find me useful, and pay me well. It's four years now, sir, since it happened."

"Just one year before I got home from Natal," casually remarked Roland.

"He sends for me sometimes," continued Mr. Jenner, pursuing his own thoughts, which were running on the clergyman. "When any fresh idea occurs to him, he'll write off for me, post haste; and when I get there he puts all sorts of questions to me, about the old times in Lincoln's Inn. You see, he has always held that Mr. Ollivera did not kill himself, and has been ever since trying to get evidence to prove he did not. The hope never seems to grow old with him, or to rest; it is as fresh and near as it was the day he first took it up."

Roland felt a little puzzled. "Did Mr. Ollivera kill himself, or didn't he? Which do you mean?"

Jenner shook his head. "I think he did, unlikely though it seemed. All the circumstances proved it, and nobody doubted it except the Rev. Mr. Ollivera. Bede Greatorex, who was the last person to see him alive, thinks there can be no doubt whatever; I overheard him say it was just one of William Ollivera's crotchets, and not the first by a good many that he had taken up. The clergyman used to be for ever coming into the office talking of it, saying should he do this or do the other, until Bede told him he couldn't have it; that it interrupted the business."

"What has Bede Greatorex to do with it? Why should Ollivera come to him?"

"Bede Greatorex has nearly as much to do with it as the clergyman. He and the two Olliveras were cousins. Bede Greatorex was awfully cut at the death: he'd be glad to see there was doubt attending it; but he, as a sensible man, can't see it. They buried Mr. Ollivera like a dog."

"What did they do that for?"

"The verdict was felo-de-se. Mr. Hurst can tell you all about it, sir; he was at Helstonleigh at the time: he says he never saw such a scene in his life as the funeral. It was a moonlight night, and half the town was there."

"I'll get it all out of him," quoth Roland, who had not lost in the smallest degree his propensity to indulge in desultory gossip.

"Don't ask him in the office," advised Jenner. "Brown would stop you at the first word. He never lets a syllable be dropped upon the subject. I asked him one day what it was to him, and he answered that it was not seemly to allude to the affair in the house, as Mr. Ollivera had been a connection of it. My fancy is that Brown must have known something of it at the time, and does not like it mentioned on his own score," confidentially added little Jenner, who was of a shrewd turn. "I saw him change colour once over it."

"Who is Brown?" questioned Roland.

"That's more than I can say," was the reply. "He's an uncommonly efficient clerk; but, once out of the office, he keeps himself to himself, and makes friends with none of us. Here we are, sir."

The eating-house, however unsuitable it might have been to one holding his own as the nephew of an English baronet, to say nothing of an Irish peer, was welcome as sun in harvest to hungry Roland. He ordered a magnificent dinner, off-hand: three plates of meat each, three of tart; vegetables, bread and beer ad libitum: paid for the whole, changing his five-pound note, and gave a shilling to the man who waited on them. Little Jenner went out with his face shining.

"We must make the best of our way back, Mr. Yorke. Time's up."

"Oh, is it, though," cried Roland. "I'm not going back yet. I shall take a turn round to see Mrs. Jenkins; there are five hundred things I want to ask her."

One can only be civil to a man who has just treated one to a good dinner, and Jenner did not like to tell Roland pointblank that he had better not go anywhere but to the office.

"They are awfully strict about time in our place," cried he; "and we are busy just now. I must make haste back, sir."

"All right," said easy Roland. "Say I am coming."

His long legs went flying off in the direction of Gower Street, Jenner having given him the necessary instructions to find it; and he burst clattering in upon Mrs. Jones in her sitting-room without the least ceremony, very much as he used to do in the old days when she was Mrs. Jenkins. Mrs. Jones had been for some time now given to wish that she had not changed her name. Doing very well as the widow Jenkins, years ago, in her little hosier's shop in High Street, Helstonleigh, what was her mortification to find one day that the large and handsome house next door, with its shop-windows of plate-glass, had been opened as another hosier's by a Mr. Richard Jones. Would customers continue to come to her plain and unpretending mart, when that new one, grand, imposing, and telling of an unlimited stock within, was staring them in the face? The widow Jenkins feared not; and fretted herself to fiddle-strings.

The fear might have had no cause of foundation: the show kept up at the adjoining house was perhaps founded on artificial bases, rather than real. Richard Jones (whom the city had already begun to designate as Dicky) turned out to be of a sociable nature; he made her acquaintance whether she would or no, and suddenly proposed to her to unite the two businesses in one, by making herself, and her stock, and her connection, over to him. Mrs. Jenkins's first impulse was to throw at his head the nearest parcel that came to hand. Familiarity with an idea, however, sometimes reconciles the worst adversary; as at length it did Mrs. Jenkins to this. To give her her due, she took no account whatever of Mr. Jones in the matter; he went for nothing, a bale of waste flung in to make weight, she should rule him just as she had ruled Jenkins; her sole temptation was the flourishing shop, à côté, and the good, well-furnished house. So Mrs. Jenkins exchanged her name for that of Jones, and removed, bag and baggage; resigning the inferior home that had so long sheltered her. It was close upon this, that one of the barristers, coming in to the summer assizes at Helstonleigh, took apartments at Mrs. Jones's. That was Mr. Ollivera: and in the following March, when he again came in, occurred his tragical ending.

Before this, long before it, Mrs. Jones had grown to realize to herself the truth of the homely proverb, All's not gold that glitters. Mr. Jones's connection did not prove to be of the most extensive kind; far from it; the large, imposing stock turned out to be three parts dummies; and she grew to believe—to see—that his motive in marrying her was to uphold his newly-established business by beguiling to it her old customers. The knowledge did not tend to soothe her naturally tart temper; neither did the fact that her husband took vast deal of pleasure abroad, spent money recklessly, and left her to do all the work. Mr. Jones's debts came out, one after the other; more than could be paid; and one morning some men of the law walked quietly in and put themselves in possession of the effects. Things had come to a crisis. Mr. Jones, after battling out affairs with the bankruptcy commissioner, started for America; his wife went off to London. Certain money, her own past savings, she had been wise enough to have secured to her separate special use, and that could not be touched. With a portion of it she bought in some of the furniture, and set up as a letter of lodgings in Gower Street.

But that Roland Yorke had not seen the parlour at Helstonleigh (which the reader had the satisfaction of once entering with Mr. Butterby), he would have gone well nigh to think this the same room. The red carpet on the floor, the small book-shelves, the mahogany sideboard with its array of glasses, the horsehair chairs, the red cloth on the centre table, all had been transplanted. When Roland bustled in, he found Mrs. Jones knitting away at lambs' wool socks, as if for her life. In the intervals of her home occupation, or when her house was slack of lodgers, she did these for sale, and realized a very fair profit.

"Now then," said Roland, stirring up the fire of his own accord, and making himself at home, as he liked to do wherever he might be, "I want to know all about everybody."

Mrs. Jones turned her chair towards him with a jerk; and Roland put question after question about the old city, which he had so abruptly quitted more than seven years before. It may be that Mrs. Jones recognized in him a kind of fellow-sufferer. Neither of them cared to see Helstonleigh again, unless under the auspices of a more propitious fate than the present. Anyway, she was gracious to Roland, and gave him information as fast as he asked for it, repeating some things he had heard before. He persisted in calling her Mrs. Jenkins, saying it came more natural than the other name.

Mr. Channing was dead. His eldest son Hamish was living in London. Arthur was Mr. Galloway's right hand; Tom was a clergyman, and just made a minor canon of the old cathedral; Charley Mrs. Jones knew nothing about, except that he was in India. The college school had got a new master. Mr. Ketch was reposing in a damp green nook, side by side with old Jenkins the bedesman. Hamish Channing's bank had come to grief, Mrs. Jenkins did not know how. In the panic, she believed.

"And that beautiful kinsman of mine, William Yorke, reigns at Hazeldon, and old Galloway is flourishing in his office, with his flaxen curls!" burst forth Roland, suddenly struck with a weighty sense of injustice. "The bad people get the luck of it in this world, Mrs. Jenkins; the deserving ones go begging. Hamish Channing's bank come to grief;—bright Hamish! And look at me!—and you! I never saw such a world as this with its miserable ups and downs."

"Ah," said Mrs. Jones with a touch of her native tartness, "it's a good thing there's another world to come after. We may find that a better one."

The prospect (probably from being regarded as rather far-off) did not appear to afford present satisfaction to Roland. He sat pulling at his whiskers, moodily resenting the general blindness of Fortune in regard to merit, and then suddenly wheeled round to his own affairs.

"I say, Mrs. J."—a compromise between the two names and serving for both—"I want a lodging. Couldn't you let me come here?"

She looked up briskly. "What kind of a lodging? I mean as to position and price."

"Oh, something comfortable," said Roland.

Perhaps for old acquaintance' sake, perhaps because she had some apartments vacant, Mrs. Jones appeared to regard the proposition with no disfavour; and began to talk of her house's accommodation.

"The rooms on the first floor are very good and well furnished," she said. "When I was about it, Mr. Yorke, I thought I might as well have things nice as not, one finds the return; and the drawing-room floor naturally gets served the best. There's a piano in the front room, and the bed in the back room is excellent."

"They'd be just the thing for me," cried Roland, rising to walk about in pleasurable excitement. "What's the rent?"

"They are let for a pound a week. Mr.—"

"That'll do I can pay it," said he eagerly. "I don't play the piano myself; but it may be useful if I give a party. You'll cook for me?"

"Of course we'll cook," said Mrs. Jones. "But I was about to tell you that those rooms are let to a clergyman. If you—"

Roland had come to an abrupt anchor at the edge of the table, and the look of blank dismay on his face was such as to cut short Mrs. Jones's speech. "What's the matter?" she asked.

"Mrs. J., I couldn't give it; I was forgetting. They are to pay me a pound a-week at Greatorex's; but I can't spend it all in lodgings, I'm afraid. There'll be other things wanted."

"Other things!" ejaculated Mrs. Jones. "I should think there would be other things. Food, and drink, and firing, and light, and wear and tear of clothes, and washing; and a hundred extras beside."

Roland sat in perplexity. Ways and means seem to have grown dark together.

"Couldn't you let me one room? A room with a turn-up bedstead in it, Mrs. Jenkins, or something of that? Couldn't you take the pound a-week, and do for me?"

"I don't know but I might make some such arrangement, and let you have the front parlour," she slowly said. "We've got a Scripture reader in the back one."

Roland started up impulsively to look at the front parlour, intending to take it, off hand. As they quitted the room—which was built out at the back, on the staircase that led down to the kitchen—Roland saw a tall, fair, good-looking young woman, who stopped and asked some question of Mrs. Jones. Which that lady answered sharply.

"I have no time to talk about trifles now, Alletha."

"Who's that?" cried Roland, as they entered the parlour: a small room with a dark paper and faded red curtains.

"It's my sister, Mr. Yorke."

"I say, Mrs. J., this is a stunning room," exclaimed Roland, who was in that eager mood, of his, when all things looked couleur-de-rose. "Can I come in today?"

"You can tomorrow, if we agree. That sofa lets out into a bedstead at night. You must not get into my debt, though, Mr. Yorke," she added, in the plain, straightforward way that was habitual with her. "I couldn't afford it, and I tell you so beforehand."

"I'll never do that," said Roland, impulsively earnest in his sincerity. "I'll bring you home the pound each week, and then I shan't be tempted to change it. Look here"—taking two sovereigns from his pocket— "that's to steer on ahead with. Does she live here?" he added, going back without ceremony to the subject of Miss Rye. "Alletha, do you call her? what an odd name!"

"The name was a mistake of the parson's when she was christened. It was to have been Allethea. I've had her with me four or five years now. She is a dressmaker, Mr. Yorke, and works sometimes at home, and sometimes out."

"She'd be uncommonly good-looking if she were not such a shadow," commented Roland with candour.

Mrs. Jones gave her head a toss, as if the topic displeased her. "Shadow, indeed! Yes, and she's likely to be one. Never was any pig more obstinate than she."

"Pigs!" cried Roland with energy, "you should see the obstinacy of Natal pigs, Mrs. J. I have. Drove 'em too."

"It couldn't equal hers," disputed Mrs. J., with intense acrimony. "She is wedded to the memory of a runaway villain, Mr. Yorke, that's what she is! A good opportunity presented itself to her lately of settling, but she'd not take it. She'd sooner fret out her life after him, than look upon an honest man. The two pigs together by the tail, and let 'em pull two ways till they drop, they'd not equal her. And for a runaway; a man that disgraced himself!"

"What did he do?" asked curious Roland.

"It's not very good to repeat," said Mrs. Jones tartly. "She lived in Birmingham, our native place, till the mother died, and then she came to me at Helstonleigh. First thing she tells me was, that she was engaged to be married to some young man in an office there, George Winter: and over she goes to Birmingham the next Christmas on a visit to her aunt, on purpose to meet him: stays there a week, and comes home again. Well, Mr. Yorke, this grand young man, this George Winter, about whom I had my doubts, though I'd never seen him, got into trouble before three months had gone by: he and a fellow-clerk did something wrong with the money, and Winter decamped."

"I wonder if he went to Port Natal?" mused Roland. "We had some queer people over there."

"It don't much matter where he went," returned Mrs. Jones, hotly. "He did go, and he never came back, and he took Alletha's common sense away with him: what with him and what with the dreadful affair at our house of that poor Mr. Ollivera, she has never been herself since. It both happened about the same time."

Roland recalled what he had recently heard from Jenner regarding the death of the barrister, and felt a little at sea.

"What was Ollivera to her?" he asked.

"What! why, nothing," said Mrs. Jones. "And she's no better than a lunatic to have taken it as she did. Whether it's that, or whether it's the pining after the other, I don't know, but one of the two's preying upon her. There's Mr. Ollivera!"

Roland went to the window. In the street, talking, stood a dark, small man in the garb of a clergyman, with a grave but not unpleasant face, and sad dark eyes.

"Oh, that's Mr. Ollivera, is it?" quoth Roland. "He looks another shadow."

"And it is another case of obstinacy," rejoined Mrs. Jones. "He has refused all along to believe that his brother killed himself; you could as soon make him think the sun never shone. He comes to my parlour and talks to me about it by the hour together, with his note-case in his hand, till Alletha can't sit any longer, and goes rushing off with her work like any mad woman."

"Why should she rush off? What harm does it do to her?"

"I don't know: it's one of the puzzles to be found out. His coming here was a curious thing, Mr. Yorke. One day I was standing at the front door, and saw a young clergyman passing. He looked at me, and stopped; and I knew him for Henry Ollivera, though we had only met at the time of the death. When I told him I had rooms to let, and very nice ones, for it struck me that perhaps he might be able to recommend them, he looked out in that thoughtful, dreamy way he has, (look at his eyes now, Mr. Yorke!) seeing nothing, I'm certain; and then said he'd go up and look at the rooms; and we went up. Would you believe that he took them for himself on the spot?"

"What a brick!" cried Roland, who was following out suggested ideas but imperfectly. "I'll take this one."

"Alletha gave a great cry when she heard he was coming, and said it was Fate. I demanded what she meant by that, but she'd not open her lips further. Talk of Natal pigs, forsooth, she's worse. He took possession of the rooms within the week; and I say, Mr. Yorke, that, Fate or not Fate, he never had but one object in coming—the sifting of that past calamity. His poor mistaken mind is ever on the rack to bring some discovery to light. It's like that search one reads of, after the philosopher's stone."

Roland laughed. He was not very profound himself, but the philosopher's stone and Mrs. Jones seemed utterly at variance.

"It does," she said. "For there's no stone to be found in the one case, and no discovery to be made in the other, beyond what has been made. I don't say this to the parson, Mr. Yorke; I listen to him and humour him for the sake of his dead brother."

"Well, I shan't bother you about dead people, Mrs. J., so you let me the room."

The bargain was not difficult. Every suggestion made by Mrs. Jones, he acceded to before it had well left her lips. He had fallen into good hands. Whatever might be Mrs. Jones's faults of manner and temper, she was strictly just, regarding Roland's interests at least in an equal degree with her own.

"Do you know," said Roland, nursing his knee as the bargain concluded, "I have never felt so much at home since I left it, as I did just now by your fire, Mrs. J.? I'm uncommon glad I came here."

He was genuine in what he said: indeed Roland could but be genuine always, too much so sometimes. Mrs. J.—as he called her—brought back so vividly the old home life of his boyhood, now gone by for ever, that it was like being at Helstonleigh again.

"My eldest brother, George, is dead," said Roland. "Gerald is grand with his chambers and his club, and is married besides, but I've not seen him. Tod is in the army: do you remember him? an awful young scamp he was, his face all manner of colours from fighting, and his clothes torn to that degree that Lady Augusta used to threaten to send him to school without any. Where's your husband number two, Mrs. J.?"

"It is to be hoped he is where he will never come away from; he went sailing off three years ago from Liverpool," she answered sharply; for, of all sore subjects, this of her second marriage was the worst. "Anyway, I have made myself and my goods secure from him."

"Perhaps he's at Port Natal, driving pigs. He'll find out what they are if he is."

Mr. Ollivera was turning to the house. Roland opened the parlour door when he had passed it; to look after him.

Some one else was there. Peering out from a dark nook in the passage, her lips slightly apart, her eyes strained after the clergyman with a strange kind of fear in their depths, stood Alletha Rye. Mr. Ollivera suddenly turned back, as though he had forgotten something, and she shrank out of sight. Mrs. Jones introduced Roland: "Mr. Roland Yorke."

Mr. Ollivera's face was thin; his dark brown eyes shone with a flashing, restless, feverish light. Be you very sure when that peculiar light is seen, it betokens a mind ill at rest. The eyes fixed themselves on Roland: and perhaps there was something in the tall, fine form, in the good-nature of the strong-featured countenance, that recalled a memory to Mr. Ollivera.

"Any relative of the Yorkes of Helstonleigh?"

"I should think so," said Roland, "I am a Yorke of Helstonleigh. But I've not been there since I went to Port Natal, seven years and more ago. Do you know them, Mr. Ollivera?"

"I know a little of the minor-canon, William Yorke, and—"

"Oh! he!" curtly interrupted Roland, with a vast amount of scorn. "He is a beauty to know, he is."

The remark, so like a flash of boyish resentment, excited a slight smile in Mr. Ollivera.

"Bill Yorke showed himself a cur once in his life, and it's not me that's going to forget it. He'd have cared for my telling him of it, too, had I come back worth a few millions from Port Natal, and gone about Helstonleigh in my carriage and four."

Mr. Ollivera said some courteous words about hoping to make Roland's better acquaintance, and departed. Roland suddenly remembered the claims of his office, and tore away at full speed.

Never slackening it until he reached the house of Greatorex and Greatorex; and there he very nearly knocked down a little girl who had just come out of the private entrance. Roland turned to apologise; but the words died on his lips, and he stood like one suddenly struck dumb, staring in silence.

In the pretty young lady, one of two who were talking together in the passage, and looked round at the commotion, Roland thought he recognised an old friend, now the wife of his cousin William Yorke. He bounded in and seized her hands.

"You are Constance Channing?"

"No," replied the young lady, with wondering eyes, "I am Annabel."

Mr. Roland Yorke's first movement was to take the sweet face between his hands, and kiss it tenderly. Struggling, blushing, almost weeping, the young lady drew back against the wall.

"How dare you?" she demanded in bitter resentment. "Are you out of your mind, sir?"

"Good gracious, Annabel, don't you know me? I am your old playfellow, Roland Yorke."

"Does that give you any right to insult me? I might have known it was no one else," she added in the moment's anger.

"Why, Annabel, it was only done in great joy. I had used to kiss you, you remember: you were but a little mite then, and I was a big tease. Oh, I am so glad to see you! I'd rather have met you than all the world. You can't be angry with me. Shake hands and be friends."

To remain long at variance with Roland was one of the impossibilities of social life. He possessed himself of Annabel Channing's hand and nearly shook it off. What with his hearty words, and what (may it be confessed, even of Annabel) with the flattery of his praises and general admiration, Annabel's smiles broke forth amidst her blushes. Roland's eyes looked as if they would devour her.

"I say, I never saw anybody so pretty in all my life. It is the nicest face; just what Constance's used to be. I thought it was Constance, you know. Was she not daft, though, to go and take up again with that miserable William Yorke?"

Standing by, having looked on with a smile of grand pity mingled with amusement, was a lady in the most fashionable attire, the amount of hair on her head something marvellous to look at.

"I should have known Roland Yorke anywhere," she said, holding out her hand.

"Why, if I don't believe it's one of the Joliffes!"

"Hush, Roland," said Annabel, hastening to stop his freedom, and the tone proved that she had nearly forgiven him on her own score. "This is Mrs. Bede Greatorex."

"Formerly Louisa Joliffe," put in that lady. "Now do you know me?"

"Well, I never met with such a strange thing," cried Roland. "That makes three—four—of the old Helstonleigh people I have met today. Hurst, Mrs. J., and now you two. I think there must be magic in it."

"You must come and see me soon, Roland," said Mrs. Greatorex as she went out. Miss Channing waited for the little girl, Jane Greatorex, who had run in her wilful manner into her uncle Bede's office. Roland offered to fetch her.

"Thank you," said Miss Channing. "Do you know which is the office?"

"Know! law bless you!" cried Roland. "What do you suppose I am, Annabel? Clerk to Greatorex and Greatorex."

Her cheeks flushed with surprise. "Clerk to Greatorex and Greatorex! I thought you went to Port Natal to make your fortune."

"But I did not make it. It has been nothing but knocking about; then and since. Carrick is a trump, as he always was, but he gets floored himself sometimes; and that's his case now. If they had not given me a stool here (which he got for me) I'm not sure but I should have gone into the hot-pie line."

"The—what?"

"The hot-pie line; crying them in the streets, you know, with a basket and a white cloth, and a paper cap on. There's a fine opening for it down in Poplar."

Miss Channing burst out laughing.

"It would be nothing to a fellow who has been over yonder," avowed Roland, jerking his head in the direction Port Natal might be supposed to lie. And then leaping to a widely different subject in his volatile lightness, he said something that brought the tears to her eyes, the drooping tremor to her lips.

"It was so good in the old days; all of us children together; we were no better. And Mr. Channing is gone, I hear! Oh, I am so sorry, Annabel!"

"Two years last February," she said in a hushed tone. "We have just put off our mourning for him. Mamma is in the dear old house, and Arthur and Tom live with her. Will you please look for the little girl, Mr. Yorke?"

"Now I vow!"—burst forth Roland in a heat. "I'll not stand that, you know. One would think you had put on stilts. If ever you call me 'Mr. Yorke' again, I'll go back to Port Natal."

She laughed a little pleasant laugh of embarrassment. "But, please, I want my pupil. I cannot go myself into the offices to look for her."

At that moment Jane Greatorex came dancing up, and was secured. Roland stood at the door to watch them away, exchanged a few light words with a clerk then entering, and finally bustled into the office.

"Am I late?" began Roland, with characteristic indifference. "I'm very sorry, Mr. Brown. I was looking at some lodgings; and I met an old friend or two. It all served to hinder me, but I'll soon make up for it."

"You have been away two hours and a half, Mr. Yorke."

"It's more, I think," said Roland. "I assure you I did my best to get back. You'll soon find what I can get through, Mr. Brown."

Mr. Brown made no reply whatever. Jenner was absent, but Hurst was at his post, writing, and the faint hum of voices in the adjoining room, told that some client was holding conference with Mr. Bede Greatorex.

Roland resumed his copying where he had left off, and wrote for a quarter of an hour without speaking. Diligence unheard of! At the end of that time he looked off for a little relaxation.

"Hurst, where do you think I am going to lodge?"

"How should I know?" responded Mr. Hurst. And Roland told him where in an undertone.

"Jenner and I were going along Tottenham Court Road, and met her," he resumed presently, after a short interlude of writing. "She looks twenty years older."

"That's through her tongue," suggested Mr. Hurst.

"In the old days down there, I'd as soon have gone to live in a Tartar's house as in hers. But weren't her teas and toasted muffins good! Here, in this desert of a place—and it's worse of a desert to me than Port Natal—to get into her house will seem like getting into home again."

Mr. Brown, looking off his work to refer to a paper by his side, took the opportunity to direct a glance at the opposite desk. Whether Roland took it to himself or not, he applied sedulously for a couple of minutes to his writing.

"I say, Hurst, what a row there is about that dead Mr. Ollivera!"

"Where's the row?"

"Well, it seems to crop up everywhere. Jenner talked of it; she talked of it; I hear that other Mr. Ollivera talks of it. You were in the thick of it, they say."

Hurst nodded. "My father was the surgeon fetched to him when he was found dead, and had to give evidence at the inquest. I went to see him buried; it was a scene. They stole a march on us, though."

"Who did?"

"They let us all disperse, and then went and read the burial service over the grave; Ollivera the clergyman, and three or four more. Arthur Channing was one."

"Arthur Channing!"

Had any close observer been in the office, he might perchance have noticed that while Mr. Brown's eyes still sought his work, his pen had ceased to play. His lips were slightly parted; his ears were cocked; the tale evidently bore for him as great an interest as it did for the speakers—an interest he did not choose should be seen. Had they been speaking aloud, he would have checked the conversation at once with an intimation that it could not concern anybody: as they spoke covertly, he listened at leisure. Mr. Hurst resumed.

"Yes, Arthur Channing. The rumour ran that William Yorke had promised to be present, but declined at the last moment, and Arthur Channing voluntarily took his place out of sympathy for the feelings of the dead man's brother."

"Bravo, old Arthur! he's the trump he always was. That's the Reverend Bill all over."

"The Reverend Bill let them have his surplice. And there they stood, and read the burial service over the poor fellow by stealth, just as the old Scotch covenanters held their secret services in caves. Altogether a vast deal of romance encircled the affair, and some mystery. One Godfrey Pitman's name was mixed up in it."

"Who was Godfrey Pitman?"

Hurst dipped his pen slowly into the ink. "Nobody ever knew. He was lodging in the house, and went away mysteriously the same evening. Helstonleigh got to say in joke that there must have been two Godfrey Pitmans. The people of the house swore through thick and thin that the real Godfrey Pitman left at half-past four o'clock and went away by rail at five; others saw him quit the house at dark, and depart by the eight o'clock train. It got to a regular dispute."

"But had Godfrey Pitman anything to do with Mr. Ollivera?"

"Not he."

"Then where was the good of bringing him up?" cried Roland.

"I am only telling you of the different interests that were brought to bear upon it. It was an affair, that death was!"

The entrance of Mr. Frank Greatorex broke up the colloquy, recalling the clerks to their legitimate work. But the attention of one of them had become so absorbed that it was with difficulty he could get himself back again to passing life.

And that one was Mr. Brown.

CHAPTER X

GOING INTO SOCIETY

The year was growing a little later; the evenings were lengthening, and the light of the setting sun, illumining the west with a golden radiance, threw some of its cheering brightness even on the streets and houses of close, smoky London.

It shone on the person of the Reverend Henry William Ollivera, as he sat at home, taking his frugal meal, a tea-dinner. The room was a good one, and well furnished in a plain way. The table had been drawn towards one of the windows, open to the hum of the street; the rosewood cabinet at the back was handsome with its sheet of plate-glass and its white marble top; the chairs and sofa were covered with substantial cloth, the pier-glass over the mantlepiece reflected back bright ornaments. Mr. Ollivera was of very simple habits, partly because he really cared little how he lived, partly because the scenes of distress and privation he met with daily in his ministrations read him a lesson that he was not slow to take. How could he pamper himself up with rich food, when so many within a stone's throw were pining for want of bread? His landlady, Mrs. Jones, gave him sound lectures on occasion, telling him to his face that he was trying to break down. Sometimes she prepared nice dinners in spite of him: a fowl, or some other luxury, and Mr. Ollivera smiled and did not say it was not enjoyed. The district of his curacy was full of poor; poverty, vice, misery reigned, and would reign, in spite of what he could do. Some of the worst phases of London life were ever before him. The great problem, "What shall be done with these?" arose to his mind day by day. He had his scripture readers; he had other help; but destitution both of body and mind reared itself aloft like a many-headed monster, defying all solution. Sometimes Mr. Ollivera did not come in to dinner at all, but took a mutton-chop with his tea; as he was doing now.

Four years had elapsed since his brother's mysterious death (surely it may be called so!) and the conviction on the clergyman's mind, that the verdict was wholly at variance with the facts, had not abated one iota. Nay, time had but served to strengthen it. Nothing else had strengthened it. No discovery had been made, no circumstance, however minute, had arisen to throw light upon it one way or the other. The hoped-for, looked-for communication from the police-agent, Butterby, had never come. In point of fact Mr. Butterby, in regard to this case, had found himself wholly at sea. Godfrey Pitman did not turn up in response to the threatened "looking after;" Miss Rye departed for London with her sister when affairs at the Jones's came to a crash; and, if the truth must be told, Mr. Butterby veered round to his original opinion, that the verdict had been a correct one. Once, and once only, that renowned officer had presented himself at the house of Greatorex and Greatorex. Happening to be in London, he thought he would give them a call. But he brought no news. It was but a few weeks following the occurrence, and there might not have been time for any to arise. One thing he had requested—to retain in his possession the scrap of writing found on the table at the death. It might be useful to him, he said, for of course he should still keep his eyes open: and Mr. Greatorex readily acquiesced. Since then nothing whatever had been heard from Mr. Butterby, or from any other quarter; but the sad facts were rarely out of the clergyman's mind; and the positive conviction, the expectation of the light, to break in sooner or later, burnt within him with a steady ray, sure and true as Heaven.

Not of this, however, was Mr. Ollivera's mind filled this evening. His thoughts were running on the disheartening scenes of the day; the difficult men and women he had tried to deal with—some of them meek and resigned, many hard and bad; all wanting help for their sick bodies or worse souls. There was one case in particular that interested him sadly. A man named Gisby, discovered shortly before, lay in a room, dying slowly. He did not want help in kind, as so many did; but of spiritual help, none could be in greater need. Little by little, Mr. Ollivera got at his history. It appeared that the man had once been servant in the house of Kene, the Queen's counsel—Judge Kene now: he had been raised to the bench in the past year. During his service there, a silver mug disappeared; circumstances seemed to point to Gisby as guilty, and he was discharged, getting subsequently other employment.

But now, the man was not guilty—as he convinced Mr. Ollivera, and the suspicion appeared to have worked him a great deal of ill, and made him hard. On this day, when the clergyman sat by his bed-side, reading and praying, he had turned a deaf ear. "Where's the use?" he roughly cried, "Sir Thomas thinks me guilty always." It struck Mr. Ollivera that the man had greatly respected his master, had valued his good opinion and craved for it still; and the next morning this was confirmed. "You'll go to him when I'm dead, sir, and tell him the truth then, that I was not guilty? I never touched the mug, or knew how or where it went."

Returning home with these words ringing in his ears, Mr. Ollivera could not get the man out of his mind. So long as the sense of being wronged lay upon Gisby, so long would he encase himself in his hard indifference, and refuse to hear. "I must get Kene to go to see the man," decided Mr. Ollivera. "He must hear with his own ears and see with his own eyes that he was not guilty, and tell him so; and then Gisby will come round. I wonder if Kene is back from circuit."

Excessively tired with his day's work, for his frame was not of the strongest, Mr. Ollivera did not care to go out that evening to Sir Thomas Kene's distant residence on the chance of not finding him. And yet, if the judge was back, there ought to be no time lost in communicating with him, for Gisby was daily getting nearer to death. "Bede Greatorex will be able to tell me," suddenly thought Mr. Ollivera, when his tea had been long over and twilight was setting in. "I'll send and ask him."

Moving to his writing-table, he wrote a short note, reading it over before enclosing it in an envelope.

"Dear Bede,—Can you tell me whether Sir Thomas Kene is in London? I wish particularly to see him as soon as possible. It is on a little matter connected with my parish work.

"Truly yours

"William Ollivera."

It was a latent thought that induced Mr. Ollivera to add the concluding sentence and the motive shall be told. He and Bede Greatorex had come to an issue twice upon the subject of his so persistently cherishing the notion that the now long-past death was anything but a suicide; or rather, that he should pursue it. Bede heard so much of it from him that he grew vexed, and at length vowed he would listen to him no more. And Mr. Ollivera thought that if Bede fancied he wanted to see Sir Thomas Kene on that subject, he might refuse to answer him.

Ringing the bell, he gave the note to the servant with a request (preferred with deprecation and a plea of his own tired state, for he was one of those who are sensitively chary of giving any extra trouble) that it should be taken to Mr. Bede Greatorex, and an answer waited for.

But when the girl got downstairs, there arose some slight difficulty; she was engaged in a necessary household occupation—ironing—and her mistress did not care that she should quit it. Miss Rye stood by with her things on, about to go out on some errand of her own. Ah me! these apparently trifling chances do not happen accidentally.

"Can't you just step round to Bedford Square, with it, Alletha?" asked Mrs. Jones. "It won't take you far out of your way."

Miss Rye's silent answer—she seemed always silent now—was to pick up the note and go out with it. She knew the house, for she worked occasionally for Mrs. Bede Greatorex, and was passing to the private entrance when she encountered Frank Greatorex, who was coming out at the other door. He wished her good evening, and she told him her errand, showing the note directed to Bede.

"He is in his office still," said Frank, throwing open the door for her. "Walk in. Mr. Brown, attend here, please."

Miss Rye stepped into the semi-lighted room, for there was only a shaded lamp on Mr. Brown's desk; and Frank Greatorex, closing the door, was gone again. Mr. Brown, at work as late as his master, came forward.

"For Mr. Bede Greatorex," said Miss Rye, handing him the note. "I will wait—"

The words were broken off with a faint, sharp cry. A cry, low though it was, of surprise, of terror, of dismay. Both their faces blanched to whiteness, they stood gazing at each other, she with strained eyes and drawnback lips, he with a kind of forced stillness on his features, that nevertheless told of inward emotion.

"Oh, my good heaven!" she breathed in her agitation. "Is it you?"

Miss Rye had heard speak of Mr. Brown, the managing clerk in the department of Mr. Bede Greatorex. Jenner had mentioned him: Roland Yorke had commented on him and his wig. But that "Mr. Brown" should be the man now standing before her, she had never suspected; no, not in her wildest dreams.

"Sit down, Miss Rye. You are faint."

She put his arm from her, as he would have supported her to a seat, and staggered to one of herself. He followed, and stood by her in silence.

"What are you called here?" she began—and, it may be, that in the moment's agitation she forgot his ostensible name and really put it as a question, not in mocking, condemnatory scorn:—"Godfrey Pitman?"

Every instinct of terror the man possessed seemed to rise up within him at sound of the name. He glanced round the room; at the desks; at the walls; as if to assure himself that no ear was there.

"Hush—sh—sh!" with a prolonged note of caution. "Never breathe that name, here or elsewhere."

"What if I were to? To speak it aloud to all who ought to hear it?"

"Why then you would bring a hornet's nest about heads that you little wot of. Their sting might end in worse than death."

"Death for you?"

"No: I should be the hangman."

"What do you mean?"

"Listen, Miss Rye. I cannot tell you what I mean: and your better plan will be never to ask me. If—"

"Better for whom?" she interrupted.

"For—well, for me, for one. The fact is, that certain interests pertaining to myself and others—certain reminiscences of the past," he continued with very strong emphasis, "have become so complicated, so interwoven as it were one with the other, that we must in all probability stand or fall together."

"I do not understand you."

"I can scarcely expect that you should. But—were any proceeding on your part, any word, whether spoken by design or accident, to lead to that fall, you would rue it to the last hour of your life. That you can at least understand."

The faintness was passing off, and Miss Rye rose, steadying herself against the railings of Mr. Hurst's desk. At that moment the inner door was unlatched, and the clerk, recalled to present duties, caught the note from her unresisting hand.

"For Mr. Bede Greatorex," he said aloud, glancing at the superscription. "I will give it to him."

It was Mr. Bede Greatorex who came forth. He took the note, and glanced at Alletha.

"Ah, Miss Rye! Is it you?"

"Our maid was busy, so I brought it down," she explained. "Mr. Ollivera is waiting for an answer."

Bede Greatorex went back to his room, leaving the intervening door open. She sat and waited. Mr. Brown, whose work was in a hurry, wrote on steadily at his desk by the light of a shaded lamp. A minute or two, and Bede Greatorex brought her a bit of paper twisted up, and showed her out himself.

With the errand she had come abroad to execute for herself gone clean out of her head, Alletha Rye went back home, her brain in a whirl. The streets she passed through were crowded with all the bustle and jostle of London life; but, had she been traversing an African desert, she could not have felt more entirely alone. Her life that night lay within her: and it was one of confused tumult.

The note found Mr. Ollivera asleep: as the twilight deepened, he had dropped, in sheer weariness, into an unconscious slumber. Untwisting the scrap of paper, he held it near a lighted candle and read the contents:—

"Dear Henry,—Kene is back, and is coming to us this evening; we expect two or three friends. Louisa will be pleased if you can join us. Faithfully yours,

"B.G."

Mr. Ollivera eschewed gaiety of all kinds, parties included. Over and over again had he been fruitlessly invited to the grand dinners and soirées of Mrs. Bede Greatorex, until they left off asking him. "Two or three friends," he repeated as he put down the note. "I don't mind that, for I must see Kene."

Dressing himself; he was on the point of setting out, when a messenger arrived to fetch him to a sick person; so that it was half-past ten when he reached the house of Mr. Greatorex. And then, but for his mission to the Judge, he would have quitted it again without entering the reception-rooms.

Two or three friends! Lining the wide staircase, dotting the handsome landing, crowding the numerous guest-rooms, there they were; a mob of them. Women in the costly and fantastic toilettes of the present day; men bowing and bending with their evening manners on. Mr. Ollivera resented the crowd as a personal wrong.

"'Two or three friends,' you wrote me word, Bede," he reproachfully said, seeing his cousin in a corner near the entrance-door. "You know I do not like these things and never go to them."

"On my word, Henry, I did not know it was going to be this cram," returned Bede Greatorex. "I thought we might be twenty, perhaps, all told."

"How can you put up with this? Is it seemly, Bede—in this once staid and pattern house?"

"Seemly?" repeated Bede Greatorex.

"Forgive me, Bede. I was thinking of the dear old times under your mother's rule. The happy evenings, all hospitality and cheerfulness; the chapter read at bedtime, when the small knot of guests had departed. Friends were entertained then; but I don't know what you call these."

Perhaps Bede Greatorex had never, amid all his provocations, felt so tempted to avow the truth as now—that he abhorred it with his whole heart and soul. Henry William Ollivera could not hate and despise it more than he. As to the good old days of sunshine and peace thus recalled, a groan well nigh burst from him, at their recollection. It was indeed a contrast, then and now: in more things than this. The world bore a new aspect for Bede Greatorex, and not a happier one.

"Is Kene here, Bede?"

"Not yet. What is it that you want with him?"

Mr. Ollivera gave a brief outline of the case; Bede left him in the middle of it to welcome fresh arrivals. Something awfully fine loomed up, in pink silk and lace, and blazing emeralds. It was Mrs. Bede Greatorex. Her chignon was a mile high, and her gown was below her shoulder-blades. The modest young clergyman turned away at the sight, his cheeks flushing a dusky red. Not in this kind of society of late years, the curiosities of fashionable attire were new to him.

"Is Bede mad?" he inwardly said, "or has he lost all control over his wife's actions?"

Somebody else, not used to society, was staring on with all the eyes of wonder he possessed. And that was Roland Yorke. Leaning against the wall in a new suit of dress-clothes, with a huge pair of white gloves on that would have been quite the proper thing at Port Natal, stood Roland. Mr. Ollivera, trying to get away from everybody, ran against him. The two were great friends now, and Roland was in the habit of running up to Mr. Ollivera's drawing-room at will.

"I say," began Roland, "this is rather strong, is it not?"

"Do you mean the crowd?"

"I mean everything. Some of the girls and women look as if they had forgotten to put their gowns on. Why do they dress in this way?"

"Because they fancy it's the fashion, I suppose," replied Mr. Ollivera, drawing down the corners of his thin lips.

"They must have taken the fashion from the Zulu Kaffirs," returned Roland. "When one has been knocked about amidst that savage lot—fought with 'em, too, men and women—one loses superfluous fastidiousness, Mr. Ollivera; but I don't think this is right."

Mr. Ollivera intimated that there could not be a doubt it was all wrong.

"Down in Helstonleigh, where I come from, they dress themselves decently," observed Roland, forgetting that his reminiscences of the place dated more than seven years back, and that fashion penetrates to all the strongholds of society, whether near or distant. "The girls there are lovely, too. Just look if they are not."

Mr. Ollivera, in some slight surprise, followed the direction of the speaker's eyes, and saw a young lady sitting back in a corner; her white evening dress, her banded hair, the soft, pure flush on her delicate face, all as simple, and genuine, and modest as herself.

"That's what the girls are in my native place, Mr. Ollivera."

"Mrs. Bede Greatorex is a native of Helstonleigh, also," observed the clergyman, dryly. And for a moment Roland was dumb. The pink robe, the tower of monstrous hair, and the shoulder-blades were in full view just then.

"No, she is not," cried he, triumphantly. "The Joliffe girls were born in barracks; they only came among us when the old colonel settled down."

"Who is the young lady?"

"Miss Channing. Her brother and I are old chums. He is the grandest fellow living; the most noble gentleman the world can show. He—why, if I don't believe you know him!" broke off Roland, as a recollection of something he had been told flashed across his mind.

"I!" returned Mr. Ollivera.

"Was Arthur Channing not at a—a certain night funeral?" asked Roland, dropping his voice out of delicacy. "You know. When that precious cousin of mine, Bill Yorke, lent you his surplice."

"Yes, yes," said Mr. Ollivera, hastily; "I had forgotten the name. And so that is Arthur Channing's sister!"

"She is governess to that provoking little wretch, Jane Greatorex," said polite Roland, forgetting in his turn that he was speaking of his listener's cousin, "and she ought to be a queen. She ought, Mr. Ollivera, and you would say so if you knew her. She looks one, does she not? She's as like Arthur as two pins, and he's fit for the noblest king in the world."

The clergyman slightly smiled. He had become accustomed to his new friend's impulsive mode of speech.

"Yes, we are both of us down just now, dependents of the Greatorex house—she teacher in it, I office-clerk," went on Roland. "Never mind: luck may turn some day. I told Annabel so just now, but she sent me away. I was talking to her too much, she said, and made people stare. Perhaps it was so: I know her cheeks turned red every other minute."

"And to make them paler, you take up your position here and gaze at her," observed Mr. Ollivera with another smile—and smiles were rare from him.

"Oh, law!" cried Roland. "I'm always doing something wrong. The fact is, there's nobody else worth looking at. See there! a yellow gown and no petticoats under it. If this is fashion I hope my mother and sisters are not going in for it! I shall go back to her," he added, after a moment's pause. "It's a shame she should sit there alone, with nothing to look at but those Models, passing and repassing right before her eyes. If Arthur were here, I believe he'd take her away, I do."

Roland, vegetating in that unfashionable region, Port Natal, had not yet become accustomed to the exigencies of modern days; and he spoke freely. Just then the throng was great in front of him, and he remained where he was. Taller than almost any one in the room, he could look at Annabel at will; Mr.

Ollivera, about up to Roland's shoulder, could get but occasional glimpses of her. Many a one glanced at Roland with interest, wondering who the fine, strong young man was, leaning against the wall there, with the big white gloves on, and the good-natured face, unsophisticated as a boy's.

Elbowing his way presently across the room something after the manner he might have elbowed through a crowd on the quay at Durban, Roland once more took up his position by Miss Channing. The old playfellows had become new friends, and Roland contrived that they should often meet. When Miss Channing was walking in the Square with her pupil, he was safe to run up, and stay talking; quite oblivious to the exigencies of the office waiting for his services. Jane Greatorex had learned to look for him, and would walk where she was likely to see him, in defiance of Miss Channing. In spite of Roland's early fever to quit his native place, in spite of his prolonged rovings, he was essentially a home-bird, and could have been content to talk of the old days and the old people with Annabel for ever.

"Where's Jane tonight?" he began, as he joined her.

"In bed. She was very naughty this evening, and for once Mr. Bede Greatorex interfered and sent her."

"Poor child! She is awfully troublesome, though, and one gets tired of that in the long run. If you—Halloa!"

Roland stopped. He was gazing in surprise at someone standing near: a man nearly his own age, tall and strong, and bearing altogether a general resemblance to himself. But the other's face had a cynical cast, expressive of ill-nature, and the lips were disagreeably full. Roland recognized him for his brother, although they had not met for more than seven years.

"That's Gerald, if ever I saw him in my life."

"Yes, it is Gerald," said Miss Channing, quietly. "He generally comes to Mrs. Bede's soirées."

"Isn't he got up!"

Roland's expression was an apt one. Gerald Yorke was in the very pink of male fashion. His manners were easy; entirely those of a man at home in society.

"He does it grand, does he not?" cried Roland, who had made one advance towards making friends with his brother since coming to London, and was not responded to in kind.

Miss Channing laughed. Gerald Yorke had entered on some kind of public career and was very prosperous, she believed, moving amidst the great ones of the land. Roland, quite forgetting where he was, or perhaps not caring, set up a whistle by way of attracting the attention of Gerald, who turned amidst others at the strange sound.

"How d'ye do, Gerald, old boy? Come and shake hands."

The voice was loud, glad, hearty; the great hand, with its great white glove drawn up over it, minus a button, was stretched above intervening heads. Gerald Yorke's face grew dark with the light of annoyance, and he hesitated before making the best of the situation, and getting near enough to shake the offered hand.

He would far rather have become conveniently deaf, and walked off in an opposite direction. Alike though the brothers were in general personal resemblance, no contrast could be greater than they presented in other respects. Gerald, fine and fashionable, with his aristocratic air and his slow, affected drawl, was the very type of all that is false of that insincerity and heartlessness obtaining in what is called society. Roland, hot, thoughtless, never weighing a word before he spoke it, impulsive, genuine, utterly unsophisticated as to the usages and manners that go to make up the meetings of fashionable life, was just as single-hearted and true.

Gerald, as Roland put it, "went in" for grandeur, and he was already prejudiced against his brother. In a communication from Lord Carrick, apologizing for not being able to answer satisfactorily Gerald's appeal for a loan, that nobleman had confidentially avowed that he could not at present assist even Roland effectually, and had got him a place as clerk temporarily, to save him from embarking in the hot-pie line. It may therefore be readily understood that Gerald did not consider an intimacy with Roland likely to conduce to his own advancement (to say nothing of respectability) and his annoyance and surprise at seeing him now where he did were about equally great.

The hands were shaken, and a few words of greeting passed; warm and open on Roland's part, cool and cautious on Gerald's. A friend of Gerald's, the Honourable Mr. Somebody, who was by his side and begged for an introduction, was more cordial than he.

"I have not seen him since we parted seven years ago, when I went off to Port Natal," explained Roland with his accustomed candour. "Haven't I had ups and downs since then, Gerald!" he continued, turning his beaming face upon his brother. "You have heard of them I dare say, through Carrick."

"You did not make a fortune," drawled Gerald, wishing he could get away.

"A fortune! Law bless you, Ger! I was glad to work on the port with the Kaffirs, unloading boats; and to serve in stores, and to drive cattle and pigs; anything for bread. You can't think how strange all this seems to me"—pointing to the waving crowd in the room, several of whom had gathered round, attracted by this fraternal meeting.

"Aw! Surprised to see you amidst them," minced Gerald, who could not resist the little ill-natured hint, in his growing rage.

"Mrs. Greatorex invited me," said Roland, his honest simplicity detecting not the undercurrent of sarcasm. "I am in Greatorex's office; I don't suppose you knew it, Gerald. They give me twenty shillings a week; and Carrick goes bail for my rigging out. I got this coat from his tailor's tonight."

The crowd laughed, the Honourable roared, and Gerald Yorke was half mad.

"I'd not acknowledge it, at any rate, if I were you," he said, imprudently, his affectation lost in a gust of temper. "After all you were born a Yorke."

"Acknowledge what, Ger?" returned Roland.

"The—the—the shame of taking a common clerkship at twenty shillings a week; and all the rest of the degradation," burst forth Gerald, setting conventionality at defiance. "My uncle, Lord Carrick, warned me of this; my mother, Lady Augusta, spoke of it in a recent letter to me," he added for the benefit of the ears around.

"Why, Ger, where's the use of being put out?" retorted Roland, but with no symptom of ill-humour in his good-natured tone. "I was down, and had nobody to help me. Carrick couldn't; old Dick Yorke wouldn't; Lady Augusta said she had all of you pulling at her: and so Carrick talked to Greatorex and Greatorex, and they put me into the place. The pound a week keeps me; in clover too; you should hear what I sometimes was reduced to live on at Port Natal. There was an opening for a hot-pie man down at Poplar, and the place was offered me; if I had gone into that line you might have grumbled."

The ladies and gentlemen shrieked with merriment: they began to think the fine young fellow, who looked every whit as independent a man as his fastidious brother, was chaffing them all. Gerald ground his teeth and tried to get away.

"You'll come and see me, old fellow?" said Roland. "I've a stunning room, bedroom and sitting-room in one, the bedstead's let out at night. It is at Mother Jones's; poor soft Jenkins's widow, you know, that we used to wot of in the days gone by."

Gerald made good his escape: and when they were quiet again. Roland had leisure to look at Miss Channing. Her bent face shone like a peony, the effect of vexation and suppressed laughter.

"Why, what's the matter>" he asked.

"You should not say such things, Roland. It was quite out of place in a room like this."

"What things?"

"About yourself. It is so different, you know, from anything young men experience here."

"But it is all true," returned Roland, unable to see the argument.

"Still it need not be proclaimed to an indiscriminate crowd. You might show more tact. Gerald was fit to die of mortification. And you who used to have so much pride!"

Roland Yorke, honestly willing to please everybody and vex none, stood looking ruefully. "As to pride, Annabel, if a fellow wants that knocked out of him, he had better go over to Port Natal, and get buffeted as I did," he concluded. "I left it all behind me there, I'm afraid. And, of tact, I don't think I ever possessed any."

Which was perfectly true.

Meanwhile Mr. Ollivera, waiting in vain to see Sir Thomas Kene enter, grew sick of the ever-changing, ever-moving panorama that jostled him, and went downstairs to his uncle's small and comfortable room, leaving word with the servants where he might be found if the Judge came in. Mr. Greatorex very rarely joined these large parties. He was sitting in quiet now, a bit of bright fire in the grate, for the evenings were still chilly, and a reading-lamp, newspapers, and books on the table. Slender, active, upright still, he scarcely looked his age, sixty-two: his face was fresh yet, and not a thread of grey mingled with the smooth brown hair.

"Henry, is it you!" he exclaimed; for he was surprised to see his nephew enter at that late hour. And Mr. Ollivera, as he took a chair, apologized for interrupting him, but said he had grown so weary of the turmoil above.

"You don't mean to say you have been making one of them!"

"I have for once, uncle. It will serve me for ten years to come. People say to me sometimes, 'Why don't you go into society?' Good heavens! to think that rational beings, God's people who have souls to be saved, can waste their precious hours in such, evening after evening! The women for the most part are unseemly to behold; their bodies half dressed, their faces powdered and painted, their heads monstrosities, their attire sinfully lavish. The men affect to be heartless, drawling coxcombs. It is a bad phase of life, this that we have drifted into, rotten at its core; men and women alike artificial. Do you like this in your house, Uncle Greatorex?"

"When Bede married, I resigned to him the mastership of the house, so far as these things were concerned," replied Mr. Greatorex.

"I know. Does Bede like it?"

"He countenances it. For myself, I trouble them but little now. Even my dinner I often cause to be served here. Bede's wife was civil enough to come down this evening and press me to join them."

"Bede looks more worried than usual—and that need not be," observed William Ollivera. "What is it, I wonder? To me he has the air of a man silently fretting himself into his grave."

"You know what it is, William," said Mr. Greatorex, in a low tone, and calling his nephew as he often did, by his second Christian name. "Bede's wife is a great worry. But there's another."

"What is it?"

"Illness," breathed Mr. Greatorex. "Symptoms that we don't like have shown themselves in him lately. However—they may pass away. The doctors think they will."

"I came here to meet Kene, whom I very particularly wish to see," resumed the clergyman, after a pause. "Bede said he expected him."

"Ay; some magnet must have drawn you, apart from that," pointing his thumb at the rooms above. And Mr. Ollivera explained why he was seeking the Judge.

"I thought something fresh might have arisen in the old case; or at least that you fancied it," observed Mr. Greatorex. "You must be coming round to our way of thinking, William. Time goes on, but that stands still."

"I shall never come round to it."

"John has been dead four years and two months, now," pursued Mr. Greatorex. "And it has stood still all that time."

William Ollivera, leaned forward in his chair, and the fire and the lamp alike played on his wasted face, on the bright flush of emotion that rose in his thin cheeks.

"Uncle! Uncle Greatorex! it is as fresh in my mind now as it was the first day I went down to Helstonleigh, and saw him lying white and cold and dead, with the ban of the coroner's verdict upon him. I cannot shake it off: and of late I am not sure but I have tried to do so, in the sheer weariness of prolonged disappointment. 'Tarry yet awhile, and wait,' a voice seems saying ever to me: and I am content to wait. I cannot rest; I find no peace. When I wake in the morning, I say, 'This day may bring forth fruit;' when I go to rest at night, the thought, that it has not, is the last upon me. There will be neither rest nor peace for me until I have solved the enigma of my brother's death; and I am always working on for it."

"Sir Thomas Kene has come, sir," interrupted a servant at this juncture, opening the door.

Henry Ollivera rose; and, wishing Mr. Greatorex good night, went forth to his interview with the Judge.

CHAPTER XI

DAY-DREAMS

The house was almost within a stone's-throw of Bedford Square; one of a good street. Its drawing-room windows were thrown open to the fine evening twilight, and a lady sat at one of them in a musing attitude. She was very nice looking, with a clear healthy colour on her cheeks, and soft bright dark eyes that had a thought in them beyond her years, which may have been six or seven-and-twenty. The features were well-formed; the shapely mouth, its rather thin and decisive lips, and the pretty pointed chin, spoke of innate firmness. Her hand, displaying its wedding-ring and keeper, was raised to support lightly her head, the slender fingers touching the smooth dark brown hair. She was perfectly still; not a movement betrayed that she heard or saw aught but her own thoughts; not a rustle stirred the folds of her soft silk dress, lying around her.

"Shall I tell him, or not?" she murmured at length. "I have never had any concealment from him yet, nor he from me; but then I know it will pain and worry him. He has certainly changed a little: in the old days it seemed that anxiety could never touch him; that he would always throw it from him with a light word. Heigho! I suppose it comes with the cares of life."

A moment's pause, during which she was again still as before, and then the soliloquy was resumed.

"I could keep it from him, if needs were: the postman gave me the letter as I was going out, and no one knows of its arrival. But still—I don't like to begin it; and he might feel vexed afterwards: for of course he must come to know of it sometime. Oh dear! I never felt so irresolute before. They used to say at home I was so very downright. I wonder which would be right to do? If I were sure he—"

The room door was pushed open with a sudden whirl, and a little child came flying in with outstretched arms and a shouting, joyous laugh.

"Mamma, mamma!"

"Nelly!"

The arms were entwined together, the golden head with its shower of silken curls, nestled on the mother's bosom. Oh, but she was of rare loveliness, this child; with the delicately fair features, the great blue eyes, the sunny hair, and ever-sunny temperament.

"Now, Nelly! You know you have been told over and over again not to be so boisterous. Fancy a little lady, just five years old, coming in like that! It might have been a great rude dog."

Another sweet, joyous laugh in answer, a host of kisses pressed by way of peace-offering on the gentle face, bent down in reproof more mock than real.

"Nurse was running to catch me. She says it's bedtime." And, to confirm the assertion, the French clock on the mantlepiece at that moment told out eight.

"So it is. Come and say goodnight to papa, Nelly."

Taking the child's hand she went out into what seemed a flood of light, after the gradually darkening room. The hall-lamp threw its rays upwards; on the gleaming silk of her pale blue dress, on the white fairy robes of the child, on the well-carpeted stairs. In the front room below, the tea stood ready by the evening fire: they went through to another room; and the mother spoke.

"Nelly has come to wish papa goodnight."

Seated at the table of this inner room was a gentleman writing fast by a shaded candle. He looked up with a sunny smile of welcome, and you saw the likeness then between the child and the father. The winning, beautiful features; the fair, bright complexion; the laughing blue eyes; the gay, happy temperament: all were the same.

It was James Channing. Sunny Hamish, as he used to be called. He was but thirty; a tall, well-proportioned, but as yet very slender man; rising over six feet, altogether attractive, handsome to look upon. Nelly, forgetting her lecture, flew into his arms with a shout and a laugh, as she had into those of her mother.

"And what may this young lady have been about that she has not come to see me before, this evening?" he asked.

"Nurse kept her out rather late, Hamish, for one thing, and I knew you were busy," came the answer; not from the child, but from Mrs. Channing.

"Yes, I am very busy. I have not any minutes to give even to my darling Nelly tonight," he fondly said, kissing the bright hair and the rosy lips. "Nelly must go to bed and dream of papa instead."

"You'll have time when the ship comes home, papa," said the child.

"Lots of time then."

"The ship is to be a book."

"Ay."

"And it will bring great luck?"

"Yes. Please God."

The last words were murmured in a tone suddenly hushed to reverence; low and happy; hopeful with a great, glad, assured hope, cheering to listen to; a trusted hope that lighted up the whole countenance of the man with its radiance, and shone forth in beams from his blue eyes. But he said no more; not even to his wife and his little child could he speak of the sanguine joy that anticipation wrought within him.

With too many kisses to be counted, with good nights spoken yet and yet again, Nelly was released and disappeared with her mother. The child had been trained well. There was some indulgence on the parents' side—perhaps that is indispensable, in the case of an only child—but there was neither trouble nor rebellion on hers. Little Nelly Channing had been taught to obey good laws; and, to do so, came to her naturally.

Mrs. Channing took her upstairs and turned into her own dressing-room, as usual. She deemed it well that the child should say her prayers in solitude, and, always when practicable, in the same place. Nelly sat down of her own accord by her mother, and was quite still and quiet while a very few easy verses from the Bible were read to her; and then she knelt down to say her simple prayers at her mother's knee.

"God bless my darling little Nelly, and make her a good girl!" said Mrs. Chaining, as she took her out and resigned her to the nurse.

"Are you ready for tea, Hamish?" she asked when she went downstairs again.

"Quite. But, Ellen, I think I shall have to trouble you to bring it to me tonight."

"Are you so very busy?"

"Ay. Look here."

He pointed with his pen to some papers on the table. "Those are proof sheets: and I must get this manuscript in tomorrow, or they will not insert it in the next month's number."

"Hamish, I hope you are not doing too much," she gravely said. "I don't like this night-work."

He laughed gleefully. "Too much! I only wish I had too much to do, Ellen. Never fear, dear."

"I wish you would teach me to correct the proofs."

"What an idea!"

"I shall teach myself, sir."

"It would be waste of time, young lady. I could not let anybody go over my proofs but myself."

"You vain fellow! I wonder if self-conceit is indigenous to you literary men? Are they all as vain as Hamish Channing?"

He took up the pen-wiper and threw it at her. But somehow Ellen was not in a mood for much jesting tonight. She put the pen-wiper—a rosette of red cloth—on the table again, and went and stood in silence with her hand on his shoulder. He turned his head.

"What is it, love?"

"Hamish, I would bring in your tea willingly; you know it; but I think it would do you more good to leave this work, if only for five minutes. And I have something to say to you."

"Very well. I can't come for a quarter of an hour. You are a regular martinet."

Ellen Channing left him and sat down in the other room to wait; and this will afford the opportunity for a word of explanation. Amidst the very very many people in all classes of life, high and low, on whom a certain recent panic had wrought its disastrous effects, was Hamish Channing. The bank, of which he had been manager in Helstonleigh, was drawn into the vortex by the failure of another bank, and went in its turn. Honourable men had to do with it; they sacrificed their own property in the emergency, and not a creditor suffered; every one was paid in full. It could not be reorganized, and it left Hamish without employment. His wife's father, Mr. Huntley, had been one of the principal shareholders, and on him had fallen the greater weight of the heavy loss. It fell, too, at a time when Mr. Huntley could not afford to sustain it. He possessed a large property in Canada, but it had latterly begun to yield him little or no return. Whether in consequence of local depreciation, or of mismanagement (or perhaps something worse) on the part of his agents there, he knew not, and he sent his son out to see. The young man (he was three or four years younger than Mrs. Channing, and quite inexperienced) seemed not to be able to grapple with the business; he wrote home most confused and perplexing accounts, of which Mr. Huntley could make nothing. At length that gentleman resolved to go out himself; and the letter we have heard Mrs. Channing alluding to today was from him. It was the second news they had received, the first having merely announced his safe arrival: and the accounts this last contained were so gloomy that Ellen Channing would fain have kept them from her husband.

It must be distinctly understood that the failure of the bank in Helstonleigh was in no way connected with ill-management. Had a quorum of the wisest business-men in the world been at its head, they could neither have foreseen its downfall nor averted it. Therefore Hamish Channing came out of that, as he had out of every untoward thing all his life, untarnished in honour and in character. A small secretaryship was offered him in London, which he accepted; and he removed to the great city, with his wife and little daughter, his goods and chattels, there to set up his tent. A very small income had been settled on Ellen when she married; the larger portion of her fortune was to accrue to her on her father's death. Whether it would be much, or little, or any, under the altered state of affairs, it was impossible now to say.

But it was not on the secretaryship that Hamish Channing depended for fame and fortune. A higher and dearer hope was his. That Hamish possessed in a high degree that rarest of all God's gifts, true genius, he had long known. Writers of talent the world has had, and had in abundance, men and women; of real genius but few. Perhaps, after all, the difference is not very distinguishable by the general mass of readers. But, to those who possess it, its characteristics are unmistakable. The divine light (is it too much to call it so?) that lies within them shines as a very beacon, pointing on to fame; to honour; above all, to appreciation: the knowledge that they are different from their fellow-mortals, of a higher and nobler and rarer order, and that the world will sometime recognize the fact and bow down in worship, is never absent from the consciousness of the inner heart.

But, with the gift, James Channing also possessed its almost invariably accompanying attribute: a refined sensitiveness of feeling. And that is a quality not too well calculated to do battle with rude, every-day life. Should the great hope within him ever meet with a stern, crushing disappointment, his inability to bear the shock would in all probability show itself in some very marked degree. No one but himself knew or suspected the extreme sensitiveness of his every feeling; it had been hidden hitherto under the nonchalant ease of manner, the sunny temper which made Hamish Channing's great charm. When the bank was broken up, and with it his home and his greater means of living, it was not felt by him as many another man would have felt it: for it seemed only to render more feasible the great aim of his life—the devoting himself to literature. Years ago he had begun to write: and the efforts were first efforts, somewhat crude, as all first efforts, whether given to the world or not, must of necessity be, but they bore unmistakably the stamp of genius. His appointment to the bank and his marriage interrupted his writing; and his genius and pen had alike lain dormant for some six years. His wife's father, Mr. Huntley, had procured his later appointment to the London secretaryship, and Hamish did not venture to decline it and devote himself wholly to literature, as he would have liked to do. The pay, though small, was sure; Ellen's income was smaller still, and they must live; so he accepted it. His duties there occupied him from nine to four: and all his available time beyond that, early and late, was devoted to writing. The day's employment was regarded as but a temporary clog, to be given up as soon as he found his income from literature would justify it. To accomplish this desirable end, he was doing a great deal more than was good for him and taking too little rest. In point of fact, he had, you see, two occupations, each one of which would have been sufficient for an industrious man. What of that? Hamish never so much as cast a thought to it.

Oh, with what a zest had he re-commenced the writing, laid aside for so long! It was like returning to some glad haven of rest. Joy filled his whole being. The past six years had been heavy with suppressed yearning; the yearning to be about the work for which he knew God had pm-eminently fitted him: but his duties had been onerous, his time nearly fully taken up; and when he would have snatched some moments from night for the dearer work, his wife and his anxious friends had risen up in arms against it, for he was not over-strong, and some delicacy of constitution was preached about. Besides, as Mr. Huntley said, a writing manager might alarm the bank's patronizers. But he had it all his own way now, and made good profit of his writings. Papers on social questions of the day, essays, stories, were in turn written, and taken by different periodicals. They had to be written, apart from other hopes and views, for the style in which they lived required additional means to support it, beyond his salary and his wife's money. It was not much style, after all, no extravagance; three maidservants, and little company; but everybody knows how money seems to melt in London.

He had been at this work now for a year. And his wife was beginning to grow anxious, for she knew he was doing too much, and told him he was wearing himself out. If he could but resign the secretaryship! was ever in her secret hopes and thoughts just as much as his; and she wished her father could get his Canadian affairs well settled, so as to allow the necessary addition to her income. Hamish laughed at this. He was living in a glad dream of future fame and fortune: that it would inevitably come, he felt as sure of as though it lay at hand now, ready to be picked up. He was writing a long work; a work of three volumes; and this was the precious gem on which all his hopes and love and visions were centred. The periodical writing had to be done, for its returns were needed; but every spare moment, apart from that, was devoted to the book. A light of gladness beamed from his eyes; a joy, sweet as the chords of some soothing melody, lay ever on his spirit. Oh, what is there of bliss and love in the world that can compare with this! And it is known to so few; so few: by all else it can never be so much as imagined. Do not mistake it, you who read, for the pleasurable anticipation of a man or woman who may from chance causes have "taken up" the profession of literature, and look for the good, substantial and otherwise, that it is to bring. The two are wholly different; the one is born of heaven, the other of earth. But that man must live, Hamish Channing amidst the rest, the thought of money being one of the returns, would be distasteful; never, as I honestly believe, accepted as such without a blush: the dross of earth mingling with the spiritualized, exalted, pure joy of Eden. It is well that this same gift of genius with its dear pleasures and its attendant after-pains—for they come—should be vouchsafed to a unit amidst tens of thousands!

Mrs. Channing sat waiting for him; the tea standing before her, herself thoughtful. The room was of good size and handsomely furnished, its chairs and curtains of rich purple cloth. Their furniture had been a present from Mr. Huntley when they married, who was not one to do things niggardly. As Mrs. Channing sat, facing the inner door, the windows were behind her; the fireplace, with its ornaments and its large chimney-glass on her left; a piano on one side it, a white marble-topped cabinet with purple silk lining to its glass-doors on the other; and on her right, stood the sideboard, and other furniture. The inner room, used exclusively by Hamish for writing, had horsehair chairs, and a bookcase running all along the side of the wall.

The door opened, and Hamish came in. He had a small bundle in his hand; proof sheets done up for the post, and sent them out at once by the maid, as he sat down to tea. Which he seemed inclined to swallow at a gulp, and to eat his piece of bread-and-butter wholesale, ever anxious to get back to his labour and the glowing visions of promise connected with it.

"Hamish, I do believe you like your writing better than you like me!" Ellen said to him one day almost passionately. And for answer, Mr. Hamish in his sauciness had said he was not sure but he did.

He sat there at tea, now, talking gaily as usual. His wife interrupted him, telling of the letter she had received, and its unfavourable news. He listened with his sunny smile.

"I had great mind not to tell you at all, Hamish," she confessed. "Papa's temperament is nearly as sanguine as yours; and if he writes in poor spirits, saying he fears it may turn out that he is a ruined man, I know things must be very bad."

"But why have hesitated to tell me, Ellen?"

"To save you anxiety. Don't you see what it implies? If papa loses his property, the fortune that would have been mine sometime will be lost too."

Had she been speaking of the probable loss of some mere trifle, he could scarcely have heard it with more equanimity. It seemed to Hamish that the future was, according to human foresight, in his own hands.

"Never mind, Ellen, we have a resource that cannot be lost. I will take care of you, Heaven aiding me; you shall have every needful and substantial good in abundance."

"Yes, that is just it. You work too much already: you would work more then."

Hamish laughed. "Do you know what I wish, Ellen? I wish the day were four-and-twenty hours long instead of twelve, and that I had two sets of brains and hands."

"How are you getting on?"

"Oh, so well. It is all right, my darling. And will be."

They were interrupted by a visitor—Mr. Roland Yorke. There had been a casual meeting once or twice, but this was the first time he had been there. They invited him to come; but Roland had the grace to be ashamed of a certain escapade of his in the days gone by, which brought disgrace for the time being on Arthur Channing, and he had rather held back from appearing. This he partially confessed.

"It would have been so different, you know, Hamish, had I returned with a few millions from Port Natal, and gone home to atone to Arthur in the face and eyes of all the town, and done honour to him for what he is, the best man living, and heaped a fortune upon him. But I have not been able to do that. I'd rather rush off again to Port Natal and its troubles, than I'd go within miles of Helstonleigh."

"And so, to mend it, you thought you would keep miles away from me," said Hamish, with his glad smile of welcome. "I think there's only one person in the world would be more glad to see you than I, and that's Arthur himself."

"I know. I know what a good fellow you always were. But I hadn't the face to come, you see. It was Annabel made me now."

Suddenly shaking both their hands in the heartiest manner, with a grip that brought pain to Mrs. Channing, who wore rings, Roland fell to at the tea. Hamish, remembering his appetite of old, rang the bell for some good things to be brought in; and Roland was speedily in the midst of the most comfortable enjoyment, mentally and bodily. He gave them his own confidence without the least reserve, both as to present and past; gravely telling everything, including the nearly embraced hot-pie scheme of commerce, which made Hamish hold his sides, and the having met Gerald at Mrs. Bede Greatorex's party.

"I rather expect Gerald here this evening," remarked Hamish.

"Do you?" said Roland, his mouth full of savoury pie. "He won't be too pleased to see me; he means to cut me, I'm nearly sure. Do you see much of him, Hamish?"

Hamish explained that he did. They were both in the literary line; and Gerald had some good engagements as a reviewer.

"Where's his wife?" asked Roland. "Yes, please, Mrs. Channing, another cup; plenty of milk and sugar."

"In the country; somewhere in Gloucestershire. Gerald is not too communicative on that score."

"Don't you think, Hamish, he must have been a great duffer to go and marry before he knew how he could keep a wife?"

Hamish raised his eyebrows with the good-natured indifferent manner that Roland so well remembered in the days gone by; but answer made he none. Where Hamish Channing could not praise, he would not blame. Even by his immediate relatives Gerald's imprudent marriage was tacitly ignored, and the Lady Augusta Yorke had threatened to box Roland's ears in Ireland, when he persisted in asking about it.

"I always knew Gerald would not go into the Church," remarked Roland. "I wouldn't; they say Tod threatened to run off to sea if they talked to him of it: somehow we boys have a prejudice against following my father's calling. I'll tell you a secret, Hamish: if a fellow wants to be made, to have his nonsense knocked out of him, he must go to Port Natal. Do you remember the morning you saw me decamping off for London on my way to it?"

"Don't I," said Hamish, his lips parting with merriment at the remembrance. "There was commotion that day at Helstonleigh, Roland; in Galloway's office especially."

"And dear old Arthur buried his wrongs and went to the rescue; and poor dying Jenkins got out of his bed to help. He was nothing but a calf, poor fellow, a reed in Mrs. J.'s hands, but he was good as gold. I say, she's altered."

"Is she?"

Roland nodded. "The going to Port Natal made me, Hamish," he resumed; and Hamish was slightly surprised at the serious tone. "I should have been one of the idlest of the family batch but for the lesson I got read to me there. I went out to make my fortune; instead of making it, I had to battle with ill-fate, and ill-fate won the day. They call it names of course; a mistaken enterprise, a miserable failure; but it was just the best thing that could have happened for me. I was proud, stuck-up ignoramus; I should have depended on Carrick, or anybody else, to get my living for me; but I mean now to earn it for myself."

When Hamish went to his work later, leaving Ellen to entertain their guest, Roland followed him with his eyes.

There was a change in Hamish Channing, apparent to one even as unobservant as Roland. The face was thinner than of yore; its refined features were paler; they looked etherealized, as it seemed to Roland. The sweet-natured temperament was there still, but some of its once gay lightness had given place to thought. The very frequent mocking tone had been nearly entirely laid aside for one of loving considerateness to all.

"What are you looking at?" questioned Ellen, struck with Roland's fixed gaze and unusual seriousness.

"At him. He is so changed."

"Older, do you mean?"

"Law bless you, no. Of course he is older by more than seven years; but he is very young-looking still; he does not look so old as I do, and I am two years his junior. I used to think Hamish Channing the handsomest fellow living, but he was nothing then to what he is now. I hope you won't consider it's wrong of me to say it, Mrs. Channing, but there's something in his face now that makes one think of Heaven."

"Mr. Yorke!"

"There! I knew what it would be. Mr. Ollivera flies out at me when I say wrong things. Other people don't say them. It must have been that Port Natal. I thought I was dead once, over there," added Roland, passing on to another topic with his usual abruptness.

Ellen smiled; she had spoken in surprise only. Roland Yorke, who had brought his chair round to the fire, sat opposite to her, his elbow on his knee, his head bent forward.

"I don't mean that it makes one think he is going to Heaven—going to die before his time; you need not be afraid, Mrs. Channing. It was not that kind of thought at all; only that the angels and people about, up there, must have just such faces as Hamish's; good, and pure, and beautiful; and just the same sweet expression, and the same loving-kindness in the tone of voice."

Roland stopped and pulled at his dark whiskers. Mrs. Channing began to think he had also changed for the better.

"Many a one, remembering the past, would have just turned their backs upon me, Mrs. Channing. Instead of that, he is as glad to see me, and makes me as cordially welcome as if I were a lord, or a prize pig sent him at Christmas. What did I nearly die of? you ask. Well, of fever; but I got all sorts of horrid torments. I had the eye-epidemic; it's caused by the dust, and I thought I was going blind. Then I had what they call Natal sores, a kind of boil; then I nearly had a sun-stroke; the heat's something awful, you know. And I got the ticks everlastingly."

"Do you mean the tic-douloureux?"

"Law bless you! A Port Natal tick is an insect. It sits on the top of the grass waiting for you to pass by and darts into your legs; and no earthly thing will get it off again, except tugging at it with tweezers. They have no wings or mouth, nothing but a pair of lancets and a kind of pipe for a body, covered with spikes. Oh, they are nice things. When I set up that store for leeches and candles and pickled pork, I used to go and get the leeches myself, to save buying; lots of them grow in the rivulets round about; but I would bring home a vast many more ticks than leeches, and that didn't pay, you know. Where's the little thing?"

"Nelly? She has gone to bed."

"She is the prettiest child I ever saw."

"She is just like her papa," said Mrs. Channing, whose cheeks were flushing softly with pardonable love and pride at the praise of her child.

"So she is. When will his book be out?"

"Ah, I don't know. He is getting on quickly, he tells me. I think he is a ready writer."

"I suppose most men of genius are that," remarked Roland. "He does not talk much about it, does he?"

"Not at all. A very little to me. These wonderful hopes and dreams that lie down deep within us, and go to make up the concealed inner life of our dearest feelings, cannot be spoken of to the world. I have none," she added, slightly laughing; "I am more practical."

"Hamish is so hopeful! It is his temperament."

"Hopeful!" repeated Mrs. Channing; "indeed he is: like nothing I ever saw. You have heard of day-dreams, Mr. Yorke; well, this book is his day-dream. He works at it late and early, almost night and day. I tell him sometimes he must be wearing himself out."

"One never does really wear out from work, Mrs. Channing. I used to think I was wearing out at old Galloway's; but I didn't know what work was until I got to Natal. I learnt it then."

"Did You sit up to work at night at Port Natal?"

"Only when I had not got a bed to go to," answered candid Roland. "Mine was not that kind of work, sitting up to burn the midnight oil; it lay in knocking about."

"That's quite different."

"What puzzles me more than anything is, that Gerald should have turned author," resumed Roland. "Henry Ollivera was talking about genius at our place the other day. Why, according to what he described it to be, Gerald Yorke must have about as much genius as a walking gander."

Ellen laughed. "Hamish says Gerald has no real genius," she said. "But he has a good deal of talent. He is what may be called a dashing writer."

"Well, I don't know," disputed Roland, who was hard of belief in these alleged qualities of his brother. "I remember in the old days at home, when Gerald was at the college-school, he couldn't be got to write a letter. If Lady Augusta wanted him to write a letter to Carrick, or to George out in India, she would have to din at him for six months. He hated it like poison."

"That may have been idleness."

"Oh, we all went in for that," acknowledged Roland. "I should have been a very lazy beggar to the end of time but for the emigration to Port Natal."

CHAPTER XII

COMMOTION IN THE OFFICE OF GREATOREX AND GREATOREX

The summer sun, scorching the walls of houses and the street pavements with its heat and its glare, threw itself in great might into the offices of Greatorex and Greatorex. Josiah Hurst and Roland Yorke were at their desk, writing side by side. Jenner was at his, similarly occupied; Mr. Brown was holding a conversation in an undertone with some stranger, who had entered with him as he came in from an errand: a man of respectable, staid appearance. Something in the cut of his clothes spoke of the provinces; and Roland Yorke, who never failed to look after other people's affairs, however pressing his own might be, decided that the stranger was a countryman, come up to see the sights of London.

"Which I can't, except from the outside," grumbled Roland to himself. "It's an awful sell to have to go about with empty pockets. I wonder who the fellow is?—he has been whispering there twenty minutes if he's been one. He looks as if he had plenty in his."

Mr. Bede Greatorex came in and took his place at his desk. The head-clerk drew his head away from close proximity with his friend's, and commenced work; a hint to the stranger that their gossip must be at an end.

The latter asked for a pen and ink, wrote a few words on a leaf he tore from his pocketbook, folded it in two, and gave it to Mr. Brown.

"That is my address in town," he said. "Let me see you tonight. I leave tomorrow at midday."

"Good," replied Mr. Brown, glancing at the writing on the paper.

The stranger went out, lifting his hat to the room generally, and Mr. Brown put the paper away in his pocket.

"Who was that?" asked Mr. Bede Greatorex.

"A gentleman I used to know, sir, a farmer," was the reply. "I met him outside just now, and he came in with me. We got talking of old times."

"Oh, I thought it was someone on business for the office" said Mr. Bede Greatorex, half in apology for inquiring. His face looked worn as usual, his eyes bright and restless. Some of the family could remember that when the late Mrs. Greatorex had first shown symptoms of the malady that killed her, her eyes had been unnaturally bright.

The work went on. The clocks drew near to twelve, and the sun in the heavens grew fiercer. Roland began to look white and flustered. What with the work and what with the heat, he thought he might as well be roughing it at Port Natal. He was doing pretty well on the whole—for him—and did not get lectures above four times a week. To help liking Roland was impossible; with his frank manners, his free good-nature, his unsophisticated mind, and his candid revelations in regard to himself, that would now and again plunge the office into private convulsions. It was also within the range of possibility that his good connections, and the fact of his being free of the house, running up at will to pay unexpected visits to Mrs. Greatorex, had their due weight in Mr. Brown's mind; for breaches of office etiquette were tolerated in Roland that certainly would not have been in any other clerk, whether he was a gentleman or not. Roland had chosen to constitute himself a kind of enfant de la maison; he and his brothers and sisters had been intimate with the Joliffe girls; he could remember once having nearly got up a fight with Louisa, now Mrs. Bede Greatorex; and, to make Roland understand that in running upstairs when he chose, darting in upon Mrs. Greatorex as she sat in her boudoir or drawing-room, darting in upon Miss Channing as she gave lessons to Jane Greatorex, he was intruding where he ought not, would have been a hopeless task. Once or twice Mr. Bede Greatorex had voluntarily invited him up to luncheon or dinner; and so Roland made himself free of the house, and in a degree swayed the office.

They were very busy today. The work which he and Hurst and Jenner had in hand was being waited for, so that Roland had to stick to it, in spite of the relaxing heat, and fully decided he could not be worse off at Port Natal. The scratching of the pens was going on pretty equally, when Frank Greatorex came in.

"I want a cheque from you, Bede."

"Where's Mr. Greatorex?" returned Bede in answer; for it was to him such applications were made in general.

"Gone out."

Bede put aside the deed he had been sedulously examining, went into his private room, and came back with his chequebook.

"How much?" he asked of his brother, as he sat down.

"Forty-four pounds. Make it out to Sir Richard Yorke."

With a simultaneous movement, as it seemed, two of those present raised their heads to look at Frank Greatorex: Roland Yorke and Mr. Brown. The former was no doubt attracted by the sound of his kinsman's name; what aroused Mr. Brown's attention did not appear, but he stared for a moment in a kind of amazement.

"Upon consideration, I don't think I'll take the cheque with me now; I will call for it later in the day, when I've been into the city," spoke a voice at the door; and Sir Richard Yorke appeared. Bede, who was just then signing the cheque, "Greatorex and Greatorex," finished the signature, and came forward to shake hands.

"How d'ye do, sir," spoke up Roland.

Sir Richard's little eyes peered out over his fat face, and he condescended to recognise his nephew by a nod. Bede Greatorex spoke a few words to the baronet, touching the matter in hand, and turned back to his desk, leaving Frank to escort the old gentleman out. Bede, about to cross the cheque, hesitated.

"Did Mr. Frank say a crossed cheque?" he asked, looking up.

"No, sir; he said simply a cheque," said Jenner, finding nobody else answered.

"Yes," broke out Roland, "it's fine to be that branch of the family. Getting their cheques for forty-four pounds! I wish I could get one for forty-four shillings."

"Have the goodness to attend to your own business, Mr. Yorke."

Bede Greatorex left the cheque uncrossed. In a few minutes, after putting things to rights on his desk, he gathered up his papers, including the cheque and chequebook, and went into his room. Putting the things altogether in his desk there,—for he had an engagement at twelve and the hour was within a minute or two of striking,—he locked it and went out by the other door, not coming into the front room again.

Now it happened that Bede Greatorex, who had expected to be absent half an hour at the longest, was unavoidably detained, so that when Sir Richard Yorke returned for his cheque it could not be given to him. Mr. Greatorex, however, was at home then, and drew out another. And the day went on.

"You must cancel that cheque, Bede," Mr. Greatorex casually observed to his son that same evening, after office-hours. "It was very unbusiness-like to leave it locked up, when you were not sure of coming back in time to give it to Sir Richard."

"But I thought I was sure. It does not matter."

"If you will bring me those title-deeds of Cardwell's, I'll go over them myself quietly, and see what I can make out," said Mr. Greatorex.

Bede crossed the passage to his private room, and unlocked his desk. The deeds Mr. Greatorex asked for were the same that he had been examining in the front office in the morning.

Some flaw had been discovered in them, or was suspected, and it was likely to give the office some trouble, which would fall on Bede's head. There they lay inside the desk, just as Bede had placed them in the morning, with the paper-weight upon them; detained at Westminster until a late hour, he had not been to his desk since. Reminded by his father to destroy the cheque—useless now—Bede thought he would do it at once.

But he could not find it. Other papers, besides the title-deeds, cheque, and chequebook, he had placed within, and he went carefully over them all, one by one. Nothing was missing, nothing had apparently been touched, but the cheque certainly was not there. He searched his desk in the front office, quite for form's sake, for he knew that he had carried the cheque with him to his private room.

"One would think you had been drawing out the deeds," remarked Mr. Greatorex when he returned.

"I can't find that cheque," answered Bede.

"Not find the cheque!" repeated Mr. Greatorex. "What do you mean, Bede?"

Bede gave a short history of the affair. He had been in a hurry: and, instead of staying to put the cheque and chequebook into his cash-box, had left them loose in his table-desk with the title-deeds and sundry other papers.

"But you locked your desk?" cried Mr. Greatorex.

"Assuredly. I have only unlocked it now. The cheque would be as safe there as in the cash-box."

"You could not have put it in, Bede; it must be somewhere about."

"I am just as certain that I put it in, as I am that it is not there now."

Mr. Greatorex did not believe it. Bede had been for some time showing himself less the keen, exact man of business be used to be. Trifling mistakes, inaccuracies, negligences, would come to light now and again; vexing Mr. Greatorex beyond measure.

"I don't know what to make of you of late, Bede," he said after a pause. "You know the complaints we have been obliged to hear. These very title-deeds"—putting his hand on those just brought in—"it was you who examined and passed them. One negligence or another comes cropping up continually, and they may all be traced to you. Is your state of health the cause?"

"I suppose so," replied Bede, who felt conscious the reproach was merited.

"You had better take some rest for a time. If—."

"No," came the hasty interruption, as though the proposal were unpalatable. "Work is better for me than idleness. Put me out of harness, and I should knock up."

"Bede," said Mr. Greatorex, in a tone of considerate kindness, but with some hesitation, "it appears to me that you get more of a changed man day by day. You have not been the same since your marriage. I fear the cause, or a great portion of it, lies in her; I fear she gives you trouble. As you know, I have never spoken to you before of this; I have abstained from doing so."

A flush, that had shown itself in the clear olive face when Mr. Greatorex began to speak, faded to whiteness; the hand, that accidentally touched his father's, felt fevered in all its veins.

"At least, my wife is not the cause of my illness," he answered in a low tone.

"I don't know that, Bede. That a great worry lies on your heart continually, that a kind of restless, nervous anxiety never leaves you by night or by day, is sufficiently plain to me; I know that it can only arise from matters connected with your wife: and I also know that this, and this alone, tells upon your bodily health. Your wife's extravagance is bringing you care: ruin will surely supervene if you do not check it."

Bede Greatorex opened his lips to speak, but seemed to think better of it, and closed them again. His brow was knitted in two upright lines.

"Unless you can do so, Bede, I shall be compelled to make an alteration in our arrangements. In justice to myself and to my other children, your name must be withdrawn from the firm. Not yourself and your profits: only the name, as a matter of safety."

Bede Greatorex bit his lips. His father's heart ached for him. For a long while Mr. Greatorex had seen that his son's unhappy state of mind (and that it was unhappy no keen observer, much with him, could mistake) arose through his wife. And he thought Bede a fool for putting up with her.

"You need not be afraid," said Bede. "I will take care the firm's interests are not affected."

"How can you take care?" retorted Mr. Greatorex, in rather a stern tone. "When debts are being made daily in the most reckless manner: debts that you know nothing of, until the bills come trooping in and you are called upon to pay, can you answer for what it will go on to? Can I? Many a richer man than either of us, Bede, has been brought to the Bankruptcy Court through less than this. Ay, and I will tell you what else, Bede—it has brought husbands to the grave. When people remark to me, 'Your son Bede looks ill,' I quietly answer 'Do you think so?' when all the while I am secretly wondering that you can look even as well as you do."

"Who remarks on it?" asked Bede.

"Who! Many people. Only the other night, when Henry Ollivera was here, he spoke of it."

"Let Henry Ollivera concern himself with his own affairs," was the fierce answer. "Does he want to be a—"

Bede's voice dropped to an inaudible whisper. But the concluding words had sounded like—"curse amongst us."

"Bede! Did you say curse?"

"I said king," answered Bede. His nostrils were working, his lips were quivering, his chest was heaving; all with a passion he was trying to suppress. Mr. Greatorex looked at him, and waited. He had seen Bede in these intemperate fits of anger before: sometimes for no apparent cause.

"We will go book to the starting-point, this cheque, Bede," he quietly said. "You must have overlooked it. Go and search your desk again."

Bede was leaving the room when he met a servant coming to it with a message. Mr. Yorke had called, and wished to see Mr. Greatorex for a couple of minutes: his business was important.

The notion of Roland Yorke and important business being in connexion, brought a smile to the face of Mr. Greatorex. He told the servant to send him in.

But instead of Roland, it was the son of Sir Richard Yorke who advanced. A very fashionable gentleman in evening dress, small and slight, with white hands, a lisp, and a silky moustache. He had come about the cheque.

Sir Richard, fatigued with his visit to the city, had gone straight home to Portland Place, after receiving the cheque from Mr. Greatorex, and sent his son to the bankers' to get it cashed: a branch office of the London and Westminster. The clerk, before he cashed it, looked at it rather attentively, and then went away for a minute.

"We have cashed one cheque before today, sir, precisely similar to this," he said on his return. "Would Sir Richard be likely to have two cheques from Greatorex and Greatorex in one day, each drawn for the same amount—forty-four pounds?"

"Greatorex and Greatorex are my father's men of business: he went to get some money for them today, I know; I suppose he chose to receive it in two cheques instead of one," replied Mr. Yorke haughtily, for he deemed the question an impertinence. "Sir Richard may have wished to pay the half of it away."

The clerk counted out the money and said no more. The cheques were undoubtedly genuine, the first made out in the well-known hand of Bede Greatorex, the last in that of his father, and the clerk supposed it was all right. Mr. Yorke sent the money up to Sir Richard when he got home, and went out again. At dinner-time, he mentioned what the clerk had said—"Insolent fellah!" and the old baronet, who knew of the fact of two cheques having been drawn, took alarm.

"He'd not let me wait an instant; sent me off here before I'd well tasted my soup," grumbled Mr. Yorke. "One of you had better come and see him if the cheque has been lost and cashed; or he'll ask me five hundred questions which I can't answer, and fret himself into a fit. He has had one fit, you know. As to the cheque, it must have got into the hands of some clever thief, who made haste to reap the benefit of it."

"And your desk must have been picked, Bede, if you are sure you put it in," observed Mr. Greatorex.

"I'm sure of that," answered Bede. "But I don't see how the desk can have been picked. Not a thing in it was displaced, and the lock is uninjured."

Bede had a frightful headache—which was the cause of his looking somewhat worse than usual that evening, so Mr. Greatorex went to Sir Richard Yorke's. And in coming home he passed round by Scotland Yard.

On the following morning, sitting in his room, he held a conference with his two sons, whom he had not seen on his return the previous night.

"They think at Scotland Yard it must inevitably have been one of the clerks in your room, Bede," said Mr. Greatorex.

"One would think it, but that it seems so very unlikely," answered Bede. "Brown and Jenner have been with us quite long enough for their honesty to be proved; and the other two are gentlemen."

"Their theory is this; that someone, possessing easy access to your private room, opened the desk with a false key."

"For the matter of that, the clerks on our side the house could obtain nearly if not quite as easy access to Bede's room through its other door," observed Frank Greatorex.

"Yes. But you forget, Frank, that none of them on our side the house knew of the cheque having been drawn out and left there. Jelf will be in by-and-by."

The morning's letters, recently delivered, lay before Mr. Greatorex in a stack, and he began to look at them one by one before opening; his common custom. He came to one addressed to Bede, marked "Private" on both sides, and tossed it to his son!

Bede opened it. There was an inner envelope, sealed, and, addressed and marked just like the outer one, which Bede opened in turn. Frank Greatorex, standing near his brother, was enabled to see that but a few lines formed its contents. Almost in a moment, before Bede could have read the whole, he crushed the letter together and thrust it into his pocket. Frank laughed.

"Your correspondent takes his precautions, Bede. Was he afraid that Mrs. Bede—"

The words were but meant in jest, but Frank did not finish them. Bede turned from the room with a kind of staggering movement, his face blanched, his whole countenance livid with some awful terror. Frank simply stared after him, unable to say another word.

"What was that?" cried Mr. Greatorex, looking up at the abrupt silence.

"I don't know," said Frank. "Bede seems moonstruck with that letter he has had. It must contain tidings of some bother or other."

"Then rely upon it, it is connected with his wife," severely spoke Mr. Greatorex.

The news relating to the cheque fell upon the office like a clap of thunder. Every clerk in it felt uncomfortable especially those attached to Mr. Bede's department. The clerk at the bank, who had cashed the cheque, was questioned. It had been presented at the bank early in the afternoon, about half-past one o'clock he said, or between that and two. He had not taken notice of the presenter, but seemed to remember that he was a tall dark man, with black whiskers. Had taken it and cashed it quite as a matter of course; making no delay or query; it was a common thing for strangers, that is strangers to the bank, to present the cheques of Greatorex and Greatorex. No; he had not taken the number of the notes, for the best of all possible reasons—that he had paid it in gold, as requested. This clerk happened also to be the one to whom Sir Richard Yorke's son had presented the second cheque; he spoke to that gentleman of the fact of having cashed one an hour or two before, exactly similar; but Mr. Yorke seemed to intimate that it was all right; in short appeared offended at the subject being named to him.

At present that comprised all the information they possessed.

It was Mr. Bede Greatorex who, made the communication to the clerks in his room. He was sitting at his desk in the front office when they arrived,—an unusual circumstance; and when all were assembled and had settled to their several occupations, then he entered upon it. The cheque he had drawn out, as they might remember, on the previous morning for Sir Richard Yorke, and which he had locked up subsequently in his table-desk in the other room, had been abstracted from it, and cashed at the bank. He spoke in a quiet, friendly manner, just in the same tone he might have related it to a friend, not appearing to cast the least thought of possible suspicion upon any one of them. Nevertheless, no detective living could have watched their several demeanours, as they heard it, more keenly than did Mr. Bede Greatorex.

The clerks seemed thunderstruck. Three of them gazed at him, unable for the moment to shape any reply; the other burst out at once.

"The cheque gone! Stolen out of the desk, and cashed al the bank! My goodness! Who took it, sir?"

The words came from nobody but Roland, you may be sure. Mr. Bede Greatorex went on to give a few explanatory details; and Roland's next movement was to rush into the adjoining room without asking permission, and give a few tugs to the lid of the table-desk. Back he clattered in a commotion.

And here let it be remarked, en passant, that it is somewhat annoying to have to apply so frequently the word "clatter" to Roland's progress, imparting no doubt a good deal of unnecessary sameness. But there is really no other graphic expression that can be found to describe it. His steps were quick, and the soles of his boots made noise enough for ten.

"I say, Mr. Bede Greatorex," he exclaimed, "it is no light hand that could open that desk without a key. I've had experience in lifting weights over at Port Natal when helping to load the ships with coal—"

"Kindly oblige me by making less noise, Mr. Yorke," came the interrupting reproof.

Which Roland seemed not to heed in the least. He tilted himself on to a high stool in the middle of the room, his legs dangling, just as though he had been at a free-and-easy meeting; and there he sat, staring in consternation.

"Will the bank know the fellow again that cashed it?"

"My opinion is that the desk was opened with a key in the ordinary way," observed Mr. Bede Greatorex, referring to a previous remark of Roland's, but passing over his present question.

"Perhaps you left your keys about?" suggested Roland. "I did not leave them about, Mr. Yorke. I had them with me."

"Well, this is a go! I say!" he resumed, with quite a burst of excitement, his eyes beaming, his face glowing, "who'll be at the loss of the money? Old Dick Yorke?"

"Ah, that is a nice question," said Bede Greatorex.

"I beg your pardon, sir," interposed Mr. Brown, who had been very thoughtful. "Don't you think you must be mistaken in supposing you put the cheque in the desk? I could understand it all so easily if—"

"I know I put it in my desk, and left it there locked up," said Mr. Bede Greatorex, stopping the words. "What were you about to say?"

"If you had carried the cheque out inadvertently, and dropped it in the street," concluded Mr. Brown, "it would have been quite easy to understand then. Some unprincipled man might have picked it up, and made off at once to the bank with it, hazarding the risk."

"But I did nothing of the sort," said Bede: and Mr. Brown shook his head, as if he were hard of conviction.

"Of course there's not much difference in the degree of guilt, but many a man who would not for the world touch a locked desk might appropriate a picked-up cheque, sir."

"I tell you, the cheque was taken from my desk," reiterated Mr. Bede Greatorex, slightly irritated at the persistency.

"Well, sir, then all I can say is, that it is an exceedingly disagreeable thing for every one of us," said the head-clerk.

"I do not wish to imply that it is," said Bede Greatorex. "Mr. Yorke, allow me to suggest that sitting on that stool will not do your work."

"I hope old Dick will be the one to lose it!" cried Roland, with fervour, as he quitted the stool for his place by Mr. Hurst. "Forty-four pounds! it's stunning. He's the meanest old chap alive, Mr. Greatorex. I'd almost have taken it myself from him."

"Did you take it?" questioned Hurst in a whisper. "What's that?" retorted Roland.

He faced Hurst as he spoke, waiting for a reply. All in a moment the proud countenance and bearing changed. The face fell, the clear eyes looked away, the brow became suffused with crimson. Hurst saw the signs, and felt sorry for what he had said; had said in thoughtlessness rather than in any real meaning. For he knew that it had recalled to Roland Yorke a terrible escapade of his earlier life.

CHAPTER XIII

TAKING THE PLACE OF JELF

"It will stick in my gizzard for ever. I can see that. An awful clog, it is, when a fellow has dropped into mischief once in his life, and repented and atoned for it, that it must be cast in his teeth always; cropping up at any hour, like a dead donkey in the Thames; I might as well have stayed at Port Natal!"

Such was the inward soliloquy of Mr. Roland Yorke as he bent over his writing after that overwhelming question of Hurst's, "Did you take it?" Hurst, really grieved at having hurt his feelings, strove to smooth away what he had said.

"I beg your pardon, old fellow," he whispered. "On my honour I spoke without thought."

"I dare say you did!" retorted Roland.

"I meant no harm, Roland; I did not indeed. Nothing connected with the past occurred to me."

"You know it did," was the answer, and Roland turned his grieved face full on Hurst. "You know you wanted to bring up that miserable time when I stole the twenty-pound note from old Galloway, and let the blame of it fall on Arthur Channing. Because I took that, you think I have taken this!"

"Hush! You'll have them hear you, Yorke."

"That's what you want. Why don't you go and tell them?" demanded Roland, who was working into a passion. "Proclaim it aloud. Ring the bell, as the town-crier does at home on a market-day. Call Greatorex and Brown and Jenner up from their desks. Where's the good of taunting me in private?"

Hurst kept his head down and wrote on in silence, hoping to allay the storm he had inadvertently provoked. In spite of his protestations, he had spoken in reference to that past transaction, and the tone showed the truth to Roland; but still he had spoken thoughtlessly. Roland, as he believed, was no more guilty of this present loss than he himself was; and he felt inclined to clip his tongue out for its haste.

Pushing his hair from his hot face, biting his lips, drawing deep breaths in his anger and emotion, stood Roland. Presently the pen was dashed down on the parchment before him, blotting it and defacing it for use, but of course that went for nothing, and Roland stalked to the desk of Mr. Bede Greatorex.

"I wish to say, sir, that I did not steal the cheque."

The words took Mr. Bede Greatorex by surprise. But he had by this time become pretty well acquainted with Roland and his impulsive ways; he liked him in spite of his faults as a clerk; otherwise he would never have put up with them. A pleasant smile crossed his lips as he answered; answered in jest.

"You know the old French proverb, I dare say, Mr. Yorke: 'Qui s'excuse s'accuse'?"

Roland made nothing of French at the best of times: at such as these, every pulse within him agitated to pain, it was about as intelligible as Hebrew. But, had he understood every word of the joking implication, he could not have responded with more passionate earnestness.

"I did not touch the cheque, sir; I swear it. I never saw it after you took it from this room, or knew where you put it, or anything. It never once came into my thoughts."

"But why do you trouble yourself to say this?" asked Mr. Bede Greatorex, speaking seriously when he noticed the anxious tone, the emotion accompanying the denial. "No one thought of supposing you had taken it."

"Hurst did, sir. He accused me."

Hurst, in his vexation, pushed his work from him in a heap. Of all living mortals, surely Roland was the simplest! he had no more tact than a child. Mr. Bede Greatorex looked from one to the other.

"I did nothing of the kind," said Hurst, speaking quietly. "The fact is, Roland Yorke can't take a joke. When he made that remark about his uncle, Sir Richard, I said to him, 'Did you take the cheque?' speaking in jest of course; and he caught up the question as serious."

"There, go to your place, Mr. Yorke," said Bede.

"I'd not do such a thing as touch a cheque for the world; or any other money that was not mine: no, not though it did belong to old Dick Yorke," earnestly reiterated Roland, keeping his ground.

"Of course you would not. Don't be foolish, Mr. Yorke."

"You believe me, I hope, sir."

"Certainly. Do go to your desk. I am busy."

Roland went back to it now, his face brighter. And Bede Greatorex thought with a smile how like a boy he was, in spite of his eight-and-twenty years, and his travels in Port Natal. These single-minded natures never grow old, or wise in the world's ways.

Another minute, and a stranger had entered the office. And yet, not quite a stranger; for Bede Greatorex had seen him some few years before, and Hurst and Roland Yorke knew him at once. It was Mr. Butterby; more wiry than he used to be, more observant about the keen eyes. He had come in reference to the loss of the cheque, and saluted Mr. Bede Greatorex who looked surprised and not best pleased to see him. Jelf, the officer expected, was a man in whom Bede had confidence; of this one's skill he knew nothing.

"It was Sergeant Jelf whom we desired to see," said Bede, speaking with curt sharpness.

"It was," amicably replied Mr. Butterby. "Jelf got a telegram this morning, and had to go off unexpected. I'm taking his place for a bit."

"Have you changed your abode from Helstonleigh to London?"

"Only tempory. My headquarters is always at Helstonleigh. And now about this matter, Mr. Bede Greatorex?"

"I think we need not trouble you. It can wait until Sergeant Jelf returns."

"It might have to wait some time then," was Mr. Butterby's answer. "Jelf is off to Rooshia first; St. Petersburgh; and it's hard to say how long he'll stay there or where he may have to go to next. It's all right, sir; I've been for this ten minutes with Mr. Greatorex, have learnt the particulars of the case, and got his instructions."

Bede Greatorex bit his lip. This man, associated in his mind with that past trouble—the death of John Ollivera, who had been so dear to him, who was so bitterly regretted still—was rather distasteful to Bede than otherwise, and for certain other reasons he would have preferred Jelf. There seemed however no help for it, as his father had given the man his instructions.

Mr. Butterby turned his attention on the clerks. As a preliminary step to proceedings, he peered at them one by one under his eyebrows, while apparently studying the maps on the walls. Hurst favoured him with a civil nod.

"How d'ye do, Butterby?" said Roland Yorke. "You don't get much fatter, Butterby."

Mr. Butterby's answer to this was to stare at Roland for a full minute; as if he could not believe his own eyes at seeing him there.

"That looks like Mr. Roland Yorke!"

"And it is him," said Roland. "He is a clerk here. Now then, Butterby!"

"I beg to state that I have full confidence in all my clerks," interposed Mr. Bede Greatorex.

"Just so," acquiesced the detective. "Mr. Greatorex senior thinks the same. But it is requisite that I should put a few questions to them, for all that. I can't see my way clear until I shall have ascertained the movements of every individual clerk this house employs, from the time the cheque was put into your desk yesterday, sir. And I mean to do it," he concluded with equable composure.

He was proceeding to examine the clerks, holding a worn note-book in his hand to pencil down any answer that might strike him, when Bede Greatorex again interposed, conscious that this might be looked upon by some of them as an unpardonable indignity.

"I cannot think this necessary, Mr. Butterby. We place every confidence in our clerks; I repeat it emphatically. Mr. Brown and Mr. Jenner have been with me for some years now; Mr. Hurst and Mr. Yorke are gentlemen."

"I know who they two are; knew them long before you did, sir; and their fathers too. Dr. Yorke, the late prebendary, put some business into my hands once. But now, just leave this matter with me, Mr. Bede Greatorex. Your father has done me the honour to leave it in my hands; and, excuse me for saying it, so must you. All these four, now present to hear you mention their names with respect, understand just as well that what I do is an ordinary matter of form the law's officers require to be gone through, as if I paid 'em the compliment to say so."

"Oh, very well," said Bede, acquiescing more cheerfully. "Step in to my private room with me for a moment first, Mr. Butterby."

He held the door open as he spoke; but, before the officer could turn to it, Mr. Greatorex came in. Bede shut the door again, and nodded to Mr. Butterby as much as to say, "Never mind now."

And so the questioning of the clerks began. Mr. Greatorex stayed for a short while to listen to it, and talked to them all in a friendly manner, as if to show that the procedure was not instituted in consequence of any particular suspicion, rather as an investigation in which the house, masters and clerks, were alike interested. The head-clerk went on with his work during the investigation as calmly as if Mr. Butterby had been a simple client; the questions put to him, as to his own movements on the previous day, he answered quietly, calmly, and satisfactorily. Roland never wrote a single line during the whole time; he did nothing but stare; and made comments with his usual freedom. When his turn came to receive the officer's polite attention, he exploded a little and gave very insolent retorts, out of what Mr. Butterby saw was sheer contrariness.

The inquiry narrowed itself to this side of the house, the rest of the clerks being able to prove, individually, that they had not been near Mr. Bede's room during the suspicious hours of the previous day. Whereas it appeared, after some considerable sifting, that each one of these four could have entered it at will, and unseen. What with the intervening dinner-hour, and sundry outdoor commissions, every one of them had been left alone in the office separately for a greater or less period of time. It also came out that, with the exception of Jenner, each had been away from the office quite long enough to go to the bank with the cheque, or to send it and secure the money. Roland Yorke, taking French leave, had stayed a good hour and a quarter at his dinner, having departed for it at a quarter past one. Mr. Brown had been out on business for the house from one till half-past two; and Mr. Hurst, who went to the stamp office, was away nearly as long. In point of fact, the chief office-keeper had been little Jenner, who came back from dinner at half-past one.

"And now," said the detective, after putting up the pocketbook, in which he had pencilled various of the above items of intelligence, "I should like to get a look at this desk of yours, Mr. Bede Greatorex."

Bede led the way to his room, and shut himself in with the detective. While apparently taking no notice whatever of the questions put to his clerks, keeping his head bent over some papers as if his very life depended on their perusal, he had in reality listened keenly to the answers of all. Handing over the key of his table-desk, he allowed the officer to examine it at will, and waited. He then sat down in his own handsome chair of green patent leather and motioned the other to a seat opposite.

"Mr. Butterby, I do not wish any further stir made in this business."

Had Mr. Butterby received a cannon-ball on his head he could scarcely have experienced a greater shock of surprise, and for once made no reply. Bede Greatorex calmly repeated his injunction, in answer to the perplexed gaze cast on him. He wished nothing more done in the matter.

"What on earth for?" cried Mr. Butterby.

"I shall have to repose some confidence in you," pursued Mr. Bede Greatorex. "It will be safe, I presume?"

Butterby quite laughed at the question. Safe! With him! It certainly would be. If the world only knew the secrets he held in his bosom!

"And yet I can but trust you partially," resumed Bede Greatorex. "Not for my own sake; I have nothing to conceal, and should like things fully investigated; but for the sake of my father and family generally. Up to early post-time this morning I was more anxious for Jelf, that he might take the loss in hand, than ever my father was."

Bede Greatorex paused. But there came no answering remark from his attentive listener, and he went on again.

"I received a private note by this morning's post which altered the aspect of things, and gave me a clue to the real taker of the cheque. Only a very faint clue: a suspicion rather; and, that, vague and uncertain: but enough to cause me, in the doubt, to let the matter drop. In fact there is no choice left for me. We must put up with the loss of the money."

Mr. Butterby sat with his hands on his knees, a favourite attitude of his: his head bent a little forward, his eyes fixed on the speaker.

"I don't quite take you, Mr. Greatorex," said he. "You must speak out more plainly."

Bede Greatorex paused in hesitation. This communication was distasteful, however necessary he might deem it, and he felt afraid of letting a dangerous word slip inadvertently.

"The letter was obscure," he slowly said, "but, if I understand it aright, the proceeds of the cheque have found their way into the hands of one whom neither my father nor I would prosecute. To do so would bring great pain upon us both, perhaps injury. The pain to my father would be such that I dare not show him the letter, or tell him I have received it. For his sake, Mr. Butterby, you and I must both hush the matter up."

Mr. Butterby felt very much at sea. A silent man by nature and habit, he sat still yet, and listened for more.

"There will be no difficulty, I presume?"

"Let us understand each other, sir. If I take your meaning correctly, it is this. Somebody is mixed up in the affair whose name it won't do to bring to light. One of the family, I suppose?"

Mr. Butterby had to wait for an answer. Bede Greatorex paused ere he gave it.

"If not an actual member of the family, it is one so nearly connected with it, that he may almost be called such."

"It's a man, then?"

"It is a man. Will you work with me in this, so as to keep suspicion from my father? Tacitly let him think you are doing what you can to investigate the affair. When no result is brought forth, he will suppose you have been unsuccessful."

"Of course, sir, if you tell me I am not to go on with it, why I won't, and it is at an end. Law bless me! Lots of things are put into our hands one day; and, the next, the family comes and says, Hush 'em up."

"So far good, Mr. Butterby. But now, I wish you, for my own satisfaction, to make some private investigation into it. Quite secretly, you understand: and if you can learn anything as to the thief, bring the news quietly to me."

Mr. Butterby thought this was about as complete a contradiction to what had gone before as it had been ever his lot to hear. He took refuge in his silent gaze and waited. Bede Greatorex put his elbow on the table and his hand to his head as he spoke.

"If I were able to confide to you the whole case, Mr. Butterby, you would see how entirely it is encompassed with doubts and difficulties. I have reason to fancy that the purloiner of the cheque out of this desk must have been one of the clerks in my room. I think this for two reasons; one is, that I don't see how anybody else could have had access to it."

"But, sir, you stood it out to their faces just now that you did not suspect them."

"Because it will not do for them to know that I do. I assure you, Mr. Butterby, this is a most delicate and dangerous affair. I wish to my heart it had never happened."

"Do you mean that the clerk, in taking it—if he did take it—was acting as the agent of some other party?"

Bede Greatorex nodded. "Yes, only that."

"But that's enough to transport him, you know," cried Butterby, slightly losing the drift of the argument.

"If we could bring him to book, yes. But that must not be done. I don't see who else it could have been," added Bede, communing with himself rather than addressing Mr. Butterby; and his face wore a strangely perplexed look.

"Could any of the household—the maidservants, for instance—get into this here room?" asked Mr. Butterby.

"There's not one of them would dare to risk it in the daytime. They are in the other house. No, no; I fear we must look to one of the young men in the next room."

Mr. Butterby nodded with satisfaction: matters seemed to be taking a more reasonable turn.

"Let's see; there's four of them," he began, beginning to tell the clerks off on his fingers. "The manager, Brown, confidential, you said, I think—"

"I did not say confidential," interrupted Bede Greatorex. "I said we placed great confidence in him. There's a distinction, Mr. Butterby."

"Of course. Then there's the little man, Jenner; and the others, Hurst and Yorke. Have you any doubt yourself as to say one of them?" quickly asked Mr. Butterby, looking full at the lawyer.

Bede Greatorex hesitated. "I cannot say I have. It would be so wrong, you know, to cast a doubt on either, when there is not sufficient cause; nothing but what may be a passing, foundationless fancy."

"Speak out, Mr. Bede Greatorex. It's all in the day's work. If there is really nothing, it won't hurt him; if there is, I may be able to follow it up. Perhaps it's one of the two gentlemen?"

"If it be any one of the four, Mr. Hurst."

The detective so far forgot his good manners as to break into a low whistle.

"Mr. Hurst! or Mr. Yorke, do you mean?" he cried, in his surprise.

"Not Mr. Yorke, certainly. Why should you think of him?"

"Oh, for nothing," carelessly answered Butterby. "Hurst seems an upright young man, sir."

"It is so trifling a doubt I have of him, the lifting of a straw, as may be said, that I should be sorry to think he is not upright. Still, I have reason for deciding that he is the most likely, of the four, for doubt to attach to."

At that moment, the gentleman in question interrupted them—Josiah Hurst; bringing a message to Mr. Bede Greatorex. An important client was waiting to see him. Mr. Butterby took a more curious look at the young man's countenance than he had ever done in the old days at Helstonleigh.

"The lawyer's wrong," thought he to himself. "He is no thiever of cheques, he isn't."

"I shall be at liberty in one minute, Mr. Hurst. Shut the door. You understand?" he added in a low tone to the detective, as they stood up together in parting. "All that I 'have said to you must be kept secret; doubly secret from my father. He must suppose you at work, investigating; whereas, in point of fact, the thing must drop. Only, if you can gain any private information, bring it to me."

Mr. Butterby answered by one of his emphatic nods. "You see there's nothing come up yet about that other thing," he said.

"What other thing?"

"The death of Mr. Ollivera."

"And not likely to," returned Bede Greatorex. "That was over and done with at the time."

"Just my opinion," said the detective. "Jenner was his clerk in chambers.".

"Yes. A faithful little fellow."

"Looks it. Who's the other one—Mr. Brown?"

"I can only tell you that he is Mr. Brown; I know nothing of his family. We have had him three or four years."

"Had a good character with him, I suppose? Knew where he'd been, and all that?"

"Undoubtedly. My father is particular. Why do you ask?"

"Only because he is the only one in your room that I don't know something of. Good morning, Mr. Bede Greatorex."

Bede shut the door, and Mr. Butterby walked away, observing things indoors and out with a keen eye, while he ruminated on what he had heard. Sundry reports, connected with the domestic life of Bede Greatorex, were familiar to his comprehensive ears.

"It's a rum go, this," quoth he, making his comments "He meant his wife, he did; I'd a great mind to say so. Hush it up? of course they must. And Madam keeps the forty-four pounds. But now—does he suspect it might have been one of the clerks helped her to it, or was it only a genteel way of stopping my questions as to how the 'member of the family' could have got indoors to the desk? She grabbed his key, she did, and took out the cheque herself: leastways I should say so. Stop a bit, though. Who cashed it at the bank? Perhaps one of 'em did help her. 'Twasn't Hurst, I know nor little Jenner, either. Don't think it was young Yorke in spite of that old affair at Galloway's. T'other, Brown, I don't know. Anyway," concluded Mr. Butterby, his thoughts recurring to Bede Greatorex, and his wife, "he has got his torment in her; and he shows it. Never saw a man so altered in all my life: looks, spirits, manners: it's just as though there was a blight upon him."

That the presence of the police-agent in the office had not been agreeable to the clerks, will be readily understood. It had to be accepted for an evil; as other evils must be for which there is no help. Roland

Yorke felt inclined to resent it openly, and thought the fates were against him still, as they had been at Port Natal. What with that unlucky question of Hurst's and the appearance of Butterby on the scene, both recalling the miserable escapade of years ago that he would give all the world to forget, Roland, alike hot-headed and hot-hearted, was in a state of mind to do any mad thing that came uppermost. And the morning wore away.

"Why don't you go to dinner, Mr. Yorke?"

The question came from the manager. Roland, in his perplexity of mind and feelings, had unconsciously let the usual time slip by. Catching up his hat, he tore through the street at speed until he reached the bank, into which he went with a burst.

"I want to see one of the principals."

What with the haste the imperative demand, and the imposing stature and air, Roland was at once attended to, and a gentleman, nearly as little as Jenner came forward.

"Look here," said Roland. "Just you bring me face to face with the fellow who cashed that cheque yesterday. The clerk, you know."

"Which cheque?" came the very natural question from the little gentleman, as he gazed at the applicant.

"The one there's all this shindy over at Greatorex and Greatorex's. Drawn out in favour of old Dick Yorke."

Of course it was not precisely the way to go about things. Before Roland's request was complied with, a little information was requested as to what his business might be, and who he was.

"I am Mr. Roland Yorke."

"Any relation to Sir Richard Yorke?"

"His nephew by blood; none at all by friendliness. Old Dick—but never mind him now. If you'll let me see the clerk, sir, you will hear what I want with him."

The clerk, standing at elbow behind the counter, had heard the colloquy. Roland dashed up to him so impulsively that the little gentleman could with difficulty keep pace.

"Now, then," began Roland to the wondering clerk, "look at me—look well. Am I the man who presented that cheque yesterday?"

"No, sir, certainly not," was the clerk's reply. "There's not the least resemblance."

"Very good," said Roland, a little calming down from his fierceness. "I thought it well to come and let you see me, that's all."

"But why so?" asked the principal, thinking Sir Richard Yorke's nephew, though a fine man, must be rather an eccentric one.

"Why! why, because I am in Bede Greatorex's office and we've had a policeman amongst us this morning, looking us up. They say the cheque was brought here by a tall fellow with black whiskers. As that description applies to me, and to none of the others, I thought I'd come and let you see me. That's all. Good morning."

Dashing out in the same commotion that he had entered, Roland, still neglecting his dinner, went skimming back to the house of Greatorex and Greatorex. Not to enter the office, but to pay a visit to Mrs. Bede's side of it.

Not very long before this hour, Mr. Bede Greatorex, all the cares of his business on his shoulders, not the least of them (taking it in all its relations) being the new one connected with the abstracted cheque went upstairs for luncheon and a few minutes' relaxation. He found his wife full of her cares. Mrs. Bede Greatorex had cards out for that afternoon, bidding the great world to a Kettle-drum and she was calculating what quantity of ices and strawberries to order in, with sundry other momentous questions.

The rooms were turned upside-down. A vast crowd was expected, and small articles of impeding furniture, holding fragile ornaments, were being put out of the way, lest they should come to grief in the turmoil.

"Yes, that quantity of ice will be sufficient; and be sure take care that you have an abundance of strawberries," concluded Mrs. Bede Greatorex to the attendant, who had been receiving her orders. "Chocolate? Of course. Where's the use of asking senseless questions? Bede," she added, seeing her husband standing there, "I know how you detest the smell of chocolate, saying it makes you as sick as a dog, and brings on headaches; but I cannot dispense with it in my rooms. Other people give it, and so must I."

"Give what you like," he said wearily "What is it you are going to hold? A ball?"

"A ball in the afternoon! Well done, Bede! It's a drum."

"The house is never free from disturbance, Louisa," he rejoined, as a man pushed by with a table.

"You should let me live away from it. And then you'd not smell the chocolate. And the doors would not be impeded forever with carriages, as you grumble they are. With a house in Hyde Park—"

"Hush!" said Bede in a whisper: "What did I tell you the other day?—That our expenses are so large, I could not live elsewhere if I would: Don't wear me out with this everlasting theme, Louisa."

It was not precisely the hearth for a min, oppressed with the world's troubles, to find refuge in; neither was she the wife. Bede sighed in very weariness, and turned to go, away, thinking how welcome to him, if he could but get transplanted to it, would be the corner of some far-off desert, never before trodden by the foot of man.

A great noise on the stairs, as if a coach-and-six were coming up in fierce commotion, followed by a smart knocking at the room door. Bede turned to escape, thinking it might possibly be the advance guard of the Drum. Nobody but Mr. Roland Yorke. And Roland (who had come up on a vain search for

Miss Channing) seeing his master there, at once began to tell of where he had just been and for what purpose. To keep his own counsel on matter whatever, would have been extremely difficult to Roland.

"It is said, you know, Mr. Bede Greatorex, that the man, who cashed the cheque and got the money, was a tall fellow with black whiskers so I thought it well to go and show myself. I am tall," drawing up his head; "I've got black whiskers," pushing one side forward with his hand; "and nobody else in your room answered to the description."

"It was very unnecessary, Mr. Yorke. You were in Port Natal."

"In Port Natal!" echoed Roland, staring. "What has Port Natal to do with this?"

Bede Greatorex slightly laughed. In his self-absorption, he had suffered his mind to run on other things.

"As to unnecessary—I don't think so, after what that ill-natured Hurst said. And perhaps you'd not, sir, if you knew all," added simple Roland, thinking of Mr. Galloway's banknote. "Anyway, I have been to the bank to show myself."

"What did the bank say to you?" questioned Bede Greatorex, his tone one of light jest.

"The bank said I was not in the least like the fellow; he was tall, but not as tall as me, and they are nearly sure he had a beard as well as whiskers. I thought I'd tell you, sir."

Mrs. Bede Greatorex, listening to this with curious ears, inquired what the trouble was, and heard for the first time of the loss of the cheque, the probable loss of the forty-four pounds. Had Mr. Butterby been present to mark her surprise, he might have put away his opinion that she was the recipient alluded to by Bede Greatorex, and perhaps have mentally begged her pardon for the mistaken thought.

"Will you come to my kettle-drum, Mr. Roland?"

"No, I won't," said Roland. "Thank you all the same," he added a minute after, as if to atone for the bluntness of the reply. "I've been put out today uncommonly, Mrs. Bede Greatorex; and when a fellow is, he does not care for drums and kettles."

However, when the kettle-drum was in full swing about five o'clock in the afternoon and the stairs were crowded with talkers and trains, Roland, thinking better of it, elbowed his way up amidst. People who did not know him, thought he must be from the Court at least; the Lord Chamberlain, or some such great man, for Roland had a way of holding his own and tacitly asserting himself, like nobody else. He caught sight of Gerald, who averted his head at once; he saw Mrs. Hamish Channing, and she was the only guest he talked to. Roland was again looking for Annabel. He found her presently in the refreshment room, seeing that Miss Jane did not make herself ill with strawberries and cream.

Into her ear, very much as though it had been a rock of refuge, Roland confided his wrongs; Mr. Hurst's semi-accusation of him in regard to the loss, his errand to the bank, and in short all the events of the morning.

"I couldn't have done it by him," said Roland. "Had he made a fool of himself when he was young and wicked, I could no more have flung it in his teeth in after-years, to twist his feelings, than I could twist yours, Annabel. When I've been repenting of the mad act ever since; never going to my bed at night or rising in the morning, without thinking of it and—dashing it: but I was going to say another word: and hoping and planning how best to recompense every soul that suffered by it! It was too bad of him."

"Yes it was," warmly answered Annabel, her cheeks flushing with the earnestness of her sympathy. "Roland, I never liked that Josiah Hurst."

CHAPTER XIV

GERALD YORKE IN A DILEMMA

Mr. Gerald Yorke stood in his chambers—as he was pleased to style the luxurious rooms he occupied in a most fashionable quarter of London. Gerald liked both luxury and fashion, and went in for both. He was occupied very much as Mrs. Bede Greatorex had been earlier in the day—namely, casting a glance round his rooms, and the supplies of good things just brought into them. For Gerald was to give a wine and supper party that night.

Running counter to the career planned for him—the Church—Gerald had embarked on one of his own choosing. He determined to be a public man; and had private ambitious visions of a future premiership. He came to London, got introductions through his family connections, and hoped to be promoted to some government appointment to start with. As a preliminary step, he plunged into society and high living; going out amidst the great world and receiving men in return. This requires some amount of cash, as everybody who has tried it knows, however unlimited the general credit may be; and Gerald Yorke laboured under the drawback of possessing none. A handsome present from Lord Carrick when his lordship was in funds, of a five-pound note, screwed out of his mother's shallow purse, constituted his resources. So Gerald did as a vast many more do—he took to writing as a temporary means of living. Of genius he had none; but after a little practice he became a sufficiently ready writer. He tried political articles, he wrote short stories for periodicals, he obtained a post on one or two good papers as a reviewer. Gerald liked to review works of fiction best: they gave him the least trouble: and no one could cut and slash a rival's book to shreds, more effectively than he. Friendly with a great many of the literary world, and with men belonging to the press, Gerald found plenty of work put into his hands, for which he was well paid. At last he began to try his hand at a book himself. If he could only get through it, he thought, and it made a hit and brought him back money, what a glorious thing it would be!

As the time went on, so did Gerald's hopes. The book progressed towards completion (in spite of sundry stumbling blocks where he had seemed stuck), and success, with its attendant golden harvest, drew almost as near to his view, as its necessity was in reality. For the ready money earned by his stray papers and reviews, was verily but as a drop of water in the great ocean of Gerald's needs.

Look at him as he stands there with his back to the fireplace; the tall, fine man in his evening dress. But there is a savage frown of perplexity and temper on his generally cynical face, for something has occurred to annoy him.

And yet, that had been in its earlier part such a red-lettered day! In the morning Gerald had put the finishing conclusion to his book, and complacently written the title. In the afternoon he had been introduced to a great literary don at Mrs. Bede Greatorex's drum, who might prove of use in the future.

Calling in later upon a friend, he had taken some dinner with him, and then returned home and dressed for the opera, his supper guests being bidden for twelve o'clock. He was just going out on his way to the opera, when two letters met his eye, which he had overlooked on entering. The one, he saw, was in the handwriting of a creditor who was becoming troublesome; the other in that of his wife and marked "Immediate."

Gerald Yorke had been guilty of one imprudent act, for which there was no cure. When only twenty-one, he had married. The young lady, Winnifred Eales, was of no family, and did not possess a fraction of money. Gerald was taken by her pretty face, and was foolish enough to marry her off-hand; saddling himself with a wife without having the wherewithal to keep one. Little did Gerald Yorke's acquaintances in London suspect that the fast and fashionable young man, (only in his twenty-sixth year now, though looking older) had a wife and three children! Had the question been put to Gerald "Are you married?" he would have briefly acknowledged it; but he never volunteered the information. His wife was his wife; he did not wish to repudiate either her or the children; but he had long ago found them an awful incumbrance, and kept them in the background. To do so was less cost. Had Gerald come into two or three thousand a year, he would have set up his tent grandly, have had his family home to it forthwith, and introduced them to the world: until that desirable time should arrive, he had meant them to remain in the little country cottage-home in Gloucestershire, where he had placed them, and where they knew nobody. But that his wife was tolerably patient and very persuadable, he would have struck long before. She did grumble; when Gerald visited her she was fretful, tearful, fractious and complaining. In fact, she was little better than a child herself, and not by any means a strong-minded one.

But the crisis had come. Gerald tore open the letter, with its ominous word Immediate, and found unwelcome news. For two or three blissful moments, he did not believe his eyesight, and then the letter was dashed down in vehement passion.

"Winny's mad!"

Whinny (as Gerald's wife was generally called) tired of her lonely home, of the monotonous care of her children, tired above all of waiting month after month, year after year, for the fulfilment of his promises to put matters upon a more satisfactory footing, had taken the initiative into her own hands. She informed her husband that she had given up the cottage, sold off its furniture by auction, and should arrive with the children in London (Paddington terminus) at three o'clock the next day, where he must meet her if he could: if not, they should drive at once to him at his chambers, or to his club, the Young England. A slight concluding hint was annexed that he need not attempt to stop her by telegraph, for the telegraph people had received orders not to bring her up any messages that might arrive.

A pretty announcement, that, for a man in society to get! Gerald stood very much as if he had received a blow that blinded him. What was he to do with them when they came? Never in all his life had he been so pushed into a corner. The clock went ticking on, on; but Gerald did not heed it.

His servant came in, under pretence of bringing a dish of fruit, and ventured to remind him of the engagement at the opera, truly thinking his master must have forgotten it. Gerald sent the opera very far away, and ordered the man to shut the door.

In truth he was in no mood for the opera now. Had there been a possibility of doing it, he would have put off his supper-party. The other letter, which he opened in a kind of desperation, contained threats of unpleasant proceedings, unless a debt, long sued for, was paid within twenty-four hours. Money,

Gerald must have and he did not know where to get it. His literary pay had been forestalled wherever it could be. He had that day applied to young Richard Yorke (or Vincent, as Gerald generally called him, being the finer name of his cousin's two baptismal ones) for a loan, and been refused. Apart from the future difficulties connected with Winny and the children, it would take some cash in pocket to establish them in lodgings.

"Winny wants a good shaking for causing me this trouble," earnestly soliloquised Gerald in his dilemma, that fashionable drawl of his, kept for the world, not being discernible in private life. "Suppose she should turn restive and insist on coming here? Good heavens! a silly, untidy wife, and three ill-kept children!"

He walked to the sideboard, dashed out a glass of some cordial with his shaking band, and drank it, for the picture unnerved him.

"If I could get my book accepted by a publisher, and an advance made upon it," thought Gerald, resuming his place on the hearthrug, "I might get along. Some of those confounded publishers are so independent; they'll keep a manuscript for twelve months and never look at it."

A short while before this, Gerald had tried his hand at a play, which ill-natured managers had hitherto refused to accept. Gerald of course thought the refusal arose from nothing but prejudice, as some others do in similar cases. He went on with his soliloquy.

"I think I'll get some fellow to look over my novel and give me an opinion upon it—which I can repeat over to a publisher. Write it down if necessary. That's what I ought to have done by the drama: one is apt to be overlooked in these days without a special recommendation. Let's see? Who is there? Hamish Channing. Nobody so good. His capabilities are first-rate, and I'll make him read it at once. If Vincent Yorke—"

The soliloquy was brought to a standstill. Some commotion outside, as if a visitor had sought to enter and was stopped, caught Gerald's startled ear; but he knew his servant was trustworthy. The next moment the door opened, and the man spoke.

"Mr. Yorke, sir."

Who should walk in, with his usual disregard to the exigencies of ceremonious life, but Roland! Gerald stared in utter astonishment; and, when satisfied that it was in truth his brother, frowned awfully. Gerald in his high sphere might find it difficult to get along; but to have an elder brother who was so down in the world as to accept any common employment that offered, and put up with one room and a turn-up bedstead, and not scruple to own it, was a very different matter. And Gerald's intention was to wash his hands of Roland and his low surroundings, as entirely as Sir Richard Yorke could do.

Roland took a survey of things in general, and saluted his brother with off-hand cordiality. He knew his presence there was unacceptable, but in his good-nature would not appear to remember it. The handsome rooms, lacking no signs of wealth and comfort, the preparations for the entertainment that peeped out here and there, Gerald himself (as Roland would have expressed it) in full fig; all seemed to denote that life was sunny in this quarter, and Roland thought it was fine to be Gerald.

Gerald slowly extended one unwilling finger in response to Roland's offered grasp, and waited for him to explain his business, not inviting him to sit. It was not he that would allow Roland to think he might be a visitor there at will. Roland, however, put himself into a comfortable velvet lounging-chair of his own accord, as easily as he might have put himself into the old horsehair thing at Mrs. Jones's: and then proceeded to tell his errand.

It was this. Upon going home that night at seven—for he had to stay late in the office to make up for the time lost at Mrs. Bede's kettle-drum—Roland found a letter from Lord Carrick, who was in the shade still. Amidst some personal matters, it contained a confidential message for Gerald, which Roland was charged to deliver in person. This was no other than a reminder to Gerald that a certain pecuniary obligation for which he and Lord Carrick were equally responsible (the latter having made himself so, to accommodate Gerald, but receiving no benefit) was becoming due, and that Gerald would have to meet it. "Tell him, my boy, that I'd willingly find the means for him if I could, and as much more at the back of it," wrote the good-natured peer; "but I'm regularly out of everything for the time being, and can't."

It may be easily conceived that the errand, when explained, did not tend to increase Roland's welcome. Gerald bit his full lips with suppressed passion, and could willingly have struck his brother. Vincent Yorke, perhaps as an ostensible plea for not responding in kind to Gerald's application for the loan of twenty pounds that day, said they might have to lose forty-four, and had disclosed to him the particulars of the appropriated cheque, adding that he should think suspicion must lie on someone of the four clerks in Bede Greatorex's office. That was quite enough for Gerald.

In anything but a temperate way he now attacked his brother, not saying, Did you steal the cheque? but accusing him of doing it, and bringing up the old transaction at Mr. Galloway's. There ensued a sharp, short quarrel: which might have been far sharper on Roland's side but for the aspersion already cast on him by Hurst: that seemed to have paved the way for this, and deadened its sting.

"Look here, Gerald," said Roland, calming down from anger, but speaking with an emotion at which Gerald stared. "My taking that twenty pound note from Galloway was an awful mistake; the one great mistake of my life, for I shall never—"

"Call it a theft," roared Gerald.

"For I shall never make such another," went on Roland, just as though he had not heard the interruption. "It will stick to me always, more or less, be cropping up everlastingly; but, for all that, it was the best thing that could have happened to me."

Gerald answered by a sneer.

"It sent me out to Port Natal. I should never have gone but for that, however much I might have talked of it. I wanted to put Arthur Channing straight with the world, and I couldn't stay and face the world while I did it. Well, I went out to Port Natal: and I stayed there, trying to get into funds, and come home with some redeeming money in my hand. I stayed long enough to knock out of me a great deal that wanted to come out; idleness, and folly, and senseless pride. I'm not one of the good and brave ones yet, such as Arthur Channing is; but I've learnt at any rate to do a little for myself and be tolerant to others; I've learned not to be ashamed to work honestly for my bread before eating it. There."

"The sooner you take yourself out of my rooms, the better," said Gerald. "I am expecting friends."

"Don't fancy I'm going to wait till they come; I'd not intrude on either you or them," retorted Roland, turning to depart. "I came up on your business, Gerald, tonight, to oblige Carrick; but I shall tell him to choose somebody else for a messenger if he wants to send again. Good night."

Gerald gave no answer. Unless the banging-to the door after Roland with his foot could be called one.

He stood ruminating for a short while alone. The message certainly tended to a further complication of Gerald's perplexities. Although he had originally assured Lord Carrick that he should not look to him to meet the bill, he really had done so: for nobody looked in vain to that imprudent and good-hearted man, when he had it in his power to help.

"There's nothing for it but the novel," decided Gerald presently. "What's the time?"

Glancing over his shoulder, he saw that it was not yet half-past nine. As his guests would not arrive until twelve, there was time, and to spare, for a visit to Hamish Channing. So, packing up his manuscript, he went forth.

Hamish sat in his writing-room as usual this evening, working closely. His face wore a weary look as the light from the candle, the shade temporarily removed, fell upon it. Ever good-humoured, ever full of sweet hope, of loving-kindness to the whole world, he cared not for his weariness; nay, was not conscious of it.

An arrival at the street door, and a bustle in the next room following closely upon it; a child's joyous laughter and light chatter. Hamish knew the cause. Little Miss Nelly had returned home from a child's party, her hands laden with fairy gifts. In she came; papa could not keep the door quite closed from her; in her white muslin frock with the broad blue sash and sleeve ribbons, and the bit of narrow blue on her neck, suspending the locket with Grandpapa Channing's likeness in it. Hamish caught up the lovely little vision and began fondling it; kissing the bright cheeks, the chattering lips, the pretty neck.

"And now Nelly must go," he said, "for I have my work to do."

"A great deal of work?"

"Oceans of it, Nelly."

"Mamma says, you work too much," returned Nelly, looking full at him with her brilliant, sweet blue eyes, so like his own.

"Tell mamma I say she knows nothing about it."

"Jane Greatorex was there, papa, and Aunt Annabel. She told me to tell you, too, not to work so much."

"Jane Greatorex did?"

"Now, papa, you know! Annabel."

"We'll have mamma and Annabel taken up for conspiracy. Good night, my little treasure: I'd keep you here always if I could."

"Let me say my prayers to you tonight, papa," whispered the child.

He was about to say no, but seemed to change his mind, and quitted the chair at the writing-table for another. Then Nelly, throwing all her gifts on the table in a heap, knelt down and put up her hands to say her prayers. When she had concluded them, he did not let her rise, but laid his hand upon her head and kept it there in silence, as if praying himself. And Nelly went out with some awe, for papa's eyes looked as if they had tears in them.

Hamish had settled to work again, and Nelly would be a myth until the next morning, when Gerald Yorke arrived, dashing up in a hansom. He came in to Hamish at once, carrying his manuscript.

"You'll do me a favour, won't you, old friend?"

"What is it?" asked Hamish, the sunny smile on his face already an earnest of compliance. And Gerald undid his manuscript.

"I want you to read this; to go over it carefully and attentively; and then give me your opinion of it. I thought once of asking Caustic, but your judgment is worth more than his, because I know you'll give a true report."

Gerald had either been in too great haste to make a fair copy for the press, or else had deemed that point superfluous. As Hamish caught sight of the blurred and blotted lines in Gerald's notably illegible hand, he hesitated. He was so full of work, and this would be indeed a task. Only for the tenth part of a moment, however; he could sit up at night and get through it.

"At once," said Gerald. "If you could put away your own work for it, I should be obliged; I have a reason for wishing to get it back directly. And Hamish, you'll mind and give me your real opinion in strict candour."

"Do you say that seriously?" asked Hamish, his tone one of grave meaning.

"Of coarse I do. Or why should I ask you to read it at all?"

"Not very long ago, a friend brought me a work he had written, begging me to look over it, and tell him what I thought of it, without disguise or flattery, just as you do now," spoke Hamish. "Well, I thought he meant it, and did as he requested. Above all, he had said, point out to me the faults. I did point out the faults. I told him my opinion candidly and kindly, and it was not a favourable one. Gerald, I lost my friend from that hour."

Gerald laughed. The cases, he thought, were totally dissimilar. Had an angel from Heaven come down and said an unfavourable opinion could be pronounced upon this work of his, he had not believed it.

"Don't be afraid, Channing. I shall thank you to give me your true opinion just as though the manuscript belonged to some stranger, who would never know what you said."

"I don't like the title," observed Hamish, accepting the conditions.

"Not like the title?"

"No."

Gerald had called it by a title more wonderful than attractive. The good sense of Hamish Channing discovered the mistake at once.

"We made it up between us one night over our drink; one put in one word and one another," said Gerald, alluding to sundry confrères of his. "After all, Hamish, it's the book that makes the success, not the title."

"But a good book should possess a good title."

"Well, the title can go for now; time enough to alter that later," concluded Gerald, rather testily. "You'll lose no time, Channing?"

"No more than I can help. To put all my work away you must know to be impracticable, Gerald. But I'll make what haste I can." Hamish went with him to the other room where Mrs. Channing was sitting, and Gerald unbosomed himself to them of his great care; the dilemma which the evening's post had put him in, as to the speedy arrival of his wife.

"What on earth to do, I can't tell," he said with a groan. "Lodgings for a family are not found in an hour; and that's the best thing I can do with them yet awhile. If Winny were not an utter simpleton, she'd at least have given me a clear day's warning. And only look at the impossibility of my getting dinner and tea for them tomorrow, and all the rest of the necessaries. I shan't know how to set about it."

Hamish glanced at his wife and she at him, and they spoke almost simultaneously.

"If you would like to bring them here first, Gerald, do so. You know we shall be happy to see Winny. It may give you a few hours more to fix on lodgings, and they need not move into them until night."

Gerald twirled his watch-chain as he stood, and did not at once accept. He was looking very cross.

"Thank you," he said at length, but not very graciously, "then they shall come here. I suppose you could not make it convenient to meet them for me at Paddington, Hamish?"

"That I certainly could not," replied Hamish. "You know my hours in the city, Gerald. If you are unable to go yourself, why don't you ask Roland? I don't suppose"—and Hamish broke into a smile—"his services are so valuable to Greatorex and Greatorex that they'd make an objection."

The mention of his brother was enough for Gerald. He called him a few contemptuous names, and went out to the cab, which had waited to drive him back to his chambers, and to the entertaining of his friends, who arrived in due course, and did not separate too soon.

Hamish finished his own work, and then he commenced for Gerald. He sighed a little wearily, as he adjusted his light. Ellen thought him long, and came in.

"Not ready yet, Hamish!"

"My darling, I must sit late tonight. I thought you had gone to bed."

"I have been waiting. You said at tea-time you had not so very much to do. It is twelve o'clock. Whatever's that?"

"Gerald Yorke's manuscript. He wants me to read it."

"Hamish! As if you had not too much work of your own!"

"One must do a little kindness now and then," he said cheerfully. "You go on, love. I'll come by-and-by."

It was of no use saying more, as Ellen knew by experience. This was not the first friend's manuscript he had toiled through: and she went upstairs. Hamish glanced at the light, saw that he had another candle in readiness, coughed a little, as he often did now, applied himself closely to his task until three o'clock, and then left off. In heart and mind ever genial, he thought nothing of the extra toil: it was to do a good turn for Gerald. Surely these unselfish, loving natures shall find their deeds recorded on high, and meet with their reward!

He was up with the lark. Six o'clock saw him in his room again, that he might give a few more hours to the manuscript before proceeding to his daily work in the city.

Hamish Channing's was no eye-service, either to heaven or to man.

CHAPTER XV

VISITORS FOR MRS JONES

When the exigencies of a story require that two parts of it should be related at once, the difficulty is, which to take first; or rather which may be delayed with the least inconvenience: and very often, as is the case with other things in life we choose the wrong.

Mrs. Jones sat in her parlour at the twilight hour and a very dark twilight, too, but light enough for the employment she was so busy over—knitting. Not woollen socks this time, but some complicated affair of silk, more profitable than the stockings. Roland Yorke had just started on that visit, already told of, to Gerald's chambers, after enjoying a sumptuous tea and toasted muffin in Mrs. Jones's parlour, where, for the sake of company, his meals were sometimes taken. Miss Rye was out at work; Mr. Ollivera had an evening service; and so the house was quiet, and Mrs. Jones at leisure to pursue her occupation.

Not for very long. A double knock at the street door gave forth its echoes, and the servant-maid came in, after answering it.

"A gentleman wants to know if there's not a room to let here, ma'am."

Mrs. Jones looked up as if she meant to snap the girl's nose off. "How should he know any room's to let? There's no bill up."

"I've asked him into Mr. Yorke's parlour," said the girl, aware that it was worse than profitless to contend with her mistress. "He has got spectacles on, and he says his name's Mr. Brown."

Mrs. Jones shook out her gown and went to the visitor: a tall gentleman with those slightly-stained glasses on that are called smoke coloured. He generally took them off indoors, wearing them in the street to protect his eyes from the sun, but on this occasion he kept them on. It was the Mr. Brown who belonged to the house of Greatorex and Greatorex; Mrs. Jones had heard his name, but did not know him personally and he had to introduce himself as well as his business.

Mr. Roland Yorke, in his confidential communications to Josiah Hurst and the office generally, touching other people's concerns as well as his own—for gossiping, as an agreeable interlude to his hard work, still held its sway over Roland—had told of the departure of the scripture reader for another district, and the vacancy, in consequence, in Mrs. Jones's household. Mr. Brown, listening to all this, but saying nothing, had come to the conclusion that the room might suit himself; hence his visit tonight. He related these particulars quite candidly, and asked to see the room if it were not already let. He should give very little trouble, he said, took nothing at home but his breakfast and tea, and had his boots cleaned out of doors.

Mrs. Jones marshalled him to the room: the back-parlour, as the reader may remember: and the bargain was concluded at once, without a dissentient voice on the stranger's part. Mrs. Jones remembered afterwards that when she held the candle aloft for him to see its proportions and furniture, he scarcely gave a single glance before saying it would do, and laid the first week's rent down in lieu of references.

"Who asked for references?" tartly demanded Mrs. Jones, not a whit more courteous to him, her lodger in prospective, than she was to others. "Time enough to speak of references when you're told they're wanted. Little Jenner has often talked of you. Take up the money, if you please."

"But I prefer to pay my rent in advance," said Mr. Brown. "It has been my custom to do so where I am."

He spoke decisively, in a tone that admitted of no appeal, and Mrs. Jones caught up the money with a jerk and put it loose in her pocket. Saying he would let her know the time of his entrance, which might probably be on the following evening, he wished her goodnight, and departed: leaving an impression on his future landlady that his voice was in some way not altogether unfamiliar to her.

"I'm not as 'cute in remembering faces as Alletha is," acknowledged Mrs. Jones to herself, while she watched him down the street from the front door, "but I'll back my ears against hers for voices any day. Not lately; I hardly think that; it's more like a remembrance of the far past. Still I don't remember his face. Heard him speak perhaps in some railway train; or—Goodness heart alive! Is it you?"

This sudden break was occasioned by the appearance of another gentleman, who seemed to have sprung from nowhere, until he halted close before her. It was the detective officer, Butterby: and Mrs. Jones had not seen him since she quitted her country home.

"I thought it looked like you," cried Mr. Butterby, giving his hand. "Says I to myself, as I strolled along, 'If that's not the exact image of my old friend, Mrs. Jones, it's uncommon like her. It is you, ma'am! And how are you? So you are living in this quarter!"

Crafty man! Mrs. Jones had assuredly dealt him a box on the ear could she have divined that he was deceiving her. He had been watching her house for some minutes past, knowing just as well as she did that it was hers. Mrs. Jones invited him indoors, and he went under protest, not wishing, he said, to intrude: but the going indoors was what he intended doing all along.

They sat gossiping of old times and new. Mr. Butterby took a friendly glass of beer and a biscuit; Mrs. Jones, knitting always, took none. Without seeming to be at all anxious for the information, he had speedily gathered in every particular about Roland Yorke that there was to gather. Not too charitably disposed to the world in general, in speech at any rate, Mrs. Jones yet spoke well of Roland.

"He is no more like the proud, selfish aristocrat he used to be than chalk's like cheese," she said. "In his younger days Roland Yorke thought the world was made for him and his pleasure, no matter who else suffered: he doesn't think it now."

"Sowed his wild oats, has he?" remarked Mr. Butterby.

"For the matter of wild oats, I never knew he had any particular ones to sow," retorted Mrs. Jones. "Whether or not, he has got none left, that I can see."

"Wouldn't help himself to another twenty-pound note," said Mr. Butterby carelessly, stretching out his hand to take a second biscuit.

"No, that he would not," emphatically pronounced Mrs. Jones. "And I know this—that there never was an act repented of as he repents of that. His thoughts are but skin-deep; he's not crafty enough to hide them, and those that run may read. If cutting off his right hand would undo that past act, he'd cut it off and be glad, Mr. Butterby."

"Shouldn't wonder," assented the officer. "Many folks is in the like case. Have you ever come across that Godfrey Pitman?"

"Not I. Have you?"

The officer shook his head. Godfrey Pitman had hitherto remained a dead failure.

"The man was disguised when he was at your house at Helstonleigh, Mrs. Jones, there's no doubt of that; and the fact has made detection difficult, you see."

The assumption as reflecting disparagement on her and her house, mortally offended Mrs. Jones. She treated Mr. Butterby to a taste of the old tongue he so well remembered, and saw him with the barest civility to the door on his departure. Miss Rye happened to be coming in at the time, and Mr. Butterby regarded her curiously with his green eyes in saluting her. Her face and lips turned white as ashes.

"What brings him here? she asked under her breath, when Mrs. Jones came back to her parlour from shutting the door.

"His pleasure, I suppose," was Mrs. Jones's answer, a great deal too much put out to say that he had come (as she supposed) accidentally. Disguised men lodging in her house, indeed! "What's the matter with you?"

Alletha Rye had sat down on the nearest chair, and seemed labouring to get her breath. The ghastly face, the signs of agitation altogether, attracted the notice of Mrs. Jones.

"I have got that stitch in my side again; I walked fast," was all she said.

Mrs. Jones caught up her knitting.

"Did Butterby want anything in particular?" presently asked Miss Rye.

"No, he did not. He is in London about some business or other, and saw me standing at the door this evening as he passed by. Have you got your work finished?"

"Yes," replied Alletha, beginning to unfasten her mantle and bonnet-strings.

"I've let the back-parlour," remarked Mrs. Jones; "so if there's any of your pieces in the room, the sooner you fetch them out the better. Brown, the managing clerk to Mr. Bede Greatorex, has taken it."

"Who?" cried Alletha, springing out of her seat.

"It's a good thing there's no nerves in this house; you'd startle them," snapped Mrs. Jones. "What ails you tonight?"

Alletha Rye turned her back, apparently searching for something in the sideboard drawer. Her face was growing paler, if possible, than before; her fingers shook; the terror in her eyes was all too conspicuous. She was silently striving for composure, and hiding herself while she did so. When it had in a degree come she faced Mrs. Jones again, who was knitting furiously, and spoke in a quiet tone.

"Who did you say had taken the room, Julia? Mr. Brown? Why should he take it?"

"You can go and ask him why."

"I would not let it to him," said Alletha, earnestly. "Don't; pray don't."

Down went the knitting with a fling. "Now just you explain yourself, Alletha Rye. What has the man done to you, that you should put in your word against his coming in?"

"Nothing."

"Oh! Then why should he not come pray? His worst enemy can't say he's not respectable—after being for years confidential clerk to Greatorex and Greatorex. Do you hear?—what have you to urge against his coming?"

Alletha Rye was at a loss for an answer. The real reason she dared not give; and it was difficult to invent one. But the taxed brain is wonderfully apt.

"It may not be agreeable to Mr. Yorke."

Mrs. Jones was never nearer going into a real passion: and, in spite of her sharp tongue, passion with her was exceedingly rare. She gave Alletha what she called a taste of her mind and it was rather a bitter one while it lasted. Mrs. Jones did not drop it easily, and it was she who broke the ensuing silence.

"Don't bring up Mr. Yorke's name under any of your false pretences, Alletha Rye. You have taken some crotchet in your head against the man, though I don't know how or when you can have seen him, just as you did against Parson Ollivera. Anyway, I have accepted Brown as tenant, and he comes into possession tomorrow night."

"Then I may as well move my work out at once," said Alletha, meekly, taking up a candle.

She went into the back parlour, and caught hold of an upright piece of furniture, and pressed her aching head upon it as if it were a refuge. The candle remained on the chest of drawers; the work, lying about, was ungathered but she stood on, moaning out words of distress and despair.

"It is the hand of fate. It is bringing all things and people together in one nucleus; just has it has been working to do ever since the death of John Ollivera."

But the events of the evening were not entirely over, and a word or two must be yet given to it. There seemed to be nothing but encounters and re-encounters. As Mr. Butterby was walking down the street on his departure, turning his eyes (not his head) from side to side in the quiet manner characteristic of him observing all, but apparently seeing nothing, though he had no object in view just now, there came up a wayfarer to jostle him; a tall, strong young man, who walked as if the street were made for him, and nearly walked over quiet Mr. Butterby.

"Halloa!" cried Roland, for it was nobody else. "It's you, is it! What do you do up here?"

Roland's tone was none of the pleasantest, savouring rather of the haughty assumption of old days. His interview with Gerald, from which he was hastening, had not tended to appease him, and Mr. Butterby was as much his bête noire as he had ever been. The officer did not like the tone: he was a greater man than he used to be, having got up some steps in the official world.

"Looking after you, perhaps," retorted Mr. Butterby. "The streets are free for me, I suppose."

"It would not be the first time you had looked after the wrong man. How many innocent people have you taken into custody lately?"

"Now you just keep a civil tongue in your month, Mr. Roland Yorke. You'd not like it if I took you."

"I should like it as well as Arthur Channing liked it when you took him," said bold Roland. "There's been a grudge lying on my mind against you ever since that transaction, Butterby, and I promise you I'll pay it off if I get the chance."

"Did you make free with that cheque yesterday, Mr. Yorke—as you did by the other money?" asked Mr. Butterby, slightly exasperated.

"Perhaps I did and perhaps I didn't," said Roland. "Think so, if you like. You are no better than a calf in these matters, you know, Butterby. Poor meek Jenkins, who was too good to stop in the same atmosphere that other folks breathed, was clearer-sighted than you. 'It's Arthur Channing, your worships, and I've took him prisoner to answer for it,' says you to the magistrates. 'It never was Arthur Channing,' says Jenkins, nearly going down on his knees to you in his honest truth. 'Pooh, pooh,' says you, virtuously indignant, 'I know a thief when I see him—'"

"Now I vow, Mr. Roland Yorke—"

"Don't interrupt your betters Butterby; wait till I've done," cried aggravating Roland, over-bearing the quieter voice. "You took up Arthur Channing, and moved heaven and earth to get him convicted. Had the wise king, Solomon, come express down from the stars on a frosty night, to tell you Arthur was innocent, you'd have pooh-poohed him as you did poor Jenkins. But it turned out not to be Arthur, you know, old Butterby; it was me. And now if you think you'd like to go in for the same mistake again, go in for it. You would, if you took me up for this second thing."

"I can tell you what, Mr. Roland Yorke—you'd look rather foolish if I walked into Mr. Greatorex's office tomorrow morning, and told him of that past mistake."

"I don't much care whether you do or don't," said candid Roland. "As good let it come out as not, for somebody or other is always casting it in my teeth. Hurst does; my brother Gerald does—I've come now straight from hearing it. I thought I should have lived that down at Port Natal; but it seems I didn't."

"You'll not live it down by impudence," said Mr. Butterby.

"Then I must live it up," was the retort, "for impudence is a fault of mine. I've heard you say I had enough for the devil. So good night to you, Butterby. I am to be found at my lodgings, if you'd like to come after me there with a pair of handcuffs."

Roland went striding off, and the officer stood to look after him. In spite of the "impudence" received, a smile crossed his face; it was the same impulsive, careless, boyish Roland Yorke of past days, good-natured under his worst sting. But whatever other impression might have been left upon Mr. Butterby's mind by the encounter, one lay very clear—that it was not Roland who was guilty this time, and he must look elsewhere for the purloiner of the cheque.

CHAPTER XVI

WINNY

Five minutes past three at the Paddington station, and all the bustle and confusion of a train just in. Gerald Yorke stood on the platform, welcoming a pretty little fair-haired woman, whose unmeaning doll's face was given to dimple with smiles one minute, and to pout the next. Also three fair-haired children, the eldest three years old, the youngest just able to walk. Mrs. Gerald Yorke was not much better than a child herself. To say the truth, she was somewhat of a doll in intellect as well as face; standing always in awe of big, resolute, clever Gerald, yielding implicitly to his superior will. But for a strong-minded sister, who had loudly rebelled against Winny's wrongs, in being condemned to an obscure country cottage, while he flourished in high life in London, and who managed privately the removal for her, she had never dared to venture on the step; but this was not to be confessed to her husband. She felt more afraid than ever of the consequences of having taken it, now that she saw him face to face.

"How many packages have you, Winny?"

"Nineteen."

"Nineteen!"

"But they are not all large, Gerald. Some of them are small bundles, done up in kitchen towels and pillowcases."

Gerald bit his lip to avoid an ugly word: to anybody but his wife on this her first arrival in London, he would have flung it out.

"Have you brought no nursemaid, Winny?"

"Good gracious, no! How could I tell I might afford to bring one, Gerald? You know I had but one maid for everything, down there."

Hurrying them into a cab, Gerald went in search of the luggage, suppressing a groan, and glancing over his shoulder on all sides. Bundles done up in kitchen towels and pillowcases! If Gerald Yorke had never before offered up a prayer, he did then: that no ill-chance might have brought any of his fashionable friends to the station that unlucky afternoon.

"Drive through the obscurest streets," he said in the cabman's ear on his return, as he mentioned Hamish Channing's address. "Never mind taking a round; I'll pay you." And the man put his whip to the bridge of his nose, and gave a confidential nod in answer: for which Gerald could have knocked him down.

"And now, Winny, tell me how you came to do this mad thing," he said sternly, when he was seated with them.

For answer, Mrs. Yorke broke into a burst of sobs. It was coming, she thought. But Gerald had no mind for a scene there; and so held his tongue to a better opportunity. But the tears continued, and Gerald angrily ordered her not to be a child.

"You've never kissed one of us," sobbed Winny. "You've not as much as kissed baby."

"Would you have had me kiss you on the platform?" he angrily demanded. "Make a family embracing of it, for the benefit of the public! I'll kiss you when we get in. You are more ridiculous than ever, Winny."

The three little things, sitting opposite, were still as mice, looking shyly at him with their timid blue eyes. Gerald took one upon his knee for a moment and pressed its face to his own, fondly enough. Fortune was very unkind to him he thought, in not giving him a fine house for these children, and a thousand or two per annum to keep them on.

"Are we going to your chambers, Gerald?"

"That is another foolish question, Winny! My chambers are hardly large enough for me. I have taken lodgings for you this morning; the best I could at a minute's notice. London is full of drawbacks and inconveniences: if you have to put up with some, you must remember that you have brought them on yourself."

"Will there be any dinner for us?" asked Winny timidly. "The poor little girls are very hungry."

"You are going to Mrs. Hamish Channing's until tonight. I daresay she'll have dinner ready for you. Afterwards you can call at the rooms, and settle with the landlady what you will want got in."

The change in Mrs. Yorke's face was like magic; a glad brightness overspread it. Once when she was ill in lodgings at Helstonleigh, before her husband removed her into Gloucestershire, her eldest child being then an infant, Hamish Channing's wife had been wonderfully kind to her. To hear that she was going to her seemed like a haven of refuge in this wilderness of a London, which she had never until now visited.

"Oh, thank you, Gerald. I am so glad."

"I suppose you have brought some money with you," said Gerald.

"I think I have about sixteen shillings," she answered, beginning to turn out her purse.

"Where's the rest?

"What rest?"

"The money for the furniture. You wrote me word you had sold it."

"But there were the debts, Gerald. I sold the furniture to pay them. How else could I have left?—they'd not have let me come away. It was not enough to pay all; there's six or seven pounds unpaid still."

An exceedingly blank look settled on Gerald's face. The one ray of comfort looming out of this checkmating step of his wife's, reconciling him to it in a small degree, had been the thought of the money she would receive for the furniture. But what he might have said was stopped by a shriek from Winny, who became suddenly aware that the cab, save for themselves, was empty.

"The luggage, Gerald, the luggage! O Gerald, the luggage!"

"Hold your tongue, Winny," said Gerald angrily, pulling her back as she was about either to spring out or to stop the driver. "The luggage is all right. It will be sent to the lodgings."

"But we want some of the things at once," said Winny piteously. "What shall we do without them?"

"The best you can," coolly answered Gerald. "Did you suppose you were going to fill Hamish Channing's hall with boxes and bundles?"

Mrs. Channing stood ready to receive them with her face of welcome, and the first thing Winny did was to burst into tears and sob out the grievance about the luggage in her arms. If Gerald Yorke had married a pretty wife, he had also married a silly and incapable one: and Gerald had known it for some years now. Just waiting to hand them over to Mrs. Channing's care, and to give the written address of the lodgings, Gerald left. He was engaged that afternoon to dine with a party at Richmond, and would not see his wife again before the morrow.

"Don't—you—mean—to live with us?" she ventured to ask, on hearing him say this, her face growing white with dismay.

"Of course I shall live with you," sharply answered Gerald. "But I have my chambers, and when engagements keep me out, shall sleep at them."

And Gerald, lightly vaulting into a passing hansom, was cantered off. Winny turned to her good friend Ellen Channing for consolation, who gave her the best that the circumstances admitted of.

Hamish, beyond his bright welcome, saw very little of Winny that evening; he was shut up with her husband's manuscript. He took her home at night. The lodgings engaged by Gerald consisted of a sitting-room and two bedchambers, the people of the house to cook and give attendance. Hamish paid the cab and accompanied her indoors. The first thing Mrs. Gerald Yorke did, was to sit down on the lowest chair, and begin to cry. Her little girls, worn out with the day's excitement and the happy play in Nelly Channing's nursery, were fit to drop with fatigue, and put themselves quietly on the carpet.

"Oh, Mr. Channing! do you think he is not going to forgive me! It is so cruel of him to send us into this strange place all alone."

"He had an engagement, you know," answered Hamish, his tone taking, perhaps unconsciously, the same kind of soothing persuasion that he would have used to a child. "London engagements are sometimes not to be put off."

"I wish I was back in Gloucestershire!" she bewailed.

"It will be all right, Mrs. Yorke," he returned gaily. "One always feels unhappy in a fresh place. The night Ellen first slept in London she cried to be back at Helstonleigh."

A servant, who looked untidy enough to have a world full of work upon her back, showed Hamish out. In answer to a question, she said that she was the only one kept, and would have to wait on the new lodgers. Hamish slipped some money into the girl's hand and bade her do all she could for the lady and the little children.

And so, leaving Gerald's wife in her new home, he went back to his work.

He, Hamish Channing, with his good looks and his courtly presence, was treading the streets gaily on the following morning. Many a man, pressing on to business, spared a moment to turn and glance at him, wondering who the fine, handsome fellow was, with the bright and good face. It was a face that would be bright always, bright in dying; but it had more than two shades of care on it today. For if any one living man hated, more than another, to inflict pain and disappointment, it was Hamish Channing. He was carrying back Gerald's manuscript, and had no good report to give of it.

However clever Gerald might be at dashing off slashing articles in the review line, he would never be able to succeed in fiction. This first attempt proved it indisputably to Hamish Channing. The story was unconnected, the plot scarcely distinguishable, and there were very grave faults besides, offending against morality and good taste. Not one reader in fifty, and that must be some school-girl, inveterate after novels, could get through the first volume. Certainly, in plunging into a long work of fiction, Gerald Yorke had mistaken his vocation. How entirely different this crude and worthless book was from the high-class work Hamish was writing, his cheeks glowed to contemplate. Not in triumph over Gerald; never a tarnish of such a feeling could lie in his generous heart; but at the consciousness of his own capability, the gift given him by God, and what the work would be to the public. But that he deemed it lay in his duty, in all kindliness, not to deceive Gerald, he would not have told him the truth; no, in spite of the promise exacted of him to give a just, unvarnished report.

Gerald sat at breakfast, in a flowery dressing-gown, in the rooms he was pleased to call his chambers, his breakfast and its appointments perfect. Silver glittered on the table, its linen was of the fairest damask, the chocolate and cream sent its aroma aloft. Gerald's taste was luxurious: he could not have lived upon a sovereign a-week as Roland was doing: perhaps Roland had never learnt to do it but for that renowned voyage of his.

"Halloa, Hamish, old fellow! What brings you here so early?"

"Oh, one or two matters," answered Hamish, keeping the manuscript out of sight at first, for he really shrank from having to report of it. "I was not sure you would be up."

"I had to be up early this morning. Tell your news out, Hamish; I suppose the gist of it is that Winny is in a state of rebellion. Stay! I'll send the things away. One has no appetite after a Star-and-Garter dinner and pipes to wind up with till three in the morning. You have breakfasted?"

"An hour ago."

"It is an awfully provoking step for Winny to have taken," said Gerald, as his servant disappeared with the breakfast tray. "She has no doubt been grumbling to you and Mrs. Channing about her 'wrongs,'— it's what she called it yesterday—but I know mine are worse. Fancy her taking such a mad start! What on earth I am to do with them in town, I can't guess. You've not got her outside, I suppose? You know, Hamish, I couldn't help myself; I had to leave her."

"Qui s'excuse s'accuse," returned Hamish, with one of his sunny smiles chancing on the very common French proverb that Mr. Bede Greatorex had applied but recently to Gerald's brother.

"Oh bother," said Gerald. "Did Winny strike last night, and refuse to go into lodgings?"

"She went all right enough but she didn't like your leaving her to go in alone. My wife seized hold of the occasion to read me a lecture, saying she should not like it at all; I'm not sure but she said 'not put up with it.'"

"Your wife is a different woman from mine," growled Gerald; for Hamish's gay, half mocking tone covering a kinder and deeper feeling, jarred somewhat on his perplexed mind. "You knew what Winny is before today. I shall go down and see her by-and-by."

"Shall you keep these chambers on?"

"Keep these chambers on!" echoed Gerald, "why, of course I must keep them on. And live at them too, in a general way. Though how I shall afford the cost of the two places, the devil only knows."

"You have been affording it hitherto. Winny has had a separate home."

"What keeps a cottage down yonder, won't pay lodgings in London. You must know that, Hamish."

Hamish did not immediately speak: if he could not agree, he would not disagree. He did not see why Gerald should not take either a small house, or apartments sufficiently commodious, in a neighbourhood good enough for his fashionable friends not to be ashamed to resort to. Hamish and Gerald understood things in so different a light: Gerald estimated people (and fashion) by their drawl, and dress, and assumption of fast life: Hamish knew that all good men, no matter though they were of the very highest rank, were proud to respect worth and intellect and sincere nature in a poor little home, as in a palace perched aloft on Hyde Park gates. Ah me! I think one must be coming near to quit this world and its frivolity, ere the curtain of dazzling gauze that falls before our eyes is lifted.

"Are you getting on with my manuscript, Hamish?"

"I have brought it," said Hamish, taking it from his pocket. "I put away my own work—"

"Oh, thank you old fellow," was the quick interruption.

"Now don't thank me for nothing, Gerald. I was about to say that one can judge so much better of a book in reading it without breaks given to other work, that I stretched a point; for my own pleasure, you know."

Gerald drew the parcel towards him, and opened it tenderly, undoing the string as if it fastened some rare treasure. Hamish saw the feeling, the glad expectation and his fine blue eyes took a tinge of sadness. Gerald looked up.

"I think I'll tell you how it is, Hamish. Upon this manuscript—"

What was it that happened? Gerald broke off abruptly and looked at the door; his mouth slightly opened, his ear was cocked in the attitude of one, listening anxiously. Hamish, unused to the sounds of the place, heard nothing whatever.

"Say I'm out, Hamish, old fellow; say I'm out," whispered Gerald, disappearing noiselessly within an invisible closet; invisible from being papered like the walls and opening with a knob no bigger than a nut. Hamish sat in a trance of inward astonishment, easy as ever outwardly, a half smile upon his face.

He opened the door in answer to a knock. A respectable-looking man at once stepped inside, asking to see Mr. Yorke.

Hamish with a gesture of his hand pointed to the empty room, indicating that Mr. Yorke was not there to be seen. The applicant looked round it curiously; and at that moment Gerald's servant came up with a rush, and glanced round as keenly as the applicant.

"My master's gone out for the day, Mr. Brookes."

"How many more times am I to have that answer given me?" demanded Mr. Brookes. "It's hardly likely he'd be gone out so soon as this."

"Likely or not, he's gone," said the servant, speaking with easy indifference.

"Well, look here; there's the account, delivered once more and for the last time," said Mr. Brookes, handing in a paper. "If it's not paid within four-and-twenty hours, I shall summons him to the county-court."

"And he means it," emphatically whispered the servant in Hamish's hearing, as Mr. Brookes's descending footsteps echoed on the stairs.

Hamish pulled back the closet-door by the knob to release Gerald. He came forth like a whirlwind—if a furious passion may be called one. Hamish had not heard so much abuse lavished on one person for many a day as Gerald gave his servant. The man had been momentarily off his usual vigilant guard, and so allowed Gerald's sanctum (and all but his person) to be invaded by an enemy.

"I owe the fellow a trifle for boots," said Gerald, when he had driven his servant from the room. "He is an awful dun, and will not be put off much longer. Seven pounds ten shillings,"—dashing open the bill. "And for that paltry sum he'll county-court me!"

"Pay him," said Hamish.

"Pay him! I should like to pay him," returned Gerald, gloomily. "I'd pay him today, and have done with him, if I could, and think it the best money ever laid out. I'm awfully hard up, Hamish, and that's a fact."

Hamish began mentally to deliberate whether he was able to help him. Gerald stood on the hearthrug, very savage with the world in general.

"I'd move heaven and earth to avoid the county-court," he said. "It would be sure to get about. Everything is contrary and cross-grained just now: Carrick's not to the fore; Vincent Yorke says he has neither cross nor coin to bless himself with, let alone me. I never got but one loan from the fellow in my life, and be hanged to him!"

"Your expenses are so heavy, Gerald."

"Who the devil is to make them lighter?" fiercely demanded Gerald. "One can't live as a hermit. I beg your pardon, old fellow; I'm cross, I know, but I have so much to worry me. Things come upon one all at once. Because I had not enough ways for my ready money just now, Winny must come up and want a heap."

"What is pressing you particularly?"

"That," said Gerald, flicking his hand in the direction of the boot bill. "There's nothing else very much at the present moment." But the "present moment" with Gerald meant the present actual hour that was passing.

"About my manuscript," he resumed, his tone brightening a little as he sat down to the table to face Hamish.

Still, for an instant or two, Hamish hesitated. He drew the sheets towards him and turned them over, as if in deliberation what to say.

"You charged me to tell you the truth, Gerald."

"Of course I did," loudly answered Gerald. "The truth, the whole truth, and nothing but the truth."

"Well, Gerald, I should not but for your earnest wish, and that it is I suppose the more real kindness to do so, as it may prevent you from wasting time upon another. I am afraid it won't do, old friend."

"What won't do?" asked Gerald, with wide-open eyes that showed the wonder in them.

Delicately, gently, considerately, as he could have imparted ill news to the dearest friend he had on earth, Hamish Channing told him the story would not do, would not, at least, be a success, and pointed out why he thought so. The book was full of mistakes and faults; these for the most part he passed lightly over: speaking rather of the defects of the work as a whole.

"Go on; let's have it all," said Gerald, when there was a pause: and Hamish saw nothing of the suppressed passion, or of the irony that lay at the bottom of the following words. "You think I cannot succeed in fiction?"

"Not in a long work—"

"Why the work's a short one," interrupted Gerald.

"Very short indeed. Some writers of fiction (and as a rule they are the best, Gerald) put as much in a volume and a half as you have written for the three volumes. I don't think you could write a successful work of fiction in even one volume, Gerald—as I count success. It must have a plot; it must have consecutiveness in the working out; it must have—"

"It must have, in short, just the qualities that my work lacks," interposed Gerald with a laugh: and Hamish felt relieved that he was receiving things so easily.

"If I thought that any hints or help of mine would enable you to accomplish a work likely to be successful, I would heartily put myself at your service, Gerald. But I don't. I am sure you have mistaken your vocation in attempting a work of fiction."

"Thank you," said Gerald. "Your work has not been tried yet. That's sure to prove a success, I suppose?"

The bright glow of anticipation lighted Hamish Manning's sensitive face. It would have betrayed the all-powerful hope lying within him, apart from the involuntary smile, checked on his lips.

"I could hardly bring myself to make the report, Gerald. And should not, I think, but that I care for your interests as for those of my own brothers. You know I do, and therefore will not mistake me. I debated whether I should not get up some excuse for giving no opinion, except that you had better submit it to a publisher. Of course you can do that still."

"Let me understand you," said Gerald. "You wish to inform me that no publisher would be likely to take it." Hamish paused slightly. "I do not say that. Publishers take all kinds of works. The chief embarrassment on my mind is this, Gerald: that, if published, it could not bring you much honour or credit; or—I think—returns."

They shook hands; and Hamish, who would be late at his office, departed, leaving Gerald alone. He went along with a light, glad step, wondering whether he could afford to help Gerald out of the money difficulty of the day. Sixteen guineas were due to him for literary work; if he got it paid, he would enclose the receipt for the boot-bill to Gerald, saying nothing.

Leaving Gerald alone. Alone with his bitter anger; with an evil look on his face, and revenge at his heart.

There was only one thing could have exceeded Gerald Yorke's astonishment at the veto pronounced, and that was the utter incredulity with which he received it. He had looked upon his book as a rara avis, a black swan: just as we all look on our productions, whether they may be bad or good. The bad ones perhaps are thought most of: they are more trusted to bring back substantial reward. Of course, therefore, Gerald Yorke could but regard the judgment as a deliberately false one, spoken in jealous envy; tendered to keep him back from fame. He made the great mistake that many another has made before him, when receiving honest advice in a similar case, and many will make again. And the book gained in his opinion rather than lost.

"Curse him for his insolence! curse him for a false, self-sufficient puppy!" foamed Gerald, rapping out unorthodox words in his passion. "Ware to yourself, Mr. Hamish Channing! you shall find, sooner or later, what it is to make an enemy of me."

But Gerald received some balm ere the day was over, for Mr. Brookes's receipted bill came to him by post in a blank envelope. And he wondered who on earth had been civil enough to pay the money.

CHAPTER XVII

AT FAULT

It was easier for Mr. Bede Greatorex to say to the police-agents "Drop the investigation," than it was for them to do it. Had he been the sole person to whom they were responsible, the thing would have lain in a nutshell; but their employer was his father. And Mr. Greatorex was pushing discovery to an issue as he had never pushed anything yet. He looked up details himself; he went backwards and forwards to Scotland Yard; he was altogether troublesome.

As the days went on, and Mr. Butterby brought forth no result, only presented himself once in a way to say there was none to bring, Mr. Greatorex grew angry. Surely such a thing was never heard of!—as for a cheque to be stolen out of one of their desks at midday, carried to the bank and openly cashed, and for the police to say they could not trace the offender! Mr. Greatorex avowed that the police ought to be ashamed to confess it; that, in his opinion, they must be getting incapable of their duties.

One thing had struck Mr. Greatorex in the matter—that his son Bede seemed not to be eager for the investigation: if he did not retard it, he certainly did not push it. Perhaps the best word to express Bede's state of mind in regard to it, as it appeared to Mr. Greatorex, was indifference. Why was this? Bede ought to be as anxious as himself. Nay, more so: it was from his possession and his desk that the cheque was taken. Mr. Greatorex supposed that the laxity in regard to business affairs, which appeared latterly to have been creeping upon his son, must be extending itself even to the stealing of money. Was he more seriously ill than he allowed them to know? The fear, that it might be so, crossed the mind of Mr. Greatorex.

The solicitor sat one morning in his private room, Jonas Butterby opposite to him. The detective was there in answer to a peremptory mandate sent by Mr. Greatorex to Scotland Yard the previous day. Whether Mr. Butterby was responsible to himself alone for the progress or non-progress of the investigation; or, if not, whether he had imparted a hint at headquarters of Bede Greatorex's private communication to him, was locked up within his own breast. One thing appeared clear—that he was at liberty to do as he pleased.

"It is not the loss of the money; it is not that the sum of forty-four pounds is of so much moment to me that I must needs trace it out, and if possible regain it," Mr. Greatorex urged, his fine, fresh, honest face bent full on the detective, sternness in its every line. "It is the unpleasantness of knowing that we have a thief about us: it is the feeling of insecurity; the fear that the loss will not stop here. Every night of my life when the offices close, I seem to prepare myself for the discovery that some other one has taken place during the day."

"Not at all an unlikely thing to happen," acknowledged Mr. Butterby, who probably felt himself less free under existing circumstances than he usually was, and therefore spoke with deprecation.

"That the cheque must have been taken by one of the clerks attached to my son's room, I think there can be little doubt of. The difficulty is—"

"Mr. Bede thinks so himself," interrupted Butterby. "He charged me specially to look after them; after one of 'em in particular."

"Which was it?"

"Hurst."

"Hurst!" repeated Mr. Greatorex in surprise.

"But Mr. Bede is mistaken, sir. It was no more Hurst than it was me."

Instincts are subtle. And one came unbidden into the mind of the detective officer as he spoke—that he had made a mistake in repeating this to Mr. Greatorex. The truth was—carrying within him his private instructions, and the consciousness that they must be kept private—he found these interviews with the head of the firm slightly embarrassing.

"Why should he suspect Hurst if he—"

The door opened, and the person in question appeared at it—Bede Greatorex. Catching a glimpse of the detective's head, he was going out of it a vast deal quicker than he had entered; but his father stopped him.

"Bede! Bede! Come in. Come in and shut the door. Here's a fine thing I have just heard—that you are suspecting one person in particular of having taken the cheque. Over and over again, you have told me there was nobody in particular to be suspected."

A lightning glance from Bede Greatorex's fine dark Spanish eyes flashed out on the detective. It said as plainly as glance could speak, "How dare you presume to betray my confidence?"

That gentleman sat unmoved, and nodded a good morning with his customary equanimity.

"Mr. Greatorex—doing me the honour to call upon me to report progress—observed that he fully thought it was one of the clerks in your room we must look to, sir," spoke Butterby in a slow calm tone. "I told him your opinion was the same; and you had charged me to look well after them, especially Mr. Hurst. That was all."

Bede Greatorex bit his lip in anger. But the communication might have been worse.

"What is there against Hurst?" impatiently asked Mr. Greatorex.

"Nothing at all," said Bede quietly. "If I said to Mr. Butterby that one of my clerks might have taken the cheque, it was only because access to my room was more obtainable by them than by anybody else I can think of. And of the four, Hurst spends the most money."

"Hurst has the most money to spend," observed Mr. Greatorex.

"Of course he has. I make no doubt Hurst is as innocent as I."

This was very different from suspecting Hurst, from desiring that he should be specially looked after, and perhaps Mr. Greatorex felt the two accounts the least in the world contradictory. The keen-sighted observer sitting by, apparently sharpening the point of his broken lead-pencil, noticed that the eyes of Bede Greatorex never once went openly into the face of his father.

"If it was my case," thought the officer, "I should tell him the truth out and out. No good going about the bush this way, saying he suspects one and suspects another, when he does not suspect 'em: far better that old Greatorex should hear the whole and see for himself that it can't be gone into. He don't care to worrit the old gentleman: that's what it is."

That is just what it was. But Mr. Butterby was not right in all his premises.

"I am fully persuaded that every clerk on my side the house is as innocent as are those on yours, sir," spoke Bede Greatorex, a kind of tremor in his tone; which tremor did not escape the officer's notice, or that it was caused by anxious, painful eagerness: and that astute man knew in a moment that old Greatorex must not have his suspicions turned actively on Bede's employés. "I believe it was Butterby who first mentioned them. Upon that, I ran them over in my mind, and remembered that Hurst was the only one spending much money—he lives in fashionable lodgings as a gentleman. Was it not so, Mr. Butterby?"

The detective was professionally prepared for most accidents. Therefore when Bede Greatorex turned upon him with startling rapidity, a second flash darting forth from his dark eyes, he never moved a muscle.

"You are right, sir."

"Bede," said Mr. Greatorex, in a still tone of meaning, "if the same facility for getting access to your room attached to the clerks on my side the house, I should not say to you so positively that they were not guilty. You seem to resent the very thought that suspicion can attach to them."

"Not at all, father. Perhaps I felt vexed that Hurst's name should have been mentioned to you without grounds."

"Understand me, Mr. Butterby," spoke the elderly gentleman sharply. "I expect to have this matter better attended to than it has been. And I repeat to you that I think the clerks in my son's room should be—I do not say suspected, but sufficiently thought of. It is monstrous to know that a theft like this can have been openly committed in a professional man's house, and you officers should avow yourselves at fault. We may be losing some of our clients' deeds next."

The detective glanced at Mr. Bede Greatorex, and was answered, as he thought, by the faintest signs in return. It was not the first time he had been concerned in cases where sons wished things kept from knowledge of fathers.

"We don't give it up, sir. Allow us more time, and perhaps we may satisfy you better."

"I shall expect you to do so," returned Mr. Greatorex with sufficient emphasis. And the officer rose to quit his presence. "Go round by the other door to my room and wait."

Surely these words were breathed into Mr. Butterby's ear! Faint though the whisper was he could not have fancied it. Bede Greatorex was crossing his path at the moment, as if he wished to look from the window.

Fancy or not, the officer acted upon it. Going round by the street to the professional entrance, and so on up the passage to the private room. When Bede Greatorex returned to it, he saw him seated against the wall, underneath the map of London.

"You did wrong to mention Mr. Hurst to my father," Bede began with imperative quickness, as he slipped the bolt of the middle door.

"That's as it may be," was the rejoinder, cool as usual. "If there's not some outlet of suspicion given to your father, it will be just this, Mr. Bede Greatorex—that he'll make one for himself. Leastways, that's my opinion."

"Be it so. I do not want it to take the direction of my clerks."

"He lays the blame on us: says we are lax, or else incapable; and it is only natural he should think so. Anyway there's no harm done about Mr. Hurst: you made it right with him there. Do you suspect Hurst still, sir?"

"Yes. At least more than I do any one of the others."

Mr. Butterby put his hands on his knees and bent a little forward. "If you wish me to do you any service in this, sir, you must not keep me quite so much in the dark. What I want to get at, Mr. Bede Greatorex, is the true reason of your pitching upon Hurst yourself."

"I cannot give it to you," said Bede promptly. "What I told you at our first interview, I repeat now—that the suspicion against him is but a faint one. Still it is sufficient to raise a doubt; and I have no reason to doubt the other three. Jenner is open and honest as the day; Brown valuable and trustworthy; and Mr. Yorke must of course be exempt."

"Oh, of course he must," dryly acquiesced the detective with a cough. He knew he was sure of Roland in this case, but he thought Bede Greatorex might not have spoken so confidently had he been cognizant of a certain matter connected with the past.

"I would not much mind answering for Jenner myself," remarked Mr. Butterby. "Brown seems all right, too."

"Brown's honesty has been sufficiently proved. Very large sums have passed through his hands habitually, and he has never wronged us by a shilling. Had he wished to help himself, he would have done it before now: he has had the opportunity."

"Then that leaves us back at Hurst again. Where is your objection, sir, to the doubt of him being mentioned to your father?"

A kind of startled look crossed Bede's face: a look of fear: and he spoke hastily.

"Have you forgotten what I said? That the fact of Mr. Hurst's knowing he was suspected (assuming he is guilty) would be attended with danger. Awful danger, too. If it were possible to disclose all to my father, he would forfeit a great deal that he holds dear in life, rather than incur it."

"Well it seems to me that I can be of little use in this matter," said Butterby, turning somewhat crusty. "I have had dangerous secrets confided to me in my lifetime, sir; and the parties they were told of are none the wiser or the worse for it yet."

"And I wish I could confide this to you," said Bede, steadily and candidly. "I'd be glad enough to get it out of my keeping, for I don't know what to do with it. If no one but myself were concerned; if I could disclose it to you without the risk of injuring others you should hear it this next minute. For their sakes, Mr. Butterby, my lips are tied. I dare not speak."

"Does he mean his wife, or doesn't he?" thought Butterby. And the question was not solvable. "I'll look after Hurst a bit," he said aloud. "Truth to tell, I considered him the safest of them all, in spite of your opinion, Mr. Bede Greatorex, and have let him be. He shall get a little of my private attention now. And so shall one of the others," the detective mentally added.

"Unsuspected by Hurst himself," enjoined Bede, a shade of anxiety in his voice.

Could Mr. Butterby have been suspected of so far forgetting professional dignity as to indulge in winks, it might have seemed that he answered by one, as he rose from his chair.

"I'll just take a look in upon them now," he remarked. "And let me advise you, sir, to get your father in a more reasonable frame of mind, if possible. If he calls in fresh aid, as he threatens, there might be the dickens to pay."

Bede Greatorex crossed the room hastily, as though he meant to guard the middle door, and spoke in a low tone.

"I do not care that they should know you have been with me. Not for the world would I let it come to their knowledge that I doubt either of them."

"Now do you suppose that I am a young gosling?" demanded Butterby. "You have done me the honour to confide this private business to my hands, Mr. Bede Greatorex, and you may safely leave it in 'em. After being at the work so many years, there's not much left for me to be taught."

He departed by the passage, treading lightly, and halted when he came to the clerks' door. He was in deep thought. This matter which, as he phrased it, Mr. Bede Greatorex had done him the honour to put in his hands, was no such great matter after all; a mere trifle in professional quarters: but few things had so much puzzled the detective. Not in his way to discovery: that, as it seemed to him, would be very easy, could he pursue it openly. Bede Greatorex puzzled him; his ambiguous words puzzled him; the thing itself puzzled him. In most cases Mr. Butterby could at least see where he was; in this he stood in a sea-encompassed fog, not understanding where he was going, or what he was in search of.

Giving the swing-door a dash backwards, as though he had just entered, he went into the room. Mr. Brown was at his desk, Roland Yorke at his; but the other two were absent. So if the visit had been intended as a special one to Josiah Hurst, it was a decided failure.

When was the great Butterby at fault? He had just looked in upon them "in passing," he said, to give the good-morrow, and enquire how they relished the present state of the thermometer, which he should pronounce melting. How did Mr. Yorke like it?

Mr. Yorke, under the circumstances of not knowing whether he stood on his head or his heels, had not thought about the thermometer. Since the receipt of a letter that morning, containing the news that one, whom he cared for more than a brother, might probably be coming to London shortly on a visit, Roland had been three parts mad with joy. He was even genial to the intruder, his bête noire.

"Is it you, Butterby? How are you getting on, Butterby? Take a stool if you like, Butterby."

"Can't stop," said Butterby. "Just meant to give a nod round and go out again. Not come in on business today. You look spruce, Mr. Yorke."

"I've got on my Sunday suit," answered Roland—who in point of fact was uncommonly well got-up, and had a rosebud in his button-hole. "Carrick's tailor has not a bad cut. You have heard of red-letter days, old Butterby: this is one for me. One should not put on one's every-day coat on such occasions: they don't come too often."

"Got a fortune bequeathed?" enquired Mr. Butterby.

"It's better than that," said enthusiastic Roland, who in these moments, when his heart and affections were touched, could but be more impulsively genuine than ever. "Somebody's coming to London; somebody that you know, Butterby."

"Mr. Galloway, perhaps."

"No; you are wrong this time," returned Roland, not in the least taken aback: though perhaps the detective, to judge by his significant tone, meant that he should be. "You'd not see me dressed up for him. There are two men in Helstonleigh I'd put on shirtsleeves to welcome rather than a good coat: the one is old Galloway, the other William Yorke. Guess again."

Instead of doing anything of the sort, by which perhaps his professional reserve might have been compromised, Mr. Butterby turned his attention on the manager. Pursuing his work steadily, he had taken no heed of Mr. Butterby, beyond a civil salute at first.

"You've not heard more of this mysterious loss, I suppose?"

"Nothing more, sir," was Mr. Brown's answer, looking up full at the speaker, perhaps to show that he did not shrink from intercourse with a detective officer. "It seems strange, though, that we should not."

"Thieves are clever when they are professional ones; and I've got to think it was no less a man did the job for Mr. Greatorex," said Butterby, in quite a fatherly tone of confidence. "There has been a regular band of 'em at work lately in London; and in spite of opinions when I was here last, I say they might have gone in through the passage straight and bold, and done the job easy, and you unsuspicious young men, shut up in this here first room, never have heard a sound of what was going on."

"I think that is how it must have been failing the other thought—that Mr. Bede Greatorex took the cheque abroad and dropped it," said the manager with quiet decision.

"Of course. And unless I'm mistaken, Mr. Bede thinks the same. I should like to have three minutes' chat with you some evening, Mr. Brown, all by our two selves. You are naturally anxious for discovery, so am I: there's no knowing but what something or other may come out between us."

Perhaps to any eye save the watchful one of a police-officer, the slight hesitation before replying might have passed unnoticed. Mr. Brown had no particular wish to be questioned; it was no affair of his, and he thought the detective and Mr. Bede Greatorex quite enough to manage the matter without him. But when his answer came, it was spoken readily.

"Whenever you please. I am generally at home by eight o'clock."

He gave his new address—Mrs. Jones's. At which the crafty detective expressed surprise, inwardly knowing the very day and hour when Mr. Brown had moved in.

"There! Do you live there? The Joneses and I used to be old acquaintances; knew 'em well when they were at Helstonleigh. Knew Dicky must be making a mess of it long before the smash came. You'll see me then, Mr. Brown, one of these first evenings."

"Don't be in a hurry, Butterby," spoke Roland, who had been amusing himself by trying how far he could tilt his stool backwards without capsizing, while he listened. "It's not old Galloway, it's Arthur Channing."

"Is there anything so remarkable in Arthur Channing's coming to London? questioned Butterby.

"To me there is. I tell you it is a red-letter day in my life, and I have not had many such since I sailed from Port Natal. If I were not in this confounded old office, with one master in the next room and another there"—flinging a ball of paper at the manager—"I should sing and dance and leap my joy off. Three copies have I begun to take of a musty old will, and spoilt 'em all. Brown says I'm out of my senses; ask him."

"You never were famous for not spoiling copies—or for particular industry, either, you know, Mr. Yorke."

The rejoinder rather nettled Roland. "I'd rather be famous for nothing than for what you are famed for in Helstonleigh, Butterby—taking up the wrong man. It was not your fault that Arthur Channing didn't get transported."

"Nor yours," quietly retorted Mr. Butterby.

"There! Go on. Bring it all out. If you've come to do it, do it, Butterby. I told you to, the other night. And when Arthur Channing is in London, you put up a prayer every morning not to meet him at Charing Cross. The sight of him couldn't be pleasant to your mind, and passers-by might see your brow redden: which for a bold, fear-nothing police-detect—"

"Is Mr. Bede Greatorex in?"

The interrupting questioner was the Reverend Henry William Ollivera. As he entered, the first man his eyes fell on was Butterby. It was a mutual recognition: and they had not met since that evening in Butterby's rooms on the occasion of the clergyman's visit to Helstonleigh.

Before a minute had well elapsed, as it seemed to the two spectators, they were deep in that calamity of the past, recalling some of its details, lamenting the non-success that had attended the endeavour to trace it out. It did not much interest Roland, and his mind also was filled to the brim with matter more agreeable. Apparently it did not interest Brown the manager, for he kept his head bent on his work. In the midst of it Bede Greatorex came in.

"I tell you, Mr. Officer, my faith has never wavered, or my opinion changed," the clergyman was saying with emotion, scarcely interrupting himself to nod a salutation to Bede. "My brother did not commit suicide. He was barbarously murdered; as every instinct warned me at the time, and warns me still. The waiting seems long; the time rolls by, day after day, year after year: weariness has to be subdued, patience cherished; but, that the hour of elucidation will come, is as sure as that you and I stand here, facing each other."

"Mr. Greatorex told me that the Reverend Ollivera stood to his opinion as strongly as he ever did," was the answering remark of the officer; and it might be that there was a shade of compassion in his tone— compassion for the mistaken folly of the man before him.

"It has occurred to me at times, that if I were a member of the detective police, endowed with all the acuteness for the discovery of crime that their occupation and (we may suppose) natural aptitude for it must give, I should have brought the matter to light long ago. Do not think I reflect on your individual skill or care, sir; I speak generally."

"Ah!" said Mr. Butterby with complacent jocularity, "we all are apt to picture to ourselves how much we'd do in other folks's skins."

"It is strange that you have never been able to find traces of the man whose name was afterwards mixed up in the affair, Godfrey Pitman."

"There you are right, sir," readily avowed the officer. "I should uncommonly like to come across that Godfrey Pitman on my own score: setting aside anything he might have had to do with the late Mr. Ollivera."

The clergyman quickly took up the words. "Do you think he had anything to do with his death?"

"I don't go as far as that. It might have been. Anyway, as circumstances stand at present, he seems the most likely to have had, of all those who were known to have been in the house that evening."

Happening to raise his eyes, Mr. Brown caught those of Mr. Bede Greatorex. They were fixed on the speaker with a kind of eager, earnest light. To many a man it might have told the tale—that he, Bede Greatorex, had also doubts of Pitman. But then, Bede Greatorex had expressed his belief in the suicide: expressed it still. One thing was certain, had Bede chosen to confess it—that Godfrey Pitman was in his mind far oftener than the world knew.

"How is it that you have never found him?" continued Mr. Ollivera, to Butterby.

"I don't know. We are not usually at fault for a tithe of the time. But the man, you see, was under false colours; his face and his name were alike changed."

"You think so?"

"Think so!" repeated Mr. Butterby with a second dose of compassion for the parson's intellect. "That mass of hair on his face was hardly likely to be real. As to the name, Pitman, it was about as much his as it was mine. However, we have not found him, and there's no more to be made of it than that. Mr. Bede

Greatorex asked me about the man the other day, whether I didn't think he might have gone at once out of the country. It happens to be what I've thought all along."

"I do not see what he could have against my brother, that he should injure him," spoke the clergyman, gazing on vacancy, the dreamy look, so often seen in them, taking possession of his eyes. "So far as can be known, they were strangers."

"Now, sir, don't you run your head again a stone wall. Nobody says he did injure him; only that it's within the range of possibility he could have done it. As to being strangers, he might have turned out to be one of Counsellor Ollivera's dearest friends, once his disguises were took off."

Under the reproof, Mr. Ollivera drew in, and there was a short pause of silence. He broke it almost immediately, to ask about the letter so often mentioned.

"Have you taken care of the paper?"

"I have," said Mr. Butterby, rather emphatically. "And I mean to do it, being permitted. This house wrote for it to be sent up, but I gave Mr. Greatorex my reasons for wishing to keep it, and he charged me not to let it go. If ever the time comes that that document may be of use, Reverend Sir, it will be forthcoming."

As the officer went out, for there was nothing more to remain for, Mr. Ollivera began speaking to Bede in a low tone. This conversation lasted but a minute or two, and was over, Bede retiring to the other room.

"Arthur Channing is coming to London, Mr. Ollivera."

That the interruption came from nobody but Roland, need not be affirmed. He was the only one in the office who presumed to interlard its business with personal matters. The clergyman, who was going out, turned his head.

"You will have the opportunity of making his better acquaintance, Mr. Ollivera. He is the noblest and grandest man the world ever saw. I don't mean in looks—though he might compete for a prize on that score—but for goodness and greatness. Hamish is at the top of the tree, but Arthur caps him."

Arthur Channing and his qualities did not bear interest for Mr. Ollivera just then; he had no time to attend to them. Saying a pleasant word in answer, he departed. Almost close upon that, Sir Richard Yorke came in, and went into the private room.

"Perhaps something has turned up about the cheque, and he's come to tell it," cried idle Roland. "I say, Mr. Brown, did you ever hear how they all keep up the ball about that Godfrey Pitman? Mrs. J. was describing him to me the other night. She and Miss Alletha came to an issue about his personal charms: the one saying his eyes were blue, the other brown. Remembering the fable of the chameleon, I decided they must have been green. I'd not like to joke about him, though"—dropping his light tone—"if he really had a hand in John Ollivera's death. What do you think?"

"What I think is this, Mr. Yorke. As the person in question has nothing to do with my work or yours, I am content to let him alone. I should be exceedingly obliged to you to get that copy done for me."

"I'll get it done," said ready Roland. "There are such interruptions in this office, you see."

He was working away at a steaming pace, when Sir Richard Yorke came forth again, talking with Bede Greatorex. Roland slipped off his stool, and brought his tall self in his uncle's path.

"How are you, Sir Richard?"

Sir Richard's little eyes went blinking out, and he condescended to recognize Roland.

"Oh, ah, to be sure. You are one of the clerks here! Hope you keep out of debt, young man."

"I try to," said Roland. "I get a pound a week, and live upon it. It is not much for all things. One has to enjoy champagne and iced turtle through the shop-windows."

"Ah," said Sir Richard slowly, rubbing his hands together as if he were washing them of undesirable connections, "this comes of being a rover. You should do as Gerald does: work to keep up a position. I read an able article in the Snarler last night, which was pointed out to me as Gerald Yorke's. He works to some purpose, he does."

"If Gerald works he spends," was on the tip of his tongue. But he kept it in: it was rare indeed that his good-nature failed him. "How is Vincent?" he asked.

Vincent was very well, Sir Richard vouchsafed to reply, and went out, rubbing his hands still.

So, with one interlude or another, Roland's morning was got through. When released, he went flying in search of Annabel Channing, to impart to her the great news contained in her brother's letter.

She was not in the schoolroom. She was not in the dining-room. She was not anywhere that Roland could see. He turned to descend the stairs again more slowly than he had gone up, when Jane Greatorex came running from the landing above.

"Jane! Jane! I told you you were not to go down."

The voice, calling after the child, would have been like Annabel's but for a choking sound in it. He looked up and saw her: saw her face inflamed with tears, heard the sobs of grief. It took Roland more completely aback than any sight he had witnessed at Port Natal. The face disappeared swiftly, and Miss Jane jumped into his arms in triumph.

"Jenny, what is it?" he asked in a kind of dumb whisper, as if motion were suddenly struck out of him. "What is amiss with Miss Channing?"

"It's through Aunt Bede. She puts herself into passions. I thought she'd have hit her this morning. She told her she was not worth her salt."

Roland's face grew white with indignation.

"Your Aunt Bede did!"

"Oh, it's nothing new," said the child carelessly. "Aunt Bede goes on at her nearly as much every day."

CHAPTER XVIII

MR BROWN AT HOME

That the managing clerk of Mr. Bede Greatorex was anything but a steady man, his worst enemy could not have said. Mr. Brown's conduct was irreproachable, his industry indefatigable. At the office to the very minute of opening, quitting it always last at night, occupying all his spare time at home in writing, except that necessary to be consumed in sleep; and of habits so moderate, that even Roland Yorke, with all his experiences of Port Natal deprivations, would have marvelled at them, it might have been surmised that Mr. Brown had set in to acquire a modest fortune. The writing he did at home was paid for. It was so thoroughly to be depended on for correctness and swift completion, that Greatorex and Greatorex were glad to give it to him, and kept it a tacit secret from the other clerks. For Mr. Brown did not care that it should be known in the office, lest he should lose his standing. To carry copying home for remuneration, might have been deemed infra dig. for the manager.

For his breakfast he took a hard-boiled egg, or a sausage, or a herring, as might be; tea, and bread. At dinner-time, the middle of the day, his food did not differ from the above, a glass of beer being substituted for the tea. He invariably called it his luncheon, saying he dined out later; and hurried over it to get to his writing. In the evening he had tea again, butter, bread, and one or other of the afore-mentioned luxuries, with radishes or some light garden production of that kind which might happen to be in season. Shrewd Mrs. Jones, after a few days' experience of her lodger's habits, came to the private conclusion, that the daily dinner out had place only in fable. On Sundays he dined at home, openly, upon potatoes and meat—generally a piece of steak. The maid found out that he blacked his boots over-night, keeping his brushes and blacking-bottle locked up; put on but one clean shirt a week, with false wristbands and fronts the rest of the time. Given to arrive at rapid decisions, Mrs. Jones set all this down, not to parsimony, but to needful economy, for which she concluded there must be some good cause; and honoured his self-denial.

Police-officer Butterby, having scraped acquaintance (of course by chance) with the landlord where Mr. Brown had previously lived, gathered sundry details over a pipe, into his capacious ears. The house, situated in an obscure quarter, was let out in rooms—chambers it might be said, of a poor and humble grade, with a wide, dark, common staircase of stone. One lodger did not interfere with another; and all the landlord and his wife had to do was to take the weekly money. Mr. Brown had been with them between three and four years, the landlord said; was most steady and respectable. Gentleman Brown they always called him. They did his room, though most of the others did their own. Never went to theatres, or smoking-places; never, in short, spent a sixpence in waste, saved up what he could for his mother and sick sister in the country, who were dependent on him. Had not the least idea why he left; might have knocked him (the landlord) down with a feather when Gentleman Brown tapped at his door one evening late, saying business was calling him away on the morrow or next day, and put down a full week's rent in lieu of notice; was the best and most regular man that ever lodged in a decent house; should be right down glad to have him back again.

A good character, certainly; as Mr. Butterby could but mentally acknowledge; steady, self-denying, working always to support a mother and sick sister! He had no cause to dispute it; having come on a fishing expedition rather than a suspicious one.

Mr. Brown sat working tonight in his room at Mrs. Jones's, the evening of the day mentioned in the last chapter: a shaded lamp was at his elbow; his spectacles, which he always took off in writing, lay on the table beside him. The room was of fair size for its situation; a folding screen standing cornerwise concealed the small bed. A high bureau stood opposite the fireplace, near it a dwarf-cupboard of mahogany with a flat top, which served for a side-table. Mr. Brown had drawn the larger table to the window, that he might catch the last light of the summer's evening. He sat sideways; the right hand cuff of his worn coat turned up. Out of doors he appeared as a gentleman; indoors he was economically careful in dress, as in other things.

A light tap at the door; followed by the entrance of Miss Rye. He rose at once, and turned down the coat-cuff. She came to bring a letter that the postman had just left. Never, unless when forced to it by the very rare absence of the maid, did Miss Rye make her appearance in his room. The servant was out this evening; and Mrs. Jones had handed her the letter with a decisive command that might not be disregarded. "Take it in, Alletha."

She put the letter on the table, and was turning out without a word. Mr. Brown went to the door, and held it close while he spoke, that the sound of voices might not be heard outside.

"What is the reason that you shun me, Miss Rye? Is it well? Is it kind?"

She suddenly lifted her hand to her bosom, as if a spasm took her, and the little colour that was in her face faded out of it.

"It is well. As to kind—you know all that is over."

"I do not know it. I neither admit it, nor its necessity. Civility at least might remain. What has been my motive, do you suppose, in coming here, but to live under the same roof that shelters you? Not to renew the past, as it once existed between us; I do not ask or wish it; but to see you now and then, to exchange an unemotional, calm word with you once in a way."

"I cannot stay. Please to let me pass, sir!"

"The old place, where I lodged so long, suited me, for it was private; and I need privacy, as you know," he continued, paying no attention to her request. "It was also reasonable enough to satisfy even me. Here I pay nearly double; here I am more liable to be seen by those who might do me harm. But I have braved it all for you. Perhaps the former friendship—I do not wish to offend even by a name, you see, Miss Rye—was a terrible mistake for you, but I at least have been true to it."

"The best and kindest thing you can do for me, sir, is to go back to your late lodgings."

"I shall stay in these. You told me, in the only interview I have held with you since I came here, that I was a man of crime. I admit it. But criminals have affections as well as other people. You are cruel to me, Alletha Rye."

"It is you who are cruel," she returned, losing in emotion the matter-of-fact reserve, as between waitress and lodger, she had been studying to maintain. "You must know the pain your presence brings me. Mrs. Jones has invited you to dine with her on Sunday next, I hear; let me implore of you not to come in."

"Off a piece of boiled beef," he rejoined in a plain, curt tone, as if her manner and words were hardening him. "The offer is too good a one to be refused."

"Then I shall absent myself from table."

"Don't drive me quite wild, Alletha Rye. You have me in your power: the only one in London who has—so far as I hope and believe. I'd almost as soon you went and gave me in charge."

"Who is cruel now?" she breathed. "You know that you can trust me; you know that I would rather forfeit my own life than put yours in jeopardy: but I take shame to myself in saying it. It is just this," she added, struggling with her agitation, "you are safe with me, but you are not welcome."

"I told you somewhat of my secrets in our last interview: I would have told you more, but you would not listen—why I am living as I do, trying to atone for the miserable sins of the past—"

"Atone!"

"Yes, it is well to catch me up. One of them, at least, never can be atoned for. It lies heavier on my mind than it does on yours. If—"

The sharp voice of Mrs. Jones, from above stairs, demanding what was the matter with Alletha's ears, that they did not hear the door-bell, put a stop to the interview. A hectic spot shone on her cheeks as she hastened to answer it.

The red glow had given place to a ghastly whiteness when she came in again. Mr. Brown had already settled to his writing and turned back his cuff. She closed the door of her own accord, and went up to him; he stood gazing in surprise at her face. Its every lineament expressed terror. The lips were drawn and cold; the eyes wild. However bad might have been the contamination of his touch, he could not help taking her trembling hands. She suffered it, entwining her lingering fingers within his.

"What has happened?" he asked in a whisper.

"That man has come; Butterby, the detective officer from Helstonleigh. He says he must see Mr. Brown—you. Heaven have mercy on us! Has the blow fallen at last?"

"There's nothing to fear. I expected a call from him. He only knows me as Mr. Brown, manager to Greatorex and Greatorex. Let him come in."

"I have shut him up in Mrs. Jones's parlour."

"You must go and send him to me. I am but your lodger to him, you know. Get a little colour into your face first."

A minute or two and Mr. Butterby was introduced, amicably telling Miss Rye, that, to judge by appearances, London did not appear to agree with her. Mr. Brown, composedly writing, put down his pen in the middle of a word, and rose to receive him.

It was a chatty interview. The great man was on his agreeable manners, and talked of many things. He made some fatherly enquiries after the welfare of Mr. Hurst; observing that some of them country blades liked their fling when in London, but he fancied young Hurst was tolerably steady. Mr. Brown quietly said he had no reason to suppose him otherwise.

"You have been from thirteen to fourteen years with the Greatorexes, I think," remarked the detective.

Mr. Brown laughed. "From three to four."

"Oh, I made a mistake. And before you came to them?"

"With a solicitor, now deceased. Mr. Greatorex can tell you anything of him you wish to know. He had me direct from him."

"Me wish to know? Not a bit. Who on earth is it walking about overhead? His boots have been on the go ever since I came in."

"It must be Mr. Ollivera. He does walk in his rooms sometimes."

"I should say his mind was restless. Thinking always of his brother, they say. It was a curious case, that, take it for all in all. Ever heard the particulars, Mr. Brown?"

"Yes, Mr. Greatorex once related them to me. The young men in the office get speaking of it."

"Ah, they had all something to do with Counsellor Myers, so to say. Jenner was the clerk in chambers. Hurst's father was the surgeon called in at the death; Yorke was in Port Natal at the time, but his folks knew him. Talkative young fellows, all the lot; like gossip, I'll be bound, better than work. I'll answer that one of 'em does—Mr. Roland Yorke."

A smile crossed the manager's face at thought of Roland's work. "When I hear them begin to speak of the late Mr. Ollivera's death, I stop it at once," he remarked. "Jenner is very much given to it, never considering whose office he is in. The name of a man who has committed self-destruction, cannot be pleasant to his relations."

"As to self-destruction," spoke Mr. Butterby, with a nod, "I don't say it was that in Ollivera's case. I don't say it was not. There's only two people have held out against it; and they've been obstinate enough in the cause for two thousand. Parson Ollivera, and the young woman in this house, Alletha Rye."

"On the other hand," observed the clerk, "some are as positive that he did commit it. Mrs. Jones for one, Mr. Bede Greatorex for another. They possess the same knowledge of the details that the other two do, and are certainly as able of conclusion."

Jonas Butterby opened his mouth, as if to let in a whiff of air to his teeth, for he closed it again without speaking. In the heat of argument his usual cautious reticence had for once nearly failed him, and he all but betrayed his private opinion—that Bede Greatorex had grown to suspect Godfrey Pitman.

"Who told you that Bede Greatorex holds to that view, Mr. Brown?"

"It is well known he does. I have heard him say so myself."

"He did, and no mistake," nodded the shrewd detective, who, upon reflection, saw no reason why he should not speak out. "He made as sure that it was suicide, at the time, as you are that that's a inkpot afore you. But if he has not drawed round a bit to the contrary opinion, my name's not Jonas Butterby. Bede Greatorex, in his innard breast, has picked up doubts of the missing man, that worthy Pitman."

Mr. Brown got up to do something to the window-blind, and the peculiar look that crossed his face—not a smile, not a spasm of pain, not a sharp contraction of fear, but something of all three—was thereby hidden from his visitor. He was calm enough when he came back again.

"Did Mr. Bede Greatorex tell you so?"

"Not he. He let a word drop or two, and I could see at once the man was on his mind. But that's not our business, Mr. Brown, neither must it be made so, you understand. What I want to talk about, is the cheque affair. Let's go over the particulars quietly together."

Not so very quietly to begin with. A swinging-open of the street door as if the house itself were being pushed back; a stamping of feet in the passage; a shouting out to everybody—Mrs. J., Miss Rye, the servant Betsey—to bring him hot water, announced the arrival at home of Mr. Roland Yorke.

CHAPTER XIX

A FOUNTAIN SHIVERED

The day is not yet over. It had been a busy one at the house of Greatorex and Greatorex. What with business, what with inward vexation, of one or two kinds, Mr. Greatorex felt cross and weary as the evening drew on.

There had been some unnecessary delay in the prosecution of a cause being tried at Westminster, for which Bede was in fault. A large bill for fripperies had been presented to the office that day, and by mistake to Mr. Greatorex instead of to Mrs. Bede's husband. The capricious treatment being dealt out to Miss Channing had been spoken of by Jane to her grandpapa; and preparations for another enormous reception for that night were in active progress. All these matters, as well as others, were trying the usually placid temper of Mr. Greatorex.

He did not appear at the dinner-table that evening, but had a chop taken to his private sitting-room. Calling for his son Bede, he found he was not forthcoming. Bede, Mr. Greatorex was told, had gone to London Bridge to meet a steamer from France, by which his wife's sister was expected. Jane Greatorex ran in to her grandpapa, and asked, spoilt child that she was, if he would not invite her and Miss

Channing to drink tea with him: Mrs. Bede not having bidden them to the soirée. Yes, Mr. Greatorex said; they should spend the evening in his room. Closed in there quietly and snugly, they heard only as from a distance the turmoil of the large gathering above, and Mr. Greatorex partially forgot his cares.

Mrs. Bede Greatorex's rooms were lighted up, shutting out the remains of daylight, when Roland Yorke entered them. For it was to get himself up for this soirée that Roland had gone home in a commotion, calling for half the people in the house to wait on him. The company was large, elbowing each other as usual, and fighting for space on the staircase and landing with the beauteous plants that lined the walls. Whatever might be Mrs. Bede's short-comings in some of the duties of life, she never failed in one—that of gathering a vast crowd at her bidding. This evening was to be great in music; and some of the first singers and performers of the day had been secured to delight the company; at what cost, was known only to Bede's pocket.

Roland's chief motive in coming to it—for he did not always attend when invited—was to get an interview with Miss Channing. The vision of her tearful face, seen in the morning, the revelation contained in the careless words of Jane Greatorex had been making a hot place in his breast ever since. Roland wanted to know what it meant, and why she put up with it. His eyes went roaming into every corner in search of Annabel; but he could not see her.

"Ill-conditioned old she-stork!" ejaculated Roland, apostrophising the unconscious Mrs. Bede Greatorex. "She has gone and kept her out of the way tonight."

In consequence of this failure in his expectations, Roland had leisure to concentrate his attention on the general company; and he did it in a slightly ungracious mood; his blood was boiling up with the awful injustice (imaginary rather than real) dealt out to the governess.

"And all because that nasty conceited little pig, Jane Greatorex, must get an education."

"What's that, Roland?"

Roland, in his indignation, had spoken so as to be overheard. He turned to see the bright face of Hamish Channing, who had entered the room with his wife on his arm.

"You here, Hamish! Well, I never!"

"I have come out of my shell for once," said Hamish. "One cannot be a hermit always, when one has an exacting wife. Mine threatened me with unheard-of penalties if I didn't bring her tonight."

"Hamish!" exclaimed Mrs. Channing. "He does nothing but talk against me, Roland. It is good for him to come out sometimes.

"I say, I can't see Annabel," cried Roland, in a most resentful tone, as he, still hoping against hope, cast his eyes in search of her over people's heads. "It's a thundering shame she is a prisoner upstairs tonight, I suppose, taking care of Jane Greatorex."

"But that's no reason why you should call the little lady names," laughed Hamish.

"I called her a little pig," avowed Roland. "I should like to call somebody else a great pig; to her face too; only she might turn me out for my bad manners. If there is one thing I hold in contempt more than another, Hamish, it is a Tyrant."

"Does that apply to Miss Annabel Channing?"

"Bad manners to you then, Hamish, for speaking such a word!" burst forth Roland. "Annabel a tyrant! You'll tell me I'm a Mormon next! She's the sweetest-tempered girl in the world; she's meek and gentle and friendless here, and so that woman puts upon her. You used to snub her at home when she was a child; they snub her here: but there's not one of the lot of you fit to tie her shoe. There."

Roland backed against the wall in dudgeon, and stood there, pulling at his whiskers. Hamish enjoyed these moods of Roland's beyond everything; they were so genuine.

"And if I were getting on as my father's son ought to be, with a decent home, and a few hundreds to keep it up, it's not long she should be left to the mercy of any of you, I can tell you that, Mr. Channing."

Hamish Channing's laugh was interrupted by Mrs. Bede Greatorex—"that woman" as Roland had just disrespectfully called her. Mr. and Mrs. Channing had been slowly threading their way to her, a difficult matter from the impeding crowd. She welcomed them with both hands. Hamish, a favourite of hers, was the courtly, sunny Hamish as of yore; making the chief attraction of whatever society he might happen to be in.

"I am very glad to see you; but I wonder you like to show your face to me," said Mrs. Bede.

"What is my offence?" enquired Hamish.

"As if you need ask! I don't think you've been to one of my gatherings for three months. If it were not for your wife. I'd leave off sending you cards, sir."

"It was my wife's doings to come this evening; she dragged me out," answered saucy Hamish. "You've no idea how she pats upon a fellow, Mrs. Greatorex."

Ellen laughed. "The real truth is, Mrs. Greatorex, that he was a little less pressed for work than usual, and came of his own accord."

"That horrid work!" spoke Mrs. Bede. "You are a slave to it."

"Wait until my fortune's made," said Hamish.

"That will be when your book's out!"

"Oh yes, of course."

The answer was given banteringly. But a slight hectic came into his face, his voice unconsciously took a deeper tone. Heaven alone knew what that anticipated book already was to his spirit.

"When will it be finished?"

"It is finished."

"How glad you must be!" concluded Mrs. Bede.

The evening went on. Roland kept his place against the wall, looking as if everybody were his natural enemy. On the whole, Roland did not like soirées; there was no room for his elbows; and the company never seemed to be in their natural manners; rather on artificial stilts. Having come out to this one for the specific purpose of meeting Annabel, Roland could but regard the disappointment in the light of a personal wrong, and resent it accordingly.

In the midst of a grand, tremendous cavatina, loud enough to split the ceiling, while the room was preparing itself to applaud, and Roland was thinking it might have been more agreeable to ears if given out of doors, say on the quai at Durban, he happened to raise his head, and saw Gerald opposite. Their eyes met. Roland nodded, but Gerald gave no response. Gerald happened to be standing next to Hamish Channing.

And the two were attracting some attention, for they were known by many present to be rising stars in the literary world. Perhaps Hamish was also gaining notice by his personal attributes; it was not often so entirely good-looking a man was seen in the polite society of soirées and drums. Side by side they stood, the aspiring candidates for literary honours, soon to be enrolled amidst the men who have written Books. Which of them—that is, which work—would be the most successful? That remained to be learnt. Hamish Channing had the advantage (and a very great one) in looks; anybody might see that: Hamish had the advantage in scholarship; and he had the advantage, though perhaps the world could not see it yet, of genius. Hamish Channing's education had been also sound and comprehensive: he was a College man. Gerald was not. Mr. Channing the elder had been straitened for means, as the public has heard of, but he had contrived to send his eldest son to Cambridge, A wonderful outward difference was there in the two men, as they stood side by side: would there be as much contrast in their books?

Gerald was looking fierce. The sight of Hamish Channing brought to his mind the adverse opinion pronounced on his manuscript. His resentment had grown more bitter; his determination, to be revenged, into a firm and fixed resolve, He could not completely cut Hamish, as it was his pleasure to cut his brother Roland, but he was haughty and distant. Hamish, of genial temper himself, and his attention distracted by the large assembly, observed it not.

The crashing came to an end, the applause also, and in the general move that succeeded, Roland got away. Seeing a vacant sofa in a comparatively deserted room, he took possession of one end of it. A fashionable young woman seated herself at the other end and took a survey of him.

"I am sure you are one of the Yorkes of Helstonleigh! Is it Roland?"

Roland turned to the speaker: and saw a general resemblance (in the chignon and shoulder-blades) to Mrs. Bede Greatorex.

"Yes, I am Roland," he answered, staring.

"Don't you remember me?—Clare Joliffe?"

"Good gracious!" cried Roland, seizing her hand and shaking it nearly off. Clare Joliffe had never been a particular favourite of his; but, regarded in the light of a home face, she was agreeably welcome. "Whatever brings you here, Miss Joliffe?"

"I am come over on a visit," said the young lady. "Louisa has invited me for the first time since her marriage. I only got here at seven o'clock tonight; we had a rough passage and the boat was late."

"Over from where? What boat?"

"Boulogne."

"Have you been staying there?"

"We are living there. We have left Helstonleigh—oh, ever so long ago. Mamma got tired of it, and so did I and Mary."

Roland's ill-humour disappeared with the old reminiscences, for they plunged into histories past and present. Home days and home people, mixed with slight anecdotes of Port Natal life. Mrs. Joliffe had quitted Helstonleigh very shortly after that occurrence that had so startled the town—the death, of John Ollivera. It was perhaps natural, perhaps only a curious accident, that the sad fact should be reverted to between them now as they talked: we all know how one subject leads to another. Clare Joliffe grew confidential about that and other things. One bond she and Roland seemed to have between them this night—a grievance against Mrs. Bede Greatorex. Roland's consisted in that lady's unkind treatment (real or fancied) of Miss Channing, the notion of which he had but picked up that selfsame day. Clare Joliffe's resentment appeared to be more general, and of longer standing.

"It's such an unkind thing of her, Roland—I may call you Roland, I suppose?"

"Call me Ro if you like," said easy Roland.

"Here's Louisa in this nice position, servants, and carriages, and company about her, no children, living like a queen; and never once has she invited me or Mary inside her doors. It's a great shame. She should hear what mamma thinks of it. I don't suppose she'd have asked me now, only she could not well avoid it, as I am passing through London to visit some friends in the country. Mamma wrote to ask her to give me a night's lodging, and then she wrote back, inviting me to stay a week or two."

"Why should she not have had you before?"

"Oh, I don't suppose there has been any reason, except that she has not thought of it. Louisa was always made up of self. We never fancied she'd marry Bede Greatorex."

"Why not?"

"At least, what we thought was, that Bede would not marry her. He must have cared for her very much, or he would not, after the affair about John Ollivera."

"What had that to do with it?" questioned Roland, opening his eyes—for he supposed the young lady was alluding to the barrister's death.

"She engaged herself to both of them."

"Who did?"

"Louisa."

"Did she!"

Clare Joliffe nodded. "We never quite understood how it was. She was up here on a visit for ever so long, weeks and weeks; it was in the time of Mrs. Greatorex; and if she did not promise herself to Bede, there was at least a good deal of flirtation going on between them. We got to know that after Louisa returned home. The next year, when John Ollivera was at Helstonleigh, she had a flirtation with him. I know she used to write to both of them. Anyway, at the time of his last visit, when the death occurred, she had managed to engage herself to the two."

"I've heard of two wives, but I never heard of two engagements going on together," observed Roland. "Which of the fellows did she like best?"

"I think she liked John Ollivera. But Bede had a good income ready made to his hand, and money went for a great deal with Louisa. She could not marry both of them, that was certain; and how she would have got out of the dilemma but for poor John Ollivera's death, it is impossible to imagine. I never shall forget her look of fright the night Bede Greatorex came in unexpectedly. We had a few friends with us; mamma had invited Mr. Ollivera, and the tea waited for him. There was a ring at the bell, and then the room-door opened for somebody to be shown in. 'Here's your counsellor,' I whispered to Louisa. Instead of him, the servant announced Mr. Bede Greatorex; Louisa's face turned ghastly."

"I don't understand," said Roland, rather at sea. "When was it?"

"It was the night that John Ollivera came by his death. He was in Helstonleigh for the assizes, you know; he was to have pleaded the next day in a cause mamma was interested in. He said he would come in to tea if he were able; and when Bede Greatorex appeared we were all surprised, not knowing that he was at Helstonleigh. We still expected Mr. Ollivera, and Louisa kept casting frightened glances to the door every time it opened. I know she felt at her wit's end; for of course with both her lovers on the scene, a crisis was inevitable, and her deceit would have to come out. Bede Greatorex was whispering to her at times throughout the evening; there seemed to be some trouble between them. Mr. Ollivera did not come—Bede told us he had left him busy, and complaining of a headache. I thought Bede seemed very angry with Louisa; and as soon as he left, she bolted herself in her chamber, and we did not see her again that night. The next morning she sent word down she was ill, and stayed in bed. Mary said she knew what it was that ailed her—worry; but I thought she only wished to avoid being downstairs if the two called. We were at breakfast when Hurst, the surgeon; came in—he was attending mamma at the time—and brought the dreadful news to us, that Mr. Ollivera had been found dead. I carried the tidings up to Louisa, and told her that she must have gone out and killed him. Nothing else could have extricated her so completely from the dilemma."

"But—you don't mean that she—that she went out and killed him?" cried Roland in puzzled wonder. "Could she have got out without being seen?"

"Of course I don't mean it; I said it to her in joke. Why, Roland, you must be stupid to ask such a thing."

"To be sure I must," answered Roland, in contrition. "It's all through my having been at Port Natal."

The last word was drowned in a shiver of glass. Both of them turned hastily. Mr. Bede Greatorex, in taking his elbow from the ormolu cabinet behind the sofa, had accidentally knocked down a beautiful miniature fountain of Bohemian glass, which had been throwing up its choice perfume.

"He certainly heard me," breathed Clare Joliffe, excessively discomfited. "I never knew he was there."

The breakage caused some commotion, and must have annoyed Mr. Bede Greatorex. He rang the bell loudly for a servant, and those who caught a view of his face, saw that it had a white stillness on it, painful as death.

Roland made his escape. The evening, so far as he was concerned, seemed a failure, and he thought he would leave the rooms without further ceremony. Leaping down the staircase a flight at a time, he met Jane Greatorex ascending attended by her coloured maid.

"Halloa! what brings you sitting up so late as this?" cried free Roland.

"We've been spending the evening with grandpapa in his room," answered Jane. "He gave us some cakes and jam, and Miss Channing made the tea. I've got to go to bed now."

"Where's Miss Channing?"

"She's there, in grandpapa's room, waiting to finish the curtain I tore."

Away went Roland, casting thought to the winds in the prospect of seeing Annabel at last, and burst into Mr. Greatorex's room, after giving a smart knock at the door. The wonder was that he knocked at all. Annabel was alone mending the crimson silk curtain of the lower bookcase. Jane, dashing it open to look after some book, had torn the curtain woefully; so Miss Channing took it from its place and set to work to repair it. To be thus unceremoniously invaded brought a flush to her cheeks—perhaps she could not have told why—and Roland saw that her eyes were red and heavy. Sitting at the table, near the lamp, she went on quietly with her work.

"Where's old Greatorex?" demanded Roland. "I thought he was here."

"Mr. Greatorex is gone into his consulting-room. Some one came to see him."

Down sat Roland on the other side of the table; and, as a preliminary to proceedings, pulled his whiskers and took a long stare right into the young lady's face.

"I say, Annabel, why are you not at the party tonight?"

"I don't always care to go in. Mrs. Greatorex gives so many parties."

"Well, I came to it only for one purpose; and that was to see you. I should not have bothered to dress myself for anybody else. Hamish and his wife are there."

"I did not feel very well this evening."

"No, I don't suppose you did. And, besides that, I expect the fact is, that Mrs. Bede never invited you. She is a beauty!"

"Roland!"

"You may go on at me till tomorrow if you like, Annabel; I shall say it. She's a tyrannical, mean-spirited, heartless image; and I shall be telling her so some day to her face. You should hear what Clare Joliffe says of her selfishness."

In the midst of her vexation, Miss Channing could not forbear a smile. Roland was never more serious in his life.

"And I want to know what it was she had been doing today, to put you into that grief."

Annabel coloured almost to tears. It was a home question, and brought back all the troubles connected with her position in the house. Whether Mrs. Bede Greatorex had taken a dislike to her, or whether that lady's temper was alone in fault, Miss Channing did not know; but a great deal of petty annoyance was heaped upon her almost daily, sometimes bordering upon cruel insult. Roland, however, was much mistaken if he thought she would admit anything of the kind to him.

"I see what it is; you are too generous to say it's true," he observed, after vainly endeavouring to get some satisfactory answer. "You are too good for this house, Annabel, and I only wish I could take you out of it."

"Oh, thank you," she said with a quiet smile, not in the least suspecting his meaning.

"And into one of my own."

"One of your own?"

The remark was elicited from her in simple surprise. She looked up at Roland.

"Yes, one of mine. But for bringing you to the fate of Gerald's wife, I'd marry you tomorrow, Annabel."

In spite of the matter-of-fact, earnest tone in which he spoke, almost as if he were asserting he'd take a voyage in the clouds but for its impossibility, Annabel was covered with confusion.

"Some one else's consent would have to be obtained to that bargain," she said in a hesitating, lame kind of way, as she bent her head low over a tangle in the red sewing-silk.

"Some one else's consent! You don't mean to say you'd not marry me, Annabel!"

"I don't say I would."

Roland looked fierce. "You couldn't perjure yourself; you couldn't, Annabel; don't you know what you always said—that you'd be my wife?"

"But I was only a senseless little child then."

"I don't care if you were. I mean it to be carried out. Why, Annabel, who else in the world, but you, do you suppose I'd marry?"

Annabel did not say. Her fingers were working quickly to finish the curtain.

"I can tell you I am looking forward to it if you are not. I vowed to Hamish tonight that you should not stay here another day if I could—good evening, sir."

Mr. Greatorex, returning to the room, looked a little surprised to see a gentleman in it, who rose to receive him. Recognising Roland, he greeted him civilly.

"Is it you, Mr. Yorke? Do you want me?"

"No, sir. Coming down from the kick-up, I met Jenny, who said Miss Channing was here; so I turned in to see her. She's as unhappy in this house as she can be, Mr. Greatorex; folks have tempers, you know; and in catching a glimpse of her face today, I saw it red with grief and tears. Look at her eyes now, sir. So I came to say that if I could help it by taking her out and marrying her, she should not be here another day. I was saying it when you came in, Mr. Greatorex."

To hear the single-minded young fellow avow this, standing there in his earnest simplicity, in his great height, was something to laugh at. But Mr. Greatorex detected the rare good-feeling.

"I am afraid Miss Channing may think your declaration is premature, Mr. Yorke. You are scarcely in circumstances to keep yourself, let alone a wife."

"That's just the misfortune of it," said candid Roland. "My pound a week does for me, and that's all. But I thought I'd let her know it was the power to serve her that was wanting, not the will. And now that it's said, I've done with the matter, and will wish you good night, Mr. Greatorex. Good night, Annabel. Hark at that squalling upstairs! I wonder the cats don't set up a chorus!"

And Mr. Yorke went out in commotion.

"He does not mean anything, sir," said Annabel Channing rather piteously to Mr. Greatorex. "I hope you will pardon him; he is just like a boy."

"I am sure he does not mean any harm," was the lawyer's answer, his lips parting with a smile. "Never were two so much alike in good-hearted simplicity as he and his Uncle Carrick. Don't let his thoughtless words trouble you, child."

Roland, clearing the streets at a few bounds, dashed home, into to Mrs. Jones's parlour, a light through the half-open door showing him that that lady was in it. It was past eleven: as a rule Mrs. Jones liked to keep early hours; but she appeared to have no intention of going to bed yet.

"Are you working for a wager, Mrs. J.?" asked Roland, in allusion to the work in her nimble fingers.

"I am working not to waste my time, Mr. Yorke, while I sit up for Alletha Rye. She is not in yet."

"Out on the spree?" cried Roland.

"She and sprees don't have much to do with each other," said Mrs. Jones. "There's a little child ill a few doors higher up, and Alletha's gone in to sit with her. But she ought to have been home by eleven. And how have you enjoyed yourself, Mr. Yorke?"

"I say, Mrs. J., don't you go talking about enjoyment," spoke Roland resentfully. "It has been a miserable failure altogether. Not a soul there; the men and women howling like mad; and one's elbows crushed in the crowd. Catch me dressing for another!"

Mrs. J. thought the answer slightly inconsistent. "If there was not a soul there, Mr. Yorke, how could your elbows get crushed?"

"There was not a soul I cared for. Plenty of idiots. I don't say Hamish Channing and his wife are that, though. Clare Joliffe was there. Do you remember her at Helstonleigh?"

"Clare? Let me see—Clare was the second: next to Mrs. Bede Greatorex. And very much like her."

Roland nodded. "She and I were sitting on a sofa, nobody to be seen within earshot, and she began talking of the night Mr. Ollivera died. You should have heard her, Mrs. J.: she went on like anything at her sister, calling her selfish and false and deceitful, and other good names. All in a minute there was a crash of glass behind us, and we turned to see Bede Greatorex standing there. I had not spoken treason against his wife, but I didn't like him to have seen me listening to it. It was an awkward situation. If I had a wife, I should not care to hear her abused."

"But what caused the crash of glass?" asked practical Mrs. J.

"Oh, Bede's elbow had touched a perfume fountain of crimson glass, and sent it over," said Roland carelessly. "It was a beautiful thing, costing I'm sure no end of money, and Mrs. Bede had filled it with scent for the evening. She'll go in a tantrum over it when the company departs. Were I Bede I should tell her it blew up of itself."

"Is Miss Clare Joliffe staying there?"

"Got there today by the boat. The Joliffes are living in France now. She says it is the first time Mrs. Bede has invited any of them inside the doors: it was the thought of that, you know, that caused her to go on so. Not that I like Mrs. Bede much better than she does. She can be a Tyrant when she likes, Mrs. J.!"

"To her husband?"

"Oh, I don't know anything about that. Bede's big enough to put her down if she tries it on with him. She is one in the house."

"Like a good many other mistresses," remarked Mrs. J. "I wish Alletha would make haste."

"She never asked Miss Channing and little Greatorex to her party tonight," continued Roland. "Not that it was any loss for Miss Channing, you know; only I went there thinking to see her. Old Greatorex had them to spend the evening in his parlour. Had I been Hamish I should just have said, 'Where's my sister that she is not present?' Oh, yes, she can be a Tyrant! And do you know, what with one cross thing and another, I forgot to ask Hamish if he had heard the news about Arthur. It went clean out of my mind."

Mrs. Jones, rather particularly occupied with a knot in her work, made no reply. Roland, thinking perhaps his revelations as to Mrs. Bede had been sufficiently extensive, sat for some minutes in silence; his face bent forward, his elbow on his knee, and pulling at his whiskers in deep thought.

"I say, Mrs. J., how much do you think two people could live upon?" he burst forth.

"That depends upon who they are, Mr. Yorke."

"Well, I mean—I don't mind telling you in confidence—me and another. A wife, for instance."

Had Roland said Me and a Kangaroo, Mrs. Jones could not have looked at him with more surprise—albeit not one to be surprised in general.

"I'd like to take her from there, for she's shamefully tyrannized over. We need not mention names, but you guess I dare say who's meant, and you are not to go and repeat it to the parish. If I could get my pay increased to three or four times what it is, by dint of doing extra work and putting my shoulder to the wheel in earnest; and if she could get a couple of nice morning pupils at about fifty pounds apiece, that would make three hundred a year. Now don't you think, Mrs. Jenkins, we might get along with that?"

"Well—yes," answered Mrs. Jones, speaking with some hesitation, and rather to satisfy the earnest, eager face waiting for her decision, than in accordance with her true belief. "The worst of it is that prospects rarely turn out as they are expected to."

"Now what do you mean, Mrs. J.? Three hundred a-year is three hundred a-year. Let us be on the safe side, if you like, and put it down at two hundred: which would be allowing for my present pay being only doubled. Do you mean to say two people could not live on two hundred a-year? I know we could; she and I."

"Two people might, when both are economically inclined. But then you see, Mr. Yorke, one ought always to allow for interruptions."

"What interruptions?" demanded Roland.

"Sickness. Or pay of pupils falling off."

"We are both as healthy as ever we can be," said Roland, heartily. "If I had not been strong and sound as a young lion, should I have stood all that knocking about at Port Natal? As to pay and pupils, we might take care to make them sure."

"There might be things to increase expenses," persisted Mrs. Jones, maintaining her ground as usual. "Children, for instance."

Roland stared with all his eyes. "Children!"

"It would be within the range of possibility, I suppose, Mr. Yorke. Your brother Gerald has some."

"Oh law!" cried Roland, his countenance falling.

"And nobody knows what a trouble they are and how much they cost—except those who have tried it. A regular flock of them may come trooping down before you are well aware."

The vista presented to Roland was one his sanguine thoughts had never so much as glanced at. A flock of children had not appeared to him less likely to arrive, than that he should set up a flock of parrots; and he candidly avowed it.

"But we shouldn't want any children, Mrs. J."

Mrs. J. gave a rather derisive sniff. "I've known them that want the fewest get bothered with the most."

Roland had not another word to answer. He was pulling his whiskers in much gloom when Miss Rye was heard to enter. Mrs. Jones began to roll her work together, preparatory to retiring for the night.

"Look here, Mrs. Jones. I'm uncommon fond of children—you should see how I love that sweet Nelly Channing—I'd not mind if I had a score about the place; but what becomes of the little monkeys when there's no bread and cheese to feed them on?"

"That's the precise difficulty, Mr. Yorke."

CHAPTER XX

GRAND REVIEWS

Gerald Yorke's book was out. An enterprising firm of publishers had been found to undertake it, and they brought it forth in due course to the public. Great reviews followed closely upon its advent, lauding its merits and beauties to the skies. Three critiques appeared in one week. The great morning paper gave one, as did the two chief weekly reviewing journals. And each one in its turn sung or said that for ages the public had not been so blest as in this most valuable work of fiction.

In his writing-room, the three glorious reviews before him, sat Hamish Channing, his heart and face alike in a glow. Had the praises been bestowed upon himself, he could scarcely have rejoiced more. How Gerald must have altered the book, he thought: and he felt grieved and vexed to have passed so uncompromising a judgment upon his friend's capabilities as a writer of fiction, when the manuscript was submitted to him. "It must have been that he wrote it too hastily, and has now taken time and consideration to his aid," decided Hamish.

Carrying the papers in his hand he sought his wife, and in the fulness of his heart read out to her the most telling sentences. Bitter though the resentment was, that Gerald was cherishing against Hamish

Channing, he could but have experienced gratification had he witnessed the genuine satisfaction of both, the hearty emphasis which Hamish gave to the laudations bestowed on the author.

"How hard he must have worked at it, Ellen."

"Yes; I did not think Gerald had the application in him."

With his arm on the elbow of his chair, and his refined face a little raised as it rested on his hand, Hamish took a few moments for thought. The eyes seemed to be seeking for something in the evening sky; the sweet light of hope pervaded unmistakably the whole bright countenance. Hamish Channing was but gazing at the vision that had become so entirely his; one that was rarely absent from him; that seemed to be depicted in all its radiant colouring whenever he looked out for it. Fame, reward, appreciation; all were stirring his spirit within, in the vivid light of buoyant expectancy.

"And, if Gerald's book has received this award of praise, what will not mine obtain?" ran his thoughts. For Hamish knew that, try as Gerald would, it was not in him to write as he himself could.

He took his hat and went forth to congratulate Gerald, unable to be silent under this great fame that had fallen on his early friend. Being late in the day, he thought Gerald might be found at his wife's lodgings, for he knew he had been there more than usual of late.

True. Gerald sought the lodgings as a kind of refuge. His chambers had become disagreeably hot, and it was only by dint of the utmost caution on his own part, and diligence on his servant's, that he could venture into them or out of them. The lodgings were less known, and Gerald felt safer there. Things were going very cross with him just now; money seemed to be wanted by his wife and his children and his creditors, all in a hurry, not to speak of the greatest want, himself; and there were moments when Gerald Yorke felt that he might have to seek some far-off city of refuge, as Roland had done, and sail for a Port Natal.

There was no one in the sitting-room when Hamish Channing entered it. The maid said Mr. Yorke had gone out; Mrs. Yorke was putting her children to bed. On the table, side by side with the papers containing the three great reviews, lay a copy of the work. Hamish took it up eagerly, anxious to see the new and good writing that had superseded the old.

He could not find it. One or two bad passages, that he specially remembered, caught his eye; they were there still, unaltered. Had Gerald carelessly overlooked them? Hamish was turning over the pages in some wonder, when Winny came in.

Came in, cross, fractious, tearful. Lonely as Mrs. Gerald Yorke's life had been in Gloucestershire, she had long wished herself back, for the one in London was becoming too trying. Winny had none of the endurance that some wives can show, and love and suffer on.

She came tip to Hamish with outstretched hand. But that he and Ellen proved the generous friends they did, she could not have borne things. Many and many a day there would have been no dinner for the poor little girls, no stop-gap for the petty creditors supplying the daily wants, no comforts of any sort at home, save for the unobtrusive, silently aiding hand of Hamish Channing.

"What is the matter, Winny?" asked Hamish, in relation to the tears. And he spoke very much as he would to a child. In fact, Mrs. Gerald Yorke had mostly to be treated as one.

"Gerald has been so cross; he boxed little Kitty's ears, and nearly boxed mine," pleaded poor Winny, putting herself into a low rocking-chair, near the window. "It is so unreasonable of him, you know, Mr. Channing, to vent it upon us. It's just as if it were our fault."

"Vent what?" asked Hamish, taking a seat at the table, and turning to face her.

"All of it," said Winny, in her childish, fractious way. "His shortness of money, and the many bothers he is in. I can't help it. I would if I could, but if I can't, I can't, and Gerald knows I can't."

"In bothers as usual?" spoke Hamish, in his gay way.

"He is never out of them, Mr. Channing; you know he is not; and they get worse and worse. Gerald has no certain income at all; and it seems to me that what he earns by writing, whether it's for magazines or whether it's for newspapers, is always drawn beforehand, for he never has any money to bring home. Of course the tradespeople come and ask for their money; of course the landlady expects to be paid her weekly rent; and when they insist on seeing Gerald, or stop him when he goes out, he comes back in such a passion you never saw. She made him savage this evening, and he took and boxed Kitty."

"She! Who?"

"The landlady—Miss Cook."

"Winny, I paid Miss Cook myself, last week."

"Oh, but I didn't tell you there was more owing to her; I didn't like to," answered helpless Winny. "There is; and she has begun to worry always. She gets things in for us, and wants to be paid for them."

"Of course she does," thought Hamish. "Where's Gerald?" he asked.

"Gone out somewhere. You know that money you let me have to pay the horrible bill I couldn't sleep for, and didn't dare to give to Gerald," she continued, putting up her hands to her little distressed face. "I've got something to tell you about it."

Hamish was at a loss. The bills he and his wife had advanced money for were getting numerous. Winny, rocking herself gently, saw he did not recollect.

"It was for the shoes and stockings for the children and the boots for me; we had nothing to our feet. Ellen brought me the money last Saturday—three pounds—though the bill was not quite that. Well, Gerald saw the sovereigns lying in the dressing-table drawer—it was so stupid of me to leave them there!—and he took them. First he asked me where I'd got them from; I said I had scraped them up to pay for the children's shoes. Upon that, he put them in his pocket, saying he had bills far more pressing than children's shoe bills, and must take them for his own use. O-o-o-o-o-oh!" concluded the young wife, with a burst of her childish grief, "I am very miserable."

"You should have told your husband the money belonged to Mrs. Channing—and was given to you by her for a special purpose."

"Good gracious!" cried Winny, astonishment arresting the tears in her pretty eyes. "As if I would dare to tell him that! If Gerald thought you or Ellen helped me, he would be in the worst passion of all. I'm not sure but he'd beat me."

"Why?"

"He would think that I was running up a great debt on my own score for him to pay back sometime. And he has such oceans of pride, besides. You must never tell him, Mr. Channing."

"How does he think the accounts get paid?" asked Hamish.

"He does not think about it," she answered, eagerly. "So long as he is not bothered, he won't be bothered. He will never look at a single bill, or hear me speak of one. As far as he knows, the people and Miss Cook come and worry me for money regularly. But oh! Mr. Channing! if I were to be worried to any degree, I should die. I should wish to die, for I could not bear it. Ellen knows I could not."

Yes; in a degree, Hamish and his wife both knew this. Winny Yorke was quite unfitted to battle with the storms of the world; they could not see her breasting them, and not help. A brother of hers—and Gerald was aware of this—who had been overwhelmed with the like, proved how ill he was fitted to bear, by putting a terrible end to them and all else.

"And so, that bill for the shoes and stockings was not paid, and they came after it today, and abused Gerald—for I had said to them it would be ready money," pursued Winny, rocking away. "Oh, he was so angry! he forbid me to buy shoes; he said the children must go barefoot until he was in a better position. If the man comes tomorrow, and insists on seeing me, I shall have to run away. And Fredy's ill."

The wind-up was rather unexpected, and given in a different tone. Fredy was the eldest of the little girls, Kitty the second, Rosy the third.

"If she should be going to have the measles, the others will be sure to catch it, and then what should I do?" went on Winny, piteously. "There'd be a doctor to pay for and medicine to be got, and I don't think druggists give credit to strangers. It may turn out to be only a bad cold."

"To be sure it may," said Hamish cheerily. "Hope for the best, Mrs. Yorke. Ellen always does."

Mrs. Yorke sighed. Ellen's husband was very different from hers.

"Gerald is in luck; he will soon I think, be able to get over his difficulties. Have you reed these reviews?" continued Hamish, laying his hand upon the journals at his elbow.

"Oh yes, I've read them," was the answer, given with slighting discontent.

"I never read anything finer—in the way of praise—than this review in the Snarler," spoke Hamish.

"He wrote that himself."

"Wrote what?"

"That review in the Snarler."

"Who wrote it?" pursued Hamish, rather at sea.

"Gerald did."

"Nonsense, Winny. You must be mistaken."

"I'm sure I'm not," said Winny. "He wrote it at this very table. He was three hours writing it, and then he was nearly as long altering it: taking out words and sentences and putting in stronger ones."

Hamish, when his surprise was over, laughed slightly. It had a little destroyed his romance.

"And two friends of Gerald's wrote the other reviews," said Winny, continuing her revelations. "Gerald has great influence with the reviewing people; he says he can get any work made or marred."

"Oh, can he?" quoth Hamish, with light good-nature. "At least, these reviews will tell well with the public and sell the book. Why, Winny, instead of being low-spirited, you have cause to be just the other way. It is a great thing to have got this book so well out. It may make Gerald's fortune."

Winny sat bolt upright in the rocking-chair, and looked at Hamish, with a puzzled, cross face. He supposed that she did not understand.

"What I mean, Winny, is that this book may lead really to fortune in the end. If Gerald once becomes known as a successful author—"

"The bringing out of the book has caused him to be ten times more worried than before," interrupted Whiny. "Of course it is known that he has a book out, and the consequence is that everybody who has got sixpence owing by either of us, is dunning him for money—just as if the book had made his fortune! He cannot go to his chambers, unless he shoots in like a cat; and he is getting afraid to come here. My opinion is, that he'd have been better off without the book than with it."

This was not a particularly pleasant view of affairs; but Hamish was far from subscribing to all Winny said. He answered with his cheering smile, that was worth its weight in gold, and rose to leave.

"Things are always darkest just before dawn, Mrs. Yorke. And I must repeat my opinion—that this book will lay the foundation of Gerald's fortune. He will soon get out of his embarrassments."

"Well, I don't understand it, but I know he says the book has plunged him into fresh debt," returned Winny, gloomily. "I think he has had to pay an immense deal to get it out."

Hamish was turning over the leaves of the book as he stood. Winny at once offered to lend it him: there were two or three copies about the house, she said. Accepting the offer, for he really wished to see the good and great alterations Gerald must have made, Hamish was putting the three volumes under his arm when the street door opened, and Gerald came running up.

"Well, old friend!" cried Hamish, heartily, as he shook Gerald's hand. "I came to wish you joy."

Winny disappeared. Never feeling altogether at ease in the presence of her clever, stern, arbitrary husband, she was glad to get away from it when she could. Hamish and Gerald stood at the window, talking together in the fading light, their theme Gerald's book, the reviews, and other matters connected with it. Hamish spoke the true sentiments of his heart when he said how glad and proud he was, for Gerald's sake.

"I have been telling your wife that it is the first stepping-stone to fortune. It must be a great success, Gerald."

"Ah, I thought you were a little out in the opinion you formed of it," said Gerald loftily.

"I am thankful it has proved so. You have taken pains to alter it, Gerald."

"Not much: I thought it did very well as it was. And the result proves I was right," added Gerald complacently. "Have you read the reviews?"

"I should think I have," said Hamish warmly. "They brought me here tonight. Reviews such as those will take the public by storm."

"Yes, they tell rather a different tale from the verdict passed by you. You assured me I should never succeed in fiction; had mistaken my vocation; got no elements for it within me; might shut up shop. What do the reviews say? Look at that one in the Snarler," continued Gerald, snatching up that noted authority, and holding it to the twilight, formed by the remnant of day and the light of the street-lamps, while he read an extract from its pages aloud.

"We do not know how to find terms of praise sufficiently high for this marvellously beautiful book of fiction. The grateful public, now running after its three volumes, cannot be supplied fast enough. From the first page to the last, attention is rapturously enchained; one cannot put the book down—"

"And so on, and so on," continued Gerald, breaking off the laudatory recital suddenly, and flinging the paper behind him again. "No good to continue, as you've read it. Yes, that is praise from the Snarler. Worth having, I take it," he concluded in unmistakable triumph over his fellow-man and author, quite unconscious that poor simple Winny had let the cat out of the bag.

"If reviews ever sell a book, these must sell yours, Gerald."

"I think so. We shall see whether your book gets such; it's finished, I hear," spoke Gerald, leaning from the window to survey a man who had just crossed the street. "One never can tell what luck a work will have while it is in manuscript."

"One can tell what it ought to have."

"Ought! oughts don't go for much now-a-days; favour does though. The devil take the fellow."

This last genial wish applied to the man, who had made for the house-door and was ringing its bell. Gerald grew just a little troubled, and betrayed it.

"Don't let these matters disturb your peace, Gerald," advised Hamish in his kindest and most impressive manner. "You cannot fail to get on now. Have the publishers paid you anything yet?"

"Paid me!" retorted Gerald rather savagely, "they are asking for the money I owe them. It was arranged that I should advance fifty pounds towards bringing the book out. And I've not been able to give it them yet."

Gerald spoke truly. The confiding publishers, not knowing the true state of Mr. Yorke's finances, but supposing there could be no danger with a man in his position—living in the great world, of aristocratic connections, getting his name up in journalism—had accepted in all good faith his plausible excuses for the non-prepayment of the fifty pounds, and brought out the book at their own cost. They were reminding him of it now; and more than hinting that a bargain was a bargain.

"And how I am to stave them off, the deuce only knows," observed Gerald. "I want to keep in with them if I can. The notion of my finding fifty pounds!"

"There must be proceeds from a book with such reviews as these," said Hamish. "Let them take it out of their first returns."

"Oh, ah! that's all very well; but I don't know," was the answer given gloomily.

"Well, good night, old friend, for I must be off; you have my best wishes in every way. I am going to take home the book for a day; I should like to look over it; Winny says you have other copies."

"Take it if you like," growled Gerald, who heard the maid's step on the stairs, and knew he was going to be appealed to. "Now then!" he angrily saluted her, as she came in. "I've told you before you are not to bring messages up to me after dusk. How dare you disobey?"

"It's that gentleman that always will see you, sir," spoke the discomfited girl.

"I am gone to bed," roared Gerald; "be off and say so."

And Hamish Channing, running lightly downstairs, heard the bolt of the room slipped, as the servant came out of it. That Gerald had a good deal of this kind of worry, there was no doubt; but he did not go the best way to work to prevent it.

As soon as Hamish got home, he sat down to his writing-table, and set himself to examine Gerald's book. Gradually, as he turned page after page of the three volumes in rotation, a perplexed, dissatisfied look, mixed with much disappointment, seated itself in his face.

There had been no alterations made at all. All the objectionable elements were there, just as they had been in the manuscript. The book was, in fact, exactly what Hamish had found it—utterly worthless and terribly fast. It had not a chance of ultimate success. Not one reader in ten, beginning the book, would be able to call up patience to finish it. And Hamish was grievously vexed for Gerald's sake; he could have set on to bewail and bemoan aloud.

Suddenly the reviews flashed over his mind; their glowing descriptions, their subtle praise, their seductive, lavish promises. In spite of himself, of his deep feeling, his real vexation, he burst into a fit of laughter, prolonged until he had to hold his sides, at the thought of how the very innocent and helpless public would be taken in.

CHAPTER XXI

ROLAND YORKE'S SHOULDER TO THE WHEEL

The weeks went on. Roland Yorke was hard at work, carrying out his resolve of "putting his shoulder to the wheel." Vague ideas of getting into something good, by which a fortune might be made, floated through his brain in rose-coloured clouds. What the something was to be he did not exactly know; meanwhile, as a preliminary to it, he sought and obtained copying from Greatorex and Greatorex, to be done in spare hours at home. Of which fact Roland (unlike Mr. Brown) made no secret; he talked of it to the whole office; and Mr. Brown supplied him openly.

It was an excessively hot evening, getting now towards dusk. Roland had carried his work to Mrs. Jones's room, not so much because his own parlour was rather close and stuffy, as that he might obtain slight intervals of recreative gossip. He had it to himself, however, for Mrs. Jones was absent on household cares. The window looked on a backyard, in which the maid, who had come out, was hanging up a red table-cover to dry, that had evidently had something spilled on it. Of course Roland arrested his pen to watch the process. He was sitting in his shirtsleeves, and had just complained aloud that it was hotter than Africa.

"Who did that?" he called out through the open window. "You?"

"Mr. Ollivera, sir. He upset some ink; and mistress have been washing the place out in layers of cold water. She don't think it'll show."

"What d'ye call layers?"

"Different lots, sir. About nineteen bowlfuls she swilled it through; and me a emptying of 'em at the sink, and droring off fresh water ready to her hand."

The hanging-out and pulling the damaged part straight took a tolerably long time; Roland, in the old seduction of any amusement being welcome as an accompaniment to work, continued to look on and talk. Suddenly, he remembered his copying, and the young lady for whose sake he had undertaken the labour.

"This is not sticking to it," he soliloquised. "And if I am to have her, I must work for her. Won't I work, that's all! I'll stick to it like any brick! But this copying is poor stuff to get a fellow on. If I could only slip into something better!"

Considering that Mr. Roland Yorke's earnings the past week, what with mistakes and other failures, had been one shilling and ninepence, and the week previous to that fifteenpence, it certainly did not look as though the copying would prove the high road to fortune. He began casting about other projects in his mind, as he wrote.

"If they'd give me a place under Government, it would be the very thing. But they don't. Old Dick Yorke's as selfish as a camel, and Carrick's hiding his head, goodness knows where. So I am thrown on my own resources. Bless us all! when a fellow wants to get on in this world, he can't."

At this juncture Roland came to the end of his paper. As it was a good opportunity for taking a little respite, he laid down his pen, and exercised his thoughts.

"There's those photographing places—lots of them springing up. You can't turn a corner into a street but you come bang upon a fresh establishment. They can't require a fellow to have any previous knowledge, they can't. I wonder if any of them would take me on, and give me a couple of guineas a-week, or so? Nothing to do there, but talk to the visitors, and take their faces. I should make a good hand at that. But, perhaps, she'd not like it! She might object to marry a man of that sort. What a difficulty it is to get into anything! I must think of the other plan."

The other plan meant some nice place under Government. To Roland that always seemed a sure harbour of refuge. The doubt was, how to get it?

"There's young Dick—Vincent, as he likes to be called now," soliloquised Roland. "I've never asked him to help me, but perhaps he might: he's not ill-natured where his pocket's not called in question. I'll go to him tomorrow; see if I don't. Now then, are you dry?"

This was to the writing. Roland rose up to get more paper, and then found that he had left it behind him at the office—some that he ought to have brought home.

"There's a bother! I wonder if I could get it by going round? Of course the offices are closed, but I'd not mind asking Bede for the key if he's in the way."

To think and to act were one with Roland. He put on his coat, took his hat, and went hastening along on his expedition. Rather to his surprise, as he drew to his walk's end, his quick eyes, casting themselves into dark spots as well as light ones, caught sight of Bede Greatorex standing in the shade opposite his house, apparently watching its lighted windows, from which sounds of talking and laughing issued forth. Roland conjectured that some gaiety was as usual going on in the house, which its master would escape. Over he went to him, without ceremony.

"You don't like all that, sir?" he said, indicating the supposed company.

"Not too much of it," replied Bede Greatorex, startled out of his reverie by the unexpected address. "The fact is," he condescended to explain to his curious clerk, perhaps as an excuse for standing there, "certain matters have been giving me trouble of late. I was in deep thought."

"Mrs. Bede Greatorex does love society: she did as Louisa Joliffe," remarked Roland, meaning to be confidential.

"I was not thinking of Mrs. Bede Greatorex, but of the loss from my office," spoke his master in a cold, proud tone of reproof.

Crossing the road, as if declining further conversation, he went in. Roland saw he had offended him, and wished his tongue had been tied, laying down his thoughtless speech as usual to the having sojourned at Port Natal. It might not be a propitious moment for requesting the loan of the office keys, and Roland had the sense to foresee it.

Who should come out of the house at that moment, but Annabel Channing, attended by a servant. The sight of her put work, keys, and all else, out of Roland's head. He leaped across, seized her hands, and learnt that she had got leave to spend the evening with Hamish and his wife.

"I'll take care of you; I'll see you safely there," cried Roland, impetuously. "You can go back, old Dalla."

Old Dalla—a middle-aged yellow woman who had brought Jane Greatorex from India and remained with the child as her attendant—made no more ado, but took him at his word; glad to be spared the walk, she turned indoors at once. And before Annabel well knew what had occurred, she found herself being whirled away by Roland in an opposite direction to the one she wished to go. It was only twilight yet. Roland had her securely on his arm, and began to pace the square. To say the truth, he looked on the meeting as a special chance, for he had not once set eyes on the young lady, save in the formal presence of others, since that avowal of his a fortnight ago, in Mr. Greatorex's room.

"What are you doing?" she asked, when she could collect herself "This is not the way to Hamish's."

"This is the way to get a few words with you, Annabel; one can't talk in the streets with its glare and its people. We are private here; and I'll take you to Hamish's in a minute or two."

In this impulsive fashion, he began telling her his plans and his dreams. That he had determined to make an income and a home for her: as a beginning, until something better turned up, he was working all his spare time at copying deeds, "nearly night and day." One less unsophisticated than Roland Yorke, might have suppressed a small item of the programme—that which related to Annabel's contributing to the fund herself, by obtaining pupils. Not he. He avowed it just as openly as his own intention of getting "something under Government." In short, Roland made the young lady a regular offer. Or, rather, did not so much make the offer, as assume that it had been already made, and was, so far, settled. His arguments were sensible; his plans looked really feasible; the day-dreams tolerably bright.

"But I have not said I would have you yet," spoke Annabel all in a flutter, when she could get a word in edgeways. "You should not make so sure of things."

"Not make sure of it! Not have me!" cried Roland, in indignant remonstrance. "Now look you here, Annabel—you know you'll have me: it is all nonsense to make believe you won't. I don't suppose I've asked you in the proper way, or put things in the proper light; but you ought to make allowance for a fellow who has had his manners knocked out of him at Port Natal. When the time arrives that I've got a little house and a few chairs and tables in its rooms, you'll come home to me and I'll try and make you happy in it, and work for you till I drop! There! If I knew how to say it better, I would: and you need not despise a man for his incapable way of putting it. Not have me! I'd like to know who you would have, if not me!"

Annabel Channing offered no farther remonstrance. That she had contrived to fall in love with Roland Yorke, and would rather marry him than anybody else in the world, she knew all too well. The home and the chairs and the tables in it, and the joint working together to keep it going, wore a bright vista to her heart, looked at from a distance with youth's hopeful eyes. But she did not speak: and Roland, mistaking her silence, regarded it as a personal injury.

"When I and Arthur are the dearest friends in the world! He'd give you to me off-hand; I know it. It is not kind of you, Annabel. We engaged ourselves to each other when you were a little one and I was a tall donkey of fourteen, and if I've ever thought of a wife at all since I grew up, it was of you. I have done nothing but think of you since I came back. I wonder how you'd feel if I turned round and said, 'I don't know that I shall have you.' Not jovial, I know."

"You should not bring up the nonsense we said when we were children," returned Annabel, at a loss what else to answer. "I'm sure I could not have been above seven. We were playing at oranges and lemons: I remember the evening quite well: and you—"

"Now just you be open, Annabel, and say what it is your mind's harbouring against me," interrupted Roland, in a tone of deep feeling. "Is it that twenty-pound note of old Galloway's?—or is it because I went knocking about at Port Natal?"

"Oh, Roland, how foolish you are! As if I could think of either!"

And there was something in the words and tone, in the pretty, shy, blushing face that reassured Roland. From that moment he looked upon matters as irrevocably settled, gave Annabel's hand a squeeze against his side, and went on to enlarge upon his dreams of the future.

"I've taken counsel with myself and with Mrs. J., and I don't think the pair of us are likely to be led astray by romance, Annabel, for she is one of the strong-minded ones. She agrees with me that we might do well on three hundred a year; and, what with my work and your pupils, we could make that easily. But, I said to her, let's be on the safe side, and put it down at only two hundred. Just to begin with, you know, Annabel. She said, 'Yes, we might do on that if we were both economical'—and I'm sure if I've not learnt to be that I've learnt nothing. I would not risk the temptation of giving away—which I am afraid I'm prone to—for you should be cash-keeper, Annabel; just as Mrs. J. keeps my sovereign a week now. My goodness! the having no money in one's pocket is a safeguard. When I see things in the shop windows, whether it's eatables, or what not, I remember my lack of cash, and pass on. I stopped to look at a splendid diamond necklace yesterday in Regent Street, and thought how much I should like to get it for you; but with empty pockets, where was the use of going in to enquire the price?"

"I do not care for diamonds," said Annabel.

"You will have them some time, I hope, when my fortune's made. But about the two hundred a year? Mrs. J. said if we could be sure of making that regularly, she thought we might risk it; only, she said there might be interruptions. It would not be Mrs. J. if she didn't croak."

"Interruptions!" exclaimed Annabel, something as Roland had interrupted Mrs. Jones, and quite as unsuspicious as he. "Of what kind?"

"Sickness, Mrs. J. mentioned, and—but I don't think I'll tell you that," considered Roland. "Let's say, and general contingencies. I'm sure I should as soon have thought of setting up a menagerie of owls, but for her putting it into my head. A fellow who has helped to land boats at Port Natal can't be expected to foresee everything. Would you be afraid to encounter the two hundred a year?"

"I fear mamma would for me. And Hamish."

"Now Annabel, don't you get bringing up objections for other people. Time enough for that when they come down with them of their own accord. I intend to speak to Hamish tonight if I can get the opportunity. I don't want you to keep your promise a secret. You are a dear good girl, and the little home shall be ours before a twelvemonth's gone by, if I have to work my hands off."

The little home! Poor Roland! If he could but have foreseen what twelve months would bring forth.

Hamish Channing's book had come out under more favourable auspices than Gerald's. The publisher, far from demanding money in advance for expenses, had made fair terms with him. Of course the result would depend on the sale. When Hamish held the first copies in his hand, his whole being was lighted up with silent enthusiasm; the joy it was to bring, the appreciation, had already set in. He sent a copy to his mother; and he sent one to Gerald Yorke, with a brief, kind note: in the simplicity of his heart, he supposed Gerald would rejoice, just as he at first had rejoiced for him.

How good the book was, Hamish knew. The publisher knew. The world, Hamish thought, would soon know. He did not deceive himself in its appreciation, or exaggerate the real worth and merits of the work: in point of fact, the praise meted out to Gerald's would have been really applicable to his. Never did Hamish, even in his moments of extremest doubt and diffidence, cast a thought to the possibility that his book would be cried down. Already he was thinking of beginning a second; and his other work, the occasional papers, went on with a zest.

He sat with his little girl, Nelly, on his knee, on this selfsame evening that Roland had pounced on Annabel. The child had her blue eyes and her bright face turned to him as she chattered. He looked down fondly at her and stroked the pretty curls of her golden hair.

"And when will the ship be home, papa?"

"Very soon now. It is nearing the port."

"But when will it be quite, quite, quite home?"

"In a few days, I think, Nelly. I am not sure, but I ought to say it has come."

"It was those books that came in the parcel last night?" said shrewd little Nelly.

"Even so, darling."

"Mamma has been reading them all day. I saw"—Nelly put her sweet face close up and dropped her voice—"I saw her crying at places of them."

A soft faint crimson stole into Hamish Channing's cheeks; his lips parted, his breath came quicker; a sudden radiance illuminated his whole countenance. This whisper of the child's brought to his heart its first glad sense of that best return—appreciation.

Company arrived to interrupt the quiet home happiness. Mrs. Gerald Yorke and her three meek children. Winny had a face of distress, and made a faint apology for bringing the little ones, but it was over early to leave them in bed. Close upon this, Roland and Annabel entered, and had the pleasure of being in time to hear Gerald's wife tell out her grievances.

They were of the old description. No money, importunate creditors, Gerald unbearably cross. Annabel felt inclined to smile; Roland was full of sympathy. Had the prospective fortune (that he was sure to make) been already in his hands, he would have given a purse of gold to Winny, and carried off the three little girls to a raree-show there and then. The next best thing was to promise them the treat: which he did largely.

"And me too, Roland," cried eager Nelly, dancing in and out amid the impromptu visitors in the highest glee, her shining curls never still.

"Of course you," said Roland to the fair child who had come to an anchor before him, flinging her arms upon his knees. "I'd not go anywhere without you, you know, Nelly. If I were not engaged to somebody else, I'd make you my little wife."

"Who is the somebody else? Kitty?"

"Not Kitty. She's too little."

"Let it be me, then."

Roland laughed, and looked across at Hamish. "If I don't ask you for her, I may for somebody else. So prepare."

"I'm sure, I hope, Roland, if ever you do marry, that you'll not be snappish with your wife and little girls, as your brother is with us," interposed Winny with a sob. "I think it is something in Mr. Channing's book that has put him out today. As soon as it came this morning, he locked himself in the room alone with it, and never came out for hours; but when he did come—oh, was he not in a temper! He pushed Winnifred and she fell on the carpet, and he shook Rosy till she cried; and nobody knows for what. I'm sure they are like mice for quietness when he's there; they are too much afraid of him to be otherwise."

It was well for Gerald Yorke that he committed no grave crimes; for his wife, in her childish simplicity, in her inability to bear in silence, would be safe to have betrayed them. She was right in her surmises—in fact, Winny, with all her silliness, had a great deal of discernment—that the cause of her husband's temper being worse than usual was Hamish Channing's book. Seizing upon it when it came, Gerald locked himself up with it, forbidding any interruption in terms that might not be disobeyed. On the surface alone he could see that it was no sham book: Gerald's book had about twenty lines in a page, and the large, wide, straggling type might have been read a mile off. This was different: it was closely printed, rather than not, as if the writer were at no fault for matter. In giving a guinea and a half for this work, the public would not find itself deluded into finding nothing to read. Gerald sat down. He was about to peruse this long-expected book, and he devoutly hoped to find it bad and worthless.

But, if Gerald Yorke could not write, he could appreciate: and with the first commencing pages he saw what the work really was—rare, good, of powerful interest; essentially the production of a good man, a scholar, and a gentleman.

As he read on and on, his brow grew dark with a scowl, his lips were angrily bitten: the book, properly noticed, would certainly set the world a-longing: and Gerald might experience some difficulty in writing it down. The knowledge did not tend to soften his generally ill-conditioned state of mind, and he flung the last volume on the table with a harsh word. Even at that early stage, some of the damnatory terms he would use to extinguish the book passed through his active brain.

Emerging from his retreat towards evening in this genial mood, he made those about him suffer from it. Winny, the non-enduring, might well wish to escape with her helpless children! Gerald departed; to keep an engagement at a white-bait entertainment; and she came to Hamish Channing's.

How different were the two men! Hamish Channing's heart had ached to pain at the badness of Gerald's book, for Gerald's sake; had he been a magician, he would have transformed its pages, with a stroke of his wand, to the brightest and best ever given to the world. Gerald Yorke put on the anger of a fiend because Hamish's work was not bad; and laid out his plans to ruin it.

"Man, vain man, dressed in a little brief authority,
Plays such fantastic tricks before high heaven
As make the angels weep."

If the world is not entirely made up of these two types of men, the bad and the good, the narrow-hearted and the wide, the kindly generous and the cruelly selfish, believe me there are a vast many of each in it.

"It's getting worse and worse," sobbed Winny, continuing her grievances over the tea-table. "I don't mean Gerald now, but the shortness of money and the worry. I know we shall have to go into the workhouse!"

"Bless you, don't lose heart!" cried Roland with a beaming face. "I can never lose that again, after the ups and downs in Africa. I'll tell you of one, Mrs. Gerald.—Another piece of muffin, Kitty? there it is.—I and another fellow had had no food to speak of for two days; awfully low we were. We went into a store and they gave us some advertising bills to paste on the walls. Well, somehow I lost the fellow and the bills, for he had taken possession of them. I went rushing about everywhere, looking for him—and that's not so pleasant when your inside's as hollow as an empty herring barrel—but he never turned up again. Whether he decamped with the bills, or whether he was put out of the way by a knock on the head, I don't know to this hour. Anyhow I had to go back to the store the next day, and tell about it. If you'll believe me they accused me of swallowing the bills, or otherwise making away with them, and called for a man to take me into custody. A day and a night I lay in their detention cell, with nothing to eat and the rats running over me. Oh, wasn't it good! One can't be nice, over there, our experiences don't let us be; but I always had a horror of rats. Well, I got over that, Mrs. Gerald."

"Did they try you for it?" questioned Mrs. Gerald, who had suspended her tea to listen, full of interest.

"Good gracious, no! They let me out. Oh, but I could tell you of worse fixes than that. You take heart, I say; and never trouble your thoughts about workhouses. Things are safe to turn round when they seem at the worst."

The tea over, Mrs. Yorke said she must take her departure: the children were weary; she scarcely knew how she should get them back. Hamish had a cab called: when it came he went out and lifted the little ones into it. Winny looked at it dubiously.

"You'll not tell Gerald that I said he was in a temper about your book, Mr. Channing?" she said pleadingly, as she took her seat.

"I'll not tell Gerald tales of any sort," answered Hamish with his gay smile. "Take heart, as Roland tells you to do, and look forward to better days both for you and your husband. Perhaps there is a little glimmer of their dawn already showing itself, though you cannot yet see it."

"Do you mean through Gerald's book?" she asked half crossly.

"Oh dear no. What I mean has nothing to do with Gerald's book. Who has the paper of cakes?—Fredy. All right. Good night. The cab's paid, Mrs. Yorke."

Mrs. Yorke burst into tears, leaned forward, and clasped Hamish's hand. The intimation, as to the cab, had solved a difficulty running through her mind. It was a great relief.

"God bless you, Mr. Channing! You are always kind."

"Only trust in God," he whispered gravely. "Trust Him ever, and He will take care of you."

The cab drove off, and Hamish turned away, to encounter Roland Yorke. That gentleman, making his opportunity, had followed Hamish out; and now poured into his ear the tale he had to tell about himself and Annabel. Hamish did not hear it with altogether the stately dignity that might be expected to attend the reception of an offer of marriage for one's sister. On the contrary, he burst out laughing in Roland's face.

"Come now! be honest," cried Roland, deeply offended. "Is it me you despise, Mr. Channing, or the small prospect I can offer her?"

"Neither," said Hamish, laughing still. "As to yourself, old fellow, if Annabel and the mother approve, I should not object. I never gave a heartier handshake to any man than I would to you as my brother-in-law. I like you better than I do the other one, William Yorke; and there's the truth."

"Oh—him! you easily might," answered Roland, jerking his nose into the air, with his usual depreciation of the Reverend William Yorke's merits. "Then why do you laugh at me?"

"I laughed at the idea of your making two hundred a year at copying deeds."

"I didn't say I should. You couldn't have been listening to me, Hamish—I wish, then, you'd not laugh so, as if you only made game of a fellow! What I said was, that I was putting my shoulder to the wheel in earnest, and had begun with copying, not to waste time. I have been thinking I'd try young Dick Yorke."

"Try him for what?"

"Why, to get me a post of some sort. I think he'll do it if he can. I'm sure it's not much I shall ask for—only a couple of hundreds a year, or so. And if Annabel secures a nice pupil or two, there'd be three hundred a year to start with. You'd not mind her teaching a little, would you, Hamish, while I was waiting for the skies to rain gold?"

"Not I. That would be for her own consideration."

"And when we shall have got the three hundred a year in secure prospect, you'll talk to Mrs. Channing of Helstonleigh for me, won't you?"

Hamish thought he might safely say Yes. The idea of Roland's "putting his shoulder to the wheel" sufficiently to earn two hundred pounds income, seemed to be amidst the world's improbabilities. He could not get over his laughing, and it vexed Roland.

"You think I can't work. You'll see. I'll go off to young Dick Yorke this very hour, and sound him. Nothing like taking time by the forelock. He is likely to be married, I hear."

"Who is?"

"Young Dick. They call him Vincent now, but before I went to Port Natal 'Dick' was good enough for him. My father never spoke of them but as old Dick and young Dick. Not that we had anything to do with the lot: they held themselves aloof from us. I never saw either of them but once, and that was when they came down to Helstonleigh to my father's funeral. He died in residence, you know, Hamish."

Hamish nodded: he remembered all the circumstances perfectly. Dr. Yorke's death had been unexpected until quite the last. Ailing for some time, he had yet been sufficiently well to enter on what was called his close residence of twenty-one days as Prebendary of the cathedral, of which he was also sub-dean. The disease made so rapid progress that before the residence was out he had expired.

"Old Dick made some promises to George that day, saying he'd get him on because George was the eldest, I suppose; he took little notice of the rest of us," resumed Roland. "It was after we came in from the funeral, in our crape scarfs and hat-bands. But he never did an earthly thing for him, Hamish—as poor George could tell you, if he were alive. My father always said his brother Dick was selfish."

"You may find young Dick the same," said Hamish.

"So I should if it were his pocket I wanted to touch. But it's not, you know. And now I'll be off to him. I had intended to spend this evening at my copying, but I left the paper in the office, and there was likely to be a hitch about my getting it I'll make up for it tomorrow night. I shall be back in time to tell you of my success, and to help you take Annabel home."

Roland's way of taking time by the forelock was to dash through the streets at his utmost speed, no matter what impediments he might have to overthrow in his way, and into the fashionable clubhouse frequented by Vincent Yorke, who dined there quite as often as he did at his father's house in Portland Place. Roland was in luck, and met him coming out.

"I say Vincent, do stay and hear me for a minute or two. It is something of consequence."

Vincent Yorke, not altogether approving of this familiar mode of salutation from Roland, although fate had made them cousins, did not quite see his way to refuse the request. As Roland had said, young Dick was sufficiently good-natured where his pocket was not attacked. He led the way to a corner in a room where they could be private, sat down, and offered a chair to Roland.

It was declined. Roland was a great deal too excited and too eager to sit. He poured forth his wants and hopes—that he wished co work honestly for just bread and cheese, and to get his own living, and be beholden to nobody: would he, Dick, help him to a place? He did not mind how hard he worked; till his shirtsleeves were wet with honest sweat, if need be; and live on potatoes and half a pint of beer a day; so that he might just get on a little, and make a sum of two hundred pounds a year: or one hundred to begin with.

The word "Dick" slipped out inadvertently in Roland's heat. Not a man living so little capable, as he, of remembering conventionalities when thus excited. Vincent Yorke, detecting the earnest purpose, the sanguine hope, the real single-mindedness of the applicant, could but stare and laugh, and excuse mistakes under the circumstances. The very boldness of the request, preferred with straightforward candour and without the slightest reticence, told on him favourably, because it was so opposite to the crafty diplomacy that most men would have brought to bear on such an application. Favourably only, you understand, in so far as that he did not return a haughty repulse off-hand, but condescended to answer civilly.

"Such things are not in my line," he said, and—face to face with that realistic Port Natal traveller, he for once put aside his beloved fashionable attribute, the mincing lisp. "I don't go in for politics; never did go in for 'em; and Government places are not likely to come in my way. You should have applied to Sir Richard. He knows one or two of the Cabinet Ministers."

"I did apply to him once," replied Roland, "and he sent me off with a flea in my ear. I said then, I'd never ask him for any thing again, though it were to keep me from starving."

Vincent Yorke smiled. "Look here," said he; "you take him in his genial moods. Go up to him now; he'll just have dined. If anything can be got out of him, that's the time."

Mr. Vincent Yorke hit upon this quite as much to get rid of Roland, as in any belief in its efficacy. In the main what he said was true—that Sir Richard's after-dinner moods were his genial ones; but that Roland had not the ghost of a chance of being helped, he very well knew. That unsophisticated voyager, however, took it all in.

"I'll run up at once," he said. "I'm so much obliged to you, Vincent. I say, are you not soon going to be married? I heard so."

"Eh—yes," replied Vincent, with frigid coldness, relapsing into himself and the fine gentleman.

"I wish you the best of good luck," returned Roland, heartily shaking the somewhat unwilling hand with a grip that he might have learned at Port Natal. "And I hope she'll make you as good a wife as I know somebody else will make me. Good night, Vincent, I'm off."

Vincent nodded. It struck him that, with all his drawbacks and deficiencies, Roland was rather a nice young fellow.

Outside the club door stood a hansom. Roland, in his eagerness and haste, was only kept from bolting into it by the slight deterrent accident of having no change in his pocket to pay the fare. He did not lose much. The speed at which he tore up Regent Street might have kept pace with the wheels of most cabs; and the resounding knock and ring he gave at Sir Richard's door in Portland Place, must surely have caused the establishment to think it announced the arrival of a fire-escape.

The door was flung open on the instant, as if to an expected visitor. But that Roland was not the one waited for, was proved by the surprise of the servant. He arrested the further entrance.

"You are not the doctor!"

"Doctor!" said Roland, "I am no doctor. Let me pass if you please. I am Mr. Roland Yorke."

"I beg your pardon, sir," said the man, recognizing the name as one borne by a nephew of the house. "You can go up, sir, of course if you please, but my master is just taken ill. He has got a stroke."

"Bless me!" cried Roland, in concern. "Is it a bad one?"

"I'm afraid it is for death, sir," whispered the man. "We left him at his wine after dinner, all comfortable; and when we went in a few minutes ago, there he was, drawed together so that you couldn't know him, and no breath in his body that we could hear. The nearest doctor's coming, and James is running to fifteen likely places to see if he can find Mr. Vincent."

"I'll go for him; I know where he is," cried Roland. And without further reflection he hailed another hansom that happened to be passing, jumped into it and ordered it to the clubhouse. Vincent was only then coming down the steps. He took Roland's place and galloped home.

"I hope he'll be in time," thought Roland. "Poor old Dick!"

He was not in time. And the next morning London woke up to the news of Sir Richard Yorke's sudden death from an attack of apoplexy. And his son, the third baronet, had succeeded to the family estates and honours as Sir Vincent Yorke.

CHAPTER XXII

A LITTLE MORE LIGHT

Something fresh, though not much, had turned up, relating to the case of the late Mr. Ollivera. That it should do so after so many years had elapsed—or, rather, that it should not have done so before—was rather remarkable. But as it bears very little upon the history in its present stage, it may be dismissed in a chapter.

When John Ollivera departed on the circuit which was destined to bring him his death, a young man of the name of Willett accompanied the bar. He had been "called," but in point of fact only went as clerk to one of the leading counsel. There are barristers and barristers just as there are young men and young men. Mr. Charles Willett had been of vast trouble to his family; and one of his elder brothers, Edmund, who was home from India on a temporary sojourn to recruit his health, had taken up the cause against him rather sharply: which induced a quarrel between them and lasting ill-feeling.

An intimacy had sprung up between Edmund Willett and John Ollivera, and they had become the closest of friends They took a (supposed) final leave of each other when Mr. Ollivera departed on his circuit, for Mr. Willett was on the point of returning to India. His health had not improved, but he was obliged to go back; he was in a merchant's house in Calcutta; and the probabilities certainly were that he would not live to come home again. However, contrary to his own and general expectations, as is sometimes the case the result proved that everybody's opinion was mistaken. He not only did not die, but he grew better, and finally lived: and he had now come to England on business matters. The minute details attendant on John Ollivera's death had never reached him, either through letters or newspapers, and he became acquainted with them for the first time in an interview with the Rev. Mr. Ollivera. When the unfinished letter was mentioned, and the fact that they had never been able to trace out the smallest information as to whom it was intended for Mr. Willett at once said that it must have been intended for himself. He had charged John Ollivera (rather against the latter's will) to carry out, if possible, an arrangement with Charles Willett upon a certain disagreeable matter which had only come recently to the knowledge of his family, and to get that young man's written promise to arrest himself in, at least, one of his downward courses towards ruin. The letter to Mr. Ollivera, urging the request, was written and posted in London on the Saturday; Mr. Ollivera (receiving it on Sunday morning at Helstonleigh) would no doubt see Charles Willett in the course of Monday. That this was the "disagreeable commission" he had spoken of to Mr. Kene, as having been entrusted to him, and which he had left the Court at half-past three o'clock to enter upon, there could be no manner of doubt. Mr. Willett had expected an answer from him on Tuesday morning—it was the last day of his stay in London, for he would take his departure by the Dover mail in the evening—which answer never came. That Mr. Ollivera was writing the letter for the nine o'clock night despatch from Helstonleigh, and that the words in the commencing lines, "should I never see you again," referred solely to Mr. Willett's precarious health, and to the belief that he would not live to return again from India, also appeared to be indisputable. If this were so, why then, the first part of the letter, at any rate, was the sane work of a perfectly sane man, and no more pointed at self-destruction than it did at self-shampooing. The clergyman and Mr. Willett, arriving at this most natural conclusion, sat and looked at each other for a few moments in painful silence. That unexplained and apparently unexplainable letter had been the one sole stumbling-block in Henry William Ollivera's otherwise perfect belief.

But, to leave no loophole of uncertainty, Charles Willett was sought out. When found (with slippers down at heel, a short pipe in his mouth, and a pewter pint-pot at his elbow) he avowed, without the smallest reticence, that John Ollivera's appointment for half-past three on that long-past Monday afternoon in Helstonleigh, had been with him; and that, in answer to Mr. Ollivera's interference in his affairs, he had desired him to mind his own business and to send word to his brother to do the same.

This left no doubt whatever on the clergyman's mind that the commenced letter had been as sensible and ordinary a letter as any man could sit down to pen, and that the blotted words were appended to it by a different hand—that of the murderer.

In the full flush of his newly-acquired information, he went straight to the house of Mr. Greatorex, to pour the story into his uncle's ear. It happened to be the very day alluded to in the last chapter—in the evening of which you had the pleasure of seeing Mr. Roland Yorke industriously putting his shoulder to the wheel, after the ordinary hours of office work were over.

Mr. Greatorex had been slightly discomposed that day in regard to business matters. It seemed to him that something or other was perpetually arising to cause annoyance to the firm. Their connection was on the increase, requiring the unwearied, active energies of its three heads more fully than it had ever done; whereas one of those heads was less efficient in management than he used to be—the second of them, Bede Greatorex. Mr. Greatorex, a remarkably capable man, always had more hard, sterling, untiring work in him than Bede, and he had it still. With his mother's warm Spanish blood, Bede had inherited the smallest modicum of temperamental indolence. As he had inherited (so ran the suspicion), the disease which had proved fatal to her.

"I cannot reproach him as I would," thought Mr. Greatorex, throwing himself into a chair in his room, when he quitted the office for the day, urged to despair almost at this recent negligence, or whatever it was, that had been brought home to them, and which had been traced to some forgetfulness of Bede's. "With that wan, weary look in his face, just as his mother's wore when her sickness was coming on, it goes against me to blow him up harshly, as I should Frank. He must be very ill; he could not, else, look as he does; perhaps already nearly past hope: it was only when she was past hope that she suddenly failed in her round of duties and broke down. And he has one misery that his mother had not—trouble of mind, with that wife of his."

It was at this juncture that Mr. Greatorex was broken in upon by Henry William Ollivera. The clergyman, standing so that the bright slanting rays of the hot evening sun, falling across his face, lighted up its pallor and its suppressed eagerness, imparted the tale that he had come to tell: the discovery that he and Edmund Willett had that day made.

It a little excited Mr. Greatorex. Truth to say, he had always looked upon that unfinished letter as a nearly certain proof that his nephew's death had been in accordance with the verdict of the jury. To him, as well as to the dead man's brother, the apparent impossibility of discovering any cause for its having been penned, or person for whom it could have been intended, had remained the great gulf of difficulty which could not be bridged over.

In this, the first moment of the disclosure, it seemed to him a great discovery. We all know how exaggerated a view we sometimes take of matters, when they are unexpectedly presented to us. Mr. Greatorex went forth, calling aloud for his son Bede: who came down, in return to the call, in dinner attire. As Bede entered, his eye fell on his cousin Henry—or William, as Mr. Greatorex generally liked to call him—whose usually placid countenance was changed by the scarlet hectic on its thin cheeks. Bede saw that something, great or little, was about to be disclosed, and wished himself away again: for some time past he had felt no patience with the fancies and crotchets of Henry Ollivera.

It was Mr. Greatorex who disclosed what there was to tell. Bede received it ungraciously; that is, in spite of disbelieving mockery. Henry Ollivera was accustomed to these moods of his. The clergyman did not resent it openly; he simply stood with his deep eyes fixed watchingly on Bede's face, as if the steady gaze, the studied silence, carried their own reproof.

"I believe, if some wight came down on a voyage from the moon, and fed you with the most improbable fable ever invented by the erratic imagination of man, you would place credence in it," said Bede, turning sharply on Mr. Ollivera.

"Edmund Willett has not come from the moon," quietly spoke the clergyman.

"But Charles Willett—lost man!—is no better than a lunatic in his drinking bouts," retorted Bede.

"At any rate, he was neither a lunatic nor drunk today."

"His story does not hold water," pursued Bede. "Is it likely—is it possible, I should almost say,—that had he been the man with whom the appointment was held that afternoon, he would have kept the fact in until now?—and when so much stir and enquiry were made at the time?"

"Edmund Willett says it is just exactly the line of conduct his brother might have been expected to pursue," said Mr. Ollivera. "He was always of an ill-conditioned temper—morose, uncommunicative. That what Charles Willett says is perfectly true, I am as sure of as I am that I stand hers, You had better see him yourself, Bede."

"To what end?"

"That you may be also convinced."

"And if I were convinced?" questioned Bede, after a pause. "What then?"

"I think the enquiry should be reopened," said Mr. Ollivera, addressing chiefly his uncle. "When I have spoken of pursuing it before, I was always met, both by Butterby and others, with the confuting argument that this letter was in my way. To say the truth, I found it a little so myself always. Always until this day."

"Don't bring up Butterby as an authority, William," interposed Mr. Greatorex. "If Butterby cannot conduct other cases better than he has conducted the one concerning our lost cheque, I'd not give a feather for him and his opinions."

For the purloiner of that cheque remained an undiscovered puzzle; and the house of Greatorex and Greatorex (always excepting one of them) felt very sore upon the point, and showed it.

"William is right, Bede. This discovery removes a mountain of uncertainty and doubt. And if, by ventilating the unhappy affair again we can unfold the mystery that attaches to it, and so clear John's name and memory, it ought to be done."

"But what can be tried, sir, or done, more than has been?" asked Bede, in a tone of reasoning.

"I don't know. Something may be. Of one thing I have felt a conviction all along—that if John's life was rudely taken by man's wicked hand, heaven will in time bring it to light. The old saying, that 'Murder will out,' is a very sure one."

"I do not think it has proved so in every instance," returned Bede, dreamily carrying his recollection backwards. "Some cases have remained undiscovered always."

"Yes, to the world," acquiesced Mr. Greatorex. "But there lies a firm belief in my mind that no man—or woman either—over committed a wilful murder, but someone or other suspected him in their secret heart, and saw him in all his naked, miserable sin."

"Don't bring woman's name in, father. I never like to hear it done."

Bede spoke in the somewhat fractious tone he had grown often to use; that it was but the natural outlet of some inward pain none could doubt. Mr. Greatorex put it down chiefly to bodily suffering.

"Women have done worse deeds than men," was the elder man's answer. And Mr. Ollivera took a step forward.

"Whether man or woman did this—that is, took my dear brother's life—and then suffered the slur to rest on his own innocent self—suffered him to be buried like a dog—suffered his best relatives to think of him as one who had forfeited Heaven's redeeming mercy, I know not," said the clergyman. "But from this time forward, I vow never to slacken heart, or hand, or energy, until I shall have brought the truth to light. The way was long and dark, and seemed hopeless; it might be that I lost patience and grew slack and weary; perhaps this discovery has arisen to reprove me and spur me on."

"But what can you do in it?" again asked Bede.

"Whatever I do in it, I shall not come to you to aid me, Bede," was the reply. "It appears to me—and I have told you this before—that you would rather keep the dark cloud on my brother's name than help to lift it. What had he ever done to you in life that you should so requite him?"

"Heaven knows my heart and wish would be good to clear him," spoke Bede, with an earnestness that approached agitation. "But if I am unable to do it,—if I cannot see how it may be done,—if the power of elucidation does not lie with me—what would you?"

"You have invariably thrown cold water upon every effort of mine. My most earnest purposes you have all but ridiculed."

"No, Henry. I have been sorry, vexed if you will, at what I thought the mistaken view you take up. Over-reiteration of a subject leads to weariness. If I was unable to see any other probable solution than the one arrived at by the coroner and jury, it was not my fault. As to John—if by sacrificing my own life, at any moment since I saw him lying dead, could have restored his, I would willingly have offered it up."

"I beg your pardon, Bede; I spoke hastily," said the man of peace. "Of course I had no right to be vexed that you and others cannot see with my eyes. But, rely upon it, the avowal now made by Charles Willett is true."

"Yes, perhaps it may be," acknowledged Bede.

"William," interrupted Mr. Greatorex, lifting his head after a pause of thought—and his voice had sunk to a whisper. "It could not be that—that—Charles Willett was the one to slink in, and harm him?"

A kind of eager light flashed into the dark eyes of Bede Greatorex, as he turned them on his cousin. If it did not express a belief in the possibility of the suggestion, it at least betrayed that the idea stirred up his interest.

"No," said Mr. Ollivera. "No, no. Charles Willett has not behaved in a straightforward manner over it, but he is cool and open now. He says he has made it a rule for many years never to interfere voluntarily in the remotest degree with other people's business; and therefore he did not mention this until questioned today. Had he never been questioned, he says, he would never have spoken. I cannot understand such a man; it seems to me a positive sin not to have disclosed these facts at the time; but I am sure he tells the whole of the truth now. And now I must wish you good evening, for I have an engagement."

Bede went along the passage with his cousin, and thence was turning to ascend the staircase. His father called him. "What is it?" Bede asked, advancing.

"What is it?—why I want to talk to you about this."

"Another time, father. The dinner's waiting."

"You would go to dinner if the house were falling," spoke Mr. Greatorex, in his hasty vexation.

"Will you not come, sir?"

"No. I don't want dinner. I shall get tea here and a chop with it. Things that are happening worry me, Bede; if they don't you."

Bede went away with a heavy sigh. Perhaps he was more worried, and had greater cause for it too, than his father; but he did not choose to let more of it than he could help be seen.

Guests were at his table this evening, only some three or four; they were bidden by Mrs. Bede, preparatory to going to the opera together. It is more than probable that the suspicion of this assembly of guests kept Mr. Greatorex away.

The dinner was elaborate and expensive as usual. Bede ate nothing. He sat opposite to his wife and talked with the company, and took viand after viand on his plate when handed to him; but only to toy with the morsel for a few moments, and send it away all but untasted. Why did his wife gather around her this continual whirl of gaiety?—he nearly asked it aloud with a groan. Did she want to get rid of care? as, heaven knew, he did. A looker-on, able to dive into Bede's heart, might rather have asked, "Nay, why did he suffer her to gather it?"

The heat of the room oppressed him; the courses were long, but he sat on—on, until quiescence became intolerable. When lights came in he rose abruptly, went to the furthermost window, and threw it wide open. Twilight encompassed the earth with her soft folds; the day's bold garishness was over for at least some welcome hours. A woman was singing in the street below, her barefooted children standing round her with that shrinking air peculiar to such a group, and she turned up a miserable, sickly, famine-stricken face to Bede, in piteous, mute appeal. It was not ineffectual. Whatever his own cares and illness might be, he at least could feel for others. Just as he flung the woman a shilling, his wife came to him in a whisper, whose tone had an unpleasant ring of taunt in it.

"Have you, as usual, the headache, tonight?"

"Headache and heartache, both, Louisa."

"I should suppose so, by your quitting the table. You might have apologized."

"And you might give the house a little rest. How far I am from wishing to complain or interfere unnecessarily, you must know, Louisa; but I declare that this incessant strain of entertaining people will drive me crazy. It is telling upon my nerves. It is telling in a different way upon my father."

"I shall entertain people every day, when I am not engaged out myself," said Mrs. Bede Greatorex. "Take a house for me away, in Hyde Park, or Belgravia; or I'd not mind Portland Place; and then we should not annoy Mr. Greatorex. As long as you are obstinate about the one, I shall be about the other."

Bede seized her hand; partly in anger, partly—as it seemed—in tenderness: and drew her nearer, that she might hear his impressive whisper.

"I am not sure but your wish, that we should quit the house, will be gratified—though not as you expect. My father's patience is being tried. He is the real owner of the house; and at any moment he may say to us, Go out of it. Louisa, I. have thought of mentioning this to you for some little time; but the subject is not a pleasant one."

"I wish he would say it."

"But don't you see the result? You are thinking of a west-end mansion. My means would not allow me to take a dwelling half so good as this one. That's the simple truth, Louisa."

She flung his hand from her with a defiant laugh of power, as she prepared to rejoin the guests. "You might not, but I would."

And Bede knew that to run him helplessly into debt would have been fun, rather than otherwise, to his wife.

Coffee came in at once, and Bede took the opportunity to escape. There was no formal after-dinner sitting this evening, or withdrawal of the ladies. As he passed along the corridor, Miss Channing was standing at the door of the study. He enquired in a kind tone if she wanted anything.

"I am waiting for Mrs. Greatorex—to ask her if I may go for an hour to my brother's," answered Annabel. "Old Dalla will take me."

"Go by all means, if you wish," he said. "Why did you think it necessary to ask? Do make yourself at home with us, Miss Channing, and be as happy as you can."

Annabel thanked him, and he went downstairs, little supposing how very far from happy it was possible for her to be, exposed to all the caprices of his wife. Halting at the door for a moment he wandered across the street, and stood there in the shade, mechanically listening to the ballad woman's singing, wafted faintly from the distance, just as he mechanically looked up at his own lighted windows, and heard the gay laughter that now and again came forth from them.

"I never ought to have married her," said the voice of conscience, breathing its secrets from the cautious depths of his inmost heart. "Every law, human and divine, should have warned me against it. I was infatuated to blindness: nay, not to blindness; I cannot plead that: but to folly. It was very wrong: it was horribly sinful: and heaven is justly punishing me. The fault was mine: I might have kept aloof from her after that miserably eventful night. I ought to have done so; to have held her at more than arm's distance evermore. Ought!—lives there another man on the face of the earth, I wonder, who would not? The fault of our union was mine wholly, not hers; and so, whatsoever trials she brings on me I will bear, patiently, as I best may. I sought her. She would never have dared to seek me, after that night and the discovery I made the day subsequently in poor John's room: and the complication of ill arising, or to arise, from our marriage, I have to answer for. I am nearly tired of the inward warfare: three years of it! Three years and more, since I committed the mad act of tying myself to her for life: for better or for worse: and it has been nothing for me but one prolonged, never-shifting scene of self-repentance. We are wearing a mask to each other: God grant that I may go to my grave without being forced to lift it! For her sake; for her sake!"

He paused to raise his hat from his brow and wipe the sweat that had gathered there. And then he took a step forward and a step backward in the dim shade. But he could not drive away, even for a moment, the care ever eating away his heart, or turn his vision from the threatening shadow that always seemed looming in the distance.

"Of all the wild infatuation that ever took possession of the heart of man for woman, surely mine for Louisa Joliffe was the worst! Did Satan lead me on? It must have been so. 'Be sure your sin shall find you out.' Since that fatal moment when I stood at the altar with her, those ominous words have never, I think, been quite absent from my memory. Every hour of my life, every minute of the day and night as they pass, does my sin find me. Knowing what I did know, could I not have been content to let her go her own way, while I went mine? Heaven help me! for I love her yet, as man rarely has loved. And when my father, or any other, casts a reflection on her, it is worse to me than a dagger's thrust. So long as I may, I will shield her from—"

It was at this moment that the soliloquy, so pregnant with weighty if vague revelation, was broken in upon by Mr. Roland Yorke. Little guessed careless Roland what painful regrets he had put a temporary stop to. Bede, as was previously seen, went indoors, and Roland departed with Miss Channing on her evening visit, dismissing Dalla without the smallest ceremony.

The carriage, to convey Mrs. Bede Greatorex and her friends abroad, drove up. Bede, somewhat neglectful of the rest, came out with his wife, and placed her in it.

"Are you not coming with us?" she bent forward to whisper, seeing he was about to close the door.

"Not tonight. I have some work to do."

"Sulky as usual, Bede?"

His lips parted to retort, but he closed them, and endured meekly. Sulky to her he had never been, and she knew it. The carriage moved away with her: and Bede lifted his hat; a smile, meant to deceive the world, making his face one of careless gaiety.

Whether he had work to do, or not, he did not get to it. Sauntering away from the door, away and away, hardly knowing and not heeding whither, he found himself presently in the Strand, and thence at the river-side. There he paced backwards and forwards with unequal steps, his mind lost in many things, but more especially in the communication made that day by Henry Ollivera.

The fragmentary letter connected with that long-past history, and the appointment spoken of by Mr. Kene, that John Ollivera went out of court to keep, had been as much of a puzzle to Bede Greatorex as it was to other people. Upon reflection, he came now to think that the present solution of the affair was the true one. Would it lead to further discovery? Very fervently he hoped that it would not. There were grave reasons, as none knew better than Bede, for keeping all further discovery back; for, if it came, it would hurl down confusion, dismay, and misery, upon innocent heads as well as guilty ones.

The river, flowing on in its course, was silent and dull in the summer's night. A line of light illumined the sky in the west where the sultry sun had gone down in heat: and as Bede looked towards it and thought of the All-seeing Eye that lay beyond that light, he felt how fruitless it was for him to plot and plan, and to say this shall be or this shall not be. The course of the future rested in the hands of one Divine Ruler, and his own poor, short-sighted, impotent will was worse than nothing.

CHAPTER XXIII

LAID WITH HIS FOREFATHERS

So great a man as Sir Richard Yorke must of course be honoured with a great funeral. He had died on a Thursday; the interment was fixed for the next Friday week: which, taking the heat of the weather and sundry other trifles into consideration, was a little longer than it need have been. Sir Vincent, his new dignity as head of the Yorke family lying upon him with a due and weighty self-importance, was determined (like Jonas Chuzzlewit of wide memory) that the public should see he did not grudge to his late father any honour in the shape of plumes and mutes and coaches and show, that it was in his power to accord to him. There were three costly coffins, one of them of lead, and at the very least three and sixty sets of towering feathers. So that Portland Place was as a gala that day, and windows and pavements were alike filled with sight-gazers.

The Rev. William Yorke, Minor Canon of Helstonleigh Cathedral, Chaplain of Hazledon, and Rector of Coombe Lee, was bidden to it. He was not very nearly related to the deceased (his father and Sir Richard had been second cousins), but he was undoubtedly a rising man in the Church, and Sir Vincent thought fit to remember the connection. The clergyman stood in the relationship of brother-in-law to Hamish Channing; and it was at Hamish's house he stayed during the brief stay—two days—of his sojourn in town.

Another, honoured with an invitation, was Gerald Yorke. Roland was not of a particularly exacting disposition, but he did think he, the eldest, ought not to have been passed over for his younger brother. Oughts don't go for much, however, in some things, as Roland knew. Gerald belonged to the great world: he had, fashionable chambers, fashionable friends, fashionable attire, and a fashionable drawl; his private embarrassments were nothing to Sir Vincent; in fact they might be said to be fashionable too: and so Gerald, the consequential, was bidden to a seat in a mourning-coach, with feathers nodding on the four horses' heads.

Roland was ignored. Not more entirely so than if Sir Vincent had never heard there was such a man in the world. A lawyer's clerk, enjoying a pound a week and a turn-up bedstead, who took copying home to do at twopence a page, and avowed he had just been nearly on the point of turning hot-pie vendor, was clearly not an individual fit to be suffered in contact with a deceased baronet, even though it were only to follow him to the tomb of his forefathers. But, though Roland was not there, his master was Mr. Greatorex. And Mr. Greatorex, as solicitor and confidential man of business to the late Sir Richard, occupied no unimportant post in the procession.

It was late in the afternoon; and the mortal remains, bereft of all their attendant pomp and plumes and scutcheons had been left in their resting-place, when a mourning coach drew up to Mr. Channing's, out of which stepped William and Gerald Yorke. Roland, happening to be there, watched the descent from the drawing-room window side by side with Nelly Channing, and it may be questioned which of the two looked on with the more unsophisticated interest. Mr. Greatorex had not been quite so unmindful of Roland's claims to be considered as Sir Vincent was, and had told him he might take holiday on the day of his uncle's funeral, by remaining away from the office.

Roland obeyed one portion of it literally—the taking holiday. It never occurred to Roland that he might turn the day to profit, by putting his shoulder to the wheel, and his fingers to copying; holiday was holiday, and he took it as such. Rigged out in a handsome new suit of black (made in haste by Lord Carrick's tailor), black gloves, and a band of cloth on his hat, Roland spent the forepart of the day in sightseeing. As many showplaces as could be gone into for nothing, or next to nothing, he went to; beginning with Madame Tussaud's waxwork, for which somebody gave him admission, and ending with a live giantess down in Whitechapel. Late in the afternoon, and a little tired, he arrived at Hamish Channing's, and was rewarded by seeing Annabel. Mrs. Bede Greatorex (gracious that day) had given Miss Channing permission to spend the evening there to meet her sister's husband, the Rev. William Yorke. Hamish, just in from his office, sat with them. Nelly Channing, her nose flattened against the windowpane, shared with Roland the delight of the descent from the coach. Its four black horses and their lofty plumes, struck on the child's mind with a sensation of awe that nearly overpowered the admiration. She wore a white frock with black sash, and had her sleeves tied up with black ribbons. Mrs. Channing, herself in black silk, possessed a large sense of the fitness of things, and deemed it well to put the child in these ribbons today, when two of the mourners would be returning there from the funeral.

They came upstairs, William and Gerald Yorke, and entered the drawing-room, the silk scarves on their shoulders, and the flowing hat-bands of crape sweeping the ground. Nelly backed into a corner, and stood there staring at the attire. It was the first time the clergyman and Roland had met for many years. As may have been gathered during back pages, Roland did not hold his cousin in any particular admiration, but he knew good manners (as he would himself have phrased it) better than to show aught but civility now. In fact, Roland's resentment was very much like that of a great many more of us—more talk than fight. They shook hands, Roland helped him to take off the scarf, and for a few moments they were absorbed in past interests. Whatever Roland's old prejudices might have been he could not deny that the Rev. William Yorke was good-looking as of yore; a tall, slender, handsome man of four-and-thirty now, bearing about him the stamp of a successful one; his fresh countenance was genial and kind, although a touch of the noted Yorke pride sat on it.

That pride, or perhaps a consciousness of his own superiority, for William Yorke was a good man and thought well of himself for it, prevented his being so frankly cordial with Roland as he might have been. Roland's many faults in the old days (as the clergyman had deemed them), and the one great fault which had brought humiliation to him in two ways, were very present to his mind tonight. Slighting remarks made by Gerald on his brother during the day, caused Mr. Yorke to regard Roland as no better than a mauvais sujet, down in the world, and not likely to get up in it. Gerald, on the contrary, he looked upon as a successful and rising man. Mr. Yorke saw only the surface of things, and could but judge accordingly.

"How is Constance?" enquired Roland. "I sent her word not to marry you, you know."

"Constance is well and happy, and charged me to bring you a double share of love and good remembrances," answered the clergyman, slightly laughing.

"Dear old Constance! I say," and Roland dropped his voice to a mysterious whisper, "is not Annabel like her? One might think it the same face."

Mr. Yorke turned and glanced at Annabel—she was talking apart with Gerald. "Yes, there is a good deal of resemblance," he carelessly said, rather preoccupied with marvelling how the young man by his side came to be so well dressed.

Roland, his resentments shallow as the wind, and as fleet in passing, would have shaken hands with Gerald as a matter of course. Gerald managed to evade the honour without any apparent rudeness; he had the room to greet and his silk scarf to unwind, and it really seemed to Roland that it was quite natural he should be overlooked.

"A magnificent funeral," spoke Gerald, glancing askance at Roland's fine suit of mourning, every whit as handsome as his own. "Seven mourning coaches-and-four, and no end of private carriages."

"But I can't say much for their manners, they did not invite me," put in Roland. "I'm older than you, Gerald."

"Aw—ah—by a year or two," croaked Gerald in his worst tone, as to affectation and drawl. "One has, I take it, to—aw—consider the position of a—aw—party on these—aw—occasions, not how old they may be."

"Oh, of course," said Roland, some slight mockery in his good-natured voice. "You are a man of fashion, going in for white-bait and iced champagne, and I'm only an unsuccessful fellow returned like a bad shilling, from Port Natal, and got to work hard for my bread and cheese and beer."

As the hour of William Yorke's return from the funeral was uncertain, but expected to be a late one, it had been decided that the meal prepared should be a tea-dinner—tea and cold meats with it. Gerald was asked to remain for it. A few minutes, and they were seated in the dining-room at a well-spread board, Mrs. Channing presiding; Hamish, with his bright face, his genial hospitality, and his courtly manners, facing her. Roland and Annabel were on one side, the clergyman and Gerald on the other. Miss Nelly, on a high chair, wedged herself in between her mamma and Roland.

"Treason!" cried Hamish. "Who said little girls were to be at table?"

"Mamma did," answered quick Nelly. "Mamma said I should have a great piece of fowl and some tongue."

"Provided you were silent, and not troublesome," put in Mrs. Channing.

"I'll keep her quiet," said Roland. "Nelly shall whisper only to me."

Miss Nelly's answer was to lay her pretty face close to Roland's. He left some kisses on it.

Gerald sat next to Hamish and opposite to Annabel. Remembering the state of that gentleman's feelings towards Mr. Channing, it may be wondered that he condescended to accept his hospitality. Two reasons induced him to it. Any quarters were more acceptable than his own just now, and he had no invitation for the evening, even had it been decent to show himself in the great world an hour after leaving his uncle in the grave. The other reason was, that he was just now working some ill to Hamish, and, wished to appear extra friendly to avert suspicion.

"I hope you have not dined, Roland," remarked Hamish, supplying him with a large plate of pigeon-pie.

"Well, I have, and I've not," replied Roland, beginning upon the tempting viand. "I bought three sausage-rolls at one o'clock, down east way: it would have been my dinner but for this."

Gerald flicked his delicate cambric handkerchief out of his pocket and held it for a moment to his nose, as if he were warding off some bad odour that brought disgust to him. Sausage-rolls! Whether they, or the unblushing candour of the avowal were the worst, he hardly knew.

"Sausage-rolls must be delicacies!" he observed with a covert sneer. And Roland looked across.

"They are not as good as pigeon-pie. But they cost only twopence apiece: and I had but sixpence with me. I have to regulate my appetite according to my means," he added with a pleasant laugh and his mouth full of crust and gravy.

"Roland—as you have, in a manner touched upon the subject—I should like to ask what you think of doing," interposed William Yorke, in a condescending but kindly tone. "You seem to have no prospects whatever."

"Oh I shall get along," cheerfully answered Roland with a side glance at Miss Channing. "Perhaps you'll see me in housekeeping in a year's time from this."

"In housekeeping!"

"Yes: with a house of my own—and, something else. I'm not afraid. I have begun to put my shoulder to the wheel in earnest. If I don't get on, it shall not be from lack of working for it."

"How have you begun to put your shoulder to the wheel?"

"Well—I take home copying to do in my spare time after office hours. I have been doing it in earnest over three weeks now."

"And how much do you earn at it weekly?" continued William Yorke.

A slight depression from its bright exultation passed over Roland's ingenuous face. Hamish saw it, and laughed. Hamish was quite a confidant, for Roland carried to him all his hopes and their tiresome drawbacks.

"I can tell you: I added it up," said Roland. "Taking the three weeks on the average, it has been two-and-twopence a week."

"Two-and-twopence a week!" echoed William Yorke, who had expected him (after the laudatory introduction) to say at least two pounds two. Roland detected the surprise and disappointment.

"Oh, well, you know, William Yorke, a fellow cannot expect to make pounds just at first. What with mistakes, when the writing has to be begun all over again, and the paying for spoilt paper, which Brown insists upon, two-and-twopence is not so much amiss. One has to make a beginning at everything."

"Are you a good hand at accounts?" enquired Mr. Yorke, possibly in the vague notion that Roland's talents might be turned to something more profitable than the copying of folios.

"I ought to be," said Roland. "If the counting up, over and over and over again, of those frying-pans I carried to Port Natal, could have made a man an accountant, it must have made one of me. I used to be at it morning and evening. You see, I thought they were going to sell for about eight-and-twenty shillings apiece, out there: no wonder I often reckoned them up."

"And they did not!"

"Law, bless you! In the first place nobody wanted frying-pans, and I had to get a Natal store-keeper to house them in his place for me—I couldn't leave them on the quay. But the time came that I was obliged to sell them: they were eating their handles off."

"With rust, I suppose."

"Good gracious, no! with rent, not rust. The fellow (they are regular thieves, over there) charged me an awful rent: so I told him to put them into an auction. Instead of the eight-and-twenty shillings each that I had expected to get, he paid me about eight-and-twenty pence for the lot, case and all. But if you ask whether I am a ready reckoner, William Yorke, I'm sure I must be that."

The Rev. William Yorke privately thought there might be a doubt upon the point. He fancied Roland's present prospects could not be first-rate.

"The copying is nothing but a temporary preliminary," observed Roland. "I am waiting to get a place under Government. Vincent Yorke I expect can put me up for one, now he has come into power; and I don't think he'll want the will, though he did pass me over today."

If ever face expressed condemnatory contempt, Gerald's did, as he turned it fall on his brother. For, this very hope was being cherished by himself. It was he who intended to profit by the interest of Sir Vincent, to be exerted on his behalf. And to have a rival in the same field, although one of so little account as Roland, was not agreeable.

"The best thing you can do, is to go off again to Port Natal," he said roughly. "You'll never get along here."

"But I intend to get along, Gerald. Once let me have a fair start—and I have never had it yet—there's not many shall distance me."

"What do you call a fair start?" asked Mrs. Channing, who always enjoyed Roland's sanguine dreams.

"A place where I can bring my abilities into use, and be remunerated accordingly. I don't ask better than to work, and be paid for it. Only let me earn a couple of hundreds a year to begin with, Mrs. Channing, and you'd never hear me ask Vincent Yorke or anybody else for help again."

"You had not used to like the prospect of work, Roland," spoke William Yorke.

"But then I had not had my pride and laziness knocked out of me at Port Natal."

William Yorke lifted his eyes. "Did that happen to you?"

"It did," emphatically answered Roland. "Oh, I shall get into something good by-and-by, where my talents can find play. Of all things, I should best like a farm."

"A farm!"

"A nice little farm. And if I had a few hundred pounds, I'd take one tomorrow. Do you know anything of butter-making, Annabel?" he stopped to ask, dropping his voice.

Annabel bent her blushing face over her plate, and pretended not to hear. Roland thought she was offended.

"I didn't mean make it, you know," he whispered; "I'd not like to see you do such a thing"—bringing his face back again to the general company. "But it's of little good thinking of a farm, you see, William Yorke, when there's no money to the fore."

"You don't know anything of farming," said Mr. Yorke, inwardly wondering whether this appeal to Annabel had meant anything, or was only one of Roland's thoughtless interludes of speech.

"Don't I?" said Roland; "I was on one for ever so long at Port Natal, and had to drive pigs. It is astonishing the sight of experience a fellow picks up over there, and the little he learns to live upon."

"Because he has to do it, I suppose."

"That's the secret. I am earning a pound a week now, regular pay, and make it do for all my wants. You'd not think it, would you, William Yorke?"

"Certainly not, to look at you," said William Yorke, with a smile. "Are clothes included?"

"Oh, Carrick goes bail for all that. I'm afraid he'll find the bills running up; but a fellow, if he's a gentleman, must look decent. I'm as careful as I can be, and sit in my shirtsleeves at home when it's hot."

"Lady Augusta has visions of your walking about London streets in a coat out at elbows. I think it troubles her."

Roland paused, stared, and then started up in impulsive contrition, nearly pulling off the table-cloth.

"What a thoughtless booby I was, never to let her know! The minute you get down home, you go to her, William Yorke. Tell her how it is—that I have the run of Carrick's people for clothes, boots, hats, and all the rest of it. This suit came home at eight this morning, with an apology for not sending it last night— the fellow thought I might be going to the funeral—and a sensible thought too! Look at it!" stretching out his arms, and turning himself about, that Mr. Yorke might get a comprehensive view of the superfine frock-coat and silken linings. "I'm never worse dressed than this: only that my things are not on new every day. You tell the mother this, William Yorke."

He had not done it in vanity; of that Roland possessed as little as any one; but in eager, earnest desire to reassure his mother, and atone to her for his ungrateful forgetfulness. Stooping for his table napkin, he at down again.

"Yes, I am well-dressed, though I do have to work. And for recreation, there's this house to come to; and dear old Hamish and Mrs. Channing receive me with gladness and make much of me, just as though I had always been good, and Nelly jumps into my arms."

"When do you mean to come to Helstonleigh?"

"Never," answered Roland, with prompt decision. "As I can't go back as I wanted to—rich—I shall not go at all. What I wish to ask is, when Arthur Channing is coming up here?"

"Arthur Channing! I cannot tell."

"It is a shame of people to get a fellow's hopes up, and then damp them. Arthur wrote me word—oh, a month ago—that he was coming to London on business for old Galloway. Close nearly upon that, comes a second letter, saying Galloway was not sure that he should require to send him. I should like to serve him out."

William Yorke smiled. "Serve out Arthur?"

"Arthur! I'd like to draw Arthur round the old city in a car of triumph, as we used to chair our city members. I mean that wretch of a Galloway. He ought to be taken up for an impostor. Why did he go and tell Arthur he should send him to London, if he didn't mean to?"

Gerald Yorke let his fork fall in a semi-passion, and nearly chipped the beautiful plate of Worcester china: was all the conversation to be monopolised by Roland and his miserable interests? It was high time to interfere. Picking up the fork with an air, he cleared his throat.

"Sir Vincent comes into about four thousand a-year, entailed property. We went in to hear the will read by old Greatorex. It's not much, is it?"

"Not to one reared to the notions Vincent Yorke has been," said Hamish. "But he has more than that, I presume?"

"Some odds and ends, I believe: I asked Greatorex. And there's the little homestead down in Surrey. Sir Richard's liabilities die with him. Perhaps he had wiped them off beforehand?"

"I'm sure he had," said Roland, with good-natured warmth. "Oh, we hear a good deal in our office. As to four thousand a-year being little for one man, you should have been at Port Natal, Gerald, and you'd estimate it differently."

"To a man about town, like myself, it seems a starvation pittance, considering what Sir Vincent will have to do out of it," returned Gerald loftily, speaking to any at table, rather than to his brother.

"That's just it," said Roland. "If I were a man about town, and had not been out to Port Natal and learnt the value of money, it might seem so to me. Dick won't find it enough, I daresay. I should think a rent of four hundred a-year riches!"

Gerald curled his lip. "No doubt; and some pigs to drive."

"I'd like a pig, Roland," cried Nelly Channing, turning to him, and unconsciously creating a diversion. "A pretty little pig, with blue ribbons."

"As pretty as you," said Roland, squeezing her. "You mean a guinea-pig, little stupid. As to driving pigs, Gerald—it's not a very good employment of course; but you see I had to do what I was put to—or starve."

"I'd rather starve than do it," retorted Gerald. "And so would any one with the instincts of a gentleman."

"You only go out there and try what starving is; you'd t good-humour ell a different tale," said Roland, maintaining his good-humour. "Starving there means starving."

Some one of those turns in conversation, which occur so naturally, brought round the subject to Mr. Ollivera. Roland, imparting sundry revelations of his home-life at Mrs. Jones's—or, as he called her still, Mrs. Jenkins—mentioned the clergyman's name.

"Don't you mean to call and see him?" he asked of William Yorke. "You'd better."

But Mr. Yorke declined. "My time in London is so very short," he said; "I go home tomorrow. Besides, I have really no acquaintance with Mr. Ollivera. We never met but on one occasion."

"When you lent him your surplice," spoke Roland. And William Yorke looked up in surprise.

"What do you know about it?"

"Oh, I know a great deal," returned Roland. "I say—why did you not attend that night yourself? You promised."

"I did not promise. All I said was that I would consider of it. Upon reflection, I thought it better not to go. The circumstances were very peculiar; and the Dean, had he come to know of it, might have taken me to task."

"Not he," said independent Roland. "The Dean's made of sterling gold."

"What sort of a chanter does Tom make?" enquired Hamish.

"Very fair; very fair, indeed," replied William Yorke, some patronage in his tone, meant for the absent young minor canon. Consciously vain of his own excellence in chanting, Mr. Yorke could but accord comparative praise to Tom Channing's. The vanity was not without cause; Mr. Yorke's sweet and sonorous voice was wont to fill the aisles of the old cathedral with its melody.

Just as the tea was over, one of the servants came in with a folded weekly review hot from the press on her silver waiter, and presented it to her master. Hamish opened it with a slight apology, and was glancing at its pages, when he folded it again with a sudden movement and quietly put it in his pocket. His sight, in the moment's happy confusion, partially faded; a bright hectic lighted his cheek; his whole heart leaped up within him, as with a rushing, blissful sense of realized hope. For he had seen that a review of his book was there.

CHAPTER XXIV

AS IRON INTO THE SOUL

The change in his face was remarkable. It was as though a blight had passed over it and withered the hopeful life out.

He sat with the journal in his hand—the authoritative "Snarler"—and read the cruel lines over and over again. When, in the solitude of his own study, they first met his eager eye, skimming them rapidly, and their purport was gathered in almost at a glance, a kind of sick faintness seized upon his heart, and he hastily put away the paper as though it were some terrible thing he dared not look further upon.

The shock was awful—and the word is not used in its often light sense; the disappointment something not to be described. After the departure of his guests, Roland and Gerald, and William Yorke had gone by his own wish to take home Annabel and to make a late call on Mrs. Bede Greatorex—if haply that fashionable dame might be found at home—Hamish Channing had passed into his study; and, there, alone with himself and his emotions, he once more unfolded the paper. All the while he had sat with it in his pocket, a sweet tumultuous hope had been stirring his bosom; he could hardly forbear, in his eagerness to realize it, telling them to make haste and depart. And when they were really going, it seemed that they were a month over it. He stood up wishing them goodnight.

"By the way, Hamish, I should think your book would soon be getting its reviews," spoke crafty Gerald, who had seen the journal brought in, and knew what was in it. "I hope you'll get good ones, old fellow."

And the wish was spoken with so much apparent genuineness, the tone of the voice had in it so vast an amount of gushing feeling, that Hamish gratefully wrung the offered hand. After that, even had he been of a less ingenuous nature, he would have suspected the whole world of abusing his book, rather than Gerald Yorke.

Shut up in his study, the lamp beside him, he unfolded the paper with trembling expectation, his heart beating with happiness. It was one of those moments, and they come in all our lives, which must stamp itself on the memory for ever. He looked, and looked. And then put the pages away in a kind of terror.

Never, in this age of bitter reviews, had a more bitter one than that been penned. But for his intense unsuspicion, for his own upright single-mindedness, he might possibly have recognized Gerald Yorke's slashing style. Gerald, as its writer, never once occurred to him. After awhile, when the first brunt of the shock had passed—and it was almost as a shock of death—he took up the paper again, and read the article through.

His hair grew damp with perspiration; his face burnt with a hot shame. With this apparently candid, but most damnatory review before his eyes, it seemed to him that his book must be indeed bad. The critique was ably written, and it attacked him from all sides and on all points. Gerald Yorke had taken pains with that as he had never taken pains with any article before. It had been, so to say, days in construction. One portion would be altered today, one tomorrow; and the result was that it told. The chief characteristic of the whole was sarcastic mockery. The scholarship of the book was attacked, (and that scholarship—that is, of its writer—formed the chief point of envy in a covert corner of Gerald's heart); its taste, its style, its every thing. The pen had been steeped five fathoms deep in gall. Rounded periods spoke of the work's utter worthlessness, and affectionately warned the public against reading it, with quite fatherly care. It called the author an impudent upstart; it demanded to know what he meant by fostering such a book on the public; it wondered how he had found a publisher; it almost prayed the gods, that preside over literary careers, to deliver unhappy readers from James Channing. Abuse and ridicule; ridicule and abuse; they rang the changes one upon another. Hamish read; he turned back and read again; and the fatal characters burnt themselves into his brain as with a ruthless fire.

What a reward it was! Speaking only as a recompense for his devotion and labour, leaving aside for the moment the higher considerations, how cruel was the return! The devoted lad, read of in history, concealed a fox in his bosom, and it repaid him by gnawing at his vitals. That reward was not more remorselessly cruel than this. Where was the use of Hamish Channing's patient industry, his persevering endurance, his burning the midnight candle, to bring forth this fruit? To what end the never-ceasing toil and care? While Gerald Yorke had been flourishing in society, Hamish Channing was toiling. Burning his candles, so to say, at both ends! The unwearied industry, the patient continuance in labour, the ever-buoyant, trustful hope!—all had been his.

Does the public realize what it is, I wonder, to exercise this brain-work day by day, and often also night by night, week after week, month after month, year after year? A book is put into the hands of a reading man—or say a woman, if you will—and he devours it with ardour or coolness, more or less of either as the case may be, and makes his comments afterwards with complaisance, and says the book is a nice book, and seems almost to think it has been brought out for his special delectation. But does he ever cast a reflection on the toil that book has cost the writer? Does he look up to him with even a thought of gratitude? Generally speaking, no. In the midst, perhaps, of very adverse circumstances, of long-continued sickness, of headache, heartache, many aches; when the inward spirit is fainting at life's bitter troubles, and it would seem in vain to struggle more, the labour must yet be done. Look at Hamish Channing—his is no ideal case. His day's work over, he got to his work—the night's—and wrote on, until his mind and body were alike weary. While others played, he toiled; when others were abroad at their banquetings and revellings, idling away their hours in what the world calls society, and Gerald Yorke making one amidst them, he was shut up in his room, labouring on persistently. And this was his reward!

The best energies of his power and intellect had Hamish Channing given to the book: the great gift of genius, which had certainly been bestowed largely upon him, was exercised and brought to bear. No merit to him for that; he could not help exercising it. It appeared to him, this writing for his fellow men, to be the one special end for which he was sent into the world—where every man has his appointed and peculiar aptitude for someone calling or duty, though it happens that a vast many never find out their own until too late. A man reared, as had been James Channing, to good; anxious to live here in the single-minded fulfilment of every duty, using the world only as a passage to a better, can but write as a responsible agent; whether he may be working at a religious tract or a story of fiction, he does it as to his Creator, imploring day by day that he may be helped in it. Had Hamish been required to write without that sense of responsibility upon him, he would have put aside his pen.

And the disappointment! the rude, pitiless, condemning shock! It might be that such was necessary; that it had been sent direct from heaven. The least sinful man on earth may have need of such discipline.

Again Hamish read the article from beginning to end. Read, and re-read it. It was as if the lines possessed the fatal fascination of the basilisk, attracting him against his will. He writhed under the executioner's knife, while he submitted to it. The book was a good and brilliant work, betraying its genius in every line, well conceived, well plotted, ably written. It was one of those that take the whole imagination of the reader captive; one that a man is all the better for reading, and rises up from with a subdued spirit, hushed breath, and a glowing heart. While enchaining man's deepest interest, it yet insensibly led his thoughts to Heaven. Simple though it was in its pure Saxon diction, its sentiments were noble, generous, and exalted. Not a thought was there to offend, not a line that, for its parity, might not have been placed in the hands of his child. Modest, as all gifted with true genius are, yet possessing (for that must always be), a latent consciousness of his great power, Hamish had looked forward for success to his book, as surely as he looked for Heaven. That it could be a failure, he had simply never thought of; that it should be badly received, ridiculed, condemned, written down, had not entered his imagination. Had he been told such might be the result, he would have quietly answered that it was impossible.

In all matters where the minds and feelings, the inward, silent hopes and fears, are deeply touched, it cannot be but that we are sensitively alive to the opinions of our fellow men, and swayed by their judgment. As Hamish Channing read and re-read, learning the cruel sentences almost by rote, his heart failed within him. For the time being, he thought he must have erred in supposing the book so good; that it must be a foolish and mistaken book, deserving only of their sharp criticism; and a sense of humiliation, than which nothing could be more intensely painful, took possession of his spirit.

But the belief could not remain. The mood changed again. The book resumed nearly its estimated place in his mind, and the sense of humiliation was superseded by the smarting conviction of cruel injustice. What had he or his book done that they should be so reviled?

"Lord, thou knowest all things! surely I have not deserved this!" irrepressibly broke from the depths of his anguish.

No, he had not deserved it. As some others have not, who yet have had to bear it. It is one of the world's hard lessons, one that very few are appointed to learn. Injustice and evil and oppression exist in the world, and must exist until its end. Only then shall we understand wherefore they are permitted. Pardon, reader, if a line or two seem to be repeated. The many months of toil, the patient night-labour, that but for the hope-spring rising in the buoyant heart might have been found too wearing; the self-denial ever exercised; the weary night watching and working—all had been thrown back upon Hamish Channing, and rendered, as it were, nugatory. Try and picture to yourselves what this labour is; its aspirations of reward, its hopes of appreciation—and for a wickedly disposed man, or simply a carelessly indifferent man, or a vain, presumptuous man, or a man who has some petty spite to gratify against author or publisher, or a rival reviewer, or a man that writes but in wanton idleness, to dash it down with a few strokes of a pen!

Such things have been. They will be again. But if Gerald Yorke, and others like him, would consider how they violate the divine law of enjoined kindness, it might be that the pen would now and then pause.

Would Gerald have to answer for it at the Great Day of Reckoning? Ah, that is a question very little thought of; one perhaps difficult to answer. He had set himself deliberately in his foolish envy, in his ill-conditioned spirit, to work ill to Hamish Channing: to put down and write down the book that he knew was depended on to bring back its return, that was loved and cherished almost as life. It was within the range of possibility that he might work more ill than he bargained for. Heaven is not in the habit of saying to man by way of reminder when he gets up in a morning, "I am looking at you:" but it has told us such a thing as that every secret word and thought and action shall be brought to light, whether it be good or whether it be evil. Gerald ignored that, after the fashion of this busy world; and was perfectly self-complacent under the ignoring.

Only upon such a mind as Hamish Channing's, with his nervous attributes of genius, his refined sensitiveness, could the review have brought home its worst bitterness. Fortunately such minds are very rare. Gerald Yorke had little conception of the extent of its fruit. He would have set on and sworn off his anger, and called the writer, who could thus stab in the dark, a false coward, and sent him by wishes to all kinds of unorthodox places, and vowed aloud to his friends that he should like to horsewhip or shoot him. Thus the brunt, with him, would have been worked off; never so much as touched the vital feelings, if Gerald possessed any. It was another thing with Hamish Channing. He could almost have died, rather than have spoken of the attack to any living man; and if forced to it, as we are sometimes forced to unwelcome things, it would have brought the red blush of shame to his sensitive brow, to his shrinking spirit.

He sat on; on, with his aching heart. One hand was pressed upon his chest: a dull pain had seated itself there. Never again, as it seemed to him, should he look up from the blow. More and more the cruelty and the injustice struck upon him. Does it so strike upon you, reader? The book was not perfection (I never met with one that was, in spite of what the reviews chose to affirm of Mr. Gerald Yorke's), but it was at least written in an earnest, truthful spirit, to the utmost of the abilities God had given him. How had it invoked this requital? Hamish pondered the question, and could not answer it. What had he done to be shown up to the public; a butt for any, that would, to pitch scorn at? There was no appeal; there could be no redress. The book had been held forth to the world—at least to the thousands of it that would read the "Snarler"—as a bad and incapable book, one they must avoid as the work of a miserably presumptive and incapable man.

A slight movement in the next room, and Mrs. Channing came in with Nelly. Miss Nelly, in consideration of the late substantial tea, had not been sent to bed at the customary hour. Hamish slipped the review inside his table-desk, and greeted them with a smile, sweet-tempered as ever under the blow. But his wife saw that some change lay on his face.

"Is anything the matter, Hamish? You look—worn; as if you had received some ill news."

"Do I? I am a little tired, Ellen. It has been very hot today."

"I thought you were not going to work tonight."

"Oh, I'm not working. Well, young lady, what now?"

Miss Nelly had climbed on his knees. She had been brought in to say goodnight.

"When's the ship coming home, papa?"

He suddenly bent down and hid his face on the child's bright one. Heaven alone knew what the moment's suffering was and how he contrived not to betray it.

"Will it come tomorrow, papa?"

"We shall see, darling. I don't know."

The subdued, patient tone had something of hopelessness in it. Mrs. Channing thought he must be very tired.

"Come, Nelly," she said. "It is late, you know."

He kissed the child tenderly as ever, but so quietly, and whispered a prayer for God to bless her; his tone sounding like one of subdued pain, almost as though his heart were breaking. And Nelly went dancing out, talking of the ship and the good things it was to bring.

Quite immediately, a gentleman was shown in. It was the publisher of the book. Late though the hour was, he had come in some perturbation, bringing a copy of the "Snarler."

"Have you any enemy, Mr. Channing?" was nearly the first question he asked, when he found Hamish had seen the article.

"Not one in the wide world, so far as I know."

"The review of your book is so remarkably unjust, so entirely at variance with fact and truth, that I should say only an enemy could have done it," persisted the publisher. "Look, besides, at the rancour of its language, its evident animus; I scarcely ever read so aggravated an attack."

But still Hamish could only reiterate his conviction. "I have no enemy."

"Well, it is a great pity; a calamity, in short. When once an author's reputation is made and he is a favourite with the public, bad reviews cannot harm him: but to a first book, where the author is unknown, they are sometimes fatal."

"Yes, I suppose they are," acquiesced Hamish.

"We must wait now for the others, Mr. Channing. And hope that they will be the reverse of this. But it is a sad thing—and, I must say, a barefaced injustice."

Nothing more could be said, nothing done. The false review was in the hands of the public, and Hamish and his publisher were alike powerless to arrest or remedy the evil. The gentleman went out, leaving Hamish alone.

Alone with his blow and its anguish. He felt like one who, living all night in a sweet dream, has been rudely awakened to some terrible reality. The sanguine hopes of years were dashed away; life's future prospects had broken themselves up. If ever the iron entered into the soul of man, it had surely passed into that of James Channing.

The injustice told upon him worse than all; the unmerited stab-wound would damage him for aye. In his bosom's bitter strife, he almost dared to ask how men could be permitted thus to prey one upon another, and not be checked by Heaven's lightning. But, to that there might be no answer: others have asked it before him.

"So I returned, and considered all the oppressions that are done under the sun: and behold the tears of such as were oppressed, and they had no comforter; and on the side of their oppressors there was power: but they had no comforter. Wherefore I praised the dead which are already dead more than the living which are yet alive."

Involuntarily, with a strange force, these words passed through the mind of James Channing.

But the wise King of Israel—and God had given him more than earthly wisdom—could give no explanation of why this should be.

PART THE THIRD

CHAPTER XXV

DURING THE AUTUMN

This must be called the third part of the story, if we may reckon the short commencing prologue as the first. The year had gone on to October, and that month was quickly passing.

The lapse of time, some three or four months, had not brought any change worth recording: people and things were in the main very much in the position that they had been: but a slight summary of progress must be given.

Bede Greatorex had been on the wing. In early August he went abroad with his wife, choosing Switzerland as his first halting-ground. Bede had proposed some place (if that could be found) less frequented by the English; and Mrs. Bede had retorted that if he wanted to vegetate in an outlandish desert, he might go to it alone. In the invariable kindness and consideration Bede observed to her, even to her whims, he yielded: and they went off in the commotional wake of a shoal of staring tourists, with another commotional shoal behind them.

Mr. Greatorex it was who had insisted on the holiday for Bede. "You are getting more incapable of hard work every day," he plainly said to him: "a rest will, I hope, restore you; and take it you must." Bede yielded. That he was very much in need of a change of some sort, he knew. And of rest also—if he could only get it. But the latter might be more hard to obtain than Mr. Greatorex suspected or imagined.

So they went to Switzerland first: Bede and his wife, and her maid Tallet. Bede thought the party would have been a vast deal more compact and comfortable without the lady's-maid, not to speak of the additional expense, and he gently hinted as much. The hint was quite lost on Mrs. Bede, who took not the smallest notice of it. In point of fact, that lady (besides being incorrigibly idle, never doing an earthly thing for herself) had absolute need of artistic aid in the matter of making-up: face and shape and hair and attire alike requiring daily renovation. From Switzerland they went rushing about to other places, not at all necessary to note, and got back home the middle of October, after rather more than two months' absence; being followed by nearly a fourgon of fashions from Paris: for that seductive capital had been their last resting-place, and Mrs. Bede had found its magazins as seductive as itself. Bede winced at the cheques he had to give.

Mr. Greatorex started with alarm when he saw his son. They got home at night, having come up by the tidal train from Folkestone, which had been somewhat delayed in consequence of the boat's rough passage. During their absence, it had been the quietest and happiest home imaginable: Mr. Greatorex, Annabel Channing, and the little girl forming it; Frank Greatorex having holiday as well as Bede. For visitors they had Henry William Ollivera and Roland Yorke, one or the other dropping in to tea twice or thrice a week. Mr. Greatorex was a very father to Annabel; and Miss Jane, subjected to regularity and desirable influences only, was on her best behaviour. The old lawyer, in the happy quiet, the relief conferred by the absence of noise and Mrs. Bede, thought the good old times must be coming back again.

All three were sitting together in the drawing-room when Bede and his wife got in. The chandelier's rays flashed full on Bede's face, and Mr. Greatorex started. Far from his son's having derived benefit from the prolonged tour, he looked worse than ever; his cheeks hollow and hectic, his face altogether worn. Perhaps for the first time it struck Mr. Greatorex, as he glanced from one to the other, that she likewise looked thin and worn, with restless eyes and hollow cheeks, hectic also. But in the hectic there was this difference: Bede's was natural, hers was put on. What would they have been without the rouge?

Bede said he was better. When Mr. Greatorex spoke seriously to him on the following morning, recommending that there should be a consultation, Bede laughed. He declared that the rest from business had done him an immense deal of good. Thin? Oh of course he was thin. So was Louisa—did Mr. Greatorex not notice it?—Tallet was the same, for the matter of that: they had gone whirling about from place to place, a little too fast, he supposed, making a toil of pleasure. And then the dreadful sea passage!—of course they looked the worse last night, but they were both all right this morning.

So spoke Bede, and went to work with a will: really with some of his old energy. He appeared fresh and tolerably well after the night's rest; and Mr. Greatorex felt reassured.

Gerald Yorke was another who had taken holiday. Gerald had managed to get an invitation to cruise in the Honourable Mr. Fuller's yacht; and Gerald, with two or three other invited guests, went careering off in it for the space of six weeks. Before starting, he had fully accomplished his reviewing work with regard to Hamish Channing's book—but that can be left until later. Gerald enjoyed himself amazingly. The yacht put into foreign ports on occasion, and they got a few days' land cruise. The honourable owner treated his friends right royally, and Gerald had not felt so much at ease since he was a boy. By a slice of luck, which Gerald hardly believed in at the time, he had induced Vincent Yorke to lend him fifty pounds before starting, and he thought himself laudably generous in dividing this with his wife.

"Now mind, Winny," he said to her on the morning of his departure, "I shall be away about five weeks. It can't take you five pounds a week to live and pay rent, so I shall expect you to have a good sum in hand when I get back. I'll drop you a letter now and then, but you'll not be able to write to me, as we shall be moving about from place to place just as the wind or mood takes us."

Therefore, on the score of his wife and children, Gerald was entirely at ease; and he quite expected, after his charge to Winny, that she would have something like eight or ten pounds left of the twenty-five; at least, that she ought to have. He was out of reach of creditors too; the future he did not allow to trouble him (he never did), and Gerald gave himself wholly up to the enjoyment of the present.

Little did Gerald Yorke suspect, as he leaned over the side of the yacht in seductive indolence, smoking his cigar and sipping his iced Burgundy, that poor Winny's money had come to an end before the second week was over. It might not have cost him a single moment's care if he had known it, for Gerald was one upon whom no earthly person's trouble made the smallest impression, unless it touched him personally. Effectually out of the way himself, Winny might just have done as she best could. Gerald would have wished he was at hand to tell her she deserved a shaking for her folly, and dismissed the matter from his mind.

The way the money went so soon, was this. Gerald's man-servant in chambers, just as glad as his master to get a respite from troublesome creditors, who went well nigh to wear his patience out, informed one of that ill-used body of men where Mr. Gerald Yorke had gone, on the very day following the departure—"Cruising over the sea in a lord's yacht to foreign parts, and likely to be away till winter." Of course this struck the applicant dumb. He happened to know that Gerald Yorke had a wife and family in town, and he set himself forthwith to learn their address; which he found not very difficult of accomplishment. His own debt was not a very heavy one, rather short of six pounds. Down he went, demanded an interview with Mrs. Yorke, and so scared her senses away by insisting upon instant payment there and then, that Winny handed out the money. Other creditors got to know of this; they went down too, and insisted upon the same prompt payment on their score. Winny had many virtues no doubt, but there was one she could certainly not boast of—courage. In all that related to debt and its attendant annoyances, she was timid as a fawn. To be pressed for an account and not pay it if she had the money in her possession, was simply impossible to Winifred Yorke. But this I think has been hinted at before. When the last fraction of the twenty-five pounds had left her (in a payment of four pounds ten to a stern-looking, but by no means abusive man). Winny burst into tears: saying aloud she did not expect her husband home for weeks, did not know where to write to him, and had not a sixpence left for herself and her poor little children. Upon that the man put the half-sovereign back into Mrs. Yorke's hand without a word, and departed.

So there was Winny, literally without a sixpence, save for this ten shillings, and Gerald not quite two weeks gone. But for Hamish Channing and his wife, she might really have starved; most certainly she would have been turned out of doors; for the landlady, nearly tired of Mr. Gerald Yorke's uncertain finances, had never kept her. Miss Cook said she could not afford to let rooms and get no rent; and no doubt that was true. Away went Winny with her grief and helplessness to Mrs. Channing. It was an awkward dilemma, an embarrassing appeal, and Ellen Channing felt it as such. On the one hand there was this poor helpless woman, and her not much more helpless children: on the other, Ellen was aware that Hamish had already aided her far more extensively than he could afford.

Oh, it was true. Many and many a little luxury (Gerald would have called it a necessary) that Hamish required in his failing health—for it had begun to fail—did he debar himself of for the sake of Gerald Yorke's wife and children. His heart ached for them. He took not the smallest pleasure, he often walked where he ought to have rode, he would eat breed and cheese for his lunch, or a dry roll where he should have had a chop, that he might give the saved money to Mrs. Yorke. In those golden dreams of fame and fortune, when his book was approaching completion, and the realization of its returns had apparently been drawing very near (months ago now, it seemed to be, since they were dreamt out), Hamish had cherished a little delightful plot: of setting Gerald on his legs again anonymously—of putting him straight with the world, and perhaps something over, that he might see his way at least a little clearer towards a more satisfactory state of household matters for himself and Winny jointly. This had been frustrated through the book's being written down, as already partially told of, and a corner of the grief in Hamish Manning's weary heart was sighing itself out for Gerald's sake. Hamish said not a word of the disappointment to a living soul—we are speaking now in regard to Gerald—Ellen had been his sole confidant, and he did not allude to it even to her. To Hamish, it seemed that there was only the more necessity for helping Gerald, in administering to the necessities of his forsaken wife.

And Gerald's wife had invented a pleasant fable. As the weeks went on after Winny came to London, it was not possible but that Gerald should see someone must help her with money. Put to it for an excuse, one day that Gerald asked the question point blank, and not daring to say it was Hamish or Ellen Channing, Winny declared it was her mother. Gerald stared a little. Mrs. Eales lived somewhere down in Wales, and existed on an annuity of sixty pounds a-year. But though he wondered how the good old mère contrived to help Winny so much, or in fact at all, he inquired no farther. She might be reducing herself to a crust and a glass of water a day; might be, for aught he knew, forestalling her income wholesale; Gerald was complacently content to let it be so.

And thus matters had been going on: Winny in want always, and Hamish taxing himself and his needs to help her. In September, the office he served offered him a fortnight's holiday, thinking he looked as if he required it. Hamish thanked them, but declined. He had no spirits for taking holiday, and the helping of Gerald's family left him no funds for it.

And when Winny burst into Mrs. Channing's one afternoon, with this last confession, that she was utterly penniless, save for the half-sovereign the man threw back, and should be so until Gerald came home, weeks hence, telling it in the hearing of her three little girls, her face woe-begone, her tears and sobs fit to choke her, Ellen Channing felt annoyed and vexed. Mixed with her compassion for Gerald's wife, there was a feeling that they had already done more for her than they were justified in doing. Ellen would have liked the fortnight's holiday very much indeed on her own score. A suspicion had begun to dawn upon her that her husband was not so strong as he might be, and one morning she spoke to him. It was only the London heat that made him feel weak, Hamish answered, perhaps really thinking so. Very well, argued Ellen, then there was all the more necessity for getting out of it to the seaside for a change. And he would have been glad enough to take the change had funds allowed it. Considering that the small amounts of help incessantly applied to the need of Mrs. Gerald Yorke would have taken them to the seaside ever so many times over, Mrs. Channing had felt it. And to have this fresh demand made, when she had supposed Winny was safe for some weeks to come, to hear the avowal that she wanted money for everything—food and lodging and washing and sundries, did strike Mrs. Channing as being a little too much.

Ellen Channing had been, as Ellen Huntley, reared to liberality. She was large-hearted by nature, open-handed by habit. To refuse to continue to aid Mrs. Yorke in her helpless need, would have gone against her inclination, but to continue to supply her at any cost was almost equally so. What to do, and what Winny would do, she could not think. The first thing was, to take Winny's things off and comfort her for the rest of the day; the next was to send the children to Miss Nelly in the nursery; the third to wait till Hamish came in.

He arrived at the usual hour, his face a little brighter than it had been of late. However James Channing might strive to conceal the curious pain—not physical yet, only mental—always gnawing at his heart-strings, and to put on a brave smile before his wife and the world, she detected that all was not right with him. Leaving Winny, on the plea that she would see whether the children were at tea yet, Mrs. Channing followed her husband into his dressing-room.

He had just dried his hands when she entered, and was turning to the glass to brush his hair. She stood by while telling him of Winny's piteous state, and the impossibility, as it seemed, that they could do much for her.

"Yes we can, Ellen," he said, turning to her with his bright smile when the recital was over. "I have had a slice of luck today."

"A slice of luck!"

"Even so. You remember Martin Pope, poor fellow, who somehow got down in the world at Helstonleigh, and borrowed a little money from me to get him up in it again?"

"Yes, I remember. It was sixty pounds."

"Well, Ellen, he has been rather long getting up, but it is really coming at last. He called in at the office this morning, and repaid me the half of the loan. Poor Martin! he is honourable as the day. He says the not being able to repay me when the bank went worried him terribly; and all the more so, because I never bothered him."

"Did you ask him for it then?"

"No. I was sure he had it not in his power to refund, and so left him in peace. Ellen, if I were dying for money—if I saw my wife and child dying for it—I think I could not be harsh with those who owed it me, where I knew they were helpless in means, though good in will, to pay."

He had put down the brush, and was taking a small packet of notes from his pocketbook, laughing rather gaily.

"I'm like a schoolboy showing his treasures. See, love. Six five-pound notes. We can help Mrs. Winny."

Ellen's fair fresh face broke into dimples. "And we can take a holiday too, Hamish?"

"Ah no. At least I can't. That's over."

"But why?"

"Because when I declined the holiday, the clerk under me was allowed to take one, and another of them is ill. I must stick to my post this year."

The dimples hid themselves: the expectant face clouded over. He noticed it.

"I am very sorry, Ellen. If you would like to go, and take Nelly and nurse—"

"Oh, Hamish, you know I would not," she interrupted, vexed that he should even suggest such a thing. "I only care for it for your sake; for the rest it would be to you."

"I don't care about it for myself, love."

He drew her to him as she passed on her way to quit the room, and kissed her fondly. Ellen let her hand rest for a moment on his neck; she never looked at him now, but a feeling of apprehension darted through her, that he was not as strong as he ought to be.

Hamish closed the door after her, finished his toilet, and then stood looking from the open window. The world had changed to him for some little time now; the sunshine had gone out of it. That one bitter, cruel review, had been followed up by others more cruel, if possible, more bitter. The leading papers were all against him. How he battled with it at the time and made no sign, he hardly knew. To heart and spirit it was a death-blow; for both seemed alike to have had their very life crushed out. He went on his way still, fulfilling every duty every daily obligation in kindly courteousness as of yore, believing that the world saw nothing. In good truth the world did not. Save that his sunny smile had always a tinge of sadness in it, that he seemed to get a trifle thinner, that his voice, though sweet as ever, was low and subdued, the world noticed nothing. Ellen alone saw it; saw that a blight had fallen upon the inward spirit.

But she little guessed to what extent. Hamish himself did not. All he knew was, that a more cruel blow had been dealt to him than he had supposed it possible to be experienced in this life. When by chance his eye would fall on a volume of his work, his very soul seemed to turn sick and faint. It was as if he had cast his whole hopes upon a die, and lost it. His dreams of fame, his visions of that best reward, appreciation, had faded away, and left him nothing but darkness. Darkness, and worse than darkness; for out of it loomed mortification and humiliation and shame. The contrast alone went well nigh to kill him. In the pursuit of his high artistic ideal, he had lived and moved and almost had his being. The ills of life had touched him not; the glorious, expectant aspirations that made his world, shielded him from life's frowns. It is ever so with those rare few whom the Divine gift of genius has made its own. As the grand hope of fruition drew nearer and nearer, it had seemed to Hamish, at moments, that realization had actually come. The laurel-crown seemed to rest upon his head; the longed-for prize all but touched his expectant lips. No wonder, when the knell of all this light and hope and blessedness boomed suddenly out, that the better part of Hamish Channing's life, his vitality, went with it.

He worked on still. His papers for the magazines were got up as before, for he could not afford to let them cease. Gerald Yorke, borrowing here, borrowing there, might go careering off in yachts, and pass weeks in idleness, sending work and care to his friend the Deuce; but Hamish and Gerald were essentially different men. Even this evening, after Hamish should have dined, he must get to his toilsome work. It was felt as a toil now: the weary pain, never quitting his bosom, took all energy from him.

He stood holding the window-curtain in his rather fragile hand; more fragile than it used to be. The sky that evening was very lovely. Bright purple clouds, bordered with an edge of shining gold, were crowding the west; a brighter sheet of gold underneath them seemed as if it must be flooding the other side of the world, to which the sun was swiftly passing, with its dazzling dawn of burnished radiance. Hamish could but notice it: it is not often that a sunset is so beautiful. Insensibly, as he gazed, thoughts stole over him of that OTHER world, where there shall be no need of the sun to lighten it: where there shall be no more bitter tears or breaking hearts; where sorrow and trouble shall have passed away. These same thoughts came to him very often now, and always with a kind of yearning.

As he took his hand from the curtain, with that deep, sobbing sigh, or rather involuntary catching of the breath, which is a sure token of some long-concealed enduring sorrow—for else it is never heard—the signet-ring fell from his little finger. It had grown too large for him—as we are all apt to say. If I don't take care, I shall lose it, thought Hamish. And that would have been regarded as a misfortune, for it had been his father's, the one Mr. Channing always wore and used. This was the third time it had slipped off with a run.

Hamish saw his wife's work-box on a table, looked in it, and found some black sewing-silk. This he wound round and round the ring hastily, for he knew dinner must be ready. Thus secured, he put it on again, and left the room. The children heard his step, and came bounding out of the nursery, Miss Nelly springing into his arms.

He kissed her very tenderly; he lovingly put back her golden hair. He took up the other little things and kissed them in turn, asking if they had had love-letters from papa. Looking into the nursery, he inquired whether they had plenty of jam and such-like good things on the tea-table, telling nurse to see that little Rosy, who could not fight for herself, got her share. And then, leaving them with his pleasant nod, his sunny smile, he went to the drawing-room, and gave their mother his arm to take her down to dinner, whispering to her—for she seemed in a low state, her tears on the point of bursting out—that he would make it all right for her until her husband came home. And it was that husband, that father, who had worked him all the ill! Hamish suspected it not. Cowards and malicious ones, such as Gerald, stab in the dark.

And so September went on, and October drew near, and by and bye Mr. Gerald Yorke arrived at home again. Winny, who had no more tact than her youngest infant, the little Rosy, greeted her husband with a flood of tears, and the news of how she had been obliged to pay away the twenty-five pounds in settling his bills. Gerald called her a fool to her face, and frowned awfully. Winny only sobbed. Next he demanded, with a few more ugly words that might have been left out, how the devil she had managed to go on. Between choking and shrinking, the answer was nearly inaudible, and Gerald bent his head to catch it: she had had a little more help from "mamma."

Was Mrs. Gerald Yorke's deceit excusable? Even under the circumstances few may think it so. And yet—it was a choice between this help, and the very worst discomfort that could fall upon her: debt. Winny was shrewd in some things: she knew all about her husband's ill-feeling to Mr. Channing: she knew about the reviews; and she really did believe that if Gerald got to hear whence her help had come, he would shake her as he shook Kitty. In her utter lack of moral courage, she could but keep up the deception.

But Gerald Yorke had come home in feather, a prize-rose in his button-hole. By dint of plausible statements to Mr. Fuller, he had got that honourable friend to lend him two hundred pounds. Or rather, strictly speaking, to get it lent to him. With this money safely buttoned up in his pocket, Winny's penniless state was not quite so harshly condemned as it might otherwise have been: but when Winny timidly asked for some money to "pay mamma back," Gerald shortly answered that he had none, mamma must wait.

And so, at this, the opening of the third part of the story, Gerald Yorke was flourishing. A great man he, in his chambers again, free from duns for a time, giving his wine parties, entering into the gaieties of social life, with all their waste of time and money. Winny got her rent paid now, regularly, and some new bonnets for herself and the children.

"I am so glad to hear you are more at ease, Gerald," Hamish Channing said, meeting him one day accidentally, and speaking with genuine kindness, but never hinting at any debt that might be due to himself. "How have you managed it, old friend?"

"Oh—aw—I—paid the harpies a—aw—trifle, and have—aw—got some credit again," answered Gerald, evading the offered hand. "Good day. I'm in a hurry."

But Gerald Yorke, though flourishing in funds, was not flourishing in temper. Upon one subject it was chronically bad, and he just as angry and mortified as he could be. And that was in regard to his future prospects in the field, of literature. Three or four days after his return, he paid a visit to his publishers, sanguinely hoping there might be a good round sum coming to him, the proceeds of his book. Alas for sublunary expectations! The acting partner met him with a severely cold face and very ill news. The flashing laudatory reviews, written (as may be remembered) by Gerald himself or his bosom friends, had not much served the book, after all, in the long run. When they appeared, it caused demands for it to flow in, and a considerable number of copies went out. But when the public got the book, they could not or would not read it; and the savage libraries returned the copies to the publishers, wholly refusing to pay for them. They sent them back in shoals: they vowed that the puffing of an utterly miserable book in the extraordinary style this one had been puffed, was nothing less than fraud: some went so far as to say that the publishers and the author and the reviewers ought all to be indicted together for conspiracy. In short, the practical result was, that the book might almost be said to be withdrawn, so few copies remained in circulation. In all respects it was an utter failure. No wonder the unhappy publisher, knowing himself wholly innocent in the matter, smarting under a considerable loss, besides the fifty pounds that ought to have been advanced by Gerald, and never yet had been, no wonder he met Mr. Gerald Yorke with a severe face. The only gratification afforded him lay in telling this, and enlarging rather insultingly on the worthlessness of the book.

"You, a reviewer, could not have failed to know it was bad, Mr. Yorke; one that was certain to fail signally."

"No I didn't," roared Gerald.

"Well, I'd recommend you never to attempt another. That field is closed to you."

"What the devil do you mean?—how dare you presume to give me such advice? I shall write books without end if I think fit. My firm belief is that the failure is your fault. You must have managed badly, and not properly pushed the book."

"Perhaps it is my fault that the public can't read the book and won't put up with it," retorted the publisher.

Gerald flung away in a temper. A hazy doubt, augmenting his mortification and anger, kept making itself heard: whether this expressed opinion of the book's merits might not be the true one? Hamish Channing, though softening the fiat, had said just the same. Gerald would very much have liked to pitch publisher and public into the sea, and Hamish Channing with them.

CHAPTER XXVI

ARRIVING AT EUSTON SQUARE

Roland Yorke had stuck to his copying. During this autumn, now rapidly passing, when all the world and his wife were off on the wing, spending their money, and taking out their fling at pleasure—which Roland thought uncommonly hard on him—he had really put his shoulder to the wheel and drudged on at his evening work. The office had him by day, the folios by night. And if he hindered an evening or two a week by dropping in upon Mr. Greatorex and somebody else who was in Mr. Greatorex's house, he sat up at his work when he got home. Truly Roland had learnt a lesson at Port Natal, for this was very different from what he would have done in the old days at Helstonleigh. It could not be said that he was gaining a fortune. The writing came to grief sometimes; Roland was as fond of talking as ever, by way of recreative accompaniment to labour, and the result would be that words were left out in places and wrong ones penned in others: upon which fresh paper had to be got, and the sheet begun again. Therefore he was advancing rather more surely than swiftly: his present earnings amounted in the aggregate to two sovereigns! And these he deposited for safety in Mrs. Jones's hands.

But Roland is not writing this October evening: which, all things considered, was destined to turn out rather a notable one. A remark was made in a former chapter, that Roland, from the state of ecstatic delight he was thrown into by the news that Arthur Channing was about to visit London, did not quite know whether he stood on his head or his heels. Most assuredly that same remark might be applied to him this evening. Upon dashing into his room, a little before six o'clock, Roland found on his tea-table a letter awaiting him that had come by the day-mail from Helstonleigh. Recognizing Arthur's handwriting, he tore it open, read the few lines it contained, and burst forth into a shout so boisterous and prolonged, that the Reverend Mr. Ollivera, quietly reading in the drawing-room above, leaped off his seat with consternation, fully believing that somebody was on fire.

Arthur Channing was coming to London! Then. That same evening. Almost at that very hour he ought to be arriving at Euston Square Station. Roland did not give himself leisure to digest the why and the wherefore of the journey, or to speculate upon why the station should be Euston Square and not Paddington. Arthur was coming, and that was sufficient for him.

Neglecting his tea, brushing himself up, startling Mrs. Jones with the suddenness of the tidings, which he burst into her room to deliver, Roland set off for the Euston Square terminus. As usual, he had not a fraction of money. That was no impediment to his arriving in time: and the extraordinary manner in which he pushed his way along the streets, striding over or through all impediments, caused a crowd of ragamuffins to collect and follow him on the run, believing that, like Johnny Gilpin, he was doing it for a wager.

Charles, the youngest of the Channing family, was coming home overland, viâ Marseilles, from India, where he had an excellent appointment. He had gone to it at eighteen, two years ago, and been very well until recently. All at once his health failed, and he was ordered home for a six months' sojourn. It was to meet him in London, where he might be expected in a day or two, and take him down to Helstonleigh, that Arthur Channing was now coming.

Panting and breathless with haste, looking wild with excitement, Roland went striding on to the platform just as the train came steadily in. It was a mercy he did not get killed. Catching sight of the well-remembered face—though it was aged and altered now, for the former stripling of nineteen had grown into the fine man of seven-and-twenty—Roland sprang forward and held on to the carriage. Porters shouted, guards flew, passengers screamed—it was all one to him.

They stood together on the platform, hand locked in hand: but that French customs do not prevail with us, Roland might have hugged Arthur's life out. The tears were in his eyes with the genuineness of his emotion. Roland's love for his early friend, who had once suffered so much for his sake, was no simulated one. The spectators spared a minute to turn and gaze on them—the two notable young men. Arthur was nearly as tall as Roland, very noble and distinguished. His face had not the singular beauty—as beauty—of Hamish's, but it was good, calm, handsome: one of those that thoughtful men like to look upon. His grey eyes were dark and deep, his hair auburn.

"Arthur, old friend, I could die of joy. If you only knew how often I have dreamt of this!"

Arthur laughed, pressed his hand warmly, and more warmly, ere he released it. "I must see after my luggage at once, Roland. I think I have lost it."

"Lost your luggage?"

"Yes; in so far as that it has not come with me. This," showing a rather high basket, whose top was a mound of tissue-paper, that he brought out of the carriage with his umbrella and a small parcel, "is something Lady Augusta asked me to convey to Gerald."

"What is it?"

"Grapes, I fancy. She charged me not to let it be crushed. I sent my portmanteau on to the station by Galloway's man, and when I arrived there myself could not see him anywhere. When we reached Birmingham it was not to be found, and I telegraphed to Helstonleigh. The guard said if it came to

Birmingham in time he would put it in the van. I only got to the station as the train was starting, and had no time to look."

"But what took you round by Birmingham?"

"Business for Galloway. I had three or four hours' work to do for him there."

"Bother Galloway! How are the two mothers?" continued Roland, as they walked arm-in-arm down the platform. "How's everybody?"

"Yours is very well; mine is not. She has never seemed quite the thing since my father's death, Roland. Everybody else is well; and I have no end of messages for you."

They stood round the luggage-van until it was emptied. Nothing had been turned out belonging to Arthur Channing. It was as he feared—the portmanteau was not there.

"They will be sure to send it on from Birmingham by the next train," he remarked. "I shall get it in the morning."

"Where was the good of your coming by this duffing train?" cried Roland. "It's as slow as an old cart-horse. I should have taken the express."

"I could not get away before this one, Roland. Galloway made a point of my doing all there was to do."

"The cantankerous, exacting old beauty! Are his curls flourishing?"

Arthur smiled. "Channing still, but growing a little thin."

"And you are getting on well, Arthur?

"Very. My salary is handsome; and I believe the business, or part of it, will be mine some day. We had better take a cab, Roland. I'll get rid of Gerald's parcel first. This small one is for Hamish. Stay a moment, though."

He wrote down the name of a private hotel in the Strand, where he intended to stay, requesting that the portmanteau should be sent there on its arrival.

Jumping into a hansom, Roland, who had not recovered his head, gave the address of Gerald's chambers. As they were beginning to spin along the lighted streets, however, he impulsively arrested the man, without warning to Arthur, and substituted Mrs. Gerald Yorke's lodgings. They were close at hand; but that was not his motive.

"If we leave the grapes at the chambers, Ger will only entertain his cronies with them—a lot of fast men like himself," explained Roland. "By taking them to Winny's, those poor meek little mites may stand a chance of getting a few. I don't believe they'd ever taste anything good at all but for Mrs. Hamish Channing."

Arthur Channing did not understand. Roland enlightened him. Gerald kept up, as might be said, two establishments: chambers for himself and lodgings for his wife.

"But that must be expensive," observed Arthur.

"Of course it is. Ger goes in for expense and fashion. All well and good if he can do it—and keep it up. I think he has had a windfall from some quarter, for he is launching out uncommonly just now. It can't be from work; he has been taking his ease all the autumn in Tom Fuller's yacht."

"I don't quite understand, yet, Roland. Do you mean that Gerald does not live with his wife and children?"

"He lives with them after a fashion: gives them one-third of his days and nights, and gives his chambers the other two. You'd hardly recognize him now, he is so grand and stilted up. He'd not nod to me in the street."

"Roland!"

"It's true. He's as heartless as an owl; Ger always was, you know."

"But you are his brother."

"Brothers and sisters don't count for much with Gerald. Besides, I'm down in the world, and he'd not take a pitch-fork to lift me up in it again. Would you believe it, Arthur, he likes nothing better than to fling in my teeth that miserable old affair at Galloway's—the banknote. The very last time we ever met—I had run into Winny's lodgings to take some dolls' clothes for Kitty from little Nelly Channing— Ger taunted me with that back affair, and more than hinted, not for the first time, that I'd helped myself to some money lost last summer by Bede Greatorex. If I'd known Ger was at home, I'd never have gone: Miss Nelly might have done her errand herself. Have you read his book?"

"Ye-es, I have," answered Arthur, in a rather dubious tone. "Have you?"

"No; for I couldn't," candidly avowed Roland. "I got nearly through one volume, and it was a task. It was impossible to make head or tail of it. I know I'm different from other folks, have not half the gumption in me I ought to have, and don't judge of things as they do, which is all through having gone to Port Natal; but I thought the book a rubbishing book, Arthur, and a bad one into the bargain: Where's the use of writing a book if people can't read it?"

"Did you read the reviews on it?"

"Oh law! I've heard enough about them. Had they been peacock's feathers, Ger would have stuck them in his cap. And he pretty nigh did. I'll tell you what book I read—and cried over it too—and got up from it feeling better and happier—and that's Hamish's."

A light, like a glow of gladness, shone in Arthur Channing's honest grey eyes. "When I read that book, I felt thankful that a man should have been found to write such," he said in a hushed tone. "I should have felt just the same if he had been a stranger."

"Ay, indeed: it was something of that I meant to say. And I wish all the world could read it!" added impulsive Roland. "And did you read the reviews on it?"

"Oh my goodness," cried Roland, a blank look taking the place of his enthusiasm. "Arthur, do you know, if those horrible reviews come across my mind when I am up at Hamish's, my face goes hot with shame. I've never said a syllable about them on my own score; I shouldn't like to. When I get rich, I mean to go against the papers for injustice."

"We cannot understand it down with us," said Arthur. "On the Saturday night that William Yorke got back to Helstonleigh after attending your uncle's funeral, I met him at the station. He had the 'Snarler' with him—and told me before he'd let me open it, that it contained a most disgraceful attack on Hamish's book: in fact, on Hamish himself. Putting aside all other feeling when I read it, my astonishment was excessive."

Roland relieved his feelings by a few stamps, and it was well that the cab bottom was pretty strong. "If I could find out who the writer was, Arthur, I'd get him ducked."

"That review was followed by others, all in the same strain, just as bad as it is possible for reviews to be made."

"The wicked old reptiles!" interjected Roland.

"What struck me as being rather singular in the matter, was this," observed Arthur: "That the selfsame journals which so extravagantly and wrongly praised Gerald's work, just as extravagantly and wrongly abused Hamish's. It would seem to me that there must have been some plot afoot, to write up Gerald and write down Hamish. But how the public can submit to be misled by reviewers in this manner, and not rise against it, I cannot understand."

"If those were not the exact words of old Greatorex!" exclaimed Roland. "He read both the books and all the reviews. It was a sin and a shame, and a puzzle, he said; a humbug altogether, and he should like, for the satisfaction of his curiosity, to be behind the scenes in the performance. But what else do you think he said, Arthur?"

"I don't know."

"That the reviews and the books would find their level in the end. It was impossible, he declared, that Gerald's book could live; all the fulsome praises in Christendom could not make it: just as it was impossible for such a work as the other to be written out; it would be sure to find its way with the public eventually. Annabel told me that; and I went off the same evening to Hamish's and told him. He and old Greatorex are first rate friends."

"What did Hamish say?"

"Oh, nothing. He just smiled in his sad way, and said 'Yes, perhaps it might be,' as if the words made no impression on him."

"Why do you say 'his sad way?' Hamish always had the sweetest and gayest smile in the world. We used, if you remember, to call him Sunny Hamish."

"I know. But somehow he has altered, Arthur. He was changing a little before, seemed thoughtful and considerate instead of gay and mocking; but that was nothing to the way he has changed lately. I'd not say it to any soul but you, old Arthur, not even to Annabel, but my belief is just this—that the reviews have done it."

"The reviews!"

Roland nodded. "Taken the shine out of him for a time. Oh, he'll come-to again soon; never fear. All the sooner if I could find out who the snake was, and kick him."

"We cannot judge for others; we cannot put ourselves in their places," observed Arthur. "Or else it seems to me that, after producing such a book as Hamish's, I should rest on its obvious merits, and be little moved by what adverse friends could say."

"I'm sure they'd not move me," avowed candid Roland. "The newspaper writers might lay hold of all my flounderings at Port Natal, and print them for the public benefit in big text-type tomorrow, and direct a packet to Annabel. What should I care? I say, how about poor Charley? He has been ill."

"Very ill. They have kindly given him six months' leave, and pay his overland passage out and home."

"And how much leave have you got for London, Arthur?"

"That depends on Charley. If he comes straight on from Marseilles, he may be here in a day or two: but should his health have improved on the voyage, he will probably make a stay in Paris. I am to wait for him here until he comes, Galloway says."

"Very condescending of Galloway! I dare say he has given you plenty of business to do as well, Arthur."

"That's true," laughed Arthur. "I shall be engaged for him all day tomorrow; I have some small accounts to settle for him amidst other things."

"Where's the money?" asked Roland, in a resentful tone.

Arthur touched the breast-pocket of his under-coat. "I have brought it up with me."

"Then I devoutly hope you'll get robbed of it tonight, Arthur, to serve him out! It is a shame! Taking up the poor bit of time you've got in London with his work! That's Galloway all over! I meant to get holiday myself, that we might go about together."

"Plenty of time for that, Roland."

"I hope so. I've got something to tell you. It's about Annabel. But we are close at Mrs. Yorke's, so I'll not go into the thing now. Oh! and, Arthur, old chum, I'm so vexed, so ashamed, I shan't know how to look you in the face."

"Why not?"

"I've no money about me to pay the cab. 'Twill be a shilling. It's awfully lowering, having to meet friends upon empty pockets. I'd like to have met you with a carriage and four, and outriders; I'd like to have a good house to bring you into, Arthur, and I've got nothing."

Arthur's good, earnest eyes fixed themselves on him with all their steady affection. "You have yourself, Roland, dear old friend. You know that's all I care for. As to funds I am rich enough to pay for you and myself, though I stayed here for a month."

"It's uncommonly mortifying, nevertheless, Arthur. It makes a fellow wish to be back at Port Natal. Mother Jenkins has got two sovereigns of mine, but I never thought of it before I came out."

The cab stopped at Mrs. Gerald Yorke's door, and Roland dashed up with the prize. Mrs. Yorke sat with her youngest child on her lap, the other two little ones being on the carpet. Roland could hardly see them in the dusk of the room.

"It's grapes," said he, "from Lady Augusta. Arthur Channing says she sent them for Gerald. If I were you, Mrs. Yorke, I should feed the three chickens on them, and just tell Gerald I had done it. Halloo! what's the matter now?"

For Mrs. Yorke broke out in sobs. "It was so lonely," she said by way of excuse. "Gerald was away nearly always. To-night he had a dinner and wine party in his chambers."

"Then I'm downright glad I didn't deposit the grapes there," was Roland's comment. "As to Gerald's leaving you always alone, Mrs. Yorke, I should just ask him whether he called that manners. I don't. Good gracious me! If I were rich enough to have a wife, and played the truant from her, I should deserve hanging. Cheer up; it will all come right; and you'd say so if you had tried the ups and downs at Port Natal. Fredy, Kitty, Rosy, you little pussy cats, tell mamma to give you some grapes."

"I'm sure I'd not dare to touch the basket, though the grapes stayed tied up in it till they were rotten," was the last sobbing sound that caught Roland's ears from Mrs. Yorke as he leaped downstairs.

Their appearance at Hamish's was unexpected—for Arthur had advertised himself to Roland only—but not the less welcome. Of course Hamish and his wife thought Arthur had come to be their guest, and were half inclined to resent it when he said no. It had been arranged that he should take up his sojourn at a private hotel in Norfolk Street, where he had stayed before; his room had been engaged in it some days past, and Charles would drive to it on his arrival in London. All this was explained at once. And in the pleasure his presence brought, Hamish Channing seemed quite like his own gay self again; his cheeks bright, his voice glad, his whole manner charming.

But later, when the excitement had worn itself away, and he calmed down to sobriety and ordinary looks, Arthur sat with hushed breath, half petrified at the change he saw. Even Roland, never famous for observation, could but mark it. As if the recent emotion were taking its revenge, the change in Hamish Channing seemed very, very marked tonight. The hollow face, the subdued voice with its ring of hopelessness, the feverish cheek and hand—all were sad to hear, to feel, to look upon.

It was but a brief visit; Arthur did not stay. He wanted to see about his room, and had one or two purchases to make; and he also expected to find at the hotel letters to answer. He promised to dine with them on the morrow, and to give them as much time as he could during his stay, which might possibly last a fortnight, he laughingly acknowledged, if Mr. Charley prolonged his stay in Paris; as he was not unlikely, if well enough, to do. "So you'll probably have enough of me, Hamish," he concluded, as they shook hands.

"Roland, he is strangely altered," were the first words spoken by Arthur, when they went out together.

"Didn't I tell you so?" replied Roland. "It is just what strikes me."

Arthur walked on in silence, saying no more of what he thought. It was just as if the heart's life had gone out of Hamish; as if some perpetual weight of pain, that would never be lifted, lay on the spirit.

They walked to the Strand, and there Arthur made his small purchases, rendered necessary by the non-arrival of his portmanteau. It was striking eight by St. Mary's Church as Roland stood with him at the door of the hotel in Norfolk Street.

"These letters that you expect are waiting for you and that you have to answer," said he, resentfully, for he thought Arthur's whole time ought to be given to himself on this, the first evening, "what are they? who are they from?"

"Only from Galloway's agents, and one or two more business people. I expect they will make appointments with me for tomorrow, or ask me to make them. There may be a letter from Galloway himself. I quitted Helstonleigh an hour before the day-mail left, and I may have to write to him."

Roland growled; he thought himself very ill-used.

"It is only eight o'clock, Arthur, and I've said as good as nothing. All you've got to do won't take you more than an hour. Can't you come at nine to lodgings? You'd have the felicity of seeing Mrs. J."

"I fear not tonight, Roland."

They talked a little while longer, shook hands, and Arthur went into the hotel. Roland, turning away, decided to air himself in the Strand for an hour, and then return to the hotel and get Arthur to come home with him. He had not the smallest objection, taking it in the abstract, to spend the time before the shop windows. The pawnbrokers and eating-houses would be sure to be open, if no others were. Roland liked the pastime of looking in. Debarred of being a purchaser of desirable things, on account of the state of his exchequer, the next best thing was to take out his fill of gazing at them.

Wandering up and down, he had got on the other side of Temple Bar, and had his face glued to the glass of an oyster shop, his mouth watering at the delicacies displayed within, when the clock of St. Clement Danes struck out nine. Springing back impulsively with its first stroke, Roland came in awkward contact with someone, bearing on towards the Strand. But the gentleman, who was as tall as himself, seemed scarcely to notice the touch, so absorbed was he in his own thoughts. Save that he put out one of his hands, cased in a lavender glove of delicate hue, and slightly pushed the awkward intruder aside, he took no further heed. The face was never turned, the eyes were never removed from the straight-out look before them. Onward he passed, seeing and hearing nothing.

"What on earth has he been up to?—He looked as scared as though he had met a ghost!" mentally commented Roland with his accustomed freedom, as he stared after the wayfarer. For in him he had recognised Mr. Bede Greatorex.

He did not suffer the speculation to detain him. Taking to his heels with the last stroke of the clock, Roland gained the small hotel in Norfolk Street; into which he bolted head foremost, with his usual clatter, haste, and want of ceremony, and nearly into the arms of a tall waiter.

"I want Mr. Arthur Channing. Which room is he in?"

"Mr. Arthur Channing is gone out, sir."

"Gone out!"

"Yes, sir. Some time ago."

"He found he had no letters to write, and so went on to me," thought Roland, as he shot out again "And I have been cooling my heels in this precious street, like a booby!"

Full speed went he home now, through all the cross-cuts and nearest ways he knew, never slackening it for a moment; arriving there with bated breath and damp hair. Seizing the knocker in one hand and the bell in the other, he worked at both frantically until the door was opened. Mr. Ollivera, flinging up his window above, put out his alarmed head; Mrs. Jones, Miss Rye, two visitors, and the maid Betsey, came rushing along the passage with pale faces, Mrs. J. herself opening the door, Betsey absolutely refusing the office. Roland, without the least explanation or apology, dashed through the group into the parlour. It was dark and empty.

"Where's Arthur Channing?" he demanded, darting out again. "Mrs. J., where have you put him?"

And when Mrs. J. could gather the sense of the question sufficiently to answer it, Roland had the satisfaction—or, rather, non-satisfaction—of finding that Arthur Channing had not been there.

CHAPTER XXVII

A PRIVATE INTERVIEW

"PRIVATE AND CONFIDENTIAL.

"Cuff Court, off Fleet Street. No. 1.

"October the twenty-second.

"MR. BEDE GREATOREX.

"Sir,—A small leaf has been turned over in the matter of your cheque, lost mysteriously in June last. Leastways in something that might turn out to be connected with it. Remembering back orders, and wishing to act in accordance with the same, I'd be glad to hold a short interview with you, and would wait upon you at any hour or place you may appoint. Or if it suited your convenience to come to me, I am to be found as above, either this evening or tomorrow evening after seven o'clock.

"Your obedient servant,

"Jonas Butterby."

The above note, amidst two or three other letters, reached Mr. Bede Greatorex about four o'clock in the afternoon. He happened to be at his desk in the front room, and was giving some directions to Mr. Brown, who stood by him. As Bede ran his eyes over the lines, a deep flush, a frown, followed by a sickly paleness, overspread his face. Mr. Brown, looking at him quite by accident, remarked the signs of displeasurable emotion, and felt curious to know what the news could be that had caused it. He had, however, no opportunity for prolonged observation, for Bede, carrying the letter in his hand, went into his room and shut the door.

The note angered Bede Greatorex as well as troubled him. Who was this Butterby, that he should be continually crossing his peace? What brought the man to London?—he had gone back to Helstonleigh in the summer, and had never, so far as Bede knew, come up from it since. Was he, Bede, ere he had been a couple of weeks home from his Continental holiday, to be followed up by this troublesome detective, and his life made a worry again? In the moment's angry impulse, Bede sat down to his desk-table, and began dashing off an answer, to the effect that he could not accord an interview to Mr. Butterby.

But the pen was arrested ere it had completed the first line. Self-preservation from danger is a feeling implanted more or less strongly within us all. What if this persistent officer, denied to him, betook himself and his news to Mr. Greatorex? Bede was as innocent in regard to the purloining of the cheque and certainly as ignorant of the really guilty party as Butterby could be; he had refunded the forty-four pounds with anything but a hand of gratification; but nevertheless there were grave reasons why the matter should not be reopened to his father.

Catching up the letter, he paced the carpet for a moment or two in deep thought; halted by the window, and read it again. "Yes, I'll see him; it will be safer," said he, with decision.

He wrote a rapid note, appointing eleven o'clock the next morning for the interview at his own office. And then again paused as he was folding it; paused in deliberation.

"Why not go to him?" spoke Bede Greatorex, his eyes fixed on the opposite wall, as if he thought the map there could solve the query. "Yes, I will; I'll go tonight. That's safest of all."

Noting down the given address, he held M. Butterby's letter and his own two answers, perfect and imperfect, over the grate lighted a match, and burnt them to ashes. There was no fire; the weather was uncertain, warm today, cold tomorrow, and the fire was sometimes let go out in a morning as soon as lighted.

Evening came. And at ten minutes past seven Bede Greatorex was on the search for Mr. Butterby. "Cuff Court, Off Fleet Street." He did not know Cuff Court; and supposed that "Off Fleet Street" might indicate some turning or winding beginning in that well-known thoroughfare, and ending it was hard to say where. Bede, however, by dint of inquiry found Cuff Court at last. No. 1 had the appearance of a small private house; as in fact it was. The great Butterby generally lodged there when he came to town. The people residing in it were connections of his and accommodated him; it was, as he remarked, "convenient to places."

Bede was shown upstairs to a small sitting-room. At a square table, examining some papers taken from his open pocketbook, by the light of two gas-burners over head, sat Jonas Butterby; the same thin wiry man as ever, in apparently the same black coat, plaid trousers, and buttoned-up waistcoat; with the same green observant eyes, and generally silent lips. He pushed the papers and pocketbook away into a heap when his visitor appeared, and rose to receive him.

"Take a seat, sir," he said, handing a chair by the hearth opposite his own, and stirring the bit of fire in the grate. "You don't object to this, I hope: it ain't hardly fire-time yet, but a morsel looks cheery at night."

"I like it," said Bede. He put his hat on a side-table, and unbuttoned a thin overcoat he wore, as he sat down, throwing it a little back from the fine white shirt front, but did not take off his lavender gloves. It had always struck Mr. Butterby that Bede Greatorex was one of the finest and most gentlemanly men he knew, invariably dressed well; it had struck him that far-off time at Helstonleigh, when they met over John Ollivera's death chair, and it struck him still. But he was looking ill, worn, anxious; and the detective, full of observation by habit, could not fail to see it.

"I'm uncommon glad you've come in, Mr. Bede Greatorex. From a fresh turn some business I'm engaged on has took today, I'm not sure but I shall have to go back to Helstonleigh the first thing in the morning. Shall know by late post tonight."

"Are you living in London?"

"Not I. I come up to it only yesterday, expecting to stop a week or so. Now I find I may have to go back tomorrow: the chances is about equal one way and t'other. But if I do, I should not have got to see you this time, sir, and must have come up again for it."

"I felt very much inclined to say I'd not see you," answered Bede, candidly. "We are busy just now, and I would a great deal rather let the whole affair relating to the cheque drop entirely, than be at the trouble of raking it up again. The loss of the money has been ours, and, of course, we must put up with it. I began a note to you to this effect; but it struck me while I was writing that you might possibly be carrying your news to my father."

"No, I shouldn't have done that. It concerns you, so to say, more than him. Been well lately, Mr. Bede Greatorex?"

"As well as I usually am. Why?"

"Well, sir, you are looking, if I might make bold to say it, something like a shadder. Might a'most see through you."

"I have been doing too much lately. Mrs. Bede Greatorex and myself were on the Continent for two months, rushing about from kingdom to kingdom, and from place to place, seeing the wonders, and taking what the world calls a holiday—which is more wearing than any hard work," Bede condescended to explain, but in rather a haughty tone, for he thought it did not lie in the detective's legitimate province to offer remarks upon him. "In regard to business, Mr. Butterby: unless you have anything very particular to communicate, I would rather not hear it. Let the affair drop."

"But I should not be doing my duty either way, to you or to me, in letting it drop," returned Butterby. "If anything worse turned up later, I might get called over the coals for it at headquarters."

"Be so good as to hasten over what you have to say, then," said Bede, taking out his watch and looking at it with anything but marked courtesy.

It produced no effect on Mr. Butterby. If his clients chose to be in a hurry, he rarely was. But in his wide experience, bringing, as he generally did, all keen observation to bear, he felt convinced of one thing— that the gentleman before him dreaded the communication he had to make, and, for that reason and no other, wished to shun it.

"When that cheque was lost in the summer, Mr. Bede Greatorex, you did me the honour to put a little matter into my hands, confiding to me your confident opinion that one of your clerks must have been the purloiner of it, if not on his own score, on somebody else's that he was acting for. You asked me to give an eye privately to the four. Not having got any satisfactory news from me up to the present time, you have perhaps thought that I have been neglecting the charge, and let it fall through."

"Oh, if it concerns them, I'll be glad to hear you!" briskly spoke Bede Greatorex; and to the acute ear listening, the tone seemed to express relief as well as satisfaction. "Have you found out that one of them did take it?"

"Not exactly. What I have found out, though, tells me that it is not improbable."

"Go on, please," said Bede impatiently. "Was it Hurst?"

"Now don't you jump to conclusions in haste, Mr. Bede Greatorex; and you must just pardon me for giving you the advice. It's a good rule to be observed in all cases; and if you'd been in my part of the law as long as I have, you'd not need to be told it. My own opinion was, that young Hurst was not one to help himself to money, or anything else that wasn't his; but of course when you—"

"Stop an instant," interrupted Bede Greatorex, starting up as a thought occurred to him, and looking round in alarm. "This house is small, the walls are no doubt thin; can we be overheard?"

"You may sit down again in peace, sir," was the phlegmatic answer. "It was a child of twelve, or so, that showed you up, wasn't it?"

"Yes."

"Well, except her, and her missis—who is as deaf as a stone post, poor thing, though she is my cousin— there's not a living soul in the house. The husband and son never get home till ten. As to the walls, they are seven times thicker than some modern ones, for the old house was built in substantial days. And if not—trust me for being secure and safe, and my visitors too, wherever I may stop, Mr. Bede Greatorex."

"It was for Hurst's sake I spoke," said Bede, in the light of a rather lame apology. "It may suit me to hush it up, even though you tell me he is guilty."

"When you desired me to look after your clerks, and gave me your reasons—which I couldn't at first make top nor tail of, and am free to confess have not got to the bottom of yet—my own judgment was that young Hurst was about the least likely of all to be guilty," pursued the officer, in his calmest and coolest manner. "However, as you persisted in your opinion, I naturally gave in to it, and looked up Hurst effectually. Or got him looked up; which amounts to the same thing."

"Without imparting any hint of my reasons for it?" again anxiously and imperatively interrupted Bede Greatorex. And it nettled the detective.

"I'd like to ask you a question, Mr. Bede Greatorex, and to have it answered, sir. Do you think I should be fit for my post unless I had more 'cute discretion about me than ordinary folks, such as—excuse me—you? Why, my whole work, pretty nigh, is made up of ruses and secresy, and pitching people off on wrong scents. Says I to my friend—him that I sets about the job?—'that young Mr. Hurst has been making a undesirable acquaintance, quite innocent, lately; he may get drawed into unpleasant consequences afore he knows it; and as I've a respect for his father, a most skilful doctor of physic, I should like to warn the young man in time, if there's danger. You just turn him, inside out; watch all he does and all he doesn't do, and let me know it.' Well, sir, Hurst was turned inside out, so to say; if we'd stripped his skin off him, we couldn't have seen more completely into his in'ard self and his doings than we did see; and the result was (leastways, the opinion I came to), that I was right and you were wrong. He had no more hand in the taking of that there cheque, or in any other part of the matters you hinted at, than this pocketbook here of mine had. And when I tell you that, Mr. Bede Greatorex, you may believe it."

A short silence ensued. Bede Greatorex's left elbow rested on the table; his hand, the glove off now, was pressing his temple as if in reflective thought, the beautiful diamond ring on his little finger glittering in the gas-light. His mother had given the ring to him when she was dying, expressing a hope that he would wear it always in remembrance of her. It appeared to Bede almost as a religious duty to obey, though few men hated ornaments in connection with himself, so much as he. His eyes were fixed on the fire; Mr. Butterby's on him.

"Well, Mr. Greatorex, Hurst being put out of the field, I naturally went on to the others. Jenner I never suspected at all, 'twas not him; and I felt morally sure, in spite of his impudence to me, that this time it was not Roland Yorke. Notwithstanding, I looked a little after both those gents; and I found that it was not either of 'em."

"What do you mean by 'this time' in connection with Mr. Yorke?" inquired Bede, catching up the words, which, perhaps, had been an inadvertent slip.

Butterby coughed. But he was not a bad man at heart, and had no intention of doing gratuitous damage even to impudent Roland.

"Oh well, come Mr. Bede Greatorex—a young fellow who has been out on the spec to Port Natal, seeing all sorts of life, is more likely, you know, to tumble into scrapes than steady-natured young fellows who have never been let go beyond their mothers' apron-strings."

"True," assented Bede Greatorex. "But in spite of his travelling experiences, Roland Yorke appears to me to be one of the most unsophisticated young men I know. In the ways of a bad world he is as a very boy."

"He is just one of them shallow-natured, simple-minded chaps that never will be bad," pronounced Butterby, "except in the matter of impudence. He has got enough of that to set up trading on in Cheapside. What he'd have been, but for having got pulled up by a unpleasant check or two, I'm not prepared to say. Well, sir, them three being disposed of—Hurst, Jenner, and Yorke—there remained only Mr. Brown, your manager. And it is about him I've had the honour to solicit an interview with you."

Bede turned his eyes inquiringly from the fire to Mr. Butterby.

"You said from the first you did not suspect Mr. Brown. No more did I. You thought it couldn't be him; he has been some years with you, and his honesty and faithfulness had been sufficiently tested. I'm sure I had no reasons to think otherwise, except one. Which was this: I could not find out anything about Mr. Brown prior to some three or four years back; his appearance on the stage of life, so to say, seemed to date from then. However, sir, by your leave, we'll put Brown aside for a minute, and go on to other people."

Mr. Butterby paused almost as though he expected his hearer to give the leave in words. Bede said nothing, only waited in evident curiosity, and the other resumed.

"There was a long-established firm in Birmingham, Johnson and Teague. Accountants ostensibly, but did a little in bill-broking and what not; honest men, well thought of, very respectable. Johnson (who had succeeded his father) was a man under forty; Teague was old. Old Teague had never married, but he had a great-nephew, in the office, Samuel Teague; had brought him up, and loved him as the apple of his eye. A nice young fellow in public, a wild spendthrift in private; that's what Sam Teague was. His salary was two hundred a year, and he lived free at his uncle's residence, outside Birmingham. His spendings were perhaps four hundred beyond the two. Naturally he came to grief. Do you take me, Mr. Bede Greatorex?"

"Certainly."

"In the office, one of its clerks, was a young man named George Winter. A well-brought-up young fellow too, honest by nature, trusted, and thought much of. He and young Teague were uncommonly intimate. Now, how much blame was due to Winter I'm not prepared to say; but when Samuel Teague, to save himself from some bother, forged a bill on the office, and got it paid by the office, Winter was implicated. He'd no doubt say, if you asked him, that he was drawn into it innocently, did say it in fact; but he had been the one to hand over the money, and the firm and the world looked upon him as the worse of the two. When the fraud was discovered, young Teague decamped. Winter, in self-defence and to avert consequences, went straight the same afternoon, which was a Saturday, to old Teague's private residence, and there made a clean breast of young Teague's long course of misdoings. It killed old Teague."

"Killed him!" repeated Bede, for the detective made a slight pause.

"Yes, sir, killed him. He had looked upon his nephew up to that time as one of the saints of this here middle world; and the shock of finding him more like an angel of the lower one touched old Teague's heart in some vital spot, and killed him. He had a sort of fit, and died that same night. The next day, Sunday, young Winter was missing. It was universally said that he had made his way to Liverpool, in the track of Samuel Teague—for that's where folks thought he had gone—with a view of getting away to America. Both were advertised for; both looked upon as alike criminal. It was for such a paltry sum they had perilled themselves—only a little over one hundred pounds! Time went on, and neither of 'em was ever traced; perhaps Mr. Johnson, when he had cooled down from his first anger, was willing to let Sam Teague be, for the old man's sake, and so did not press the search. Anyway Samuel Teague is now in open business in New York, and doing well."

"And the other—Winter?"

"Ah, it's him I'm coming to," significantly resumed Mr. Butterby. "It seems that Winter never went after him at all. In the panic of finding old Teague had died, and that no quarter was to be expected from Johnson (as it wasn't then) he took a false name, put on false hair and whiskers, and stole quietly off by the train on Sunday afternoon, carrying a shirt or two in a blue bag. It was to Helstonleigh he went, Mr. Bede Greatorex, and he called himself Godfrey Pitman."

Bede Greatorex started from his seat. Up to that period he had been perfectly calm; interested of course, but as if in something that did not concern him.

"Yes, sir, Godfrey Pitman. The same that was in Mrs. Jones's house at the time of Mr. Ollivera's death; the man that Helstonleigh made so much mystery of; who was, so to say, accused of the murder. And Godfrey Pitman, sir, or George Winter, whichever you may please to call him, is one and the same with your managing clerk Mr. Brown!"

"No!" shouted Bede Greatorex.

"I say YES, sir. The very selfsame man."

Bede Greatorex, looking forward in a kind of wild manner, over Mr. Butterby's head against the opposite wall, seemed to be revolving within him various speculations connected with the disclosure.

"Why Brown has always—" He brought the words to a sudden standstill. "Brown has always unpleasantly puzzled me," had been on the tip of his tongue. But he let the words die away unspoken, and a sickly hue overspread his features. Taking his eyes from the wall and turning them on the fire, he sat as before, his brow pressed on his fingers, quite silent, after the manner of a man who is dreaming.

"I see the disagreeable doubt that is working within you, Mr. Bede Greatorex," remarked the observant detective, upon whom not a sign was lost. "You are ready to say now it was Pitman did that there deed at Helstonleigh.

"How did you find out all this about him?" asked Bede Greatorex.

"Well, I got a clue accidental. Don't mind saying so. I was about some business lately for a gentleman in Birmingham, named Foster, and in a packet of letters he put into my hand to look over, I found a note from George Winter, written from your office this past summer. It was just one of them curious chances that don't happen often; for Foster had no notion that the letter was there, thought he had destroyed it.

It was but a line or two, and them of no moment, but it showed me that Mr. Brown and George Winter was the same man, and I soon wormed out his identity with Godfrey Pitman."

"Johnson and Co. will be for prosecuting him, I suppose?" observed Bede, still as if he were dreaming.

"No," said Mr. Butterby. "I've seen Johnson and Co.: leastways Johnson. In regard to that past transaction of theirs, his opinion has changed, and he thinks that Winter, though culpably careless, and unpardonably blind as to the faith he reposed in Samuel Teague, had not himself any guilty knowledge. Anyway, Winter has been doing what he can since to repair mischief: been living on a crust and working night and day, to transmit sums periodically to Johnson in an anonymous manner—except that he just let it be known they came from him, by giving no clue to where he was, or how he gained them—with a view to wipe off the money Sam Teague robbed them of. Teague has been doing the same from his side the Atlantic," added Mr. Butterby with a knowing laugh; "so that Johnson, as he says, is paid twice over.

"Then they don't prosecute?"

"Not a bit of it. And I'm free to confess that, taking in all aspects of affairs—Brown's good conduct since, and the probability that Sam Teague was the sole offender—the man has shown himself in all ordinary pecuniary interests, just as honest and trustworthy as here and there one."

"Did he—" Bede Greatorex hesitated, stopped, and then went on with his sentence—"take my cheque?"

"That must be left to your judgment, sir. I've no cause myself to make sure of it. The letter to Foster was written about the time the cheque was lost, or a few days later; it made an allusion to money, Brown saying he was glad to be out of his debt, but whether the debt was pounds or shillings, I've no present means of knowing. Foster wouldn't answer me a syllable; was uncommonly savage at his own carelessness in letting the letter get amid the other. Living close and working hard, Brown would have money in hand of his own without touching yours, Mr. Bede Greatorex."

Bede nodded.

"On the other hand, a man who has lain under a cloud is more to be doubted than one who has walked about in the open sunshine all his life. The presenter of that cheque at the bank had a quantity of black hair about his face, just as the false Godfrey Pitman had on his at Helstonleigh. But it would be hardly fair to suspect Brown on that score, seeing there's so many faces in London adorned with it natural."

Again Bede nodded in acquiescence.

"Of course, sir, if you choose to put it to the test, you might have Mr. Brown's face dressed up for it, and let the bank see him. Anyway, 'twould set the matter at rest."

"No," said Bede, quite sharply. "No, I should not like to do it. I never thought of Brown in the affair; never. I—can't—don't—think of him now."

Did he not now think of him? Butterby, with his keen ears, fancied the last concluding sentence had a false ring in it.

"Well, sir, that lies at your own option. I've done my duty in making you acquainted with this, but I've no call to stir in it, unless you choose to put it officially into my hands. But there's the other and graver matter, Mr. Bede Greatorex."

"What other?" questioned Bede, turning to him.

"That at Helstonleigh," said the detective. "All sorts of notions and thoughts—fanciful some of 'em—come crowding through my mind at once. I don't say that he had any hand in Mr. Ollivera's death; but it might have been so: and this, that has now come out, strengthens the suspicion against him in some points, and weakens it in others. You remember the queer conduct of Alletha Rye at the time, sir—her dream, and her show-off at the grave—which I had the satisfaction of looking on at myself—and her emotion altogether?"

Bede Greatorex replied that he did remember it: also remembered that he was unable to understand why it should have been so. But he spoke like one whose mind is far away, as if the questions bore little interest.

"George Winter and Alletha Rye were sweethearts: she used to live in Birmingham before she came to Helstonleigh. But for his getting into trouble, they'd soon have been married."

"Oh, sweethearts were they," carelessly observed Bede. "She is a superior young woman."

"Granted, sir. But them superior women are not a bit wiser nor better than others when their lovers is in question. Women have done mad things for men's sakes afore today; and it strikes me now, that Alletha Rye was just screening him, fearing he might have done it. I don't see how else her madness and mooning is to be accounted for. On the other hand, it seems uncommon droll that George Winter, hiding in that top room until he could get safely away, should set himself out to harm Mr. Ollivera; a man he'd never seen. Which was the view I took at the time."

"And highly improbable," murmured Bede.

"Well, so I say; and I can't help thinking he'll come out of the fiery ordeal unscorched."

"What ordeal?"

"The charge of murder. Mr. Greatorex is safe to give him into custody upon it. I don't know that the Grand Jury would find a true bill."

All in a moment, Bede's face took a ghastly look of fear. It startled even the detective, as it was turned sharply upon him. And the voice in which he spoke was harsh and commanding.

"This must not be suffered to come to the knowledge of my father."

"Not suffered to come to his knowledge!" echoed Butterby, agape with wonder.

"No, NO! You must not let him know that Brown is Godfrey Pitman. He must never be told that Pitman is found."

"Why, Heaven bless you, Mr. Bede Greatorex! my honour has been engaged all along in the tracing out of Pitman. That one man has given me more in'ard trouble than any three. We detectives get hold of mortifying things as well as other people, and that's been one of mine. Now that I have trapped Pitman, I can't let the matter drop: and I'm sure Mr. Greatorex won't."

Bede looked confounded. He opened his month to speak, and closed it again.

"And if us two was foolish enough, there's another that wouldn't; that would a'most make us answer for it with our lives," resumed the detective, in a low, impressive tone—"and that is Parson Ollivera."

"I tell you, Butterby, this must be hushed up," repeated Bede, his agitation unmistakable, his voice strangely hollow. "It must be hushed up at any cost. Do nothing."

"And if the parson finds Pitman out for himself?" asked Butterby, his deep green eyes, shaded by their overhanging eyebrows, looking out steadily at Bede.

"That is a contingency we have nothing to do with yet. Time enough to talk of it when it comes."

"But, Mr. Bede Greatorex, if Pitman really was the—"

"Hush! Stay!" interrupted Bede, glancing round involuntarily, as if afraid of the very walls. "For Heaven's sake, Butterby, let the whole thing drop; now and for ever. There are interests involved in it that I cannot speak of—that must at all risks be kept from my father. I wish I could unburthen myself of the whole complication, and lay the matter bare before you; but I may not bring trouble on other people. To accuse Pitman would—would re-open wounds partially healed; it might bring worse than death amidst us."

It truly seemed, bending over the table in his imperative, realistic earnestness, that Bede was longing to pour out the confidence he dared not give. Butterby, revolving sundry speculations in his mind, never took his eyes for an instant from the eager face.

"Answer me one question, Mr. Bede Greatorex—an' you don't mind doing it. If you knew that Pitman was the slayer of your cousin, would you still screen him?"

"If I knew—if I thought that Pitman had done that evil deed, I would be the first to hand him over to justice," spoke Bede, breathing quickly. "I feel sure he did not."

Butterby paused. "Sir, as you have said so much, I think you should say a little more. It will be safe. You've got, I see, some other suspicion."

"I have always believed that it was one person did that," said Bede, scarcely able to speak for agitation. "If—understand me—if it was not an accident, or as the jury brought in, why then I think I suspect who and what it really was. Not Pitman."

"Can the person be got at?" inquired Butterby.

"Not for any practical use; not for accusation."

"Is it any one of them I've heard mentioned in connection with the death?"

"No; neither you nor the world. Let that pass. On my word of honour, I say to you, Mr. Butterby, that I feel sure Pitman had no hand in the matter for that reason, and for other involved reasons, I wish this information you have given me to remain buried; a secret between you and me. I will take my own time and opportunity for discharging Mr. Brown. Will you promise this? Should you have incurred costs in anyway, I will give you my cheque for the amount."

"There has not been much cost as yet," returned the detective, honestly. "We'll let that be for now. What you ask me is difficult, sir. I might get into trouble for it later at headquarters."

"Should that turn out to be the case, you can, in self-defence, bring forward my injunctions. Say I stopped proceedings."

"Very well," returned Butterby, after a pause of consideration. "Then for the present, sir, we'll say it shall stand so. Of course, if the thing is brought to light through other folks, I must be held absolved from my promise."

"Thank you; thank you truly, Mr. Butterby."

Bede Greatorex, the naturally haughty-natured man, condescended to shake hands with the detective. Mr. Butterby attended him downstairs, and opened the door for him. It was after he had gained Fleet Street, that Bede came in contact with the shoulders of Roland Yorke, never noticing him, bearing on in his all-powerful abstraction, his face worn, anxious, white, scared, like that of a man, as Roland took occasion to remark, who has met a ghost.

Back up the stairs turned Mr. Butterby, and sat down in front of the fire, leaving the gas-burners to light up his back.

There, with a hand on either knee, he recalled all the circumstances of John Ollivera's death with mental accuracy, and went over them one by one. That done, he revolved surrounding interests in his silent way, especially the words that had just fallen from Bede Greatorex one single sentence, during the whole reverie, escaping his lips.

"Was Louisa Joliffe out that evening, I wonder?"

And the clock of St. Clement Danes had moved on an hour and a quarter before he ever lifted his hands or rose from his seat.

CHAPTER XXVIII

DISAPPEARED

"I am waiting for that, Mr. Yorke."

But for the presence of Bede Greatorex, who sat at his desk in the front office, Roland might have retorted on Mr. Brown that he might wait, for he felt in just as bad a humour as it was well possible for Roland, or anybody else, to feel. Ceasing his covert grumbling to Hurst, who had the convenient gift of listening and writing away by steam at one and the same time, Roland's pen resumed its task.

Never, since Roland had joined the house of Greatorex and Greatorex, did he remember it to have been so pressed as now, as far as Bede's room was concerned. There was a sudden accumulation of work, and hands were short. Little Jenner had been summoned into Yorkshire by the illness of his mother, and Mr. Bede Greatorex had kindly said to him, "Don't hurry back if you find her in danger." They could not borrow help from the other side, for it happened that a clerk there was also absent.

Thus it fell out that not only Mr. Brown had to stay in the office the previous night until a late hour, but he detained Roland in it as well, besides warning that gentleman that he must take twenty minutes for his dinner at present, and no more. This was altogether an intense grievance, considering that Roland had fully purposed to devote a large amount of leisure time to Arthur Channing. One whole day, and this one getting towards its close, and Roland had not set eyes on Arthur. Since the moment when he left him at the door of the hotel in Norfolk Street, the last evening but one, Roland had neither seen nor heard of him. He was resenting this quite as much as the weight of work: for when his heart was really engaged, anything like slight or neglect wounded it to the core. Somewhat of this feeling had set in on the first night. After startling the street and alarming the inmates of the house, through the bell and knocker, to find that Arthur Channing had left his hotel and not come to him, was as a very pill to Roland. He had been kept all closely at work since, and Arthur had not chosen to come in search of him.

Whatever impression might have been made on the mind of Bede Greatorex by the police officer's communication, now nearly two days old, he could not but estimate at its true value the efficiency of Mr. Brown as a clerk. In an emergency like the present, Mr. Brown did that which Roland was fond of talking of—put his shoulder to the wheel. Whatever the demands of the office, Mr. Brown showed himself equal to them almost in his own person; this, combined with his very excellent administrative qualities, rendered him invaluable to Bede Greatorex. In a silent, undemonstrative kind of way, Mr. Brown had also for some months past been on the alert to watch for those mistakes, inadvertent neglects, forgetfulness in his master, which the reader has heard complained of. So far as he was able to do it, these were at once silently remedied, and nothing said. Bede detected this: and he knew that many a night when Mr. Brown stayed over hours in the office, working diligently, it was to repair some failure of his. Once, and once only, Bede spoke. "Why are you so late tonight, Mr. Brown?" he asked, upon going into the office close upon ten o'clock and finding Mr. Brown up to his elbows in work. "I'm only getting forward for the morning, sir," was the manager's quiet answer. But Bede, though he said no more, saw that the clerk had taken some unhappy error of his in hand, and was toiling to remedy it and avert trouble. So that, whatever might be Mr. Brown's private sins, Bede Greatorex could scarcely afford to lose him.

Once more, for perhaps the five hundredth time, Bede glanced from his desk at Mr. Brown opposite. No longer need, though, was there to glance with any speculative view; that had been set at rest. The eyes that had so mystified Bede Greatorex, bringing to him an uneasy, puzzling feeling, which wholly refused to elucidate itself, tax his memory as he would, were at length rendered clear eyes to him. He knew where and on what occasion he had seen them: and if he had disliked and dreaded them before, he dreaded them ten times more now.

"Ah, how do you do, Mr. Channing?"

Bede, leaving his desk, had been crossing the office to his private room, when Hamish entered. They shook hands, and stood talking for a few minutes, not having met since Bede returned from his continental tour. Just as a change for the worse in Bede struck Mr. Butterby's keen eye, so, as it appeared, did some change in Hamish Channing strike Bede.

"Are you well?" he asked.

"As well as London and its hard work will let me be," replied Hamish, with one of his charming smiles, which really was gay and light, in spite of its tinge of sadness. "It is of no use to dream of green fields and blue waves when we cannot get to them, you know."

"That's rest—when you can sit down in the one and idly watch the other," remarked Bede. "But to go scampering about for a month or two at railroad speed, neither body nor eye getting holiday, wears out a man worse than working on in London, Mr. Channing."

With a slow, lingering gaze at Hamish's refined face, which was looking strangely worn, and, so to say, etherealised, Bede passed on to his room Hamish turned to the desk of Hurst and Roland Yorke.

"How are you?" he asked of them conjointly.

"As well as cantankerous circumstances and people will let me be," was the cross reply of Roland, without looking up from his writing.

Hamish laughed.

"Just because I wanted a little leisure just now, I've got double work put on my shoulders," went on Roland. "You remember that time at old Galloway's, Hamish, when Jenkins and Arthur were both away together, throwing all the work upon me? Well, we've got a second edition of that here."

"Who is away?" inquired Hamish.

"Little Jenner. And he is good for three of us any day in point of getting through work. The result is, that Mr. Brown"—giving a defiant nod to the gentleman opposite—"keeps me at it like a slave. But for Arthur's being in London, I'd not mind some extra pressure, I'd be glad to oblige, and do it. Not that Arthur misses me, if one may judge by appearances," he continued in a deeply-injured tone. "I would not be two days in a strange place without going to see after him."

"Have you not seen Arthur, then?" inquired Hamish.

"No, I have not seen him," retorted Roland, with emphasis. "He has been too much taken up with you and other friends, to think of me. Perhaps he has gone over to Gerald's interests: and his theory is, that I'm nobody worth knowing. Mother Jenkins has had her best gown on for two days, expecting him. Live and learn—and confound it all! I'd have backed Arthur Channing, for faith and truth, against the world."

Hamish laughed slightly: any such interlude as this in Roland's generally easy nature, amused him always.

"You and I and Mrs. Jenkins are in the same box, old fellow, for Arthur has not been to me."

"Oh, hasn't he?" was Roland's answer, delivered with lofty indifference, and an angry shake of the pen, which blotted his work all over. "It's a case of Gerald, then. Perhaps he is taking him round to the Tower, and the waxwork, and the wild beasts—as I thought to do."

"I expect it is rather a case of business," remarked Hamish. "You know what Arthur is: when he has work to do, that supersedes all else. Still I wonder he did not come round last night. We waited dinner until half-past seven."

Roland was occupied in trying to repair the damage he had wilfully made, and gave no answer.

"I came in now to ask you for news of him, Roland. Where is he staying?"

"He has not called yet to see Annabel," broke in Roland. "And that I do think shameful."

"Where is he staying?"

"Staying! Why at the place in Norfolk Street. He told you where."

"Yes," assented Hamish, "but he is not staying there. I have just come from the hotel now."

"Who says he is not?"

"The people at the hotel."

"Oh, they say that, do they?" retorted Roland, turning his resentment on the people in question. "They are nice ones to keep an hotel."

"They say he is not there, and has not been there."

"Then, Hamish, I can tell you that he is there. Didn't I take him down to it that night from your house, and see him safe in? Didn't he order his missing portmanteau to be sent to the place as soon as it turned up? They had better tell me that he is not there!"

"What they say is this, Roland. That Arthur went there, but left again the same night, never occupying his bed at all: and they can give me no information as to where he is staying. I did not put many questions, but came off to you, thinking you would know his movements."

"And that is just what I don't know. Arthur has not chosen to let me know. He is at the hotel safe enough: why, he was expecting letters and telegrams and all kinds of things there! They have mistaken the name and given you the wrong answer."

Hamish did not think this. He stood in silence, feeling a little puzzled. And in that moment a faint shadow, not of evil yet, but of something or other that was wrong, first dawned on his mind.

"I want to find him," said Hamish. "If it shall turn out that he is really not at the hotel and they can give me no information, I shall not know where to look for him or what to think. But for your being busy, Roland, I would have asked you to go back with me to Norfolk Street."

Roland looked across at Mr. Brown, the light of eagerness illumining his face. He did not ask to go, but it was a strong silent appeal. Not that he had any doubt on the score of Arthur; but the walking to Norfolk Street was in prospective a very delightful interlude to the evening's hard work. But no answering look of assent did he receive.

"We'd be back in an hour, Brown, and I'd set to work like a brick. Or in less than that if we take a cab," briskly added Roland. "I have some money to pay for one; I've gone about since yesterday morning with a sovereign in my pocket, on the chance of standing treat for some sights, in case I found the chance of going out with Arthur Channing. Didn't Mrs. J. read me a lecture on not spending it in waste when she handed it over!"

"If you would promise to be back within the hour, Mr. Yorke, and really set to work with a will, you should go with Mr. Channing," was the manager's answer, who had of course heard the whole colloquy. In Roland's present restless temper, he was likely to retard work more than to advance it, especially if denied the expedition to Norfolk Street: as nobody knew better than Mr. Brown. Roland could work with a will; and no doubt would on his return, if allowed to go. So that it was policy to let him.

"Oh, thank you, Brown; that is generous," said he gratefully, as he leaped off his stool and got his hat. "I'll work away till morning light for you if it's necessary, and make no mistakes."

But Arthur was not to be found at the hotel in Norfolk Street. And the tale told there was rather a singular one. Of course Roland, darting in head-foremost in his impetuous way, demanded to see Mr. Arthur Channing, and also what they meant by denying that he was staying at it. The waiter came forward in the absence of the principal, and gave them the few particulars (all he knew) that Hamish had not before stayed to ask. In fact, Hamish had thought that Arthur must have taken some prejudice against the hotel and so quitted it for another. The following was the substance of the tale.

Mr. Arthur Channing had written from Helstonleigh to desire that a room should be prepared for him, and any letters that might come addressed to him be taken care of. Upon his arrival at the hotel (which must have been when Roland left him at it) he was informed that his room was ready, and asked if he would like to see it. Presently, he answered, and went into the coffee-room. The man (this same one telling the story) left him in it reading his letters, after supplying him with writing materials, Arthur saying that when he wanted anything he would ring. It was an exceedingly quiet hotel, not much frequented at any time; the three or four people staying in it were out that evening, so that Arthur was quite alone. By-and-by, the man said, he went in again, and found the room empty. From that time they had neither seen nor heard of Arthur.

This was the substance of the account, and it sounded somewhat incredible. Had Arthur been like Roland Yorke for instance, liable to dart about in random impetuosity, without the smallest concern for others, it might have been thought that he had taken himself off in a freak and forgotten to give notice; but Arthur was not likely to do such a thing. Hamish stood quietly while he listened to this: Roland had put himself upon a table, and sat there pulling fiercely at his whiskers, his long legs dangling downwards.

"I came with him to the door my own self," burst forth Roland before the man had well finished, as if that were a disputed point. "I watched him come right into it. That was at eight o'clock."

"Yes, sir; it was about that time, sir, that Mr. Arthur Channing got in," answered the waiter, who gave them his name as Binns.

"And when I came down, an hour later, you told me Mr. Arthur Channing had gone out; you know you did," spoke Roland, who seemed altogether out of his reckoning at the state of affairs, and wanted to blame somebody. "You never said he had gone for good."

"Well, sir, but how was I to think he had gone for good?" mildly inquired the waiter. "It have puzzled the house sir: we don't know what to suppose. Towards eleven o'clock, when the gentleman did not come in, I began to think the chambermaid must have showed him to his room, being tired, perhaps; but she said she had not, and we went up and found the room unoccupied. We have never heard of him at all since, gentlemen."

The shadow looming over Hamish grew a little darker. He began to think all this was very strange.

"The railway people were to have sent his portmanteau here," cried Roland; who, when much put out, could not reason at all, and spoke any thought that came uppermost.

"Yes, sir, the portmanteau came the next morning, sir. I carried it up to his room, sir, and it is there still."

"What! unopened!" exclaimed Hamish. "I mean, has Mr. Arthur Channing not come here to claim it?"

"No, sir; it's waiting for him against he do."

It grew serious now. Whatever abode Arthur might have removed to, he would not fail to claim his portmanteau, as common sense told Hamish Roland, hearing the answer, began to stare.

"Have you any idea how long he remained in, writing?" asked Hamish.

"No, sir. It might have been half-past eight or so, when I came back into the room, and found him gone. But I don't think he had written at all, sir, for the ink and things was on the table just as I placed them; they didn't seem to have been used."

"Were many letters waiting for him?"

"Four or five, sir. And there was a bit of a mishap with one of them, sir, for which I am very sorry. In taking them out of the rack to give to him, sir, I accidentally overlooked one, and left it in, so that Mr. Arthur Channing never had it. It's in there now."

"Be so kind as to bring it to me."

The man went for the letter, and gave it to Hamish. It was in Charles Channing's handwriting, and bore the Marseilles post-mark. A proof that Charley had arrived there safely: which was a bit of gladness for Hamish.

"I suppose you will not grumble at my opening this?" he said to the man, with a smile, as he took out his card and handed it to him. "I am Mr. Arthur Channing's brother."

"Oh, sir! I can see that by the likeness; no need to tell it to me," was the answer. "It's all right, sir, I'm sure. These other three letters have come since, sir. The big one by this morning's post, the other two later."

The big one, as the man called it, a thick, official-looking, blue envelope, was in Mr. Galloway's handwriting. Roland knew the proctor's seal too well. That one Hamish did not feel at liberty to open, but the others he did, and thought the circumstances fully justified it. Running his eyes over Charles's first, he found it had been written on board, as the steamer was nearing Marseilles. It stated that he was feeling very much better for the voyage, and thought of staying quite a week in Paris as he came through it. So far, that was good news; and now Hamish opened the other two.

Each of them, dated that morning, proved to be from a separate firm of solicitors in London and contained a few brief words of inquiry why Mr. Arthur Channing had not kept the appointment with them on the previous day.

Was Arthur lost, then? Hamish felt startled to tremor. As to poor Roland, he could only stare in helpless wonder, and openly lament that he had been such a wicked jackanapes as to attribute unkindness to Arthur.

"When I knew in my heart he was the best and truest man, the bravest gentleman the world ever produced, Hamish. Oh! I am a nice one."

Remaining at the hotel would not help them, for the waiter could tell no more than he had told. Hamish pointed to his address on the card already given, and they walked away up Norfolk Street in silence. Roland broke it as they turned into the Strand, his low voice taking a tone of dread.

"I say, Hamish! Arthur had a lot of money about him."

"A lot of money!" repeated Hamish.

"He had. He brought it up from old Galloway. You—you—don't think he could have been murdered for it?"

"Hush, Roland!"

"Oh, well—But the roughs would not mind doing such a thing at Port Natal."

CHAPTER XXIX

RESTLESS WANDERINGS

The commotion was great. Six days had elapsed since Arthur Channing's singular disappearance, and he had never been heard of.

Six days! In a case of this nature, six days to anxious friends will seem almost like six weeks. Nay, and longer. And, while on the topic, it may be well and right to state that these circumstances, this loss, occurred just as written; or about to be written; and are not a réchauffé from a dish somewhat recently served to the public in real life.

Arthur Channing arrived at the Euston Square Station on a certain evening already told of, and was met there by Roland Yorke. Later, soon after eight, he went to the private hotel in Norfolk Street, in which a room had been engaged for him, and where he had stayed before. Roland saw him go in: the waiter, Binns, received him, and left him in the coffee-room reading his letters. Upon the waiter's entering the room nearly half an hour subsequently, he found it empty. A small parcel and an umbrella belonging to him were there, but he himself was not. Naturally the waiter concluded that he had but stepped out temporarily. He was mistaken, however. From that moment nothing had been seen or heard of Arthur Channing.

If ever Roland Yorke went nigh to lose his mind, it was now. Strangers thought he must be a candidate for Bedlam. Totally neglecting the exigencies of the office, he went tearing about like a lunatic. From one place to another, from this spot to that, backwards and forwards and round again, strode Roland, as if his legs went on wires. His aspect was fierce, his hair wild. The main resting-posts, at which he halted by turns, were Scotland Yard, Waterloo Bridge, and the London docks. The best that Roland's dark fears could suggest was, that Arthur had been murdered. Murdered for the sake of the money he had about him, and then put quietly out of the way. Waterloo Bridge, bearing a reputation for having been a former chosen receptacle for mysterious carpet-bags, was of course pitched upon by Roland as an ill-omened element in the tragedy now. It had also just happened that a man, drowned from one of the bridges, had been found in the London docks: having drifted in, no doubt, with an entering or leaving ship. This was quite enough for Roland. Morning after morning would find him there; and St. Katharine's docks, being nearer, sometimes had him twice in the day.

Putting aside Roland's migrations, and his outspoken fears of dark deeds, others, interested, were to the full as much alarmed as he. The facts were more than singular; they were mysterious. From the time that Arthur Channing had entered the hotel in Norfolk Street, or—to be strictly correct—from a few minutes subsequent to that, when the waiter, Binns, had left him in the coffee-room, he seemed to have disappeared. The police could make nothing of it. Mr. Galloway, who had been at once communicated with by Hamish Channing, was nearly as much assailed by fears as Roland, and sent up letters or telegrams every other hour in the day.

The first and most natural theory taken up, as to the cause of the disappearance, was this—that Arthur Channing had received some news, amidst the letters given to him, that caused him to absent himself. But for the circumstance of the letter (written by Charles Channing on board the P. and O. steamer, and posted at Marseilles) not having been handed to Arthur, it might have been assumed that it had contained bad news of Charles, and that Arthur had hastened away to him. As the letter was omitted to be given to him—and it was an exceedingly curious incident in the problem that it should so have fallen out—this hope could not be entertained: Charles was well; and by that time, no doubt, in Paris enjoying himself. But, even had circumstances enabled them to take up this hope, it could not have lasted long: had Arthur been called suddenly away, to Charles, or elsewhere, he would not have failed to let his friends know it.

His portmanteau remained at the hotel unsought for; with his umbrella and small parcel, containing the few articles he had bought earlier in the night; full proof that when he quitted the hotel, he had meant to return to it. Now and again, even yet, a letter would reach the hotel from some stray individual or other, whom he ought to have seen on business during his sojourn in London, and had not. The letters, like the luggage, remained unclaimed, except by Hamish. In reply to inquiries, Mr. Galloway stated that the amount of money brought up to town by Arthur from himself, was sixty pounds; chiefly in five-pound notes. This was, of course, exclusive of what Arthur might have about him of his own. Mr. Galloway, in regard to the transmission of money, seemed to do things like nobody else: who, save himself, but would have given Arthur an order on his London bankers, Glyn and Co.? Not he. He happened to have the sixty pounds by him, and so sent it up in hard cash.

The first thing the police did, upon being summoned to the search, was to endeavour to ascertain what letters Arthur had received that night upon entering the hotel in Norfolk Street, and whom they were from. The waiter said there were either four or five; he was not sure which, but thought the former. He fancied there had been five in all; and, as the one was accidentally left in the rack, it must, he felt nearly sure, have been but four he delivered over. One of them—he was positive of this—had arrived that same evening, only an hour or two before Mr. Arthur Channing. The young person who presided over the interests of a kind of office, or semi-public parlour, where inquiries were made by visitors, and whence orders were issued, was a Miss Whiffin. She was an excessively smart lady in a rustling silk, with frizzy curls of a light tow on the top of her forehead, and a remarkable chignon behind that might have been furnished by the coiffeur of Mrs. Bede Greatorex. Miss Whiffin could not, or would not, recollect what number of letters there had been waiting for Mr. Channing. Being a supercilious young lady—or, at least, doing her best to appear one—she assumed to think it a piece of impertinence to be questioned at all. Yes she remembered there were a small few letters waiting for Mr. Arthur Channing; foreign or English; she did not notice which: if Binns said it was five, no doubt it was five. She considered it exceedingly unreasonable of any customer, not to say ungentlemanly, to write and order a bedroom, and walk into the house and then walk out again, and never occupy it: it was a thing she neither understood nor had been accustomed to.

And that was all that could be got out of Miss Whiffin. Binns' opinion, that the number of letters given to Arthur had been four, was in a degree borne out: for that was just the number they had been able to trace as having been written to him. Three of them were notes from people in London, making appointments for Arthur to call on them the next day; the fourth (the one spoken of by Binns as having arrived just before Arthur himself) was known to be from Mr. Galloway, that gentleman having despatched it by the day-mail from Helstonleigh.

What could have taken Arthur out again? That was the point to be, if possible, solved. Unless it could be, neither the police nor anybody else had the smallest clue as to the quarter their inquiries should be directed to. Had he quitted London again (which seemed highly improbable), then the railway stations must be visited for news of him: had he but strolled out for a walk, it must be the streets.

One of the three notes mentioned came from a firm of proctors in Parliament Street. It contained these words from the senior partner, who was an old friend of Mr. Galloway's:—"If it were convenient for you to call on me the evening of your arrival in town, I should be glad, as I wish to see you myself, and I am leaving home the following morning for a week. I shall remain at the office until nine at night, on the chance that you may come."

That Arthur, on reading the note, might have hastened to make a call in Parliament Street, was more than probable.—He knew London fairly well, having been up on two previous occasions for Mr. Galloway.—But Arthur never made his appearance there. Though of course that did not prove that he did not set out with the intention of going. Another feasible conjecture, started by Roland Yorke, was, that he might have forgotten some trifling article or other amidst his previous purchases, and gone out again to get it. Allowing that one or other of these suppositions was correct, it did not explain the mystery of his subsequent disappearance.

What became of him? If, according to this theory, he walked, or ran, up Norfolk Street to the Strand, and turned to the right or the left, or bore on across the road in pursuance of his purposed way, wherever that might be, how far did he go on that day? Where had his steps halted? at what point had he turned aside? How, and where, and in what manner had he disappeared? It was in truth a strange mystery, and none was able to answer the questions. A thousand times a day Roland declared he had been murdered—but that assertion was not looked upon as a satisfactory answer.

Upon a barrel, which happened to stand, end upwards, in a corner of an outer office at one of the police stations, into which he had gone dashing with dishevelled hair and agitated mien, sat Roland Yorke. Six days of search had gone by, and this was the seventh. With every morning that rose and brought forth no news of Arthur, Roland's state of mind grew worse and worse. The police for miles round were beginning to dread him, for he bothered their lives out. The shops in the Strand could say nearly the same. When it was found beyond doubt that Arthur was really missing, Roland had gone to the shops ringing and knocking frantically, just as he had done at Mrs. Jones's door, and bursting into those accessible. It happened to be evening: for a whole day was wasted in inquiring at more likely places, proctors' and solicitors' offices, Gerald's chambers, and the like: and so a great many of the shops were closed. Into all that he could get, dashed Roland, asking for news of a gentleman; a "very handsome young fellow nearly as tall as himself, who might have gone in to buy something." Every conceivable article, displayed or not displayed for sale, did Roland's vivid imagination picture as having possibly been needed by Arthur, from "candied rock" at a sweet-stuff mart to a stomach-pump at the doctor's. Some, serving behind the counters, thought him mad; others that he might have designs on the till; all threatened to give him into custody. In the excited state of Roland's mind it was not to be expected that he could tell a quiet, coherent tale. When Hamish Channing went later, with his courteous explanation and calm bearing, though his inward anxiety was quite as great as Roland's, it was a different thing altogether, and he was received with the utmost consideration. Threats and denial availed not with Roland: day by day, as each day came round, the shops had him again. In he was, like a man that stood head downwards and had no mind left; begging them to try and recall every soul who might have gone in to make purchases that night. But the shops could not help him. And, as the days went on, and nothing came of it, Roland began to lay the fault on the police.

"I never heard of such a thing," he was saying this morning as he sat tilting on the high barrel, and wiping his hot face after his run; which might have been one of twelve miles, or so, comprising Scotland Yard, and in and out of every shop in the Strand and Fleet Street, and all round the docks and back again. "Six days since he was missing, and no earthly news of him discovered yet! Not as much as a scrap of a clue! Where's the use of a country's having its police at all, unless they can do better than that?"

He spoke in an injured tone; one that he would have liked to make angrily passionate. Roland's only audience was a solitary stout policeman, with a prominent, buttoned-up chest and red face, who stood with his back against the mantelpiece, reading a newspaper.

"We have not had no clue to work upon, you see, Mr. Yorke," replied the man, who bore the euphonious name of Spitchcock, and was, so to say, on intimate terms with Roland, through being invaded by him so often.

"No skill, you mean, Spitchcock. I know what the English police are; had cause to know it, and the mistakes they make, years ago, long before I went to Port Natal. I could almost say, without being far from the truth, that it was the pig-headed, awful bungling of one of your lot that drove me to Africa."

"How was that, sir?"

"I'm not going to tell you. Sometimes I wish I had stayed out there; I should have been nearly as well off. What with not getting on, and being picked short up by having my dearest friend murdered and flung over Waterloo Bridge—for that's what it will turn out to be—things don't look bright over here. I know this much, Spitchcock: if it had happened in Port Natal, he would have been found ere this—dead or alive."

"Yes, that must be a nice place, that must, by your description of it, sir," remarked Spitchcock with disparagement, as he turned his newspaper.

"It was nicer than this is just now, at any rate," returned Roland. "I never heard at Port Natal of a gentleman being pounced upon and murdered as he walked quietly along the public street at half-past eight o'clock in the evening. Such a villainous thing didn't happen when I was there."

"You've got to hear it of London yet, Mr. Yorke."

"Now don't you be pig-headed, Spitchcock. What else, do you suppose, could have happened to him? I can't say he was actually murdered in the open Strand: but I do say he must have been drawn into one of the alleys, or some other miserable place, with a pitch-plaster on his mouth, or chloroform to his nose, and there done for. Who is to know that he did not open his pocketbook in the train, coming up, and some thief caught sight of the notes, and dodged him? Come, Spitchcock?"

"He'd be safe enough in the Strand," remarked the man.

"Oh, would he, though!" fiercely rejoined Roland, panting with emotion and heat. "Who is to know, then, but he had to dive into some bad places where the thieves live to do an errand for old Galloway, perhaps pay away one of his notes—and went out at once to do it? Do you mean to say that's unlikely?"

"No, that's not unlikely. If he had to do anything of the sort that took him into the thieves' alleys, that's how he might have come to grief," avowed Mr. Spitchcock. "Many a one gets put out of the way during a year, and no bones is made over it."

Roland jumped up with force so startling that he nearly upset the barrel. "That's how it must have been, Spitchcock! What can I do in it? I never cared for any one in the world as I cared for him, and never shall. Except—except somebody else—and that's nothing to anybody."

"But this here's altogether another guess sort of thing," remonstrated Mr. Spitchcock. "Them cases don't get found out through the party not being inquired for: his friends, if he's got any, thinks he's, may be, gone off on the spree, abroad or somewhere, and never asks after him. This is different."

He spoke in a cool calm kind of way. It produced no effect on Roland. The fresh theory had been started, and that was enough. So many conjectures had been hazarded and rejected in their hopelessness during the past few days that to catch hold of another was to Roland something like a spring of water would have been, had he come upon one during his travels in the arid deserts of Africa. Ordering Spitchcock to propound this view to the first of his superiors that should look in, Roland went speeding on his course again to seek an interview with Hamish Channing.

Making a detour first of all down Wellington Street: for, to go by Waterloo Bridge without inquiring whether anything had "turned up," was beyond Roland. Perhaps it was because Arthur seemed to have disappeared within the radius of what might be called its vicinity, taken in conjunction with its assumed ill-reputation—as a convenient medium over which dead cats and the like might be pitched into the safe, all-concealing river—that induced Roland Yorke to suspect the spot. It haunted his thoughts awake, his dreams asleep. One whole night he had sat on its parapet, watching the water below, watching the solitary passengers above. The police had got to know him now and what he wanted; and if they laughed at him behind his back, were civil to him before his face.

Onward pressed Roland, his head first in eagerness, his long legs skimming after. How many wayfarers and apple-stalls he had knocked over (so to say, walked through) since the search began, he would have had some difficulty to reckon up. As to bringing him to account for damages, that was simply impracticable. Before the capsized individual could understand what had happened to him, or the bewildered apple-woman so much as looked at her fallen wares, Roland was out of sight and hearing. A young shoe-black at the corner had got to think the gentleman, pressing onwards everlastingly up and down the street, never turning aside from his course, might be the Wandering Jew; and would cease brushing to gaze up at Roland whenever he passed.

Look at him now, reader. The tall, fine, well-dressed young fellow, his pale face anxious with not-attempted-to-be-concealed care, his arms swaying, the silk-lined breasts of his frock-coat thrown back, as he strides on resolutely down Wellington Street! Neither to the right nor the left looks he: his eyes are cast forth over the people's heads, towards the bridge and the river that it spans, as if staring for the information he is going to seek. One great feature in Roland was his hopefulness. Each time he started for Waterloo Bridge, or Scotland Yard, or Hamish Channing's, or Mr. Greatorex's, or any other place where news might possibly be awaiting him, renewed hope was to the full as buoyant in his heart as it had been that memorable day when he had anchored in the beautiful harbour of Port Natal, and gazed on the fair shore with all its charming scenery that seemed to Roland as a very paradise. Bright with hope as his heart had been then, so was it now in the intermittent intervals. So was it at this moment as he bore on, down Wellington Street.

"Well," said he to the toll-keeper. "Anything turned up?"

"Not a bit on't," responded the man. "Nor likely to." Roland went through, perched himself on the parapet, and took his fill of gazing at the river. Now on this side the bridge, now leaping over to that. A steamer passed, a rowing-boat or two; but Arthur Channing was not in them. Roland looked to the mud on the sides, he threw his gaze forwards and backwards, up and down, round and about. In vain. All features were very much the same that they had been from the day of his first search: certainly returning to him no signs of Arthur. And down went hope again, as completely as the pears had gone, earlier in the day, at a corner stall. Despair had possession of him now.

"You say that no suspicious character went on to the bridge that night, so far as you can recollect," resumed Roland in the gloomiest tone, when he had walked lingeringly back to the man at the gate. Lingeringly, because some kind of clue seemed to lie with that bridge and he was always loth to quit it. If he did not suspect Arthur might be lying buried underneath the stone pavement, it seemed something like it.

"I didn't say so," interrupted the gate-keeper, in rather a surly tone. "What I said was, as there warn't nothing suspicious chucked over that night."

"You can't tell. You might not hear."

"Well, I haven't got no time to jabber with you today."

"If I kept this turnstile, I should make it my business to mark all suspicious night characters that went through; and watch them."

"Oh, would you! And how 'ud you know which was the suspicious ones? Come! They don't always carry their bad marks on their backs, they don't; some on 'em don't look no different from you."

Roland bit his lips to keep down a retort. All in Arthur's interest. Upon giving the man, on a recent visit, what the latter had called "sauce," his migration on and off the bridge had been threatened with a summary stoppage. So he was careful.

"Well, I've just had a clue given me by the police. And I don't hold the smallest doubt now that he was put out of the way. And this is the likeliest place for him to have been brought to. I don't think it would take much skill, after he had been chloroformed to death, to shoot him over, out of a Hansom cab. Brought up upon the pavement, level with the parapet, he'd go as easily over, if propelled, as I should if I jumped it."

The toll-keeper answered by a growl and some sharp words. Truth to say, he felt personally aggrieved at his bridge being subjected to these scandalizing suspicions, and resented them accordingly. Roland did not wait. He went off in search of Hamish, and ere he had left the bridge behind out of sight, hope began again to spring up within him. So buoyant is the human heart in general, and Roland's in particular. Not—let it always be Understood—the hope that Arthur would be found uninjured, only some news of him that might serve to solve the mystery.

Shooting out of a Hansom cab (not dead, after the manner of a picture just drawn, but alive) came a gentleman, just as Roland was passing it. The cab had whirled round the corner of Wellington Street, probably on its way from the station, and pulled up at a shop in the Strand. It was Sir Vincent Yorke. Roland stopped; seized his hand in his impulsive manner, and began entering upon the story of Arthur Channing's disappearance without the smallest preliminary greeting of any kind. Every moment Roland could spare from running, he spent in talking. He talked to Mrs. Jones, he talked to Henry William Ollivera, he talked to Hurst and Jenner, he would have talked to the moon. Mr. Brown had been obliged to forbid him the office, unless he could come to it to work. In his rapid, excited manner, he poured forth the story, circumstance after circumstance, in Sir Vincent's ear, that gentleman feeling slightly bewildered, and not best pleased at the unexpected arrest.

"Oh—ah—I dare say he'll turn up all right," minced Sir Vincent. "A fella's not obliged to acquaint his friends with his movements. Just got up to town?—ah—yes—just for a day or two. Good day. Hope you'll find him."

"You don't understand who it is, Vincent," spoke Roland, resenting the want of interest; which, to say the best of it, was but lukewarm. "It is William Yorke's brother-in-law, Annabel's brother, and the dearest friend I've ever had in life. I've told you of Arthur Channing before. He has the best and bravest heart living; he is the truest man and gentleman the world ever produced."

"An—yes—good day! I'm in a hurry."

Sir Vincent made his escape into the shop. Roland went on to Hamish Channing's office. Hamish could not neglect his work, however Roland might abandon his.

But Hamish would have liked to do it. In good truth, this most unaccountable disappearance of his brother was rendering him in a measure unfit for his duties. He might almost as well have devoted his whole time just now to the interests of the search, for his thoughts were with it always, and his interruptions were many. To him the police carried reports; it was on him Roland Yorke rattled in half a dozen times in the course of the day, upsetting all order and quiet, and business too, by the commotion he raised. To see Roland burst in, breath gone, hair awry, face white, chest heaving with emotion, was nothing at all extraordinary; but Hamish did wish, as the doors swung back after Roland, once more, on this morning, that he would not burst in quite so often. Perhaps Roland was a little more excited than usual, from the full belief that he had at length got hold of the right clue.

"It's all out, Hamish," he panted. "Arthur's as good as found. He went out of the hotel to do some errand for Galloway; it took him into those bad, desperate, pick-pocketing places where the police dare hardly go themselves, and that's where it must have been done."

Hamish laid down his pen. The colour deserted his face, a faintness stole over his heart.

"How has it been discovered, Roland?" he inquired, in a hushed tone.

"Spitchcock did it. You know the fellow,—red face, fat enough for two. I was with him just now; and in consequence of what he said, it's the conclusion I have come to."

Naturally, Hamish pressed for details. Upon Roland's supplying them, with accuracy as faithful as his state of mind allowed, Hamish knew not whether to be most relieved or vexed. Roland had neither wish nor thought to deceive; and his positive assertion was made only in accordance with the belief he had worked himself into. To find that the present "clue," as Roland called it, turned out to be a supposititious one of that impulsive gentleman's mind, on a par with the theory he entertained in regard to Waterloo Bridge, was a relief undoubtedly to Hamish; but, nevertheless, he would have preferred Roland's keeping the whole to himself.

"I wish you'd not take up these fancies, Roland," he said, as severely as his sweet nature ever allowed him to speak. "It is so useless to bring me unnecessary alarms."

"You may take my word for it that's how it will turn out to have been Hamish."

"No. Had Mr. Galloway charged him with any commission to unsafe parts that night—or to safe ones, either—he would have written up since to tell me."

"Oh, would he, though!" cried Roland, wiping his hot brow. "You don't know Galloway as I do, Hamish. He's just likely to have given such a commission (if he had it to give) and to think no more about it. Somebody ought to go to Helstonleigh."

Hamish made no reply to this. He was busy with his papers.

"Will you go, Hamish?"

"To Helstonleigh? Certainly not. There is not the slightest necessity for it. I am quite certain that Mr. Galloway holds no clue that he has not imparted."

"Then if nobody goes down, I will go," said Roland, his eyes lighting with earnestness, his cheeks flushing. "I never thought to show myself in Helstonleigh again until fortune had altered with me; but I'd despise myself if I could let my own feelings of shame stand in old Arthur's light."

"Don't do anything of the kind," advised Hamish. "Believe me, Roland, it is altogether an ideal notion you have taken up. Your impulsive nature deceives you."

"I shall go, Hamish. I am not obliged to carry your consent with me."

"I should not give it," said Hamish, slightly laughing, but speaking in an unmistakably firm accent.

He was interrupted by a hacking cough. As Roland watched him, waiting until it should cease, watched the hectic colour it left behind it, a sudden recollection came over him of one who used to cough in much the same way before he died.

"I say, old fellow, you've caught cold," he said.

"No, I think not."

"I'd get rid of that cough, Hamish. It makes me think of Joe Jenkins. Don't be offended: I'm not comparing you together. He was the thinnest and poorest lamp-post going, a miserable reed in the hands of Mrs. J.; and you are bright, handsome, fastidious Hamish Channing. But you cough alike."

With the last words Roland went dashing out. When he had a purpose in view, head and heels were alike impetuous, and perhaps no earthly power, unless it had been the appearance of Arthur, could have arrested him in the end he had in view—that of starting for Helstonleigh.

CHAPTER XXX

A NEW IDEA FOR MR OLLIVERA

The Reverend Henry William Ollivera sat in his room at a late breakfast: he had been called abroad to a sick parishioner just as he was about to sit down to it at nine in the morning. With his usual abandonment of self, he hastened away, swallowing a thimbleful of coffee without milk or sugar, and carrying with him a crust of bread. It was nearly one when he came back again, having taken a morning service for a friend, and this was his real breakfast. Mrs. Jones, who cared for the comforts of the people about her in her tart way, had sent up what she called buttered eggs, a slice of ham, and a hot roll. The table-cloth was beautifully white: the coffeepot looked as good as silver.

But, tempting as the meal really was, hungry as Mr. Ollivera might be supposed to be, he was letting it get cold before him. A newspaper lay on the stand near, but he did not unfold it. The strangely eager light in his eyes was very conspicuous as he sat, seeing nothing, lost in a reverie; the fevered hands were still. Some months had elapsed now since his wild anxiety, to unfold the mystery enshrouding his brother's death, had set-in afresh, through the disclosure of Mr. Willett; a burning, restless anxiety, that never seemed wholly to quit his mind, by night or by day.

But nothing had come of it. Seek as Mr. Ollivera would, he as yet obtained no result. An exceedingly disagreeable and curious doubt had crossed his thoughts at times—whence arising he scarcely knew—of one whom he would have been very unwilling to suspect, even though the adverse appearances were greater than at present. And that was Alletha Rye. Perhaps what first of all struck him as strange, was Miss Rye's ill-concealed agitation upon any mention of the subject, her startling change of colour, her shrinking desire to avoid it. At the time of Mr. Willett's communication the clergyman had renewed his habit of going into Mrs. Jones's parlour to converse upon the topic; previously he had been letting it slip into disuse, and then it was that the remarkable demeanour of Miss Rye dawned gradually on his notice. At first he thought it an accident, next he decided that it was strange, afterwards he grew to introduce the topic suddenly on purpose to observe her. And what he saw was beginning to make a most unpleasant impression on him. A very slight occurrence, only the unexpected meeting of Mr. Butterby that morning, had brought the old matter all back to him. As he was hastening home from church, really wanting his breakfast, he encountered Jonas Butterby the detective. The latter said he had been in town nearly a week on business (the reader saw him at the commencement, in conjunction with Mr. Bede Greatorex), but was returning to Helstonleigh that night or on the morrow. For a few minutes they stood conversing of the past, Butterby saying that nothing had "turned up."

"Have you not heard of Godfrey Pitman?" suddenly asked Mr. Ollivera.

The question was put sharply: and for once the clever man was at fault. Did Mr. Ollivera mean to imply that he had heard of Pitman?—that he, the clergyman, was aware that he had heard? Or, was it but a simple question? In the uncertainty Mr. Butterby made a pause, evidently in some kind of doubt or hesitation, and glanced keenly at the questioner from under his eyebrows. Mr. Ollivera marked it all.

"Have you heard of him, then?"

"The way that folks's thoughts get wandering!" exclaimed Butterby, with a charming air of innocence. "Pitman, says you: if I wasn't a running of my head on that other man—Willett. And he has got an attack of the shivers from drinking; that's the last gazetted news of him, sir. As to that Godfrey Pitman—the less we say about him, the better, unless we could say it to some purpose. Good morning, Reverend Sir; I've got my work cut out for me today."

"One moment," said Mr. Ollivera, detaining him. "I want your opinion upon a question I am going to ask. Could a woman, think you, have killed my brother?"

Perhaps the question was so unexpected as slightly to startle even the detective. Instead of answering it, his green eyes shot out another keen glance at Mr. Ollivera, and they did not quit his face again. The latter supposed he was not understood.

"I mean, could a woman, think you, have had the physical strength to fire the pistol?"

"Do you ask me that, sir, because you suspect one?"

"I cannot say I go so far as to suspect one. It has occurred to me latterly as being within the range of possibility. I wish you would answer my question, Mr. Butterby?"

"In course, from the point you put it, it might have been a woman just as well as a man; some women be every bit as strong, and a sight bolder," was Mr. Butterby's answer. "But I can't wait, sir, now," he added, as he turned away and said good morning once more.

"It was queer, his asking that," very softly repeated Mr. Butterby, between his lips, as he walked on at a quicker pace than usual.

Mr. Ollivera got home with his head full of this; and, as usual under the circumstances, was letting his late breakfast grow cold before him. Mrs. Jones, entering the room on some domestic errand, gave him the information that Roland Yorke had just come in in a fine state of commotion (which was nothing unusual), saying Arthur Channing was as good as found murdered; and that he was, in consequence, off to Helstonleigh. Before Mr. Ollivera, setting to his breakfast then with a will, could get downstairs, Roland had gone skimming out again. So the clergyman turned his steps to the house of Greatorex and Greatorex.

It could not be but that the singular and prolonged disappearance of Arthur Channing should be exciting commotion in the public mind. Though it had not been made, so to say, a public matter, at least a portion of the public knew of it. The name did not appear in the papers; but the "mysterious disappearance of a gentleman" was becoming quite a treasure to the news-compilers. Greatorex and Greatorex had taken it up warmly, as much from real intrinsic interest in the affair itself, as that Annabel was an inmate of their house. Arthur Channing had stood, unsolicited, over John Ollivera's grave at the stealthy midnight burial service; and Mr. Greatorex did not forget it. He had offered his services at once to Hamish Channing. "We have," he said, "a wide experience of London life, and will do for you in it all that can be done." Bede, though kindly anxious, wished the matter could be set at rest, for it was costing him a clerk. Roland candidly avowed that he was no more fit for his work at present, than he would be to rule the patients in St. Luke's; and Bede privately believed this was only truth. Little Jenner was home again, and took Roland's work as well as his own.

One very singular phase of the attendant surroundings was this—so many people appeared to be missing. The one immediately in question, Arthur Channing, was but a unit in the number. Scarcely an hour in the day passed but the police either received voluntary news of somebody's disappearance; or, through their inquiries after Arthur, gained it for themselves. If space allowed, and these volumes were the proper medium for it, a most singularly interesting account might be given of the facts, every word of which would be true.

Henry Ollivera found Mr. Greatorex in the dining-room finishing his luncheon. In point of fact it was his dinner, for he was going out of town that afternoon and would not be home until late. Bede, who rarely took luncheon, though he sometimes made a pretence of going up for it, was biting morsels off a hard biscuit, as he stood against the wall by the mantelpiece, near the handsome pier-glass that in his days of vanity he had been so fond of glancing in. Mrs. Bede Greatorex was at table; also the little girl, Jane, whose dinner it was. The board was extravagantly spread, displaying fish and fowl, and other delicacies, and Mrs. Bede was solacing herself with a pint of sparkling hock, which stood at her elbow. She looked flushed; at least, as much as a made-up face can look, and in her eyes there shone an angry light: perhaps at the non-appearance of two visitors she had expected, perhaps because she had just come from one of her violent-tempered attacks on Miss Channing. Mr. Greatorex, like his son Bede, did not appear to appreciate the good things: he was making his dinner off one plain dish and a glass of pale ale.

"You will sit down and take some, William?"

Mr. Ollivera declined; he had just swallowed his breakfast. From the absence of Miss Channing at the table, he drew an augury that the ill news spoken of by Mrs. Jones must be correct. But Mr. Greatorex said he was not aware of anything fresh; and a smile crossed his lips upon hearing that Roland was the author of the report. Bede laughed outright.

"If you only knew how often he has come in, startling us with extraordinary tales, you'd have learnt by this time what faith to have put in Roland Yorke," said Bede. "A man more sensitively nervous than he is, or ever will be, would have had brain-fever with all this talking and walking and mental excitement."

"He says, I understand, that he is going down to Helstonleigh, to get some information from Mr. Galloway," said the clergyman.

"Oh, is he? As good go there as stay here, for all the work he does. He'd start for the moon if there were a road to convey him to it."

"I wonder you give him so much holiday, Bede," remarked Mr. Ollivera.

"He takes it," answered Bede. "He is of very little use at his best, but we don't choose to discharge him, or in fact make any change until Lord Carrick comes over, who may now be expected shortly. I believe one thing—that he tries to do his utmost: and Brown puts up with him."

"Do you know," began Mr. Ollivera, in a low, meaning tone, when the door Closed upon the luncheon-tray, and the three gentlemen stood around the fire, Mrs. Bede having betaken herself to a far-off window, "I have half a mind to go to Helstonleigh myself."

"In search of Arthur Channing, William?"

"No, uncle. In quest of that other search that has been upon my mind so long. An idea has forced itself upon me lately that it—might have been a woman."

"For heaven's sake drop it," exclaimed Bede, with strange agitation. "Don't you see Louisa?"

She could not have heard—but Bede was always thus. He had his reasons for not allowing it to be spoken of before her. One of them was this. In the days gone by, just before their marriage, Clare Joliffe, suddenly introducing the subject of Ollivera's death, when Bede was present, said to her sister in a tone between jest and earnest, that she (Louisa) had been the cause of it. Clare meant no more than that her conduct had caused him to end his life—as it was supposed he did. But Louisa, partly with passion, had gone into a state of agitation so great as to alarm Bede. Never, from that time, would he suffer it to be mentioned before her if he could guard against it.

"But, William what do you mean about a woman?" asked Mr. Greatorex, dropping his voice to a low key.

"Uncle Greatorex, I cannot explain myself. I must go on in my own way, until the time to speak shall come. That the clearance of the past is rapidly advancing I feel sure of. A subtle instinct whispers it to me. My dreams tell it me. Forget for the present what I said. I ought not to have spoken."

"You are visionary as usual," said Bede, sarcastically.

"I know that you always think me so," was the clergyman's answer, and he turned to depart.

There was a general dispersion. Only Mr. Greatorex remained in the room: and he had fallen into deep thought: when Roland Yorke, in his chronic state of excitement, dashed in. Without any ceremony he flung himself into a chair.

"Mr. Greatorex, I am nearly dead-beat. What with cutting about perpetually, and meeting depressing disappointments, and catching up horrible new fears, it's enough to wear a fellow out, sir."

Roland looked it: dead-beat. He had plenty of strength; but it would not stand this much overtaxing. In the last six days it may be questioned if he had sat down, with the exception of coming to a temporary anchor on upright barrels or parapets of bridges; and then he and his legs were so restless from excitement that a spectator would have thought he was afflicted with St. Vitus's Dance.

"Been taking a round this morning as usual, I suppose, Mr. Yorke," said the lawyer.

"Ever so many of them, sir. I began with the docks: I can't help thinking that if anything was done with Arthur in conjunction with a carpet-bag, he might turn up there, after drifting down. Then I walked back to Scotland Yard, then looked into a few shops and police-stations. Next I went to Waterloo Bridge, then down to Hamish Channing's, then back to Mrs. Jones's; then to Vincent Yorke's; and now I'm come here to tell you I'm going down to Helstonleigh, if you don't mind sparing me."

If you don't mind sparing me! For the use he was of to the house, it did not matter whether he went or stayed. But that Roland had improved in mind and manners, he had surely not asked it. Time was when he had gone off on a longer journey than the one to Helstonleigh and never said to his master, With your leave or by your leave; but just quitted the office impromptu, leaving his compliments as a legacy.

"And if you please I'd like to see Miss Channing before I start, sir; to tell her what I'm doing, and to ask if she has any messages for her people."

Mr. Greatorex rang the bell. He fancied Miss Channing might be out, as she had not appeared at luncheon.

Not out, but in her bedroom. The pretty bedroom with its window-curtains of chintz and its tasty furniture. When gaiety or discord reigned below, when Mrs. Bede Greatorex's temper tried her as with a heavy cross, Annabel could come up here and find it a sure refuge. In one of the outbreaks of violence that seemed to be almost like insanity, Mrs. Bede had that morning attacked Miss Channing—and for no earthly reason, There are such tempers, there are such women in the world. Some of us know it too well.

Weeping, trembling, Annabel gained her chamber, and there sobbed out her heart. It had needed no additional grief today, for Arthur's strange disappearance filled it with a heavy, shrinking, terrible weight. Jane ran up to say luncheon was ready—their dinner; Annabel replied that she could not eat any. Taking the child in her arms, kissing her with many gentle kisses, she whispered a charge not to mention what had passed: if grandpapa or uncle Bede happened to remark on her absence from table, Jane might say she had a headache, and it would be perfectly true, for her head did ache sadly. It was ever thus; even Mrs. Bede Greatorex she endeavoured to screen from condemnation. Trained to goodness; to return good for evil whenever it was practicable: to bear sweetly and patiently, Annabel Channing strove to carry out certain holy precepts in every action of her daily life. Too many of us keep them for the church and the closet. Annabel had learnt the one only way. Praying ever, as she had been taught from childhood, for the Holy Spirit spoken of by Jesus Christ to make its home in her heart, and direct and restrain her always, she certainly knew the way to Peace as well as it can be known here; and practised it. "The fruit of righteousness is sown in peace of them that make peace."

But it was hard to bear. Her nature was but human. There were times, as on this day, when she thought she could not endure it; that she must give up her situation. And that she was loth to do. Loth for more reasons than one. Putting aside these trying outbreaks, the place was desirable. She was regarded as an equal, treated as a lady, well paid: and, what weighed greatly with Annabel in her extreme conscientiousness, she was unwilling to abandon Jane Greatorex. For she was doing the child good: good in the highest sense of the word. Left to some governesses (conscientious ones too in a moral and scholastic point of view) Jane would grow up a selfish, careless, utterly worldly woman: Annabel was ever patiently working by gentle degrees to lead her to wish to be something better; and she had begun to see a little light breaking in on her way. For this great cause she wished to remain: it seemed to be a duty to do so.

Drawing her desk towards her, she had sat down to write to her sister Constance, William Yorke's wife. Constance was her great resource. To her, when the world's troubles were pressing heavily, Annabel poured out her sorrow—never having hinted at any particular cause, only saying the situation "had its trials"—and Constance never failed to write by return of post an answer that cheered Annabel, and helped her on her way. The very fact of writing seemed often to do her good as on this day, and the tears had dried on her cheeks, and her face grew cheerful with hopeful resolution, as she folded the letter.

"I must balance the good I enjoy here against the trouble," she said; "that will help me to bear it better. If Jane—"

She was interrupted by the young lady in question; who came running in, followed by one of the maids.

"Miss Channing, Roland Yorke wants to see you in the dining-room."

"Roland Yorke!" repeated Annabel, dubiously. With all his lack of attention to conventionalities, Mr. Roland had never gone so far as to send up for her.

"It was Mr. Greatorex who desired me to tell you, miss," spoke up the servant, possibly thinking Miss Jane's news needed confirmation. "He rang to know whether you were at home, and then told me to come and say that Mr. Yorke wished to see you."

Annabel smoothed down the folds of her grey silk dress, and looked to see that her pretty auburn hair was tidy. She saw something else; her swollen eyes, and the vivid blushes on her cheeks.

"I'll come with you," whispered Miss Jane. "I'll tell him about Aunt Bede."

And the conviction that she might tell, in spite of all injunction against it, startled Annabel. Roland was the young lady's prime favourite, regarded by her as a big playfellow.

"You cannot come with me, Jane. Mary, be so kind as to take Miss Jane to Dalla. Say that she must remain in the nursery until I am at liberty."

Roland was alone in the dining-room when she entered it. With a delicacy that really was to be commended in one who had been to Port Natal, he would not tell her of the theory he had caught up, or why he was going to Helstonleigh; only that he was about to start for that city.

"But what are you going for, Roland?" was the very natural question that ensued.

"To see old Galloway," he replied, standing by her on the hearthrug where Mr. Greatorex and Henry Ollivera had been standing but just before. "I think Galloway must have given—at least—that is—that he could find some clue to Arthur's movements, if he were well pumped; and I am going to do it. Somebody ought to go; Hamish won't, and so it falls upon me."

Annabel made no answer.

"I shan't like appearing in the old place," he candidly resumed. "I said I never would until I could take a fortune with me; but one has to do lots of things in this world that go against the grain; one soon lives long enough to find that boasting turns out to be nothing but emptiness."

"Oh Roland!" she said, as the utter fallacy of the expectation struck upon her, "I fear it will be a lost journey. Had Mr. Galloway been able to furnish ever so small a clue, he would have been sure to send it without being asked."

"That's what Hamish says. But I mean to try. I'd be off today to the North Pole as soon as to Helstonleigh, if I thought it would find him. And to think, Annabel, that while he was being kept out of the way by fate or ruffians, I was calling him proud!—and neglectful!—and hard-hearted! I'll never forgive myself that. If, through lack of exertion on my part, he should not be found, I might expect his ghost to come back and stand at the foot of my bed every night."

"But—Roland—you have not given up all hope?" she questioned, her clear, honest hazel eyes cast up steadily and beseechingly at his.

"Well, I don't know. Sometimes I think he's sure to turn up all right, and then down I go again into the depths of mud. Last night I dreamt he was alive and well, and I was helping him up some perpendicular steps from a boat moored under Waterloo Bridge. When I awoke I thought it was true; oh! I was so glad! Even after I remembered, it seemed a good omen. Don't be down-hearted, Annabel. Once, at Port Natal, a fellow I knew was lost for a year. His name was Crow. We never supposed but what he was dead, but he came to life again with a good crop of red whiskers, and said he'd only been travelling. I say! what's the matter with your eyes?"

The sudden question rather confused her. She answered evasively.

"You've been crying, Annabel. Now, you tell me what the grievance was. If Mrs. Bede Greatorex makes you unhappy—good gracious! and I can't help you, or take you out of here! I do not know when I shall: I don't get on at all. It's enough to make a man swear."

"Hush Roland! I am very unhappy about Arthur."

"Why, of course you are—how came I to forget it?" he rejoined, easily satisfied as a child. "And here am I, wasting the precious time that might be spent in looking after him! Have you anything to send to Helstonleigh?"

"Only my love. My dear love to them all. You will see mamma?"

Roland suddenly took both her hands in his, and so held her before him, stooping his head a little, and speaking gently.

"Annabel, I shall have to see your mamma, and tell her—"

She did not mean that at all; it had not so much as occurred to her. Naturally the cheeks became very vivid now. Without further ado, asking no leave, bold Roland kissed the shrinking face.

"Good bye, Annabel. Wish me luck."

Away he clattered, waiting for neither scolding nor answer, and was flying along the street below, before Annabel had at all recovered her equanimity.

To resolve to go to Helstonleigh was one thing, to get to it was another; and Roland Yorke, with his customary heedlessness, had not considered ways and means. It was only when he dashed in at his lodgings that morning (as, we have heard, was related by Mrs. Jones to Mr. Ollivera), that the question struck him how he was to get there. He had not a coin in the world. Roland's earnings (the result of having put his shoulder to the wheel these three or four months past) had been deposited for safety with Mrs. Jones, it may be remembered, and they amounted to two sovereigns. These had been spent in the search after Arthur. In the first commotion of his disappearance, Roland had wildly dashed about in Hansoms; for his legs, with all their length and impatience, would not carry him from pillar to post fleet enough. He made small presents to policemen, hoping to sharpen their discovering powers; he put two advertisements in the Times, offering rewards for mysterious carpet-bags. But that a fortunate oversight caused him to omit appending any address, it was quite untellable the number of old bags that might have been brought him. All this had speedily melted the gold pieces. He then got Mrs. Jones to advance him (grumblingly) two more which went the same way, and were not yet repaid. So there he was, without money to take him to Helstonleigh, and nobody that he knew of likely to lend him any.

"I can't walk," debated he, standing stock-still in his parlour, as his penniless state occurred to him. "They'd used to call it a hundred and eleven miles in the old coaching days. It would be nothing to me if I had the time, but I can't waste that now. Hamish has set his face against my going, or I'd ask him. I wonder—I wonder whether Dick Yorke would let me have a couple of pounds?"

To "wonder," meant to do, with Roland. Out he went again on the spur of the moment, and ran all the way to Portland Place. Sir Vincent was not at home. The man said he had been there that morning on his arrival from Sunny Mead (the little Yorke homestead in Surrey), but had gone out again directly. He might be expected in at any moment, or all moments, during the day.

Roland waited. In a fine state of restlessness, as we may be sure, for the precious time was passing. He was afraid to go to the club lest he might miss him. When one o'clock had struck, Roland thought he might do his other errand first: which was to acquaint Greatorex and Greatorex with his departure, and see Miss Channing. Therefore, he started forth again, leaving a peremptory message for Sir Vincent should he return, that he was to wait in for him.

And now, having seen Mr. Greatorex and Annabel, he was speeding back again to Portland Place. All breathless, and in a commotion, of course; driving along as if the pavement belonged to him, and nobody else had any claim to it. Charging round a corner at full tilt, he charged against an inoffensive foot-passenger, quietly approaching it: who was no other than Mr. Butterby.

Roland brought himself up. It was an opportunity not to be missed. Seizing hold of the official button-hole, he poured the story of Arthur Channing's disappearance into the official ear, imploring Mr. Butterby's good services in the cause.

"Don't you think any more of the uncivil names I've called you, Butterby. You knew all the while I didn't mean anything. I've said I'd pay you out when I got the chance, and so I will, but it shall be in gold. If you will only put your good services into the thing, we shall find him. Do, now! You won't bear malice, Butterby."

So impetuous had been the flow of eloquence, that Mr. Butterby had found no opportunity of getting a word in edgeways: he had simply looked and listened. The loss of Arthur Channing had been as inexplicable to him as to other people.

"Arthur Channing ain't one of them sort o' blades likely to get into a mess, through going to places where drinking and what not's carried on," spoke he.

"Of course he is not," was Roland's indignant answer. "Arthur Channing drink! he'd be as likely to turn tumbler at a dancing-booth! Look here, Butterby, you did work him harm once, but I'll never reproach you with it again as long as I live, and I've known all along you had no ill-meaning in it: but now, you find him this time and that will be tit for tat. Perhaps I may be rich some day, and I'll buy you a silver snuffbox set with diamonds."

"I don't take snuff," said Mr. Butterby.

But it was impossible to resist Roland's pleading, in all its simple-hearted energy. And, to give Mr. Butterby his due, he would have been glad to do his best to find Arthur Channing.

"I can't stay in London myself," said he; "I've been here a week now on private business, and must go down to Helstonleigh tomorrow; but I'll put it special into Detective Jelf's hands. He's as 'cute an officer, young Mr. Yorke, as here and there one, and of more use in London than me."

"Bless you, Butterby!" cried hearty Roland; "tell Jelf I'll give him a snuffbox, too. And now I'm off. I won't forget you, Butterby."

Mr. Butterby thought the chances that Roland would ever have tin snuff-boxes to give away, let alone silver, were rather poor but he was not a bad-natured man, and he detained Roland yet an instant to give him a friendly word of advice.

"There's one or two folks, in the old place, that you owe a trifle to, Mr. Yorke—"

"There's half-a-dozen," interrupted candid Roland.

"Well, sir, I'd not show myself in the town more than I could help. They are vexed at being kept out of their money thinking some of the family might have paid it; and they might let off a bit if you went amid 'em: unless, indeed, you are taking down the money with you."

"Taking the money with me!—why, Butterby, I've not got a sixpence in the world," avowed Roland, opening his surprised eyes. "If Dick Yorke won't lend me a pound or so, I don't know how on earth to get down, unless they let me have a free pass on the top of the engine."

There was no time for more. Away he went to Portland Place, and thundered at the door, as if he had been a king. But his visit did not serve him.

Sir Vincent Yorke had entered just after Roland departed. Upon receiving the peremptory message, the baronet marvelled what it could mean, and whether all the Yorke family had been blown up, save himself. Nothing else, he thought, could justify the scapegoat Roland in desiring him, Sir Vincent, to stay in. To be kept waiting at home when he very particularly wanted to be out—for Sir Vincent had come to town to meet the lady he was shortly to marry, Miss Trehern—made him frightfully cross. So that when Roland re-appeared he had an angry-tempered man to deal with.

And, in good truth, had Roland announced the calamity, so pleasantly anticipated, it would have caused Sir Vincent less surprise; certainly less vexation. When he found he had been decoyed into staying in for nothing but to be asked to lend money to take Mr. Roland careering off somewhere by rail—he was in too great a passion to understand where—Sir Vincent exploded. Roland, quietly braving the storm, prayed for "just a pound," as if he were praying for his life. Sir Vincent finally replied that he'd not lend him a shilling if it would save him from hanging.

So Roland was thrown on his beam ends, and went back to Mrs. Jones's with empty pockets, revolving ways and means in his mind.

CHAPTER XXXI

MR GALLOWAY INVADED

It was night in the old cathedral town. The ten o'clock bell had rung, and Mr. Galloway, proctor and surrogate, at home in his residence in the Boundaries, was thinking he might go to rest. For several days he had been feeling very much out of sorts, and this evening the symptoms had culminated in what seemed a bad cold, attended with feverishness and pain in all his limbs. The old proctor was one of those people whose mind insensibly sways the body; and the mysterious disappearance of Arthur Channing was troubling him to sickness. He had caused a huge fire to be made up in his bedroom, and was seated by it, groaning; his slippered feet on a warm cushion, a railway rug enveloping his coat, and back, and shoulders; a white cotton nightcap with a hanging tassel ornamenting gracefully his head. One of his servants had just brought up a basinful of hot gruel, holding at least a quart, and put it on the stand by his easy chair. Mr. Galloway was groaning at the gruel as much as with pain, for he hated gruel like poison.

Thinking it might be less nauseous if disposed of at an unbroken draught, were that possible—or at least soonest over—Mr. Galloway caught up the basin and put it to his lips. With a cry and a splutter, down went the basin again. The stuff was scalding hot. And whether Mr. Galloway's tongue, or teeth, or temper suffered most, he would have been puzzled to confess.

It was at this untoward moment—Mr. Galloway's face turning purple, and himself choking and coughing—that a noise, as of thunder, suddenly awoke the echoes of the Boundaries. Shut up in his snug room hearing sounds chiefly through the windows, the startled Mr. Galloway wondered what it was, and edged his white nightcap off one ear to listen. He had then the satisfaction of discovering that the noise was at his own front door. Somebody had evidently got hold of the knocker (an appendage recently made to the former naked panels), and was rapping and rattling as if never intending to leave off. And now the bell-handle was, pulled in accompaniment—as a chorus accompanies a song—and the alarmed household were heard flying towards the door from all quarters.

"Is it the fire-engine?" groaned Mr. Galloway to himself. "I didn't hear it come up."

It appeared not to be the fire-engine. A moment or two, and Mr. Galloway was conscious of a commotion on the stairs, some visitor making his way up; his man-servant offering a feeble opposition.

"What on earth does John mean? He must be a fool—letting people come up here!" thought Mr. Galloway, apostrophising his many years' servitor. "Hark! It can never be the Dean!"

That any other living man, whether church dignitary or ordinary mortal, would venture to invade him in his private sanctum, take him by storm in his own chamber, was beyond belief. Mr. Galloway, all fluttered and fevered, hitched his white nightcap a little higher, turned his wondering face to the door, and sat listening.

"If he is neither in bed nor undressed, as you say, I can see him up here just as well as below; so don't bother, old John," were the words that caught indistinctly the disturbed invalid's ear: and somehow the voice seemed to strike some uncertain chord of memory. "I say, old John, you don't get younger," it went on; "where's your hair gone? Is this the room?—it used to be."

Without further ado the door was flung open; and the visitor stepped over the threshold. The two, invader and invaded, gazed at each other. The one saw an old man, who appeared to be shrunk in spite of his wraps, with a red face, surmounted by a cotton nightcap, a flaxen curl or two peeping out above the amazed eyes, and a basin of steaming gruel: the other saw a tall, fine, well-dressed young fellow, whose face, like the voice, struck on the chords of memory. John spoke from behind.

"It's Mr. Roland Yorke, sir. He'd not be stayed: he would come up in spite of me."

"Goodness bless me!" exclaimed the proctor.

Putting down his hat and a small brown paper parcel that he carried, Roland advanced to Mr. Galloway, nearly turning over the stand and the gruel, which John had to rush forward and steady—and held out his hand.

"I don't know whether you'll shake it, sir, after the way we parted. I am willing."

"The way of parting was yours, Mr. Roland, not mine," was the answer. But Mr. Galloway did shake the hand, and Roland sat down by the fire, uninvited, making himself at home as usual.

"What's amiss, sir?" he asked, as John went away. "Got the mumps? Is that gruel? Horrid composition! I think it must have been invented for our sins. You must be uncommon ill, sir, to swallow that."

"And what in the world brings you down here at this hour, frightening quiet people out of their senses?" demanded Mr. Galloway, paying no heed to Roland's questions. "I'm sure I thought it was the parish engine."

"The train brought me," replied matter-of-fact Roland. "I had meant to get here by an earlier one, but things went cross and contrary."

"That was no reason why you should knock my door down."

"Oh, it was all my impatience: my mind's in a frightful worry," penitently acknowledged Roland. "I hope you'll forgive it, sir. I've come from London, Mr. Galloway, about this miserable business of Arthur Channing. We want to know where you sent him to?"

Mr. Galloway, his doubts as to fire-engines set at rest, had been getting cool; but the name turned him hot again. He had grown to like Arthur better than he would have cared to tell; the supposition flashed into his mind that a discovery might have been made of some untoward fate having overtaken him, and that Roland's errand was to break the news.

"Is Arthur dead?" he questioned, in a low tone.

"I think so," answered Roland. "But he has not turned up yet, dead or alive. I'm sure it's not for the want of looking after. I've spent my time pretty well, since he was missing, between Waterloo Bridge and the East India Docks."

"Then you've not come down to say he is found?"

"No: only to ask you where you sent him that night, that he may be."

When the explanation was complete, Roland discovered that he had had his journey for nothing, and would have done well to take the opinion of Hamish Channing. Every tittle of information that Mr. Galloway was able to give, he had already written to Hamish: not a thought, not a supposition, but he had imparted it in full. As to Roland's idea, that business might have carried Arthur to dishonest neighbourhoods in London, Mr. Galloway negatived it positively.

"He had none to do for me in such places, and I'm sure he'd not of his own."

Roland sat pulling at his whiskers, feeling very gloomy. In his sanguine temperament, he had been buoying himself with a hope that grew higher and higher all the way down: so that when he arrived at Mr. Galloway's he had nearly persuaded himself that—if Arthur, in person, was not there, news of him would be. Hence the loud and impatient door-summons.

"I know he is at the bottom of the Thames! I did so hope you could throw some light on it that you might have forgotten to tell, Mr. Galloway."

"Forgotten!" returned Mr. Galloway, slightly agitated. "If I remembered my sins, young man, as well as I remember all connected with him, I might be the better for it. His disappearance has made me ill; that's what it has done; and I'm not sure but it will kill me. When a steady, honourable, God-fearing young man like Arthur Channing, whose heart I verily believe was as much in heaven as earth; when such a man disappears in this mysterious manner at night in London, leaving no information of his whereabouts, and who cannot be traced or found, nothing but the worst is to be apprehended. I believe Arthur Churning to have been murdered for the large sum of money he had about him."

Mr. Galloway seized his handkerchief, and rubbed his hot face. The nightcap was pushed a little further off in the process. It was the precise view Roland had taken; and, to have it confirmed by Mr. Galloway's, seemed to drive all hope out of him for good.

"And I never had the opportunity of atoning to him for the past, you see, Mr. Galloway! It will stick in my memory for life, like a pill in the throat. I'd rather have been murdered myself ten times over."

"I gave my consent to his going with reluctance," said Mr. Galloway, seeming to repeat the fact for his own benefit rather than for Roland's. "What did it signify whether Charles was met in London, or not? if he could find his way to London from Marseilles alone, surely he might find it to Helstonleigh! Our busy time, the November audit, is approaching: but it was not that thought that swayed me against it, but an inward instinct. Arthur said he had not had a holiday for two years; he said there was business wanting the presence of one of us in London: all true, and I yielded. And this is what has come of it!"

Mr. Galloway gave his face another rub; the nightcap went higher and seemed to hang on only by its tassel, admitting the curls to full view. In spite of Roland's despairing state, he took advantage of the occasion.

"I say, Mr. Galloway, your hair is not as luxuriant as it was."

"It's like me, then," returned Mr. Galloway, whose mind was too much depressed to resent personal remarks. "What will become of us all without Arthur (putting out of sight for a moment the awful grief for himself) I cannot imagine. Look at his mother! He nearly supported the house: Mrs. Channing's own income is but a trifle, and Tom can't give much as yet. Look at me! What on earth I shall do without him at the office, never can be surmised!"

"My goodness!" cried modest Roland. "You'll be almost as much put to it, sir, as you were when I went off to Port Natal."

Mr. Galloway coughed. "Almost," assented he, rather satirically. "Why, Roland Yorke," he burst forth with impetuosity, "if you had been with me from then till now, and abandoned all your lazy tricks, and gone in for hard work, taking not a day's holiday or an hour's play, you could never have made yourself into half the capable and clever man that. Arthur was."

"Well, you see, Mr. Galloway, my talents don't lie so much in the sticking to a desk as in knocking about," good-humouredly avowed Roland. "But I do go in for hard work; I do indeed."

"I hear you didn't make a fortune at Port Natal, young man!"

Roland, open as ever, gave a short summary of what he did instead—starved, and did work as a labourer, when he could get any to do and drove pigs, and came back home with his coat out at elbows.

"Nobody need reproach me; it was worse for me than for them—not but what lots of people do. I tried my best; and I'm trying it still. It did me one service, Mr. Galloway—took my pride and my laziness out of me. But for the lessons of life I learnt at Port Natal, I should have continued a miserable humbug to the end, shirking work on my own score, and looking to other folks to keep me. I'm trying to do my best honestly, and to make my way. The returns are not grand yet, but such as they are I'm living on them, and they may get better. Rome was not built in a day. I went out to Port Natal to set good old Arthur right with the world; I couldn't bring myself to publish the confession, that you know of, sir, while I stopped here. I thought to make my fortune also, a few millions, or so. I didn't do it; it was a failure altogether, but it made a better man of me."

"Glad to hear it," said Mr. Galloway.

He watched the earnest eager face, bent towards him he noted the genuine, truthful, serious tone the words were spoken in and the conclusion he drew was that Roland might not be making an unjustifiable boast. It seemed incredible though, taking into recollection his former experience of that gentleman.

"And when I've got on, so as to make a couple of hundred a year or so, I am going to get married, Mr. Galloway."

"In—deed!" exclaimed Mr. Galloway, staring very mach. "Is the lady fixed upon?"

"Well, yes; and I don't mind telling you, if you'll keep the secret and not repeat it up and down the town: I don't fancy she'd like it to be talked of yet. It's Annabel."

"Annabel Channing!" uttered Mr. Galloway, in dubious surprise. "Has she said she'll have you?"

"I am not so sure she has said it. She means it."

"Why she—she is one of the best and sweetest girls living; she might marry almost anybody; she might nearly get a lord," burst forth Mr. Galloway, with a touch of his former gossiping propensity.

Roland's eyes sparkled. "So she might, sir. But she'll wait for me. And she does not expect riches, either; but will put her shoulder to the wheel with me and be content to work and help until riches come."

Mr. Galloway gave a sniff of disbelief. He might be pardoned if he treated this in his own mind as a simple delusion on Roland's part. He liked Annabel nearly as well as he had liked Arthur; and he looked upon Mr. Roland as a wandering knight-errant, not much likely to do any good for himself or others. Roland rose.

"I must be off," he said. "I've got my mother to see. Well, this is a pill—to find you've no clue to give me. Hamish said it would be so."

"I hear Hamish Channing is ill?"

"He is not ill, that I know of. He looks it: a puff of wind you'd say would blow him away."

"Disappointed in his book?"

"Well, I suppose so. It's an awful sin, though, for it to have been written down—whoever did it."

"I should call it a swindle," corrected Mr. Galloway. "A barefaced, swindling injustice. The public ought to be put right, if there were anyway of doing it."

"Did you read the book, Mr. Galloway?"

"Yes; and then I went forthwith out and bought it. Ana I read Gerald's."

"That was a beauty, wasn't it?" cried sarcastic Roland.

"Without paint," pursued Mr. Galloway, in the same strain. "It was just worth throwing on the fire leaf by leaf, that's my opinion of Gerald's book. But it got the reviews, Roland."

"And be shot to it! We can't understand the riddle up in London, sir."

"I'm sure we can't down here," emphatically repeated Mr. Galloway. "Well, good night: I'm not sorry to have seen you. When are you going back?"

"Tomorrow. And I'd rather have gone a hundred miles the other way than come near Helstonleigh. I shall take care to go and see nobody here, except Mrs. Channing. If—"

"You must not speak of Arthur to Mrs. Channing," interrupted the proctor.

"Not speak of him!"

"She knows nothing of his loss: it has been kept from her. She thinks he is in Paris with Charles. In her weak state of health she would hardly stand the prolonged suspense."

"It's a good thing you told me," said Roland, heartily. "I hope I shan't let it out. Good night, sir. I must not forget this, though!" he added, taking up the parcel. "It has got a clean shirt and collar in it."

"Where are you going to sleep?"

Roland paused. Until that moment the thought had never struck him where he was to sleep.

"I dare say they can give me a shake-down at the mother's. The hearthrug will do: I'm not particular. I'd used to go in for a feather bed and two pillows. My goodness! what a selfish young lunatic I was!"

"If they can't, perhaps we can give you a shake-down here," said Mr. Galloway. "But don't you ring the house down if you come back."

"Thank you, sir," said Roland, gratefully. "I wonder all you old friends are so good to me."

He clattered down in a commotion, and found himself in the Boundaries. When he passed through them ten minutes before, he was bearing on too fiercely to Mr. Galloway's to take notice of a single feature. Time had been when Roland would not have cared for old memories. They came crowding on him now the dear life associations, the events and interests of his boyhood, like fresh green resting-places 'mid a sandy desert. The ringing out of the cathedral clock, telling the three-quarters past ten, helped the delusion. Opposite to him rose the time-honoured edifice, worn by the defacing hand of centuries. Renovation had been going on for a long while; the pinnacles were new; old buildings around, that formerly partially obscured it, had been removed, and it stood out to view as Roland had never before seen it. It was a bright night; the moon shone as clearly as it had done on that early March night which ushered in the commencing prologue of this story. It brought out the fretwork of the dear old cathedral; it lightened up the gables of the quaint houses of the Boundaries, all sizes and shapes in architecture; it glittered on the level grass enclosed by the broad gravel walks, which the stately dames of the still more stately church dignitaries once cared to pace. But where were the tall old elm-trees—through whose foliage the moonbeams ought to have glittered, but did not? Where were the rooks that used to make their home in them, wiling the poor college boys, at their Latin and Greek hard by, with the friendly chorus of caws? Gone. Roland looked up, eyes and mouth alike opening with amazement, and marvelled. A poor apology for the trees was indeed left; but topped and lopped to discredit. The branches, towering and spreading in their might, had been removed, and the homeless rooks driven away, wanderers.

"It's nothing but sacrilege," spoke bold Roland, when he had done staring. "For certain it'll bring nobody good luck."

He could not resist crossing the Boundaries to the little iron gate admitting to the cloisters. It would not admit him tonight: the cloister porter, successor to Mr. John Ketch of cantankerous memory, had locked it hours ago, and had the key safely hung up by his bed-side in his lodge. This was the gate through which poor Charley Channing had gone, innocently confiding, to be frightened all but to death, that memorable night in the annals of the college school. Charley, who was now a flourishing young clerk in India (at the present moment supposed to be enjoying Paris), and likely to rise to fame and fortune, health permitting. Many a time and oft, had Roland himself dashed through the gate, surplice on arm, in a white heat of fear lest he should be marked "late." How the shouts of the boys used to echo along the vaulted roof of the cloisters! How they seemed to echo in the heart of Roland now! Times had changed.

Things had changed. He had changed. A new set of boys filled the school: some of the clergy were fresh in the cathedral. The bishop, gone to his account, had been replaced by a better: a once great and good preacher, who was wont in times long gone by to fill the cathedral with his hearers of jostling crowds, had followed him. In Mr. Roland's own family, and in that of one with whom they had been very intimately associated, there were changes. George Yorke was no more; Gerald had risen to be a great man; he, Roland, had fallen, and was of no account in the world. Mr. Channing had died; Hamish was dying—

How came that last thought to steal into the mind of Roland Yorke. He did not know. It had never occurred to him before: why should it have done so now? Ah, he might ask himself the question, but he could not answer it. Buried in reflections of the past and present, one leading on to another, it had followed in as if consecutively, arising Roland knew not whence, and startling him to terror. He shook himself in a sort of fright; his pulse grew quick, his face hot.

"I do think I must have been in a dream," debated Roland, "or else moonstruck. Sunny Hamish! as if the world could afford to lose him! Nobody but a donkey whose brains had been knocked out of him at Port Natal, would get such wicked fancies."

He went back at full gallop, turned the corner, and looked out for the windows of his mother's house. They were not difficult to be seen, for in every one of them shone a blaze of light. The sweet white radiance of the moon, with its beauteous softness, never to be matched by earthly invention, was quite eclipsed in the garish red of the flaming windows. Lady Augusta Yorke had an assembly—as was plain enough by the signs.

"Was ever the like bother known!" spoke Roland aloud, momentarily halting in the quiet spot. "She's got all the world and his wife there. And I didn't want a soul to know that I was at Helstonleigh!"

He took his resolution at once, ran on, and made for a small side door. A smart maid, in a flounced gown and no cap to make mention of, stood at it, flirting with a footman from one of the waiting carriages. Roland went in head foremost, saying nothing, passing swiftly through tortuous passages and up the stairs. The girl naturally took him for a robber, or some such evil character, and stood agape with wonder. But she did not want for courage, and went after him. He had made his way to what used to be his sister's schoolroom in Miss Channing's time; the open door displayed a table temptingly set out with refreshments, and nobody was in it. When the maid got there, Roland, his hat on a chair and parcel on the floor, was devouring the sandwiches.

"Why, what on earth!" she began. "My patience! who are you sir? How dare you?"

"Who am I?" said Roland, his mouth nearly too full to answer. "You just go and fetch Lady Augusta here. Say a gentleman wants to see her. Tell her privately, mind."

The girl, in sheer amazement, did as she was bid: whispering her own comments to her mistress.

"I'd be aware of him, my lady, if I were you, please. It might be a maniac. I'm sure the way he's gobbling up the victuals don't look like nothing else."

Lady Augusta Yorke, slightly fluttered, took the precaution to draw with her her youngest son, Harry, a stalwart King's Scholar of seventeen. Advancing dubiously to the interview, she took a peep in, and saw the intruder, a great tall fellow, whose back was towards her, swallowing down big tablespoonfuls of custard. The sight aroused Lady Augusta's anger: there'd be a famine; there'd be nothing left for her hungry guests. In, she burst, something after Roland's own fashion, words of reproach on her tongue, threats of the police. Harry gazed in doubt; the maid brought up the rear.

Roland turned, full of affection, dropped the spoon into the custard dish, and flew to embrace her.

"How are you, mother darling? It's only me."

And the Lady Augusta Yorke, between surprise at the meeting, a little joy, and vexation on the score of her diminishing supper, was somewhat overwhelmed, and sunk into a chair in screaming hysterics.

CHAPTER XXXII

IN THE CATHEDRAL

The college bell was tolling for morning prayers: and the Helstonleigh College boys were coming up in groups and disappearing within the little cloister gate, with their white surplices on their arms, just as Roland Yorke had seen them in his reminiscential visions the previous night. It was the first of November: a saint's day; and a great one, as everybody knows; consequently the school had a holiday, and the king's scholars attended divine service.

Roland was amidst them, having come out after breakfast to give as he said a "look round." The morning was well on when he awoke up from the conch prepared for him at Lady Augusta's—a soft bed with charming pillows, and not a temporary shake-down on the hearthrug. They had sat up late the previous night, after Lady Augusta's guests had left, talking of old times and new ones. Roland freely confessed his penniless state, his present mode of living, with all its shifts and drawbacks, the pound a week that Mrs. Jones made do for all, the brushing of his own clothes, the sometimes blacking of his own boots: which sent his mother into a fit of reproachful sobs. In his sanguine open-heartedness he enlarged upon the fortune that was sure to be his some time ("a few hundreds a-year and a house of his own"), and made her and his two sisters the most liberal promises on the strength of it. Caroline Yorke turned from him: he had lost caste in her eyes. Fanny, with her sweet voice and gentle smile, whispered him to work on bravely, never to fear. The two girls were essentially different. Constance Channing had done her utmost with them both: they had gone to Hazledon with her when she became William Yorke's wife; but her patient training had borne different fruit.

Roland dashed first of all into Mr. Galloway's, to ask if he had news of Arthur. No, none, Mr. Galloway answered with a groan, and it "would surely be the death of him." As Roland left the proctor's house, he saw the college boys flocking into the cloisters, and he went with them. Renovation seemed to be going on everywhere; beauty had succeeded dilapidations, and the old cathedral might well raise her head proudly now. But Roland did wonder when the improvements and the work would be finished; they had been going on as long as he could remember.

But the cloisters had not moved or changed their form, and Roland lost himself in the days of the past. One of the prebendaries, a fresh one since Roland's time, was turning into the chapter-house; Roland, positively from old associations, snatched off his hat to him. In imagination he was king's scholar again, existing in mortal dread, when in those cloisters, of the Dean and Chapter.

"I say—you," said he, seizing hold of a big boy, who had his surplice flung across his shoulder in the most untidy and crumpled fashion possible, "show me Joe Jenkins's grave."

"Yes, sir," answered the boy, wondering what fine imperative gentleman had got amidst them, and speaking civilly, lest it might be a connection of someone of the prebendaries. "It's round on the other side."

Running along to the end of the north cloister, near to the famous gravestone "Miserrimus," near to the spot where a ghost had once appeared to Charles Channing he pointed to an obscure corner of the green grave-yard, which the cloisters enclosed. Many and many a time had Roland perched himself on those dilapidated old mullioned window-frames in the days gone by.

"It's there," said the boy. "Old Ketch, the cloister porter, lies on this side him."

"Oh, Ketch does, does he! I wonder whose doings that was! It's a shame to have placed him, a cross-grained old wretch, side by side with poor Jenkins."

"Jenkins was cross-grained too, for the matter of that," cried the boy. "He was always asking the fellows for a tip to buy baccy, and grumbling if they did not give it."

Roland stared indignantly. "Jenkins was! Why, what are you talking of? Jenkins never smoked."

"Oh; didn't he though! Why, he died smoking; he was smoking always. Pretty well, that, for an old one of seventy-six."

"I'm not talking of old Jenkins," cried Roland. "Who wants to know about him?—what a senseless fellow you are! It's young Jenkins. Joe; who was at Galloway's."

"Oh, him! He was buried in front, not here. I can't go round to show you, sir for time's up."

The boy took to his heels, As schoolboys only can take to them, and Roland heard him rattle up the steps of the college hall to join his comrades. Propped against the frame-work, his memory lost itself in many things; and the minutes passed unheeded by. The procession of the king's scholars aroused him. They filed along the cloisters from the college hall, two and two, in their surplices and trenchers, his brother Harry, one of the seniors nearly the last of them. When they had disappeared, Roland ran round to the front grave-yard. Between the cathedral gates and those leading to the palace, stood a black-robed verger, with his silver mace, awaiting the appearance of the Dean. Roland accosted the man and asked him which was Joe Jenkins's grave.

"That's it, sir," and the verger indicated a flat stone, which was nearly buried in the grass. "You can't miss it his name's there."

Roland went into the burial-ground, treading down the grass. Yes, there it was. "Joseph Jenkins. Aged thirty-nine." He stood looking at it for some minutes.

"If ever I get rich, Joe, poor meek old fellow, you shall have a better monument," spoke Roland aloud. "This common stone, Mrs. J.'s no doubt, shall be replaced by one of white marble, and we'll have your virtues inscribed on it."

The quarter-past ten chimed out; the bell ceased, and the swell of the organ was heard. Service had begun in the cathedral. Roland went about, reading, or trying to read, other inscriptions; he surveyed the well-remembered houses around; he shaded his hand from the sun, and looked up to take leisure notice of the outer renovations of the cathedral. Tired of this, it suddenly occurred to him that he would go in to service; "just for old memories' sake."

In, he went; never heeding the fact that the service had commenced, and that it used not to be the custom for an intruder to enter the choir afterwards. Straight on, went he, to the choir gates, not making for either of the aisles, as a modest man would, pushed aside the purple curtain, and let himself into a stall on the decani side; to the intense indignation of the sexton, who marvelled that any living man should possess sufficient impudence for it. When Roland looked up, and had opened the large prayer-book lying before him, the chanter had come to that portion of the service, "O Lord, open Thou our lips." It was a melodious, full, pleasant voice. A thorough good chanter, decided Roland, reared to be critical in such matters; and he took a survey of him. The chanter was on the cantons side, nearly opposite to Roland; a good-looking, open-countenanced young clergyman, with brown hair, whose face seemed to strike another familiar chord on Roland's memory.

"If I don't believe it's Tom!" thought Roland.

Tom it was. But it slightly discomposed the equanimity of the Reverend Thomas Channing to find the stalwart, bold disturber, at whom everybody had stared, and the Dean himself glanced at, telegraphing him a couple of nods, in what seemed the exuberance of gratified delight. The young chanter's face turned red; he certainly did not telegraph back again.

Thus tacitly repulsed, Roland had leisure to look about him, and did so to his heart's content, while the Venite and the Psalms for the day were being sung. Nearly side by side with himself; at the chanting desk, but not being used for chanting today, he discovered his kinsman, William Yorke. And the Reverend William kept his haughty shoulder turned away; and had felt fit to faint when Roland had come bursting through the closed curtains. He, and Tom Channing, and the head-master of the school, were the three minor canons present.

Oh, how like the old days it was! The Dean in his stall; the sub-dean on the other side, and the new prebendary, whom Roland did not know. There stood the choristers at their desks; here, on the flags, extended the two facing lines of king's scholars, all in their white surplices. There was a fresh head-master in Mr. Pye's place, and Roland did not know him. The last time Roland had attended service in the cathedral—and he well remembered it—Arthur Channing took the organ. He had ceased for several years to take it now, except on some chance occasion for pleasure. Where was Arthur now? Could it be that he "was not?" What with the chilliness of the thought and the chilliness of the edifice, Roland gave a shiver.

But they are beginning the First Lesson—part of a chapter in Wisdom, William Yorke reading it. With the first sentences Arthur was brought more forcibly into Roland's mind.

"But the souls of the righteous are in the hand of God, and there shall no torment touch them. In the sight of the unwise they seemed to die: and their departure is taken for misery, and their going from us to be utter destruction: but they are in peace."

And so on to the end of the verses. Sitting back in his stall, subdued and quiet now, all his curiosity suppressed, Roland could not but think how applicable the Lesson was to Arthur. Whether living or dead, he must be at peace, for God had surely proved him and found him worthy for Himself. Roland Yorke had not learnt yet to be what Arthur was; but a feeling, it might be called a hope, stole over him then for the first time in his life that the change would come. "Annabel will help me," he thought.

When service was over, Roland greeted all he cared to greet of those who remembered him. Passing back up the aisle to join Tom Channing in the vestry (where the first thing he did was to try on the young parson's surplice and hood), he met his kinsman coming from it. Roland turned his shoulder now, and his cold sweeping bow, when the minor canon stopped to speak, would have done honour to a monarch. William Yorke walked on, biting his lips between amusement and vexation. As Roland and Thomas Channing were passing through the Boundaries, a rather short, red-faced, pleasant looking young man met them, and stayed to shake hands with the minor canon. It was Stephen Bywater. Roland knew him at once: his saucy face had not altered a whit. Bywater had come into no end of property in the West Indies (as Roland heard explained to him by Tom afterwards), and was now in Europe for a short sojourn.

"How's Ger? asked Bywater, when they had spoken of Arthur and general news.

"A great man," answered Roland. "Looks over my head if he meets me in the street. I might have knocked him down before now, Bywater, but for having left my manners at Port Natal."

"Oh, that's it, is it?" cried Bywater. "Ger is Ger still, I see. Does he remember the ink-bottle?"

"What ink-bottle?"

"And the tanning of birch Pye gave him?"

Roland did not understand. The termination of that little episode of schoolboy life had taken place after he had quitted Helstonleigh, and it was never imparted to him. Stephen Bywater recited it with full flavour now.

"Ger's not so white himself, then," remarked Roland. "He's always throwing that banknote of Galloway's in my teeth."

"Is he? I once told him he was a cur," added Bywater, quietly. "Goodbye, old fellow; we shall meet again, I hope."

Mrs. Channing was delighted to see Roland. But when he spoke to her of Annabel she burst out laughing, just as her son Hamish had done; which slightly disconcerted the would-be bridegroom. Considering that in three or four months, as he now openly confessed, he had saved up two pounds towards commencing housekeeping (and those were spent), Mrs. Channing thought the prospect for him and Annabel about as hopeless a one as she had ever heard of. Roland came to the private conclusion that he must be making the two hundred a year before speaking again. He remembered the warning Mr. Galloway had given him in regard to Arthur, and got away in safety.

Home again then to Lady Augusta's, where he stayed till past midday, and then started for the station to take the train for London. Fearing there might be a procession to escort him off, the old family barouche ordered out, or something of that, for Roland remembered his mother of old, he stole a march on them and got out alone, his brown paper parcel in his hand and three or four smaller ones, containing toys and cakes that Fanny was sending to Gerald's children. His intention had been to dash through the streets at speed, remembering Mr. Butterby's friendly caution. But the once well-known spots had charms for Roland, and he halted to gaze at nearly every step. The Guildhall, the market-house, the churches: all the old familiar places that had grown to his memory when far away from them. Before Mrs. Jenkins's house he came to a full stop: not the one in which Mr. Ollivera had met his death, but the smaller dwelling beside it. From the opposite side of the way stood Roland, while he gazed. The shop sold a different kind of wares now; but Roland had no difficulty in recognising it. In the parlour behind he had revelled in the luxurious tea and toasted muffins; in that top room, whose windows faced him, poor humble Jenkins had died. Away on at last up the street, he and his parcels, looking to the right and the left. Once upon a time the Lady Augusta Yorke, seduced by certain golden visions imparted to her by Roland, had gone to bed and dreamt of driving about a charming city whose streets were paved with malachite marble, all brilliant to glance upon; many a time and oft had poor Roland dreamt of the charms of these Helstonleigh streets when he was fighting a fight with starvation at Port Natal. Looking upon them now, he rubbed his eyes in doubt and wonder. Could these be the fine wide streets of the former days? They seemed to have contracted to a narrow width, to be mean and shabby. The houses appeared poor, the very Guildhall itself small. Ah me! The brightness had worn off the gold.

Roland walked on with the slow step of disappointment, scanning the faces he met. He knew none. Eight years had passed since his absence, and the place and the people were changed to him. Involuntarily the words of that ever beautiful song, which most of us know by heart, came surging up his memory, as he gazed wistfully from side to side.

"Strange to me now are the forms I meet
When I visit the dear old town."

Strange enough. Was it for this he had come back? Often and often during his wanderings in the far-away African land, had other lines of the same sweet song beaten their refrain in his brain when yearning for Helstonleigh. There was a certain amount of sentiment in Roland Yorke, for all his straightforward practicability.

"Often I think of the beautiful town
That is seated by the sea;
Often in thought go up and down
The pleasant streets of that dear old town,
And my youth comes back to me.
And a verse of a Lapland song
Is haunting my memory still:
'A boy's will is the wind's will,
And the thoughts of youth are long, long thoughts.'"

"I can see the shadowy lines of its trees,

And catch in sudden gleams
The sheen of the far-surrounding seas
And islands that were the Hesperides
Of all my boyish dreams.
And the burden of that old song,
It murmurs and whispers still:
'A boy's will is the wind's will,
And the thoughts of youth are long, long thoughts.'"

There were no seas around Helstonleigh, but the resemblance was near enough for Roland, as it has been for others. Other verses of the song seemed to be strangely realized to him now, as he walked along.

"There are things of which I may not speak;
There are dreams that cannot die;
There are thoughts that make the strong heart weak.
And bring a pallor into the cheek,
And a mist before the eye.
And the words of that fatal song
Come over me like a chill:
'A boy's will is the wind's will,
And the thoughts of youth are long, long thoughts.'"

"I can see the breezy dome of groves,
The shadows of Deering's woods;
And the friendships old and the early loves
Come back with a Sabbath sound, as of doves
In quiet neighbourhoods.
And the verse of that sweet old song,
It flutters and murmurs still:
'A boy's will is the wind's will,
And the thoughts of youth are long, long thoughts.'"

"And Deering's woods are fresh and fair,
And with joy that is almost pain
My heart goes back to wander there;
And among the dreams of the days that were
I find my lost youth again.
And the strange and beautiful song,
The groves are repeating it still:
'A boy's will is the wind's will,
And the thoughts of youth are long, long thoughts.'"

Believe it or not as you will, of practical, matter-of-fact Roland, these oft-quoted lines (but never too often) told their refrain in his brain as he paced the streets of Helstonleigh, just as they had done in exile.

He went round by Hazledon; and William Yorke came forward in the hall to meet him, with outstretched hand.

"I knew you would not leave without coming in."

"It's to see Constance, not you," answered Roland.

Constance was ready for him; the same sweet woman Roland in his earlier days had thought the perfection of all that was fair and excellent. He thought her so still. She had her children brought down, and took the baby in her arms. Roland made them brilliant offerings in prospective, in the shape of dolls and rocking-horses: and whispered to their mother his romance about Annabel. She wished him luck, laughing all the while.

"When William was in London this summer he thought Hamish was looking a little thin," said Constance. "Is he well?"

"Oh, he's well enough," answered Roland. But his face flushed a dusky red as he spoke, for the question recalled the strange idea that had flashed into his mind, unbidden, the past night; and Mr. Roland thought himself guilty for it, and resented it accordingly. "You never saw such a lovely little fairy as Nelly is."

But he had no time to stay. Roland went out on the run; and just fell into the arms of a certain Mr. Simms: one of the few individuals he had particularly hoped to avoid.

Mr. Simms knew him. That it was a Yorke there could be no doubt; and a minute's pause sufficed to show him that it was no other than the truant Roland. Civilly, but firmly, Mr. Simms arrested progress.

"Is it you, Mr. Roland Yorke?"

"Yes, it's me," said Roland. "I'm only at Helstonleigh for a few hours and was in hopes of getting off again without meeting any of yon," he candidly added. "You're fit to swear at me, I suppose, Simms, for never having sent you the money?"

"I certainly expected to be paid long before this, Mr. Yorke."

"So did I," said Roland. "I'd have sent it you had I been able. I would, Simms; honour bright. How much is it? Five pounds?"

"And seven shillings added on to it."

"Ay, I've got the list somewhere. It's over forty pounds that I owe in the place altogether, getting on for fifty: and every soul of you shall be paid with interest as soon as I can scrape the money together. I've had nothing but ill-luck since I left here, Simms, and it has not turned yet."

"It was said you went to foreign parts to make your fortune, sir. My lady herself told me you were safe to come home with one."

"And I thought I was," gloomily answered Roland. "Instead of that, Simms, I got home without a shirt to my back. I've gone in for work this many a year now, but somehow fortune's not with me. I work daily, every bit as hard and long as you do, Simms; perhaps harder; and I can hardly keep myself. I've not been able to do a stroke since this dreadful business about Arthur Channing—which brought me down here."

"Is he found, sir? We shouldn't like to lose such a one as him."

"He's neither found nor likely to be," said Roland, shaking his head. "Old Galloway declares it will be his death: I'm not sure but it'll be mine. And now I must be off, Simms, and I leave you my honest word that I'll send you the money as soon as ever it is in my power. I'd like to pay you all with interest. You shall be the first of them to get it."

"I suppose you couldn't pay me a trifle off it now, Mr. Yorke? A pound or so."

"Bless your heart!" cried Roland, in wide astonishment. "A pound or so! I don't possess it. I pawned my black dress-suit for thirty shillings to come down upon, and travelled third class. Goodbye, old Simms; I shall lose the train."

He went off like a shot. Mr. Simms looking after the well-dressed gentleman, did not know what to make of the plea of poverty.

Roland went whirling back to London again, third class, and arrived at the Paddington terminus in a fever. That the worst had happened to Arthur, whatever that worst might be, he no longer entertained a shadow of doubt. His thirty shillings (we might never have known he had been so rich but for the candid avowal to Mr. Simms) were not quite exhausted, and Roland put his parcels into a hansom and drove down to Mrs. Gerald Yorke's.

To find that lady in tears was nothing unusual; the rule, in fact, rather than the exception; she was seated on the floor by the firelight in the evening's approaching dusk, and the three little girls with her. The grief was not much more than usual. Gerald had been at home, and in a fit of bitter anger had absolutely forbidden her to take the children to drink tea with little Nelly Channing at four o'clock, as invited. Four o'clock had struck; five too; and the disappointed mother and children had cried through the hour.

"It is too bad of Gerald," cried sympathising Roland, putting his parcels on the table.

"Yes, it is; not to let us go there," sobbed Mrs. Yorke. "All Gerald's money is gone, too, and he went off without answering me when I said I must have some. I don't possess as much as a fourpenny-piece in the world; and we've not got an atom of tea or butter in the house and can have no tea at home, and we've only one scuttle of coals left, for I've just rung for some and the girl says so, and—oh, I wish I was dead!"

Roland felt in his pockets, and found three shillings and twopence. It was all he possessed. This he put on the table, wishing it was fifty times as much. His heart was good to help all the world.

"I'm ashamed of its being such a trifle," said he, pulling at his whiskers in mortification. "If I were rich I should be glad to help everybody. Perhaps it'll buy a quarter of butter and a bit of tea and half a hundred of coals."

"And for him to deny our going there!" repeated Winny, getting up to take the money, and then rocking herself violently. "You know the state we were in all the summer: Gerald next door to penniless and going about in fear of the bum-bailies," she continued, adhering in moments of agitation to her provincial expressions. "We wanted everything; rent, and clothes, and food; and if it had not been for a friend who continually helped us we might have just starved."

"It was your mother," said Roland.

"But it was not my mother," answered Mrs. Yorke, ceasing her rocking to lean forward, and her cheeks and her eyes looked alike bright in the flashing firelight. "It was Mr. Chaining."

"What?"

She could not be reticent, and explained all. How Hamish, or his wife for him, had helped them, even to the paying of boot-bills for Gerald. Roland sat amazed. Things that had somewhat puzzled even his careless nature were becoming clear.

"And Gerald not know of this?"

"As if I should dare to tell him! He thinks it all comes from my mother. Oh, Roland, you don't know how good and kind Hamish Channing is! he is more like one of Heaven's angels. I think, I do really think, I must have died, or come to a bad end, but for him. He is the least selfish man I ever knew in the world; the most thoughtful and generous."

"I know what Hamish is," assented Roland, with energy. "And to think that he has got to bear all this awful sorrow about his best brother—Arthur!"

"Oh, Arthur is found. He is all right," said Mrs. Yorke, quietly.

"What!" shouted Roland, starting from his chair.

"Arthur has been at Marseilles all the while. Hamish had a letter from him this morning."

A prolonged stare; a rubbing of the amazed face that had turned to a white heat; and Roland caught up his hat, and went out with a bang. Half a moment, and he was back again, sweeping his parcels from the table to the children on the carpet.

"It's cakes and toys from Fanny," said he. "Go into them, you chickens. That other's a shirt, Mrs. Yorke: I can't stay for it now."

On the stairs, as he was leaping down, Roland unfortunately encountered the servant maid carrying up a scuttle of coals. It was not a moment to consider maids and scuttles. Down went the coals, down went the maid. Roland took a flying leap over the débris, and was half way on his road to Hamish Channing's before the bewildered landlady, arriving on the scene, could understand what the matter was.

The explanation of what had been a most unpleasant mystery was so very simple and natural, that the past fright and apprehension seemed almost like a take-in. It shall be given at once; though the reader will readily understand that at present Hamish knew nothing of the details, only the bare fact that Arthur was alive and well. He would have to wait for them until Arthur's return.

Amidst the letters handed to Arthur Channing by the waiter of the hotel that night in Norfolk Street, was one from Marseilles, stating that Charles, just before landing, had had a relapse, and was lying at Marseilles dangerously ill—his life despaired of. Perhaps in the flurry of the moment, Arthur did not and could not act so reasonably as he might have done. All his thoughts ran on the question—How could he in the shortest space of time get to Marseilles? By dint of starting on the instant—on the instant, mind—and taking a fleet cab, he might get to London Bridge in time to catch the Dover mail-train. Taking up his hat and letters, he ran out of the coffee-room calling aloud for the waiter. Nobody responded: nobody, as it would appear, was at that moment in the way to hear him. Afraid of even an instant's detention, he did not wait, but ran out of the hotel, up Norfolk Street, hailed a passing hansom, and reached London Bridge Station before the train started. From Dover to Calais the boat had an exceedingly calm passage, and Arthur was enabled to write some short notes in the cabin, getting ink and paper from the steward: one to the hotel that he had, as may be said, surreptitiously quitted, one to Hamish, one to Roland, one to Mr. Galloway, one to Mr. Galloway's London agents. Arthur, always considerate, ever willing to spare others anxiety and pain, did not say why he was hastening to Marseilles, but merely stated that he had determined on proceeding thither, instead of awaiting Charles in London. These letters he gave to a French commissionaire on landing in Calais, with money to buy the necessary stamps, and a gratuity to himself; ordering him to post them as soon as might be. Whether the man quietly pocketed the money and suppressed the letters, or whether he had in his turn entrusted them to someone else to post, who lost, or forgot them, would never be ascertained. Arthur, all unconscious of the commotion he was causing at home, arrived quietly at Marseilles, and there found Charles very ill, not quite out of danger For some days he was wholly occupied with him, and did not write at all: as he had said nothing about the illness, he knew there could be no anxiety. Now that he did write, Charles was getting better rapidly. It may just be observed, that the letter left in the rack of the hotel (that came on with the rest of the steamer's letters from Marseilles) had served to complicate matters; but for that letter it would have been surmised that Arthur had received unfavourable news of Charles, and had gone on to him. The accident was indeed a singular one, which left that letter in the rack: and even the thought that there should have been a second from Marseilles never occurred to them. All these, and other details, Hamish Channing would have to wait for. He could afford to do so—holding that new letter of relief in his hand, which stated that Charles was eager to continue his journey homewards, so that they would probably be in London soon after its receipt.

"Oh, Hamish, it is good!" cried Roland, who had sat listening with all his heart and eyes. "It's like a great bright star come down from Heaven. It's like a gala-day."

"I dare say there is a letter waiting for you at Mrs. J.'s, friend."

"Of course there is," decided Roland. "As if Arthur would forget me! Old Galloway won't die yet."

But, even in that short absence of a day and a night, Roland seemed to see that Hamish Channing's face had grown thinner: the fine skin more transparent, the genial blue eyes brighter.

CHAPTER XXXIII

A STARTLING AVOWAL

Cuff Court, Fleet Street; and a frosty day in December. The year has gone on some six or seven weeks since the last chapter, and people are beginning to talk of the rapidly-advancing Christmas.

Over the fire, in the little room in Cuff Court, where you once saw him by gas-light, sits Mr. Butterby. The room is bright enough with sunlight now; the sunlight of the cold, clear day; a great deal brighter than Mr. Butterby himself, who is dull as ditch-water, and in a sulky temper.

"I've been played with; that's what I've been," said Butterby in soliloquy. "Bede Greatorex bothers me to be still, to be passive; and when I keep still and passive, and stop down at Helstonleigh, taking no steps, saying nothing to living mortal, letting the thing die away, if it will die, he makes a mull of it up in town. Why couldn't he have kept his father and Parson Ollivera quiet? Never a lawyer going, but must be sharp enough for that. Not he. He does nothing of the sort, but lets one or both of 'em work, and ferret, and worry, and discover that Godfrey Pitman has turned up, and find out that I knew of it, and go to headquarters and report me for negligence I get a curt telegram to come to town, and here's the deuce to pay."

Mr. Butterby turned round, snatched up a few papers that lay on the table, glanced over the writing, and resumed his soliloquy when he had put them down again.

"Jelf has it in hand here, and I've not yet got to see him. Not of much use my seeing him before I've heard what Bede Greatorex has to say. One thing they've not been sharp enough to discover yet— where Godfrey Pitman is to be found. Foster in Birmingham holds his tongue, Johnson shows Jelf the door when he goes to ask about Winter: and there they are, Jelf and the Parson, or Jelf and Mr. Greatorex—whichever of them two it is that's stirring—mooning up and down England after Pitman, little thinking he's close at home, right under their very noses. I and Bede Greatorex hold that secret tight; but I don't think I shall feel inclined to hold it long. 'Where is Pitman?' says the sergeant to me yesterday, at headquarters. 'Ah!' says I, 'that's just the problem we are some of us trying to work out.'"

Mr. Butterby stopped, cracked the coal fiercely, which sent up a blaze of sparks, and waited. Resuming after a while.

"And it is a problem; one I can't make come square just yet. There's Brown—as good call him by one alias as another—keeping as quiet as a mouse, knowing that he is being looked after for the murder of Counsellor Ollivera. What's his motive in keeping dark? The debts he left behind him in Birmingham are paid; Johnson and Teague acknowledge his innocence in that past transaction of young Master Samuel's; they are, so to say, his friends, and the man knows all this. Why, then, don't he come forward and reap the benefit of the acquittal, and put himself clear before the world, and say—Neither am I guilty of the other thing—the counsellor's death? Of course, when Jeff and Jeff's masters know he is hiding himself somewhere, and does not come forward, they assume that he dare not, that he was the man who did it. I'd not swear but he was, either. Looking at it in a broad point of view, one can't help seeing that he must have some urgent motive for his silence—and what that motive is, one may give a shrewd guess at: that he is screening himself or somebody else. There's only one other in the world that he would screen, I expect, and that's Alletha Rye."

A long pause. A pause of silence. Mr. Butterby's face, with all his professional craft, had as puzzled a look on it as any ordinary mortal's might wear.

"I suspected Alletha Rye more than anybody at the time. Don't suspect her now. Don't think it was her; wouldn't swear it wasn't, though. And, in spite of your injunction to be still, Mr. Bede Greatorex, I'll go into the thing a bit for my own satisfaction."

Looking over the papers on the table again, he locked them up, and sat down to write a letter or two. Somebody then came in to see him on business—which business does not concern us. And so time passed on, and when the sunlight had faded into dusk, Mr. Butterby put on a top pilot-coat of rough blue cloth, and went out. The shows were lighted, displaying their attractions for the advancing Christmas, and Mr. Butterby had leisure to glance at them with critical approval as he passed.

These past few weeks had not brought forth much to tell of in regard to general matters. Arthur and Charles Channing had passed through London on their way to Helstonleigh; Roland Yorke had resumed his daily and evening work, and had moreover given his confidence to Sir Vincent Yorke (nothing daunted by that gentleman's previous repulse) on the subject of Annabel Channing, and in his sanguine temperament was looking ever for the place Vincent was to get him; and James Channing drew nearer and nearer to another world. But this world was slow to perceive it—Hamish, the bright! Three or four times a week Roland snatched a minute to dart down to the second-hand furniture shops in Tottenham Court Road, there to inquire prices and lay in a stock of practical information as to the number and nature of articles, useful and ornamental, indispensable for a gentleman and lady going into housekeeping.

But Mr. Butterby was on his way to Mrs. Jones's residence, and we must follow him. Halting opposite the house to take a survey of it, he saw that there was no light in Mr. Ollivera's sitting-room; there was no light anywhere, that he could see. By which fact he gathered that the clergyman was not at home: and that was satisfactory, as he did not much care to come in contact with him just at the present uncertain state of affairs.

Crossing the street, he knocked gently at the door. Miss Rye answered it, nobody but herself being in the house. A street gas-lamp shone full on her face, and the start she gave was quite visible to Mr. Butterby. He walked straight in to Mrs. Jones's parlour, saying he had come to see her; her, Alletha Rye. Her work lay on the red table-cover by the lamp; Mr. Butterby sat down in the shade and threw back his coat; she stood by the fire and nervously stirred it, her hands trembling, her face blanching.

"When that there unhappy event took place at Helstonleigh, the death of Counsellor Ollivera, now getting on for five years back, there was a good deal of doubt encompassing it round about, Miss Rye," he suddenly began.

"Doubt?" she rejoined, faintly, sitting down to the table and catching up her work.

"Yes, doubt. I mean as to how the death was caused. Some said it was a murder, and some said it was his own doing—suicide."

"Everybody said it was a suicide!" she interrupted, with trembling eagerness, her shaking fingers plying the needle as if she were working for very life. "The coroner and jury decided it to be one."

"Not quite everybody," dissented Mr. Butterby, listening with composure until she had finished. "You didn't. I was in the churchyard when they put him into the ground, and heard and saw you over the grave."

"But I had cause to—to—alter my opinion, later," she said, her face turning hectic with emotion. "Heaven alone knows how bitterly I have repented of that night's work! If cutting my tongue out afterwards, instead of before, could have undone my mistake—"

"Now look here; don't you get flurried," interposed Mr. Butterby. "I didn't come here to put you out, but just to have a rational talk on a point or two. I thought at the time it was a suicide, as you may remember: but I'm free to confess that the way in which the ball has been kept rolling since has served to alter my opinion. Counsellor Ollivera was murdered!"

She made no reply. Taking up her scissors, she began cutting away at the work at random, and the hectic red faded away to a sickly whiteness.

"There was a stranger lodging at Mrs. Jones's at the time, you remember, one Godfrey Pitman. Helstonleigh said, you know, Miss Rye, that if anybody did it, it was him. That Godfrey Pitman is an uncommonly sharp card to have kept himself out of the way so long! Don't you think so?"

"I don't think anything about it," she answered. "What is it to me?"

"Well, Miss Rye, I've the pleasure of telling you that Godfrey Pitman's found!"

The little presence of mind left in Alletha Rye seemed to quit her at the words. Perhaps she was no longer so capable of maintaining it as she once had been: the very best of our powers wear out when the soul's burthen is continued long and long.

"Found!" she gasped, her hands falling on her work, her wild eyes turned to Mr. Butterby.

"Leastways so near found, that it mayn't be a age afore he's took," added the detective, with professional craft. "Our friends in the blue coats have got the clue to him. I'd not lay you the worth of that silver thimble of yours, Miss Rye, that he's not standing in a certain dock next March assizes."

"In what dock? What for?" came from her trembling lips.

"Helstonleigh dock For what le did to Mr. Ollivera. Come, come, I did not want to frighten you like this, my good young woman. And why should it? It is not certain Pitman will be brought to trial, though he were guilty. Years have gone by since, and the Greatorexes and Parson Ollivera may hush it up. They are humane men; Mr. Bede especially."

"You don't believe Godfrey Pitman was guilty?" she exclaimed, and her eyes began to take a hard look, her voice a defiant tone.

"Oh, don't I!" returned Butterby. "What's more to the purpose, Miss Rye, the London officers and their principals, who have got it in hand, believe it."

"And what if I tell you that Godfrey Pitman never was guilty; that he never raised his hand against Mr. Ollivera?" she broke forth in passionate accents, rising to confront him. "What if I tell you that it was I?"

Standing there before him, her eyes ablaze with light, her cheeks crimson, her voice ringing with power, it was nearly impossible to disbelieve her. For once, the experienced, cool man was taken aback.

"You, Miss Rye!"

"Yes, I. I, Alletha Rye. What, I say, if I tell you it was I did that terrible deed? Not Godfrey Pitman. Now then! you must make the most of it, and do your best and worst."

The avowal, together with the various ideas that came crowding as its accompaniment, struck Mr. Butterby dumb. He sat there gazing at her, his speech utterly failing him.

"Is this true?" he whispered, when he had found his tongue.

"Should I avow such a thing if it were not? Oh, Mr. Butterby! hush the matter up if it be in your power," she implored, clasping her hands in an attitude of beseeching supplication, and her breath came in great gasps, so that the words were jerked out, rather than spoken. "In pity to me, hush it; it has lain at rest all these years. Let Godfrey Pitman be! For my sake, let him be! I pray you in Heaven's name!"

She sat down in her chair, tottering back to it, and burst into a flood of hysterical tears. Mr. Butterby waited in silence till they were over, and then buttoned his coat to go out. Putting out her timid hand, she caught his arm and held it with a nervous grasp.

"You will promise me Mr. Butterby?"

"I can't promise anything on the spur of the moment," said he in a grave, but not unkind tone. "You must let me turn things over in my mind. For one thing, neither the hushing of the matter up, nor the pursuing of it, may lie with me. I told you others had got it in hand, Miss Rye, and I told you truth. Now there's no need for you to come to the door; I can let myself out."

And Mr. Butterby let himself out accordingly, making no noise over the exit.

"I'm blest if I can see daylight," he exclaimed with energy, as he went down the street at a brisk pace. "Did she do it herself?—or is she trying to screen Master George Winter? It's one of the two; and I'm inclined to think it is the last. Anyway, she's a brave and a bold woman. Whether she did it, or whether she didn't, it's no light matter to accuse herself of mur—"

Mr. Butterby came to a full stop: both in words and steps. It was but for a second of time; and he laughed a little silent laugh at his own obtuseness as he passed on.

"I forgot her avowal at the grave. If she had done it herself, she'd never have gone in for that public display, lest it should turn attention on her. Yes, yes; she is screening Winter. Perhaps the man, hiding in that top floor, with nothing to do but torment his wits, got jealous of the counsellor below, fancying she favoured him, and so—"

The break in Mr. Butterby's sentence this time was occasioned by his shooting into an entry. Approaching towards him came Mrs. Jones, attended by her servant with a huge market-basket: and as he had neither time nor wish for an encounter with that lady at the present moment, he let her go by.

CHAPTER XXXIV

A TELEGRAM TO HELSTONLEIGH

That same evening, just as suddenly as Detective Butterby had shot into the entry, did he seem to shoot into the private room of Mr. Bede Greatorex. The clerks had just left the office for the evening; Bede, putting things straight on his desk, was thinking of going upstairs to dinner. To be thus silently invaded was not pleasing: but Bede could only resign himself to his fate.

In a spirit of reproach Mr. Butterby entered on the business of the interview, stating certain facts. Bede took alarm. Better, as he thought, that the earth should be arrested in its orbit, than that the part Godfrey Pitman played in connection with his cousin's death at Helstonleigh should be brought to light.

"It is the very charge, above all others, that I gave you, Mr. Butterby—the keeping secret what you had learnt about the identity of Godfrey Pitman," broke forth Bede.

"And it is because I obeyed you and did keep it, that headquarters have put it into others' hands and are hauling me over the coals," spoke Mr. Butterby in an injured tone.

"Have you told them that it was by my desire you remained passive?"

"I have told them nothing," was the answer. "I let 'em think that I was looking after Godfrey Pitman still myself, everywhere that I could look, high and low."

"Then they don't know yet that he and my clerk Brown are the same?" said Bede, very eagerly.

"Not a bit on't. There's not a living soul of the lot has been sharp enough to turn that page yet, Mr. Bede Greatorex."

"And it must be our business to keep it closed," whispered Bede. "I will give you any reward if you can manage to do it."

"Look here, sir," spoke Butterby. "I am willing to oblige you as far as I can in reason; I've showed you that I am; but to fill you up with hopes that that secret will be a secret long, would be nothing but wilful deceit: and deceit's a thing that don't answer in the long run. When I want to throw people off a scent, or worm things out of 'em for the law's purposes, I send their notions off on all sorts of air journeys, and think it no wrong: but to let you suppose I can keep from the world what I can't keep, and take your thanks and rewards for doing it, is just the opposite case. As sure as us two be a talking here, this matter won't stand at its present page; there'll be more leaves turned in it afore many days is gone over."

Leaning forward, his face and eyes wearing their gravest look, his elbow on the table that was between them, his finger and thumb pointed to give force to his argument, there was that altogether in the speaker's aspect, in his words, that carried a shiver of conviction to the mind of Bede Greatorex. His heart grew faint, his face was white with a sickly moisture.

"You may think to stop it and I may think to stop it, Mr. Bede Greatorex: but, take my word, it won't be stopped. There's no longer a chance of it."

"If you—could get—Brown out of the way?" spoke Bede, scarcely knowing what it was he said, and speaking in a whisper. Mr. Butterby received the suggestion with severity.

"It's not to me, sir, that you should venture to say such a thing. I've been willing to help your views when it didn't lie against my position and duty to do it; but I don't think you've seen anything in me to suppose I would go beyond that. As good step into Scotland Yard and ask them to help a criminal to escape, as ask me. We'll let that drop, sir; and I'll go on to a question I should like to put. What do you want Godfrey Pitman out of the way for?"

Bede did not answer. His hand was pressed upon his brow, his eyes wore their saddest and most dreamy look.

"If Pitman had any share in the business at Helstonleigh, you ought to be the one to give him into custody, sir."

"For the love of Heaven, don't pursue Pitman!" spoke Bede earnestly. "I have told you before, Mr. Butterby, that it was not he. So far as I believe, he never lifted his hand against John Ollivera; he did not hurt a hair of his head. Accuse any one in the world that you please, but don't accuse him."

"What if I accuse a woman?" spoke Mr. Butterby, when he had gazed at Bede to his satisfaction.

Their eyes met. Bede's face, or the detective fancied it, was growing whiter.

"Who?—What woman?" asked Bede, scarcely above his breath.

"Alletha Rye."

With a sadden movement, looking like one of relief, Bede Greatorex dropped his hand and leaned back in his chair. It was as if some kind of rest had come to him.

"Why should you bring in Alletha Rye's name? Do you suspect her?"

"I'm not clear that I do; I'm not clear that I don't. Anyhow, I think she stands a chance of getting accused of it, Mr. Bede Greatorex."

"Better accuse her than Pitman," said Bede, who seemed to be again speaking out of his uncomfortable dream.

Mr. Butterby, inwardly wondering at various matters and not just yet able to make them meet in his official mind, rose to conclude the interview. A loud bell was ringing upstairs; most probably the announcement of dinner.

"Just a parting word, sir. What I chiefly stepped in to say, was this. So long as the case rested in my hands, and Mr. Godfrey Pitman was supposed to have finally disappeared from the world, I was willing to oblige you, and let it, and him, and the world be. But from the moment that the affair shall be stirred publicly, in short, that action is forced upon me by others, I shall take it up again. Counsellor Ollivera's case belongs of right to me, and must be mine to the end."

With a civil goodnight, Mr. Butterby departed, leaving Bede Greatorex to his thoughts and reveries. More unhappy ones have rarely been entertained in this world. Men cannot strive against fate forever, and the battle had well nigh warn him out. It almost seemed that he could struggle no longer, that he had no power of resistance left within him. Mind and body were alike weary; the spirit fainted, the heart was sick. Life had long been a burden to Bede Greatorex, but never did its weight lie heavier than tonight in its refined and exquisite pain.

He had to bear it alone, you see. To lock the miserable secret, whatever might be its precise nature, and whoever might have been guilty, within his own bosom. Could he but have spoken of it to another, its anguish had been less keen; for, when once a great trouble can be imparted—be it of grief, or apprehension, or remorse; be it connected with ourselves, or (worse) one very near and dear to us—it is lightened of half its sting.

But that relief was denied to Bede Greatorex.

It had been the dinner-bell. Bede did not answer to it; but that was not altogether unusual.

They sat around the brilliantly-lighted, well-appointed banquet. Where Mrs. Bede Greatorex procured her fresh hothouse flowers from daily, and at what cost, she alone knew. They were always beautiful, charming to the eye, odoriferously pleasant to the senses. At the head of the table tonight was she, wearing amber silk, her shoulders very bare, her back partially shaded by the horse's tail that drooped from her remarkable chignon. It was not a dinner-party; but Mrs. Bede was going out later, and had dressed beforehand.

The place at her left-hand was vacant—Bede's—who never took the foot of the table when his father was present. Mr. Greatorex supposed his son was detained in the office, and sent a servant to see. Judge Kene sat on the right of Mrs. Bede; he had called in, and stayed to dinner without ceremony. Clare Joliffe and Miss Channing sat on either side Mr. Greatorex. Frank was dining out. Clare was returning to France for Christmas, after her many months' stay in the country. Her chignon was more fashionable than a quartern loaf, and certainly larger, but lacking that great achievement, the tail. Annabel's quiet head presented a contrast to those two of the mode.

Bede came up. Shaking hands with Sir Thomas Kene, he passed round to his chair; his manner was restless, his thin cheeks were hectic. The judge had not seen him for some little time. Gazing at him across the table, he wondered what malady he could be suffering from, and how much more like a shadow he would be able to become—and live. Mr. Greatorex, anxiously awake to every minute glance or motion bearing on his son's health, spoke.

"Are you thinking Bede looks worse, Sir Thomas?"

"He does not look better," was the reply. "You should see a doctor and take some tonics, Bede."

"I'm all right, Judge, thank you," was Bede's answer, as he turned a whole lot of croûtons into his purée de pois—and would afterwards send it away nearly untested.

Dinner was just over when a servant whispered to Mr. Greatorex that he was wanted. Going down at once to his room he found Henry William Ollivera.

"Why did you not come up, William? Kene is there."

"I am in no fit mood for company, uncle," was the clergyman's reply. "The trouble has come at last."

In all the phases of agitation displayed by Henry Ollivera, and when speaking of the affair he generally displayed more or less, Mr. Greatorex never saw him so much moved as now. Leaning forward on his chair, his eyes bright, his cheeks burning as with the red of an autumn leaf, his hands feverish, his voice sunk to a whisper, he entered on the tale he had to tell.

"Do you remember my saying to you one day in the dining-room above, that I thought it was a woman? Do you remember it, uncle?"

"Quite well."

"In the weeks that have gone by since, the suspicion has only gained ground in my mind. Without cause: I am bound to say it, without further cause. Nay almost in the teeth of what might have served to diminish suspicion. For, if Godfrey Pitman be really somewhere in existence, and hiding himself, the natural supposition would be, as Jelf thinks, that he was the one."

Mr. Greatorex nodded assent. "And yet you suspect the woman! Can you not say who she is, Henry?

"Yes, I can say now. I have come here to say it—Alletha Rye!"

Mr. Greatorex evinced no surprise. He had fancied it might be upon her that his nephew's doubts had been running. And he deemed it a crotchet indeed.

"I think you must be entirely mistaken," he said with emphasis. "What little I know of the young woman, tends to give me a very high opinion of her. She appears to be almost the last person in the world capable of such a crime as that, or of any crime."

"She might have done it in a moment's passion; she might have been playing with the pistol and fired it accidentally, and then was afraid to avow it; but she did it, uncle."

"Go on."

"I have been distracted with doubt. Distracted," emphatically repeated Mr. Ollivera. "For of course I knew that my suspicions of her, strong though they have been growing, did not prove her guilty. But tonight I have heard her avow it with her own lips."

"Avow what?"

"That she murdered John!"

"What!—has she confessed to you?" exclaimed Mr. Greatorex.

"No. I heard it accidentally. Perhaps I ought to say surreptitiously. And, hearing it in that manner, the question arises in my mind whether or not I should make use of the knowledge so gained. I cannot bear anything like dishonourable or underhand dealing; no, not even in this cause, uncle."

Mr. Greatorex made no reply. He was taken up with noting the strangely eager gaze fixed upon him. Something in it, he knew not what, recalled to his memory a dead face, lying alone on the border of a distant churchyard.

"It is some few weeks ago now that Mrs. Jones gave me a latchkey," resumed Mr. Ollivera. "In fact, I asked her for it. Coming in so often, and sometimes detained out late at night with the sick, I felt that it would be a convenience to me, and save trouble to the maid. This evening upon letting myself in with it about tea-time, I found the passage in darkness; the girl, I supposed, had delayed to light the lamp. My movements are not noisy at any time, as you know, and I went groping on in silence, feeling my way: not from any wish to be stealthy—such a thought never entered my head—but because Mr. Roland Yorke is given to leaving all kinds of articles about and I was afraid of stumbling over something. I was making for the table at the end of the passage, on which matches are generally kept, sometimes a chamber-candle. Feeling for these, I heard a voice in Mrs. Jones's parlour that I have not heard many times in my life, but nevertheless I knew it instantly—Butterby's, the detective."

"Butterby's!" exclaimed Mr. Greatorex. "I did not know he was in London."

"Uncle! It was Alletha Rye's voice that answered him. Her voice and no other's, disguised with agitation though it was. I heard her say that it was herself who killed my brother; that Godfrey Pitman had never raised a hand against him."

"You—really heard her say this, William?" breathed Mr. Greatorex.

"It is true as that I am a living man. It seemed to me that the officer must have been accusing Godfrey Pitman of the crime. I heard the man's surprised answer, 'You, Miss Rye!' 'Yes, I,' she said, 'I, Alletha Rye, not Godfrey Pitman.' I heard her go on to tell Butterby that he might do his best and his worst."

Mr. Greatorex sat like one bereft of motion. "This confounds me, William," he presently said.

"It confounded me," replied Mr. Ollivera. "Nearly took my senses from me, for I'm sure I had no rational reason left. The first thought that came to me was, that they had better not see me there, or discover they had been overheard until I had decided what my course should be. So I stepped silently up to my room, and the detective went away; and, close upon that, Mrs. Jones and the maid came in together. Mrs. Jones called her sister to account for not having lighted the hall-lamp, little thinking how the darkness had served me."

"But for you telling me this yourself, William, I had not believed it."

"It is true as Heaven's gospel," spoke the clergyman in his painful earnestness. "I sat a short while in my room, unable to decide what I ought to do, and then I came down here to tell you of it, uncle. It is very awful."

"Awful that it should have been Alletha Rye, you mean?"

"Yes. I have been praying, seeking, working for this discovery ever since John died; and, now that it has come in this most sudden manner, it brings nothing but perplexity with it. Oh, poor helpless mortals that we are!" added the clergyman, clasping his hands. "We set our hearts upon some longed-for end, spend our days toiling for it, our nights supplicating for it; and when God answers us according to our short-sighted wish, the result is but as the apples of Sodom, filling our mouths with ashes. Anybody but Alletha Rye; almost anybody; and I had not hesitated a moment. But I have lived under the same roof with her, in pleasant, friendly intercourse; I have preached to her on Sundays; I have given her Christ's Holy Sacrament with my own hands: in a serious illness that she had, I used to go and pray by her bed-side. Oh, Uncle Greatorex, I cannot see where my duty lies; I am torn with conflicting doubt!"

To the last words Mr. Ollivera had a listener that he had not bargained for—Judge Kene. About to take his departure, the Judge had come in without ceremony to say Goodnight to Mr. Greatorex.

"Why, what is amiss?" he cried, noting the signs of agitation as well as the words.

And they told him; told him all; there was no reason why it should be kept from him; and Mr. Ollivera begged for his counsel and advice. The Judge gave it, and most emphatically; deciding as a Judge more than as a humane man—and Thomas Kene was that.

"You cannot hesitate, Ollivera. This poor unhappy woman, Alletha Rye, must be brought to answer for her crime. Think of him, your brother, and my once dear friend, lying unavenged in his shameful grave! Humanity is a great and a good virtue, but John's memory must outweigh it."

"Yes, yes; I am thinking of him always," murmured the clergyman, his face lighting.

The initiative was taken by Mr. Greatorex. On the departure of the Judge and the clergyman, who went out together, Mr. Greatorex dropped a line to Scotland Yard. Butterby happened to be there, and answered it in person. Shortly and concisely Mr. Greatorex gave his orders.

"And I have no resource but to act upon them," coolly observed the imperturbable Butterby. "But I don't think the party was Alletha Rye."

"You don't!" exclaimed Mr. Greatorex.

"No, sir, I don't. Leastways, to my mind, there's grave reasons against it. The whole affair, from beginning to end, seems encompassed with nothing but doubts; and that's the blessed truth."

"I would like to ask you if Alletha Rye has or has not made a confession to you this evening, Mr. Butterby—to the effect that she was the one who killed Mr. Ollivera?"

"If nobody was in the house but her—as she said—she's been talking," thought the detective. "Confound these women for simpletons! They'd prate their necks away."

But Mr. Greatorex ins looking at him, waiting for the answer.

"I was with Alletha Rye this evening; I went there for my own purposes, to see what I could get out of her; little suspecting she'd say what she did. But I don't believe her any the more for having said it. The fact is Mr. Greatorex, that in this case there's wheels within wheels, a'most more than any I've ever had to do with. I can't yet disclose what they are even to you; but I'm trying to work them round and make one spoke fit into another."

"Do you know that Alletha Rye was not guilty of it?"

"No, sir, I do not."

"Very good. Lose no time. Get a warrant to apprehend Alletha Rye, and execute it. If you telegraph to Helstonleigh at once, the warrant may be up, and she in custody before midday tomorrow."

No more dallying with the law or with fate now. That was over. Mr. Butterby went straight to the telegraph office, and sent a message flying to Helstonleigh.

And Bede Greatorex went out to take part in an evening's gaiety with his wife, and came home to his rest, and rose the next morning to go about his occupation, unconscious of what the day was destined to bring forth.

CHAPTER XXXV

LIFE'S SANDS RUNNING ON

A cold brisk air, with suspicion of a frost. It was a day or two previous to the one told of in the last two chapters, when Mr. Butterby was paying visits. Being convenient to record that renowned officer's doings first, we yielded him the precedence, and in consequence have to go back a little.

The brightness of the afternoon was passing. In his writing-room, leaning back in a large easy-chair before the fire, sat Hamish Channing. Some papers lay on the table, work of various kinds; but, looking at Hamish, it almost seemed as though he had done with work for ever. A face less beautiful than Hamish Channing's would have appeared painfully thin: his, spite of its wasted aspect, had yet a wonderful charm. The remark was once made that Hamish Channing's was a face that would be beautiful always; beautiful to the end; beautiful in dying. See it now. The perfect contour of the features is shown the plainer in their attenuation; the skin seems transparent, the cheeks are delicately flushed, the eyes are very blue and bright. If the countenance had looked etherealized earlier in the history, and any cavilled at the word, they would scarcely have cavilled at it now. But in the strangely spiritual expression, speaking, one knew not how, of Heaven there was an ever-present sadness, as if trouble had been hard at work with him; as if all that was of the earth, earthy, had been crucified away.

Nobody seemed certain of it yet—that he was dying. He bore up bravely; working still a little at home; but not going to the office; that was beyond him. The doctors had not said there was no hope: his wife, though she might inwardly feel how it was, would not speak it. He sat at the head of his table yet; he was careful of his appearance as of yore. His smile was genial still; his loving words were cheerful, sometimes gay; his sweet kindliness to all around was more marked. Oh, it was not in the face only that the look of Heaven appeared: if ever a spark of the Divine spirit of love and light had been vouchsafed to man's soul, it surely had been to that of Hamish Channing.

He wore a coat of black velvet, a vest of the same, across which his gold chain passed, with its drooping seal. The ring, formerly Mr. Channing's, no longer made believe to fit the little finger; it was worn on the second. His hair, carefully brushed as ever, looked like threads of dark gold in the sunlight. Certainly it could not be said that Hamish gave in to his illness. Whatever his complaint might be, the medical men did not call it by any name; there was a little cough, a strange want of tone and strength a quick, continual, almost perceptible wasting. Whether Hamish had cherished visions of recovery for himself could not be known; most earnestly he had hoped for it. If only for the sake of his wife and child, he desired to live: and existence itself, even in the midst of a great and crushing disappointment, is hard to resign. But the truth, long dawning on his mind, had shown itself to him fully at last, as it does in similar cases to most of us; whether Hamish's weakness had taken a stride and brought conviction of its formidable nature, or whether it might be that he was temporarily feeling worse, a sadness, as of death itself, lay upon him this afternoon.

It had been a short life—as men count lives; he had not yet numbered two and thirty years. But for the awful disappointment that was drying its fibres away, he might say that it had been a supremely happy one. Perhaps no man, with the sweet and sunny temperament of Hamish Channing, possessing the same Christian principles, could be otherwise than happy. He did not remember ever to have done ill wilfully to mortal man, in thought, word, or deed. It had been done to him: but he forgave it. Nevertheless, a sense of injustice, a bitter pang of disappointment, of hopeless failure as to this world, lay on his heart, when he recalled what the past few months brought him. Leaning there on his chair, his sad eyes tracing figures in the fire, he was recalling things one by one. His never-ceasing, ever-hopeful work, and the bright dreams of future fame that had made its sunshine. He remembered, as though it were today, the evening that first review met his eye—when he had been entertaining his brother-in-law, the Reverend William Yorke, and others—and the shock it gave him. Think of it when he would even now, it brought him a sensation of sick faintness. Older men have become paralyzed from a similar shock. The first review had been so closely followed by others, equally unjust, equally cruel, that they all seemed as one blow. After that there appeared to be a sort of pause in his life, when time and events stood still, when he moved as one in a dream of misery, when all things around him were as dead, and he along with them. The brain (as it seemed) never stopped beating, or the bosom's pain working; or the sense of humiliation to quit him. And then, as the days went on, bodily weakness supervened; and—there he was, dying. Dying! going surely to his God and Saviour; he felt that; but leaving his dear ones, wife and child, to the frowns of a hard world; alone, without suitable provision. And the book—the good, scholarly, attractive book, upon which he had bestowed the best of his bright genius, that he had written as to Heaven—was lying unread. Wasted!

"Papa, shall I put on her blue frock or her green? She is going out for a walk."

This interruption came from Miss Nelly, who sat on the hearthrug, dressing her doll. There was no reply, and Nelly looked up: she wore a blue frock herself; its sleeves and the white pinafore tied together with blue ribbon. Her pretty little feet in their shoes and socks were stretched out, and her curls fell in a golden shower.

"Shall baby wear her blue frock or her green, papa? Papa, then! Which is prettiest?"

Hamish, aroused, looked down on the child with a smile. "The blue, I think; and then baby-doll will be like Nelly."

But Mrs. Channing, sewing at the window, turned her head. Something in her husband's face or in his weary tone struck her.

"Do you feel worse, Hamish?"

"No, love. Not particularly."

Sadder yet, the voice; a kind of hopeless, weary sadness, depressing to hear. Ellen quitted her seat, and came to him. "What is it?" she whispered.

"Not much, dear. The future has cleared itself; that's all."

"The future?"

"I cannot struggle any longer, Ellen. I have preached faith and patience to others, but they seem to have deserted me. I—I almost think the very strife itself is helping on the end."

Sharp though the pang was, that pierced her breast, she would not show it. Miss Nelly chattered below, asking questions of her doll, and making believe to answer.

"The—end, Hamish!"

He took her hand and looked straight in her face as she stood by him. "Have you not seen it, Ellen?"

With a heart and bosom that alike quivered,—with a standing still of all her pulses,—with a catching-up of breath, as a sob, Mrs. Churning was conscious of a stab of pain. Oh yes—yes—she had seen it; and the persuading herself that she had not, had been but a sickly, miserable pretence at cheating.

"But for leaving you and the little one, Ellen, there would be no strife," he whispered, letting his forehead rest for a moment on her arm. "It is a long while now that my dreams—I had almost said my visions—have been of that world to which we are all journeying, which every one of us must enter sooner or later. There will be no pain, or trouble, or weariness there. Only the other night, as I lay between sleep and wake, I seemed to have passed its portals into a soft, bright, soothing light, a haven of joyous peace and rest."

"And if dolly's good, and does not spoil her new blue frock, she shall go out for a walk," was heard from the hearthrug. Hamish put his elbow on the arm of the chair, and covered his face with his slender fingers.

"But when I think of my wife and child—and I am always thinking of them, Ellen,—when I realize the bitter truth that I must leave them, why then at times it seems as if my heart must break with its intense pain. Ellen, my darling, I would not, even yet, have spoken, but that I know you must have been waiting for it."

"I could have borne any trouble better than this," she answered, pressing her hands together.

"It will be softened to you, I am sure, Ellen. I am ever praying that it may."

"But—"

Visitors in the drawing-room: Mrs. Bede Greatorex and Miss Joliffe. A servant came to announce them. She had said that her mistress was at home, and Ellen had to go up. Hamish, with his remaining strength, lifted Miss Nelly on his knee, doll and all.

"Hush, papa, please! Baby is fatigued with making her toilette. She wants to go to sleep."

"What would Nelly say if papa told her he also wanted to go to sleep?"

Miss Nelly lay back in papa's arms while she considered the question, the doll hushed in hers. Ah me, it is ever thus! We clasp and love our children: they love others, who are more to them than we are.

"Why? Are you tired, papa?"

"A little weary, dear."

"Then go to sleep. Doll shall be quiet."

"The sleep's not coming just yet, Nelly. And—when it does come—papa may not awake from it."

"Not ever, ever, ever?" asked Nelly, opening her blue eyes in wonder, but not taking in at all the true sense of the question.

"Not ever—here."

"The princess went into a sleep in my tale-book, and lay on the bed with roses in her hair, and never awoke, never, never, till the good old fairy came and touched her," said Miss Nelly.

There ensued a pause. Hamish Channing's lip quivered a little; but no one, save himself, could have guessed how every fibre of his heart was aching.

"Nelly," he resumed, his voice and manner alike gravely earnest, his eyes reading hers, "I want to give you a charge. Should papa have to go on a long journey, you would be all that mamma has left. Take you care, my child, to be ever dutiful to her; to be obedient to her slightest wish, and to love her with a double love."

"A long, long, long journey?" demanded Miss Nelly.

"Very long."

"And when would you come back again to this house?"

"Not ever."

"Where would it be to, papa?"

"Heaven," he softly whispered.

Nelly rose up in his arms, the blue eyes more wondering than before.

"But that would be to die!"

"And if it were?"

Down fell the doll unheeded. The child's fears were aroused. She threw her little arms about his neck.

"Oh papa, papa, don't die! Don't die!"

"But if I must, Ellen?"

Only once in her whole life could she remember that he had called her by her true name, and that was when her grandpa died. She began to tremble.

"Who would take care of me, papa?"

"God."

She hid her face upon his velvet waistcoat, strangely still.

"He would guide, and guard, and love you ever, Ellen. Loving Him you would be His dear child always, and He would bring you in time to me. Look up, my dear one."

"Must you go the journey?"

"I fear so."

"Oh, papa!—and don't you care—don't you care for mamma and me, that you must leave us?"

"Care!"

He could say no more; the word seemed to put the finishing stroke to his breaking heart. Sobs broke from his lips; tears, such as man rarely sheds, streamed down on the little nestling head. A cry of anguish, patient and imploring, that the parting might be soothed to them all, went up aloft to his Father in Heaven.

After dusk came on, when the visitors were got rid of,—for Clare Joliffe had stayed an unconscionable time, talking over old interests at Helstonleigh—Mrs. Channing found her husband asleep in his chair. Closing the door softly on him, she sat down by the dining-room fire, and the long pent-up tears burst forth. Hamish Channing's wife was a brave woman but there are griefs that go well-nigh, when they fall, to shatter the bravest of us. Miss Nelly, captured ever so long ago by nurse, was at tea in the nursery.

Roland Yorke surprised Mrs. Channing in her sorrow. Roland never came into the house with a clatter now (at least when he thought of its master's sick state), but with as softly decorous a step as his boots could be controlled to. Down he sat in silence, on the opposite side of the hearth, and saw the reflection of Mrs. Channing's tears in the firelight.

"Is he worse?" asked Roland, when he had stared a little.

"No," she answered, scarcely making a pretence to conceal her grief. "I fear there will not be very much 'worse' in it at all, Roland: a little more weakness perhaps, and that will be all. I am afraid the end is very near. I fancy he thinks so."

Roland grew hot and cold; a dart took him under his waistcoat.

"Let's understand, Mrs. Channing. Don't play with a fellow. Do you mean that Hamish is—going—to die?"

"Yes, I am sure there is no more hope."

"My goodness!"—and Roland rubbed his hot and woe-stricken face. "Why he was better yesterday. He was laughing and talking like anything."

"Not really better. It is as I say, Roland."

"If ever I saw such a miserable world as this!" exclaimed Roland: who, though indulging at times some private despondency upon the case, had perhaps not realized its utter hopelessness until now, when the words put it unmistakably before him. "I never thought—at least, much—but what he'd get well again: the fine, good, handsome man. I'd like to know why he couldn't, and what has killed him."

"The reviews have done it," said Ellen, in a low tone.

Roland groaned. A suspicion, that they must have had something to do with the decay, had been upon himself. Hamish had never been quite the same after they appeared: his spirit had seemed to fade away in a subdued sadness, and subsequently his health followed it.

"The cruel reviews broke his heart," resumed Mrs. Channing. "I am certain of it, Roland. A less sensitive man would not have felt it vitally; a man, physically stronger, could not have suffered in health. But he is sensitive amidst the most sensitive; and he never, with all his bright face and fine form, was physically strong. And so—he could not bear the blow, and it has killed him."

Roland sat pulling at his whiskers in desperate gloom. Mrs. Channing shaded her eyes with her hand.

"If I could but pitch into the reviewers!" he cried. "Were I rich, I'd offer a thousand pounds' reward to anybody who would bring me their names. Hang the lot! And if you were not by, Mrs. Channing, it's a worse word than that I'd say."

She shook her head. "Pitching into the reviewers, Roland, would not give him back his life. The publisher thinks that one man wrote them all: or got them written. Some one who must have had a grudge against Hamish. It does seem like it."

Roland's picture might have been taken as an emblem of Despair. Suddenly the face brightened a little, the sanguine temperament resumed its sway.

"Don't you lose heart, Mrs. Channing. I'll tell you something that happened to me at Port Natal. Uncommon hard-up, I was, and lying in a place with a strong fever upon me. I thought I was dying; I did indeed. I was dreaming of Helstonleigh and all the old people there; I seemed to see Arthur and Hamish, and Hamish smiled at me in his bright way, and said, 'Cheer up, it will be all right, old friend.' Upon that, somebody was standing by the bed—which was nothing but a sack of sand that you roll off unpleasantly—laying hold of my pulse and looking down at me. I mean really, you know. A chap in the room said it was a doctor; perhaps it was; but he got me nothing but some herb-tea to drink. 'Take courage,' says he to me, 'it's half the battle!' I got well in time, and so may Hamish. You take courage, Mrs. Channing."

She smiled a little. "My taking courage would not help my husband, Roland."

"Well—no; perhaps it mightn't," acknowledged Roland, resuming his gloom. "Where is he?"

She pointed to the other room. "Asleep before the fire."

Roland softly opened the door and looked in. The firelight played on Hamish Channing's wasted features; and his dreams seemed to be of a pleasant nature, for a smile sat on the delicate lips: lips that had always shown so plainly the man's remarkable refinement. Nevertheless, sleeping and dreaming peacefully, there was something in the face that spoke of coming death. And Roland could have burst into sobs as he stood there.

Going back again, and closing the door quietly, Roland found the company augmented in the person of his brother Gerald. For some time past Gerald Yorke had heard from one and another of Hamish Channing's increased illness, which made no impression upon him, except a slightly favourable one; for, if Hamish were incapacitated from writing, it would be a rival removed from Gerald's path. This afternoon he was told that Hamish was thought to be past recovery; in fact, dying. That did arouse him a little; the faint spark of conscience Gerald Yorke possessed took a twinge, and he thought as he was near the house he'd give a call in.

"You are quite a stranger," Mrs. Channing was saying, meeting Gerald with a cordial hand and a grasp of welcome. "What has kept you away?"

"Aw—been busy of late; and—aw—worried," answered Gerald, according a distant nod to Roland. "What's this I hear about Hamish?—That he is dying!"

"Well, I don't think you need blurt out that strong word to Mrs. Channing, Gerald," interposed hot Roland. "Dying, indeed! Do you call it manners? I don't."

"I beg Mrs. Channing's pardon," Gerald was beginning, half cynically; but Ellen's voice rose to interrupt.

"It makes no difference, Roland," she kindly said. "It is the truth, you know; and I am not blind to it.

"What's the matter with him?" asked Gerald.

The matter with him? Ellen Channing told the brief story in a few words. The cruel reviews had broken his heart. Gerald listened, and felt himself turned into a white heat inside and out.

"The reviews!" he exclaimed. "I don't understand yon, Mrs. Channing."

"Of course you read them, Gerald, and must know their bitter, shameful injustice," she explained. "They were such that might have struck a blow even to a strong man: they struck a fatal one to Hamish. He had staked his whole heart and hope upon the book; he devoted to it the great and good abilities with which God had gifted him; he made it worthy of all praise; and false men rose up and blasted it. A strong word you may deem that, Gerald, for me to use; but it is a true one. They rose up, and—in envy, as I believe—set themselves to write and work out a deliberate lie: they got it sent forth to the world in effectual channels, and killed the book. Perhaps they did not intend also to kill the writer."

Gerald's white face looked whiter than usual. His eyes, in their hard stare, were very ugly.

"Still I can't understand," he said. "The critiques were, of course rather severe: but how can critiques kill a man?"

"And if you, being a reviewer yourself, Gerald, could only get to find out who the false-hearted hound was,—for it's thought to have been one fellow who penned the lot—you'd oblige me," put in Roland. "I'd repay him, as I've seen it done at Port Natal. His howling would be something fine."

"You do not yet entirely understand, I see, Gerald," sadly answered Ellen, paying no attention to Roland's interruption, while Gerald turned his shoulder upon him. "In one sense the reviews did not kill. They did not, for instance, strike Hamish dead at once, or break his heart with a stroke. In fact, you may think the expression, a broken heart, but a figure of speech, and in a degree of course it is so. But there are some natures, and his is one, which are so sensitively organized that a cruel blow shatters them. Had Hamish been stronger he might have borne it, have got over it in time; but he had been working beyond his strength; and I think also his strangely eager hope in regard to the book must have helped to wear out his frame. It was his first work, you know. When the blow came he had not strength to rally from it; mind and body were alike stricken down, and so the weakness set in and laid hold of him."

"What are these natures good for?" fiercely demanded Gerald, in a tone as if he were resenting some personal injury.

"Only for Heaven, as it seems to me," she gently answered.

Gerald rubbed his face; he could not get any colour into it, and there ensued a pause. Presently Ellen spoke again.

"I remember, when I was quite a girl, reading of a somewhat similar case in one of Bulwer Lytton's novels. A young artist painted a great picture—great to him—and insisted on being concealed in the room while a master came to judge of it. The judgment was adverse; not, perhaps, particularly harsh and cruel in itself, only sounding so to the painter; and it killed him. Not at the moment, Gerald; I don't mean that; he lived to become ill, and he went to Italy for his health, his heart gradually breaking. He never spoke of what the blow had been to him, or that it had crushed out his hope and life, but died hiding it. Hamish has never spoken."

"What I want to know is, where's the use of people being like this?" pursued Gerald. "What are they made for?"

"Scarcely for earth," she answered. "The too-exquisitely-refined gold is not meant for the world's coinage."

"I'd rather be a bit of brittle china, than made so that I couldn't stand a review," said Gerald. "It's to be hoped there's not many such people."

"Only one in tens of thousands, Gerald."

"Does it—trouble him?" asked Gerald, hesitatingly.

"The advance of death?—yes, in a degree. Not for the death, Gerald: but the quitting me and Nelly."

"I'm not yet what Hamish and Arthur are, safe to be heard up there when they ask for a thing," again interrupted Roland, jerking his head upwards: "but I do pray that from the day that bad base man hears of Hamish Channing's death, he'll be haunted by his ghost for ever. My goodness! I'd not like to have murder on my conscience. It's as bad as the fellow who killed Mr. Ollivera."

Gerald Yorke rose. Ellen asked him to wait and see Hamish, but he answered, in what seemed a desperate hurry, that he had an engagement.

"You might like to take a peep at him, Gerald," spoke Roland. "His face looks as peaceful as if it were sainted."

Gerald's answer was to turn tail and go off. Roland, who had some copying on hand that was being waited for, stayed to shake hands with Mrs. Channing.

"Look here," he whispered to her. "Don't you let him worry his mind about you and Nelly: in the way of money, you know. I shall be sure to get into something good soon; Vincent will see to that; and I'll take care of both of you. Goodbye."

Poor, penniless, good-hearted Roland! He would have "taken care" of all the world.

With a run he caught up Gerald, who was striding along rapidly. Oblivious of all save the present distress, even of Gerald's past coldness, Roland attempted to take his arm, and got repulsed for his pains.

"My way does not lie the same as yours, I think," was Gerald's haughty remark. Roland would not resent it.

"I say, Ger, is it not enough to make one sad? It wouldn't have mattered much had it been you or me to be taken: but Hamish Channing! we can't afford to lose such a one as him."

"Thank you," said Gerald. "Speak for yourself."

"And with Hamish the bread and cheese dies. She has but little money. Perhaps she'll not feel the want of it, though. I'd work my arms off for that darling little Nelly and for her too, for Hamish's sake."

"I don't believe he is dying at all," said Gerald. "Reviews kill him, indeed! it's altogether preposterous. Women talk wretched nonsense in this world."

Without so much as a parting Goodnight, Gerald struck across the street and disappeared. By the time he arrived at chambers, his mind had fully persuaded itself that there was nothing serious the matter with Hamish Channing; and he felt that he could like to shake Winny (who had been his informant) for alarming him.

His servant brought him a letter as he entered, and Gerald tore it open. It proved to be from Sir Vincent Yorke, inviting Gerald down to Sunny Mead on the morrow for a couple of days' shooting.

"Hurrah!" shouted Gerald. "Vin's coming round, is he! I'll go, and get out of him a hundred or so, to bring back with me to town. That's good. Hurrah!"

CHAPTER XXXVI

GERALD YORKE AT A SHOOTING PARTY

It was a pretty place; its name, Sunny Mead, an appropriate one. For the bright sun (not far yet above the horizon) of the clear and cold December day, shone on it cheerily: on the walls of the dwelling-house—on the green grass of the spreading lawn, with its groups of flowering laurestina and encompassing trees, that in summer cast a grateful shade. The house was small, but compact; the prospect from the windows, with its expanse of wood and hill and dale, a charming one. At its best it was a simple, unpretending place, but as pleasant a homestead for moderate desires as could be found in the county of Surrey.

In a snug room, its fire blazing in the grate, its snowy breakfast cloth, laden with china and silver, drawn near the large window that looked upon the lawn, sat the owner, Sir Vincent Yorke, and his cousin Gerald. As soon as breakfast should be over, they were going out shooting; but the baronet was by no means one who liked to disturb his morning's comfort by starting at dawn: shooting, as well as everything else in life, he liked to take easily. Gerald had arrived the previous night: it was the first time Gerald had seen Sunny Mead: and the very unpretending rank it took amidst baronets' dwelling-places, surprised him. Sir Vincent's marriage was fixed for the following month, January; and he gratified Gerald much by saying that he thought of asking him to be groomsman.

"Aw!—very happy—immensely so," responded Gerald with his most fashionable drawl, that so grated on a true and honest ear.

"Sunny Mead has this advantage; one can come to it and be quiet," observed Sir Vincent. "There's not room for more than three or four servants in it. My father used to call it the homestead: that's just what it is, and it doesn't pretend to be aught else. More coffee? Try that partridge pie. Have you seen Roland lately?"

The cynical expression of disparagement that pervaded Gerald's face at the question, made Sir Vincent smile.

"Aw—I say, don't you spoil my breakfast by bringing up him," spoke Gerald. "The best thing he can do is to go out to Port Natal again. A capital pie!"

"This devilled turkey's good, too. You'll try it presently?" spoke the baronet. "How is Hamish Channing?"

Gerald's skin turned of a dark hue. Was Sir Vincent purposely annoying him? Catching up his coffee-cup to take a long draught, he did not answer.

"I never saw so fine a fellow in all my life," resumed Sir Vincent. "Never was so taken with a face at first sight as with his. William Yorke was staying there at the time of my father's funeral, and I went next day to call. That's how I saw Channing. He promised to come and see me; but somebody told me the other day he was ill."

"Aw—yes," drawled Gerald. "Seedy, I believe."

"What's the matter with him?"

"Temper," said Gerald. "Wrote a book, and had some reviews upon it, and it put him out, I hear."

"But it was a first-rate book, Gerald; I read it, and the reviews were all wrong: suppose some contemptible raven of envy scrawled them. The book's working its way upwards as fast as it can now."

"Who says so?" cried Gerald.

"I do. I had the information from a reliable source. By-the-way, is there anything in that story of Roland's—that he is engaged to Channing's sister? or is it fancy?"

"I do wish you'd let the fellow's name be; he's not so very good to talk of," retorted Gerald, in a rage.

But Roland was not so easily put out of the conversation. As luck had it, when the servant brought Sir Vincent's letters in, there was one from Roland amidst them. Vincent laughed outright as he read it:—

"Dear Vincent,—I happened to overhear old Greatorex say yesterday that Sir Vincent Yorke wanted a working bailiff for the land at Sunny Mead. I! wish! to! offer! myself! for! the! situation! There! I put it strong that you may not mistake. Of course, I am a relative, which I can't help being; and a working bailiff is but a kind of upper servant. But I'll be very glad of the place if you'll give it me, and will do my duty in it as far as I can, putting my best shoulder to the wheel; and I'll never presume upon our being cousins to go into your house uninvited, or put myself in your way; and my wife would not call on Lady Yorke if she did not wish it. I'll be the bailiff—you the master.

"I don't tell you I'm a first hand at farming; but, if perseverance and sticking to work can teach, I shall soon learn it. I picked up some experience at Port Natal; and had to drive waggons and other animals. I'm great in pigs. The droves I had to manage of the grunting, obstinate wretches, out there, taught me enough of them. Of course I know all about haymaking; and I'd used to be one of the company at old Pierce's harvest homes, on his farm near Helstonleigh. I don't suppose you'd want me to thresh the wheat myself; but I'm strong to do it, and would not mind. I would be always up before dawn in spring to see to the young lambs; and I'd soon acquire the ins and outs of manuring and draining. Do try me, Vincent! I'll put my shoulder to the wheel in earnest for you. There'd be one advantage in taking me—that I should be honest and true to your interests. Whereas some bailiffs like to serve themselves better than their masters.

"As to wages, I'd leave that to you. You'd not give less than a hundred a year to begin with; and at the twelvemonth's end, when I had made myself qualified, you might make it two. Perhaps you'd give the two hundred at once. I don't wish to presume because I'm a relative; and if the two hundred would be too much at first (for, to tell the truth, I don't know how bailiffs' pay runs), please excuse my having named it. I expect there are lots of pretty cottages to be hired down there; may be there's one on the estate appropriated to the bailiff. I may as well mention that I am a first-rate horseman, and could gallop about like a fire-engine; having nearly lost my life more times than one, learning to ride the wild cattle when up the country at Port Natal.

"I think that's all I have to say. Only try me! If you do, you will find how willing I am. Besides being strong, I am naturally active, with plenty of energy: the land should not go to ruin for the want of being looked after. My object in life now is to get a certainty that will bring me in something tolerably good to begin, and go on to three hundred a year, or more; for I should not like Annabel to take pupils always. I don't know whether a bailiff ever gets as much.

"Bede Greatorex can give you a good character of me for steadiness and industry. And if I have stuck to this work, I should do better by yours; for writing I hate, and knocking about a farm I'd like better than anything.

"You'll let me have an answer as soon as convenient. If you take me I shall have to order leggings and other suitable toggery from Carrick's tailor; and he might be getting on with the things.

"Wishing you a merry Christmas, which will soon be here (don't I recollect one of mine at Port Natal, when I had nothing for dinner and the same for supper), I remain, dear Vincent, yours truly,

"Roland Yorke.

"Sir Vincent Yorke."

To watch the curl of Gerald's lip, the angry sarcasm of his face, as he perused this document, which the baronet handed to him with a laugh, was amusing. It might have made a model of scorn for a painter's easel. Dropping the letter from his fingers, as if there were contamination in its very touch, he flicked it across the table.

"You'll send it back to him in a blank envelope, won't you?"

"No; why should I?" returned Sir Vincent, who was good-natured in the main, easy on the whole. "I'll answer him when I've time. Do you know, Gerald, I think you rather disparage Roland."

Gerald opened his astonished eyes. "Disparage him! How can he be disparaged?—he is just as low as he can be. An awful blot, nothing else, on the family escutcheon."

"The family don't seem to be troubled much by him—saving me. He appears to regard me as a sheet-anchor—who can provide for the world, himself included. I rather like the young fellow; he is so genuine."

"Don't call him young," reproved Gerald; "he'll be twenty-nine next May."

"And in mind and manners he is nineteen."

"He talks of pigs—see what he has brought his to," exclaimed Gerald, somewhat forgetting his fashion. "The—aw—low kind of work he condescends to do—the mean way he is not ashamed to confess he lives in! Every bit of family pride has gone out of him, and given place to vulgar instincts."

"As Roland has tumbled into the mire, better for him to be honest and work," returned Sir Vincent, mincing with his dry toast and one poached egg, for he was delicate in appetite. "What else could he do? Of course there's the credit system and periodical whitewashings, but I should not care to go in for that kind of thing myself."

"Are you in want of a bailiff?" growled Gerald, wondering whether the last remarks were meant to be personal.

"Greatorex has engaged one for me. How are you getting on yourself, Gerald?"

"Not—aw—at all. I'm awfully hard up."

"You always are, Ger, according to your story," was the baronet's remark, laughing slightly.

And somehow the laugh sounded in Gerald's ear as a hard laugh—as one that boded no good results to the petition he meant to prefer before his departure—that Sir Vincent would accommodate him with a loan.

"He's close-fisted as a miser," was Gerald's mental comment. "His father all over again. Neither of them would part with a shilling save for self-gratification: and both could spend enough on that. I'll ask him for a hundred, point blank, before I leave; more, if I can feel my way to do it. Fortune is shamefully unequal in this life. There's Vin with his baronetcy, and his nice little place here and every comfort in it, and his town house, and his clear four thousand a-year, and no end of odds and ends of money besides, nest eggs of various shapes and sizes, and his future wife a seventy thousand pounder in her own right; and here's myself by his side, a better man than he any day, with not a coin of my own in the whole world, nor likely to drop into one by inheritance, and afraid to venture about London for fear of being nabbed! Curse the whole thing! He is shabby in trifles too. To give me a miserable two days' invitation. Two days! I'll remain twenty if I can."

"You don't eat, Gerald."

"I've made a famous breakfast, thank you. Do you spend Christmas down here, Vincent?"

"Not I. The day after tomorrow, when you leave me, I start for Paris."

"For Paris!" echoed Gerald, his mouth falling at the sudden failure of his pleasant scheme.

"Miss Trehern and her father are there. We shall remain for the jour de l'an, see the bonbon shops, and all that, and then come back again."

"And I hope the bonbon shops will choke him!" thought kindly Gerald.

Sir Vincent Yorke did not himself go in for keepers and dogs. There was little game on his land, and he was too effeminate to be much of a sportsman. He owned two guns, and that comprised the whole of his shooting paraphernalia. Breakfast over, he had his guns brought, and desired Gerald to take his choice.

Now the handling and understanding of guns did not rank amidst Gerald Yorke's accomplishments. Brought up in the cathedral town, only away from it on occasions at Dr. Yorke's living (and that happened to be in a town also), the young Yorkes were not made familiar with outdoor sports. Dr. Yorke had never followed them himself, and saw no necessity for training his sons to them. Even riding they were not very familiar with. Roland's letter had just informed Sir Vincent that he had nearly lost his life learning to ride the wild horses when up the country at Port Natal. Probably he had learnt also to understand something about guns: we may be very sure of one thing, that if he did not understand them, he would have voluntarily avowed it. Not so Gerald. Gerald, made up of artificialisms—for nothing seemed real about him but his ill-temper—touched the guns here, and fingered the guns there, and critically examined them everywhere, as if he were the greatest connoisseur alive, and had invented a breech-loader himself; and finally said he would take this one.

So they went out, each with his gun and a favourite dog of the baronet's, Spot, and joined a neighbour's shooting party, as had been arranged. Colonel Clutton's land joined Sir Vincent's; he was a keen lover of sport, always making up parties for it, and if Sir Vincent went out at all, it was sure to be with Colonel Clutton.

"To-day and tomorrow will be my last turn out this season," observed the baronet, as they walked along. "Not sorry for it. One gets a large amount of fatigue: don't think the slaughter compensates for that."

Reaching the meeting-place, they found a party of some three or four gentlemen and two keepers. Gerald was introduced to Colonel Clutton, an elderly man with snow-white hair. The sport set in. It was late in the season, and the birds were getting scarce or wary, but a tolerably fair number fell.

"The gentleman don't seem to handle his gun gainly, sir, as if he'd played with one as a babby," observed one of the keepers confidentially in Sir Vincent's ear.

He alluded to Gerald Yorke. Sir Vincent turned and looked. Though not much addicted to shooting, he was thoroughly conversant with it: and what he saw, as he watched Gerald, a little surprised him.

"I say, Gerald Yorke, you must take care," he called out. "Did you never handle a gun before?"

The suggestion offended Gerald: the question nettled him. His face grew dark.

"What do you mean, Sir Vincent?" was his angry answer. He would have liked to affirm his great knowledge of shooting: but his chief practice had been with a pop-gun at school.

Sir Vincent laughed a little. "Don't do any mischief, that's all."

It might have been that the public caution caused Gerald to be more careless, just to prove his proficiency; it might have been that it tended to flurry him. Certainly he would not have caused harm wilfully; but nevertheless it took place.

Not ten minutes after Sir Vincent had spoken, he was crossing a narrow strip of open ground towards a copse. Gerald, leaping through a gap in the hedge not far behind, carrying his gun (like a senseless man) on full cock, contrived, in some inexplicable manner, to discharge it. Whether his elbow caught in the leafless branches, or the trigger caught, or what it was, Gerald Yorke never knew, and never will know to his dying day. The charge went off; there was a cry, accompanied by shouts of warning, somebody on the ground in front, and the rest running to surround the fallen man.

"You have no right to come out, sir, unless you can handle a gun properly!" spoke Colonel Clutton to Gerald, in the moment's confusion. "I have been watching your awkwardness all the morning."

Gerald looked pale with fear, dark with anger. He made no reply whatever only pressed forward to see who was down, the men, in their velveteen coats and leggings, looking much alike. Sir Vincent Yorke.

"It's not much, I think," said the baronet good-naturedly, as he looked up at Gerald. "But I say, though, you should have candidly answered me that you were not in the habit of shooting, when I sent you the invitation."

No, it was not much. A few shots had entered the calf of the left leg. They got out pocket-handkerchiefs, and tied them tightly round to stop the hemorrhage. The dog, Spot, laid his head close to his master's face, and whined pitiably.

"What sense them dumb animals have!—a'most human!" remarked the keeper.

"This will stop my Paris trip," observed Sir Vincent, as they were conveying him home.

"Better that was stopped than your wedding," replied Colonel Clutton, with a jesting smile. "You keep yourself quiet, now, that you may be well for that. Don't talk."

Sir Vincent acquiesced readily. At the best of times he was sensitive to pain, and somewhat of a coward in regard to his own health. At home he was met by a skilful surgeon. The shots were extracted, and Sir Vincent was made comfortable in bed. Gerald Yorke waylaid the doctor afterwards.

"Is it serious? Will he do well? Sir Vincent is my cousin."

"Oh—Mr. Yorke; the gentleman whose gun unfortunately caused the mishap," was the answering remark. "Of course these accidents are always serious, more or less. This one might have been far worse than it is."

"He will do well?"

"Quite well. At least, I hope so. I see nothing to hinder it. Sir Vincent will be a tractable patient, you see; and a good deal lies in that."

"There's no danger, then?"

"Oh no: no danger."

Gerald, relieved on the score of apprehension of consequences, had the grace to express his regret and sorrow to the baronet. Sir Vincent begged him to think no more about it: only recommended him not to go out with a party in future, until he had had some practice. Gerald, untrue to the end, said he was a little out of practice; should soon get into it again. Sir Vincent made quite light of the hurt; it was nothing to speak of, the doctor had said; would not delay his marriage, or anything. But he did not ask Gerald to remain: and that gentleman, in spite of his hints, and his final offer to stay, found he was expected to go. Sir Vincent expressed his acknowledgments, but said he wished for perfect quiet.

So on the day following the accident, Gerald Yorke returned to town; which was a day sooner than, even at the worst, he had bargained for; and arrived in a temper. Taking one untoward disappointment with another, Gerald's mood could not be expected to be heavenly. He had fully intended to come away with his pockets lined—if by dint of persuasion Sir Vincent could be seduced into doing it. As it was, Gerald had not broached the subject. Sir Vincent was to be kept entirely quiet; and Gerald, with all his native assurance, could not ask a man for money, whom he had just shot.

CHAPTER XXXVII

IN CUSTODY

Pacing his carpet, in the worst state of perturbation possible, was the Rev. Mr. Ollivera. He had so paced it all the morning. Neglecting his ordinary duties, staying indoors when he ought to have been out, unable to eat or to rest, he and his mind were alike in a state of most distressing indecision. The whole of the night had he tossed and turned, and rose up again and again to walk his room, struggling with his conscience. For years past, he had, so to say, lived on the anticipation of this hour: when the memory of his dear brother should be cleared of its foul stain, and the true criminal brought to light. And, now that it had come, he was hesitating whether or not to take advantage of it: whether to let the stain remain, and the criminal escape.

Torn to pieces with doubt and pain, was he. Unable to see where his duty lay, more than once, with lifted hands and eyes and heart, a cry to Heaven to direct him broke from his lips. Passages of Scripture, bearing both ways, crowded on his mind, to puzzle him the more; but there was one great lesson he could not ignore—the loving, merciful teaching of Jesus Christ.

About one o'clock, when the remembrance of the miserable grave, and of him who had been so miserably put into it, lay very strong upon him, Alletha Rye came into the room with some white cravats of the parson's in her hand. She was neat and nice as usual, wearing a soft merino gown with white worked cuffs and collars, her fair hair smooth and abundant.

"I have done the best I could with them, sir: cut off the edges and hemmed them afresh," she said. "After that, I passed the iron over them, and they look just as if fresh got up.

"Thank you," murmured Mr. Ollivera, the colour flushing his face, and speaking in a confused kind of manner, like a man overtaken in a crime.

"Great heaven, can I go on with it?" he exclaimed, as she went out, leaving the neckerchiefs on the table. "Is it possible to believe that she did it?—with her calm good face, with her clear honest eye?" he continued in an agony of distress. "Oh, for guidance! that I may be shown what my course ought to be!" As a personal matter, to give Alletha Rye into custody would cause him grievous pain. She had lived under the same roof with him, showing him voluntarily a hundred little courtesies and kindnesses. These white cravats of his, just put to rights, had been undertaken in pure good will.

How very much of our terrible seasons of distress might be spared to us, if we could but see a little further than the present moment; than the atmosphere immediately around. Henry William Ollivera might have been saved his: had he but known that while he was doubting, another was acting. Mr. Greatorex had taken it into his own hands, and the house's trouble was, even then, at the very door. In after life, Henry Ollivera never ceased to be thankful that it was not himself who brought it.

A commotion below. Mr. Roland Yorke had entered, and was calling out to the house to bring his dinner. It was taken to him in the shape of some slices of roast mutton and potatoes. When Mrs. Jones had a joint herself, Roland was served from it. That she was no gainer by the bargain, Mrs. Jones was conscious of; the small sum she allowed herself in repayment out of the weekly sovereign, debarred it: but Roland was favoured for the sake of old times.

Close almost upon that, there came a rather quiet double knock at the street door, which Miss Rye went to answer. Roland thought he recognised a voice, and ran out, his mouth full of mutton.

"Why, it's never you, old Butterby! What brings you in London again?"

Whatever brought Mr. Butterby to London, something curious appeared to have brought him to Mrs. Jones's. A policeman had followed him in, and was shutting the street door, with a manner quite at home. There escaped a faint cry from Alletha, and her face turned white as ashes. Roland stared from one to the other.

"What on earth's the matter?" demanded he.

"I'd like to speak to you in private for a minute, Miss Rye," said Mr. Butterby, in a low civil tone. "Tompkins, you wait there."

She went higher up the passage and looked round something liked a stag at bay. There was no unoccupied room to take him to. Mr. Brown's frugal dinner tray (luncheon, as he called it) was in his, awaiting his entrance. That the terrible man of law with his officer had come to arrest him Alletha never doubted. A hundred wild ideas of telegraphing him some impossible warning, not to enter, went teeming through her brain. Tompkins stood on the entrance mat; Roland Yorke, with his accustomed curiosity, put his back against his parlour door-post to watch proceedings.

"Miss Rye, I'd not have done this of my own accord, leastways not so soon, but it has been forced upon me," whispered Mr. Butterby. "I've got to ask you to go with me."

"To ask me?" she tremblingly said, while he was showing her a paper: probably the warrant.

"Are you so much surprised: after that there avowal you made to me last night? If I'd gone and told a police officer that I had killed somebody, it would not astonish me to be took."

Her face fell. The pallor of her cheeks was coloured by a faint crimson; her eyes flashed with a condemning light.

"I told you in confidence, as one friend might speak to another, in defence of him who was not there to defend himself," she panted. "How could I suppose you would hasten treacherously to use it against me?"

"Ah," said Mr. Butterby, "in things of that sort us law defenders is just the wrong sort to make confidants of. But now, look here, Miss Rye, I didn't go and abuse that confidence, and though it is me that has put the wheels of the law in motion, it is done in obedience to orders, which I had no power to stop. I'm sorry to have to do it: and I've come down with the warrant myself out of respect to you, that things might be accomplished as genteel as might be."

"Now then, Alletha! Do you know that your dinner's getting cold? What on earth are you stopping there for? Who is it?"

The interruption was from Mrs. Jones, called out through the nearly closed door of her parlour. Alletha, making no response, looked fit to die.

"Have you come to arrest me?" she whispered.

"Well, it's about it, Miss Rye. Apprehend, that is. We'll get a cab and you'll go in it with my friend there, all snug and quiet. I'm vexed that young Yorke should just be at home. Tried to get here half an hour earlier, but—"

Mrs. Jones's door was pulled open with a jerk. To describe the aggravated astonishment on her face when she saw the state of affairs, would be a work of skill. Alletha with a countenance of ghastly fear; Mr. Butterby whispering to her; the policeman on the door mat; Roland Yorke looking leisurely on.

"Well, I'm sure!" exclaimed Mrs. Jones. "What may be the meaning of this?"

There could be no evasion now. Had Alletha in her secret heart hoped to keep it from her tart, condemning, and strong-minded sister, the possibility was over. She went down the few steps that led to the room, and entered it; Mr. Butterby close behind her. The latter was shutting the door, when Roland Yorke walked in, taking French leave.

Which of the two stared the most, Mrs. Jones or Roland, and which of the two felt inclined to abuse Mr. Butterby the most, when his errand became known, remains a question to this day. Roland's championship was hot.

"You know you always do take the wrong people, Butterby!"

"Now, young Mr. Yorke, just you concern yourself with your own business, and leave other folk's alone," was the detective's answering reprimand. "I don't see what call you have to be in this here room at all."

In all the phases of the affair, with its attendant conjectures and suspicions, from the first moment that she saw John Ollivera lying dead in her house, the possibility of Alletha's being cognisant of its cause, much less connected with it, had never once entered the head of Mrs. Jones. She stared from one to the other in simple wonder.

"What is it you charge my sister with, Butterby?—the death of Counsellor Ollivera?"

"Well, yes; that's it," he answered.

"And how dare you do it?"

"Now, look you here, Mrs. Jones," said Butterby, in a tone of reason, putting his hand calmly on her wrist, "I've told Miss Rye, and I tell you, that these proceedings are instituted by the law, not by me; if I had not come to carry them out, another would, who might have done it in a rougher manner. A woman of your sense ought to see the matter in its right light. I don't say she's guilty, and I hope she'll be able to prove that she's not; but I can tell you this much, Mrs. Jones, there's them that have had their suspicions turned upon her from the first."

Being a woman of sense, as Mr. Butterby delicately insinuated, Mrs. Jones began to feel a trifle staggered. Not at his words: they had little power over her mind, but at Alletha's appearance. Leaning against the wall there, white, faint, silent, she looked like one guilty, rather than innocent. And it suddenly struck Mrs. Jones that she did not attempt a syllable in her own defence.

"Why don't you speak out, girl?" she demanded, in her tartest tone. "You can, I suppose?"

But the commotion had begun to cause attention in the quiet house. Not so much from its noise, as by that subtle instinct that makes itself heard, we cannot tell how; and Mr. Ollivera came in.

"Who has done this?" he briefly asked of the detective.

"Mr. Greatorex, sir."

"The next thing they'll do may be to take me up on the charge," spoke Mrs. Jones with acrimony. "What on earth put this into their miserable heads? You don't suspect her, I hope, Mr. Ollivera?"

He only looked at Mrs. Jones in silence by way of answer, a grave meaning in his sad face. It spoke volumes: and Mrs. Jones, albeit not one to give way to emotion, or any other kind of weakness, felt as if a jug of cold water were being poured down her back. Straightforward, always, she put the question to him with naked plainness.

"Do you suspect her?"

"I have suspected her," came the low tones of Mr. Ollivera in answer. "Believe me, Mrs. Jones, whatever may be the final result of this, I grieve for it bitterly."

"I say, why can't you speak up, and say you did not do it?" stamped Roland in his championship. "Don't be frightened out of your senses by Butterby. He never pitches upon the right person; Mrs. J. remembers that."

"As this here talking won't do any good—and I'm sure if it would I'd let it go on a bit—suppose we make a move," interposed Butterby. "If you'd like to put up a few things to take with you, Miss Rye, do so. You'll have to go to Helstonleigh."

"Oh law!" cried Roland. "I say, Butterby, it's a mistake, I know. Let her go. Come! you shall have all my dinner."

"Don't stand there like a statue, as if you were moonstruck," said Mrs. Jones, seizing her sister to administer a slight shaking. "Tell them you are innocent, girl, if you can; and let Butterby go about his business."

And in response, Alletha neither spoke nor moved.

But at this moment another actor came upon the scene. A knock at the front door was politely answered at once by the policeman, glad, no doubt, to have something to do, and Mr. Brown entered, arriving at home for his midday meal. Roland dashed into the passage.

"I say, Brown, here is a stunning shame. Old Butterby's come to take up Alletha Rye."

"Take her up for what?" Mr. Brown calmly asked.

"For the killing and slaying of Counsellor Ollivera, he says. But in these things he never was anything but a calf."

Mr. Brown turned into his room, put down his hat and a small paper parcel, and went on to the scene. Before he could say a word, Alletha Rye burst forth like one demented.

"Don't come here Mr. Brown. We've nothing to do with strangers. I can't have all the world looking at me."

Mr. Brown took a quiet survey of matters with perfect self-possession, and then drew Mr. Butterby towards his room, just as though he had possessed the authority of Scotland Yard. Mrs. Jones was left alone with her sister, and caught hold of her two hands.

"Now then! What is the English of this? Had you aught to do with the death of Mr. Ollivera?"

"Never," said Alletha; "I would not have hurt a hair of his head."

Mrs. Jones, at the answer, hardly knew whether to slap the young woman's face or to shriek at her. All this disgrace brought upon her house, and Alletha to submit to it in unrefuting tameness! As a preliminary, she began a torrent of words.

"Hush!" said Alletha. "They think me guilty, and at present they must be let think it. I cannot help myself: if Butterby conveys me to Helstonleigh, he must do it."

Mrs. Jones was nearly staggered out of her passion. The cold water went trickling down again. Not at once could she answer.

"Lord help the wench for a fool! Don't you know that! if you are conveyed to Helstonleigh it would be to take your trial at the next assizes? Would you face that?"

"I cannot tell," wailed Alletha, putting up her thin hand to her troubled face. "I must have time to think."

But we must follow Mr. Brown. As he passed into his room and closed the door, he took a tolerably long look into Butterby's eyes: possibly hoping to discover whether that astute officer knew him for Godfrey Pitman. He obtained no result. Had Mr. Butterby been a born natural he could not have looked more charmingly innocent. That he chose to indulge this demand for an interview for purposes of his own, those who knew him could not doubt. They stood together before the fireless hearth; however cold the weather might be, Mr. Brown's fire went out after breakfast and was not re-lighted until night.

"I beg your pardon, Mr. Butterby. With so much confusion in there"—nodding in the direction of Mrs. Jones's parlour—"I am not sure that I fully understood. Is it true that you are about to take Miss Rye into custody on suspicion of having caused the death of John Ollivera?"

"I have took her," was the short answer. "It is nothing to you, I suppose."

"It is this much to me: that I happen to be in a position to testify that she did not do it."

"Oh, you think so, do you," said Butterby, in a civil but slightly mocking tone. "I've knowed ten men at least swear to one man's innocence of a crime, and him guilty all the while. Don't say it was perjury: appearances is deceptive, and human nature's soft."

"I affirm to you, in the hearing of Heaven, that Alletha Rye was innocent of the death of John Ollivera," said Mr. Brown in a solemn tone that might have carried conviction to even a less experienced ear. "She had nothing whatever to do with it. Until the following morning, when she found him, she was as ignorant as you that he was dead."

"Then why don't she speak up and say so? Not that it could make any difference at the present stage of affairs."

"Will you let me ask who it is that has had her apprehended? Mr. Bede Greatorex?"

"Bede Greatorex has had nothing to do with it. 'Twas his father."

"Well now, I have a favour to ask you, Mr. Butterby," continued the other after a pause. "The good name of a young woman is a great deal easier lost than regained, as no one can tell better than yourself. It will be an awful thing if Alletha Rye, being innocent—as I swear to you she is—should be accused of this dreadful crime before the world. You have known her a long while: will you not stretch a point to save it?"

"That might depend a good deal upon what the point was," replied Mr. Butterby.

"A very simple one. Only this—that you would stay proceedings until I have had time to see Bede Greatorex. Let her remain here, in custody of course—for I am not so foolish as to suppose you could release her—but don't molest her; don't take her away. In fact, treat her as though you knew she were wrongfully accused. You may be obliged to me for this later, Mr. Butterby—I won't say in the interests of humanity, but of justice."

Various thoughts and experiences of the past, as connected with Bede Greatorex, came crowding into the mind of Butterby. His lips parted with a smile, but it was not a favourable one.

"I think that Bede Greatorex could join with me in satisfying you that it was not Miss Rye," urged the petitioner. "I am almost sure he can do this if he will.

"Which is as much as to say that both he and you have got your suspicions turned on some other quarter," rejoined Butterby. "Who was it?"

That Mr. Brown's cheeks took a darker tinge at the direct query, was plain to be seen. He made no answer.

"Come! Who did that thing? You know."

"If I do not know—and I am unable to tell you that I do, Mr. Butterby—I can yet make a shrewd guess at it."

"And Bede Greatorex too, you say?"

"I fancy he can."

Looking into each other's eyes, those two deep men, there ensued a silence. "If it wasn't this woman," whispered Butterby, "perhaps it was another."

The clerk opened his lips to speak in hasty impulse: but he closed them again, still looking hard at the officer.

"Whether it was or not, the woman was not Alletha Rye."

"Then," said Mr. Butterby, following out his own private thoughts, and giving the table an emphatic slap, which caused the frugal luncheon tray to jingle, "this thing will never be brought to trial."

"I don't much think it will," was the significant answer. "But you will consent to what I ask? I won't be away long. A quarter of an hour will suffice for my interview with Bede Greatorex."

Weighing chances and possibilities, as it lay in the business of Mr. Butterby to do; knowing who the man before him was, with the suspicion attaching to him, he thought it might be as well to keep him under view. There was no apparent intention to escape; the clerk seemed honest as the day on this present purpose, and strangely earnest; but Mr. Butterby had learnt to trust nobody.

"I'll go with yon," said he. "Tompkins will keep matters safe here. Come on. Hang me if this case ever had its fellow: it turns one about with its little finger."

CHAPTER XXXVIII

BETWEEN BEDE AND HIS CLERK

They stood near each other, Bede Greatorex and his managing clerk, while Mr. Butterby paced the passage outside.

When interrupted, Bede had his elbow on the mantelpiece, his brow bent on his thin fingers. A good blazing fire here, the coal crackling and sparkling cheerily. Bede dropped his elbow.

"What is it, Mr. Brown?" he rather languidly asked.

Mr. Brown, closing the door, went straight up and said what it was: Alletha Rye had been apprehended. But he looked anywhere, as he spoke, rather than into the face of his master. A face that grew suddenly white and cold: and Mr. Brown, in his delicacy of mind, would not appear to see it.

"What a cursed meddler that Butterby is!" exclaimed Bede.

"I fancy he had no option in this, sir; that it was not left to his choice."

"Who did it, then?"

"Mr. Greatorex. This must be remedied at once, sir."

By the authoritative manner in which he spoke, it might have been thought that Bede Greatorex was the servant, Brown the master. Bede put his elbow on the shelf again, and pushed back his hair in unmistakable agitation. It was growing thin now, the once luxuriant crop; and silver threads were interwoven with the black ones.

"She must be saved," repeated Mr. Brown.

"I suppose so. Who is to do it?"

"I must, sir. If no one else does."

Bede raised his eyes to glance at his clerk; but it was not a full free glance, and they were instantly dropped again.

"You are the Godfrey Pitman, they tell me, who was in the house at the time."

"Yes, I am. But have you not known it all along, Mr. Bede Greatorex?"

"All along from when?"

Mr. Brown hesitated. "From the time I came here as clerk."

"No; certainly I have not."

"There were times, sir, when I fancied it."

A long silence. Even now, whatever secret, or association, there might be between these two men, neither was at ease with the other. Bede especially seemed to shrink from farther explanation.

"I have known but for a short while of your identity with Godfrey Pitman," he resumed. "And with George Winter. I have been waiting my own time to confer with you upon the subject. We have been very busy."

We have been very busy! If Bede put that forth as an excuse, it did not serve him: for his hearer knew it was not the true one. He simply answered that they had been very busy. Not by so much as a look or a syllable would George Winter—let us at last give him his true name—add to the terrible pain he knew his master to be suffering.

"About Miss Rye, sir? She must be extricated from her unpleasant position."

"Yes, of course."

"And her innocence proved."

"At the expense of another?" asked Bede, without lifting his eyes.

"No," answered the other in a low tone. "I do not think that need be."

Bede looked straight into the fire, his companion full at the window-blind, drawn half way down; neither of them at one another.

"How will you avoid it?" asked Bede.

"I think it may be avoided, sir. For a little while past, I have foreseen that some such a crisis as this would come: and I have dwelt and dwelt upon it until I seem to be able to track out my way in it perfectly clear."

Bede cracked the coal in the grate; which did not require cracking. "Do you mean that you have foreseen Miss Rye would be taken? Such a thought in regard to her never crossed my mind."

"Nor mine. I allude to myself, sir. If once I was discovered to be the so-called Godfrey Pitman—and some instinct told me the discovery was at last approaching—I knew that I should, in all probability, be charged with the murder of Mr. Ollivera. I—an innocent man—would not suffer for this, Mr. Greatorex; I should be obliged, in self-defence, to repel the accusation: and I have been considering how it might be done without compromising others. I think it can be."

"How?" repeated Bede shortly.

"By my not telling the whole truth. By not knowing—I mean not having recognized the—the one—who would be compromised if I did tell it. I think this is feasible, sir."

Just a momentary glance into each other's eyes; no more; and it spoke volumes. Bede, facing the fire again, stood several minutes in deep consideration. George Winter seemed occupied with one of his gloves that had a refractory button.

"In any case it must now be known who you are," said Bede.

"That will not signify. In throwing the onus of the—" he seemed to hesitate, as he had once hesitated in the last sentence—"the death off Miss Rye, I throw it equally off my own shoulders. I have for some months wished that I could declare myself."

"Why have you not done it?"

George Winter looked at his master, surprise in his eyes. "It is not for my own sake that I have kept it concealed, sir."

No. Bede Greatorex knew that it was for his; at least for his interests; and he felt the obligation in his heart. He did not speak it; pride and a variety of other unhappy feelings kept him silent. Of all the miserable moments that the death of John Ollivera had entailed upon him, this confidential interview with his clerk was not the least of them. Forced though he was to hold it, he hated it with his whole soul.

"You took that cheque from my desk," said Bede. "And wrote me the subsequent letter."

"I did not take it from the desk, sir. Your expressed and continuous belief—that you had put it in—was a mistaken one. It must have slipped from your hands when about to lock up the other papers you held, and fluttered under the desk table. Perhaps you will allow me to give you the explanation now."

Bede nodded.

"In the morning of the day that the cheque was lost, you may remember coming into the front room and seeing a stranger with me. His name was Foster; a farmer and corn-dealer near Birmingham. I had been out on an errand; and, on turning in again, a gentleman stopped me to enquire the way. While I was directing him there ensued a mutual recognition. In one sense I owed him some money: forty-four pounds. Samuel Teague, of whom you may have heard—"

"I know," interrupted Bede.

"Samuel Teague, just before he ran away, had got me to put my name to a bill for him; Mr. Foster, in all good faith, had let him have the money for it. It had never been repaid. But upon Mr. Foster's meeting me that morning, he gave me my choice—to find the money for him before he left London, or be denounced publicly as George Winter. I thought he would have denounced me then. He came into the office and would not be got rid of: saying that he had looked for me too long to let me go, now that I was found. What I was to do I did not know. I had no objection to resume my own name, for I had cleared myself with Johnson and Teague, but it must have involved the exposure relating to the affair at Helstonleigh. The thought occurred to me of declaring the dilemma to you, letting you decide whether that exposure should come, or whether you would lend me the forty-four pounds to avert it. But I shrank from doing that."

"Why?" again interposed Bede.

"Because I thought you would dislike my entering upon the subject, sir. I have shrunk from it always. Now that the necessity is forced upon me, I am shrinking from it as I speak."

Ah, but not so much as Bede was. "Go on."

"While I sat at my desk, inwardly deliberating, Mr. Frank came in, asking you to draw out a cheque for Sir Richard Yorke for forty-four pounds. The strange coincidence between the sum and the money demanded of me, struck me as being most singular. It strikes me so still. Later in the morning, I came into this room with some deeds, and saw a piece of paper lying under the table. Upon picking it up— which I did simply to replace it on the desk—I found it was the cheque. My first thought was that it must be a special, almost a supernatural, intervention in my favour; my second, that it was just possible you had left it there for me to take. Both ideas very far-fetched and imaginatory, as I saw at once. But I used the cheque, Mr. Bede Greatorex. I went home, put on the false hair I had worn as Godfrey Pitman, for I have it by me still, and got the cheque cashed in gold. It was not for my sake I did this; I hated it bitterly. And then I hesitated to use the money. At night I went to Mr. Foster's hotel, and told him that I would get the money for him by the following night if I could; if I could not, he must carry out his threat of denouncing me to the public and Mr. Greatorex. Foster consented to wait. I returned to my lodgings and wrote that anonymous note to you, sir, not telling you who had taken the cheque; merely saying that exposure was threatened of the private circumstances, known only to one or two, attendant on Mr. Ollivera's death at Helstonleigh; that the money had been taken to avert the exposure, and would be applied to that purpose, provided you were agreeable. If not, and you wished the money returned, you were requested to drop a note without loss of a moment to a certain address: if no such note were written, the money would be used in the course of the day, and things kept silent as heretofore. You sent no answer, and I paid it to Foster in the evening. I have never been able to decide whether you suspected me as the writer, or not."

"No. I fancied it might be Hurst."

"Hurst!" exclaimed George Winter in great surprise.

Bede looked up for a moment. "I felt sure the cheque must have been taken by one of you in the next room. Not knowing you then for Godfrey Pitman, my thoughts fell on Hurst. His father was the attendant surgeon, and might have made some critical discovery."

"I don't see how he could have done that, sir," was the dissenting answer.

"Nor did I. But it is the doubt in these cases that causes the fear. I should like to ask you a question—was it by accident or purposed design that you came to our house as a clerk?"

"Purely by accident. When the misfortunes fell upon me in Birmingham, and I was unwise enough to follow Samuel Teague's example and run away, I retained one friend, who stood by me. After quitting Helstonleigh on the Monday night, I concealed myself elsewhere for three or four days, and then went to him in Essex, where he lived. He procured me a clerkship in a lawyer's office in the same county, Mr.

Cale's, with whom I stayed about a year. Mr. Cale found me very useful, and when his health failed, and he retired in consequence from practice, he sent me up here to Mr. Greatorex with a strong recommendation."

"You have served us well," said Bede. "Was not your quitting Birmingham a mistake?"

"The worst I ever made. I solemnly declare that I was entirely innocent. Not only innocent myself, but unsuspicious of anything wrong on the part of Samuel Teague. He took me in, as he took in everybody else. Johnson and Teague know it now, and have at length done me the justice to acknowledge it. I knew of young Teague's profuse expenditure: he used to tell me he had the money from his uncle old Mr. Teague, and it never occurred to me to doubt it. Where I erred, was in going to the old man and blurting out the truth. He died of the shock. I shall never forgive myself for that: it seemed to me always as though I had murdered him. With his dead form, as it seemed, pursuing me, with the knowledge that I was to be included in the charge of forgery, I lost my sober senses. In my fright, I saw no escape but in flight; and I got away on the Sunday afternoon as far as Helstonleigh. It was in the opposite direction to the one Samuel Teague was thought to have taken, and I wanted to see Alletha Rye, if it were practicable, and assure her before we finally parted, that, though bad enough, I was not quite the villain people were making me out to be. There—there are strange coincidences in this life, Mr. Bede Greatorex."

"You may well say that," answered Bede.

"And one of the strangest was that of my accidentally meeting Alletha Rye five minutes after I reached Helstonleigh. Forgetting my disguise, I stopped to accost her—and have not forgotten her surprise yet. But I had not courage then to tell her the truth: I simply said I was in trouble through false friends, and was ill—which was really the case—and I asked her if she could shelter me for a day or two, or could recommend me to a place where I might be private and to myself. The result was, that I went to Mrs. Jones's house, introduced as a stranger, one Godfrey Pitman. I hit upon the name haphazard. And before I left it I was drawn into that business concerning Mr. Ollivera."

Bede Greatorex made no answer. A coincidence! one of heaven's sending.

"Why so much ill-luck should have fallen upon me I cannot tell," resumed George Winter. "I started in life, hoping and intending to do my duty as conscientiously as most men do it; and I've tried to, that's more. Fate has not been kind to me."

"There are others that it has been less kind to," spoke Bede, his tone marked with ill-suppressed agitation. "Your liabilities in Birmingham? Are they wiped out?"

"Others' liabilities you mean, sir; I had none of my own. Yes, I have scraped, and saved, and paid; paid all. I am saving now to repay you the forty-four pounds, and have about twenty pounds towards it. But for having my good old mother on my hands—she lives in Wales—I should have been clear earlier."

"You need not trouble yourself about the forty-four pounds," said Bede, recognising the wondrous obligations he and his were under to this silent, self-denying man.

"If it were forty-four hundred, sir, I should work on until I paid it, life being granted me."

"Very well," replied Bede. "I may be able to recompense you in another way."

If Bede Greatorex thought that any simple order of his would release Miss Rye from custody, he found himself mistaken. Butterby, called into the conference, was almost pleasantly derisive.

"You'll assure me she was not guilty! and Mr. Brown there can assure me she was not guilty! And, following them words up, you say, 'Let her go, Butterby!' Why, you might about as well tell me to let the stars drop out of the sky, Mr. Bede Greatorex. I've no more power over one than I have over the other."

"But she is innocent," reiterated Bede. "Mr. Brown here—you know who he is—can testify to it."

Butterby gave a careless nod in the direction of Mr. Brown—as much as to say that his knowing who he was went for a matter of course. But he was sternly uncompromising.

"Look here, Mr. Bede Greatorex. It's all very well for you to say to me Miss Rye's innocent; and for that there clever gentleman by your side to say she's innocent—and himself too, I suppose he'd like to add; but you, as a lawyer, must know that all that is of no manner of use. If you two will bring forward the right party, and say, 'This is the one that was guilty,' and prove it to the satisfaction of the law and Mr. Greatorex, that would be another thing. Only in that case can Miss Rye be set at liberty."

"You—you do not know what family interests are involved in this, Mr. Butterby," Bede said, in a tone of pain.

"Can guess at 'em," responded Butterby.

Bede inwardly thought the boast was a mistaken one, but he let it pass.

"If my father were acquainted with the true facts of the case," spoke he, "he would never bring it to a public trial; I tell you this on my honour."

"You know yourself who the party was; I see that," said Butterby.

"I do—Heaven spare me!"

There was a strange tone of helplessness mingling with the anguish of the avowal, as if Bede could contend with fate no longer. Even the officer felt for him. George Winter looked round at him with a glance of caution, as much as to say there was no necessity to avow too much. Bede bent his head, and strove to see, as well as the hour's trouble and perplexity would allow him, what might and what might not be done. Butterby, responsible to the magistrates at Helstonleigh who had granted the warrant, would have to be satisfied, as well as Mr. Greatorex.

Another minute, and Bede went forth to seek an interview with his father, who was alone in his room. Bede, almost as though he were afraid of his courage leaving him, entered upon the matter before he had well closed the door. Not in any torrent of words: he spoke but a few, and those with almost painful calmness: but his breath was laboured, himself perceptibly agitated.

"Give my authority to Butterby to release Alletha Rye from custody, because you happen to know that she is innocent!" exclaimed Mr. Greatorex in surprise. "Why, what can you mean, Bede?"

Bede told his tale. Hampered by various doubting fears lest he might drop an unsafe word, it was rather a lame one. Mr. Greatorex leaned back in his chair, and looked up at Bede as he listened. They held, unconsciously, much the same position as they had that March day nearly five years ago in another room, when the tale of the death was first told, Bede having then just got up with it from Helstonleigh Mr. Greatorex sitting, Bede standing with his arm on the mantelpiece, his face partly turned away. Bede had grown quite into the habit of standing thus, to press his hand to his brow: it seemed as though some weight or pain were always there.

"I don't understand you, Bede," spoke Mr. Greatorex frankly. "You tell me that you know of your own cognisance Alletha Rye was innocent? That you knew it at the time?"

"Almost of my own cognisance," corrected Bede.

"Which must be equivalent to saying that you know who was guilty."

"No; I don't know that," murmured Bede, his face growing damp with the conscious lie.

"Then what do you know, that you should wish to interfere? You have always said it was a case of suicide."

"It was not that, father," was Bede's low, shrinking answer. But he looked into his father's eyes with thrilling earnestness as he gave it.

Mr. Greatorex began to feel slightly uncomfortable. He detested mystery of all kinds; and there was something unpleasantly mysterious in Bede's voice and looks and words and manner.

"Did you know at the time that it was not suicide?" pursued Mr. Greatorex.

How should Bede get through this? say what he must say, and yet not say too much? He inwardly asked himself the question.

"There was just a suspicion of it on my mind, sir. Anyway, Alletha Rye must be set at liberty."

"I do not understand what you say, Bede; I do not understand you. Your manner on this subject has always been an enigma. William Ollivera holds the opinion that you must be screening someone."

A terrible temptation, hard to battle with, assailed Bede Greatorex at the charge—to avow to his father who and what he had been screening ever since the death. He forced himself to silence until it had passed.

"What is troubling you, Bede?"

Mr. Greatorex might well ask it; with that sad countenance in front of him, working with its pain. In his grievous perplexity, Bede gave the true answer.

"I was thinking if it were possible for Pitman's explanation to be avoided, father."

"What! Is Pitman found?"

"Yes, he is found," quietly answered Bede. "He—"

The room door was opening to admit some visitors, and Bede turned. Surely the propitious star to the House of Greatorex could not be in the ascendant. For they were Judge Kene and Henry William Ollivera.

And the concealment that he had striven and toiled for, and worn out his health and life to keep; fighting ever, mentally or bodily, against Fate's relentless hand, was felt to be at an end by Bede Greatorex.

CHAPTER XXXIX

NEARER AND NEARER

On a sofa, drawn at right angles with the fire, lay Hamish Channing; his bright head raised high, a crimson coverlid of eider down thrown over his feet. In the last day or two he had grown perceptibly worse; that is, weaker. The most sanguine amidst his friends, medical or others, could not say there was hope now. But, as long as he could keep up, Hamish would not give in to his illness: he rose in the morning and made a pretence of going about the house; and when he was tired, lay on the sofa that had been put into his writing-room. It was the room he felt most at home in, and he seemed to cling to it.

On the other side the hearth, bending forward in his chair, staring at Hamish with sad eyes, and pulling at his whiskers in grievous gloom, sat Roland Yorke. Roland had abandoned his home-copying for the past two days, and spent all his spare time with Hamish. Mrs. Jones, snatching a moment to go and visit Mr. Channing for old association's sake, had been very much struck with what she saw in him, and carried home the news that he was certainly dying. Roland, believing Mrs. J. to be as correct in judgment as she was tart in speech, had been looking out for death from that moment. Previously he was given to waver; one moment in despair; the next, up in the skies with exultation and thinking recovery had set in. The wind could not be more variable than Roland.

It was the twilight hour of the winter's day. The room was not lighted yet, but the blaze from the fire played on Hamish's face as he lay. There was a change in it tonight, and it told upon Roland: for it looked like the shadow of death. Things seemed to have been rather at sixes and sevens in the office that afternoon: Mr. Brown was absent, Hurst had gone home for Christmas, Bede Greatorex did not show himself, and there was nobody to tell Roland what work to be about. Of course it presented to that gentleman's mind a most valuable opportunity for enjoying a spell of recreation, and he took French leave to abandon it to itself and little Jenner. Rushing home in the first place, to see what might be doing there—for it was the day that Miss Rye had been captured by Butterby. Roland had his run for his pains. There was nothing doing, and his curiosity and good nature alike suffered. Miss Rye was a prisoner still; she, and Mrs. Jones, and the policeman left in charge, being shut up in the parlour together. "It's an awful shame of old Butterby!" cried Roland to himself, as he sped along to Hamish's. There he took up his station in his favourite chair, and watched the face that was fading so rapidly away. With an etherealized look in it that spoke of Heaven, with a placid calm that seemed to partake of the fast approaching rest; with a sweet smile that told of altogether inward peace, there the face lay; and Roland thought he had never seen one on earth so like an angel's.

Hamish had dropped into a doze; as he often did, at the close of day, when darkness is silently spreading over the light. Nelly Channing, who had learnt—by that subtle warning that sometimes steals, we know not how, over the instinct of little ones about to be made orphans—that some great and sad change was looming in the air, sat on a stool on the hearthrug as sedately as any old woman. Nelly's boisterous ways and gleeful laugh had left her for awhile: example perhaps taught her to be still, and she largely profited by it.

On her lap lay a story book: papa had bought it for her yesterday that is, had given the money to Miss Nelly and nurse when they went out, and wrote down the title of the book they were to buy, and the shop they might get it at, with his own trembling fingers, out of which the strength had nearly gone. It was one of those exquisite story books that ought to be in all children's hands, Mrs. Sherwood's; belonging of course to a past day, but nothing has since been written like them.

With every leaf that she silently turned, Nelly looked to see that it did not wake the invalid. When she grew tired, and her face was roasted to a red heat, she went to Roland, resting the open book upon his knee. He lifted her up.

"It is such a pretty book, Roland."

"All right. Don't you make a noise, Nelly."

"Margaret went to heaven in the book: she was buried under the great yew tree," whispered Kelly. "Papa's going there."

Roland caught the little head to him, and bent his face on the golden hair. He knew that what she said was true: but it was a shock nevertheless to have it repeated openly to him even by this young child.

"Papa talks to me about it. It will be so beautiful; he will never be tired there, or have any sorrow or pain. Oh, Roland; I wish I was going with him!"

Her eyes were filled with tears as she looked up; Roland's were filled in sympathy. He had cried like a schoolboy more than once of late. All on a sudden, happening to glance across, he saw Hamish looking on with a smile.

"You be off, Nelly," said arbitrary Roland, carrying her to the door and shutting it upon her and her book. "I'm sure your tea must be ready in the nursery."

"Don't grieve, Roland," said Hamish, when he sat down again.

"I wish you could get well," returned Roland, seeing the fire through a mist.

"And I have nearly ceased to wish it, Roland. It's all for the best."

"Ceased to wish it! How's that?"

"Through God's mercy, I think."

The words silenced Roland. When anything of this kind was mentioned it turned him into a child, so far as his feelings went; simple as Miss Nelly, was he, and a vast deal more humble-minded.

"Things are being cleared for me so wonderfully, Roland. But for leaving some who are dear to me, the pain would be over."

"I wish I could come across that fiend who wrote the reviews!" was Roland's muttered answer to this. "I wish I could!"

"What?" said Hamish, not catching the words.

"I will say it, then; I don't care," cried impetuous Roland—for no one had ever spoken before Hamish of what was supposed to have caused him the cruel pain. Roland blurted it all out now in his explosive fashion; his own long-suppressed wrath, and what he held in store for the anonymous reviewer, when he should have the good fortune to come across him.

A minute's silence when he ceased, a wild hectic spreading itself into the hollow cheeks—that it should so stir him even yet! Hamish held out his hand, and Roland came across to take it. The good sweet eyes looked into his.

"If ever you do 'come across' him, Roland, say that I forgive," came the low, earnest whisper. "I did think it cruel at the time; well nigh too hard to bear; but, like most other crosses, I seem to see now that it came to me direct from heaven."

"That is good, Hamish! Come!"

"We must through much tribulation enter into the kingdom," whispered Hamish, looking up at him with a yearning smile. "You have in all probability a long life before you, Roland: but the time may come when you will realize the truth of those words."

Roland swallowed down a lump in his throat as he turned to the fire again. Hamish resumed, changing his tone for one almost of gaiety.

"I have had good news today. Our friend the publisher called; and what do you think he told me, Roland? That my book was finding its way at last."

"Of course it will. Everybody always thought it must. If you could but have put off for a time your bother over the reviews, Hamish!" Roland added piteously.

"Ay. He says that in three months' time from this, the book will be in every one's hands. In the satisfaction of the news, I sat down and ate some luncheon with him and Ellen."

"Don't you think the news might be enough to cure you?" asked sanguine Roland.

Hamish shook his head. "If I were able to feel joy now as I felt the sorrow, it might perhaps go a little way towards it. But that is over, Roland. The capability of feeling either in any degree was crushed out of me."

Roland rubbed up his hair. If he had but that enemy of his under his hand, and a spacious arena that admitted of pitching-in!

"And now for some more good news, Roland. You must know how I have been troubled at the thought of leaving Ellen and the child unprovided for—"

"I say, don't you! Don't you trouble, Hamish," came the impulsive interruption. "I'll work for them. I'll do my very best for them, as well as for Annabel."

"It won't be needed, dear old friend," and Hamish's face, with its bright, grateful smile, almost looked like the sunny one of old. "Ellen's father, Mr. Huntley, is regaining the wealth he feared he had lost. As an earnest of it, he has sent Ellen two hundred pounds. It was paid her today."

"Oh, now, isn't that good, Hamish!"

"Very good!" answered Hamish, reverently and softly, as certain words ran through his mind: "So great is His mercy towards them that trust in Him."

"And so, Roland, all things are working round pleasantly that I may die in peace."

Mrs. Channing, coming in with her things on, for she had been out on some necessary business, interrupted the conversation. She mentioned to Roland that she had seen Gerald drive up to his wife's rooms, and that he had promised to come round.

"Why I thought he was at Sunny Mead with Dick!"

"He told me he had just returned from it," said Mrs. Channing.

"I say, Hamish, who knows but he may have brought me up a message!" cried Roland.

Hamish smiled. Roland had disclosed the fact in family conclave, of his having applied for the place of bailiff to Sir Vincent; Annabel being present. He had recited, so far as he could remember them, the very words of the letter, over which Hamish had laughed himself into a coughing-fit.

"To be sure," answered Hamish, with a touch of his old jesting spirit. "Gerald may have brought up your appointment, Roland."

That was quite enough. "I'll go and ask him," said Roland eagerly. "Anyway he may be able to tell me how Dick received it."

Away went Roland, on the spur of the moment. It was a clear, cold evening, the air sharp and frosty; and Roland ran all the way to Mrs. Gerald Yorke's.

That lady was not in tears this evening; but her mood was a gloomy one, her face fractious. The tea was on the table, and she was cutting thick bread-and-butter for the three little girls sitting so quietly round it, before their cups of milk-and-water. Gerald had gone out again; she did not know where, whether temporarily, or to his chambers for the night, or anything about him.

"I think something must have gone wrong at Sunny Mead," observed Winny. "When I asked what brought him back so soon, he only swore. Perhaps Sir Vincent refused to lend money, and they had a quarrel. I know Gerald meant to ask him: he is in dreadful embarrassment."

"Mamma," pleaded a little voice, "there's no butter on my bread."

"There's as much as I can afford to put, Kitty," was Mrs. Yorke's answer. "I must keep some for the morning. Suppose your papa should find no butter for breakfast, if he comes home to sleep tonight! My goodness!"

"Bread and scrape's not good, is it, Kitty?" said Roland. "No," plaintively answered the child.

Roland clattered out, taking the stairs at a leap. Mrs. Yorke supposed he had left without the ceremony of saying goodnight.

"Just like his manners!" she fractiously cried. "But oh! don't I wish Gerald was like him in temper!"

Roland had not gone for the night. He happened to have a shilling in his pocket, and went to buy a sixpenny pot of marmalade. As he was skimming back with it, his eye fell on some small shrimps, exposed for sale on a fishmonger's board. The temptation (with the loose sixpence in his hand) was not to be resisted.

He carried in the treasures. But that the three little ones were very meek spirited, they would have shouted at the sight. Roland lavishly spread the marmalade on the bread-and-scrape, and began pulling out shrimps for the company round, while he talked of Hamish.

"They are saying that those reviews that were so harsh upon his books have helped to kill him," said Mrs. Yorke, in a low tone, turning from the table to face Roland.

"But for those reviews he'd not have died," answered Roland. "I never will believe it. Illness might have come on, but he'd have had the spirit to throw it off again."

"Yes. When I sit and look at him, Roland, it seems as if I and Gerald were wretches that ought to hide ourselves. I say to myself, it was not my fault; but I feel it for all that."

"Why, what do you mean?" asked Roland.

"About the reviews. I can't bear to go there now."

"What about the reviews?"

"It was Gerald who wrote them."

Roland, for convenience sake, had the plate of shrimps on his knee during the picking process. He rested from his work and stared in a kind of puzzle. Winny continued.

"Those reviews were all Gerald's doings. That dreadful one in the Snarler he wrote himself; here, and was two days over it, getting to it at times as ideas and strong words occurred to him to make it worse and worse—just as he wrote the one of praise on his own book. The other reviews, that were every bit as bad, he got written. I read every word of the one in the Snarler in manuscript. I wanted to tell him it was wicked, but he might have shaken me. He said he owed Hamish Channing a grudge, and should get his book damned. That's not my word, you know, Roland. And, all the while, it was Hamish who was doing so much for me and the poor children; finding us in food when Gerald did not."

No whiter could Hamish Channing's face look when the marble paleness of death should have overshadowed it, than Roland's was now. For a short while it seemed as though the communication were too astounding to find admittance to his mind. Suddenly he rose up with a great cry. Down went shrimps, and plate, and all; and he was standing upright before Mrs. Yorke.

"Is it true? Is it true?"

"Why of course it's true," she fractiously answered, for the movement had startled her. "Gerald did it all. I'd not tell anybody but you, Roland."

Throwing his hat on his head, hind part before, away dashed Roland. Panting, wild, his breath escaping him in great sobs, like unto one who has received some strong mental shock, he arrived at Mr. Channing's in a frantic state. Vague ideas of praying at Hamish's feet for forgiveness were surging through his brain—for it seemed to Roland that he, as Gerald's brother, must be in a degree responsible for this terrible thing.

The door opened, he turned into the dining-room, and found himself in the presence of—Gerald. Hamish, feeling unusually weak, had gone up to bed, and Gerald was waiting the signal to go to him. As he supposed he must call to see Hamish before it should be too late—for Ellen had told him how it was, that afternoon—he had come at once to get the visit over.

Of all the torrents of reproach ever flung at a man, Gerald found himself astounded by about the worst. It was not loud; loudness might have carried off somewhat of the sting; but painfully sad and bitter. Roland stood on the hearthrug in front of Gerald as he had but now stood before Gerald's wife; with the same white and stricken face; with the same agitation shaking him from head to foot. The sobbing words broke from him in jerks: the voice was a wail.

"Was it not enough that I brought disgrace on Arthur Channing in the years gone by, but you, another of us ill-doing Yorkes, must destroy Hamish?" panted Roland. "Good Lord! why did heaven suffer us two to live! As true as we are standing together here, Gerald, had I known at the time those false reviews were yours, I should have broken your bones for you."

"You shut up," retorted Gerald. "It's nothing to you."

"Nothing to me! Nothing to me—when one of the best men that ever lived on earth has been wilfully sent to his grave? Yes; I don't care how you may salve over your conscience, Gerald Yorke; it is murder, and nothing less. What had he done to you? He was a true friend, a true, good friend to you and to me: what crime against us had he committed, that you should treat him like this?"

"If you don't go out of the house, I will," said Gerald. But Roland never seemed to so much as hear it.

"Who do you suppose has been helping you all this year?" demanded Roland. "When you were afraid of the county-court over a boot bill, somebody paid the money and sent you the receipt anonymously: who has kept your wife and children in rent and clothes and food, and all kinds of comforts, while you gave wine parties in your chambers, and went starring it over the seas for weeks in people's yachts? Hamish Channing. He deprived himself of his holiday, that your wife and children might be fed, you abandoning them: he has lived sparingly in spite of his failing health, that you and yours might profit. You and he were brought up in the same place, boys together, and he could not see your children want. They've never had a fraction of help but what it came from Hamish and his wife."

"It is a lie," said Gerald. But he was staggered, and he half felt that it was not.

"It is the truth, as heaven knows," cried Roland, breaking down with a burst. "Ask Winny, she told me. I'd have given my own poor worthless life freely, to save the pain of those false and cruel reviews to Hamish."

Sheer emotion stopped Roland's tongue. Mrs. Channing, entering, found the room in silence; the storm was over. Roland escaped. Gerald, amazingly uncomfortable, had a mind to run away there and then.

"Will you come up, Gerald?" she said.

Hamish lay in bed in his large cheerful chamber, bright with fire and light. His head was raised; one hand was thrown over the white coverlid; and a cup of tea waited on a stand by the bed-side. Roland stood by the fire, his chest heaving.

"But what is it, old fellow?" demanded Hamish. "What has put you out?"

"It is this, Hamish—that I wish I could have died instead of you," came the answer at last, with a burst of grief.

He sat down in the shade in a quiet corner, for his brother's step was heard. As Gerald approached the bed, he visibly recoiled. It was some time since he had seen Hamish, and he verily believed he stood in the presence of death. Hamish held out his hand with a cheering smile, and his face grew bright.

"Dear old friend! I thought you were never coming to see me."

Gerald Yorke was not wholly bad, not quite devoid of feeling. With the dying man before him, with the truths he had just heard beating their refrain in his ears, he nearly broke down as Roland had done. Oh, that he could undo his work! that he could recall life to the fading spirit as easily as he had done his best to take it away! These regrets always come rather late, Mr. Gerald Yorke.

"I did not think you were so ill as this, Hamish. Can nothing be done?"

"Don't let it grieve you, Gerald. Our turns must all come, sooner or later. Don't, old fellow," he added in a whisper. "I must keep up for Ellen's sake. God is helping me to do it: oh, so wonderfully."

Gerald bent over him: he thought they were alone. "Will you forgive me?"

"Forgive you!" repeated Hamish, not understanding what there was to forgive.

And Gerald, striving against his miserably pricking conscience, could not bring himself to say. No, though it had been to save his own life, he dared not confess to his cowardly sin.

"I have not always been the good friend to you I might, Hamish. Do say you forgive me, for Heaven's sake!"

Hamish took his hand, a sweet smile upon his face. "If there is an anything you want my forgiveness for, Gerald, take it. Take it freely. Oh, Gerald, when we begin to realize the great fact that our sins are forgiven, forgiven and washed out, you cannot think how glad we are to forgive others who may have offended us. But I don't know what I have to forgive in you."

Gerald's chest heaved. Roland's, in his distant chair in the shade, heaved rebelliously.

"I had ambitious views for you, Gerald. I meant to do you good, if I could. I thought when my book was out and brought funds to me, I would put you straight. I was so foolishly sanguine as to fancy the returns would be large. I thought of you nearly as much as I thought of myself: one of my dear old friends of dear old Helstonleigh. The world is fading from me, Gerald; but the old scenes and times will be with me to the last. Yes, I had hoped to benefit you, Gerald, but it was otherwise ordained. God bless you, dear friend. God love and prosper you, and bring you home to Him!"

Gerald could not stand it any longer. As he left the room and the house, Roland went up to the bed with a burst, and confessed all. To have kept in the secret would have choked him.

Gerald was the enemy who had done it all; Gerald Yorke had been the one to sow the tares amid wheat in his neighbour's field.

A moment of exquisite pain for Hamish; a slight, short struggle with the human passions, not yet quite dead within his aching breast; and then his loving-kindness resumed its sway, never again to quit him.

"Bring him back to me, dear Roland; bring him back that I may send him on his way with words of better comfort," he whispered, with his ineffable smile of peace.

CHAPTER XL

GODFREY PITMAN'S TALE

Shut in with closed doors, George Winter told his tale. Not quite all he could tell; and not the truth in one very important particular. If that single item of fact might be kept secret to the end, the speaker's will was good for it.

They were all standing. Not one sat. And the room seemed filled with the six men in it, most of whom were tall. The crimson curtain, that Annabel Channing had mended, was drawn before the bookcase: on the table-cover lay pens and ink and paper, for Mr. Greatorex sometimes wrote at night in his own room. He and Judge Kene were near each other; the clergyman was almost within the shadow of the window curtain; Bede a little farther behind. On the opposite side of the table, telling his tale, with the light of the bright winter's day falling full upon him, illuminating every turn of his face, and, so to say, every word he uttered, was George Winter. And, at right angles with the whole assemblage, his keen eyes and ears taking in every word and look in silence, stood the detective, Jonas Butterby.

Mr. Greatorex, in spite of his son Bede's protestations, had refused to sanction any steps for the release of Alletha Rye from custody. As for Butterby, in that matter he seemed more inexorably hard than a granite stone. "Show us that the young woman is innocent before you talk about it," said they both with reason. And so George Winter was had in to relate what he knew; and Mr. Greatorex—not to speak of some of the rest—felt that his senses were temporarily struck out of him when he discovered that his efficient and trusted clerk, Brown, was the long-sought after and ill-reputed Godfrey Pitman.

With a brief summary of the circumstances which had led him, disguised, and under the false name of Pitman, to Mrs. Jones's house at Helstonleigh, George Winter passed on to the night of the tragedy, and to the events which had taken him back to the house after his departure from it in the afternoon. If ever Mr. Butterby's silent eyes wore an eager light, it was then; not the faintest turn of a look, not the smallest syllable was lost upon him.

"When I had been a week at Mrs. Jones's, I began to think it might be unsafe to remain longer," he said; "and I resolved to take my departure on the Monday. I let it transpire in the house that I was going to Birmingham by the five o'clock train. This was to put people off the scent, for I did not mean to go by that train at all, but by a later one in an opposite direction—in fact, by the eight o'clock train for Oxford: and I had thought to wait about, near the station, until that hour. At half-past four I said good day to Mrs. Jones, and went out: but I had not gone many yards from the door, when I saw one of the Birmingham police, who knew me personally. I had my disguises on, the spectacles and the false hair, but I feared he might recognize me in spite of them. I turned my back for some minutes, apparently looking into a shop window, and when the officer had disappeared, stole back to Mrs. Jones's again. The door was open, and I went upstairs without being seen, intending to wait until dusk."

"A moment if you please," interrupted Mr. Greatorex. "It would seem that this was about the time that Mr. Ollivera returned to Mrs. Jones's. Did you see him?"

"I did not, sir; I saw no one."

"Go on."

"I waited in my room at the top of the house, and when night set in, began to watch for an opportunity of getting away unseen by the household, and so avoid questionings as to what had brought me back. It seemed not too easy of accomplishment: the servant girl was at the street door, and Alfred Jones (as I had learnt his name to be) came in and began to ascend the stairs. When half-way up, he turned back with some gentleman who came out of the drawing-room—whom I know now, but did not then, to be Mr. Bede Greatorex. Alfred Jones saw him to the front door, and then ran up again. I escaped to my room, and locked myself in. He went to his own, and soon I heard him go down and quit the house. In a few minutes I went out of my room again with my blue bag, ready for departure, and stood on the stairs to reconnoitre—"

"Can you explain the cause of those grease spots that we have heard of?" interrupted Bede Greatorex at this juncture. And it might almost have seemed from the fluttering emotion of his tone, which could not be wholly suppressed, that he dreaded the revelation he knew must be coming, and put the question only to delay it.

"Yes, sir. While Alfred Jones was in his room, I dropped my silver pencil-case, and had to light a candle to seek it. I suppose that, in searching, I must have held the candle aside and let the drops of tallow fall on the carpet."

"Go on," again interposed Mr. Greatorex, impatiently. "You went out on the stairs with your bag. What next?"

The witness—if he may be termed such—passed his hand slowly over his forehead before answering. It appeared as though he were recalling the past.

"As I stood there, on the top of the first flight, the sound of voices in what seemed like angry dispute, came from the drawing-room. One in particular was raised in passionate fury; the other was less loud. I did not hear what was said; the door was shut—"

"Were they both men's voices?" interrupted Mr. Ollivera—and it was the first question he had put.

"Yes," came the answer; but it was given in a low tone, and with somewhat of hesitation. "At least, I think so."

"Well."

"The next thing that I heard was the report of a pistol, followed by a cry of pain. Another cry succeeded to it in a different voice, a cry of horror; and then silence supervened."

"And you did not go in?" exclaimed Mr. Ollivera in agitation, taking a step forward.

"No. I am aware it is what I ought to have done; and I have reproached myself later for not having done it; but I felt afraid to disclose to any one that I was yet in the house. It might have led to the discovery of who and what I was. Besides, I thought there was no great harm done; I declare it, upon my honour. I could still hear sounds within the room as of someone, or more, moving about, and I certainly heard one voice speaking low and softly. I thought I saw my opportunity for slipping away, and had crept down nearly to the drawing-room door, when it suddenly opened, very quietly, and a face looked out. Whoever it might be, I suppose the sight of me scared them, for they retreated, and the door was reclosed softly. It scared me also, sending me back upstairs; and I remained up until the same person (as I supposed) came out again, descended the stairs, and left the house. I got out myself then, gained the railway station by a circuitous route, and got safely away from Helstonleigh."

As the words died upon the ear, there ensued a pause of silence. The clergyman broke it. His mind seemed to be harping on one string.

"Mr. Brown, was that person a man or a woman?"

"Oh, it was a man," answered Mr. Brown, looking down at his waistcoat, and brushing a speck off it with an air of carelessness. But something in his demeanour at that moment struck two people in the room as being peculiar—Judge Kene and Mr. Butterby.

"Should you recognize him again?" continued the clergyman.

"I cannot say. Perhaps I might."

"And you can stand there, Mr. Brown and deliberately avow that you did not know a murder had been committed?" interposed the sternly condemning voice of Mr. Greatorex.

"On my sacred word of honour, I declare to you, sir, that no suspicion of it at the time occurred to me," answered the clerk, turning his eyes with fearless honesty on Mr. Greatorex. "When I got to learn what had really happened—which was not for some weeks—I wondered at myself. All I could suppose was, that the fear and apprehension I lay under on my own score, had rendered me callous to other impressions."

"Was it you who went in, close upon the departing heels of Mr. Bede Greatorex, and did this cruel thing?" asked Judge Kene, with quiet emphasis, as he gazed in the face of the narrator.

"No," as quietly, and certainly as calmly, came the answer. "I had no cause to injure Mr. Ollivera. I never saw him in my life. I am not sure that I knew there was a barrister of the name. I don't think I ever heard of him until after he was in the grave where he is now lying."

"But—you must have known that Mr. Ollivera was sojourning in Mrs. Jones's house at the same time that you were?

"I beg your pardon, Sir Thomas; I did not know that anyone was lodging there except myself. Miss Rye, whom I saw for a few minutes occasionally, never mentioned it, neither did the servant, and they were the only two inmates I conversed with. For all I knew, or thought, Mrs. Jones occupied the drawing-room herself. I once saw her sitting there, and the maid was carrying out the tea-tray. No," emphatically concluded the speaker, "I did not know Mr. Ollivera was in the house: and if I had known it, I should not have sought to harm him."

The words were simple enough; and they were true. Judge Kene, skilled in reading tones and looks, saw that much. The party felt at a non-plus: as far as Alletha Rye went, the taking her into custody appeared to have been a mistake.

"You will swear to this testimony of yours, Mr.—Winter?"

"When you please. The slight amount of facts—the sounds—that reached me in regard to what took place in Mr. Ollivera's room, I have related truthfully. Far from Miss Rye's having had aught to do with it, she was not even in the house at the time: I affirm it as before heaven."

"Who was the man?" asked Judge Kene—and Mr. Butterby, as he heard the question, gave a kind of derisive sniff. "Come; tell us that, Mr. Winter."

"I cannot tell you," was George Winter's answer. "Whoever it was he went down the stairs quickly. I was looking over top balustrades then, and caught but a transient glimpse of him."

"But you saw his face beforehand?—when he looked out of the room?"

"I saw someone's face. Only for a minute. Had I known what was to come of it later, I might have noticed better."

"And this is all you have to tell us?" cried Henry William Ollivera in agitation.

"Indeed it is all. But it is sufficient to exonerate Miss Rye."

"And now, Bede, what do you know?" suddenly spoke Mr. Greatorex. "You have acknowledged to me that you suspected at the time it was not a case of suicide."

Bede Greatorex came forward. All eyes were turned upon him. That he was nerving himself to speak, and far more inwardly agitated than appeared on the surface, the two practised observers saw. Judge Kene looked at him critically and curiously: there was something in the case altogether, and in Bede himself, that puzzled him.

"It is not much that I have to tell," began Bede, in answer to his father, as he put his hand heavily on the table, it might be for a support to rest on: and his brow seemed to take a pallid hue, and the silver threads in his once beautiful hair were very conspicuous as he stood. "A circumstance caused me to suspect that it was not a case of suicide. In fact, that it was somewhat as Mr. Brown has described it to be—namely, that someone else caused the death."

A pause of perfect silence, It seemed to Bede that the very coals, cracking in the grate, sounded like thunder.

"What was the circumstance?" asked Mr. Greatorex, for no one else liked to interrupt. "Why did you not speak of it at the time?"

"I could not speak of it then: I cannot speak of it fully now. It was of a nature so—so—so—." Bede came to a full stop: was he getting too agitated to speak, or could he not find a word? "What I would say is," he continued, in a firm low tone, rallying his nerves, "that it was sufficient to show me the facts must have been very much as Mr. Brown now states them."

"Then you only think that, Bede?"

"It is more than thinking. By all my hopes of Heaven, declare that Alletha Rye had not, and could not have had, anything to do with John's death," he added with emotion. "Father, you may believe me: I do know so much."

"But why can you not disclose what it is you know?"

"Because the time has not come for it. William, you are looking at me with reproachful eyes: if I could tell you more I would. The secret—so much as I know of it—has lain on me with a leaden weight: I would only have been too glad to disburthen myself of it at first, had it been possible."

"And what rendered it impossible?" questioned the clergyman.

"That which renders it so now. I may not speak; if I might, I should be far more thankful than any of you who hear me."

"Is it a secret of trust reposed in you?"

Bede paused. "Well, yes; in a degree. If I were to speak of what I know, I do not think there is one present"—and Bede's glance ran rapidly over each individual face—"but would hush it within his own breast, as I have done."

"And you have a suspicion of who the traitor was?"

"A suspicion I may have. But for aught else—for elucidation—you and I must be content alike to wait."

"Elucidation!" spoke the clergyman in something like derision. "It will not, I presume, ever be allowed to come."

"Yes, it will, William," answered Bede, quietly. "Time—events—heaven—all are working rapidly on for it. Alletha Rye is innocent; I could not affirm that truth to you more solemnly if I were dying. She must be set at liberty."

As it was only on the question of her guilt or innocence that the council had been called, it seemed that there was nothing more to do than to break it up. An uncomfortable sensation of doubt, dissatisfaction, and mystery, lay on all. The clergyman stalked away in haughty displeasure. Bede Greatorex, under cover of the crowd, slid his hand gratefully for a moment into that of George Winter, his sad eyes sending forth their thanks. Then he turned to the Judge.

"You can give the necessary authority for the release, Sir Thomas."

"Can I?" was the answer, as Sir Thomas looked at him. "I'll talk about it with Butterby. But I should like to have a private word first with Mr. Winter."

"Why! you do not doubt that she is innocent?"

"Oh dear no; I no longer doubt that. Winter," he added in a whisper, laying his hand on the clerk's shoulder to draw him outside, "whose face was it that you saw at the door of the room?"

"Tell him," said Bede suddenly, for he had followed them. "You will keep the secret, Kene, as I have kept it?"

"If it be as I suspect, I will," emphatically replied the Judge.

"Tell him," repeated Bede, as he walked away. "Tell him all that you know, Winter, from first to last."

It caused Mr. Greatorex and Butterby to be left alone together. The former, not much more pleased than William Ollivera, utterly puzzled, hurt at the want of confidence displayed by Bede in not trusting him, was in a downright ill-temper.

"What the devil is all this, Butterby?" demanded he. "What does it mean?"

Mr. Butterby, cool as a cucumber, let his eyelashes close for a moment over his non-betraying eyes, and then answered in meek simplicity.

"Ah, that's just it, sir—what it means. Wait, says your son Mr. Bede; wait patiently till things has worked round a bit, till such time as I can speak out. And depend upon it, Mr. Greatorex, he has good cause to give the advice."

"But what can it be that he has to tell? And why should he wait at all to tell it?"

"Well, I suppose he'd like to be more certain of the party," answered Butterby, with a dubious cough. "Take a word of advice from me too, Mr. Greatorex, on this here score, if I may make bold to offer it— do wait. Don't force your son to disclose things afore they are ripe. It might be better for all parties."

Mr. Greatorex looked at him. "Who is it that you suspect?"

"Me!" exclaimed Butterby. "Me suspect! Why, what with one odd thought or another, I'd as lieve say it must have been the man in the moon, for all the clue we've got. It was not Miss Rye: there can't be two opinions about that. I told you, sir, I had my strong doubts when you ordered her to be apprehended."

"At any rate, you said she confessed to having done it," sharply spoke Mr. Greatorex, vexed with everybody.

"Confound the foolish women! what would the best of 'em not confess to, to screen a sweetheart? Alletha Rye has been thinking Winter guilty all this while, and when it came to close quarters and there seemed a fear that he'd be taken up for it, she said what she did to save him. I see it all. I saw it afore Godfrey Pitman was half way through his tale: and matters that have staggered me in Miss Rye, are just as clear to read now as the printing in a big book. When she made that there display at the grave— which you've heard enough of, may be, Mr. Greatorex—she had not had her doubts turned on Godfrey Pitman; she'd thought he was safe away earlier in the afternoon: when she got to learn he had come back again in secret, and was in the house at the time, why then she jumped to the conclusion that he had done the murder. I remember."

Mr. Butterby was right. This was exactly how it had been. Alletha Rye had deemed George Winter guilty all along; on his side, he had only supposed she shunned him on account of the affair at Birmingham. There had been mutual misunderstanding; tacit, shrinking avoidance of all explanation; and not a single word of confidence to clear it all up. George Winter could not seek to be too explicit so long as the secret he was guarding had to be kept: if not for his own sake, for that of others, he was silent.

"As to what Bede's driving at, and who he suspects, I am in ignorance," resumed Mr. Greatorex. "I am not pleased with his conduct: he ought to let me know what he knows."

"Now, don't you blame him afore you hear his reasons, sir. He's sure to have 'em: and I say let him alone till he can take his own time for disclosing things." Which won't be of one while, was the detective's mental conclusion.

"About Miss Rye? Are you here, Butterby?"

The interruption came from Judge Kene. As he walked in, closing the door after him, they could but be struck with the aspect of his face. It was all over of a grey pallor; very much as though its owner had received some shock of terror. "What is the matter, Judge?" hastily asked Mr. Greatorex. "Are you ill?"

"Ill? No. Why do you ask? Look so!—Oh, I have been standing in a room without fire and grew rather cold there," carelessly replied the Judge.

CHAPTER XLI

A TELEGRAM FOR ROLAND YORKE

Lounging quite back in the old elbow horsehair chair, his feet stretched out on the hob on either side the fire, which elegant position he had possibly learnt at Port Natal, sat Mr. Roland Yorke. He had just come home to his five o'clock tea, and took the occasion to indulge in sundry reminiscences while waiting for it to be brought to him. Christmas had passed, these two or three days now; the brief holiday was over, and working days were going on again.

Roland's mood was a subdued one. All things seemed to be, more or less, tinted with gloom. Hamish Channing was dying; a summons had been sent for his friends; the last hour could not now be very far off: and Roland felt it deeply. The ill, worked by his brother Gerald, seemed never to go out of his mind for a moment, sleeping or waking. Vexation of a different kind was also his. Day after day in his sanguine temperament he had looked for a letter from Sir Vincent Yorke, appointing him to the post of bailiff; and no such letter came. Roland, who had heard nothing of the slight accident caused by Gerald (you may be very sure Gerald would not be the one to speak of it), supposed the baronet was in Paris with Miss Trehern. A third source of discomfort lay in the office. Bede Greatorex, whose health since the past few days had signally failed, avowed himself at last unequal to work, and an extra amount of it fell upon his clerks. Roland thought it a sin and a shame that before Christmas Day had well turned, he should have, as he phrased it, to "stick to it like any dray-horse." A rumour had arisen in the office that Bede Greatorex was going away with his wife for change and restoration, and that Mr. Brown was to be head of the department in Bede's place. Roland did not regard the prospect with pleasure: Mr. Brown being a regular martinet in regard to keeping the clerks to their duty.

The grievance that lay uppermost on his mind this evening, was the silence of Sir Vincent. For Hamish he had grieved until it seemed that he could grieve no longer; the rumoured change in the office might never be carried out but on the score of Sir Vincent's neglect there was no palliation.

"I'd not treat him, so," grumbled Roland, his complaint striving to find relief in words. "Even if the place was gone when I applied, or he thought I'd not suit, he might write to me. It's all very fine for him kicking up his heels in Paris, and dining magnificently in the restaurants off partridges and champagne, and forgetting a fellow as he forgets me; but if his whole hopes in life lay on the die, he'd remember, I know.

If I knew his address over there, I'd drop him another letter and tell him to put me out of suspense. For all the answer that has come to me, one might think he had never had that first letter of mine. He has had it though, and it's a regular shame of him not to acknowledge it, when my heart was set on being able to carry Hamish the cheering news, before he died, that Annabel was provided for. If Dick would only give us a pretty little cottage down yonder and a couple of hundreds a-year! It wouldn't be much for Dick to give, and I'd serve him bravely day and night. I declare I go into Hamish's room as sheep-faced as a calf, with the shame of having no news to tell. Annabel says—Oh, it's you, Miss Rye, is it! Precious cold tonight!"

Miss Rye had come in with the small tea-tray: the servant was busy. She wore a knot of blue ribbon in her hair, and looked otherwise bright. Since a private interview held with Mr. Butterby and George Winter, when they returned to release her from custody, she had appeared like a different woman. Her whole aspect was changed: the sad, despairing fear on her face had given place to a look of rest and hope. Roland had taken occasion to give Mr. Butterby a taste of what that gentleman called "sauce," as to his incurable propensity for apprehending the wrong person, and was advised in return to mind his own business. While Mrs. Jones had been existing since in a chronic state of tartness; for she could not come to the bottom of things, and Alletha betrayed anything but a readiness to enlighten her.

"What's for tea?" asked Roland, lazily, turning his head to get a view of the tray.

"They have boiled you an egg," replied Miss Rye. "There was nothing else in the house. Have you seen your letter, Mr. Yorke?"

"A letter!" exclaimed Roland, starting up with so much alacrity as to throw down the chair, for his hopes suddenly turned to the vainly-expected communication from Sir Vincent. "Where is it? When did it come? Good old Dick!"

It had come just as he went out after dinner, she answered, as she took the letter—which bore a foreign post-mark—from the mantelpiece to hand to him. And eager Roland's spirits went down to zero as he tore it open, for he recognized the writing to be, not Dick Yorke's, but Lord Carrick's.

"Oh, come though, it's rather good," said he, running his eyes down the plain and sprawling hand—very much like his own. "Carrick has come out of his troubles; at least, enough of them to show himself by daylight again in the old country; he will be over in London directly. I say, Miss Rye, I'll bring him here, and introduce him to you and Mrs. J."

And Miss Rye laughed as she left the room more freely than she had laughed for many a day.

"Perhaps Carrick can put me into something!" self-communed Roland, cutting off the top of his egg, and taking in a half-slice of inch-thick bread-and-butter at a bite. "I know he'll not want the will when I tell him about Annabel."

The last morsel was eaten, and Roland was on the point of demanding more, for his appetite never failed, when he heard someone come to the house and inquire for Mr. Yorke. Visions of the arrival of Lord Carrick flashed over him; he made a dash to the passage, and very nearly threw down a meek little gentleman, who was being shown into his room.

"Holloa!" said Roland, the corners of his mouth dropping with disappointment. "Is it only you?"

For the visitor was nobody but little Jenner. He had brought a communication from Mr. Greatorex, and took off his hat while he delivered it.

"You are to go back with me to the office at once, if you please, Mr. Yorke. Mr. Greatorex wants you."

"What have I done now?" questioned Roland, anticipative of a reprimand.

"It is not for anything of that sort, sir. I believe Sir Vincent Yorke has telegraphed for you to go down to him at Sunny Mead. The despatch said you were to lose no time."

Whether Roland leaped highest or shouted loudest, the startled house could not have decided. The anticipated bailiff's place was, in his imagination, as surely his, as though he had been installed in it formally. To wash his hands, brush his hair, and put on a superfine coat took but a minute, before he was striding to the office little Jenner on the run by his side, and to the presence of Mr. Greatorex.

Into which he went with a burst. The lawyer received him calmly and showed the message from Surrey.

"Sir Vincent Yorke to Mr. Greatorex.

"Send Roland Yorke down to me by first train. Lose no time."

"Good old Dick!" repeated Roland in the fulness of his heart. "I thought he'd remember me; and there was I reproaching him like an ungrateful Tom-cat! It is to appoint me to the bailiff's place, Mr. Greatorex."

"Well—it may be," mused Mr. Greatorex. "But I had fancied the post was filled up."

"Not it, sir. Long live Dick! When did he come back from Paris?"

"I know nothing about Sir Vincent's recent movements, Mr. Yorke. You had better be getting to the Waterloo Station. Have you money for the journey?"

"I've got about sevenpence-halfpenny, sir."

Mr. Greatorex took a half-sovereign from his desk, and ten shillings in silver. "I don't know how often the trains run," he observed, "but if you go at once to the station, you will be all right for the first that starts."

Not to the station, let it start as soon as it would, without first seeing Annabel, and telling her of his good fortune. Away up the stairs went Roland, in search of her, leaping over some boxes that stood packed in the hall: and there he encountered Mr. Bede Greatorex. It was four whole days since Roland had met him, and he thought he had never seen a face so changed in the short space of time. Annabel was not at home, Bede said; she had gone to Mr. Channing's.

"You don't look well, sir."

"Not very, I believe. I am about to try what a month or two's absence will do for me."

"And leave us to old Brown!—that will be a nice go!" exclaimed Roland in blank dismay. "But I may not have to stay," he added more brightly, as recollection returned to him "Vincent Yorke has telegraphed for me, sir, and I and Mr. Greatorex think that he is about to appoint me his bailiff."

A smile crossed the haggard face of Bede. "I wish you success in it," he kindly said.

"Thank you, sir. And I'm sure I wish you and Mrs. Greatorex heaps of pleasure, and I heartily hope you'll come home strong. Oh! and, Mr. Bede—Carrick's coming back."

Bede nodded in answer. Greatorex and Greatorex knew more of the matter than Roland, since it was they who had intimated to the peer that the coast was now sufficiently clear for him.

Roland leaped into a cab, and was taken to Mr. Channing's. He waited in the empty dining-room; and when Annabel came to him, told her hurriedly of what had happened. The cab was waiting at the door, Roland was eager, and her pale cheeks grew rosy with blushes as he talked and held her hands.

"It can't be for anything else, you know, Annabel. He is going to instal me off-hand for certain, or else he would have written and not telegraphed: perhaps the new bailiff (if he did appoint one) has turned out to be no good. There'll be a pretty cottage, I daresay, its walls all covered with roses and lilies, with two hundred a year; and we shall be as happy as the day's long. You'll not mind trying it, will you?"

No, Annabel whispered, the cheeks deepening to crimson, she would not mind trying it. "I think—I think, Roland," she added, bending down her pretty face, "that I might have a pupil if I liked; and be well paid for her."

"That's jolly," said Roland. "We might do, with that, if Dick only offered me one hundred. He is uncommonly close-fisted. There'd be a house free, and no end of fruit and garden-stuff; and living in the country is very cheap."

"It is Jane Greatorex."

"Oh she," cried Roland, his countenance falling. "She is a regular little toad, Annabel. I'd not like you to be bothered with her."

"She would be always good with me. Mr. and Mrs. Bede are going away, and Mr. Greatorex does not want us there any longer. He said a few words to me today about my returning home to mamma at Helstonleigh and taking Jane with me: that is, if mamma has no objection. He said he would like Jane to be with me better than with any one; and he'd make it worth my while in point of salary."

"Then, Annabel, if you don't object to the young monkey, that's settled, and I shall look upon it that we are as good as married. What a turn in fortune's wheel! Won't I serve Dick with my best blood and marrow! I'll work for him till my arms drop. I say! couldn't I just see Hamish? I'd like to tell him."

He ran softly up the stairs as he spoke. Hamish was in bed; and just now alone, save for Miss Nelly, who had rolled herself upon the counterpane like a ball, her cheek close to his. Roland whispered all the items of good news exultantly: it never occurred to him to think that they might turn out to be castles in the air. A smile, partaking somewhat of the old amused character, flitted across Hamish's wasted but still beautiful face, and sat in his blue eyes as he listened.

"You'll leave Annabel especially to me, won't you, Hamish; and wish us both joy and happiness?"

"I wish you both the best wishes I can wish, Roland—God's blessing," was the low, earnest answer. "His blessing through this life, and in that to come."

Roland bent his face down to Nelly's to hide its emotion, and began kissing her. His grief for Hamish Channing sometimes showed itself like any girl's.

"I have left you her guardian, Roland."

"Me!" exclaimed Roland, the surprise sending him and his wet eyes bolt upright.

"You and Arthur jointly. You will take care of her interests, I know."

"Oh, Hamish, how good of you! Nelly's guardian! Won't I take care of her! and love her, too. I'll buy her sixpen'orth of best sugared almonds every day."

Hamish smiled. "Not her personal guardian, Roland; her mother will be that. I meant as to her property."

"Never mind; it's all one. Thank you, Hamish, for your trust in me. Oh, I am proud! And mind that you are a good girl, Miss Nelly, now that I shall have the right to call you to order."

Roland did not seem quite to define the future duties in his own mind. Nelly raised her tear-stained face, and looked at him defiantly.

"I'm going away with papa."

"Not with him, my child," whispered Hamish. "You must stay here a little while. You and mamma will come later."

Nelly burst into sobs. "Heaven is better than this. I want to go there."

"We shall all get there in time, Nelly," observed Roland in much gloom, "but I wish I could have gone now in his stead. Oh, Hamish, I do I do indeed! Gerald's black work will never be out of my heart. And there's your book getting its crown of laurels at last, and you not living to wear them!"

The gentle face, bright with a light not of this world, was turned to Roland. "A better crown is waiting for me," he murmured. "My Lord and Master knows how thankfully I shall go to it."

A stamping outside as of an impatient cab-horse on the frosty street, reminded Roland that he was bound on a non-delayable mission. On the stairs he met Annabel, caught hold of her without ceremony, and gave her shrinking face a few farewell kisses.

"Goodbye, darling. When I come back it will be as bailiff of Sunny Mead."

Roland's delay had been just enough to cause him to miss a train, and the evening was considerably later when he was at length deposited at the small station near Sunny Mead.

Looking up the road and down the road in the cold moonlight, uncertain which was his way, he found himself accosted by a man in the garb of a groom.

"I beg pardon, sir: are you Mr. Yorke."

"Yes."

"I've got the dog-cart here, sir."

"Oh, have you?" returned Roland; "I thought Sunny Mead was close to the station."

"It's a matter of ten minutes' walk, sir; but they gave me orders to be down, and wait for every train until you came."

"How long has Sir Vincent been back from Paris?" questioned Roland, as they bowled along.

"From Paris, sir? He haven't been to it: not lately. The accident stopped his going."

"What accident?"

Ah! what accident! Roland's eyes opened to their utmost width with surprise, as he listened to the answer.

"Good heavens! And it was caused, you say, by Gerald Yorke?"

"That it was, sir."

"Why, he's my brother."

"Well, sir, accidents happen unintentional to the best of us," observed the man, striving to be polite. "Some of 'em said that the gentleman didn't show himself 'cute at handling of a gun."

"I don't believe he ever handled one in his life before," avowed impulsive Roland. "What a fool he must have been! How is Sir Vincent going on? I'm sure I hope it was no great damage."

"Sir Vincent was going on all right till today, sir; and as to the damage it was not thought to be much. We hear now that it has taken a turn for the worse. They talk of erysipelas."

"Oh, that's nothing," said Roland. "I knew a fellow who got erysipelas in the face at Port Natal till it was as big as a pumpkin, but he did his work all the same. That's it," he mentally decided, as they approached the house. "Poor Dick, confined indoors, can't look after things himself, and is going to put me to do it."

Upon a flat bed, or couch, in the downstairs room, where we saw him breakfasting with Gerald, lay Sir Vincent Yorke, his dog beside him. He held out his hand to greet Roland. Impulsively and rather explosively, that unsophisticated African traveller burst out with regrets on the score of the accident, and the more especially that it should have been caused by Gerald.

"Ay, it was a bad job," said Sir Vincent, quietly. "Sit down Roland. Here near to me. I am in a good bit of pain, and don't care to talk at a distance."

Roland took the chair pointed to, not a yard off Sir Vincent as he lay, and the two looked at each other. A kind of honest shame was on Roland's face: he was inwardly asking himself how much more disgrace Gerald meant to bring on him. The moderator lamp, a soft, thin perforated paper thrown over to subdue its brightness, was behind the invalid.

"I hope you'll soon be about again, Vincent."

"I hoped so, too, until this morning," was Sir Vincent's answer. "My leg was very uneasy all last night, and I sent at daybreak for the surgeon. He came, and was obliged to tell me that an unfavourable change had taken place: in fact, that dangerous symptoms had set in."

"But you can be cured?" cried Roland.

"No, not now."

"Not be cured!" exclaimed Roland, starting up with wild eyes, and hardly knowing what to understand. "Do you mean, that it will be long first?"

"I mean, that I shall never be cured at all in this world. Sit down, Roland, and listen quietly. The wound, regarded at first as a very simple one, and apparently continuing to progress well, has taken a turn for the worse; and must shortly end in death. Now, do be tranquil, old fellow, and listen. You are my heir, you know, Roland."

Roland, constrained to patience and his chair, stared, and pulled at his whiskers, and stared again.

"Your heir?"

"Certainly. My heir."

The contingency had never, in the whole course of his life, entered into the imagination of simple Roland. He sat in speechless bewilderment.

"The moment the breath goes out of this poor frail body—and the doctors tell me it will not be many more hours in it now—you will be Sir Roland Yorke. The fourth baronet, and the possessor of the Yorke estates—such as they are."

"Oh, my gracious!" uttered Roland, a vast deal more startled at the prospect than he had been at that of crying hot-pies in Poplar. "Do you mean it, Vincent?"

"Mean it! Where are your wits gone, that you need ask? You must know as well as I do that you come next in succession."

"I never thought of it; never once. I don't want it, Vincent, old fellow; I don't, indeed. I hope, with all my heart, you'll get well, and hold it for yourself. Oh, Dick, I hope you will!"

Roland had risen and caught the outstretched hand. As Sir Vincent heard the earnest tones, and saw the face of genuine concern shining out in all its guileless simplicity, the tears in the honest eyes, he came to the conclusion that Roland had been somewhat depreciated among them.

"Nothing can save me, Roland; the doctors have pronounced me to be past human skill, and I feel for myself that I am so. It has not been long, one day, 'to set my house in order,' has it?"

Amidst Roland's general confusion, nothing had struck him more than the change in Vincent's tone. The old, mincing affectation was utterly gone. A man cannot retain such when brought face to face with death.

"If you could but get well!" repeated poor Roland, rubbing his hot face as he got back to his chair.

"Doctors, lawyers, and parsons—I have had them all here today," resumed Sir Vincent. "The first man I sent for, after the fiat was pronounced, was a lawyer from the village hard by: there might not be time, I feared, to get down old Greatorex. He made a short will for me: and it was only when I began to consider what its provisions should be, that I (so to say) remembered you as my heir and successor."

Roland sat, hopelessly listening, unable to take in too much at once.

"The entailed property lapses to you; but there is some, personal and else, at my own disposal. With the exception of a few legacies, I have bequeathed it all to you, Roland—and you'll be poor enough: and I've appointed you sole executor. But I think you will make a better man, as the family's head, than I might have made in the long run; and I am truly glad that it is you to succeed, and not Gerald."

Roland gave a groan.

"I allude to his disposition, which I don't think great things of, and to his propensity for spending," continued Sir Vincent. "Gerald would have every acre of the estate mortgaged in a couple of years: I think you will be different. Don't live beyond your means, Roland; that's all.

"I'll try to do my very best by everybody," replied Roland. "As to living beyond my means, Annabel will see to that, and take care of me. Dick! Dick! it seems so wicked of me to talk coolly of it, as if I were speculating on your death. I wish you'd try and live! I don't want the estate and the money; I never thought of such a thing as coming in to it. I rushed down here tonight, hoping you were going to make me your bailiff; and I thought how well I'd try to serve you, and what a good fellow you were for doing it."

"Ah," was the dying man's slight comment, as he drew himself a trifle higher in the bed. "You will be master instead of bailiff; that's all the difference. I had just engaged a bailiff when you wrote: and I'd advise you to keep him on, Roland, unless you really feel competent to the management yourself."

"I'll keep him on until I've learnt it; that won't be long first. I must have something to employ my time in, Vincent."

"True: I wish I had had it. An idle man must, almost of necessity, glide into various kinds of mischief: of which debt is one."

"You need not fear debt for me, Vincent," was the earnest answer. "I have lived too long on empty pockets, and earned a crust before I ate it, to have ill ways for money or inclination to spend. Why, my best dress suit has been in pawn these two months: and old Greatorex had to advance me twenty shillings to bring me down here."

Something like a smile flitted over Sir Vincent's lips. He pointed to a desk that stood on a side-table.

"When I am gone, Roland, you can open that: there's a little loose cash in it. It will be enough to repay Greatorex and redeem your clothes."

"But I'd not like to take it, Vincent, thank you. I'd not, indeed."

"Why, man! it will be your own then."

"Oh, well—I never!" cried Roland softly: quite unable to realize his fast-approaching position.

"The danger to some people might lie in being thus suddenly raised from poverty to affluence," remarked Sir Vincent. "It has shipwrecked many a one."

"Don't fear for me, or for the estate either, Vincent. Had this happened some seven or eight years ago, when I was a lazy, conceited, ignorant young fool, nearly as stuck-up as Gerald, I can't say how it might have been. But I went to Port Natal, you know; and I gained my life's lesson there. Hamish Channing has left me guardian to Nelly. I can guess why he did it, too—that the world may see he thinks me worthy to be trusted at last. He had always the most delicately generous heart in Christendom."

"Hamish and I!" murmured Sir Vincent, in self-communing, "on the wing nearly together."

Yes, it was so. And Roland, with all his lamentation, could not alter the fiat.

"What was the lesson you learnt at Port Natal?"

"Not to be a reckless spendthrift; not to be idle and useless. Vincent," added Roland, bending his face forward in its strange earnestness, and dropping his voice till it was scarcely louder than a whisper, "I learnt in Port Natal that there was another world to live for after this: I learnt that our time was not our own to waste in sin, but God's time, given us to use for the best. A chum of mine out there, named Bartle, was struck down by an accident; the doctor said he'd not live the day out—and he didn't. It was a caution to hear his moans and groans, Vincent. He had not been very bad, as far as I knew, in the ways that the world calls bad; he had only been careless and idle, and wasted his days, and never thought of what was to come after. I wish everybody that's the same had seen him die, Vincent, and heard his dreadful cries for mercy. If ever I forget to remember it, I think God would forget me. I saw many such sudden deaths, and plenty of remorse for them, but none as trying as his. It taught me a lesson: brought me to thought, you know. Don't you fear for me, Vincent; it will be all right, I hope: and if I could ever be so foolhardy as to look at a step on the backward route, Annabel would not let me take it."

Roland had spoken in characteristic oblivion that the case, as to the sudden striking down, bore so entire an analogy to the one before him. Sir Vincent recalled it to him.

"Yes. Just as it is with me, Roland."

"Oh—but—you've got time yet, you know, Dick," he said, a little confused. "A parson, who was knocking about, over there, in a threadbare coat, came in and saw Bartle, and talked to him about the thief on the cross. Bartle couldn't see it; his fears didn't let him; you may."

"Yes, yes," replied Sir Vincent, with a half smile, but Roland thought it looked like a peaceful one. "I have had a parson with me also, Roland."

Roland's face lighted up with a kind of reverence. Sir Vincent put out his hand and stroked the dog.

"You'll be kind to him, Roland?"

"Oh, won't I, Dick! What's his name?"

"Spot."

"Here! Spot, Spot!"

"Go, Spot. Go to your future master."

"Come, then, old fellow. Spot! Spot!"

The dog made a sudden leap to the side of Roland at the call, and rubbed his nose against the extended hand.

"I'll be as good to him as if he were a child," spoke Roland, in his earnestness. "See! we are friends already, Vincent."

And this simple-hearted young fellow was the scapegoat they had all despised! Sir Vincent caught the strong hand and clasped it within his delicate one.

CHAPTER XLII

A WIDE BLACK BAND ON ROLAND'S HAT

Early in the afternoon and the Waterloo Railway Station. A gentleman got out of a first-class carriage, and made his way to one of the waiting hansoms.

"Stop at the first hatter's you come to," he said to the driver.

Leaping out when his directions were obeyed, he entered the shop and asked for a mourning band to be put on his hat; a "deep one." You do not need to be told who it was, and what the black band was for. Vincent had died about eight o'clock in the morning, and the Natal traveller was Sir Roland Yorke.

Save for the fact that he had some money in his pockets, in actual reality, which afforded a kind of personal ease to the mind, he was anything but elated at the change of position. On the contrary, he felt very much subdued. Roland could not be selfish, and the grief and shock brought him by the unexpected death of his cousin Vincent, outweighed every thought of self. He had already tasted some of the fruits of future power. Servants and others had referred to him that morning as the new baronet and their master; his pleasure had been consulted in current matters touching the house and estate, his orders been requested as to the funeral. Roland was head of all now, the sole master. Setting aside the sadness that filled his heart to the exclusion of all else, the very suddenness of the change would prevent him as yet realizing it in his own mind.

With the conspicuous band on his hat, stretching up rather above the top of the crown, Roland entered the cab again, and ordered it to the office. There he presented himself to Mr. Greatorex.

"Well?" said the lawyer, turning round from his desk "So you are back again! What did Sir Vincent want with you? Has he made you his bailiff?"

Roland sadly shook his head. And Mr. Greatorex saw that something was wrong.

"What's amiss?" he hastily inquired.

"If you please sir, I am Sir Roland now."

"You are what?" exclaimed Mr. Greatorex.

"It's only too true," groaned Roland. "Poor Vincent is dead. Mr. Greatorex, I'd work on all fours for a living to the end of my days if it could bring him to life again. I never thought to come in, I'm sure; and I wouldn't willingly. He died at eight o'clock this morning."

Mr. Greatorex leaned back in his chair and relieved his mind by a pastime he might have caught from Roland—that of staring. Not having heard of Sir Vincent's accident, this assertion of his death sounded only the more surprising. Was Roland telling the truth? He almost questioned it. Roland, perceiving the doubt, gave a summary of particulars, and Mr. Greatorex slowly realized the facts.

Sir Roland Yorke! The light-headed, simple-minded clerk, who had been living on a pound a week and working sufficiently hard to get it, suddenly transformed into a powerful baronet! It was like a romance in a child's fairy tale. Mr. Greatorex rose and held out his hand.

"I must congratulate you on your succession, Sir Roland, sad though the events are that have led to it."

"Now don't! please don't!" interrupted Roland. "I hope nobody will do that, sir: it sounds like a wrong on poor Dick. Oh, I'd bring him to life again if I were able."

"I trust you will make us your men of business, Sir Roland," resumed Mr. Greatorex, still standing. "We have been solicitors to the head of the Yorke family in succession for many years now."

"I'm sure if you'll be at the trouble of acting for me, I should like nothing better, sir: bad manners to me if I could have any different thought! And I've put your name and Mr. Bede's down in the list for the funeral, if you'll please attend it. There'll be but a few of us in all. Gerald (though I shouldn't think he will show his face at it), William Yorke, Arthur Channing, two or three of Dick's friends, and you and Mr. Bede. Poor Dick said to me when he was dying not to have the same kind of show he had for his father's funeral, he saw the folly of it now, but the quietest I could order. I think he has gone to heaven, Mr. Greatorex."

But that the subject was a solemn one, Mr. Greatorex had certainly laughed at the quaint simplicity of the concluding sentence. One reminiscence in connection with the past funeral rose forcibly in his mind—of the slighting neglect shown to the young man now before him. He, the real heir-presumptive, only that nobody had the wit to think of it, was not deemed good enough to follow his uncle to the grave. But stood in his place now.

Bede would not be able to attend the ceremony, Mr. Greatorex said aloud: he was already in France, having crossed over with his wife by the last mail train.

"What is the matter with him?" asked Roland. "He looked as ill as he could look yesterday."

"I don't know what the matter is," said Mr. Greatorex. "He has an inward complaint, and I fear it must be making great strides. His name will be taken out of the firm tomorrow, and give place to Frank's. It was Bede's own request: it is as if he fears he may never be capable of business again."

"I'm sure I hope he will," cried Roland in his sympathy. "About me, Mr. Greatorex? Of course I'd not like to leave you at a pinch; I'll come to the office tomorrow morning and do my work as usual for a day or two, until you've found somebody to replace me. I should like to take this afternoon for myself."

But Mr. Greatorex with a smile, thought they should not need to trouble Sir Roland: which was no doubt an agreeable intimation: and Roland really had a good deal to do in connection with his new position.

"If I'm not forgetting!" he exclaimed, just as he was taking his departure. "There's the money you lent me, sir, and I thank you for the loan of it."

In taking the sovereign from his pocket, he pulled out several. Mr. Greatorex jokingly remarked that he had apparently no longer need to borrow.

"It is from poor Dick's desk," sadly observed Roland. "He told me there was enough money in it to repay the pound to you and get my clothes out of pawn, and that it would be all my own when he died. Well, what do you think I found there when I opened it today?—Nearly a hundred pounds in gold and bank notes!"

"But you have not got all that about you, I hope?"

"Yes I have, sir; it was safer to bring it up than to leave it. I shall pay it into the banker's. I've got to show myself there, I suppose, and leave my signature in their books; it won't be so neat a one as poor Dick's."

Roland departed. Looking in for a moment at the office as he went out, and announcing himself as Sir Roland Yorke, upon which Mr. Hurst burst out laughing in his face. He dashed in on Mrs. Jones with his news, ate nearly the whole of a shilling Madeira cake that happened to be on the table, while he talked, and made a voluntary promise to that tart and disbelieving matron to refurnish her house from top to bottom.

Then the cab was ordered to the banker's, where his business was satisfactorily adjusted. Gerald's chambers were not far off, and Roland took them next. The servant met him with the bold assertion that his master was out.

"Don't bother yourself to deny him, my good man; I saw his face at the window," said Roland, with frankness. "You may safely show me in: I am not a creditor."

"Well, sir, we are obliged to be excessively cautious, just now, and that's the truth," apologized the man in a tone of confidence. "Mr. Yorke, I think?"

"Sir Roland Yorke," corrected Roland.

"Sir?" returned the man, looking at him as if he thought he saw a lunatic.

"Sir Roland Yorke," was the emphatic repetition. "Have the goodness to announce me."

And the servant opened the room door and did it.

As Roland saw Gerald's quick look of surprise, he would, under other circumstances, have shaken in his shoes at the fun. But sadness wholly reigned over him today. And—if truth must be told—a terrible aversion to Gerald for his work and its fruits held possession of the new heir.

"Oh, it's you," cried Gerald, roughly. "What on earth possessed the fellow?"

"The fellow did right, Gerald. I gave him my name, and he announced it."

"Don't come here with your fool's blabber. He said 'Sir Roland Yorke.'"

"And it is what I am."

Gerald's face grew dark with passion. He had an especial dislike to be played with.

"Vincent's dead, Gerald."

"It is a lie."

"Vincent died this morning at eight o'clock," repeated Roland. "I was with him: he telegraphed for me yesterday. Look at this mourning band"—showing his hat—"I've just been to get it put on. Do you think I'd have the face to invent a jest on this subject? Vincent Yorke is dead, poor fellow, and I have come into things as Sir Roland. Not that I can fully believe it myself yet." The tone of the voice, the deep black band, and a kind of subtle instinct within himself brought conviction of the truth home to Gerald Yorke.

Had it been to save his fame, he could not have helped the loud brazen tone from going out of his voice, or the dread that took possession of his whole aspect.

"What—has—he—died—of?"

"The gunshot wound."

A pause. Gerald broke it.

"It was going on well. I heard so only two days ago."

"But it took a sudden turn for the worse; and he is dead."

Gerald's face assumed a tinge as of bluish chalk. Was he to have two lives on his soul? Hamish Channing's had surely been enough for him without Vincent Yorke's. Pushing back his damp hair, he met Roland's steady look, and so made believe to feel nothing, went to the fire, and stirred it gently.

"Why did the doctors let it take this turn?" he asked, flinging down the poker. "It was as simple a wound as ever was given."

"I suppose they'd have helped it if they could."

Another pause.

"Well—of course—as you have succeeded, I must congratulate you," said Gerald stiffly and lamely. Absently, too, for he was buried in thought, reflecting on what an idiotic policy his, to Roland, had been: but this contingency had never occurred to him more than it had to Roland.

"Vincent had a good lot of property that was not entailed," resumed Gerald. "Do you know who he has willed it to? Did he make a will?"

"He made a will yesterday, before telegraphing for me," Gerald lifted his face with a transient hope.

"I wonder if he has remembered me?"

"I think not. Except some legacies to the servants, and a keepsake for Miss Trehern—his watch and diamond ring, I fancy—he said nobody's name was mentioned in the will but mine. It has not been opened: I thought I'd leave it till after the funeral. I am the executor."

"You!—you don't want his ready money as well as his inheritance, spoke Gerald, in a foam.

"I'm sure I didn't want any of it, I only thought to be his bailiff; but I can't help it if it has come to me," was Roland's quiet answer, as he turned to depart. "Good afternoon, Gerald. I thought it right to call and tell you of his death: you may like to draw your blinds down."

"Thanks," said Gerald, sarcastically.

"You will receive an invitation to the funeral, Gerald. But I'd like to intimate that if you do not care to attend, I shall not look upon it in the light of a slight," added candid Roland, who really spoke in simple good nature. "We shall be enough without you if you'd rather stay away."

Before Gerald's awful rage at the speech was over, for he looked upon it as bestowed in a patronizing light from the new baronet, Roland was vaulting into the waiting cab. Gerald had the pleasure of peeping on from the window.

"Sir Roland Yorke!—Sir Roland Yorke!" he spoke aloud in his horrible mortification. "Sunny Mead for his home, and four thousand a year landed property, and heaps of ready money. Curse the beggar! Curse the shot that has brought him the luck of the inheritance! I'd sell my soul for it to have been mine. I should wear the honours better than he. I wish to Heaven he could die tonight!"

And Mr. Gerald Yorke, looking after the receding cab with a dark and sullen countenance, could indeed have sold his soul; if by so doing he might have annihilated his brother and stepped into his place. He was in that precise frame of mind for which some few men in the world's actual history, and a vast many in fiction, have stained their hands with crime for the greed of gain.

Tread lightly, speak softly; for death is already hovering in the chamber. As Roland enters on tiptoe he takes in the scene at a glance. Hamish lying, with closed eyes, and the live ball, Miss Nelly, tucked outside beside him her golden curls mingling with his damp hair. A sea of old Helstonleigh faces seems to be gathered round; save that Roland silently clasps Arthur's hand, he takes notice of none. Edging himself between Annabel and Tom Channing, as they stand side by side, he bends his face of concern downwards. The slight stir arouses Hamish, he opens his eyes, and holds up his feeble hand with a remnant of the old smile.

"Back again! Head bailiff?"

Roland bit his lip. His chest was heaving with emotion, his face working. Hamish, who retained his keenest perceptive faculties to the last, spoke again in his faint voice.

"Is it good news?"

"It's good news. Good news, Hamish, and at the same time awfully bad. Vincent's dead, and I'm—I'm in his shoes."

Hamish did not seem to understand. Neither did the others.

"It's me to come after him, poor fellow, you see. I am Sir Roland now."

As the words fell upon the previously silent room, you might have heard a pin drop. Cheeks flushed, eyes looked out their questioning surprise at the speaker. Upon Hamish alone the communication seemed to make no impression: earthly interests were to him now as nothing.

"You will give me Annabel with a will, Hamish, now that I have come into the family inheritance?"

"I had already given her to you, so far as my best will was good to do it. Roland—"

The voice seemed to be fading away altogether, but in the eyes there was an eager gaze. Roland bent his head lower to catch the sounds about to issue from the lips.

"There's a different and a better inheritance, Roland; one of love, and light, and everlasting peace. You will both of you strive for that."

"Yes, that we will. And gain it too. Oh, Hamish, if you could but stop with us a bit longer!" burst forth Roland, letting his suppressed emotion come out with a choking sob. "It's nothing all round but dying. First Vincent, and now you! I never knew such a miserable world as this. I'd have laid down my own life to keep either of you in it."

There stole a smile of ineffable peace over the dying face. It seemed to have caught a ray of the heavenly light in which it would so soon be shining.

CHAPTER XLIII

DREAMS REALIZED

It is certainly not often in this life that improbable dreams of fame and fortune get to be realized as they were in the case of Roland Yorke. Down he went to his native place, Helstonleigh, in all the glory of fame and fortune that his imagination had been wont to picture: the dog, Spot, with him. He paid his creditors their debts twice over he made presents to his mother and the world; he went knocking at old Galloway's door, and caused himself to be fully announced, as he had at Gerald's—Sir Roland Yorke. He ran in and out of the proctor's office at will, took possession of his former stool there, and answered callers as if he were the veritable clerk he used to be. He promised a living to Tom Channing, promotion in India to Charley; made a sweeping bow to William Yorke the first time he met him in the street, and called out to know whether he might be considered a scapegoat still. He put up a tombstone to commemorate the virtues of Jenkins. Meeting Harry Huntley, he nearly cried over Hamish. Hamish Channing's book was at length in every heart and home—ah, that he had lived to see it! The good had all come too late for him. Ellen would be wealthy from henceforth, for her father had regained his fortune; her aunt, stiff Miss Huntley, had died, and bequeathed to her the whole of hers; and little Miss Nelly was an heiress.

Not immediately, however, had Roland hastened to quit London for Helstonleigh, and there's something to tell about it. He had affairs to attend to first; and it took him some time to forget his daily sorrow for the dead. Roland's private belief was that he should never cease to mourn for Hamish; should never rise in the morning, or go to rest at night, without thinking of him and Gerald's miserable work. He entered on his abode at Sunny Mead, his home from henceforth, made himself acquainted with his future position, and what his exact revenues would be. In his imperfect way, but honest wish to do right, he apportioned out plenty of work for himself, and not much to spend, resolving above all things to eschew a life of frivolity and idleness. Roland would rather have followed the plough's tail day by day, than sink to that.

The first few weeks he divided his time between Sunny Mead and London. When in town, he dropped in upon his old friends with native familiarity: prosperity and a title could not change Roland. The office and clerks saw him very often; Mrs. Jones's tea and muffins occasionally suffered by a guest who had a large appetite. He refurnished that tart lady's house for her after a rather sharp battle; for at first Mrs. J. would not accept the boon. The first visitor Roland had the honour of entertaining was Lord Carrick. His white-haired lordship was flourishing in London again, and gave Roland a whole week of his hearty, genial good-natured company at Sunny Mead.

The thorn in the flesh was Gerald, and it happened that Mr. Gerald's career came to a crisis during the week of Lord Carrick's stay at Sunny Mead. On the last day of it, when they were out in the frost, and the peer was imparting to his nephew sundry theories for the best cultivation of land, a servant ran out to announce the arrival of a lady, who had come in great haste from the railway station. She appeared to be in distress, the man added, and said she must at once see Sir Roland.

In distress beyond doubt: for when Roland went clattering in, wondering who it could be, there met him the tear-stained face of Winny. She had brought down a piteous tale. Gerald, arrested the previous day, had lodgings in that savoury prison, Whitecross Street; he had boldly sent her to ask Roland to pay his debts and set him free. Winny, sobbing over some luncheon that Roland good-naturedly set her down to at once, protested that she felt sure one at least of the three little girls would be found in the fire when she got back to them.

Lord Carrick drew Roland aside.

"I'm not ill-natured, me boy, as ye knew long ago, and I'd do a good turn for anybody; but I'd like to give ye a caution. Don't begin by paying Gerald's debts. If ye do, as sure as ye're a living man, ye'll never have a minute's peace for him to the last day of ye're life. Set him free now, and all his thanks would be to run up more for ye to pay. In a year's time he'd be in the same plight again; and he or his creditors would be bothering ye always. Don't begin it. Let him fight out his debts as he best can."

"It's just what I'd like to do," said Roland. "I'd not mind allowing a couple of hundred a year, or so, for Winny and the children. I meant to offer it. It might be paid to her weekly, you know, uncle, and I could slip something more into her hand whenever we met. She might get a bit of peace then. But I don't think it would be doing Gerald any real kindness in the long run to release him from his debts."

Lord Carrick nodded most emphatically.

"I need not tell Winny this, Uncle Carrick—only that she and the kittens shall be taken care of from henceforth. She can carry a sealed note back to Gerald."

"I'll see to him," said Lord Carrick. "If he is to get any help at all, it must be from me. Ye can write the note to him. It would be the worst day's work ye ever entered on if ye attempted to help him. It is nothing else but helping people, Roland, me boy, that has kept me down, and I'd not like to see you begin it. If Gerald can't get clear without assistance, I may come to the rescue later. But he'll have to try."

"Perhaps I might be got to allow him a hundred a year, or so, for himself later," added relenting Roland. "But I'll never have anything to do with his debts, or suffer him to look to me to pay them."

Could Gerald in his distant and gloomy abode, but have heard this, he had surely been ready to shoot the pair of speakers; and with more intentional malignity, too, than he had shot Sir Vincent.

But we began the chapter at Helstonleigh. For once in its monotonous life that faithful city had found something to arouse it from its jog-trot course; and people flew to their doors and windows to gaze after Sir Roland Yorke. It did not seem much less improbable that the time-honoured cathedral might some night disappear altogether, than that the once improvident schoolboy of not too good repute, the careless run-a-gate who had made a moonlight flitting, and left some fifty pounds' worth of debts behind him, should come back Sir Roland, like a hero of romance.

Fruition never answers to anticipations—as Roland found, now that his golden visions came to be realized. The romantic charm of the oft-pictured dream was wanting; the green freshness of sanguine boyhood no longer threw its halo on his heart; the vivid glow of imaginative hope had mellowed down to a sober tint. In manner, in gleeful frankness, Roland was nearly as impulsive and boyish as ever; but his mind had gained a good deal of experience, and reflection had come to him. The chances and changes of the world had worked their effect; and the deaths caused directly or indirectly by Gerald, sat heavily on his generous heart. Adam's curse lies on all things, and there can be no pleasure without pain.

Roland did not miss it. Enough of charm was left to him. Annabel was staying with her mother, and things seemed to have gone back again to the dear old days before Roland had known the world, or tasted of its cares. Roland went calling upon his acquaintance continually, distant and near, making himself at home everywhere. Ellen Channing, worn to a thread-paper with grief, was visiting her father in her maiden home. Nelly made its charm now. The young widow would probably take up her abode at Helstonleigh, in spite of Roland's strong advice that it should be near Sunny Mead.

"I told you I should be sure to get on and make my fortune sometime, Mr. Galloway."

The old proctor, whose health was failing hopelessly, returned a slighting answer. Roland, without ceremony as usual, had dashed into the office, and was sitting on a high desk with his legs dangling. The remark was given in return for some disparaging observation as to Roland's former doings.

"You made it! Ugh! A great deal of that."

"Oh—well—I've come into one, at any rate."

"The only way you were ever likely to attain to one. Left to your own exertions, you'd have got back here with holes in your breeches."

"Now don't you be personal, sir," was the laughing rejoinder. "I'm Sir Roland Yorke, you know."

"And a fine Sir Roland you'll be!"

"I'll try and be a good one," said Roland emphatically, as he caught Arthur's eye—who was seated in the place of state as the head of the office, for the proctor had virtually resigned it. "Arthur knows he can trust me now: ask him, else, sir. Hamish knew it also before he died."

"I should like to hear what business he had to die, and who killed him?" cried old Galloway explosively. "It was done amongst you, I know. A nice thing for my old friend Mr. Huntley to get back to England and find his son-in-law dead: the bright, true young fellow that he loved as the apple of his eye."

"Yes, I think he was killed among us, up there," sadly avowed Roland, his honest face kindling with shame. "But I did not help in it, Mr. Galloway; I'd have given my life to save his. I wish I could!"

"Wishes won't bring him back. I saw his wife yesterday—his widow, that is. I'm sure I couldn't bear to look at her."

"Did you see sweet little Nelly?" cried Roland eagerly, his thoughts taking a turn. "If ever I have a girl of my own I hope she'll be like that child."

"Now just you please to take yourself off, Sir Roland, and come in when we're a little less busy," returned the proctor, who was very much out of sorts that morning. "You are hindering business, just as you used to do."

But perhaps the greatest of all small delights was that of encountering Mr. Butterby. Roland had just emerged from the market house one Saturday, where he had been in the thick of the throng, making himself at home, and inquiring affably the price of butter of all the faces he remembered, and been seduced into buying a tough old gander, on the grave assurance that it was a young and tender goose, when he and the detective met face to face.

"Well?" said Roland, dangling the goose in his hand, as unblushingly as though it had been a bouquet of choice flowers.

"Well?" returned Mr. Butterby. "How are you, sir? I heard you were down here."

"Ay. I've come to set things straight that I left crooked. And glad to be able to do it at last. You've heard about me, I suppose, Butterby?"

"I've heard," assented Butterby. "You are Sir Roland Yorke, and have come into the family estates and honours, through the untimely death of Sir Vincent. A lucky shot for you, sir."

"Lucky?" groaned Roland. "Well, in one sense I suppose it was: but don't go and think me a heartless camel, Butterby. I declare to you that if I could bring Sir Vincent back, though I had to return to my work again, and the turn-up bedstead at Mrs. J.'s, I'd do it this minute cheerfully. When I sat by, watching him die, knowing he was going to make room for me, I felt downright wicked: almost as bad as my nice brother must have felt, who shot him. Did you read about it in the newspapers?—they had got it all as pat as might be. I can't think, for my part, how they lay hold of things."

Butterby nodded assent. There was little he did not read, if it could in the remotest degree concern him.

"I'm paying up, Butterby. Paying everybody, and something over. If ever I get into debt again call me an owl. Galloway groans and grunts, and says I shall; but I fancy he knows better. What do you think? He took his hat off to me in the street yesterday! formerly he'd hardly nod to me over his shoulder sideways."

"How were the folks up yonder, Sir Roland, when you left?" asked Butterby, jerking his head in the direction of London. "Is Miss Rye all right?"

"Oh, she's uncommon jolly. The last day I called there, Mrs. J. said she supposed she and Winter—they call him Winter now—would be making a match of it. Upon that, I told Miss Rye I'd buy her the wedding dress. Instead of being properly grateful, she advised me not to talk so fast. I say, Butterby, that was a mistake of yours, that was—the taking her into custody for the one that killed John Ollivera."

"Ay," carelessly returned Mr. Butterby, with a kind of sniff. "The best of us go in for mistakes, you know."

"I suppose you can't help it, just as some people can't help dreaming," observed Roland with native politeness. "I went up and saw his grave yesterday. I say, shall you ever pitch upon the right one?"

But that Mr. Butterby turned his eyes away towards the Guildhall opposite before he answered, Roland might have observed a peculiar shade cross their steady light. Whatever curious outlets his speculations had drifted to in the course of years, as to the slayer of Mr. Ollivera, he knew the truth now.

"Shan't try at it, sir. Take it from first to last, it has been about the queerest case that over fell under mortal skill; and we are content for the future to let it be."

"I won't forget you, Butterby. You've not been a bad one on the whole. A snuffbox would be of no use, you said; but you shall have something else. And look here, if ever you should come within range of my place in Surrey, I'd be glad to see you there for half an hour's chat. Good-day, old Butterby. Isn't this a prime goose? I've just been giving seven shillings for it."

He and his ancient goose went vaulting off. Roland frequently took articles home to help garnish Lady Augusta's dinner-table; very much to the wrath of the cook, who found she had double work.

But it must not be thought Roland led entirely an idle life at Helstonleigh. Apart from personal calls on his friendship, in the shape of dropping in upon people, he had work on his hands. By Mrs. J.'s permission he was replacing the plain stone on poor Jenkins's grave with one of costly marble. Roland himself undertook the inscription. Not being accustomed to composition, he found it a puzzling task.

"Here's to the memory of Joseph Jenkins. He was too good for this world, inoffensive as a young sparrow, and did everybody's work as well as his own. Put upon by the office and people in general, he bore it all meekly, according to his nature, never turning again. A cough took him off to Heaven, leaving Mrs. J. behind, and one or two to regret him, who knew his virtues. This tribute is erected by his attached friend, (who was one of the worst to put upon him in life,) and sorrowful, Roland Yorke."

Such was the inscription for the marble tombstone, as it went in to the sculptor. That functionary suggested some slight alterations, which Sir Roland was reluctant to accede to. There ensued writing and counter writing, and the epitaph, finally inscribed, contained but little (like some bills that pass through Parliament) of the original.

And so the sweet days of spring glided on, and the time came for Roland to depart. To depart until June, when he would return to claim his bride. Tom Channing should marry them, and nobody else, avowed Roland; and if the Reverend Bill put up his back at not having the first finger in the pie, why he must put it up. Annabel was his confidant in all things; and Annabel thought she should rather be married by her brother, than by William Yorke.

The once happy home of the Channings bore the marks of time's chances and changes. The house was the same, as were its elements for peace, but some of its inmates had quitted it for ever. Mrs. Channing, Arthur, Tom, Charles, and Annabel: they moved about in their mourning garments, with their regretful faces, thinking ever of him who had whilom made its sunshine, Hamish the bright. He had gone to a better world, where there was neither pain nor tears, neither cruel injustice nor heart-breaking sorrow; but this consolation is always hard to realize, and their grief was lasting. Mrs. Channing looked aged and worn; the boys and girls had grown into men and women; in old Judith and her snow-white mob-cap, there alone appeared to be no change.

It was at length the day of Roland's departure, and he was holding a final interview with Annabel. They stood at the glass doors of the study window, open to the garden, and the warm May sun shone in gaily, making the crape on Annabel's silk dress look hot and rusty. The once untidy study, when they were all boys and girls together, had been renovated with a green carpet and delicately-papered walls; the young parson now called it his.

Considering Roland's deficiencies on the score of forethought, he had really organized the plans for his future life with a great deal of wisdom. Sunny Mead was to be their sole home, and Annabel chief cash-keeper in regard to ready money. On that he was resolved, honestly avowing that he was not to be trusted with money in his pocket: it was sure to go. The residence in Portland Place, which Sir Richard had only held on a lease, had been given up: there was to be no town house, no fashion, no gaiety. Annabel seconded him in all, urging moderation strenuously. He was going up now to make his bow to the Prince of Wales at a leéve: and it was to be hoped he would accomplish it with passable decorum: and Annabel would be presented to the Queen on the first favourable opportunity, after she should be Lady Yorke. So far, that was due from their position; but there the exigencies of fashionable society would for them end. Sunny Mead would be their home; and, it could not be doubted, a very happy one. They are talking of the prospect, now as they stand together: and to both it is one of rose colour.

"But for going to Port Natal, Annabel, there's no knowing how I might have turned out—a regular drawling idler about town, as some of the Yorkes have been before me. I might have gone in for all kinds of folly, and come to no end of grief. We shall be safe down at Sunny Mead, and live like—like—" Roland stops for a simile.

"Rational people," puts in Annabel with a smile.

"Fighting-cocks," says Roland. "I shall make a good farmer."

"But, Roland," she rejoins, dubiously, "I hope you'll not discharge the bailiff until you feel that you are fully competent to the management. You don't know much of farming yet."

"Not know much of farming!" exclaims Roland, his eyes opening with surprise. "After all my experience at Port Natal! Look at the pigs I had to manage—obstinate, grunting animals—and the waggons and carts I was put to drive—filled with calves sometimes! I'm not obliged to take the threshing and mowing myself, you know. As to the bailiff, he shall stay on until you send him away, if it's two years to come."

She bends her blushing face a little forward, plucking an early rosebud. Roland takes it from her and puts it in his coat. On her finger flashes a valuable diamond ring, the pledge of their engagement.

"We won't have a frying-pan in the house, Annabel. I can't bear to see one since that failure at Port Natal."

She turns her laughing eyes on him. Roland honestly thinks they are the truest, sweetest, best the world ever contained, and feels he can never be thankful enough that he is to call them his.

CHAPTER XLIV

CONCLUSION

The summer and the day were alike on the wane. It was the end of July, and a dull evening. Mr. Greatorex was sitting alone in the coming twilight, in the large and handsome dining-room, where we first saw him at the beginning of this history. Haggard he had looked then waiting to hear the particulars of his favourite nephew's death; far more haggard he looked now, for the truth in regard to it was at length disclosed to him.

He wore deep mourning. The son, whose appearance of ill health had of late given him so much concern, was dead: Bede. Alas! it was not illness of body that had ailed Bede Greatorex, and turned his days to one ever-moving, never-ceasing tumultuous sea of misery, but that far worse affliction, illness of mind. In bodily sickness there may arise intervals of light, when the suffering is not felt so keenly, or the heavenly help is nearer for support; in mental sickness, grave as Bede's was, such intervals never come.

After quitting home at the turn of Christmas, and travelling for a month or two hither and thither, Bede settled down in a remote French town. There was a very small colony of English in it, and an English chaplain, who did the duty for nothing. Bede had not intended to make it a permanent halting place, but his weakness increased greatly, and he seemed never willing to attempt another move onwards. Mrs. Bede grumbled woefully: she called the town a desert and their lodgings a barn: truth to say, the rooms were spacious and had as good as nothing in them. She amused herself—such amusement as it was—by taking drives in the early spring freshness, and talking French, for improvement, with a fashionable Parisian femme de chambre, whom she had found herself lucky enough to engage. In June, Bede died: and the date of his death happened, by a rather singular coincidence, to be that of Roland Yorke's wedding day. But that can pass.

With Bede's death, a month ago now, things in the office had undergone some fresh arrangements. Frank Greatorex was his father's sole partner in the practice. Frank was soon to bring home his wife and it was to be hoped she would make a happier home of the dwelling than its late mistress had done. There could be little doubt of it: and Mr. Greatorex stood a fair chance of regaining some of his domestic comforts. The prospects of Bede's widow were not flourishing. Bede had not left a shilling behind him; a little debt, in fact, instead; that is, she was in debt: and the bills for his funeral and other incidental expenses, had come over to Mr. Greatorex. There had been no marriage settlement on Louisa Joliffe: she was now left to the mercy of her father-in-law: and though a generous man by nature and habit, Mr. Greatorex was not showing himself generous in this. In a cool, business-like letter, conveyed to her personally by a trustworthy clerk, Mr. Greatorex had informed her that henceforward she would be allowed two hundred pounds a year. One hundred pounds in addition he made her a present gift of. The clerk, despatched with the letter and money, was Mr. Brown, who had entirely resumed his name of Winter: the office, not getting into the new habit readily, usually called him Mr. Brown-Winter. Mr.

Winter was commissioned to discharge the above-mentioned bills, and to see a stone placed over the grave, the inscription for which had been written down by Mr. Greatorex. It was short as might be: only the following words, with the date of death.

BEDE GREATOREX.
AGED THIRTY-NINE.

"Come unto me all ye that labour and are heavy laden."

Mr. Winter had executed his charges, and was back again. The clerks heard with very little surprise that he was to be promoted amidst them: the confidential manager in future under Mr. Greatorex and his son; one whom the office would have to look up to as a master. Rumour went that Mr. Winter was about to become a qualified solicitor: not from any view of setting up for himself, but that he might be more efficient for his duties in the house of Greatorex and Greatorex. His salary would be handsome: it had been already considerably augmented since the month of January last. Mr. Winter had taken a small, pretty house, and would, soon bring a wife home to it: Alletha Rye was to change her name to Alletha Winter. The clerks in general looked upon it that Mr. Winter's promotion took its rise in his undoubted business merit and capacity: but in point of fact it was owing to a few lines written by Bede to his father.

"The man is of sterling merit: he has forgotten self in striving patiently to benefit and shield me: reward him for my sake. I am sure he will repay in faithfulness all you can do for him."

Little more than this did Bede say; not a word as to the nature of what the benefit or the shielding had been. Mr. Greatorex knew now, for a revelation had been made to him through Judge Kene. Bede, only the day before his death, had posted a letter to Sir Thomas Kene, one that he had spent a week in writing, getting to it at intervals.

The anguish that communication, and other things, brought to Mr. Greatorex, was very sharp still. He was feeling it as he sat there in the evening twilight. Bede's death he had, in one sense, almost ceased to mourn: knowing now what a happy release from mental pain it must have been. But he could not think with the smallest patience of Bede's wife: never again, never again. She had been the primary author of all the misery: but for her, his son—ay, and someone else, dear to him as a son—had been, in all human probability, living now, happy, peaceful, and playing a good and busy part on the world's stage.

"Will you admit visitors sir?"

"Eh! what!"—and Mr. Greatorex started up half in alarm as the servant spoke, so deeply had he been buried in far-away thoughts. "Visitors this evening!—no. Stay, Philip. Who are they?"

"Sir Roland and Lady Yorke, sir."

"Oh, I'll see them," said Mr. Greatorex. "Ask them to walk up."

Roland and his wife, passing through London from their wedding tour, part of which had been spent in Ireland, at Lord Carrick's, had halted for a night at one of the hotels.

"To see old friends," said Roland. Not that he had many to see: Mrs. J. and Mr. Greatorex nearly comprised them. Whinny Yorke and her children were in Wales with her mother. Gerald had sent them, "as a temporary thing," till he could get "a bit straight." When that desirable epoch might be expected to dawn, was hidden in the mystery of the future. Gerald had been a good month in Whitecross Street prison, done to death pretty nearly with his creditors' reproaches, who used to go down in a body to abuse him when they found there was no chance of their getting a farthing. He and his chambers had been sold up; and altogether Gerald had come to considerable grief. Just now he was in Paris, enjoying himself on a sum of money that Lord Carrick had been induced to give him, and on the proceeds from an article that he supplied twice a week to a London newspaper. He thought himself terribly hard worked; and slightly relieved his bile by telling everybody that his brother Roland was the greatest villain under the sun. Roland meant to find him a post if he could, and meanwhile took care of Winny and the little ones: Gerald quietly ignored that.

"Sir Roland and Lady Yorke."

Mr. Greatorex met them with outstretched hands, giving Annabel a fatherly kiss on her blushing face. He quite forgot her new elevation, remembering her only as the sweet and simple girl who had made sunshine in his house at odd moments. She looked sweet and simple still, quite unaltered. Roland, on his part, had not attained the smallest additional dignity: he clattered in just as of yore. They were going to Sunny Mead on the morrow, and he began telling of his future plans for the happy home life.

Mr. Greatorex smiled as he listened. "I don't fancy you will give us much work, Sir Roland, in the way of incurring debts and trouble, and coming to us to get you clear of them," he observed.

"No thank you, I leave that to Gerald. Mr. Greatorex," added Roland, his eyes shining with honest light, his face meeting that of his ex-master, "I promised Vincent when he was dying that I'd keep clear of trouble; I as good as promised Hamill: I'd not go from my word to them, you know. And, what's more, I shall never wish to."

"I see. You will be a dead loss to us. The Yorkes in general have been profitable clients."

Roland took the words seriously, and his mouth fell a little.

"I'm very sorry, sir. I—I'll give you a present every year to make up for the deficiency, if you'll accept it. A golden inkstand, or something of that sort."

Mr. Greatorex looked at him with a smile, never speaking. Roland resumed, thoroughly in earnest, his voice low.

"It's such an awful deal of money, you see; four thousand a year, besides a house and lots of other things. Two people could never spend it, and if we could, we don't think it would be doing right. Annabel and I see things alike. We mean to put aside half of our income; against a rainy day, say; or—there are so many people who want help. You see, Mr. Greatorex, we have both learnt to live on little. But I'm sure I shall be sorry, if you look upon me as a loss."

"You can repay me, Roland, better than by a golden inkstand," said Mr. Greatorex, laying his hand on the young man's shoulder. "Let me come to you for a week annually when the summer roses are in bloom; and do you tell me, year by year, that you have adhered to your proposed simple mode of life."

Roland was in the skies at once. "It is a bargain, mind that," he said. "You will come to us always with the summer roses. As to a week only, we'll talk about that."

"And Jane shall meet you, sir," interposed Annabel with shy joy. "She is very happy at her school; I often have letters from her. Roland and I were thinking of having her at Christmas, if you don't mind."

"And Nelly Channing too, if her mother will spare her," put in Roland. "And we have talked about those three little mites in Wales. It would be good to have the lot together, and give them a bit of pleasure. They should have a jolly Christmas tree; and we'd get over some boxes of lumps of delight from Turkey, by one of the P. and O. steamers; and I'd bring them up to the waxwork. Annabel and I both love children."

"And I hope to my heart you may have some of your own to bless you!" rejoined Mr. Greatorex with unaccountable emotion. "To bless you when they are young; to bless you when they—when they—shall be grown. God grant you may never have cause to weep for them in tears of blood! Many of earth's sorrows are hard to bear, but that is the weightiest that Heaven can inflict upon us."

Roland stared a little. The thing seemed nearly as incomprehensible to his view of social life as that he should have to weep for some defect in the moon.

"We'd bring them up in the best way, Mr. Greatorex," was the simple answer. "Annabel would, you may be sure, and I'd try to. I don't think I got brought up in the best way myself: there was too much scuffling and scrambling. Mrs. J. once said—I beg your pardon, Annabel."

For Annabel was trying to express to Mr. Greatorex their regret at his son's death. The strange emotion that had shaken him she knew must be felt for Bede.

"We are both of us very sorry, sir, for him and for you," she said.

"My dear, you need not be," spoke Mr. Greatorex, in a low sad tone. "His life had grown weary; and death, to him must have been like a welcome rest at the close of day. A little sooner, a little later—what does it matter?"

"And for the muffs of doctors not to be able to cure him! Mr. Greatorex, when I remember him, and Vincent Yorke, and Hamish Channing, my respect for the medical profession does not go up. Halloa! who's this?" broke off Roland.

Philip was coming in with a cloud of surprise on his face, while a rustle as of extensive petticoats might be heard in his rear. He addressed his master with deprecation, conscious of something to tell that might not be very agreeable.

"It is Mrs. Bede Greatorex, sir."

"Who?" hurriedly exclaimed Mr. Greatorex.

"Mr. Bede's widow, sir. She has arrived with a French maid and a cab full of boxes."

No need to reiterate the news, for Mrs. Bede stood in view. Mr. Greatorex seized his servant by the coat like one in alarm, and gave a private order.

"Keep the cab. Don't unload the boxes. Mrs. Bede Greatorex will not remain here."

Mrs. Bede Greatorex, a widow of a month, was not less fashionable in appearance than when she was a wife. Rather more so, of the two. Her dress of rich silk and crape was a model for the mode books, her hair was wonderful to behold. A small bob of something white peeped out atop of the chignon; looking close, it might be discovered to be an inch of quilled net: and its wearer called it a widow's cap with all the brass in life.

She held out her hand to Mr. Greatorex, but he seemed not to see it. That his resentment against this woman was one of bitterness, could not be mistaken. Mrs. Bede did not appear to notice the coldness of the greeting. Brushing past Annabel, she cast a rather contemptuous look towards her, and said some slighting words.

"What! are you here again? I thought the house was rid of you."

"This is my wife; Lady Yorke," spoke Roland in as haughty a tone as it was possible for him to assume. "Don't forget it, if you please, Mrs. Bede Greatorex."

She looked from one to the other of them. That Roland had succeeded to the family honours, she knew, but she had not heard of his marriage. The poor young governess, whom she had put upon and made unhappy, Lady Yorke! A moment's pause: Mrs. Bede's manner changed as if by magic, and she kissed Annabel on both cheeks, French fashion. Nobody knew better than she on which side her bread was buttered.

"Ah, dear me, it's fine to be you, Annabel! What changes since we last met. You a wife, and I a widow."

Mr. Greatorex took an impatient step forward, as if to speed her departure. She turned to him, speaking of her husband.

"I think Bede might have got well if he would. I used to tell him so. The doctors made an examination afterwards, and found, as you have heard, that there was no specific disease whatever. He wasted away; wasted and wasted; it was like as though there were a consuming fire ever within him burning him away to death."

"My goodness!" cried Roland. "Poor Bede."

"It was most unsatisfactory: I never saw anything like it in my life before," tartly retorted Mrs. Bede, for her husband's death had not pleased her, and she resented it openly. Not for the loss or love of him, but for the loss of his means. "I think he might have got well had he struggled for it. If you'll believe me, only the day before he died, he went out in a carriage to the post office, that he might post a letter himself to Sir Thomas Kene."

No one answered her, or made any comment.

"Is my old room ready for me?"

Mr. Greatorex, to whom the question was more particularly put, motioned her towards the door, and moved thither himself. "I wish to speak with you in private for a minute," he said. "Pardon me Sir Roland, I will be back directly."

That Mrs. Bede Greatorex had come to take the house by storm, hoping thereby to resume her late footing in it, Mr. Greatorex knew just as well as she. His letter to her, delivered by George Winter, was unmistakably plain; and he did wonder at the hardihood which had brought her hither, after its receipt.

"You cannot have misunderstood my communication," he said to her as they turned into the room that had once been her boudoir. "I must beg to refer you to it. This house can never shelter you again."

"But it must," she answered.

"Never again; never again."

"At least, I must stay here for some days, until I can decide where my residence shall be," she persisted, her voice taking the unpleasant shriek that it always took in anger. "You can't deny me that."

Mr. Greatorex raised his hand as if to waive off the argument and the words. "Philip shall see you to an hotel, if you feel incompetent to drive to one with your maid," he said, slightly sarcastic. "But, under my roof; it once sheltered in happiness my poor son; you may not remain."

"I was your son's wife," she passionately said.

"I will tell you what you were to him, if you wish. I don't press it."

"Well?"

"His curse."

"Thank you."

"His curse before marriage; his curse after it."

As he stood there, with his face of pain, speaking not in an angry tone, but one mournfully subdued, certain items connected with the past rose up to fill the mind of Mrs. Bede Greatorex. She was aware then that he knew all; she had some little shame left in her, and her very brow grew crimson.

"I cannot imagine what you may have heard, or be suspecting," she said, falteringly. "The past is past. I did nothing very wrong. Nothing but what plenty of other girls do."

"May God forgive you, Louisa Greatorex; as I know He has forgiven him."

It was surging up in her mind like angry waves, that far gone-by time, one event replacing another. During her prolonged visit to this very house as Louisa Joliffe, she had suffered Bede to become passionately attached to her. Suffered?—it was she who drew him and drew him on. She engaged herself to him privately; a solemn engagement; and Bede acceded to her request that it should be kept secret for a time. She did not like Bede; she was playing an utterly false part; she coveted the good income and position that would be hers as his wife, but she rather disliked him. Her motive in demanding that their engagement should be concealed, was a hope that some offer more desirable might turn up. Oh that Bede had suspected it! He looked for her to be his wife as surely as he looked for Heaven. After her return home from her visit, and John Ollivera, was sojourning at Helstonleigh, she played exactly the same game over with him. Drawing him on to love her, and engaging herself to him in private. She liked him, but she did not like to have to wait an indefinite number of years, until the young barrister should find himself in a position to marry. Which of the two she would eventually have chosen, was a matter that must remain in uncertainty for ever; most likely (she acknowledged so to herself) Bede and his wealth. Things went on smoothly enough, she corresponding ardently with both of them in secret, until the time of the March assizes—so often told of—and the fatal night when Bede Greatorex came down to Helstonleigh on a mission to his cousin. The contretemps, the almost certainty of discovery, the very probable fear that she should lose both her lovers, nearly drove Louisa out of her senses. That something in connection with it had passed between Bede and his cousin, she knew from Bede's manner that evening at her mother's; how much, she did not dare to ask. The following morning, when the news was brought to her that Mr. Ollivera had destroyed himself, she felt like a guilty woman. Whatever might have been the mystery of the death: whether he had really committed suicide, or whether Bede had shot him in the passion of his hot Spanish blood—and it was impossible but that she should have her latent doubts—she was the primary cause; and she knew it, and felt it. Had she gone out and killed him herself, she could not have felt it more. She became aware of another thing—that Bede Greatorex, searching amidst the effects of the dead on the following day, must have found her love-letters: more impassioned letters than she was wont to write to him. Bede did not visit her again during his stay at Helstonleigh, and she would not have dared to seek him. Some months later they met by accident in London: were thrown together three or four times. Bede renewed his offer of marriage, and she accepted him at once; the doubt in her mind, as to the part he might have taken in John Ollivera's death, never having been solved. She conveniently ignored it, for the glowing prospect of an establishment was all in all. But what sort of a wife did she make him?—how much did Bede, in his chivalric devotion, have to bear? She alone knew; she knew it now as she stood there; and her attempt to carry it off with a high hand to Mr. Greatorex failed signally. If ever the true sense of her sin should be brought home by Heaven to Louisa Greatorex, its weight, as connected with the treatment of her husband, would be well-nigh greater than she could bear. A curse to him before marriage; a curse to him after: Mr. Greatorex had well said it.

"Am I to starve in future, that you won't give me a home?" she burst forth, driving other thoughts away from her. "What's two hundred a year? How am I to live?"

"My recommendation to you was, that you should live in Boulogne; with or near your mother," Mr. Greatorex answered calmly. "The two hundred pounds will be amply sufficient for that."

"Two hundred pounds!" she retorted, rudely. "I shall spend that on my dress."

"As you please, of course. It is the sum that will be paid you in quarterly instalments of fifty pounds, as long as I live. At my death, the half of it only would be secured to you. Should you marry again, the payments would altogether cease. All this I stated to you in my letter: I repeat it now. Not another shilling will you receive from me—in life, or after death."

She saw her future; saw it all laid out before her as on a map; and her face took a blank look, betraying mortification and despair. No more ravishing toilettes or French waiting maids; no more costly dinnergivings, or magnificent kettle-drums. Mrs. Bede Greatorex and society must henceforth live tolerably far apart. The home she had so despised, this that she was now being turned from, would be a very palace compared with the lodgings in Boulogne.

"To prolong this interview will not be productive of further result," spoke Mr. Greatorex, taking a step towards the door. "I must beg to remind you that friends are waiting for me."

"And my clothes, that I left here? And the ornaments that were mine?"

"Everything belonging to you has been packed ready for removal. The cases shall be all sent to whatever place you may name."

She turned away without another word. Mr. Greatorex rang the bell. Outside, sitting underneath one of the white statues, near the small conservatory, was the French maid, inwardly railing against the want of politeness of these misérable Anglishe. Trusty Philip had warned her that she need not go up higher.

The cab drove away with them, and Mr. Greatorex returned to the dining-room with a relieved heart.

"She is done with at last, thank Heaven! Let us have tea together, Roland," he added, with a hearty smile. "Lady Yorke will take off her bonnet, and make it for us; as she did when she was my little friend Annabel Channing."

Copy of the letter received by Judge Kene from Bede Greatorex.

"As you know so much, Sir Thomas, I owe it to you and to myself to afford some further explanation. You have shown yourself a true friend: add to the obligation, by imparting the details I now write to Henry William Ollivera.

"When I was despatched to Helstonleigh on that fatal mission, I was engaged to be married to Louisa Joliffe, and loved her passionately. The engagement had existed several months, but it was at her request kept a secret to ourselves. After delivering the message and business I was charged with to John, we sat on, in his room, talking of indifferent matters. I said that I should spend the evening with the Joliffes: John laughed a little, and said perhaps he should. One word led to another, and at last he told me, premising it must be in confidence, that he was engaged to Louisa. I thought he was joking; my answer annoyed him; and he went on to say things about Louisa's love for him and their future marriage that nearly drove me wild. What, I hardly know now. It seemed to me that he had treacherously stepped in to strive to take my bride from me, to win her for himself, my one little ewe lamb. We recriminated on each other: she had deceived us both, but neither of us suspected it then: and we felt something like rival tiger cats; at least I know I did. Whenever my Spanish blood got up I was a madman—as you may remember, Kene, for you saw me so once or twice in earlier days—I was nothing else that wicked evening. At some taunt of his, or it sounded like one to me, I took up the pistol, that lay on the table underneath my hand, and fired it at him. Before Heaven, where I shall so soon stand, I declare that I had no deliberate intention of killing him. I did not know whether the pistol was loaded or not. I do not even think I knew what I was doing, or that I had caught up the pistol: in my mad rage I was conscious of nothing. The shot killed him instantaneously, even in the midst of his cry. I cried out too—with horror at what I had done; my passion faded and I stood still as he was. Before I crossed the step or two to his succour, I saw that he was dead. How horribly I have repented since that I did not fling open the door and call out for assistance, none, save myself, can know. Self-preservation lies instinctively within us all, and I suppose that stopped me. Oh, the false coward that I have since ever called myself!—the years of concealment and misery it would have saved All I thought of then, was—to get away. A short while I listened, but no sound told that any one had been within earshot; I softly opened the door to escape, putting out my head first to reconnoitre; and—found myself nearly face to face with a man. He stood on the stairs in an attitude of listening, and our eyes met in the gas-light. I never forgot his; they seemed to shine out from a mass of black hair; those same eyes afterwards puzzled my memory for years. When the eyes of my subsequent clerk, Mr. Brown, had used to strike some unpleasant chord on my memory, but what I could not fathom, I never connected them with those other eyes; for Brown had put off his disguise then, and looked entirely another person. Ah, Kene! don't you see the obligation I lie under to this man, George Winter? Not at that moment did he know I had committed murder, but in a short period of time, as soon as the newspapers supplied details of the night's doings, he could but become aware of it. Had a doubt remained on his mind, when he entered our office and knew me for Bede Greatorex, the thing must have been made clear to him as daylight. To shield me he has remained under a cloud himself: I hope my father will reward him. Even when he was giving his evidence before you and the rest, he told a lie to save me. For he said that when he saw the face at the door it was after the departure of Mr. Bede Greatorex. It was my face he saw, Kene; no other. All through these years he has watched my misery; and in his great compassion for what he knew my sufferings must be, has been silently lightening life to me where he could. But, to go back to the time.

"I should think we gazed at each other for the space of half a minute, the man on the stairs and I: the fright of seeing someone there nearly paralyzed me; and then I went in again and shut the door. It was perhaps the sight of him that caused me to attempt to throw the suspicion off myself: certainly I had not thought of it before. I put the pistol on the carpet by the chair, as if it had fallen from John's right hand; and next, looking about on the table, I found the unfinished letter, and added the lines you know of. I seemed to be doing it in a dream; that it was not myself but somebody else, and all in a desperate hurry, for I grew afraid of stopping. Then it occurred to me to put out the lamp; I don't know why; and, upon that, I went out resolutely, for I did not like the dark. Luck seemed to be against me. As I opened the door this second time, some young man (not the first) was passing by. Instinct caused me to turn round and make believe to be speaking to John. What words I really said, I should never have remembered but for hearing the young man, Alfred Jones, repeat them at the coroner's inquest. They served me more than I thought: for Alfred Jones unconsciously took up the natural supposition that John was also speaking to me; this version went forth to the public, and it was assumed that what happened, happened after my departure. There's no doubt that it was the chief element in throwing suspicion off me. He showed me out of the house, and thenceforward I had to try and act the part of an innocent man. I went to the Star and Garter and drank some brandy-and-water: I went thence to Mrs. Joliffe's: how I did it all, with that horrible thing upon me, I have never known. I said a few cautious words to Louisa, and by her answers, I felt sure that John's boast had been (at least in part) a vain one. As I returned up High Street, some tradesman was standing just within his side-door. He did not know I saw him. Halting, I looked at John Ollivera's windows, just opposite, and said something to the effect that John must have gone to bed—all for the man to hear me. Just afterwards I met you, Kene,—do you remember it? You were going to call on John, but I said he had gone to bed and the people of the house, too, I supposed, as there was no light to be seen. I shrank from the discovery, and would fain have put it off for ever. What a night that was for me! As I had stirred the tea at Mrs. Joliffe's, as I stirred the brandy-and-water at the hotel, John's face seemed to be in the liquid, staring up at me. In the dark of the bedroom, after the candle had burnt out, I saw him in his chair, just as I had left him. I had not dared to ask for a night-light, lest it might excite suspicion; how could I answer for it that the hotel would not get to learn I was not in the habit of burning one?

"You know the rest: the discovery and the inquest that followed. Did I act my part well, Kene? I suppose so, by the result. That day—the first—you were with me when we examined John's desk: it was advised that I should look over his letters for any clue that perhaps they might show to the motive of his self-inflicted death. The large bundle of letters, Kene, came, I found, from Louisa Joliffe, and poor John's was no vain boast: she had been all to him that she had professed to be to me, and a traitor to both.

"Why did I marry her, you will naturally ask. Ah, why! why! Because my love for her fooled me into it: because, if you will, I was mad. When we met again, months afterwards, the passion that I thought I had killed within me, rose up with ten-fold force, and I yielded to it. To do so was not much less sinful (looking at it as I look now) than the other and greater crime. I saw it even as I stood with her before the altar, I saw it afterwards clearer and clearer. But I loved her even in spite of my better judgment; I love her even yet: and I have striven to do my duty by her in all indulgence, to shield her from the cares of the world.

"And there's my life's history. Oh, Kene, if I have been more sinful than other men, my merciful God knows what my expiation has been. Can you even faintly picture it to yourself? From a few minutes after the breath went out of poor John's body, my punishment set in. It was only fear just at first; it was the bitterest remorse afterwards that ever made a wreck of mortal man. I am not a murderer by nature, and John and I were dear friends. My days have been one long, wearing penance: regret for him and his shortened life, dread of my crime's discovery; one or the other filling every moment: remorse and repentance, repentance and remorse: and that it has been so is owing to Heaven's mercy. Not an hour of the day or night, but I would gladly have given up my own life to restore his. After the first confused horror had passed, I should have declared the truth at the time but for my mother's sake: in her state of health it would have killed her. When she died, the time had gone by for it: I had my father and my wife to consider later, and remained perforce silent. My father has thought my bodily health failed: in one sense so it did, for I have been wasting away from the first, dying slowly inch by inch.

"And that's all, Kene. When you shall have heard news of my death—it will be with you very close upon this letter—disclose the whole to Henry William Ollivera. With regard to my father, I leave the matter to you. If he in the slightest degree suspects me—and I can but think he must, after Winter's confession, and from the easy acquiescence he gave to my coming on the Continent for an indefinite period—then tell him the whole. Heaven bless you all, and grant you the peace that can spring alone of Jesus Christ's atonement! I have dared to think it mine for some little time now.

"Bede Greatorex."

When the tidings of Bede's death reached him, Sir Thomas Kene went out to seek an interview with Mr. Ollivera. The clergyman read the letter, and bent his head in prolonged silence.

"After all, I suppose John's grave will have to remain undisturbed," spoke the Judge. "Winter cleared his memory."

"Yes; better so, perhaps," was the slow, thoughtful reply. "If I had never before been thankful that I read the burial service over him, I should be so now. You see, I was right, Kene. God be merciful to us all, for we are all miserable sinners!"

Danesbury House (1860)

East Lynne (1861)

The Elchester College Boys (1861)

A Life's Secret (1862)

Mrs. Halliburton's Troubles (1862)

The Channings (1862)

The Foggy Night at Offord: A Christmas Gift for the Lancashire Fund (1863)

The Shadow of Ashlydyat (1863)

Verner's Pride (1863)

Lord Oakburn's Daughters (1864)

Oswald Cray (1864)

Trevlyn Hold; or, Squire Trevlyn's Heir (1864)

William Allair; or, Running away to Sea (1864)

Mildred Arkell: A Novel (1865)

The Argosy (1865)

Elster's Folly: A Novel (1866)

St. Martin's Eve: A Novel (1866)

Lady Adelaide's Oath (1867)

Orville College: A Story (1867)

The Ghost of the Hollow Field (1867)

Anne Hereford: A Novel (1868)

Castle Wafer; or, The Plain Gold Ring (1868)

The Red Court Farm: A Novel (1868)

Roland Yorke: A Novel (1869)

Bessy Rane: A Novel (1870)

George Canterbury's Will (1870)

Dene Hollow (1871)

Within the Maze: A Novel (1872)

The Master of Greylands (1872)

Johnny Ludlow (1874)

Bessy Wells (1875)

Told in the Twilight: Containing 'Parkwater' and nine short stories (1875)

Adam Grainger: A Tale (1876)

Edina (1876)

Our Children (1876)

Parkwater: With four other tales (1876)

Pomeroy Abbey (1878)

Lady Adelaide (1879)

Johnny Ludlow, Second Series (1880)

A Tale of Sin and Other Tales (1881)

Court Netherleigh: A Novel (1881)

About Ourselves (1883)

Johnny Ludlow. Third Series (1885)

Lady Grace and Other Stories (1887)

The Story of Charles Strange (1888)

Featherston's Story. A Tale by Johnny Ludlow (1889)

The Unholy Wish and Other Stories (1890)
The House of Halliwell. A Novel (1890)
Ashley and Other Stories (1897)
Victor Serenus (1898)
Johnny Ludlow. Fifth series (1899)
Johnny Ludlow. Sixth series (1899)

Translations
Les Channing. Traduit de l'Anglais par Mme Abric-Encontre (1864)
Les Filles de Lord Oakburn: Roman traduit de l'anglais par L. Bochet (1876)
La Gloire des Verner: Roman traduit de l'anglais par L. de L'Estrive (1878)
Le Serment de Lady Adelaïde: Roman traduit de l'anglais par Léon Bochet (1878)